PLUNDER
OF GOR

PLUNDER OF GOR

GOREAN SAGA * BOOK 34

JOHN NORMAN

OPEN ROAD

INTEGRATED MEDIA

NEW YORK

All rights reserved, including without limitation the right to reproduce this book or any portion thereof in any form or by any means, whether electronic or mechanical, now known or hereinafter invented, without the express written permission of the publisher.

This is a work of fiction. Names, characters, places, events, and incidents either are the product of the author's imagination or are used fictitiously. Any resemblance to actual persons, living or dead, businesses, companies, events, or locales is entirely coincidental.

Copyright © 2016 by John Norman

978-1-5040-3406-7

Published in 2016 by Open Road Integrated Media, Inc.
180 Maiden Lane
New York, NY 10038
www.openroadmedia.com

PLUNDER OF GOR

CHAPTER ONE

I knelt before him, head down, as was appropriate.

"Beat me, if I am not pleasing," I said.

"Lie here, to my side," he said, "the bara position will do."

I lay then beside him, prone, my hip to his left knee, my head forward, away from him as he sat, cross-legged, perusing a scroll. My ankles were crossed, and my wrists, too, were crossed, and held behind my back. In such a position one may be conveniently bound. My head was turned to the side, that my right cheek might be on the carpet.

"Would you like clothing?" he asked.

"It will be as Master pleases," I whispered.

He returned to his reading.

I had made the mistake, once, of begging clothing too zealously, even the clothing such as I might be granted, as humiliating, brief, and revealing as it would be.

He had kept me as I was even in the streets, in which I had heeled him, wrists bound behind me, without even the dignity of being leashed.

How free women in their robes had mocked me, and sometimes struck me. He had not seen fit to shield me from such abuse.

Why should he? Was it not clear what I was?

Too, I was a barbarian, a woman of Earth.

In those days I did not know if I most hated him, or feared him. But I most feared him.

But that had been the way with many of my masters.

They had been very different, but they were all masters. They treat us as they will, and they do with us as they will. We are slaves.

"You have not yet earned clothing," I had been informed. I had then been switched.

I had known so little of this world!

I lay beside him.

Would he touch me?

I was such that he might do with me as he pleased.

I had come to long for his touch. I had not realized, once, such men could exist. I had not known what it was to be grasped, and owned, to be seized and mocked, and thrown to his feet, to be handled with such authority. I had not known such men could exist.

I had come to need his touch. It was that for which I lived. What had been done to me? I lived for his touch.

I had been acquired months ago.

Certainly it was not the first time I had been acquired.

Once I had been free, but that was in another place, one far away.

As I lay beside him, obedient, in bara, my mind wandered.

The subject matter of the ensuing accounts began better than a year ago, in another place, on another world.

It began with my first master.

I did not realize, at first, that he was a master. And surely I did not realize that he would be my master, my first master.

It was he who taught me that I was a woman, and what it was to be a woman.

I had not, at that time, in full consciousness, save in dreams, and intrusive thoughts, realized that I was of the slave sex, and that I required a master, that I would be empty, incomplete, forlorn, meaningless, desolate, and useless without one. What is a slave without her master, and what is a master without his slave?

How he hated the women of Earth!

Why did he hate us?

How wrong that was!

Why did he not simply take us in hand, and collar us?

I would, were it in my power, he had said, bring ten thousand of the best to a better world, to ascend the block, to learn the whip and chains.

They would look well on the block.

Let them be bought and sold!

They deserve chains, and the collar.

Alas, I was not one of the best.

It was not my fault that I had been lied to. It was not my fault that I had been acculturated as I had. It was not my doing. It was an accident of time and place. I had no way of knowing, at that time, on Earth, that he was a master and I was a slave. Fool that I was, I had thought him another man of Earth, a mere man of Earth. Why had I not seen the master in his eyes, in his mien, in the nature of his regard?

In my vanity, and pride, I had displeased him.

How foolish I had been!

I was a barbarian, I could not even speak the language, I had no Home Stone, and yet I had dared to stand before him!

How natural it had seemed then; how frightful it would seem now!

But I do not think I should have been blamed. I had been taught to deny the most obvious and profound biological realities, to dismiss or despise patent differences, to deny nature, the very nature of which I was an outcome. Were humans not essentially unreal, a fraud, unlike the lion and the hawk, more honest forms of life? Were human beings not a counterfeit currency of sorts, masquerading as a genuine life form? Were they not shallow sociological artifacts, nothing in themselves, only clay waiting to be shaped, simple nondescript matter waiting to be formed as society might decree, empty vessels waiting to be filled with whatever contents were currently brewed, following the approved recipes of the day? Glory to the engineers who design automobiles and people. Hail the managers who assemble and produce the new improved model of the human being. Men were to be dethroned, from a throne they had not occupied for millennia. They were to be put aside, diminished, reduced, crippled, confused, and conflicted. Let them be meaningless and homeless in what was once their world. Teach them to spill their own blood. Let them tear their own flesh. Let them pretend to be weak and small. Let them make themselves weak and small. Let them deny and doubt themselves. Make them their own worst enemy. Who can defeat a man but himself? Let lies be spoken with confidence and authority, and repeated frequently. Is it not the case that the lie heard many times comes to wear the mask of truth? And how dangerous it is to speak truth in a world of lies!

I slipped the folder into the drawer of the filing cabinet and thrust shut the door. It was summer, and late in the afternoon. The others had gone. It was late in the week, and toward what we spoke of as "the week-end." I would close the office. I was looking forward to the beach tomorrow. I turned about, and, startled, realized he had entered the office. I had not heard the door open. He had closed it behind him, as well, an act which, for some reason, I found disturbing.

"We are closed," I told him.

"It is early," he said. "The hours posted on the door—"

"Everyone is gone," I said.

"You are not," he said.

He was a large man. I could not place the accent, if it was an accent, for the matter was subtle. Perhaps it was only that he spoke carefully, and clearly. I suspected the idiom in which he spoke might not be native to him.

"Everyone is gone," I said. "I am closing the office. Come back on Monday."

"You are a secretary, a receptionist, something like that?" he said.

"A secretary," I said.

"You can make appointments?" he said.

"The office is closed," I said. "I am leaving."

"You do not even have a moment to make an appointment?" he asked.

"Come back on Monday," I said.

He made no move to go.

"Did you hear me?" I asked.

"Yes," he said.

"You may leave," I said.

"It is true," he said, "as I was informed. You are what on this world is termed a 'bitch'."

"'On this world'?" I said. "A bitch?"

"Yes," he said.

"Get out!" I said.

"The whip takes that out of a woman," he said.

"The whip?" I said.

"Yes," he said.

I was alone with him in the office, and even the shades had been drawn, against the sun, and heat.

"I am sorry," I said. "I will make an appointment for you. Did you wish to see Mr. Wilson, or Mr. Barrett?"

"Neither," he said.

"I do not understand," I said.

"I am here to see you," he said.

"Me?"

"Yes."

"I am not an officer of the company," I said.

"I realize that," he said.

"I am not important," I said.

"That is true," he said, "but you were noticed, and I have been delegated to make a preliminary assessment."

"'Assessment'?" I said.

"Yes," he said.

"I do not understand," I said.

"It is not necessary that you do," he said.

"You are considering a girl?" I said.

"Precisely," he said.

"I am content here," I said.

"No, you are not," he said.

"Perhaps not," I said.

I then regretted some short, tart, uncomplimentary remarks I had made to some of my friends, friends of a sort, other girls, other employees, working in the same building, with whom I often lunched. These remarks had appertained, largely, to my views of the firm, my employers, and some of the other gentlemen in the building, with some of whom our firm had dealings. But it seemed unlikely he would be apprised of such things. On the other hand, he may have heard something of this sort of thing, one way or another, doubtless through the other girls, they speaking to others, and others to others. And, I was surely open to an improvement in my circumstances.

"I do not come cheap," I said.

One must be prepared to bargain.

"You might," he said.

"I might be available," I said. "It is possible. What sort of position do you have in mind?"

"One of docility, subservience, and meaninglessness," he said.

"I do not understand," I said. "What company do you represent?"

"No company, at least as you are thinking of it," he said.

"Some business?"

"In a sense, yes," he said.

"I may be available," I said. "Perhaps we can arrange an interview."

"This is an interview," he said.

"Surely this has to do with clerical skills, with office work," I said.

"No," he said, "nothing like that."

"I do not understand," I said.

"This has more to do with you, you as you are, your hair, your eye color, your carriage, your figure, your appearance, what I sense about you, such things," he said.

"Oh!" I said, delighted. "I see! It is a different sort of thing!"

"Yes," he said, "altogether."

"You are a talent scout for a motion-picture company?" I said. "You are representing a modeling agency?"

I knew that I was attractive. Certainly the other girls, those catty chits, had resented that. That had never been hard to tell. It was not my fault that I was more beautiful than they, far more beautiful.

"Would you please step over here, to the center of the room and turn before me?" he asked.

"Certainly," I said.

"Again," he said.

I turned about, once more.

I felt delightfully brazen.

I trusted he liked what he saw. Had I not auditioned for plays? Had I not submitted a portfolio to more than one agency? With good fortune I might soon be able to leave behind the hated office, the dictatorship of clocks and calendars, the endless routines, the instructions of boring superiors, phrased as requests or suggestions, the pretentious prattle of inane companions. And soon I could rid myself, too, I supposed, of this troublesomely masculine oaf, this menial, who dared to presume to speak of "assessment."

"Why are you standing?" he asked.

"I do not understand," I said.

"I am a free man," he said.

"I do not understand," I said.

"You are in the presence of a free man."

"What do you expect of me?"

"You should be on your knees," he said.

"I beg your pardon," I said.

"Kneeling," he said, "before me."

"Why?" I asked.

"Is it not obvious?" he asked.

"I do not understand," I said.

"You are a slave."

"I am not a slave!"

"Do you think I do not know a slave when I see one? You lack only the collar."

"Get out!" I said.

"You might look fetching in a slave rag, or a slave tunic," he said, "and, perhaps better, clad only in your collar."

"Get out!" I said.

"I can visualize you on a slave block," he said.

"Get out!" I said, again, tears in my eyes.

"On a slave block," he said, "it is clear that a woman is a woman."

"Go away!" I said.

"You are not yet on your knees."

"Get out! Go away!" I said.

"That will be remembered," he said.

"Why are you looking at me in that fashion?"

"It is the way one looks upon a slave," he said.

"Get out!" I demanded.

"I am perusing your lineaments."

"How dare you!" I said.

"It is not hard to conjecture their nature," he said.

"Beast!" I said.

"They will make a difference in your price."

"Price?"

"A pot girl, a kettle-and-mat girl, at best," he said.

"I do not understand."

"Fit for rep-cloth, not silk," he said.

"I do not understand," I said.

"A girl of modest market value, not much market value."

"Market value?"

"What you might sell for."

"Sell?"

"Yes."

"As a slave, I suppose," I said, angrily.

"Of course," he said. "What else?"

"I am beautiful. I am very beautiful," I said. "Many men have told me so!"

"They have seen no better."

I was then infuriated, and I slapped his face, sharply. It must have stung, and I had surely intended that it should.

Then I was frightened, for I feared he might return the blow, and I did not doubt that such a blow, even if merely with the flat of his hand, that of a male, given his size, his strength, so much more than mine, might strike me to the side of the room.

But he merely touched the side of his face, where I had struck him, and smiled. "That was a mistake," he said. "Another mistake."

"Another mistake?" I said.

"Your first, failing to kneel, failing to kneel instantly, before a free man," he said.

I stepped back.

"The blow was more serious, of course," he said. "But you are ignorant. It will not be necessary to cut off your hand, this time."

I was then even more afraid.

I moved backward, retreating step by step, and half tripped, and turned, stumbling, and struck my thigh against the edge of the desk. I winced, and turned back to face him.

"That will not do," he said. "You were clumsy. You are to move with the grace and beauty of the female, of the slave."

I feared I had made a fool of myself.

He had not moved.

But I had never before been in the vicinity of such a man.

"Have you heard of Gor?" he asked.

"No!" I said, perhaps too earnestly.

To be sure, I had heard something of Gor, the Antichthon, or Counter-Earth. But then I suppose many have heard something of it.

One hears of such things.

How can one help it?

Do not rumors rustle about? Are not strange stories borne on surprising winds? Are not unusual thoughts found in green places, amongst trees?

But I had never read a Gorean book.

I had been afraid to read a Gorean book.

I now wonder why that was.

I think I feared what might be found there.

What was there to be afraid of?

Surely I had had a course in anthropology in college, and was aware of variations in human cultures. What then is another culture? So what was so different about Gor? Why should I have been afraid, so unaccountably, to do something so simple as to read a certain book, or books? Surely there was nothing to fear. What could possibly be so disturbing about the mere thought of apprising oneself of unfamiliar possibilities? Can ideas draw blood? Surely truth is unavailing against mighty walls. Was I afraid I would find myself in such books, in such a world, that I would find myself somehow therein? Did I fear I might learn something which, in some sense, I feared I already knew?

"You have never heard of Gor?" he asked.

"No," I said.

"I think that what you are saying is false," he said. "One such as you is not permitted to lie. Only a free woman may lie. One such as you may be punished."

"'Punished'"?

"Certainly," he said. "You are a slave."

"I am not a slave!" I said.

Again he smiled.

"Gor is only in stories!" I said.

"I thought you had not heard of Gor," he said.

"It is only in stories," I said.

"So many such as you have thought," he said, "who are now on Gor, and, as they should be, in collars."

"'Collars'?"

"Slave collars."

"I shall call the police!" I said.

"They would be pleased to see such as you, naked, at their feet, in a collar," he said.

"Get out!"

He went to the door and opened it, and then turned, paused in the threshold. "As for Gor, my dear," he said, "inquire further into the matter. Normally one such as you would not be selected, but I think we may make an exception in your case. You have not been fully pleasing. And Gor, after all, has a use for its pot girls, and its kettle-and-mat girls, as well as for better, more delicious merchandise."

"You cannot demean me!" I cried. "I tell you I am beautiful, very beautiful!"

"Vain bitch," he said.

"'Bitch'?"

"As of now," he said. "The whip, as I mentioned, takes that out of a woman. It is hard to be a bitch, on your knees, your head down, fearfully kissing and licking the feet of a man."

"Beautiful!" I cried. "Beautiful!"

He stood in the portal, paused. "It is true," he said. "In a collar, you might become more beautiful. In a collar, a woman becomes far more beautiful."

"Get out!" I cried. "Get out!"

"Do not be afraid," he said. "At least, not yet. This is a preliminary assessment. No decision has been made."

"I am not afraid!" I said, trembling.

"We may meet again," he said.

"Get out!" I cried.

He then turned about, and left. Behind him he had closed the door, quietly. I heard him descend the stairs, his step placid and measured.

I then turned about, and bent over the desk, distraught, clinging to it. My thigh hurt where I had stumbled against the wood. I would probably, shortly, have a bruise there. Perhaps it was there already. After a few minutes I had become far more calm. I had very little sense of what had just occurred. Had I called the police what could they have done? What could I have told them? Was I hysterical? Was I the victim of some delusion? Had I misunderstood some brief unpleasantness, or misremembered it? Was I not making much out of little, or nothing? Might they not credit my account to some aberration? I did not know the man. I had never seen him before. I presumed that I would never see him again. He was not in our records. He was not a client, even a prospective client. There was no name, and even the description might have fit any number of large men. I had sensed an accent, but was not even sure of that.

And I was beautiful, very beautiful!

I had planned to go to the beach the next day.

Would I do so?

When I went to the beach, it was not to swim, but to relish the sun, the warm sand, the sight of the water and sky, the crowd, the sound of the surf, and sense the impression one such as I would make in such a milieu, on the young men, so many of them furtive and diffident, so frightened to be noticed in their noticing. How ashamed my culture had made so many of them to be male. Was that not to be a secret, denied even to oneself? In my sunglasses they would not even know if I noticed them or not, not until I turned to them, directly, and they quickly turned away.

It was one of the small pleasures allowed to a young woman in the culture, that of intimidating and shaming men, teasing them, taunting them, torturing them, particularly those suitably acculturated, conditioned to view the most natural promptings of their blood with trepidation and remorse. Who did we fear and hate more, I wondered, they, or ourselves?

I considered changing my plans for the morrow but then decided I would not do so. I would go forward and do exactly what I had intended to do. Also, the bruise on my thigh was high enough to be covered by the skirt of my white bathing suit.

The next incident that I might recount occurred the following afternoon, at the beach. It was not clear to me at the time, but it proved later to be connected with the unpleasantness that had occurred the day before, about closing time, at the office. I was leaning back against a rented wood-and-canvas backrest, set in the sand. I wore a broad-brimmed sun hat and sunglasses. The sand was warm, and my knees were drawn up. My beach bag was beside me, bulging with its miscellany, ranging from brushes and combs to towels and lotions. I had dismissed the incident of the preceding afternoon in the office. It was meaningless. To be sure, certain mnemonic tatters of the interaction did intrude now and then, like the stirring of leaves, like a rustling in brush, scarcely noted, where something might have moved, like whispers, whose source eluded consciousness.

I became aware, abruptly, of a presence.

A young man was standing nearby, regarding me. He wore blue slacks, and a white shirt, open at the throat.

When one is beautiful, one is used to being regarded.

I suppose it is flattering, but, too, it can be annoying.

Or is it really annoying, I wonder.

Do we tell ourselves that it is annoying, feeling we should adopt such a posture, that it is expected of us?

Would we not be more distressed, if we were not regarded?

I feigned displeasure.

It was the thing to do.

How dare he regard me so, regard me in that way, as he was!

Is one a mere object?

How horrifying to be regarded as an object, as something which might be assessed, and bought and sold!

But how accustomed I would become to such an appraisal! And, in time, I would realize that I was an object, a sentient, aware, feeling, fearing, hoping, obeying, and needful object.

It was a way of being.

I would be collared, as what I would then be, an animal, an object.

I would be bought and sold, as the mere animal, the mere object, I would then be.

I looked away, a tight gesture, signaling annoyance.

Surely that should send him on his way.

Surely that should be enough!

But when I looked back, he had remained where he was.

Usually, it is only necessary to convey, by the slightest of movements or expressions, a tincture of impatience, or disdain, and the moment would be done with. A hint of displeasure, or a frown, should be sufficient. The intrusive regard, discovered, is withdrawn, and the offending party, apprised of his oafish vulgarity, withdraws in embarrassment.

I turned to face him, boldly, letting him know I was well aware of his attention.

I almost removed my sunglasses.

He had not left.

I glared at him, allowing my disapproval to be clear, unmistakable.

He did not move.

I became angry, and apprehensive.

I did not know what was going on.

Then I suddenly thought he must know me. That must be it, or something like it. Why had he not melted away, quickly, shame-faced, looking down, or to the side? Surely he would not be where he was, continuing to regard me so intently, if he did not know me, or did not think he knew me.

"Kajira," he said.

That is it, I thought. It was a simple case, certainly an unpleasant one, of mistaken identity.

"I am sorry," I said. "That is not my name."

I drew back, tightly, against the backrest, for he knelt in the sand beside me, and reached to my sunglasses, and drew them away.

"I am not who you think I am," I said.

"Kajira," he said.

"No," I said. "I may look like her, but I am not her. My name is not 'Kajira' but 'Phyllis'. You are mistaken."

I did think that 'Kajira' was a lovely name for a girl. I was vaguely aware that I had heard the name, or word, before, but I could not recall the context, or the place, or the time.

He reached forth and brushed my sun hat from my head, and it fell back, to the sand, to my right.

"I do not know you," I said. "And you do not know me. You are mistaken."

I then became aware of a second man, and a third man. The second man held a small digital camera, and was, apparently, snapping a number of pictures. I was apparently being photographed, a number of times, and, I feared, from a variety of perspectives. The third man, somewhat more mature, perhaps in his thirties, was standing to my right.

"I do not know who you think I am," I said. "But I do not know you, and you do not know me. I am not well known. I am not a celebrity, not a famous person, or such, and my name is not 'Kajira'."

"Kajira?" he said, glancing to his more mature fellow.

The older fellow nodded. "Yes," he said, "kajira, clearly."

"My name is Phyllis," I said. "Stop!" I said.

The younger man beside me, in the sand, had brushed away my sandals, and grasped my ankles, one in each hand.

His grip was strong.

I felt helpless.

"Her ankles will shackle well," said the younger man.

"Yes," said the more mature man.

"Let me go!" I said.

"I conjecture a number-two ankle-ring size," said the younger man.

"It can be measured exactly in the pens," said the more mature man.

"Let me go!" I said.

He released me, and I drew my legs back, beneath me, frightened.

How I had been handled!

With such simple authority!

A beast might have been so handled!

"Say, '*La kajira*'," said the more mature man.

"*La kajira*," I said.

The men then left.

I did not understand the import of what I had said until later.

I was much shaken by this strange, meaningless interlude.

I slipped back into my sandals, and, reaching into my beach bag, pulled forth my cover-up, which I hastily wrapped about me.

The men had disappeared.

I saw only others on the beach, some reclining, some coming and going, moving amongst the towels, blankets, and umbrellas.

I bent down and retrieved my sun hat from the sand, and my sunglasses. The glasses seemed important. Perhaps I felt a need for some sort of shielding. What a frail wall to hide behind! But I felt the need to seek a sense of anonymity, of security, even be it so little as might be obtained by a bit of colored glass. In a short while, the wood-and-canvas backrest returned, I, fully clothed, uneasy, and frightened, left the beach.

The third incident prior to my acquisition occurred a month later. In the intervening days, and weeks, I had managed to regain much of my equilibrium. Nothing new and untoward had occurred. Life continued in the repetitious, quotidian patterns with which I was so familiar. I had assured myself, if not convinced myself, again and again, that the two incidents just recounted, however disturbing, were unrelated and negligible. Certainly the second incident, that on the beach, was a simple case of mistaken identity. I had tried to make that clear to them. I dismissed both incidents, to the extent I could.

I was not clear on the motivation of the third incident. Perhaps it was merely to let me know that I had not been forgotten, or to let me know I was still under "consideration," or, perhaps, merely, to let me know that, in a very real sense, I was not free, but theirs, and that they could apprehend me when they wished, and do with me what they pleased.

I wondered if I were a slave, already, without my knowledge. I feared so. How frightful to realize that one is a slave! It was only that I had not yet been acquired, had not yet been "gathered in," or "harvested," had not yet, so to speak, been picked from Earth's orchard of young women, picked as slavers pick fruit, "girl fruit." I was not yet in my collar!

One collar is fastened on one's neck, commonly, before the other is removed. In this way, even in a transition of masters, I remained collared. It was fitting. I was a slave.

Certainly there was little ambiguity about the third incident.

I twisted about, and awakened, suddenly.

I sat up in bed, and cried out with misery.

I jerked at my wrists.

They were encircled with metal!

I could scarcely part my hands!

I was handcuffed!

I struggled from bed. I stood, unsteadily, fighting to keep my balance. I was still clothed, in my long, blue, silken nightgown. It had not been removed. Did those who had put the metal on my wrists, who presumably could have done anything with me, not care to see me naked? Was this some sort of insult? Was I not beautiful? Was I not one in a thousand! In rage I tried to part my wrists. They were well held! I tried to thrust the cuffs from my wrists, and could not do so. I would only abrade my wrists. I thought of the ruffian who had so discomfited me in the office. I could not part my wrists, no more than the single link I was permitted! My hands, at least, were cuffed before my body! Had they been cuffed behind my body I would have been even more helpless, and my figure, despite what I might wish, and to my frustration and dismay, would have been emphasized. Were they not interested in emphasizing my helplessness? Were they not, in their brutal arrogance, interested in emphasizing my figure?

Surely I was beautiful!

I was suddenly affrighted by a possibility.

I wondered if I were still a virgin.

I was sure I was.

Was this yet another insult?

Anything might have been done with me in the night, but apparently nothing had been done. I had only been put in handcuffs!

I recalled that the gross boor in the office had dared to use expressions like "pot girl" and "kettle-and-mat girl" of me, whatever those terms might mean. He had referred to me as a "bitch." He had said I was fit for "rep-cloth," whatever that was, and not silk. But I was in silk, and I was still in silk. Surely they had seen that!

I was sure I was still a virgin.

I was sure this had not been taken from me.

If not, why?

Surely this omission was not inadvertent.

Had they no interest in this?

Could I believe that?

Did they not want my virginity, but left it to me, perhaps contemptuously, rather as they had not stripped me, but left me clothed, as they had left my hands fastened before me, not behind?

Were these things to show their scorn of me?

Were these things to show me that I was not special?

To me my virginity was of momentous consequence. How could it not be of such consequence to others?

Could it be they did not want it?

Could it be that they had no interest in it, that it was not important to them?

How could they regard as negligible so remarkable and precious a prize?

How was it possible that they had not imposed their will upon me? Surely I would be amongst the most beautiful women they had ever seen.

But I had not been bared, I had been but modestly restrained, I had been left, I was sure, my virginity; I did not think it had been reaped.

How was I to understand these things?

Was I not appealing, was I not desirable?

Consider my virginity. Was it, so momentous to me, of little, or no, concern to them, no more, perhaps, than that of a pig or dog?

How then could they view women, or women such as I?

I was accustomed to being regarded, even to being sought. I was not accustomed to being ignored.

I was angry.

But I had not been ignored, not wholly! There were metal circlets on my wrists!

I shook the cuffs.

I was not a "pot girl," a "kettle-and-mat girl," whatever such things might be!

I was not much interested in men.

They were nothing, or had been made so. Those I was familiar with, those with whom I commonly associated, were refined, effete, tentative, weak, apologetic, reluctant, well-trained, correct, embarrassed by their sex, taught to suspect it, if not despise it, so concerned they were to conform to the required stereotypes of the lubricated, well-tooled, socially acceptable interchangeable part, to whom sex and nature were irrelevant, even inimical, as they might threaten the functioning of the great, shiny beast, the immense machine, sharp-eyed and vigilant, like a vast, jealous, carefully constructed, watchful metal cat.

How swiftly that metal paw might reach out and strike any small, scurrying errant creature, should it presume to be careless of its assigned, tiny proprieties.

Where men were not men how could I be a woman?

I tried to gather my thoughts together, to control myself, to think clearly. I was afraid I might fall. I sank to my knees, on the carpet beside the bed, my head down. How secure and stable is such a posture! I must think clearly. I must decide what to do.

I was bewildered.

I felt vulnerable.

I was vulnerable.

I could call out, and perhaps others, in the hall, or adjoining apartments, might hear, and hurry to relieve my distress. Surely I could open the door for their entry. The door, I was sure, was locked, or had been relocked. Suppose neighbors, whom I knew only casually, only by sight, should enter the apartment, admitted, in answer to my cries? What would they think? Casting about, there was no sign of a forced entry. How, then, had the apartment been entered, how could it be that I was fastened, as I was? Must I not then have admitted, even welcomed, those who had so discomfited me? Surely some would think so. Perhaps all would think so. Too, how could I dare to appear before them, as I was? How could I explain my appearance, lightly gowned, my wrists in handcuffs? Would they take my plight seriously? Would they dismiss it, would they scorn me, with wise looks, would they find it amusing, no more than an embarrassing contretemps? And what if a man should see me as I was, so provocatively clad, so helpless, so restrained? Perhaps they had fantasized seeing me so, perhaps they would be pleased to see me so, while hastening, of course, to appear otherwise, feigning sympathy, and concern? Could I bear that? What would neighbors or strangers, or the police, or anyone, think? There was no sign in the apartment of violence, no broken latches, no door chains or bolts broken from the wall, no broken glass, no sign of robbery, no sign of anything rifled, or amiss, no sign of physical abuse on my body, no cuts, no marks, no bruises. My gown was not even awry, or rent or torn.

But I must elude these restraints, with the single link between the cuffs, my hands held so closely together.

But how?

Yes, I thought. I must call the police. I must prepare myself to endure their skepticism, their scarcely suppressed mockery. They would have tools, or access to tools. They might even have keys which might unclasp the impediments which so snugly enclosed my wrists! No, I thought, I could not endure the embarrassment. Surely such an appeal would be a recourse of last resort!

Better, I thought, perhaps I might open these locks, or one of them, myself. I rose, and hurried to my vanity, and flung open a drawer, and rummaged about. There were straight pins and safety pins, a small nail file, hairpins, bobby pins. An hour later I was sick with frustration. Perhaps a second person might have managed something but my hands were so closely pinioned that I could scarcely angle a pin into a lock, let alone address one directly, and the nail file was too short, as I could hold it, to do more than rest on the metal, and my fingers were too weak to exert more than a modicum of pressure on the steel.

I looked at the phone.

Perhaps a locksmith could be relied upon for discretion, though I doubted it. A locksmith might or might not possess a suitable key or keys for opening the cuff locks, but he might have, at least, tools, a file or hacksaw, which might eventually free me from the restraints. But how could I receive a locksmith, clad as I was, armed with no excuse that might not border on the inane or transparently meretricious? Too, might he not suspect my motivations? Might he not even fear a fraud, a scandal or extortion, of some sort, a girl who might suddenly struggle and scream, this outburst followed promptly by the arrival of male colleagues, seemingly outraged, threatening, and righteous?

Again I looked on the phone.

It seemed far away.

I felt weak, so weak.

I sank to my knees. I feared I might faint.

I fought to retain consciousness.

Surely I must contact someone.

But who?

It would be difficult to make the call, but it could be done. I could lay the receiver to the side, brace the phone, and press the numbers, carefully, with my right hand.

But I was miserable. I wore only the long, blue, sheer, silken nightgown. It would be almost impossible to dress. I could not even draw on a bathrobe or coat. Perhaps I could draw something up about me? Perhaps I could adjust a sheet or blanket about me, and clutch it in place?

I would manage.

Something must be done.

Then I realized what might be easily, and sensibly, done, something which would be less embarrassing, something unlikely to have negative repercussions. I must call someone I knew, whom I could trust, someone intelligent and reliable, someone who, I was sure, would listen to me sympathetically and do her best to help me. Such a person might obtain tools, expeditiously enough, innocently enough, arousing no suspicions, at a hardware store. I had few, if any, friends, for I am particular in the choosing of friends, and who, after all, would be worthy of being my friend, but I had several acquaintances. I knew several of the girls who worked in the same building that I did. Indeed, I frequently lunched with some of them. One was quiet, plain Paula, short, and sweetly bodied, simply and conservatively dressed, who seemed to live much within herself, shy, serious Paula, who listened well, so patiently, Paula, who refrained from participating in our gossip, often so frivolous and cruel, Paula, who, of all things, read books. I, and, I am sure, several of the others, rather pitied Paula. She did not carry herself with elegance or style. Despite the prescriptions and expectations of the day, she seemed unconcerned with wit and verve, with projecting a culturally recommended image. Did she not know how to do so? Surely she must wish to do so. Why, then, did she not do so or, at least, strive to do so? Too, she was clearly uninformed of many things of obvious importance. She seemed unaware of which journalists and politicians, which motion-picture and television personalities, and such, were to be approved, and, as important, those which were to be disapproved. We were not sure, at all, in many areas, that she had the right views, opinions, and attitudes. She seemed to make up her own mind about things, naturally with dismal results. Worst perhaps, as I have hinted, she seemed deplorably uninformed of fashion. I did not think she knew one designer or house from another. Such ignorance was inconceivable. I do not think she was really stupid, but what can one expect of someone who reads books? Still I was sure I could trust Paula, certainly more than the others. I sensed this about her. She seemed different from the others, somehow deeper, or more sound, or more aware, than the others. I was sure I could count on her to be compassionate and understanding. I could make use of her. She would listen carefully, strive to be of any assistance possible, and could be depended upon to keep a secret. So I would call her, and, when she arrived, which she would, I was sure, acquaint her with my surprising, untoward predicament, and send her forth to obtain what tools might be appropriate to free my wrists.

How easily then might things proceed!

I looked down at the handcuffs, so large, thick, heavy, and plain. How clumsy, simple, and ugly they were. How disproportionate they seemed to my wrists. How unlike they would be from the light, lovely restraints, so attractive, and perhaps even more secure, designed with the enhancement of beauty in mind, in which I would later, frequently, find myself helplessly emplaced.

I must call Paula.

I was so distraught I feared I might stumble, were I to stand.

I crawled toward the telephone on the night stand near the bed. It was an awkward business, my wrists pinioned before me. But I could move, a bit at a time, reaching forth, again and again. Then I was at the phone. I reached up and placed it on the floor, before me.

Next I must find Paula's number.

This would be easy.

In the drawer to the night stand was a small notebook containing my personal numbers. It contained, amongst others, the numbers of my frequent luncheon companions. Once, early in our luncheons, held in one restaurant or another, but usually in the restaurant on the fourth floor of the building, we had exchanged numbers. We had supposed this might prove a convenience for our small group, if it might prove desirable to contact one another, as if we would ever be interested in doing so. Certainly, hitherto I had never used any of these numbers. But Paula's number, I recalled, would be amongst them.

It was only necessary, now, to call her. I was sure she would be accommodating. It was her way. Surely, too, she, poor, plain Paula, should be flattered to receive a call from me, for I was smart and chic, and I stood near the pinnacle of our small hierarchy. If she were otherwise engaged, or had other plans, she must change them. That must be clear. Yet I should tell her nothing. My tone would be pleasant and social, and betray no inkling of my distress. The matter should be as if no more than if I were thinking of her, and felt like chatting, which chat could then lead naturally to an invitation, and a proposed afternoon's outing. We could meet at my apartment, perhaps for coffee, first. I might then, she having arrived, reveal my discomfiture to her, and explain, as I could, what I needed. If necessary, over the phone, though I trusted it would not be necessary, I might give her some sense of my earnestness.

I reached to the drawer of the night stand.

At that moment I cried out, startled, for the phone, placed before me on the carpet, rang.

I lifted the receiver. It was Paula!

"I hope I am not disturbing you," she said.

"No," I said, "not at all."

"Are you all right?" she asked.

"Yes," I said. "Of course. Why do you ask?"

"Something strange has happened," she said.

"What?" I said.

"You sound different," she said.

"How so?" I asked.

"Upset," she said.

"No, no," I said. "I'm fine."

"Good," she said.

"It is nice of you to call," I said, struggling to speak calmly.

"I don't mean to bother you," she said. "But I thought I should call. Something strange has happened. A messenger delivered an envelope to me, only moments ago, and inside the envelope was a smaller envelope, with a note, that the smaller envelope was to be delivered to you. Do you know anything about this?"

"No," I said.

"Do you want me to open the envelope?" she asked.

"Is it a letter?" I asked.

"I do not think so," she said. "It seems to contain something, a small, solid object."

"Hold it up to the light," I said.

"The envelope is opaque," she said.

"What does it feel like?" I asked.

"I am not sure," she said.

"A key?" I said.

"I am not sure," she said.

"I lost a key," I said.

"It might be a key," she said.

"—to the lock on my suitcase," I said.

"It's not a flat key," she said.

"Please open the envelope," I said.

A minute or two later, Paula spoke again. "It is a key," she said. "I do not think it is a suitcase key."

"Bring it to my apartment, please, and hurry!" I begged.

"Are you all right?" Paula asked, again.

"Yes, yes!" I said. "Please hurry." I gave her my address.

"Why should someone give it to me, if it is yours?" asked Paula.

"Just bring it!" I pleaded.

"You are not all right," said Paula. "Something is wrong."

"Bring it," I said. "I will tell you all I know. I must speak to someone. I am afraid. I do not know what is going on!"

"Tell me, tell me, please," said Paula.

"You must tell no one," I said.

"You are afraid," said Paula.

"Hurry," I said. "I understand little of this, but I will tell you what I can."

"Should I call a doctor, an ambulance?" asked Paula, frightened.

"No, just hurry!" I said.

CHAPTER TWO

I fear," said Paula, "it is not all nonsense."

"It must be!" I demanded.

"Those are not nonsense," said Paula, pointing to the opened hand-cuffs lying on the kitchen counter.

We were sitting about the kitchen table.

"You believe me?" I asked, plaintively.

"Many would not," said Paula, "but I do."

"But surely you do not believe all this about another world, another planet, one secretly in our own system, shielded by the sun, concealed by gravitational adjustments, an Antichthon, a Counter-Earth?"

"It is hard to know what to believe," said Paula. "But the claims of a Counter-Earth have been familiar for millennia. There are difficult-to-explain signals, and many sightings, perhaps of ships harboring in unknown ports, not those of Terra, not those of Earth."

"Such things are mythical," I said.

"Perhaps," said Paula. "But who knows from what seeds myths might first have sprung? Perhaps the smoke of legend hints at the fire of distant, forgotten fact. Data is real. It may be diversely understood."

I had recounted to Paula, who had almost immediately freed me of the homely devices in which I was so helpless, the incident in the office, and the talk of slaves, of "pot girls," of "kettle-and-mat girls," and such. I had not, of course, recounted to Paula that I had been so character-ized by the surly, uncouth ruffian I had encountered in the office. She had listened intently, even breathlessly, her eyes shining. "It may be so," she had whispered. "How lovely, how meaningful, how glorious!" she whispered. "How fearful, how frightful, how horrifying!" I had exclaimed. "No, no," she had whispered. I had then recounted to her the incident on the beach, the rude conversation, the photographing, it done without my permission, I unwilling to be photographed, the speculation as to measurements, the use of the word 'kajira'. "Are you sure of the word?" she inquired, eagerly. "Yes," I said, "they mistook me for someone else. I told them my name was not 'Kajira' but 'Phyllis'."

"Oh, dear Phyllis," she said, "how I envy you! You may be amongst the kajirae and, as yet, know nothing of it."

"I told them my name was 'Phyllis'," I said.

"Why do you think you were put in handcuffs?" she asked.

"I do not know," I said.

"Perhaps to accustom you to helplessness," she said.

"I do not understand how the apartment could have been entered," I said. "The doors and windows were locked."

"There are devices," said Paula. "I have read of them."

"I sometimes have the sense that I am being watched," I said.

"Gorean slavers," said Paula, "often scout 'slave fruit', before it is picked."

"If there were such," I said, "doubtless."

"They choose carefully," she said. "They select for intelligence, beauty, and passion."

"I am highly intelligent," I said, "and obviously extremely beautiful. But I do not care for men."

"Slave fires," she said, "may be lit in the coldest of bellies, turning them helplessly needful, beggingly needful."

I feared this might be true.

Had I not dreamed of such need, of such helplessness? Could I be turned into such a needful, helpless thing?

Surely not!

Yet had I not longed for this?

"How helpless then," she said, "would a woman be!"

"Do not speak so," I begged.

"What could she be then," she said, "but a man's slave, the slave of men."

"I would not permit it," I said. "And who could respond to the men we know?"

"Your wishes in the matter need not be considered," she said. "And all men may not be such as those with whom we are disappointingly familiar. I am sure, dear Phyllis, your libido, rendered helpless, dominated and mastered, will respond overwhelmingly to the lust of masters."

"I understand little, if anything, of this," I said.

"I think they are considering you, Phyllis," she said, "for a Gorean collar."

"Do not be absurd," I said, uneasily.

"You might be fetching," she said, "slave clad, if clad, collared, and owned."

"I am a free woman," I said, angrily.

"I suspect so," said Paula, "but who knows what the future might hold."

"What do you know of these things?" I asked.

"I read, I think, I wonder," said Paula. "I am familiar with the Gorean world, as I suspect you are not."

"I have heard of it," I said, "a little."

"I have lived in the books," said Paula. "They have spoken to me. I have found myself barefoot in those green fields, I have glimpsed far horizons from the bow of a swift galley, knelt trembling before a master."

"In your imagination!" I said.

"Yes, alas, only so," she said.

"I did not know you were like this," I said.

"I have often wondered," she said, "if there is a Counter-Earth, traversing its orbit, plying its silent way about our star, a world with its own gods and beasts, its own seasons and tides, its own strifes and wars."

"Absurd," I said.

"If there was such a world," she said, "might it not hint its presence in a hundred ways, content even to be perceived as fiction?"

"Absurd!" I said, angrily.

"Strange beasts, unwilling to be seen, might prowl in surprising precincts," she said. "Reality might wear many concealments."

"If Gor is real," I said, "let it show itself, openly!"

"It, or its custodians, may not care to do so," she said. "What would be the value or purpose of such a disclosure? How would it benefit either world? Would it not shatter comfortable visions, disrupt cultures, shake civilizations, alarm and unsettle populations, produce social, economic, and intellectual chaos? No, it is better for Gor to conceal itself, to the extent it can; it is better for it to maintain its privacy, its reticence. It is better for all that way."

I looked away, angrily.

"Besides," she said, "perhaps it is not such a well-kept secret. I am sure, if it exists, that hundreds, perhaps thousands, on this world know of it, even have dealings with it."

"It does not exist," I said.

"Perhaps not," she said. "But you have had your experiences."

"There must be an alternative explanation for them," I said, desperately.

"Perhaps," she said, "but I am not sure of that. Indeed, I hope that your experiences are precisely what they seem to be. On this world I feel I am a stranger. For years, since I was a girl, I have dreamed of a richer, more honest, more beautiful, more natural world, and of strong, owning men, who would own me and treat me as the woman I am!"

"Do not speak so!" I cried, dismayed. "Do not dare to speak so!"

"Forgive me," she said.

"I am afraid," I said.

"Perhaps there are surveillance devices, even in your apartment," said Paula, looking about, "hidden cameras, secretly installed recording devices."

"Impossible," I said.

Paula sprang suddenly to her feet, wildly, hopefully.

"What are you doing?" I asked.

"I want to look!" she said.

She began where we were, in the kitchen, and then went to the living room, and then to the bedroom. She was concerned, thorough. She opened drawers, moved furniture, looked about lamps, looked behind chests.

I followed her, dismayed.

"Here," she said, "perhaps here!"

"Paula!" I cried.

"No, nothing!" she said, at last, in frustration.

"There is nothing, Paula," I insisted.

"Nothing," she whispered, "nothing," tears in her eyes.

"Nothing," I said.

"But perhaps?" she said.

"No," I said.

"Do we know?" she asked.

"Nothing," I said.

She looked about.

"Paula?" I said.

She lifted her head to the ceiling.

What was it but a flat, opaque, plain surface, a familiar, meaningless, inert expanse?

"Paula?" I said.

"*La kajira*!" she cried.

"Paula!" I said.

"*La kajira!*" she cried again, and then, sobbing, cried so again and again, to one side of the living room and then to the other, and even to the carpeted floor, and then, once more, she lifted her head to the ceiling. "I pronounce myself kajira!" she cried.

"What are you doing?" I said.

"I am begging for the privilege of being allowed to submit myself to a master, to be the slave that I know in my heart I am."

"Paula!" I cried, in protest.

"I long for a man to put me in his collar," she said. "I want to be marked. I long to wear the chains of my master. I want to submit to men, to kneel before them, and serve, and love, and please them!"

"What sort of woman are you?" I cried.

"The one that I am," she said.

"We are alone," I said.

"I fear so," she said.

"There are no devices," I said.

"I fear not," she said, softly. "And why would they need such things? And they would scarcely wish to risk their discovery."

"Your secret is safe with me," I said.

"What secret?" she said.

"What you said," I said.

"Alas," she said, "that the world is such, that need, and wanting, and honesty, and truth must be concealed."

We returned to the kitchen table.

I was afraid she would leave.

"I will tell no one," I said.

"I feel at ease," said Paula, "to have confessed it. I am now at peace with myself. I have admitted to myself what I have long known, and what I have long longed to express."

"Do not fear," I said. "I will tell no one."

Paula looked at me.

"Why do you smile?" I asked.

"Because I know you, Phyllis," she said. "You are bright, but self-centered and shallow. Even now you are thinking of the attention you will receive, the gratification you will derive, from regaling the other girls with an account of what you regard as a juicy tidbit, fit for dessert gossip, at one of our luncheons."

"No, never!" I said.

"Your promise," she said, "is worthless, however intent you may be now to keep it. You can no more hold a promise than a sieve water, you can no more resist the temptation to gossip than straw, seeking one excuse or another, can resist flame."

"I assure you that that is not so," I averred.

"Perhaps I should have left you in those," she smiled, nodding toward the handcuffs reposing on the kitchen counter.

"No!" I said. "I am your friend. You are my friend."

"I like you," said Paula. "I am your friend. But you are not my friend. You are not capable of being a friend. Perhaps one day you will be capable of being a friend. One might hope so. Perhaps once you have learned to kneel, and lick and kiss a whip, and feel metal on your limbs, and know yourself owned and helpless, you will be capable of friendship. One does not know."

"I see," I said.

"Forgive me," she said.

"Perhaps now," I said, angrily, "I will tell! Now perhaps I will let the others know what sort of woman you are!" Then I grew frightened. "Or would you deny it?" I asked.

"I suppose few would believe it of me," said Paula, "but I would not deny it."

"Then," I said, "you are at my mercy."

"Oh?" she said.

"Yes," I said, "you must do what I wish!"

"Or you would tell?"

"Yes," I said.

"In any event," she said, "I must do what you wish."

"Why?" I asked.

"Because of what I am," she said.

"I do not understand," I said.

"I have learned what I am," she said. "I have found myself. I have confessed myself before another. The war is done."

"I might not tell," I said.

"It does not matter to me, one way or another," she said, "not any longer. But I would warn you that in denouncing me you may be denouncing others, as well, despite what they might profess. You may not know those to whom you speak. Do you know their wants, their fantasies, their dreams and needs? I do not think myself unique. Many, perhaps all, have visited, so to speak, the shores of Gor, even if they did not know the continent on which they touched, nor the names of its ports."

"I do not understand," I said.

"We are women. We need a master."

"No," I said. "No!"

"I wonder if a master would want you," she said.

"I am beautiful!" I said.

"It requires more than beauty to be an acceptable slave," she said. "Perhaps you would be fed to sleen."

"What is a sleen?" I asked.

"Hope that you will never learn," she said.

"I will never be a slave!" I said.

"So have said many who are now in their collars," she said.

"Why would a master not want me?" I asked, angrily.

"Do not fear," she said, "you would be kept anyway, as a slave."

"No!" I said.

"Masters keep their slaves," she said. "They want them. Slaves are not to be freed, no more than other beasts."

"Paula!" I protested.

"It is said that only a fool frees a slave girl," she said.

"'Slave girl'!" I said, angrily.

"But one such as you would be kept," she said.

"Oh?" I said, archly.

"Yes," she said, "collared, you will stay in a collar."

"Why?" I asked, angrily.

"Because you belong in a collar," she said.

"No!" I said.

"And once your slave fires have been ignited," she said, "you would fear only that you might be freed. You would treasure your collar. You would kiss your fingertips and press them gratefully to the brand that marks you slave. You would beg to be kept."

"Not I!" I said.

"But do not fear," she said, "you would not be freed, but would merely be sold, or given away, as might be any other domestic animal."

"How horrifying!" I cried.

"We are women," she said.

"How dare you speak so!" I chided.

"You are pretty, Phyllis," she said.

"Beautiful!" I insisted.

"But what are you good for, really?" she asked.

"'Good for'?" I asked.

"Yes," she said, "what are you good for, really? Do you not know yourself? Are you so far from yourself, so invisible to yourself? Have you not thought about yourself, and what you are?"

"I need not do so," I said. "I am popular and witty. I have a good education. I wear clothes well. I am a good dancer. I am desirable. Men like me. Women envy me. I am intelligent and beautiful. I am special."

"Forgive me, dear Phyllis," she said.

"For what?" I asked.

"You are the most worthless, and meaningless young woman I know," she said. "You are vain and shallow, self-absorbed, pretentious, rootless, a shred of paper in a park, cast about pointlessly by the wind. You have no purpose, no depth. Your views are superficial and duplicative. Your values are cheap and gaudy, the predictable plastic lies produced for mass consumption. Your relationships to others, such as they are, are dictated by instrumental concerns, those of convenience and profit, by what use they might be to you to further your own projects and enhance your own meretricious self-image. There is no authenticity or genuineness in you. You are a manufactured article, an artifact, not even aware of the machine that created you, and its purpose in doing so, that you might mindlessly consume goods and fuel the engines of others. There is no more meaning, purpose, or weight to you than to a handful of confetti. You are essentially nothing."

"Paula," I whispered, aghast.

"But perhaps you would be good for something, a little something, as a slave," she said. "It is hard to tell."

Paula rose, and turned toward the door.

"Don't leave me," I said.

"Then," she said, "someone might get some good out of you."

"Don't go!" I begged.

"You are a paper doll," she said, "something cute, and pretty, which might be dressed in a hundred ways, but a thing of but one dimension, a thing lacking substance."

"Stay a bit!" I begged. "I do not want you to go. I am afraid."

Paula looked to the door of the apartment. "I am afraid, too," she said.

"Stay, a little," I said.

"I should be leaving," she said.

"Don't go!" I said.

"Call the police," she said.

"They would think I was mad or hysterical," I said. "They would not believe me."

"Tell them then only that you are afraid of someone," she said.

"But who?" I said.

"Tell them you do not know," she said.

"They might protect me for a time," I said, "but not indefinitely."

"And," said Paula, "if there is anything to this, slavers need only be patient, and await their opportunity."

"I am afraid," I said.

"I fear," said Paula, "if they want you, they will have you. It is a business with them. We are women, and not their exalted free women, women possessing Home Stones, who would despise us even more than the men, but women with whom they can do as they please, Earth women, barbarian women, women to be trained, and bought and sold. To the slavers, we are no more than objects, no more than stock, no more than cattle of a sort."

"Stay," I said, plaintively.

"I must be going," she said.

"Then I will tell your shameful secret!" I said. "I will ruin your reputation! I will force you, in misery, to lose your job, to change your work, perhaps to leave the city, and state!"

"There is nothing shameful in being a woman, and having needs, and desiring to serve a master," she said.

"Stay with me, if only for a bit, or I will tell!" I said.

"Poor Phyllis," she said. "It does not matter to me anymore, one way or the other, not any longer."

"I am sorry," I said. "I will not tell! I will not tell! But stay, please stay!"

"I am sorry," she said.

"But," I said, desperately, frightened, "earlier you said, I remember, that in any event, despite whether I would tell or not, that you must do what I wish!"

Paula seemed struck by that.

"Yes," she said, softly. "That is true. I now know myself. I have acknowledged what I am. I will stay."

"If only for a little bit," I said, desperately.

"As you wish," she said, softly.

Poor plain Paula, I thought.

"I'll make coffee," I said.

"No," she said. "I will do it."

I watched while Paula busied herself with the coffee. After a time, the bright, stirring aroma of coffee excited and charmed the kitchen.

"Would you like cream and sugar?" asked Paula.

"Both," I said.

"May I drink, as well?" she asked.

"Certainly," I said, puzzled.

Then, to my astonishment, she bent down, and placed both cups on the floor, each wrapped in a napkin. She then knelt, by the table, and lifted one of the cups, wrapped in its napkin, to me, holding it with both hands.

"What are you doing?" I said.

"You are a free woman," she said.

"I do not understand," I said.

"Mistress," she said.

I took the cup with both hands, it wrapped in the napkin, and put it on the table.

"'Mistress'?" I said.

"All free women are as mistress to me," she said, "as all free men are as master to me."

"You are kneeling," I said.

"As is fitting," she said. "A slave often kneels before free persons. It is my honor and joy to serve a free person."

"I am Phyllis," I said.

"You are free. You are Mistress," she said. "A slave may not address a free person by their name."

"You are not a slave," I said.

"I am a slave, Mistress," she said. "I have said the words."

I sipped the coffee, brushing the napkin aside, holding the cup by the handle.

"May I drink, Mistress?" she asked.

"Certainly," I said.

"Thank you, Mistress," she said, and lifted the cup, wrapped in its napkin, to her lips.

"Sit beside me," I said.

"I dare not, Mistress," she said, head down, frightened. "I am a slave, in her place, at the feet of Mistress."

"You are not a slave," I said.

"When I said '*La kajira*'," she said, "I became a female slave."

"I said that on the beach," I said.

"Oh?" she said.

"Yes," I said.

"Then it is done," she said. "The words were spoken."

"I do not understand," I said.

"Then you, too, are a female slave," she said.

"I did not know what they meant," I said.

"But it is done," she said. "The words were spoken, Phyllis. You, too, are now a female slave."

"No," I said.

"You, too, should be on your knees," she said.

CHAPTER THREE

The large, heavy hand was clasped firmly over my mouth. My head was pulled back. I was helpless.

"This one," said the fellow holding me, "thinks she is going to be troublesome. Gag her."

"She looks pretty, squirming," said the second man.

"Shall we remove the nightgown?" asked the third man.

"No," said the fellow in whose grasp I was, "she is not of great interest. That can be done later."

Tears sprang to my eyes.

"She might have promise," said the second man, "given slave gruel and the whip."

I could not speak, so held.

Paula was kneeling to the side, frightened. When the men had appeared, so suddenly, the bolts flashed to the side, she had gone instantly to her knees, startled, her eyes wide.

Had she welcomed this intrusion?

Why had she not screamed, not run?

I had been so startled I had not had time to scream. Almost immediately I had been seized, turned, and the massive hand clapped over my mouth.

Instantly I knew myself helpless, the prisoner of such strength!

I looked wildly at Paula.

Even now, no one held her!

Why did she not scream, cry out, run?

Did she not see the plea in my eyes, that she should scream, run?

"Shall I use a readied gag?" asked the second man, "a slave bit?"

"No," said he in whose grasp I was, "let her know that materials suitable for rendering a woman helpless are conveniently at hand. Perhaps she will find that instructive."

"What of this one?" asked the third man, gesturing to Paula.

I, helpless, struggling, wanted to cry out to Paula, to rise up, run to the door, scream, anything. But she remained kneeling, trembling.

"Let her alone," said the man holding me. "She is clearly intelligent. Certainly more so than this one."

"Shall we leave her clothed?" asked the third man.

"For now," said he in whose grasp I was.

"She looks extremely interesting," said the third man.

"I look forward to seeing her stripped," said the second man.

"She should bring us good coin," said the brute, appreciatively, in whose arms I was helpless.

Paula seemed startled.

"Plain Paula," I thought to myself. "Surely she was too short, too widely hipped, too amply bodied! Did she not dress poorly? Did she not lack flair, and dash?"

I could see now that the second man had gone into the bedroom and was rummaging through drawers. In a bit he had returned to the living room, some cloth in his hand, and, apparently, two pairs of my nylon stockings.

The heavy hand was removed from my mouth, and I opened my mouth widely, wildly, to scream, but, at the same time, a wadding of cloth, silken panties, was thrust into my mouth, stifling any sound, and a moment thereafter it was bound in place by loops of two of my nylon stockings, drawn back tightly between my teeth.

"There," said the fellow, standing back, who had gagged me.

I shook my head, protestingly, tears in my eyes.

My protests, muted, scarcely audible, were unavailing.

How frightful it was then, to be silenced by the will of others. This was the first time I had had that experience. I had never been gagged before. I would grow familiar with such an experience. And how conveniently it had been done, and with familiar, approved garmenture! Did we not, in a sense, then, carry our own bonds with us? I had been effectively silenced, and with my own garments! Later, of course, a mere look, or word, would silence me. Indeed, I would soon learn to request permission before I might dare to speak.

Men would decide if and when a woman, or, better, a woman such as I, would be permitted to speak.

I was then put to my belly on the carpet, and my hands were taken behind me, and fastened together, closely, by means of one member of the second pair of nylon stockings. My ankles were then crossed and bound together by the last stocking. I tried to turn. I felt a man's shoe on my back, pressing down, pinning me to the floor. "Lie still, kajira," said a voice.

That word, again. Gagged, I could not even disabuse them of the notion that my name was not Kajira, but Phyllis.

I lay still. I could not part my hands, nor my ankles. The man's foot was then removed from my back.

How dare he treat me so? I lay prone, bound, hand and foot, gagged, helpless. How I was treated! What did he think I was? Did he think I was nothing, a slave?

How could they be so stupid, I wondered, to think Paula was more interesting, or attractive, than I!

What fools they were!

There was no comparison.

I was far more beautiful!

"It is early," said the largest man, he who had held me, he whom I took to be first amongst the three men. "We will wait a time, and depart after dark."

"There is coffee," said the second man, glancing into the kitchen, noticing the pertinent vessel.

"Good," said the third man.

At a gesture Paula rose, hurried to the kitchen, and knelt beside the stove.

The men then followed her, repairing to the kitchen.

I was dragged by the arm onto the linoleum of the kitchen and thrust to one side, by the table.

"May I speak?" asked Paula, kneeling by the stove.

"Yes," said the second man.

"Gor?" she asked, timidly.

"Yes," he said.

"*La kajira*," she said.

"We know," he said. "We heard."

"I beg to be collared, marked, and mastered," she said.

"You will be," he said.

"Thank you," she said, softly, "—Master."

"Now," said the large fellow, he who had held me, "serve coffee."

"Yes, Master," she said.

"Appropriately," he said.

"Yes, Master," said Paula, and rose to busy herself with this task.

Shortly thereafter, having ascertained the preferences of our captors, she served the coffee to them, as she had to me, kneeling, lifting the cups.

Is that how a slave serves, I wondered, so subserviently, so submissively?
Did she not know she was the same as a man?

Or was she, or I, the same as a man?

What if we were not, profoundly, really?

"How is it that a beauty like you, kajira, is keeping company with such
a mediocrity?" asked the third man. I felt his shoe nudge me in the ribs.

"Oh, Master," she protested, "do not speak so! She is not a mediocrity! She is my friend. She is bright. She is chic. She wears clothes
well. She is extremely beautiful! She is popular. She may be the most
beautiful woman I know."

The third man laughed.

"Now, now," said the second man, "she is not that bad."

"A pot girl," said the third man.

"We would not have picked her up," said the leader, "were it not
for Kurik. She is the one he called a 'bitch'. Apparently he found her
annoying, displeasing, or such, and so decided to have her picked up
and sent to Gor."

"She will be less displeasing there," said the second man.

"She will learn her sex there, its meaning and uses," said the leader,
"or be fed to sleen."

I had heard Paula refer to "sleen" before, but she had not clarified
the reference. I gathered that, for some reason, she had thought it better not to do so.

"It seems a shame to waste a capsule on her," said the third man.

"Kurik was annoyed," said the leader.

"You are too critical," said the second man. "Many kettle-and-mat
girls, and pot girls, are extremely attractive in their way, and they are as
begging, and hot, and helpless, on the mat as a two-silver-piece pleasure slave."

"We need not use a capsule on her," said the third man. "We could
keep her in a girl cage on the ship."

"We will let Kurik decide," said the leader.

"I think she has promise," said the second man. "Consider the
ankles, the wrists."

"Her homeliness," said the leader, "has nothing to do with her coloring, her figure, or such, for many men are found of such a configuration, but with her character, her impatience, her personality, her vanity,
her nastiness, her pride."

"The whip and slave gruel," said the second man.

"Yes," said the leader, "she might have possibilities."

"Kurik is not a fool," said the second man. "He might have been annoyed, but I am sure there was more to it than that. Certainly he would not recommend that every woman who is a nuisance, or bother, should be transported to Gor. He is a good judge of collar meat."

"Possibly," said the third man.

"Well," said the leader, with satisfaction, looking down at Paula, "the afternoon has not been wasted."

"Indeed not," said the third man. "We are fortunate. How often, when one stoops to pick up a pretty pebble, a common gem, will one find a diamond, as well?"

I struggled, in fury.

"Lie still," I was told.

"More coffee," suggested the leader.

"Yes, Master," said Paula.

I lay on the linoleum, helpless. Later, Paula knelt, humbly, head down, to the side.

The hands on the kitchen clock moved, sometimes it seemed slowly, sometimes rapidly.

The men played cards, at the kitchen table.

It was growing dark outside. After dark, I feared that Paula and I were to be taken somewhere. I was much aware of the time. I was much afraid. After dark, late, a metal-and-leather apparatus was drawn forth from a small case. It had a bit. It was put on Paula, from behind, and fastened in place. I do not know if they feared she might, at last, cry out, on the street, or they merely wished to familiarize her with her helplessness in a slave bit. I was angry! How willingly she submitted, even eagerly, to her bitting! I was drawn upright, rudely, to my knees, still in my bonds. They let me stay that way for a few moments, they looking down at me, perhaps that I would better know myself kneeling, and bound, before men. I put my head down. My ankles were freed, and I was drawn to my feet. My improvised gag was removed, and then I, too, was bitted. The device was forced into my mouth, and thrust back between my teeth. It locked behind the back of my neck. I realized that I could not tear it from my mouth, even had my hands been free. I wondered if slaves sometimes served in such devices, perhaps at suppers with free women present. Well then would they be reminded that they were slaves, and well then would the free women be reminded, to their pleasure, of their difference from, and their superiority to, slaves, such lowly, humble, marketable, negligible beasts. I would later learn that there were several varieties of slave bits, which differ considerably, aesthetically, and in comfort, while being uniform in their efficiency, that with respect to rendering a slave incapable of speech. A major difference amongst such bits is with respect to their closure. That in which Paula had been placed, and that in which I was shortly thereafter placed, once snapped shut, could be opened only by a tool or key. In that sense they were much like slave collars. Such bits are commonly used when one or both hands of a girl are free. Most bits, however, indeed almost all I would become familiar with, are intended, like the common gag, to be used with a bound or brace-leted slave who, given her securing, cannot reach the device. In such a case, a keyed lock, most often, is not deemed necessary. It might, of course, be used in some cases, as when one wishes to preclude certain possibilities, say, a secured slave's responses, once relieved of the device, to a stranger's questions. Also, any attempt to adjust, ease, or remove a bit or gag is cause for discipline. Accordingly, gagged or bitted slaves, even if their hands are free, would seldom dare to touch the gag or device. It was put on them by a master. Thus, they must wait until the master sees fit to relieve them of the impediment. Such things help a girl better understand her slavery. The keyed devices in which Paula and I were placed were doubtless intended to make it impossible for us, should we attempt to do so, to dislodge the bits. My wrists were still bound behind me, tightly, with one of my nylon stockings. A handcuff was snapped about Paula's right wrist, and she was drawn toward me. The other cuff was then snapped about my left wrist, after which I was unbound. We then stood before the men, bitted, and handcuffed together, her right wrist to my left wrist. The cuffs were the same as those in which I had earlier awakened. We were then hooded, blankets thrown over us, and belted about our necks.

"You will be fed in the van," said the leader.

"Slave biscuits," laughed the third man.

The simplicity of his remark startled me, and dismayed me. I did not fully understand it, but I was frightened. Slave biscuits! Did he think I was an animal? To be sure, when I was hungry, I would learn to accept such fare, even beg for it.

"The trip," said the leader, "will take several hours. There will be a sheet on the floor of the van. I trust you will be comfortable. You may have to be caged for a time in the warehouse, as additional stock is expected."

I was not stock, I wished to protest, but could not do so, as I was bitted. And, too, I feared I was now stock.

CHAPTER FOUR

In the van, after the first hour, we were unhooded and unbitted. We were given small, thick disks of what I took to be some sort of unleavened bread.

"Eat," said one of our captors, who rode with us in the back of the van.

We obeyed.

We were given water, as well.

We were not permitted speech.

We were kept handcuffed together.

This very much displeased me, for I had taken a great dislike to Paula. She was not more attractive than I! I had rather scorned her, and even felt sorry for her before. Now I resented her. One needed only examine the models in the fashion magazines, watch television commercials, watch beauty pageants, attend to the standardized ideals of womanhood promoted in our culture, so much at odds with the normal, typical woman, to recognize the naivety and ignorance of our captors. They knew no more about beauty than sculptors and painters, from ancient Greece and Rome to the Renaissance, to the Eighteenth and Nineteenth Century, and so on. But, too, if she was really so beautiful, I was not that different from her, really! I suppose she was intelligent, but surely not more intelligent than I. She could not be too intelligent; she read books. There was likely to be little there, in such reading, having to do with enhancing your appearance, improving your popularity, manipulating others, advancing your career, or such.

"May we speak, Master?" asked Paula.

"No," he said.

"Well, I will speak," I informed him.

"Do you wish to wear a slave bit?" he asked.

"No," I said, "no!"

I had had more than enough of that hideous device. I would do much to avoid it. I would be very obedient. I would try to be pleasing. I would smile. If worse came to worst, I might even let one of those insensitive brutes kiss me.

"In another hour," said the fellow, after a time, glancing at his watch, "we will arrive at the embarkation point. You will be briefly housed there, with others, in a well-lit subterranean warehouse, prior to your shipping. You will not be shipped immediately, as other merchandise is currently *en route* to the embarkation point. You will receive a briefing, a short orientation, such that you will understand what you now are and what you are now for, and some preliminary training. We want you to survive your first week on Gor."

"Gor!" I thought. "Surely he does not expect us to believe that there is such a place, supposedly another planet, supposedly another world!"

"Your serious training will take place in one of several houses," he said. "We supply such houses. Some houses conduct their own sales; others commonly have arrangements with independent markets."

I shuddered.

"Are you cold?" he asked.

I nodded. I wore only the silk nightgown.

He removed his jacket, and put it about me.

We then remained silent, as before. We had not been permitted to speak.

The van sped on.

CHAPTER FIVE

The van had slowed, and turned, and was now jolting over a rough surface. We drove for some twenty or thirty minutes. There were apparently dips in the road. We occasionally heard branches brush the sides and roof of the vehicle.

The van stopped.

"We must clear the gate," said the fellow with us. "There are hidden surveillance cameras, the fence is charged."

I assumed that this, the clearing or whatever it might be, would be done from the outside, or that the men in the cab would attend to it. Certainly our captor showed no indication of leaving us alone in the van. Unattended, even handcuffed together, might we not have attempted flight?

But I was afraid that Paula, even given such an opportunity, might have dallied, or, if she ran, it would have been merely for my sake, that I might not have been impeded.

Did she long to be on a chain? Did she hope to belong to a man, categorically, as no more than his possession?

He lifted the lid of a box to his left.

I did not understand this.

We heard a creaking, as of the swinging of two large objects, presumably the leaves of a gate.

The man with us reached into the box to his left, and withdrew two objects, apparently of pliant, folded leather.

The van moved a little ahead, and then stopped again.

One of the two men in the cab, I gathered, had left the vehicle.

"We have cleared the gate," said the man with us. He shook out the two objects he had removed from the box to his left. They were leather and sacklike; each had a short belt threaded through leather belt loops. I noted, as well, on each object, two rings, and what appeared to be a small lock of some sort.

I was uneasy.

We heard the creaking sound again, followed by a sound of joining and locking metal, and a rattle of chain.

"You are going to be hooded," said the man with us. "Hold still."

The leather, sacklike thing was drawn over my head, and, with the belt, drawn shut under my chin. It was apparently buckled shut. Then I heard a tiny sound of metal, and the click of a small lock.

I could see nothing. I felt helpless. I wanted to scream with fear. I put my right hand to the apparatus, fumbling at the buckle behind my neck.

"Put your hand down, kajira," he said. "You cannot remove it. It is locked on you."

I would soon grow accustomed to such devices, and how helpless I would be in them.

I lowered my hand. My name was not 'Kajira'. It was 'Phyllis', 'Phyllis'!

I could clearly hear Paula being served with a similar device.

A moment or two later the fellow who had left the vehicle returned. We heard the door of the cab close.

The van then lurched ahead, again.

A minute or two later it stopped, again, and, a moment later, we sensed the fellows in the cab leave the vehicle.

I felt the jacket removed from my shoulders. I felt chilly. I wore only the nightgown. My knees were drawn up, as I sat on the van floor. I was barefoot. I supposed our captor then donned the jacket.

Shortly thereafter we heard the gate at the back of the van lifted. I felt cold air rush into the vehicle. It might still be dark. I did not know. I shivered.

"Two," said a voice.

"On your feet, kajirae," said our captor. "Move to the door; you will be lifted to the walkway."

I moved gingerly toward the opening, Paula drawn hesitantly, cautiously, after me, by her right wrist.

I was taken into someone's arms, powerful, masculine arms, and lifted from the van, and placed on a wooden surface. Almost simultaneously, my left wrist fastened to her right wrist, Paula, doubtless similarly in someone's arms, was deposited beside me.

I heard the fellow who had been with us in the van descend to the walkway. "You are going to be ankleted," he said, "placed in numbered anklets. Do not try to remove the anklets. You will not be able to do so.

They will be locked on you. We will keep track of you by means of the numbers. They will identify you in our records, where your hair and eye color, your measurements, and such, will be recorded. It is important to keep track of one's stock. If it is helpful, you may begin to think of yourselves as what you now are, objects, or animals, stock, only that. You no longer have names, unless we choose to give you names. I wish you well, sweet beasts. May you find yourselves well collared, and subject to the whips of strong masters."

How helpless we were, where we knew not, hooded and handcuffed together.

"This way," said a voice, and I felt a hand grasp my upper right arm.

We were conducted along a wooden walkway. I could hear the shoes, or boots, of the men on the boards. We were then stopped. I heard the sound of a key in a lock, and a hasp being freed from its staple. Shortly thereafter I heard a door, I think a wooden door, swung back, and we were led within what I supposed might be a shed. The floor was of wood, as had been the walkway. Then we were stopped again. The next sound I heard seemed incongruous with the others. It did not fit in with the apparent primitiveness, or rurality, I had assumed characterized my surroundings.

"Step ahead," said the fellow with us.

I then felt, surprising me, carpeting under my feet, and sensed, below that, a metal surface.

I gasped, startled.

"Steady," said the male voice.

The elevator was descending.

"The holding area is underground," said the man, "some floors below. Do not be concerned. It is large, well-lit, pleasant, warm, comfortable."

After a bit, the elevator stopped.

I heard a door, or panel, slide to the side.

"Move ahead," said the male voice.

We left the elevator.

"Kneel," said the male voice, "your heads to the floor."

I knelt down, and put my head to the floor.

The handcuffs were removed from us, but my hands were drawn up, behind my back. Metal encircled my wrists. I heard two small, decisive clicks. I jerked at my wrists, but could not part them. They were fastened in place, closely together, behind my back. It was the first time I had been placed in such things. I would grow familiar with them. They are designed for women. Many are plain, but many, too, are lovely, designed, like jewelry, to set off, and enhance, not only the utter helplessness, but the beauty of their occupant. So I wore, for the first time, though I did not know it, slave bracelets. I heard two similar clicks, to my left, and I gathered that Paula was similarly secured.

I felt something of metal, heavy and sturdy, put about my left ankle, and snapped shut. A moment later, to my left, I heard a similar sound.

"They are ankleted," said a man.

"Let us examine the catch," said another.

"Kneel up," said a third man.

I obeyed.

I felt hands about my neck, from behind. The lock was undone, and the hood was unbuckled, and then pulled away.

I looked wildly about, blinking against the light, my eyes half closed, kneeling, my hands confined behind my back.

It was a large, rectangular area, uncarpeted, low-ceilinged, lit with fluorescent light. About its periphery, as I was facing, were several doors, doubtless leading to other halls, or rooms. Behind me, though I did not realize it at the time, were several cells, with closely set bars. There were also, here and there, some small kennels or cages, in which I would suppose dogs, or other animals, might be confined. Occasionally, too, some chains dangled down from the low ceiling.

"This one is a beauty," said a voice.

"Of course, I was a beauty," I thought. "Doubtless they had seldom seen a woman so beautiful!"

I lifted my head, arrogantly.

"But it was mine to withhold, or bestow, as I might," I thought. "It would open doors for me. It was my device, fortune, and weapon. Men, the smitten fools, strove to please me. It could be exploited, to my advantage. I had often done so, as a matter of routine and practice, in minor matters, biding my time, awaiting the special opportunity, which must eventually appear, the wealthiest, most handsome, most charming suitor. I could auction it off, when it pleased me, so to speak, to the highest bidder. When one has beauty, what more is needed?"

But I knelt on a cement floor, barefoot, clad only in a nightgown, my hands fastened behind me!

"Marvelous," said one of the men.

"Of course!" I thought.

"What is your name?" asked one of the men.

"Whatever Masters please," said Paula.

The men were not regarding me! They had gathered about Paula, plain, shy Paula!

"Two, silver," said one of the men.

"On a first sale?" asked another.

"Why not?" said the first.

"What of the other one?" asked a fellow, looking toward me.

"Copper tarsks," said a man.

"She is not bad," said another.

"She may do," said another, "once she has been taught her collar."

I wanted to cry out with indignation, and rage, but I dared not speak. We had been warned to silence. These men were of the sort a woman knows she must obey.

At that time I did not realize that I would, indeed, and soon, be taught my collar, indeed, would be well taught my collar.

"She is the one Kurik said was a bitch," said one of the men.

"What is a 'bitch'?" asked another of the men, who seemed to have some sort of accent.

He was answered by a phrase I did not understand, as it seemed to be in a language I did not recognize.

"Oh," said the one who had asked the question, seemingly satisfied.

"Are you a bitch?" asked the fellow who had answered the first fellow's question.

"No!" I said.

"Lying is not permitted to one such as you," he said.

"I do not think I am a bitch," I said. "I hope I am not a bitch."

I recalled that the fellow who had appeared unexpectedly in the office, that warm afternoon, near closing time, when the shades were drawn against the light and heat, had dared to use that expression of me. How rude, how insulting! And then I recalled, further, uneasily, that he informed me that a whip could take that out of a woman.

"Is it true," asked the fellow with the accent, "that when Kurik appeared before you, you did not immediately fall to your knees?"

"Yes," I whispered.

"Do not be concerned," said one of the men. "She is a stupid, spoiled woman of Earth. She did not know any better."

"She must learn quickly," said the fellow with the accent.

"She will," he was assured.

"More amusingly," said another, "she struck Kurik."

"Surely not," said the fellow with the accent.

"I wish I had seen it," said another.

"And her hand was not cut off?" asked the man with the accent.

"She thought herself a free woman," said a man.

"Mistakenly," said the man with an accent.

"True," said another. "One can look at her, and see that she is a slave. Regard her face, and lineaments."

"She knew no better," said a man. "Let her keep both hands. She will then be better able to please a master in the thousand modalities of the kajira."

"Let us chain and lash her now," said the man with the accent.

"She did not then know she was a slave," said a man.

"Many females do not," said another.

"But they are of Earth," said the man with the accent.

"Even so," said another.

"Very well," said the man with the accent. "Put them in a cell, cell six, with the others."

"Stand up," said a man. "Turn about."

We stood and turned, and I gasped, for I saw a row of cells, which had been behind us, and, here and there, some small cages or kennels, empty. In some of the cells, I could see some young women. I was very conscious then of the confinement of my wrists, and the heavy metal band locked on my left ankle.

"This way," said one of the men.

At the door of the cell our impediments, the bracelets, were removed, and we were ushered within. The door was then shut behind us, and I turned, and grasped the bars, looking out, across the large, plain room.

I did not know if we might speak or not. We had not been told.

CHAPTER SIX

The fellow approached the cell door.

"Step back," he said.

There were five in the cell, other than Paula and myself. We were all clothed, to one degree or another. Paula wore a skirt, blouse, and sweater. She had apparently drawn on this attire quickly, in order to hurry to my apartment, in response to my unusual call. It seemed she did not care much how she might look on the street. She had, as I have earlier indicated, little sense of fashion. It is hard to wear a blouse, skirt, and sweater smartly. She had not even used lipstick. Had I responded to such a call, if choosing to do so, I would have done so more particularly. Of the five others in the cell two wore jeans and sweatshirts, perhaps ill at ease with their femininity, or perhaps fearing it, or feeling it appropriate to discount it, or protest it. Their garments would have been more appropriate to adolescent males. Another wore what I supposed might be a maid's uniform, black with white trim; I wondered from what penthouse or estate she might have been seized or obtained; perhaps her employer had hired a succession of such girls, to be observed, and examined, and, if found satisfactory, to be remanded here; the fourth wore a chic, expensive business jacket, with skirt, rather as I myself commonly wore to work; and the fifth wore the remains of an evening dress. It had been muchly torn from her. My nightgown, I suspect, was more concealing.

We moved back, toward the rear of the cell and the man unlocked, and opened, the cell door.

A few yards away, before the cell, facing it, there were four other men, two of whom carried switches, useful in the disciplining of women. The fellow who had opened the cell then joined them, and all were facing us.

"Emerge," he called, "and form a line, facing us, abreast."

We left the cell, and formed the line, as we had been told. I looked about, and could see the elevator door. I did not know how many floors we had descended to reach this level.

Suddenly one of the girls, she who wore the chic business jacket with skirt, cried out, miserably, ran to the elevator, fumbled about it, and pounded on it, futilely.

"You lack the key," called the fellow who had opened the cell door, who seemed to be the leader, or spokesman for the others.

Then, after a few moments, she put her head against the elevator door, sobbing, and was still.

"There is no escape," she was informed. "There are barriers, guards, gates, bars. Outside, there are dogs. The area is remote. You might die at the fence."

She turned to regard him, dully, defeated, her cheeks stained.

"You are a female," he called to her. "That is the single most important thing about you. From that, all else follows. Return to your place in line, directly and obediently."

The girl did so.

We then stood quietly, uneasily, regarding the fellow.

"You are before men," said the fellow. "Get on your knees."

All of us knelt, except the woman who had run to the elevator. I was suffused with strange, indescribable emotions.

In the kitchen, on the linoleum, I had been on my knees before the men, for a few moments, but this seemed quite different. That had been, however disturbing, little more than a brief transition between the attitude of a prone, bound prisoner, and that of a wrist-tied, standing prisoner. It was natural that I would have been knelt, that the bonds on my ankles could be removed, making it possible for me to stand upright, before my bitting. There had been little or nothing of anything expected, fitting, or institutionalized in that posture.

This, however, was quite different.

"You are before men," had said the fellow. "Get on your knees."

Why should we, women, or, at least, our sort of women, be on our knees before men?

I recalled the brute from the office, he spoken of as Kurik. "Why are you standing?" he had asked, and had informed me that, as he was a free man, I should have been kneeling before him, as I was a slave. I had denied that I was a slave, of course.

"Do you think I do not know a slave when I see one? You lack only the collar," he had said.

"Get out!" I had said.

"You might look fetching in a slave rag, or a slave tunic," he had said, "and, perhaps better, clad only in your collar."

"Get out!" I had said.

I was kneeling.

I was shaken, half fainting. I had never felt such emotions, such feelings. I was kneeling before men. Could it be, I wondered, that I belonged so?

Could it be that I was a slave?

I do not mean, of course, in some legal sense, but in some far more profound sense, a sense in which an explicit legal imposition of servitude would be little more than a technicality, however fearful a technicality, which would recognize, acknowledge, and confirm, in a formal manner, something ancient, something underlying, deeper, and more basic, more real, than statutes, pronouncements, and rulings, something true of my very being.

"I will not kneel, no, no, never, never!" cried the woman who had run to the elevator.

"Remove her clothing, and lash her," said the man.

Two of his fellows, those without switches, started forward.

"No, no!" she cried. "I am on my knees! I am on my knees!"

At a gesture from the leader, the two fellows stepped back, being then as they had been before.

"You are women," said the leader. "It is time you learned what you are for."

Several of us looked wildly to one another. But Paula's eyes were bright. Her lips were slightly parted. She looked ecstatic.

"There are many worlds," said the man. "You are now familiar only with one, a polluted, dismal world spoiled by selfishness, thoughtlessness, and greed, a barbarian world defiling nature and poisoning seas, a world in which men and women must be fitted to the machine, rather than the machine to men and women. But there are other worlds, better worlds, other civilizations, better civilizations, higher civilizations, civilizations in which nature is not abhorred and denied but celebrated and accepted, civilizations not opposed to nature but allied with her, supportive of her, promotive of her, civilizations in which, recognized, abetted, and enhanced, nature may flourish."

I could make little of these words.

How could one understand such things?

"One such world," he said, "is Gor. It is to that world you will be transported, shipped as the merchandise you are for her markets. You are being transmitted to Gor not because of your guilt, understand, though it might be deservedly so, not for your naive contributing to the desecration of a world, nor for your mindless participation in a pathology that mocks nature, but in virtue of the simple right of the stronger to acquire, own, and master the weaker. Each of you has been assessed for Gorean bondage. Each of you has been found suitable for Gorean bondage. Each of you has been selected for Gorean bondage. As soon as this determination was made you were no longer yours, but ours. You will learn the whip, collar, and chain. You are now, as in the case of diverse high civilizations, ancient and modern, merchandise, goods, properties."

I almost reeled on my knees. I could scarcely believe what I was hearing.

"You are to keep your bodies clean, and well-groomed," he said. "You now exist to serve and please the free."

Another fellow then stepped forward. "You will remain on your knees," he said, "and repeat what I say, aloud and clearly."

He then issued a set of utterances which we, as bidden, frightened, repeated verbatim.

These utterances, which I recall well, were as follows:

I know nothing of what it is to be a slave.
I will be taught.
I will learn.
I am now worthless.
That is true, and I acknowledge it freely.
But I may be permitted to attain some minimal worth, as a slave.
That is my hope.
It is the only hope for me.
Accordingly, I beg to be a slave.
I beg to be permitted to serve masters, in all ways, instantly, perfectly, and unquestioningly.
I am a slave.
Embond me, legally, that I may serve openly, as the slave I am.

"An interesting lot," said one of the men, one of those without a switch.

"Process them," said the leader, turning away.

"On your feet, kajirae," said the fellow who had just commented on us. "Return to the cell."

We were then soon again in the cell.

The door was then closed, and locked.

"You may speak," said the fellow, turning about, paying us no more attention.

We looked at one another, and then, suddenly, gratefully, words and cries, and sobs, like the issuance of hitherto blocked fountains suddenly freed, rushed forth, cascades of speech, torrents of confusion, fears, tremblings, threats, pleas, lamentations, and protests. Some of the girls ran to the bars, seizing them, demanding succor, release, consideration.

Only Paula, sitting on the floor, with her back to a wall of the cell, seemed content, more curious than apprehensive.

I sat down beside her.

"What are kajirae?" I asked.

"Slaves," she said, "female slaves."

"And what is the meaning of 'kajira'?" I asked.

"It is a common word in Gorean for a slave, a female slave," she said.

"And in the apartment," I said, "you said '*La kajira*'. What does that mean?"

"Did you not tell me you said that some days ago, on the beach?" she asked.

"Yes," I said.

"It means," she said, "'I am a slave', 'I am a female slave', 'I am a slave girl', such things."

"I see," I said.

"When you said it," she said, "you became a slave, a slave girl. I told you that, in the apartment."

Much had rushed past me. I was confused, frightened. She had said something of this sort in the apartment. It came back to me now, frighteningly, clearly.

"I did not know what it meant," I said.

"That does not matter," she said, smiling, adding, "kajira."

I glared at her, angrily.

"I thought, often," she said, "that you belonged at a man's feet, that you would make a good slave for a man."

"You seem calm," I said, reproachfully, "in a cell, abducted."

"I have long hoped," she said, "to be noticed, to be acquired, to be picked, to be harvested, as slave fruit, to love and serve, to belong lovingly, selflessly, wholly to another. That was my dream. But I thought myself too plain, of too little interest."

I did not say so, of course, but I, too, found the apparent interest of men, some men, at least, in Paula unaccountable. I supposed she was acceptable, but what could one see in her beyond that? She was far removed from the linear, svelte ideals presented to us by costumers and designers. Even I fell far short of such an ideal, though much could be done with clothing and carriage.

"I am afraid," I said.

"At least it is warm in the cell," she said.

She had opened her sweater.

"Are you not afraid?" I asked.

"A little," she said.

"I should hope so," I said.

"I am more excited, and thrilled, than afraid," she said.

"How is that?" I asked, skeptically.

"I know something of Gor," she said, "from my reading."

"Surely we are in danger," I said.

"I do not think so," she said. "We are in the hands of Goreans, or, more likely, men much like Goreans. Such men relish, celebrate, and desire women, so much so that they will possess them, will own and master them, will have them in the way of nature, uncompromisingly."

"I am afraid," I said.

"We are in no danger," she said, "if we are diligent, devoted, earnest, pleasing, and obedient."

"That we should be so to men!" I cried, indignantly.

"We are theirs," she said. "We are women."

"Paula!" I cried.

"They are men," she said.

"Not like the men we know!" I said.

"No," she said, "not like the men we know, or knew. They are different. They will not be content with a smile, or a crumb. They will want, and will expect, and will have, everything from a woman, and the woman herself."

"A chain was spoken of," I said, "a collar, a whip!"

"We are slaves," she said. "Of course we must expect to be collared, as other beasts. We must expect to be suitably identified as what we are. We are not free women. And surely we must expect to know the shackles and chains which are our due as slaves. And we must expect to be branded."

"'Branded'," I said.

"Certainly," she said, "we are beasts. A collar might be removed."

"They spoke of a whip," I said.

"Surely," she said. "As slaves we will be subject to the whip. And, Phyllis," she said, "you may rest assured it will be used on your pretty skin if you are in the least bit displeasing."

"You find that amusing?" I said.

"Knowing you," she said, "yes. But strive to be pleasing to your master. Slaves are seldom whipped. Occasionally they might be whipped just to remind them that they are slaves."

"I am still afraid," I said.

"You are much safer than a free woman," she said. "It could be death for a free woman to fall into the hands of an enemy, unsated, wild, hot with killing, thirsting for blood, carrying fire and sword into a village, town, or city. You are a beast. Understood loot. You would simply be roped or leashed, put in a coffle, herded into a pen, to change collars or chains."

Paula put back her head, and laughed.

"Why do you laugh?" I asked, annoyed.

"I was thinking of the apartment," she said, "and your threats, that you would hold a part of me over me, that you would threaten, if I were not cooperative, if I would not stay with you, to reveal my secret, that I longed for a master."

"I would not have done so," I said.

"No," she said, "you would have done so. It would be too juicy a tidbit of gossip to let languish. You could not have resisted the temptation, sooner or later, to shine before the others, to be the center of attention, as you so often were, they hanging on your words."

"No," I said, angrily.

"But," she said, "I think your small revelation might have proved less appealing to others than you had anticipated. It is not unusual for a woman to long for a master. It is a very common wish. Thus, in their tepid, or embarrassed, or hostile, responses, or lack of responses, you might have learned something about other women, and, if you were to permit yourself to look into your own heart, you might have learned something about yourself, as well."

"Do not speak foolishness," I said.

"Have you never dreamed of yourself naked, in chains, at a man's feet?" she asked.

"One cannot help such thoughts," I said, angrily.

"Nor should one," she said.

"I see," I said, angrily.

"In any event," she said, "that is why I laughed. It seems you will never reveal my little secret, a common secret amongst women, to the others. Poor Phyllis! Soon you will be on your own chain."

"I hate you!" I cried, and lunged toward her, and slapped her, viciously, across her left cheek.

She looked at me, startled, drawing back, and put her right hand to her reddened, doubtless stinging cheek.

I looked away, angrily.

"I like you, Phyllis," she said. "I am your friend."

"I am not yours," I said, not looking at her.

When I had slapped Paula, the others in the cell, startled, had turned to regard us.

"If you were a free woman," said Paula, "I must be pleased to endure your abuse uncomplainingly, but you are not a free woman, Phyllis. You are only kajira, only another kajira."

"So?" I said.

"I care for you, I am your friend," said Paula, softly, "but I need not accept abuse from you."

"You always have," I said. "You will take it, and like it."

"I am sorry," she said. "Please forgive me, but you must be taught a lesson."

"What?" I asked, puzzled, turning, just in time to glimpse her hands reaching for me. "Stop!" I cried. "Stop! Stop! Let me go! Release me!"

My head seemed to burst with fire. Paula's two hands, fistlike, behind me, were knotted in my hair, and then, to excruciating pain, I felt my head forced down to the floor of the cell. I could not, reaching back, dislodge her hands, and they twisted yet more fiercely in my hair, twisting it. I could not rise. What was there to do but feel the pain? It was like a thousand tiny, burning daggers thrust into my scalp. "Please, please, Paula!" I begged. "Stop! Stop!"

"Tear out her hair," said the woman in the expensive jacket and skirt, she who had run to the elevator.

"No, no!" I wept, trying not to move in the slightest.

"Tear it all out!" said the woman in the torn evening dress.

"Be quiet," said Paula, "or I will set the others on you."

The young woman in the evening dress gasped, and stepped back. Apparently she was not used to being so addressed. Surely inferiors would not have been likely to do so.

"I am sorry," said Paula, "but you, too, are kajira, only that."

"Please Paula," I wept, "let me go!"

"I am sorry, Phyllis," she said. "But you must learn respect for others."

"You are hurting me, Paula!" I said. "I am your friend. Your dear, loving friend! Let me go. Ai! Ai! Please, stop! Please, stop!"

Paula stopped twisting my hair, but did not release me. I was helpless.

"Clearly there must be order in the cell," said the woman in the expensive jacket and skirt. "I will be first." I assumed she arrogated this role to herself in view of her more expensive, more fashionable attire. It was not much different from that which I normally wore to work. It was not my fault that I wore only a nightgown. Did that make me less than she? Surely we were of similar age. I could think of three or four in the cell who would be more plausible leaders than she.

"Why you?" asked the young woman who wore what seemed a maid's uniform.

"Be quiet, menial," said the woman in the jacket and skirt. Then she looked down at me. "Have you learned your lesson?" she asked.

"Yes! Yes!" I said.

"Truly?" asked Paula.

"Yes, yes!" I said.

Paula then removed her hands from my hair, and I lay still, very still, hurting, trying to understand, through the pain, what had occurred. "I am sorry, Phyllis," she said, "but it is important for you to learn that you cannot do whatever you wish, without consequences."

I was now frightened, of Paula, and, even more, of the others in the cell.

"If there is to be order here," said Paula, "it will be imposed by men. That is the way it is done. They will decide, they will pick, they will choose. They are masters. We are women."

"No," said the woman who wore the expensive jacket and skirt.

"My status is highest," said the woman in the torn evening dress. "I am wealthy."

"You are no longer wealthy," said Paula. "You are now a slave. You own nothing. It is you who are owned."

"I am the leader," announced the woman in the jacket and skirt.

"You went quickly enough to your knees," said the woman in the maid's uniform.

The woman in the jacket and skirt leapt at the woman in the maid's uniform, reaching for her hair. In a moment they were rolling about on the floor, screaming, biting, and scratching.

The woman in the muchly torn gown cried out, "No, I am first, I will be first, me, me!" and began to strike at the rolling pair with her small fists. Almost at the same time one of the young women in jeans and a sweatshirt seized the remains of the woman's gown, trying to pull her away from the others, and the woman cried out in dismay, half stripped, left with little but shreds of her garment. "Let them fight!" said the other woman who wore jeans and a sweatshirt, reaching out to impede the other, she who had interfered, who still held a piece of the evening dress in her hand. Then she, the one with a handful of the evening dress, cried out, turning angrily, and then she and the other began to push and shove at one another.

"Stop! Please, stop!" cried Paula.

But Paula's protests were unavailing.

I kept my head down, to the floor of the cell. I trembled. I was reluctant to move. My scalp still flamed, and I sobbed, trying to catch my breath. I now realized what might be done to me. I was at the mercy of others. And what if my hair had been seized not by Paula, with her woman's strength, but in the single hand of a man? Might I not have hastened to be placed anywhere, to be conducted anywhere? Would I not have begged to serve, eagerly and piteously, in any manner I might? I had not realized until then how I might be controlled by means of my hair, controlled as though I might be a slave. And then I realized I was a slave. I was afraid. It was the first time I had known such pain.

"Please, stop!" cried Paula.

But the disorder in the cell, with cries and buffetings, and strugglings, continued, unabated.

"Please!" cried Paula.

At that moment, startling and shocking us, there was a sudden, unexpected ringing of metal on metal, a loud, sharp staccato of sound at the bars, consequent on the dragging of a metal bar back and forth against them. Instantly all activity in the cell ceased.

We all then, unbidden, fearfully, fell to our knees. Later I pondered the alacrity and uniformity that had characterized that response. How unthought-out, and natural, it had been. We had all immediately, fearfully, knelt. How could that be explained? But, of course, we were slaves in the presence of the free. How natural then that we should have assumed that posture of subservience, deference, and submission, the posture of slaves!

Surely we were learning what we were.

The fellow with the metal bar then stepped back, and another man stepped forward, who carried a small bundle of white, folded cloths.

"You are kajirae," he said, "kajirae are owned. Your clothing, if you are granted clothing, is at the discretion of masters. Most masters, if they permit you clothing, will dress you for their pleasure. You have nothing to say about such things. You are not free women. We have no interest at the moment in examining you carefully, fully, as slaves. You will grow well enough acquainted with that experience later. What I have in my hand are seven tunics, slave tunics, garments designed to be worn by slaves, if they are permitted clothing. Each of you will take one, and don it. It is the only thing you may wear. You will discover that in a slave tunic there is no doubt that you are a woman. You may, at first, find it distressing, to be so briefly, and charmingly, exhibited. Later, however, you will become shamelessly proud of your sex and beauty, fearing only the contempt, wrath, and chastisement of free women, who will loathe, hate, and envy you. Men will be your only protection against them. So strive well to be pleasing, and fully pleasing, to your masters. They might sell you to a woman. I shall shortly take my leave, to return toward supper, to attend to your feeding, your feeding as slaves. You will proceed as follows. You will remove every stitch and thread of your clothing, even to hairpins, barrettes, ribbons, and such, and cast it well beyond the bars, so that you may not reach it, should you be so inclined. Every stitch and thread means every stitch and thread. You will discover that the slave tunic has no nether closure. That helps you keep in mind that you are slaves, and are always to be at the convenience of masters. How simple it is to thrust it up, over your hips, or to remove it from you, altogether. If you are wearing cosmetics, lipstick, eye shadow, or such, wipe it off. Goreans buy women raw, without artifices. Some of you flaunt nail polish or dyed hair. That can be removed later, in your house of training. As suggested, it is the pure, unadorned woman who is put on sale. After your purchase, cosmetics, enhancements, and such, as with clothing, will be at the discretion of the master. I will now leave and you may attend to your delicate and delightful transformations in all modesty."

He then slipped the small bundle of white, folded cloths through the bars, where it fell to the floor.

We regarded the small bundle.

He paused, before turning away.

"I think none of you are stupid," he said. "You are all quite intelligent. Indeed, one of the criteria in terms of which you were selected is high intelligence. Obviously highly intelligent, needful women make the best slaves. Goreans do not care for stupid slaves. They want something worthwhile in their collars. But, if, when I return, I should find any slave has failed to comply, perfectly and completely, with my instructions, that slave will be stripped and lashed."

He then turned away and, followed by the man with the metal bar, who had smote it so alarmingly against the bars, left the large room, disappearing through one of the doors across the way.

Paula cast her sweater through the bars, some feet away, and began to unbutton her blouse.

Shortly thereafter a miscellany of garments was cast from the cell.

Paula handed me a tunic.

"Thank you," I said.

"It won't take you long to strip," said the woman in the expensive jacket and skirt.

"Get your own clothes off," I snapped.

She drew back her hand to strike me, but then her head was drawn back, by the hair. "Oh!" she said, smarting.

"Please do not make a scene," said Paula. Then she released the woman's hair who, angrily, moved away, and stripped off her jacket.

"Surely they do not mean everything," said one of the two young women in jeans and a sweatshirt.

"Every stitch and thread," said Paula, kindly. "Do not be upset. You are very lovely. You will discover, happily, after all, that you are a female, and that it is a desirable, lovely thing to be. Rather than denying your sex, you will rejoice in it, for by means of it you will find and fulfill yourself and please masters."

"I cannot wear this!" exclaimed a woman, shaking, and holding out, the tiny garment. It was she who had worn the torn evening dress. "It is too short!"

"You have long, lovely legs," said Paula. "Men will like to see them."

"They are my legs!" she exclaimed.

"No," said Paula, softly, slipping from her panties. "They will belong to whoever buys you."

I pulled on the tunic. I had never worn such a thing before. I wondered if one might not be more naked in such a thing than without it. I cast the blue nightgown out, through the bars. Then I turned to face Paula. "Paula!" I said, tears in my eyes.

"You are so beautiful," whispered Paula.

I smiled, through my tears. I did think I would sell well. I wondered what I would bring. Surely the bidding would be fierce, fervid. I had no idea what currencies might be involved. Perhaps I would sell for ten thousand gold pieces.

"What of me?" asked Paula, anxiously.

"Very nice," I said, actually impressed.

Paula may have been one of the many women whose attractiveness seems to vary inversely with the complexity and abundance of her garmenture, or, perhaps better, with the sort of garments worn. Surely she did not seem to have the sort of body for which so many modern fashions appeared to be designed. Her body was too much like that of the average woman, a bit short, nicely hipped, sweetly and richly curved. Modern designs did not flatter such a body, but its beauty would lie nonetheless beneath, of course, even if obscured by an uncongenial garmenture, as if waiting. If it were to be clothed, surely its beauty would be better served by simpler, looser, more natural garments.

"Such a garment, of course," said Paula, "is designed to flatter a woman, to set her off, not to hide her, but to reveal her."

"It certainly reveals one," I said.

"You are extremely attractive in such a garment," she said.

"In what there is of it," I said, ruefully.

"You are beautiful," she said, "so beautiful, even slave beautiful."

"Is that a compliment?" I asked.

"The highest," she said.

"Do you think men would like to buy me?" I asked.

"Oh, yes!" she said.

"Well," said the woman who had worn the expensive jacket and skirt, now tunicked, "it seems they will soon have the opportunity."

"And to buy you, as well," I said.

"If anyone would wish to do so," said another now briefly tunicked beauty, the young woman who had worn the maid's uniform.

The woman who had worn the torn evening gown tried to pull down the hem of her tunic.

"Why bother?" asked the woman who had worn the maid's uniform. "Men will like to see your legs. Perhaps they will improve your price."

"Be quiet, you disgusting servant, you menial," snarled she who had worn the torn evening dress. "I could buy and sell you."

"Now," said she who had worn the maid's uniform, "it is you who can be bought and sold."

"Harlot!" hissed she who had worn the torn evening gown.

"We are less than harlots," said Paula. "We are slaves."

"Your wealth no longer rules," said the former maid to she who had worn the torn gown. "It once elevated you, and exalted you, and made you formidable, but it is no longer yours. It is gone. You are now no different from the rest of us. You are now but one female, one slave, amongst others."

"No, no, no!" she wept.

"Sisters!" cried Paula. "Kneel! A man approaches!"

Instantly we knelt.

He who had brought the tunics to the cell now stood outside the bars, looking within. Behind him were two other men.

"Excellent!" he said, approvingly. "A considerable improvement. A nice lot of kajirae."

He then called one after another of us to the bars, and had us turn before him. I remembered how the boorish fellow in the office had had me turn before him, when I had thought him in the service of some agency, say, a modeling or theatrical agency. Now I again turned before a man, again being assessed. But now I wore a slave tunic.

We were then returned to our knees in the cell.

"A good lot," he said. He then addressed us. "You are now slaves," he said. "Commonly you will find yourself owned by a single master or mistress. Nonetheless, you will address all free men as 'Master', all free women as 'Mistress'. When you reach your destination, you will begin to learn the language of your masters. Learn it as swiftly and perfectly as you can. Much can depend on this, even your life. Keep always in mind, clearly, what you are, barbarians, from a benighted world, permitted to serve your masters in a higher civilization. Be grateful. In your house of training you will be taught the basics of serving and pleasing men, of pleasing them inordinately, as women. Attend well to the lessons of the kajirae who will teach you such things. Your life, too, may depend on this. Even before you leave this enclave, you will be given slave wine. It cannot be administered too soon to slaves. It will prevent conception. As you are now animals, you are doubtless well aware that you will be bred, if bred, as any other animal, at your master's discretion and convenience. The effects of slave wine are counteracted by a drink called a 'Releaser'. If you are administered such a potion, you may expect, shortly thereafter, to be hooded and conducted to a breeding stall."

We exchanged frightened, miserable glances. Even Paula seemed distraught.

The fellow who had been addressing us then turned away and, with the side of his foot, swept our discarded clothing into a heap, a few feet from the door of the cell.

We observed it.

"You will not be needing this," he informed us. He then drew a small metallic device from his pocket, and trained it on the heap of clothing. He must then have pulled a trigger, or depressed a switch, or something. We cried out, startled. There had been a dazzling burst of light. At the same time there was a sudden blast of heat, wavelike, which swirled about and pressed against us, even in the cell, even where we knelt. I felt my tunic whip briefly about my body. I could not see for a moment, from the light, and the obtrusive afterimage. Then I, and others, cried out with surprise, and dismay, for the heap of clothing was gone. I had no doubt that such a device, if turned on a man, would leave little behind, saving perhaps a clutter of charred, smoking bones.

I suppose that this small exhibition was less than random. Certainly it would not be without its purpose, or purposes. Certainly it proved to us that a fearsome capacity for destruction, even within so small a compass as a handheld device, was at the disposal of our captors. We were confronted with an example, doubtless a trivial example, suggesting an awesome technology with which we were not acquainted. I recalled how swiftly, and apparently simply, the bolts on the apartment door had been undone. I recalled, too, one of our captors informing Paula that they had heard her enunciation "*La kajira*," even though we had searched the apartment diligently and had discovered no listening devices. I wondered if I, and doubtless others, had been under a visual and auditory surveillance of which we were unaware. Were there such devices, I did not doubt but what they had been removed from the apartment, probably after we had been handcuffed together and hooded in the two blankets, before being conducted to the waiting van. But one supposes there might have been another purpose, as well, to that seemingly small, but surely awesome, demonstration. There seemed something abrupt, decisive, significant, and final about the destruction of our clothing. It was the clothing of free women, blasted away, to which we were no longer entitled. The clothing of free women was gone, and, in its place, was the brief, humiliating, degrading garb of slaves. And, too, that clothing represented a tie with our old world. Might one not have hoped to don it again, and return to our familiar reality? Was not such a hope real as long as it lay there, even outside our bars? But then it was gone! We had nothing to wear now save what we had been given. How important clothing is to a woman! How much her sense of self, her sense of importance, of worth, of status, of what she is, depends on her garmenture! But we were naked now, stark naked, save for the tunics of slaves. How our clothing expresses us, and how we understand ourselves in its terms, and now we had not chosen our clothing, but others had done so. What would this new clothing do to us? How, in the tunic of a slave, can one be other than a slave? Do we not become congruent with our clothing? Do we not fit ourselves to our clothing? Do we not learn our self-image from our clothing? Do we not think of ourselves in terms of our clothing? Do we not become one with it? And now we found ourselves in the clothing of slaves! And I tried, wildly, to force a thought from my mind, persistent and intrusive. I was not displeased to be in the garb of a slave! "No, no!" I thought. But how frank, simple, and appealing it was, that garb, how honest, blatant, and unapologetic. I was fond of my body, and, despite my pretenses, delighted with its display. Further, though I had found few men in my former experiences of great interest, I found myself reacting differently to my captors. They were so naturally, and unassumingly, masculine, so sure of themselves. I had the sense in them of ambition, possessiveness, aggression, strength, and will. Now, clothed so briefly, and simply, before them, so obviously displayed as a woman, indeed, as a purchasable prize, I became intensely, sometimes excruciatingly, aware of them as men. How aware I was now of how I might be viewed, and viewed as I now hoped I would be viewed, as a slave!

I tried to force such thoughts from my mind.

But I could not do so.

I was tunicked.

On my left ankle was a locked, steel anklet. On it something was inscribed. It was a number, I gathered, but I was unfamiliar with the script.

I dared not conjecture what might be my responses, my helplessness, my feelings, if I found myself collared.

The fellow who had been addressing us turned and said something to the two fellows with him, and they withdrew, to return shortly with some metal bowls which they placed in a lateral line, before the fellow who had been addressing us. There were seven such bowls. The two men then withdrew again, only to soon return, one bearing a trough, some five feet in length, and the other two buckets, in one of which was a utensil, which proved to be a ladle.

"I gather," said the fellow who had been addressing us, "that you may be thirsty, and hungry."

Surely we were. Particularly, I was hungry.

"I will now ask you if you are hungry and thirsty," he said. "If you are hungry and thirsty, you may respond, 'Yes, Master'. Are you hungry and thirsty?"

"Yes, Master," we said.

"Would you like to be fed and watered?" he asked.

"Yes, Master," we said.

At a nod from the spokesman one of the men with him poured the contents of one of the buckets into the trough, that some five feet in length.

"We will open the door of the cell," said the spokesman. "The trough contains water. You will emerge from the cell on all fours, and, on all fours, slake your thirst at the trough. You may not use your hands. You will drink as dogs drink, though you are less than dogs. You are slaves. You will also note that, before me, are seven bowls, one for each of you. While you are drinking, these bowls will be filled with slave gruel. Slave gruel is bland but it is hardy and extremely nourishing. It is designed for the health and vitality of stock. When you are finished drinking, you will approach the bowls, remaining at all times on all fours. When you reach the bowls you will wait for further instructions."

The door of the cell was opened and we approached the trough, gathering about it, and then, putting down our heads, began lapping the water. I had almost forgotten how thirsty I was, from my hunger. I recalled that the man in the office, who had been so rude to me, had called me a bitch. And here I was drinking, indeed, as might a dog, a female dog, a bitch. And then I remembered I was less than a bitch, for I was a female slave. How pleased I was that he could not see me!

"Enough!" said the fellow, sharply.

It was not difficult to recognize that tone of voice. It was the voice of a master. We responded instantly, lifting our heads, frightened.

He had been generous, of course.

He had not hurried us.

I viewed one of the bowls, and approached it, and remained before it, on all fours.

In it was some sort of mush.

I would discover later it was warm.

I was terribly hungry.

"If you are pleasing," said the fellow, "we will put a biscuit in the gruel, and perhaps a bit of meat."

I determined that I would be as pleasing as I could. I wanted the biscuit, I wanted the meat.

I was at the fifth bowl, counting from the right, as I faced the line of bowls. A short ceremony, or ritual, took place, before her feeding, with each slave, seriatim, beginning on the right, and so I, given my position, by the time of my turn, was well apprised of its nature.

I was on all fours, as were the others.

Then one of the masters was before me, between me and the metal bowl, in which was a few ounces of some moist, warm, granular substance, provender, slave provender.

"Look up," he said.

I did so, and began to kiss and lick the whip which was held to my lips. I did this as humbly and earnestly as I could, for several seconds. Two of the preceding girls, one the girl who had worn the expensive jacket and skirt and the other the girl who had worn the torn evening gown, apparently had not performed this gesture of obeisance promptly enough or satisfactorily enough, for each was forced to repeat the action, again and again, until the master was satisfied. "No biscuit, no meat," he said to his fellow, who accompanied him, carrying a small pail. He then moved to the next girl in line. I had noted earlier that Paula, who had apparently performed this simple ritual satisfactorily had been awarded a biscuit and a bit of meat, as had been one of the other girls, she who was next in line.

The whip was drawn away from my lips.

"Thank you for enslaving me, Master," I said. I then bent down and placed my lips on his shoes, kissing each.

"Biscuit and meat," he said to his fellow, and, to my delight, I saw a biscuit and a bit of meat tossed into my bowl. He then moved on to the sixth girl. She was one of those who had worn jeans and a sweatshirt. The last girl in the line was she who had worn the maid's uniform.

Each, I noted, received both a biscuit and a bit of meat.

We dared not touch the food, of course, for we had not been given permission to feed.

"You may eat," said the fellow with the whip, stepping away from us, followed by his fellow.

We put down our heads and addressed ourselves gratefully to the provender in the bowls. We might not, of course, use our hands.

Such small restrictions are not uncommon, particularly in a girl's training. Most slaves, of course, feed themselves, and in the vicinity of the master. If he sits at a table, she will kneel near him. If he sits cross-legged, at one of the low, small tables found in many Gorean domiciles, indeed, almost universally, she will also kneel, usually to his right, at the same table. She may not, of course, as she is a slave, feed until permitted, just as she may not dress herself or speak without permission. To be sure, it is common in many households that she has a standing permission to do such things, which standing permission may, of course, be instantly revoked. It might be of interest to note that even Gorean free women, given the usual absence of chairs or benches in Gorean households, often regarded as awkward, unaesthetic clutter, will kneel. Sitting cross-legged is expected of men, kneeling of women. Sometimes the wild women of the forests, particularly in the north, will sit cross-legged. But when captured or enslaved they, too, will kneel. In collars they quickly, gratefully, learn their womanhood.

Following our watering and feeding, we were returned to our cell, on all fours. When we arrived in the cell, and the door was closed and locked, we were further informed that whereas we might sit in the cell, lie down, recline, kneel, or such, we were not permitted to stand. Our heads were to be kept at or below a man's belt. Further, we were not permitted to speak, though we were free to express ourselves, if we wished, by small sounds, animal noises, whimpers, and such.

I was pleased to note that in our absence from the cell, it had been supplied with a wastes pail.

I think these strictures had two purposes; one was to punish us for our hitherto unruly behavior in the cell, regarded as inappropriate for kajirae, and, secondly, perhaps, to familiarize ourselves with a modality of discipline. It is well to for a slave to learn quickly she is not a free woman.

That night several more women were brought to the enclave, perhaps thirty, or so, in two separate lots, but they were housed in other cells.

Doubtless they, too, would soon be in their tunics.

"We have enough now for the capsules," we heard one of the masters say to another.

"It is soon, is it not?" said the other.

"You are new?" said the first.

"Yes," said the other.

"It is not so soon," said the first. "Two-legged cattle are easy to acquire."

I did not understand.

What could he mean, 'two-legged cattle'?

Then I recalled that I and the others were now stock, beasts, animals, and so, I supposed, 'two-legged cattle'!

I understood better then how we were viewed, what we were. We were slaves.

"I gather then," said the other. "The ship will soon embark."

"Yes," said the first.

I was frightened to hear of a ship. Surely they were joking. Surely there was no ship. Surely there was no such place as Gor. "There is no place such as Gor," I told myself. "There is no place such as Gor!"

CHAPTER SEVEN

I lay quietly.

I was afraid to open my eyes, and look about me.

I had the sense I lay on a closely woven straw mat. I did not know where I was.

Surely I was not on my bed, in the apartment. I pressed my eyelids closely together. I had the sense that there was metal on my neck. Memories rushed back, the incident in the office, that on the beach, my awakening in my own bed, in the apartment, in my blue silken nightgown, discovering I could scarcely part my wrists, that they were handcuffed together, closely. I recalled Paula's appearance at the apartment, her freeing me of the handcuffs, and, later, the sudden, swift ingress of three men into the apartment, the simplicity and ease of our capture, the ride in the van, the arrival at the warehouse or storage facility, the cell, the taking of our clothing, our tunicking, our feeding.

I grimaced, recalling a horrid, foul taste.

Our hands had been tied behind us, and we had been knelt; then our heads had been pulled back by the hair. I recalled the plain roof of the storage facility. A drain of a plastic funnel had been forced between my teeth, and a man had pinched shut my nostrils. I could breathe only through my mouth. In a moment the funnel was flooded with some vile liquid. I felt it fill my oral cavity. As I was held by the hair and my nostrils pinched shut I could not cast out the liquid. Then I must breathe but I could breathe only through my mouth, and, to do so, to breathe, I had no option but to clear the passage of the intervening blockage. I swallowed down the liquid, swallow by repulsive swallow, shuddering.

"Every drop, kajira," said one of the men.

"Good little kajira," said another.

I was then permitted to rise, and run to the cell. I hurried to the wastes pail and put my head over it, sick, but I could not disgorge the liquid. I wanted to put my finger down my throat, to gag it out, but my hands were tied behind me. Paula was already in the cell, her hands, too, tied behind her.

"Do not struggle, dear Phyllis," she said. "Be patient, be grateful. It is for your own good."

"They torture us!" I wept.

"No," she said. "They control us. They are our masters."

"Torture!" I wept.

"No," she said, "it is slave wine."

"What is slave wine?" I asked, tears in my eyes.

"The masters spoke of it," she said. "It is brewed from sip root. It prevents conception. Be pleased you are not a white kajira owned by the red savages of the Barrens, who do not care for white men or white women. There you must chew and swallow the root, raw."

"I cannot now become pregnant?" I said.

"No," she said, "not until masters decide you are to be bred, and with whom."

"Paula!" I wept.

"The breeding of slaves is supervised," she said, "as is the case with other domestic animals."

"No!" I said.

"Now try to sleep, lovely kajira," she said.

I now twisted about, on the mat, unwilling to bring myself fully awake. My hands touched a chain; it was attached, somehow, to the metal on my neck.

It was a horrid memory, the taste of the brew. And yet I was pleased that it had been administered to me. The slave may be bought and sold, and must expect to be frequently used. She is to be always at the convenience of the master.

One other memory forced itself upon me.

My group, the seven of us, were chained together by the neck and our hands were fastened together behind us, in slave bracelets, and then we were conducted down a long tunnel, until we reached a large, domed chamber. In this chamber there was a large, disklike object, perhaps forty yards in diameter, and eight to ten feet in depth, or height.

"This is one of our ships," said our guide. "The domed roof parts."

"Surely it cannot be a ship," I thought. "There are no wings, no tail. I see no visible engines. Surely this is some gross imposture foisted upon us, but for what reason? What purpose would such a charade serve?"

"We are proud of her," said our guide. "We like to show her off. Many units simply render a kajira unconscious, after which she is encapsuled and transmitted to Gor. Indeed, she may go to sleep one night, suspecting nothing, not even being aware that she has been scouted and selected, and not awaken until she finds herself in a Gorean slave pen, naked and shackled. That is a pity. She has never even seen the ship. You, on the other hand, we choose to favor. Perhaps it is a vanity on our part, but it is one that appeals to us. If you will now ascend the ramp, we will give you a sense of the interior of the ship, its bridge, its crew quarters, its galley, the propulsion chamber, and such. Too, of course, you might be interested in seeing the tiered capsules that you will occupy."

That night, after our feeding, in which we were allowed to use our fingers, I spoke to Paula.

"You are intelligent," I said to her.

"Perhaps, a little," she said.

"These men must think we are fools," I said.

"How so?" she asked.

"They insult our intelligence," I said.

"I do not understand," she said.

"Surely you do not believe that was a real ship," I said. "Surely you do not believe there is a world, Gor."

"Go to sleep, sweet Phyllis," she said.

I twisted on the mat, unwilling to open my eyes, fearing to do so. The last thing I remembered was kneeling, in the cell, with the others, and being handed a small metal bowl, which I was to hold in both hands. Few Gorean cups, I would learn, have handles. Too, a slave's holding the cup in two hands not only affords greater stability, making it less likely that the drink might be spilled, which can be a punishable offense, but it is an aesthetic modality, as well, as it accentuates and frames the slave's beauty.

In the cup, from a decanter, was poured a small amount of an aromatic ruby beverage. It must have been spiced.

"Drink, kajirae," we were told, and we drank.

I had never tasted so delicious a beverage.

We were kneeling, in our tunics, holding the small bowls. Some of the masters were about, in the cell. They did not seem concerned with us. The door of the cell was open.

We did not attempt to leap to our feet, and run. Where would we run? Where would we go? What would we do? Too, it is not easy to leap to one's feet from a kneeling position, for one is muchly helpless on one's knees. Surely it is a suitable position for a slave before her master. And I would learn later that it is even more difficult to leap to one's feet, if one were placed in the position of the pleasure slave. But I would be taught, as well, how to rise gracefully from either position, either from the lovely, modest position of the tower slave or from the more blatant, though similarly beautiful, position of the pleasure slave, which position leaves a girl in little doubt as to what she is for and how she is viewed. The slave, in either case, is expected to be beautiful. She is a slave.

The members of my small group looked uneasily at one another. Hitherto, we had had nothing to drink but water. But now, though we were but kneeling kajirae, we had been privileged to imbibe a liquid, clearly a wine, which exceeded in bouquet and flavor any I had ever tasted. I had no way of conjecturing the vintage or year. It was a wine unlike any I had ever tasted. I supposed it would have been exorbitantly expensive if purchased in some exclusive establishment catering to an affluent and discerning clientele, and yet, here, it was being given to us, only objects and goods, only kajirae.

"On your feet, pretty beasts," said one of the masters. "We are going for a little walk."

Momentarily there seemed a little darkness about the edges of my vision. Perhaps the light in the warehouse, the storage facility, had been momentarily dimmed. I shook my head, to clear it. I rose to my feet, and caught my balance.

"It is not a long walk," said the master. "Indeed, it will be familiar to you."

I heard one of my group whimper.

"Order, single file," said the master. "Tallest girl first, thence in descending height, the shortest last".

We knew the order. It was the same as our coffle order. Slaves are often arranged aesthetically, or purposefully. The descending-height arrangement is typical. Surely it is simple and lovely. Too, in selling lines, as in sales generally, arrangements are seldom accidental. One may mix hair and eye colors, heights, complexions, figures, slender, fuller, and so on. Men vary in their interests and tastes. Sometimes two or three plainer girls, comparatively speaking, are used to lead up to, or frame, a less plain girl, in order that her beauty may seem even, by contrast, more striking.

One of our group, one of those who had worn jeans and a sweat-shirt, now briefly tunicked in white, half stumbled.

"Steady, kajira," said a master, kindly.

"Hands behind your backs, wrists crossed," said another master, a handful of laces dangling from his hand.

I felt my hands fastened together, behind my back. I did not know why we were being bound. One does not inquire. One is kajira. A kajira is often rendered helpless. It is part of being kajira.

I shook my head, again.

Why had we been bound?

"The door is open," said a master. "Go that way, as you did before. Proceed."

"Surely, pretty cattle," said another, "you need not be whipped, switched, or prodded."

The first girl, she who had worn the expensive jacket and skirt, leaned against the side of the door, to steady herself, and then, a moment later, moved through the opening.

The second in line was she who had worn the maid's uniform, or what seemed such a uniform; third was she whom I had first seen in the torn evening gown; her legs were well revealed in her short tunic; then came the taller of the two young women who had worn the frivolous, boyish garb, apparently adopted to conceal, or diminish, her sex; but in the tunic there was no doubt as to her sex; the sex of slaves is never to be in doubt; in slave garb it is clear that a woman is a woman; Paula was fifth; I was sixth; and the second of the two girls who had worn jeans and a sweatshirt was last. She was of the sort that some men characterized as "cuddly." I supposed she would make a graspable, delicious "slave armful." It was she who had half stumbled, but moments before.

I wondered if they were deliberately lowering the lights in the building.

One of my steps was unsteady.

"Surely it will not be necessary to fasten you in coffle," said a master. "Hurry, proceed."

"Surely you do not expect us to carry you," said a master.

"It is not far," said another.

"Move, move, kajirae," said another.

I had taken only a few steps when I realized that we had been drugged.

"Move along, kajirae," said the man. "It is not far."

My head swirled, I almost stumbled. I saw the bound hands of Paula before me.

I now realized why our hands had been bound behind us. We

would soon realize we had been drugged. Now we were unable to take action, dared we do so, to expel the beverage. It was in us, working the will of masters.

"Keep moving," said one of the masters. "Do not be concerned. It is scarcely a trace of tassa powder. The common dose renders a woman unconscious almost immediately. You can imagine how useful it is to slavers, in their collections. A free woman accepts a drink from a stranger and, when she awakens, some Ahn later, she discovers herself stripped, and in his chains."

I knew nothing of tassa powder. I did not know what an Ahn might be, other than that it was clearly some unit of time.

I pulled at my bound wrists, weakly. I must strive to keep my place in line.

"The matter is delicate," the man continued. "The amount to be administered must be estimated. It must be small enough to permit, for a time, the prolongation of consciousness and the practicality of movement, as in walking, and large enough to assure an eventual effective sedation. Some consideration is given to apparent body weight. Larger women get a bit more than a dusting of the powder. The matter is further complicated by the fact that movement, your walking, for example, hastens the action of the drug."

I was not fully cognizant of my surroundings.

I followed Paula, mechanically, unthinkingly, before me.

Yet the way seemed somehow familiar.

Then I knew I was in a tunnel, the sides were about, the tunnel. I remembered the tunnel. I supposed it must be the same tunnel. Before it had been brightly lit, even painfully so, but now, though the bulbs were surely illuminated, that one could note, they seemed dim. I did not remember the margins of the encircling shadows. That was different. The focus of my consciousness now seemed small, a circle within a circle, a circle within a circle, that of an encroaching, menacing hue. I sensed redness about, but nothing was red. The walls of the tunnel were white. I recalled that. The line then stopped, and I wavered. I struggled to remain on my feet. I was sure now I knew where we were. I sensed the proximity of the large, disklike object, silverish in the light; I had seen it before. It is not a ship, I told myself. It cannot be a ship. I had seen no engines, no wings, no tail. What would the point of building such a thing? What could it be for? We were still now. I was unsteady. I feared I might fall. I think one of the girls may have slumped to the floor. I had the sense that she was being lifted, and carried.

"Move ahead, up, up the ramp," said a master, almost at my elbow.

I did not think that Paula was before me now.

I did not know where she was.

I think she had preceded me, in her turn.

I was sure of very little.

My knees felt weak.

I struggled to retain consciousness.

"Up the ramp," I was told.

I felt the corrugated steel flooring of the ramp beneath my bare feet. I do not think I will ever forget that sensation. It seemed the clearest thing to me, the surface of the ramp, cold, hard, rippled, the most real thing. I began to climb, step by step.

"Good girl," said a fellow, beside me.

"Watch her," said a man. "She is hardly on her feet."

"I will," said the fellow beside me.

Some of us, I was sure, surely Paula, were already within that structure, walking, or carried.

Then I was at the opening, the door, the portal, the hatch, at the height of the ramp. I had the sense of the space before me, far, deep, the interior of the disklike object, the relatively low ceiling, some lights in the ceiling.

I shook my head. "No, no!" I said, and then I felt myself being steadied by a man's hand. "No, please," I said. "No, please!" Then I felt myself being lifted, lightly, one arm behind the back of my knees, the other behind my back. "No," I whimpered. I put my head back. I was being carried within. Everything seemed red, and it turned, slowly, and then, suddenly, it turned black.

I lay quietly.

I was afraid to open my eyes, and look about me.

I had the sense I lay on a closely woven straw mat.

Surely I was not on my bed, in the apartment. I pressed my eyelids closely together. I had the sense that there was metal on my neck. I put my hands to my neck, and felt the thick metal encirclement there, that close encirclement, perhaps two inches in height, and a half inch in thickness, within which my neck was clasped. I felt a heavy ring in the front, attached to the encirclement, and a chain was linked about that ring. I did not know where lay the other terminus of that chain. It took only a moment more to determine that I was absolutely naked.

Even the anklet had been removed from my left ankle.

I did not understand the meaning of this.

I lay quietly.

I felt a heavy, bootlike sandal nudge my right thigh.

"Kneel, bitch," said a voice, "head down, head to the floor, in your appropriate collar and chain. I anticipated seeing you so. It pleases me." I was sure I had heard that voice before.

In this moment, I could not help but apprise myself, to some extent, however inadequately, of my surroundings. I was kneeling on a closely woven straw mat, at the foot of a massive stone couch, covered with furs, in what appeared to be a large, plain, primitive room. The chain from my collar ring, about a yard long, ran to another ring, a heavy ring, which ring was fixed in the stone couch. I was thus naked, chained to the foot of a couch, kneeling, my head to the floor.

The air, even in the room, seemed wondrously clear. I could not recall having breathed such air. Perhaps I had not done so. I doubt that it was much more highly oxygenated than the air to which I was hitherto accustomed, air I had never hitherto questioned. But it was cleaner, fresher, less gray, less contaminated, I suppose. Too, I sensed something different, slightly so, something hard to place. I would learn this had to do with gravity. I supposed I weighed somewhat less here. I sensed I might move more easily, more freely here. Interestingly, in a few hours I would physically and psychologically adjust to such changes, and would behave, feel, and move here as unconsciously and naturally as I had before, on a different orb. I would learn the gravity of Gor, for it was on this world I now was, was less than that of Earth, the planet being somewhat smaller, though it would have more land surface than Earth, as it possessed only one mighty ocean, not two, that ocean being restless, turbulent, gleaming Thassa, the sea.

"Surely you understand that you are a slave," he said.

I kept my head down. I was sure I knew the voice.

"You were annoying," he said. "I decided you would be a slave. I thought it would amuse me to own you. For a time, of course. You are not worth keeping."

I said nothing.

"Perhaps you surmised that your flanks might be of interest to a man. Consider the matter."

I tried to deal with the tumult within me.

"Now, worthless bitch," he said, "I have you as I desired. I have you as you ought to be, stark naked, kneeling at a man's feet, on his chain."

I shook with emotion.

"Lift your head," he said. "Yes," he said, "it is I."

It was he whom I had not seen since that afternoon in the office, late, toward closing time.

"Yes," said he, "be afraid. Yes, tremble, pretty bitch. You are owned. You are now a slave."

I looked away, terrified to meet his eyes.

"Yes," he said, "a slave, a pot girl, a kettle-and-mat girl, perhaps not even a kettle-and-mat girl. Perhaps only a pot girl, one for the laundries, the kitchens, for turning a mill beam."

I fought strange feelings within me. I was from a barbarian world, and this man was Gorean.

"Women such as you," he said, "belong on your knees before men."

There was a wildness within me. Could what he said be true? I felt strange sensations. I feared I was secretly thrilled, kneeling so. I had never before felt such feelings. Could I be in my place, my rightful place, kneeling before a man? Surely not!

"What do you want of me?" I whispered.

"Everything," he said.

"Release me," I said. "Return me to Earth."

"Alas," he said, "you are even more stupid than I feared."

"I am not stupid," I said.

"You are now a Gorean slave girl," he said. "Rather than return you to Earth, you would be thrown to sleen."

I recalled that Paula, in the apartment, had spoken of 'sleen'. "What are sleen?" I said.

"Perhaps I will one day show you," he said. "I do not think you would like to be cast into a pit of sleen. But sleen, at least, are quick. Perhaps leech plants would be preferable for you, to be cast naked and bound amongst them, and feel them swarm over you, fasten their tendrils and vines about you, and puncture you with their fangs, and draw out the blood, noisily, minim by minim."

I shuddered.

"I am intelligent," I stammered.

He sat on the foot of the bed, those heavily sandaled feet but a foot from me. "You are now a slave girl, a barbarian slave, on the planet Gor," he said. "You exist for the pleasure and service of masters. You have learned, I trust, that all free men are to be addressed as 'Master', all free women as 'Mistress'. You may be bought and sold. As any other slave, you are subject to bonds and discipline. It is on your papers that you have been administered slave wine. Excellent.

We would not wish you becoming pregnant, unless at the decision of your master. You belong, of course, to your master, as a possession, his in all things. It is up to him whether or not you will be clothed, and in what way, and to what extent. You must not expect us to speak English to you, as I am now doing. As a slave, you must learn the language of your masters, Gorean, and learn it as quickly and as well as you can. That will be to your advantage. Indeed, it may save your life. Its rudiments, of vocabulary and grammar, will be taught to you in your house of training, to which, in a day or two, I will remit you. It will not do to bring an ignorant girl to the block. You will also, in your house of training, receive a set of injections. These constitute what we refer to as the 'stabilization serums'. Some centuries ago the caste of Physicians addressed itself to what is sometimes known as the drying and withering disease, what one might call in English, "ageing." This was regarded on Gor not as an inevitability, as commonly on Earth, but as a medical issue, susceptible to treatment and, later, to prevention. The stabilization serums are complex and have, I am told, a number of special applications and variations. You need not, however, concern yourselves with these. You will receive the basic series, which, in effect, in most cases, assures pattern stability. I see you do not understand. To simplify matters, your body will remain much as it is as long as you live. You will, thus, retain, indefinitely, your youth and beauty, your beauty such as it is, of course. I see you are surprised. Do not be confused. You remain vulnerable and mortal. You are spared merely the miseries and degradations of age, only those. Yes, such things would doubtless be highly prized on your former world, doubtless to the extent of billions in various currencies, but here they are inexpensive and widely available. They are commonly administered to slaves, as well as free persons. Do not think this shows any special consideration to such as you, a despised slave. It is done on behalf of the free, that their slaves will retain their vitality, passion, youth, beauty, and health, this serving to keep them more attractive and appealing, which, of course, aside from a number of obvious advantages to the master, personal and aesthetic, has a number of economic consequences as well, as his goods will then, on the whole, keep their market value, their resale value, and such."

Could it be true, what he said, I wondered. If so, what an inordinate gift I might receive, and yet it would not be a gift, truly, but merely something done in the interests of the free, that their properties, such as I, might remain more valuable!

I dared to meet his eyes. Then, frightened, I quickly lowered my eyes.

"Would you like to lick and kiss my feet," he asked, "a suitable act of deference from one such as you?"

I shook my head negatively, timidly.

"You will be a good girl, will you not?" he asked.

"Yes," I whispered.

"'Yes'?" he said.

"Yes," I said, "I will be a good girl."

"'Yes'?" he said.

"Yes, I will be a good girl—Master," I said.

"You may now beg to be beaten, if you are not pleasing," he said.

I did not speak. I was afraid to speak.

"How stupid she is," he said, wearily.

"I am not stupid," I said, adding, "Master."

He rose from the couch on which he had been sitting, and went to the wall to my left. From a peg there he removed an object, with a long leather handle, which might be grasped with two hands, and five broad, soft blades, which he shook free.

"I beg to be beaten if I am not pleasing," I said.

"You will be," he said.

"But I am a woman," I said.

"But a slave," he said.

"Yes," I whispered.

"'Yes, Master'," he said.

"Yes—Master," I said.

"Turn about, and put your head to the floor," he said, "and clasp your hands behind the back of your neck."

"Master?" I said.

"Now," he said.

I complied.

"What are you going to do?" I asked.

"We will get this over as quickly as possible," he said.

"I am a virgin!" I said. "Ai!"

He was quick, and then he thrust me from him. I shuddered from the rude, callous, repetitive, brutal, plunging violence to which I had been briefly subjected. Then he crouched beside me. I whimpered. Then, a moment later, his hand was drawn across my lips and pushed into my mouth. I tasted secretions, and my own blood. I lay on my side, he now above me, now standing beside me.

"Perhaps you should have been more courteous, when a stranger entered your office," he said.

I was silent, trying to realize what had been done to me.

"Should you not have been more courteous?" he asked.

"Yes, Master," I whispered.

"I then envisaged," he said, "having you in this way, and seeing you as you are now, so before me."

"Yes, Master," I said.

"I am," he said, "of the caste of Slavers."

"I did not know, Master," I said.

He stepped away from me.

I knew, of course, that a slave is entitled to no consideration. Yet I think I had not understood that simple matter so well until now. I was an object, a beast. And I had been used as such.

My body shook.

Two strange, conflicting emotions warred within me. One was a violent rage at what had been done to me, a rage rife with shame, degradation, humiliation, frustration, and an acute sense of a lack of recourse, a sense of an utter helplessness, and the other, even stronger, was a sense of its fittingness. Was I not a slave? Was this not what could be done with me? Too, I had the terrifying sense that if he had been a little patient, taken his time, caressed me a little, put his teeth to me, spoke his mastery, I might have cried out, grateful, yielding. I had received the sense of what might be done with me, and what I might become. How horrifying if I might find myself a yielding, begging slave in the arms of her master! How could I think of myself then as other than a moaning, worthless, subdued, conquered, pleading kajira? I trusted he had no sense of this torment within me. I lay at his feet, naked, on his chain. Surely I must prove to him that I was not a slave, that I was proud, noble, and independent, not a woman who belonged at a man's feet, not a slave!

Without speaking, he left the room.

He had replaced the whip on the wall. This pleased me. I would learn, happily, that most Gorean masters are sparing with the whip. But it is always there. I did not know what it would feel like. It had not been used on me. I was not anxious to feel it. I determined to do much to avoid its stroke. Later, once I had felt it, I would be shudderingly, keenly, desperately anxious to avoid its stroke. It is designed to punish, to punish terribly, but not to mark. It is useful in the disciplining of slaves.

He returned a bit later, with some water, and two biscuits. He put a wastes bucket within reach.

He then left the room, again.

I resolved, after he had left, in the midst of conflicting emotions, despite my profound inclinations to the contrary, as I was beginning to sense what I might be, and perhaps had always been, to behave in a way which certain militant factions in my society, with their self-serving agendas, might approve. They did not know me, of course, but they apparently took for granted their right to impose their particular values and views on me, and millions of others, by a variety of means, including those of the state.

After a bit he returned to the room.

"Have you fed and relieved yourself?" he said.

"Yes," I said.

"You omitted the word 'Master'," he said.

"Apparently," I said.

"You are a bitch, are you not?" he said.

I was silent.

"You are stupid," he said.

"No," I said, "I am not stupid."

"In any event," he said, "you have not yet learned your collar."

"I do not expect to learn it," I said.

"That is typical, at first," he said, "with some, with the more stupid ones."

"I am not stupid," I said.

"It is soon, of course," he said.

I looked away. I put my hands on the chain dangling down from the ring on the metal collar about my neck. The chain seemed heavy. It would doubtless have held a man.

"Have you ever been whipped?" he asked.

"No," I said.

"That is sometimes helpful," he said.

"Doubtless," I said.

"In any event," he said, "tomorrow I will remand you to a training house. There you will be trained."

"I will not be trained," I said. "I am not an animal!"

He looked at me.

"What you did to me!" I cried.

"It was good to get it out of the way," he said. "Accustom yourself to such things. You are a slave. Free women will envy you."

"I was a free woman!" I said.

"Not really," he said. "I have a good eye for such things."

"Free!" I said.

"In some trivial, legal sense, perhaps," he said. "But you are not a free woman now. You are a different sort of woman now."

"Free!"

"Once you are collared and branded," he said, "you may see things differently."

"I will not accept being trained as an animal," I said.

He looked down at me, wearily. I lowered my eyes, sullenly, defiantly. He then turned and went to a chest, at the side of the room. Such things are much more common in Gorean domiciles than closets and cabinets. He put back the lid of the chest, and reached within it, withdrawing a handful of what appeared to be shackles, and manacles, and a few short lengths of chain, apparently adjustable.

He dropped this paraphernalia beside me, and, kneeling beside me, grasped my right wrist, which he twisted behind my back. I felt one of the manacles clasped about it. Then my left ankle was seized and drawn back, and shackled, fastened to my right wrist.

"What are you doing?" I asked, uneasily. "Oh!" I said, as my left wrist was pulled back, close to my right ankle.

I heard a snap, as it was fastened there.

"'Master'?" he asked.

"Master," I said.

"You use the word 'Master'," he said. "But you do not yet understand it."

"Master?" I asked.

"But you will," he said, "girl."

"What are you doing, Master?" I asked. "Oh!" I said, as another adjustment was made.

"Putting you in close chains," he said.

"I do not understand," I said.

"You require discipline," he said.

"Oh!" I said, wincing.

"In the morning," he said, "you will beg training."

"Never!" I said. "Never!" I could scarcely move. "Release me!" I demanded. "Oh!" I cried, as, with snaps, he further adjusted the apparatus in which he had seen fit to place me, even more tightly.

"Release me!" I said. "Release me!" I then begged. "Please, please release me, now!"

He stood up, towering over the knot of slave at his feet.

"Until the morning," he said.

"Do not leave me like this!" I cried.

"You are chained," he said, "close chained. As in any chaining you cannot free yourself. But do not struggle, do not fight the chains. I do not want you marked, bloodied, or scarred. If you are marked, your profitability, such as it is, will be reduced, and I will be displeased. Indeed, if I find you marked, you will be whipped as few women have been whipped. It is yours to lie quietly, and endure. You have now been warned."

"Do not leave me like this!" I begged, again, more piteously.

I heard the door close.

I squirmed, scarcely capable of movement.

CHAPTER EIGHT

He tossed a sandal to the floor, some feet to my right.

"Go to it, on all fours, kiss it, and bring it to me, on all fours, in your teeth," he said.

"Yes, Master," I said.

It is easy to move so, in a slave tunic.

He then cast the second sandal to the floor, some feet to my left, and I fetched it, similarly, and, putting down my head, deposited it, too, at his feet.

I then knelt before him.

"In your training," he said, "were you taught how to lace a master's sandals?"

"Yes, Master," I said.

"You may sandal me," he said.

"Thank you, Master," I said.

In a few moments I had laced the sandals in place.

A slave is grateful for the privilege of serving her master.

"What did they call you in the training house?" he asked.

"'Phyllis'," I said. It is not unusual for a girl's former name, in a sense, particularly in the case of barbarians, to be kept on her. To be sure, technically, it is not the same name, as the legal name vanishes with the girl's freedom. 'Phyllis' was now a slave name, bestowed at the discretion of a master or mistress, as any animal might be named by its master or mistress. The retention of a former name is convenient, of course, as easily solving a naming problem, and a barbarian slave is well identified by being given a barbarian name, which is commonly done, her former name, or another such name. Sometimes an enslaved Gorean woman is given a barbarian name, to enforce upon her the lowliness, the humiliation, and degradation, of her new status. The societal position of the Gorean free woman, incidentally, particularly in the high cities, is far higher than that of the average free woman of

Earth. Accordingly her reduction to bondage is likely to be far more devastating to her than such a reduction in the case of the average woman of Earth. Many of the women of Earth, for example, think little of baring their features, and their ankles, in public, an exhibitionism which would be unthinkable for most Gorean free women, and certainly for those of the higher castes. One can well imagine the feelings of a former Gorean free woman, who might have, in daring, scandalous boldness, occasionally allowed a glove to slip a little, affording a glimpse of wrist, finding herself exposed in public, tunicked and collared, only another slave.

"It has a Cosian ring to it," he said.

I did not understand this.

"I am told some free women have that name," I said.

"Cosians, perhaps," he said.

I knew little of Gor at that time. I would later learn that Cos was a major state, somewhere to the east. At that time I did not even know where I was. Curiosity, I had been told, is not becoming in a kajira.

"Your Gorean is coming along nicely," he said.

"In the training house, the switch often abetted my learning," I said.

"You must strive to become adept in the language of your masters," he said.

"Yes, Master," I said.

"Do you hope to please your master?" he asked.

"Yes, Master," I said. I well knew the penalties for being displeasing. Yet, interestingly, I found I wanted to be pleasing to men, and that I hoped to become more so. It seemed to me, now, right and fitting that I should be owned, that I should submit, and serve.

I was different from men, very different.

This very obvious difference, on my former world, had been ignored, or denied. Here I found myself in a place where such differences were recognized. Men were not women, and women were not men. Is it not strange that there are worlds where such an observation should appear surprising, and be hailed as a profound insight? And this, I would learn, that men were not women, and women were not men, was the case amongst even the free. But for women such as I, in this place, women who were not free, such differences were profound. Our differences from men were not only acknowledged by society, but, by brand, collar, and tunic, confirmed and celebrated. Women such as I, not being free, were not permitted to deny or dismiss the truths, needs, and passions of our sex. For women such as I, such pretenses would be no more than a laughable hypocrisy. Needs and passions, desires and yearnings, should be no more things of shame than health and beauty. Too, women such as I were not encased in proprieties and conventions, not hedged in by society, not permitted to hide ourselves behind veils, or within cumbersome robes, not permitted to bargain, to tease and taunt, to barter our favors for social or economic advancement. We could be bought and sold. We were the most female of all women, the most basic and fundamental of all women, and would find ourselves in our natural place, there where we belonged, at the feet of men, their slaves.

"Brand!" he snapped.

Instantly, without even thinking, I shifted my weight to my right knee and extended my left leg, fully, drawing the tunic to the hip.

"Excellent," he said.

I had been marked my first morning in the house of training, and a house collar, a training collar, had been hammered about my throat.

Female slaves on Gor are commonly collared.

I hated the training collar.

I now wore a light metal band, flat, and close-fitting, on my throat, secured with a small lock at the back of the neck.

It was a very common Gorean collar. I would later learn that, in the south, collars were often rounded, and looser. These are usually referred to, in their varieties, as "Turian collars." Turia, I would learn, was a large city in the southern hemisphere.

"You may kneel again," he said.

I did so.

"You kneel," he said, "with your knees closely together."

That was commonly referred to, for some reason, as the position of the tower slave. Girls, of course, may be commanded to one position or another. I did not know, at that time, why the position was referred to as the position of the tower slave. From the training house I had been brought to the domicile of my master, hooded.

"Yes, Master," I said. I felt a tear form at my left eye. I feared it might move down my cheek. My master showed little inclination to beat me, but I had no desire to do anything that might prompt him to do so.

"What do you think of your collar?" he asked.

"It is attractive, Master," I said.

"Women look well in collars," he said.

"Yes, Master," I said.

"Is it comfortable?" he asked.

"Yes, Master," I said. "It is light, and comfortable. Commonly I do not even know it is on me."

"But it is," he said.

"Yes, Master," I said.

"Do many women on your former world wear collars?" he asked.

"No, Master," I said. Surely he knew that.

"That is unfortunate," he said. "A collar much enhances the beauty of a woman."

"Yes, Master," I said.

"Do slaves on your world wear collars?" he asked.

"I do not think so," I said.

"At least not publicly," he said.

"Perhaps not," I said.

How did I know what might occur when a door was closed?

"Every slave should have her collar," he said. "It reminds them they are slaves."

"Yes, Master," I said.

"On Gor," he said, "it would not do for a slave to forget that she is a slave."

"No, Master," I said.

"So she wears her collar," he said.

"Yes, Master," I said.

"It marks her well," he said.

"Yes, Master," I said.

"It would not do to have her confused with a free woman," he said.

"No, Master," I said.

I did not speak, but there seemed little doubt, as well, that a woman clad in a slave tunic would not be likely to be confused with a free woman. Too, there was always the brand. My brand was small and delicate, but unmistakable. It had been placed high on my left thigh, just below the hip. It was an attractive mark. It had a vague resemblance to a cursive 'k' in English. I was told it was a 'Kef', which is the first letter in the Gorean expression, 'kajira'. It was also, apparently, a very common brand. I was, accordingly, not privileged, or distinguished, by a special or unusual brand.

"I gather you cannot read your collar," he said.

"No, Master," I said. "Perhaps Master will teach me to read, or have me instructed."

"No," he said.

"Yes, Master," I said.

"You know what it says?" he said.

"I have been told," I said. I had been told it read 'I am the slave of Kurik of Victoria'. At that time I knew little or nothing of my surroundings. I would later learn that Victoria was a large river port. Amongst other things it was a large clearing station for the handling of slaves. It was difficult to trace slaves through Victoria, most of whom were sold without papers. Indeed, many slaves in her holding pens wore no more than chain collars, or capture collars, which suggested dubious origins, at best. Victoria was a trading port in which few questions were either asked or answered.

I put down my head, before my master.

Once he had suggested I did not know the meaning of the word 'Master', but that I would learn it.

I had learned it, in his case, and in the case of any man.

The morning after I had been "close chained," at the foot of my master's couch, he had entered, and stood over me.

He did not speak.

"I beg training!" I had said, tensely, piteously.

"What sort of training?" he asked.

"Slave training," I said.

"The training of a slave?" he asked.

"Yes!" I said.

"Why?" he asked.

"I do not know," I said.

He then prepared to turn away.

"Because I am a slave!" I cried.

"Your response seems incomplete," he said.

"Because I am a slave—Master!" I wept.

He then began to undo the fastenings.

"Thank you," I whispered, "thank you, Master."

I wept, trembled, and moaned, and cried out, inadvertently, with tiny cries of pain. I could scarcely move my limbs. His hands on my limbs were firm, and strong, and unhurried. He slowly stretched out my legs and arms, and, gently, carefully, rubbed them alive. I had fantasized that I might never be able to walk again, that I could not rise, that I had been crippled for life.

He then desisted in his work, and sat on the edge of the couch, and I lay at his feet.

I may have lain there for the better part of an hour.

He was patient. He did not hurry me.

At last, by the use of my hands, I managed to struggle, slowly, painfully, to my knees, before him, my head over his feet.

"I beg to lick and kiss the feet of my master," I whispered.

"Very well," he said.

I then addressed myself to this humble task, hoping that he would be pleased. I belonged to him. I now knew what I was, a property, an animal, an owned animal. I suppose I had been an animal on my own world, as well, but not an owned animal. And now I was an owned animal.

After a time, I looked up, tears in my eyes.

"Is Master pleased?" I asked.

"You have much to learn," he said.

"I trust I will be taught," I said.

"On Earth," he said, "I called you a 'bitch'."

"Yes, Master," I said.

"On Earth you were a bitch," he said.

"I trust I am no longer a bitch," I said.

"You cannot be a bitch in a collar," he said. "The whip sees to that."

"Yes, Master," I said.

"Perhaps you think yourself still a bitch," he said.

"I hope not," I said. "But if so, I am surely Master's bitch."

"You are no longer a bitch," he said.

"Thank you, Master," I said.

"But not for the reason you might think," he said. "A slave is far less than a bitch."

"Yes, Master," I said. Doubtless it was so.

"Shortly," he had said, "I will hood you and take you to your house of training. It is not far. This training will take only a few days, and, at the end, you will be poorly trained, as we have little time, but well enough trained, I shall hope, to survive the block and your first weeks of bondage, in which time, applying yourself, you must strive earnestly to become a better and better, and a more and more pleasing, slave. The first several days will doubtless be the hardest, the most frightening, the most harrowing, the most difficult, but, if you are intelligent, diligent, devoted, hot, and dutiful, things should go well. You will have begun to learn your collar. Masters, of course, differ, and most will train a slave to their own tastes. You must attend well to such lessons. You will discover that a man wants everything from his kajira, and that is why he has purchased her, but you will also discover that he who has everything from his kajira is likely to be pleased, contented, and happy. Why not? What can a man want, beyond everything? Some men, fools, even become fond of their kajira. That is indeed difficult to understand."

"Yes, Master," I said.

"Incredible," he said.

"Yes, Master," I said.

"If you suspect your master is becoming fond of you," he said, "you may expect to be beaten, or sold."

"Yes, Master," I said.

"One is not to care for a slave," he said.

"Yes, Master," I said.

"Slaves are worthless," he said. "They are to be despised."

"I understand, Master," I said.

I had then been hooded and taken to the house of training.

"May I speak?" I asked.

"Yes," he said.

"I know that curiosity is not becoming in a kajira," I said, "but, as Master is doubtless aware, curiosity is not unknown amongst kajirae."

"I am aware of that," he said.

"I am of Earth," I said. "Yet I was brought here, and put in a collar to serve masters."

"So?" he said.

"I gather I am not unique," I said.

"Certainly not," he said.

"Clearly, on this world," I said, "female slavery exists."

"And male slavery," he said, "but male slavery is less obvious, as most male slaves are utilized in the quarries, on the galleys, on the great farms, in such places. Occasionally a male is taken from your former world, a typical male of your former world, suitably conditioned, and thus reduced and tamed, to be sold as a silk slave to a Gorean mistress. Such can be perilous though, for they sometimes, on this world, learn their manhood, and may thus constitute a danger to the mistress, who might find herself gagged and put in a slave sack, to be sold, or even, collared, to find herself at the feet of her former slave. Accordingly most slaves brought to Gor are women, namely, members of the slave sex."

"The slave sex?" I said.

"Yes," he said, "though it would not do to say that to a Gorean free woman."

"I see," I said.

"But, enslaved, they learn their collars quickly enough," he said.

"There is a slave traffic with Earth?" I said.

"There is an extensive slave traffic, an extensive slave trade, on Gor," he said. "Indeed, wars have been fought to obtain slaves. There are Slave Roads. There are hundreds of markets, large and small. Cities may exchange slaves. Tributes are often levied in terms of female slaves, and so on. But there is nothing like a slave traffic, or slave trade, where Earth is concerned, not recently, at any rate. Rather, Earth is regarded as a breeding ground for female slaves, a place from which suitable stock may be easily obtained."

I trembled, at his feet.

"The women of Earth," he said, "sell well in our markets. Some men prefer them even to Gorean women. They have never had a Home Stone. One need not be concerned with them. They are nothing. Too, they make excellent slaves. They are soon grateful for their collars."

I was silent.

"Women have needs," he said, "slave needs. The women of Earth, familiar only with the typical men of Earth, confused, crippled, timid, diffident, apologetic, diminished, eager to conform, zealous to please those who hate them, are frequently starved for sex. How can they be fulfilled by half men, by nonmen?"

"Surely there are true men on Earth," I said.

"Are they not against the law?" he asked.

"Perhaps they exist, in secret," I whispered.

"That is doubtless wise," he said.

"Master?" I said.

"Why should they not keep manhood secret?" he asked.

"Master?" I said.

"A thousand squeaking urts," he said, "could eat a tethered kailiauk alive."

I did not understand what he said.

"Goreans," he said, "regard the women of Earth as self-acknowledged, self-confessed, slaves. Consider the lack of veiling and concealment, the brazen display of their faces, the frequent flaunting of ankles and calves, even of arms and shoulders, the styles of summer wear, the garments of beaches, the nature of night wear, the sheerness of hose, the pleasantries of lingerie, the use of cosmetics and perfumes, which a master might enforce upon a slave. These delicious and delightful adornments are the obvious vanities of slaves. Do they not beg, in their way? Do they not say, 'Consider me! I am here! I am lovely! Have me! Own me! Collar me!'?"

"I wore an anklet," I said. "When I awakened, at the foot of your couch, it was gone."

"It was no longer needed," he said.

"I know little of your world," I said.

"There are things about this world," he said, "of which many Goreans, themselves, know nothing."

"I do not understand," I said.

"Dark forces are afoot," he said. "Worlds are at stake. Species, equipped and resolute, are at war. Laws are ignored, at great peril. Mysterious ships stalk the night."

"I understand nothing of this," I said, frightened.

"Do not be concerned," he said.

"But I would know!" I said.

"Curiosity," said he, "is not becoming in a kajira."

"Yes, Master," I whispered, lowering my head.

I sensed he was considering me. Even on Earth many women are sensitive to such things. How can some, I wondered, pretend to be ignorant of the tensions, the cords of interest and desire, which attend the interactions of the sexes? Are they unaware of the radical centrality of sexuality to the human condition? Do they lie, or are they somehow ignorant, or inert, simply blind to the turbulence of invisible torrents rushing about them? Have they never experienced seemingly small things, betokening broad, sweeping currents, tiny things hinting at looming storms, the lifting of eyes, the catching of breath, the pounding of a heart, the unsteadiness of a body? Have their bodies and emotions never responded to having been viewed with interest, even desire? Have they never trembled, knowing they were wanted, and have they never admitted to themselves, as well, their own desires, that they, too, hope, and want? These things, so natural, so vital, and healthy, so frequently denied on Earth, subject to even fearful, pathological denials or dismissals, things taught on Earth to be soiled by shame and hypocrisy, are accepted and welcomed on Gor. Goreans, male and female, are not conditioned to dread and fear nature, to abet the agendas of the weak, strange, and ill-constituted, those who would seek power by means of imposing values and disvalues, those who would strive to instill and manipulate guilt to their own advantage. In any event, Goreans, male and female, slave and free, by whatever glimpse of wisdom and truth, or by whatever stroke of fortune, have never been taught to suspect themselves of some shameful unworthiness for the crime of being alive and human. It would no more occur to them to do so than it would to denounce breathing, or the circulation of the blood.

I did not speak.

Even I, from childhood on, I suspected, had been taught a sort of treachery to myself.

To be sure, one is taught, as well, not to ask questions, not to notice that views and values may have origins, histories, and purposes.

But perhaps they do.

Surely it was not difficult to detect the work of militant factions on my former world, intending to advance their own interests by distorting, denying, diminishing, and even nullifying nature. Surely there was an agenda behind the project of cultivating suspicion and hostility toward men in females and striving to devirilize males, so that the 'true male', the male to be societally approved, would be the least like a man.

But surely one must sympathize with those who would commit themselves to so ambitious a project, to so arduous an endeavor!

How brave and noble they are!

It is not easy to do away with nature.

It is not an easy thing to destroy, even if one wishes earnestly to do so.

Nature, unlike self-serving political programs, is not the product of ideologically motivated committees; who would seize control of education and the means of communication, to bend innocent, trusting children, and even unwitting populations, to their views; nature is an obstacle to such programs; it is not contrived to serve the interests of a particular group on a particular afternoon. It is real, and tenacious. It lurks in secret places, in each gene in the human body.

And not all cultures and societies need view her as an enemy, to be denounced, and done away with as soon as possible.

I suspected there were other ways to live.

And I feared that one such way had been found on Gor.

In any event, on Gor, as far as I could determine, the realities of sex not only existed, as they must, but, too, more significantly, they were acknowledged, and welcomed.

The mightinesses of nature, and the profound, interrelated, complementary differences between men and women were recognized and celebrated.

Considering these things, I shook with terror, for here I was not a free woman, exalted in society, possessed of a Home Stone. I was the most vulnerable of all women, the female slave, in a world in which men had never relinquished their sovereignty, their nature as men, their possessiveness, their aggression, their claimancy, and lust, a world in which they might do as they wished with one such as I.

And yet I feared I had a place on such a world, a natural place, one for which I might be fitted, and one in which I belonged.

"What is wrong?" he asked.

"Nothing, Master," I said.

I recalled the words of one of my instructresses, she switch bearing and herself collared, in the house of training. "You are a slave," she said, "behave as a slave, move as a slave, speak as a slave, think as a slave, feel as a slave, be honestly and openly, in every bit of your body and mind, what you are, and want to be, a slave."

"Is something wrong?" he said.

"No, Master," I said.

The differences between men and women, profound as they were anywhere, I would learn, were far more intensified, far more visible, far more open, on Gor than on my former world, even amongst the free, and so would they not be multiplied a thousandfold between the free and slave, and I was slave.

I was sure he was thinking of me, kneeling before him, tunicked. What man would not?

"You are frightened," he said.

"Yes, Master," I said.

"That is fitting," he said.

"Yes, Master," I said.

"I think you will make the transition into slavery easily," he said.

"Master?" I said.

"You were born to be a slave," he said, "to wear a collar, to be a man's work beast and plaything."

"Master?" I said.

"Consider your body, its smallness, its slightness and softness, your features, their vulnerability, their delicacy and sensitivity, their expressiveness, your lips, your eyes, your wrists, your shoulders and throat, your dispositions and emotions."

"I thought," I said, "I was only a pot girl, only a kettle-and-mat girl."

"That is all you are," he said, angrily.

I was frightened to see him angry. I did not know why he was angry. I was muchly uneasy. On the wall, to my left, on its peg, hung a five-stranded Gorean slave whip.

I put my head down.

He was large, and strong.

I sensed that his blood was quickening and heating, and I was before him, collared.

I was desperately frightened.

"Master," I said.

"Yes," he said.

"I was brought to Gor with others," I said, "to be the slave I am, branded and collared. What of the others?"

"There are commonly a hundred, certainly in the typical consignment, sometimes a few more or a few less. You were in capsule ninety-seven."

"We were looked upon, while we were sedated," I said.

"There is monitoring," he said.

"In the house of training," I said, "I saw no members of my party."

"Probably not," he said. "The stock is distributed to a variety of markets; sometimes one answers orders. It is thought wise to scatter stock. In that way their origin is not easily traced, which might lead to the discovery of sensitive information, even a ship."

"There is much danger?" I said.

"The rulers of the world of Gor," he said, "object to violations of their technology laws. Certain forms of technology are denied to humans, certainly technology of the sort that would be involved in such a ship. What is perilous, then, is bringing such a ship to the shores of Gor. Great care, and stealth, is involved."

"And thus the anklets were removed, and your captures distributed about?"

"Yes," he said.

"You spoke of the rulers of the world of Gor," I said, "who would be concerned with certain forms of technology."

"They are called Priest-Kings," he said. "I know little about them. They are the gods of Gor. I assume they are large, and handsome, and much like us, that they are glorious, formidable manlike things."

"You spoke of war, and of species, before," I said.

"I have seen beasts," he said, "foes of Priest-Kings."

"Beasts?" I said.

He shuddered. "Kurii," he said. "Let us not speak of them. Do not concern yourself. You are no more likely to see one than a Priest-King."

"Curiosity is not becoming in a kajira," I said.

"No," he said.

"War?" I said.

"Between Priest-Kings and beasts," he said. "Few on Gor even know it exists. Its waging is subtle. It is largely invisible."

"I am frightened," I said.

"I, too," he said.

"How is it that you have ships?" I asked.

"Both Priest-Kings and Kurii," he said, "enlist human allies. And Kurii have no objection to arming, and equipping, humans, provided we prove to be of service, transporting envoys and agents, carrying messages, probing defenses, obtaining rare materials, metals, chemicals, and such, scarce in the Kur worlds."

"Kur worlds?" I said.

"Large worlds, but constructed worlds," he said, "steel worlds."

"They have no planet?" I asked.

"Once, perhaps," he said. "But it seems it was destroyed, or rendered sterile."

"How could it be?" I asked.

"I do not know," he said.

"How could a planet be ruined?" I asked.

"I do not know," he said.

I feared I could conjecture how such things might take place. Might not an axis be tilted, following fearful explosions, might not a core be split, might not such a world, sundered, be driven from its star, might not an atmosphere be poisoned? I supposed a world might die quickly, or slowly, perhaps by inches, almost unnoticed.

"Kurii now want Gor," I said.

"Of course," he said.

"Are you not particular whom you serve?" I asked.

"Who knows where right and wrong lie?" he said. "Priest-Kings are tyrants. Kurii give us power, and gold."

"Master," I said.

"Yes?" said he.

"Do you know the fate of a slave named Paula?"

"She would not be easy to miss," he said. "All approved her. Who would not remember her? She was the beauty of your shipment."

"Surely not," I said, "not simple, plain Paula!"

"She will be disposed of in Ar," he said, "on a high block, at the Curulean, perhaps even from the Central Block. I would not be surprised if she went for five silver pieces, in a first sale. It will be a lucky sleen who gets his chain on her."

"I do not understand," I said.

"Surely you do not presume to compare yourself with her," he said.

"Surely I am far more beautiful!" I said.

Kurik threw back his large head and laughed. "Naive pot girl," he said.

I reddened, angrily. Surely anyone could tell I was far more beautiful than Paula. How could these lustful, powerful brutes of Gor not see that? Indeed, I was clearly the most attractive of our luncheon group, which met in the cafeteria in the building where we worked. To be sure, one or two of the girls might have thought themselves, mistakenly, my equal, or superior.

"What is she to you?" he asked.

"She was my friend," I said. "I think she was the only true friend I ever had."

"You were fortunate," he said, "to have a friend. Such as you are likely to have few friends, and to deserve none."

Tears came to my eyes. I had not treated Paula well, and had often expressed my contempt of her, veiled, of course, as well-meaning, constructive suggestions, or piquant witticisms. Yet, despite my treatment of her, which she must have understood, she had always been pleasant, patient, attentive, tolerant, accommodating, faithful, and kind. She was a reliable person, who would do much for another, asking nothing in return. I suppose, in a way, she was the only friend I had ever had.

"Forget her," he said. "She will have a thousand masters and a hundred names. She will be lost in the markets. You will never see her again."

Tears burst from my eyes.

"Wipe your face," he said.

"Yes, Master," I said, and drew my forearm across my eyes.

I think I had never felt more alone than I did then.

I looked up at my master.

"May I speak?" I asked.

One of the first things I had learned in the house of training was that a slave girl may not speak without permission. To be sure, with most masters, she has a standing permission to speak, a permission which may, of course, be bestowed or revoked, as the master may please.

"Yes," he said.

"I am yours," I said.

"Yes?" he said.

"Will you keep me?" I asked.

"For a time," he said, "perhaps a few Ahn."

I was still not clear on the length of an Ahn, a measure of time. There were several such, I had learned, in the Gorean day.

"Paula is beautiful?" I asked.

"Very much so," he said.

"Does Master find this slave attractive?" I asked.

"Stand up," he said, "and face me." I was then standing before him. He then rose to his feet, and he towered over me.

"Have you been taught to remove your tunic gracefully before a man?" he asked.

"Yes, Master," I whispered.

"Do so," he said.

I was then before him, inches from him, clad only in my collar.

"Oh!" I said.

I was thrust to the floor at his feet.

I looked up, frightened.

"Do you object to being handled so?" he asked.

I lay before him, at his feet, naked, my legs drawn up, my gaze averted. "Master will do with me as he pleases," I said. "I am collared."

"I think I will chain you," he said.

"Master will do with me as he pleases," I said. "I am collared."

A shackle was snapped shut about my left ankle. I was then on a short chain, it fastened to a ring in the foot of his couch.

"You look well on a chain," he said.

"Thank you, Master," I said.

"I am now going to have you," he said.

"Yes, Master," I said.

CHAPTER NINE

I could scarcely move in such a thing.

I was on my knees, bent down, clutching the bars, looking up through them. How tall, and large, seemed the robed figures of the men about, they not noticing me. How could I not be noticed, so close to them? Did they not know I was here? Had they no feeling for me? Would no one pity me? Would someone not bring me clothing? My neck and body were bare. My thigh was not. It wore the Kef.

What madness it seemed that I should be here, naked, marked, helpless, grasping bars, caged.

To be sure, my cage was only one of several on the wharf.

How helpless, pale, and pathetic seemed the occupants of those other devices! Could I appear similarly to them?

Surely not!

They were doubtless Gorean women, mere barbarians.

I was civilized, educated, sophisticated, informed.

I did not belong with barbarians!

I clutched the bars in frustration.

How had this come about?

I had not even known there was a world, Gor. And I had not known that the tall, sullen, complacent stranger who had entered the office late that summer afternoon was not a man of my world, but a Gorean. Had I known then what I knew now I would have immediately knelt in his presence, fearfully, and put my head to his feet. But I had treated him as a man of Earth, briefly and badly, treated him curtly, rudely, impatiently, contemptuously. Had he not come to the office too late, too near closing time? Had I not been interrupted, when preparing to leave the office early? To me he had been understood as no more than an annoyance, an inconvenience, delaying me, interfering with my intended early departure. What my employers did not know would not hurt them. It was summer. Did we not often leave early? It was not unusual. Though I had sensed he was different in some way, in some frightening way, I did not understand what might be transpiring. Surely I had no way of realizing he was not a man of Earth. I knew nothing of Gor, of Goreans. And he was not merely Gorean, but of the caste of Slavers! And I had dared to strike him! Now my hands might be cut off for such an act, if I were not to be disposed of altogether, doubtless in such a way as to apprise me of my error and constitute a warning to others. And now I was caged, on another world! How did I know that he had come to appraise me, to consider whether or not I might do, turned and exhibited, on a slave block? I gathered that, incredibly, despite my obvious beauty and desirability, which was generally recognized, and of which I had been frequently assured, could I not see the illustrations in the magazines and on the billboards, I was assessed as a mere pot girl, or kettle-and-mat girl. Indeed, I gathered that I was "borderline" in his view, if one could believe that, but, as my behavior had irritated him, had he not called me a "bitch," he had decided, perhaps for his amusement, that I would be taken to Gor, there to be marked, and learn the whip, chain, and collar. I had not known he was not a man of Earth. I was a woman of Earth. I had not realized that my behavior might have consequences. It had never happened before. I had not understood that he was not to be treated as would be a typical male of Earth, with shortness, condescension, and contempt. One may treat a man of Earth as badly as one wishes, and with impunity. But, woe, he was not a man of Earth, and he saw me as a slave. It was then, I gathered, he pondering me, pondering me as a slave, that my behavior, and the annoyance it must have provoked, swayed his view. Thus, despite the fact that I had not behaved other than would have any other young woman of Earth in the circumstances, I am sure, I was, without my knowledge, added to a list in preparation, a slave list. I would be transmitted to Gor.

I grasped the bars.

I could not stand upright. I could not fully extend my body.

Many times last night Kurik, my master, had put me to his pleasure. What seasons, and climates, and thunders, and tides, he had wreaked in my frame! He had not used me again as he had the first time, but I was left in no doubt that I was a slave. The Gorean master does not request or petition but owns and takes. He handles his slave with assurance and authority, sometimes treating her as though she were in a bit and harness, and other times as though she were a vibrating, responding musical instrument from which he draws out tunes, tiny whimpers, soft moans, and cries, as he wishes. I had thought of myself on Earth as being inert and frigid, and my master's first rude, forcible depriving me of my virginity had done little to alter that conviction. On Earth my sense of sex had extended to little more than displaying my beauty and using it to obtain attention. It is pleasant to bask in the admiration of men, even men of Earth. Occasionally I would amuse myself by arousing desires I had no intention of satisfying. It is easy to do that. Aside from the psychological gratification attendant on such, and similar, behaviors, the garnering of free entertainments and dinners is negligible. Always I was in control. I was the mistress of any such relationship. But then I had found myself helpless in the arms of a Gorean master. In his arms I was meaningless. I did not count. I was no more than a pleasure beast with which he would unilaterally slake the flames of his lust. I was a slave. Even in his first abrupt penetration of me, his holding of me, and his plunging use of me, despite the discomfort and shock, I had had some dim, frightening sense of what might be done with me, what I might become. I had then, later, when he again addressed his attentions to me, fearing I might succumb, attempted to hold myself inert. I must try to refuse to feel. I must be cold! I heard tiny sounds escape me. I was helpless in his hands. He lifted me, and turned me about, to his convenience, as he wished. In the training house I had heard of slave fires. I must not let them burn within me! But what if I could not help it, I asked myself, in anguish. And, I asked myself, why should I try to help it, why should I try to resist? Was I not a slave? Why should I not feel as a slave, yield as a slave? I heard myself gasp, and moan. "Steady, slut," he said. What if he should, as I feared he could, simply light those fires within me, fires that I could not control, and that I feared I would come to need, even to beg for? I could remember the cries of my instructresses at night, lifting their chained wrists to passing guards. "Do you wish to have your hands bound behind your back?" he asked. "No, Master," I said. "Then hold your left wrist with your right hand, behind your back," he said. "Yes, Master," I said, seizing my left wrist in my right hand, behind my back. Then he began to caress me, carefully, gently. "Oh!" I said, softly, eagerly. "Steady," he said. "Please, please," I whispered. "Steady" he said, "steady." "I cannot feel this," I protested. "I am frigid, frigid!" "You are not frigid," he said. "We do not bring frigid sluts to Gor. Men do not like them." "I fear I am a slave," I said. "You are a slave," he said. "Are these slave fires?" I asked, frightened. "You are weeks, months, from slave fires," he said. "It would doubtless be amusing to see you, when you are in their grasp." "Oh, please, Master," I cried. "Do not stop! Do not stop!" "I have no intention of stopping," he said, "until I wish to do so." "Ohhh!" I cried, and my arms clasped him. Later, when we were spent, he took me by the hair, and slapped me, thrice, sharply, across the face. "Master?" I said. "I did not give you permission to release your hands," he said. "Forgive me, Master," I said. We then lay beside one another, at the foot of the couch. I was still fastened to it, by the shackle on my left ankle. I turned to him, rising on my elbow. "I love you," I whispered, "—Master." He then rose, and, without speaking, dressed, and left the room. "Master?" I said, plaintively.

I shrank back in the cage, and the hem of the fellow's robes, as he passed, brushed the bars.

I was caged, or, I suppose, in a way, kenneled. The thought crossed my mind, "I was a bitch. Was it not appropriate for a bitch to be kenneled?" But then I recalled that I was less than a bitch, far less than a bitch. I was a slave.

"May I speak, Master?" I implored, as white and gold robes passed my cage. But I was given no notice. Not having been given permission to speak, I remained silent.

Is there no one here to rescue me, I wondered. No one to pity me? No one to save me, and return me to Earth?

But then I realized I was not such as to be saved. I was such as to be bought, sold, and owned.

One does not rescue slaves. One chains them. One keeps them at one's feet, where one wants them.

I had no money.

But I had my beauty, which had smoothed many a way on my own world, and opened many doors. Might it not be of use here? Could I not barter it, could I not accord its favors judiciously, purchasing rescue, and a prompt return to Earth? But then I realized my beauty was no longer a good with which I might bargain. It was no longer mine to bestow or withhold as I might choose. It was no longer mine. I was a slave. It belonged to whoever might own me. Were I thought to attempt to negotiate with, or sell, my favors, I might, if interest had been aroused, be simply purchased, and then, doubtless, put under the whip for my stupidity and impudence.

Kajirae are not bought to be freed; they are bought to be owned.

"No, no," I thought.

My beauty had never failed me.

A fellow in a short, brown tunic, a sack upon his shoulder, made his way between the cages. "No," I thought. "He does not look prosperous. I shall not appeal to him." In those days I could not even read the caste colors of Gor, not that all members of a caste could be depended on to appear only in caste robes, which, in many cases, were most likely to appear on caste holidays and city holidays. The fellow in brown, I would later learn, would most likely have been of the Peasantry. The colors of the five high castes were white, yellow, blue, green, and red, for the Initiates, Builders, Scribes, Physicians, and Warriors, respectively. Sometimes the indications of caste were subtle, marked by a pair, or a trio, of short ribbons on the left sleeve, near the wrist. For example, the colors of the Slavers were blue and yellow, but these colors were often displayed, when the slaver was not hunting, merely on the left sleeve, rather than in a full regalia. The colors of the Merchants, which merchants frequently claim to be a high caste, were white and yellow, or white and gold. Some regard the Slavers as a subcaste of the Merchants and others identify it as an independent caste. The caste structure apparently lends a great deal of stability to Gorean society, as most Goreans respect their caste and recognize the nature of, and the value of, its role in society. In this way, self-esteem, pride, and high intelligence tends to be spread rather evenly throughout the population, rather than being drained, over generations, into a limited number of professions. Also, allegiance to a Home Stone, and frequent internecine warfare, tends to keep the Gorean population decentralized, so that ambition and intelligence does not, over time, gravitate toward particular cities, say, larger, wealthier population centers, to the detriment of other municipalities. Whereas caste change is not prohibited, and legal provisions exist for its effectuation, it is seldom sought. The typical Gorean cares for his caste, and takes great pride in it. It does not occur to him to relinquish it. Indeed, he may look down upon, or pity, other castes. He is unlikely to desert the caste that is his own. To some, that would doubtless, however mistakenly, be construed as a betrayal of sorts. To be sure, very different societal arrangements are possible. For example, one might have a large, undifferentiated, individually competitive population in which millions struggle for a tragically limited quantity of desiderata, which must, mathematically, be beyond the reach of the vast majority, for example, a limited number of favored professions, a limited number of favored locations, and so on. It is rather as if thousands were encouraged to run in a race that could, in the nature of things, have few winners. Thus most must fail,

a situation likely to result in unhappiness, disgruntlement, frustration, resentment, and envy. To be sure, these negative emotions pave
a smooth, convenient road to power for those willing to exploit them.

I looked about, holding the bars.

Two men, tunicked, clad in red, made their way amongst the cages.
Each had a short blade slung at his left hip, suspended by a shoulder
strap. Each was helmeted. I shook with fear. I was suddenly reminded
of something I had seen long ago. It had been in a museum, on a vase.
I had thought little of it. Two helmeted men, figures on the vase, were
sharp and prominent, clearly delineated, red, on a black background.
I now, in my memory, saw the image on the vase very differently than
I had earlier. I saw it now for what it was, what it betokened, saw it as
something real, something frightening. It is, of course, one thing to see
images, or pictures, and quite another to see the thing pictured, and
sense its reality, its purposiveness, what it would be to see the thing as
it actually is. One might compare the picture of a beast, with the beast
met, unexpectedly, alive, in the wild. The experiences are quite different. And so, suddenly shaken, I realized that the imagery I had casually
noted long ago, in passing, and to which I had given little thought, was
an image of an authentic reality, and that I had now, for the first time,
experienced that reality, or something much like it. Each helmet, of
leather and metal, crested with a mane of animal hair, with its y-shaped
opening, muchly enclosed a face, a face that might, in a moment, I
supposed, be fearsome, and menacing, that might, peering out, aware
of risk and war, of danger, of the moment that might part life from
death, scrutinize a field or foe.

"Master!" cried a girl in the second cage to my right, extending a
hand through the bars. "Buy me!"

One of the young men in red turned, to regard the supplicant.

"Buy me!" she urged, again.

Neither the dealer, nor his men, were about. Perhaps that had
encouraged the girl whose cry, otherwise, if noted, might have been
construed as an importunity.

His hand moved to the wallet slung at his belt. As he held it, and
lifted it, I heard, within it, the small sounds of jostled metal.

"Yes, yes, Master!" she cried.

A fellow in white and yellow, the dealer, then seemed to appear
from nowhere, and stood beside the cage. "Shall I bring her forth, Master," he inquired, "to be looked upon?" He carried in his hand, looped,
a leash.

"No, no!" said the young man's companion, striking his fellow on the back, jovially. "Save your money! To the tavern! See the dancers! Pick out a paga girl, and bind her, and switch her to an alcove! Come away from here. Save your money for something good. This is a cheap market, with inferior slaves."

The girl drew her hand back, within the cage.

The young man then turned to look at me, and I put my head down, swiftly.

"Inferior slaves!" said his companion. "Come away! Come away!"

When I looked up, they had gone.

Last night he who had been my master, Kurik, of Victoria, had much used me. Toward morning I had found myself, if I had not been before, a conquered, subdued slave, as I could not help being, and, I fear, wished to be. I found myself surrendered, and wanting to be owned. On Earth I would have denied, in my vanity and pride, that I could be mastered, but I had found on Gor that I could be mastered, and would be mastered, and wanted to be mastered, and was mastered. I now knew any man could master me. I now knew myself a slave.

Toward morning I had turned to him, rising on my elbow, and had addressed him. "I love you," I had whispered, "—Master." He had then risen, and, without speaking, had dressed, and left the room. "Master?" I had said.

An hour or so later he had returned, bringing with him another man, unknown to me. I was still naked, and chained, by the left ankle, to the foot of his couch. The other man turned me about, and tested the soundness of my flesh. I was not even asked to rise. I then lay on my stomach, over a portion of the straw mat. I heard coins change hands. "Master?" I said. "Master?" "Be silent," he snapped. "Yes, Master," I said. I felt my hands drawn behind me, and thonged together. My left ankle was then freed of its shackle. Then, as I lay prone, my hands bound behind me, my collar was removed, and another was snapped about my neck, and then a slave hood was drawn over my head, and buckled shut, behind the back of my neck. I then felt leather about my neck, and the snap of a leash.

"Get up," I was told.

I then felt the draw of the leash against the leash collar-ring. I was apparently to be conducted from the room.

"No, Master!" I cried, wildly, miserably, unable to see, from within the hood. "Please, no, Master!"

"Be silent," he said.

"Master!" I begged.

I then felt, against the back of my thighs, several times, sharp, and stinging, the lash of a switch.

"Forgive me, Master!" I wept. "Forgive me, Master!"

I was then, on the tether, led from the room.

I heard a cry of anguish, and, to my right, a cage was opened. Its occupant, on all fours, was ordered forth, and, bending down, the dealer fastened a leash about her neck, following which he led her, she on all fours, to a space on the wharf, amongst the cages.

Shortly thereafter she was ordered to stand in that space, within a yellow circle, with her feet widely spread, and her hands clasped behind the back of her neck. Four men then assessed her.

I saw coins change hands.

Shortly thereafter her hands were tied behind her, and the dealer's leash was replaced with a new leash, of collar and chain, and I saw her led away, her head bowed.

In a cage to my left, a girl whispered to another, to her left, "I recognize the livery," she said. "She is being bought for the looms, in the mills of Mintar."

"*Ela*," said her confidant, in the next cage, "and she was the most beautiful of us all."

I was unnerved by this, and muchly uneasy. It was the first time I had seen a woman sold. I was annoyed, too, and puzzled, that they spoke of her as the most beautiful of all, for, as far as I could see from my sturdy, small, snug, barred confinement, I was far more beautiful.

In the late afternoon, surprising me, there was a sudden cessation of activity on the wharf in our vicinity, and, as precipitately, a lull in conversation. Vendors were quiet, men ceased calling out to one another, stevedores put down their bundles, men ceased speaking, and all drew to the sides, clearing a path between the bales and crates, and the cages.

One figure, alone, high sandaled, clad in a black tunic, caped, a blade at his left hip, a black helmet cradled in his left arm, approached. The hitherto-crowded aisle, the linear center of the wharf, now seemed abandoned. Men on each side watched the stranger's approach. His gait was unhurried, measured. Something about him suggested an animal, in human form, a panther. As he approached, he looked from side to side, as though with a feline intentness. It seemed he might be searching for one face in that throng. He stopped before the dealer. "Tal," he said, quietly. "Tal, Master," said the dealer, his voice shaking. Indeed, his entire body trembled. Men on either side of the dealer drew away from him. "I am recently in Victoria," said the man in black. "I would reach the tavern of Tasdron." "A thousand paces farther, Master," said the dealer, pointing to his right, with a shaking hand. "My thanks," said the fellow in black. "I wish you well." "I trust you do not seek me?" said the dealer. "No," said the stranger, "only he whose name is on the paper, folded about gold, in my wallet." "May I know his name?" asked the dealer. "Perhaps I might be of help." "Who inherits your business?" asked the stranger. "My brother," said the dealer, uncertainly. "Do you care for him to do so soon, perhaps this evening?" inquired the tall, lean, sable-clad stranger. "No!" said the dealer. "No, Master!" "So do not inquire," said the stranger. "Is he expecting you?" asked the dealer. "No," said the stranger. "I was merely curious," said the dealer. "Do not be concerned," said the stranger. "In the morning, his name will be known." "Perhaps then," said the dealer, "we shall meet again, in the morning." "In the morning," said the stranger, "I shall be gone." He then turned away, and continued on his way, down the wharf. When he had passed, as though a sigh had escaped a single man, the activities on the wharf resumed, and, once again, the bustle and hum of conversation, of cries and calls, rang out, about us.

"Have you enemies?" asked one of the dealer's assistants.

"I trust not," said the dealer. "I am an honest fellow, and I endeavor to treat all with understanding, sympathy, and fairness."

His assistant laughed.

"No rich enemies, at least," said the dealer.

"None who could pay the black fee?"

"I do not think so," said the dealer.

"Sometimes," said the assistant, "one has enemies, even rich enemies, of which one knows not."

"That is always possible," said the dealer.

Certainly the general appearance of the stranger was not something that would be likely to invite familiarity. Still I failed to understand the effect his presence had had on the wharf. I saw little that would have justified such regard. I noted, aside from his somber livery, only one oddity in his appearance. On the center of his forehead was a small sign; an emblem or device; it was black; I supposed it had been affixed, or imprinted, there, with ink or paint; I was not clear as to its purport; it seemed to be a schematic representation of a particular object, an unsheathed dagger.

I was furious that Kurik, he of Victoria, to whom I had belonged, who had so peremptorily, so routinely, so ruthlessly deprived me of my virginity, not that a slave's virginity is of more worth than that of a pig, and who had, despite my will, dared to caress me into eager, helpless, begging servitude, had sold me. Would not another man have given kingdoms for me? How could I have been sold? Could he not see how beautiful I was? He had dismissed me, even on Earth, as a pot girl, or a kettle-and-mat girl. Was he mad? Could he not see what a beauty I was, and I was in his collar! He had dared to suggest that I was not worth keeping! And then he had not kept me! On Earth I had been able to pick and choose. Offers of dates had abounded. Certainly I knew my power. Men sought my attention. I could elevate with a smile, or crush with a frown, as the moment might seize me. It was I who would, at as little as a whim, permit or terminate relationships. I ruled, smugly, and imperiously. Then I had found myself in the arms of a Gorean male, a mere slave, and then it was I, I feared, who had begged, pleaded, and hoped!

How weak is the slave, how helpless, how much at the mercy of the free!

There are many differences between a free woman and a slave. The free woman rules; the slave kneels, and hopes to please.

So I decided I would be a free woman, once again.

It would be necessary only to appeal to a free person, to win my freedom. This person, obviously, might be either a male or female.

To whom then might I most productively appeal?

Surely my instructresses in the house of my training had been mistaken. They had warned me against Gorean free women, and encouraged me to look to men for protection and comfort.

But I knew something of the lust of men.

They seemed unlikely redemptors. If a man sees a beautiful woman, naked and collared, will he rush to free her? Perhaps a suitably conditioned male of Earth, taught to betray his blood, might, sweating, trembling, and averting his gaze, consider doing so, but I did not think a Gorean male would be likely to do so. He has better things to do with a beautiful slave than free her. He would rather have her wait upon him, hand and foot, docile to his bidding, submissive to his least wish, would rather have her at his feet, would rather own her, would rather put her to use, in a thousand ways, that she may know herself owned, owned as only a woman can be owned, and he her master.

Considering the satisfactions, delights, and pleasures attendant on the mastery, men, in my view, were not the most auspicious candidates for the purpose I had in mind.

Were not free women our sisters? Might one not depend on a woman to understand the harrows of slavery, and sympathize with another woman, one of her own sex, one so unfortunate as to be collared?

My instructresses, then, were wrong.

Few free women wandered unescorted on the wharf, but they occasionally made their appearance. I thought it best to avoid a woman who was in the company of a male. I wanted to make my appeal to the woman, as woman to woman, uncomplicated by the possibly inhibiting presence of a male. It was on the wharf that I saw my first Gorean free women. How well they moved, so gracefully! There was no mistaking those movements, those of graceful forms, within those colorful, layered, beautifully draped robes, so flowing, so feminine, and it was easy to conjecture the exquisite features that, doubtless in many cases, might be concealed behind those colorful, silken, matched veils, or, if it were worn, the lengthier, heavier street veil. What man would not want to tear aside those veils, of either sort, to remove those flowing, concealing robes, to have such a thing naked, chained at his feet? Occasionally I saw slippers, not sandals, beneath the hem of those robes. Surely there was no danger of confusing such creatures with the occasional slave who sped past, tunicked, hurrying amongst the cages, sometimes hooted at by the stevedores. I was particularly concerned to choose with care. The richer the robes, I reasoned, the more likely the wealth.

A free woman would understand me, and my helplessness!

Alas, how little I knew of such women!

I should have considered more carefully a matter of possible relevance, that several of these visions held, in their small, gloved hand, an object, about a yard in length, of supple leather, and though of a much richer quality, familiar to me from the house of training, an object much like that often carried by the instructresses. Too, if I had been more aware, and more familiar with Gor, I would have noted that the slaves, as much as possible, went to great lengths to avoid finding themselves in the proximity of such women, often turning about, and hurrying away, or slipping to the side, sometimes even hastening to conceal themselves amongst the boxes and bails, the assorted cargoes, on the wharf, removed from, or waiting to be loaded upon, the long, brightly painted galleys moored but yards away.

Later there approached a free woman, alone, resplendent, one I assumed would well answer to my purposes. It would be easy to sway her, I was sure, with my tale of woe. I could not see her features, for the public veiling, the long street veil wrapped about her head and features, and extending to the golden cord low upon her waist, from which dangled an ample, embroidered purse, but I trusted they would be understanding, and kindly.

I scarcely noticed that, in her right hand, she carried a switch.

As she passed by, I called out, "Dear sister, pray attend me!"

She looked about, startled, intently, expectantly, scanning the wharf. Clearly she did not recognize the source of that unhappy solicitation. It had apparently not occurred to her that such a cry might have had its origin from within one of the tiny, barred enclosures strewn to her right, as she was passing. Surely that surprising cry could not be traced to so unlikely a venue. Such a linkage would be unthinkably preposterous. What marked beast would dare, unsolicited, to address a free woman?

"Dear sister!" I called. "I am such as you, a woman, but, hapless, have fallen upon hard times. Behold, I am afflicted by a most grievous plight! I find myself in the throes of misery and helplessness. See how I am! See what has been done to me! I would be free. Free me! Have pity! Have mercy upon me! Buy me, and restore me to freedom!"

I noted, but scarcely registered it at the time, that the girls in the cages about, those in the vicinity, had knelt, and pressed their heads fearfully to the metal floors of their tiny, sturdy confinements.

The free woman approached, seemingly incredulously. Her robes seemed hardly to move. Might not a looming rainbow of ice, floating in some arctic sea, have moved so, with such even, sedate, chill menace? She looked down. I looked up, through the bars. The sun was high, and I felt the warmth of the metal bars I grasped.

"Yes, dear sister," I said. "It was I who called. I am one such as you, but in desperate need of succor."

"'Sister'?" she said. "One such as I?"

"Yes, dear sister," I said. "I appeal to you with confidence, relying on the commonality we share, our sweet sex, that you will relieve me of my predicament, that you, in your gentleness, and profound sympathy, will beneficently and generously buy and free me, your sister."

"I have no sister," she said.

"A figure of speech," I said.

She moved a bit to the side. "You are marked," she said.

"It was done with an iron," I said. "I could not help it."

"Marked!" she said.

"Yes," I said.

"You," she said, "a slave, a stinking slave, dare to call yourself 'sister', and compare yourself with me?"

"Do not be offended," I said, and, thinking it judicious, I added, "Mistress."

"I have a Home Stone," she said, "that of Victoria, jewel of the mighty Vosk!"

"Yes, Mistress," I said. I did not really know what a Home Stone was, but it was apparently something of importance. As far as I knew, I did not have a Home Stone. Certainly no one had told me I had one.

I would later learn that slaves, no more than other animals, had Home Stones, no more than tarsks and verr, though they, like tarsks and verr, would often find themselves the properties of those who did.

Indeed, it is something of an honor for a slave, I suppose, to be the property of one who possesses a Home Stone.

"I beg to be bought and freed," I said.

"Bought, and freed?" she said, disbelievingly.

"Yes, Mistress," I said.

"Why you?" she asked.

"I am wrongly caged!" I said.

"I can see by your lineaments," she said, "you belong in a cage. You are suitably caged."

"No!" I said.

"Your Gorean is strange," she said. "You are not from the valley of the Vosk. Perhaps you are from Ti, or mountainous Thentis, or distant Turia. I do not mark it as Cosian."

"I am from far away," I said.

"Merchant! Merchant!" cried the free woman.

"How may I be of service?" inquired the dealer, hurrying to us, not pleased.

"I have been accosted by this stinking slave," she said, pointing, accusingly, to me. I saw the veil move, as she spoke so forcibly, so intensely, within it.

"*Ela!*" cried the dealer, as if horrified.

"I dare not bespeak the insults to which I have been subjected," she said. Her voice suggested youth. She may not have been much older than I, perhaps even a bit younger, but she was Gorean, and free. "I want her fed to eels," she said, "flayed, cast to sleen, honeyed and bound down for urts! Let her sleep this night with leech plants!"

"Is it true, girl," asked the dealer, "you spoke to this fine lady?"

"Yes, Master," I said.

"Without having been addressed?"

"Yes, Master," I said.

"At least you show respect to a male!" said the free woman.

"Forgive me, Master!" I said.

"What did she say?" asked the dealer.

"One of high caste, with intent, could not have insulted me more grievously," she said. "I dare not repeat it, lest I swoon with shame."

"Unfortunate, piteous, wronged, delicate lady," said the dealer, sympathetically. He spread his hands widely in a gesture of apology, and futility. What action or what words, I gathered, could make amends for so dreadful an offense. How could so profound a distress be soothed?

The dealer turned to me. "Perhaps you are sorry for your transgression?" he asked.

"Yes, yes!" I cried. "Forgive me, dear Master! Forgive me, dear, noble Mistress!"

"Do not mind the slave, noble lady," said the dealer. "She is simple, she is stupid, her wits are addled."

"She does not seem so to me," said the woman, acidly.

"Yet she spoke to you without permission," said the dealer.

"That is true," she said. "But what would men want with a simple, stupid, wit-addled slave?"

"As you know, delicate lady," said the dealer, "men are inclined to overlook such things. Consider her ankles."

"Men are stupid," said the free woman.

"I fear that is well-known amongst free women," said the dealer.

"What will it be," she asked, "urts, sleen, leech plants, nailing to a slave board, the flaying knife?"

"Perhaps you would care to buy her?" he asked.

"I do not wish to buy her," she said.

"You must understand my position," said the dealer. "I have an investment."

"I do not have money for buying slaves," she said. "What do you want for her?"

"Five gold tarsks of Ar," he said.

I thought I heard the girl, a new girl now, caged to my right, suppress a laugh. I did not understand what might precipitate such a response. Surely any amount would be a bargain, for one such as I.

"She is not worth that much," said the woman.

"Doubtless not," said the dealer. "But you know men. Look upon her ankles."

"I do not care to look upon her ankles," she said. "Let men do that."

"*Ela,*" said the dealer. "They might do so."

"You do not think she knew what she was doing?" said the woman.

"Certainly not," said the dealer.

"Perhaps then," she said, seemingly mollified, "she need only be lashed to within a bit of a hort of her life."

"That could easily be arranged," said the dealer, "though one must measure such things exactly, calculating to the portion of a hort."

"Surely you are adept at such judgments," she said.

"We do our best," he said.

"Perhaps you would error on the behalf of leniency, or mercy," she said.

"Do not think such a thing," he said, shuddering with disbelief that such a thought might have occurred to her. "But there is one thing in this sad affair I do not understand."

"What is that?" she asked.

"How one as wise as you, as refined as you, and doubtless as lovely as you, how one free in condition and noble in mien, could possibly be insulted by a slave?"

"I do not understand," she said.

"A slave, even were she so inclined, could not possibly insult one such as you," he said. "Surely you might be stung by a gnat, but you could not be insulted by a gnat. For an insult to take place there must be a commonality of levels, free to free, person to person, citizen to citizen, even slave to slave, even beast to beast, but levels cannot be crossed. Only an equal can insult an equal."

"Oh," she said.

"Surely," he said. "One might step upon an ost and suffer, but one cannot be insulted by an ost. The urt who nibbles the cheese of a Ubar, even from his plate, does not insult the Ubar. Would the Ubar not be thought strange, or even mad, if he thought himself insulted by the urt? The sleen who hisses at a hunter does not thereby become the equal of the hunter."

"Of course not," she said.

He bowed to her. "I wish you well," he said. He then turned politely away.

The free woman's eyes glared down upon me.

"You cannot insult me," she said, "stinking slave."

"No, Mistress," I said.

"I am not insulted," she said.

"No, Mistress," I assured her.

"But I am displeased," she said.

"Forgive me, Mistress," I said.

She then, in rage, lashed at the cage with her switch, striking it on the roof, and across the bars, again and again. I heard the whistle of the disciplinary device, and its shattering ringing about the cage. I drew back, frightened. None of the blows, of course, had touched me.

She then spun about, and hurried away.

A moment later the dealer appeared, who must have been attendant to the matter, watchfully, at a discreet distance.

"Free persons," he said, "are not to be addressed, unless, mayhap, it be in response to some invitation, inquiry, or such."

"Yes, Master," I said. I had known that of course, from the house of training, but the dealer may not have realized that. If he had, I would doubtless have been punished. As of now, of course, I had been informed, officially, so to speak.

"It is fortunate you were caged," he said. "If such an incident had occurred on the street, you might have had a tunic cut to pieces on your body."

I shuddered.

"I would not want your value reduced," he said. "I would not want you maimed or blinded."

"Am I truly worth only five pieces of gold?" I asked.

The dealer regarded me, startled. The girl in the cage to my right laughed aloud, and I heard sounds of mirth from the other cages. These kajirae, I gathered, had not been unaware of the recently transpired incident.

"Five pieces of gold?" said the dealer, disbelievingly.

"Only five pieces?" I asked.

"You are all only copper-tarsk girls," he said. "I had most of you for a pittance, and certainly you, from a low dealer. The girl was young. She does not yet know her robes and veils, let alone her embroidered slippers. She has no concept of the values of slaves. She had probably never been permitted to attend a sale. I said five gold tarsks, to assure myself that she would not buy you, as the price is absurd."

"Master was kind," I whispered.

"Had I set a realistic price," he said, "I feared she might buy you. Would you have cared to belong to her?"

"No, Master!" I said.

"Beware free women," he said.

"Yes, Master," I said.

"There are better things to do with a slave than abuse them, beat them, hate them, and torture them."

"Yes, Master," I said.

I recalled then my instructresses, and their admonitions with respect to free women, and their encouragement to look to men for comfort and protection. There was safety in wearing a man's collar. Men were fond of kajirae; free women were not.

What, I wondered, might account for the alleged reservations of free women pertaining to slaves?

"Copper-tarsk girls?" I said.

"Yes," he said.

"But my ankles, Master," I said.

"The girl was young, naive," he said. "And what does a free woman know of men, or of what men might prize in the ankles of slaves?"

"But they are attractive, my ankles, are they not?" I said.

"They will do," he said. "But they are too slim. They are the ankles of a pot girl."

"I thought such ankles were desirable," I said. Surely my experiences on Earth would suggest that, my awareness of public images, countless pictures in fashion magazines, and such.

"Some men may find them of interest, like the rest of you," he said.

"I see," I said.

I would later learn that the taste of Gorean men, rather as that of most men throughout Earth's history, given the evidence of mosaics, statues, paintings, and such, tended to favor the more familiar forms of womanhood, the statistically familiar woman, young, lovely, nicely curved, apparently the result of thousands of generations of sexual selections. To be sure, there are countless intriguing, exciting variations of the feminine symmetries, producing wondrous diversities of beauty. Many types ascend the blocks on Gor, and fetch remunerative prices.

"She believed me," said the dealer. "And though it is difficult to tell, I suspect she has similar ankles."

"I see," I said. Perhaps then, I thought, she and I were not so different after all. "I suspect," I then said, "she was exquisitely lovely."

"Perhaps," said the dealer. "Perhaps I will have her in a cage one day, and see."

"A cage?" I said, aghast. She was, after all, a free woman.

"Quite possibly," he said. "Being a free woman can be a precarious thing to be, particularly if one is lovely. There are wars, raids, seizures, abductions, predatory slavers, as opposed to trading slavers, and such. One of a young tarnsman's first ventures is to procure a free female from an enemy city and bring her home to his family and friends as his slave."

I did not know what a tarnsman was, no more than some other things I had heard of on this world, such as sleen or tarsks. But I did not think it an opportune time to inquire. Doubtless the master thought I knew. Should I exhibit what might be construed as profound ignorance? That would scarcely put me in good with him. Might it not seem to confirm possible suspicions of stupidity? Too, curiosity, I recalled, was not becoming in a kajira.

I was sure the whip would be unpleasant.

"Surely she was extremely beautiful," I said. I certainly supposed so, if she were rather like me.

"Who knows," he said. "She might be quite average on a sales block. She was veiled. She might have the face of a tarsk."

"Surely free women are safe on this world," I said.

"'World'?" he said.

"Here," I said, "in this place."

"Where do you think slaves come from?" he said. "It takes time to breed them. Too, it is pleasant to take a free woman and teach her that she is now a slave."

"Oh," I said.

"Why do you think they are veiled, and hidden inside robes?" he said. "And why do you think, on the other hand, veils are forbidden to slaves and slaves are scarcely clad, if clad at all?"

"I do not know, Master," I said.

"Do you think the only reason slaves are slave-clad, in brief tunics, and such, is because men enjoy seeing them so?"

"I do not know, Master," I said.

"Too," he said, "to distract attention from free women. Why should a raider or slaver risk his life to carry off a free woman, who might turn out to be more ugly than a tharlarion, when he might steal a slave, where he can see what his capture rope encircles?"

"I see," I said.

"To be sure," he said, "a former free woman's first sale may bring a good price. Some men enjoy teaching them what they now are. This is particularly the case if she is beautiful."

I had now heard of tharlarion, whatever they might be. I gathered, from the context, that it was not to a woman's advantage to resemble one.

"You must, indeed, be from far away," he said.

"Yes, Master," I said.

"Still I think she must have been a great beauty," I said.

"The quality, and desirability, of slaves," he said, "is seldom a matter of surfaces. Do not confuse the outside slave with the inside slave. They may not be identical. Cities have been bartered for a woman you might adjudge plain. One buys, and desires, the whole slave. There are many beauties. There is the beauty of a slave's joy, that of her passion, and service, that of her submission, that of her lively, vital intelligence, so stimulating to encounter, she kneeling before you, that of her emotions and feelings, that of the all of her, that of the entire fair beast, now collared."

"Yes, Master," I said.

What man, I wondered, would truly prize such things, a Gorean, I supposed, before whom she knelt, her lips pressed to his whip.

The dealer then turned about, and left.

I was now prepared to accept the views of my instructresses, to avoid free women, and placate, cultivate, and please free men.

It would then be, as I would not have earlier surmised, a man who would be most likely to buy and free me.

I was pleased.

I had always managed men, quite well.

It was the next morning.

The tarpaulin that had been cast over my cage the night before had now been drawn aside.

The day, again, was bright, and the boards of the wharf, as I could tell, placing my hands through the bars, once again, were, like the cage and bars, warm to the touch.

I looked about, after my watering and feeding, and my use of the waste trough.

This fellow looked prosperous.

His robes were white and gold. His sandals were fastened with golden straps. A weighty purse was suspended from a broad belt, encircling a portly belly.

"I am a free woman, wrongly caged!" I said. "I crave rescue. Be understanding, be noble, be kind. Buy me, restore me to freedom!"

Small eyes peered down at me, from within folds of fat.

"I doubt we shared a Home Stone," he said. "And even so, if we once did, we no longer do. That is all in the past. It is gone. It is wiped away. You are now nothing. You are now a slave. You are marked."

I did not even know, as noted, what Home Stones were.

"But what if I were once a compatriot," I said, "once of your city!"

"It matters not," he said. "You are now no more than a beast, a slave."

"What is going on here, Master?" inquired our dealer, politely, he also in robes of white and gold, though, I fear, his were rather ragged, and soiled.

The Merchant class is undoubtedly the richest of the Gorean castes, which doubtless has played its role in its pretensions to constitute a high caste, but there are low merchants as well as high merchants, poor merchants as well as rich merchants. To be sure, the sharing of caste remains important. Even a lowly peddler, I would learn, if a Home Stone is shared, thinks nothing of expecting a free meal and a night's lodging from a high merchant, who may own caravans, mines, and fleets.

"This one," said the fellow I had accosted, "wishes to be purchased, and then freed. I see little profit in that. Is she insane, or stupid?"

The dealer looked at me, narrowly. Doubtless he remembered quite well yesterday's interlude with the free woman.

Had I then, despite his injunction, dared to address myself to a free person?

"Did she speak to you first, Master?" inquired the dealer.

"Yes," said the portly fellow.

"More likely, merely naive, Master," said the dealer. "She may not yet have noticed her thigh is marked."

"She was recently free?"

"I fear so."

"She speaks oddly," said the portly fellow.

"She is from far away, a barbarian," said the dealer.

"Interesting," said the portly fellow.

"You can tell," said the dealer. "There is a tiny bit of metal embedded in one of her back teeth. One must look carefully to detect it. It is not likely to be noticed. Would you like me to bring her out of her cage?"

"Look at her upper left arm, the scar," said the portly fellow. "She is marred, disfigured."

"But not seriously, Master," said the dealer.

I did not understand what they were talking about. Later, I realized they might be referring to my vaccination mark.

"You deal in damaged goods," said the portly fellow.

"Now and then, but at bargain prices," said the dealer. "Would you like to look at her?"

"No," said the portly fellow, and turned away.

"I am not pleased with you," said the dealer, looking down upon me.

"Forgive me, Master," I said.

"You are a slave," he said. "Do you think you will be freed?"

"No, Master," I said.

"Then why speak of it?" he asked.

"Forgive me, Master," I said.

"Should slaves not be kept as slaves?" he asked.

"Yes, Master," I said.

"You are a slave," he said.

"Yes, Master," I said.

"So you should be kept as a slave," he said.

"Yes, Master," I said.

"Do you think you should be freed?" he asked.

I hesitated, as though on some fearsome brink. I feared to look within my most secret thoughts.

"Speak," he said.

I began to shake with emotion. I trembled. I shuddered.

"Must I speak?" I whispered.

"Yes," he said.

What I said then startled me. I, a woman, had been in the arms of a master.

"No, Master," I said. "I do not think I should be freed."

"Why?" he asked.

"Because I am a slave, Master," I said.

I had the sense then that an internal war was done, not that it mattered much, what I might think or feel, for I was marked and caged.

What did it matter, what I thought of such things?

I was powerless. I was a slave.

And yet, I had now acknowledged, openly and honestly, to myself, that I did not think I should be freed. How could I have said that? How could I have done so? Was I a true slave? Could that be? I feared it was so. I recalled the mighty arms of Kurik, enfolding me helplessly in the grip of the master, a helplessness and bliss I could not forget. I then understood, naked, and confined in that tiny cage, in which I could scarcely move, that it was right, and appropriate, that I be a slave. In that moment I knew I was, and should be, a slave. I was a woman, and was the rightful belonging of men. I had discovered myself, and was not discontent, but was overwhelmed with a sense of truth and joy, and, oddly perhaps, with liberation.

The internal war was done.

How fitting then that one such as I should be bought and sold, should be owned, and mastered!

How else could I find myself? How else could I realize myself?

Then misery surged up within me. Surely such things could not be true. I must not permit them to be true. I must deny them. I must pretend they could not be true! But they were true, I knew.

The internal war was done.

But must I not deny that?

But I could not do so.

I now knew myself, and had felt a master's arms.

I shuddered, a caged slave.

"Did you speak first?" he asked. "He said you did."

"No, Master!" I said.

He looked to the other cages about.

"She did, Master!" said several voices. "We heard her! She spoke first."

"Yes," cried others.

The dealer turned back to me. "Did you?" he asked.

"Yes, Master," I said, weakly.

"Barbarian!" hissed the girl caged to my right. "Barbarian!" said others.

"Then," said the dealer, "you have not only disobeyed, but you have lied."

"Yes, Master," I said. "But please do not punish me!"

"You disobeyed, and lied, and do not expect to be punished?" he said.

"I am helpless," I said. "You are a kindly, noble Master. Please be kind to me."

He straightened up, and stepped back.

"Master?" I said.

"Would you like to bathe?" he asked.

How relieved I felt.

I had feared the whip might have been put to me.

I had been forgiven!

Surely I would rejoice to be permitted to bathe. Kajirae are to keep themselves clean, neat, and well-groomed, that they might be more pleasing to masters. They are not free women.

"Oh, yes! Yes, Master!" I said.

"Bathe her," said the dealer to his two assistants, who stood about.

To my surprise, a stout rope was fastened to a ring on the top of my cage. The rope was some yards in length. It trailed back, on the wharf.

"Masters?" I said, uncertainly.

The two assistants to the dealer then lifted the cage and carried it to the edge of the wharf.

"No!" I cried.

The cage was swung back, and then heaved from the wharf. Metal, it sunk swiftly. I, its occupant, could do nothing to alter its descent. The cold waters of the river plunged through the bars, and swirled about me, and then, as I tried to rear up, and lift my head, as I could, it swirled about my head, and over my head. Some seconds later, three or four, sinking, the cage grated on sand, at the bottom of the river, near the pilings of the wharf. My eyes stung. I felt grit in my mouth, doubtless from where the bottom had been disturbed by the impact of the sinking cage. I fought, frenziedly, the desire to breathe. I shook the bars, helplessly. I was conscious of bubbles, emerging, bursting about me, near me, from my mouth. I must not breathe in. To do so would be to drown. I sensed I could not long hold my breath. A moment or two more, I was sure, and I would strangle. "Do not breathe!" I told myself. "Hold your breath! Do not breathe!" Things started to go black, within the blackness. If I fell unconscious, I knew I would automatically breathe, and that would be the end. I did not think they intended to kill me. Surely my offenses, however grievous in this world, had not warranted such a punishment. But might they kill me, as an object lesson to the others? I did not think so. Wild thoughts coursed through my head. The swirling water was cold. I felt my hair lifted about, in the current. Surely they would not wish to kill me. Was I not, in some way, however negligible, of some value, an investment of sorts, as the dealer had reminded the free woman? What if they miscalculated? What if I could not hold my breath as long as they expected? I began to despair. Strange memories, from the past, flashed about me, as though swirling in the water. I must breathe! Then I felt the cage shift, jerk, and begin to be drawn toward the surface. I must not breathe! I must not

breathe! And then the cage broke the surface of the water and, sputtering, I expelled air, and sucked into my lungs the glory of an unpolluted
world's air. I gasped. I tried to rub the water from my eyes. "No!" I
cried out, as the cage, again, released, descended into the water. Three
times I was wholly immersed for what seemed years, but could have
been only a matter of two or three minutes, at most. At last, the cage
was drawn upward to the point where it had emerged some four or
five inches from the water. It was then, apparently, tied in place. If I
turned my head to the side, and knelt in the cage, I could, between the
laps of the water against the pilings, snatch a breath. But it was painful to kneel so, my head turned as it was, the right side of my head,
and then the left side of my head, held closely against the steel ceiling
of the cage. "Forgive me, forgive me, Master!" I cried, as I could, my
mouth half full of water. I was conscious of men and women moving
over the wharf, as before, above me. I trusted the rope would hold. If
it did not, I would surely drown. I was helpless, confined in the tiny
cage. "Masters!" I cried. "Be silent," said a voice from above me. I think
it was that of one of the assistants to the dealer. My ill-fated interview
with the portly fellow in white and yellow, or gold, had taken place
rather early, in the morning, not long after the tarpaulins had been
removed from our cages, and our simple needs had been attended to.
Toward noon, my misery was intense. I was cold from the river, and in
pain, given how I must hold my body to access the narrow plate of air
between the water and the ceiling of the cage. Often I had to spit out
water. Then, a bit after noon, I shrieked with horror, for something,
long, and snakelike, had slid between the bars and brushed across my
body. "Help! Help!" I cried. Then the thing, with a snap of its long,
smooth body, had darted away. "Help!" I screamed. "What is wrong?"
asked a voice from above. I knew not who it was. "A snake," I cried, "a
water snake!" "There are no water snakes here," called the voice. "The
current discourages them. It is most likely an eel, a Vosk eel." "Help!" I
cried. "Call my master. Save me!" But I received no response to my cry.
Toward nightfall another such intruder passed between the bars of the
cage. I felt its body slide over my left leg. During the night four more
such visitants traversed the cage. Once, during the night, something
smote the cage, twice, prodding it, pushing against the bars, and then
it withdrew, unseen. In the morning, shortly after dawn, I heard activity taking place above me, men walking, carts trundling. I also smelled
food cooking, probably in pans, set on the small wheeled stoves some
vendors moved about the wharf.

I heard the dealer's voice from above me.

"Are you bathed?" he inquired.

"Yes, Master!" I said. I had not slept, except for a momentary lapse, when my head sank beneath the water, and I awakened, and raised it again, immediately, to gasp for breath.

"Are you cold, and miserable?" he asked.

"Yes, Master," I said.

"Excellent," he said. "Would you care to spend another such night?" he asked.

"No, Master!" I said.

"You did not behave well of late," he said. "You dared to speak to free persons, not once, but twice, and the second time after having been warned. You were insufficiently deferent. You were displeasing. That is not acceptable in a slave. Too, you lied. A kajira is not a free woman. A kajira is not permitted to lie. Try that when you are in a man's collar, and see what you get."

"Forgive me, Master," I said.

"Perhaps you know better now that you are a slave," he said.

"Yes, Master," I said.

"What are you?" he asked.

"A slave," I said, "only a slave." I knew that answer from the house of training. But this time I knew it was true. I was a slave, only a slave.

"I gather you are new to bondage," he said.

"Yes, Master," I said.

"You have much to learn," he said.

"Yes, Master," I said.

"Have you ever been in close chains?" he asked.

"Yes, Master," I said.

"That is far worse, is it not, than what I did to you?"

"Yes, Master," I said. It was true. In the cage, I had been able to move about somewhat, to relieve my pain.

"In the light of your newness to bondage, I was extremely merciful to you," he said. "I trust that you understand that."

"Yes, Master," I said. "Thank you, Master."

"I did not even put you under the slave whip," he said.

I had never felt the slave whip.

"A slave is grateful," I said.

"Draw her up," I heard.

A bit later, the cage, shedding water, was drawn up to the wharf, and then dragged across the boards, and placed where it had been before. There was a slight breeze over the wharf, moving amongst the boxes, and bales, and cages, and, though the day itself was warm, I shivered with cold. For a moment my teeth chattered. A small blanket was thrust through the bars, and I dried myself, as I could, and then wrapped it, gratefully, about me. Later, a pan of hot mush was thrust through the narrow opening between the gate of the cage and its flooring. I lifted it to my mouth, with both hands, and ate, eagerly.

An hour or so later, as the day continued to warm, the blanket was drawn away from me, and I was handed a wide-toothed wooden comb.

"Make yourself presentable," said one of dealer's men.

"Stupid barbarian," said the girl caged to my left.

When I had combed my hair, as I could, I lay down in the cage, my legs drawn up. Men walked to and fro about the wharf.

The cage to my right was empty. Its occupant had been sold.

CHAPTER TEN

I will look upon that one," he said.

Some days had passed, since I had been 'bathed'.

"Surely, Master," said the dealer.

I heard the key inserted into my cage lock. I looked up, frightened. The dealer thrust back the gate. "Out," he said. "On all fours, head down."

I was then leashed.

I felt the leash pulled up. "Look up," said the dealer. I was still on all fours. The leash was taut. I looked up, as I must, the leash collar tight under my chin.

"She is not a bad-looking slut," said the dealer. "I am sure you could make her squirm well on a mat. It is easy to get them to squeak and beg."

"Get her to the yellow circle," he said.

He was bearded.

"I see Master is interested," said the dealer.

I then noted, to my unease, that the fellow carried a whip.

"She is too scrawny," he said.

"Not scrawny," said the dealer, "but lithe, sweetly slender."

"Her ankles are small," said the fellow.

"Not small," said the dealer, "but slim, in lovely proportion to her slender body. And it is well known that such ankles look well in shackles."

"Any woman's ankles look well, shackled," he said.

"To be sure," said the dealer.

"Her hair is too short," said the fellow.

"Not so short," said the dealer. "And it will grow, and it may be groomed, of course, to the master's preference, with the same ease as that of the mane of a kaiila."

"To the yellow circle," suggested the man.

"Come along, slim, meaningless slut," said the dealer. "Perhaps we can find you a master."

I then, on all fours, obedient to the leash, as had been the other girl, was conducted to the yellow circle. It had been drawn in chalk, crudely, on the boards of the wharf.

"Perhaps you should return her to her cage," said the fellow, skeptically.

"At least look at her," said the dealer.

"Very well," he said.

"Stand," said the dealer.

I winced. I moaned. I had not been out of the cage since I had first been inserted into it.

"I trust she is capable of an upright posture," said the man.

"Her body has been cramped," said the dealer. "Small cages take up less space."

"They are useful, too," said the man, "for disciplinary and monitory purposes."

"Very true," said the dealer. "Also, they are less expensive."

"You deal with cheap slaves," said the fellow.

"My market is well known for its bargains," said the dealer.

"You put your cages where you wish," said the man.

"Thus, I need neither buy nor rent a building, a shelf, a cell," said the dealer. "The money saved, applied to the prices of the merchandise, redounds obviously to the benefit of the customers."

"There may be advantages, too," said the fellow, "in the way of mobility."

"Sometimes it is judicious to change a venue," acknowledged the dealer.

"Doubtless," said the man.

"It is so," said the dealer.

"Remove the leash," said the man.

This was done. I gathered that not even so small a thing was to be allowed to interfere with my perusal.

I was still on all fours, at the feet of the masters.

"Can you stand, kajira?" inquired the dealer.

"Yes, Master," I said. "I think so. I will try."

Slowly, painfully, with the assistance of the dealer, he steadying me, I rose to my feet. I was not sure I could stand, without falling.

In the meantime, several men had gathered around, some of them stevedores. Men are often attracted to the sales of women. It is not unusual for them to find such sales of interest. To be sure, in most markets spectators will outnumber bidders.

I stood, unsteadily.

"Examination position," said the dealer.

I had been taught two or three of the most common examination positions in the training house, one of which I assumed, a bit unsteadily, feet widely spread, hands clasped behind the back of the head, head up, and back, looking upward. A woman may be examined in any position, of course, and it is not unknown for a potential buyer to instruct her to assume a variety of positions. Obviously a given item of merchandise may be displayed in any number of ways.

It is difficult to move when one's feet are widely spread. One remains in place, and feels helpless. With the hands clasped together, behind the head, the hands are immobilized, and there is nothing to interfere with the customer's vision, or the assessments of his touch. The breasts are also lifted, as is the behind-the-neck tie or the behind-the-neck braceleting. The head being back, and lifted, it is difficult for the slave to be aware of the eyes and expressions of the examiner, and thus of his interests or intentions. It is also difficult, of course, to anticipate and prepare for any evaluative testing or handling.

Wild thoughts went through my head. Could this be I?

In the office, and in my former life, generally, in all of its quotidian commonplaces, in all of its prosaic routines, banalities, repetitions, and boredoms, it had never occurred to me that I might one day be standing naked on a wharf, on another world, a slave, goods, being sold. What would my friends, my luncheon friends, have thought, could they see this? Would they be horrified? I doubted it. I thought, rather, they would be amused, even delighted, thinking it a well-deserved fate for their doubtless resented, smartly dressed, pretentious, vain, snobbish, shallow luncheon fellow. Or would they too long to stand in a yellow circle, so displayed, knowing that they then must be women, and will be women, as men want them. I wondered how my employers might have reacted. I had seen them look at me. I suspected they might have been bid on me.

"She is too short," said the man.

"Not at all," said the dealer. "Why should you say so? I do not understand. She is not short, nor is she tall. She is a pleasant average height, much the same height as most slaves. Her legs are spread widely. As you well know, that makes them seem a bit shorter."

"That is true," said a stevedore.

The man looked about, annoyed.

"Can you not conjecture," said the dealer, "what she would be in your arms, what she would look like on your chain, or roped hand and foot at the foot of your couch, in your furs, or kneeling before you, licking your ankles?"

"What is this mark, on her shoulder?" asked the man. "A slave mark?"

"Scarcely," said the dealer. "She wears the Kef."

"A blemish," he said.

"Scarcely noticeable," said the dealer.

It was my vaccination mark. This time the reference was clear. I remained silent. Indeed, I had not been given permission to speak.

"Open your mouth," said the man.

I opened my mouth, widely.

"I forgot to mention," said the dealer, hastily, "she is a barbarian."

"I see," said the man. "It slipped your mind."

"I fear so," said the dealer.

"You may close your mouth," said the man.

I did so.

"How is her Gorean?" asked the man.

"Flawless," said the dealer.

"Adequate?" asked the man.

"Yes, adequate," said the dealer, "for her time with the tongue."

My instructresses, as I recalled, had been pleased with my Gorean, at least to that point. I had profited from the skill and diligence of their instruction, and, doubtless, from the attentions of their switches. One is less likely to commit grammatical mistakes when one is punished for them.

"Buy her," suggested one of the stevedores.

"Please be quiet," said the man.

The fellow touched me, slapping me lightly, here and there, with the coiled whip.

"I trust she is satisfactory, and Master is pleased," said the dealer.

"A poor slave," said the man.

"But a bargain," said the dealer.

"She is not Gorean," said the man.

"Thus you need have no reservations with respect to her treatment," said the dealer.

"One need have no reservations where any slave is concerned," said the man.

"So true," said the dealer.

"She is a barbarian," said the man.

"*Ela*," said the dealer. "It is true."

"Gorean women are beautiful," said the man.

"How true," said the dealer. "Yet, say, one in a thousand is less beautiful."

"Possibly," said the man.

"And barbarians," he said, "are selected carefully, with an eye to intelligence, beauty, and passion. In many markets they sell quite as well as Gorean women."

"I have heard so," said the man.

"Too," said the dealer, "they are cheap. One need not risk one's life for them, raid caravans, fight wars, sack and burn cities, and so on. Indeed, one does not even pay for them. As I understand it, one simply picks them up, as one might please, much as one would pick flowers in the wild or pluck fruit from unguarded orchards."

"Then you should let them go very cheaply," said the man.

"Yet one must buy feed for them, keep chains on hand, buy cages, and such," said the dealer.

"Four tarsk-bits," said the man.

"A silver tarsk," said the dealer.

The man turned abruptly away.

"I misspoke," called the dealer. "Forgive me. I meant fifty copper tarsks, say, of the weight of the copper tarsk of Brundisium."

This meant little to me at the time, but I would learn that coinages might differ considerably from city to city. In some cities, there are eight copper-tarsks to a silver tarsk, and, in others, as in Brundisium, where many land and sea routes converge, and business tends to be brisk, one hundred copper tarsks to a silver tarsk. This facilitates small transactions. Too, coinages, certainly gold and silver, are often weighed when the coinage is of one city and the transaction takes place in another. This is sometimes done even when the coinage has been minted in the same city in which the transaction takes place, apparently because of the possibility of a private debasement of coins, the shaving of coins, and such. In the northern hemisphere of Gor it is common to standardize weights against the silver and gold coinages of Ar, the silver tarsk of Ar and the golden tarsk and tarn of Ar. In the southern hemisphere, the coinage of mighty Turia serves a similar purpose.

"Five copper tarsks," said the man.

"But consider her lineaments," said the dealer, "her flanks, her wrists, her shoulders, her throat."

"I am not looking for a pleasure slave," he said. "I am buying work slaves, to sell south of the Vosk."

"Even a work slave may be attractive," said the dealer. "Forty copper tarsks."

"Perhaps ten," he said.

"You carry a whip," said the dealer. "May I inquire your caste?"

"The blue-and-yellow caste," he said.

"I suspected as much," said the dealer. "You are then a shrewd judge of collar meat, a skilled appraiser of girl stock. Surely then you must recognize that forty copper tarsks is a splendid buy for this lovely beast."

"Ten," said the man.

"What of thirty?" inquired the dealer.

"I do not need to buy, not here," said the man. "Ten."

"Thirty does not seem unreasonable," said the dealer.

"Ten," said the man. "I would hope to sell her for thirty."

"Would you consider twenty?" asked the dealer.

I sensed the man had moved behind me. I thought little of it. A customer, or client, often views an article from more than one perspective. A slave expects to be so considered. Indeed, many slaves, after a sale or two, not only expect to be well displayed, but, in their vanity, enjoy it, and look forward to it. Who does not wish to be beautiful, and excite desire? On a block, of course, the girl is likely to be turned for the buyers.

"Aii!" I cried, suddenly, reacting, involuntarily, spasmodically, wildly, reflexively, helplessly.

What had been done to me!

I could not believe what had been done to me, how, by another, without my permission, I had been forced to reveal myself, to betray my needs and sex.

I was horrified, outraged, and shamed, to the core of my being, and then I recalled I was a slave. I was a beast, an object. Anything might be done to me.

Men laughed.

My body, I feared, was a raging storm of scarlet tissue.

I struggled to return to the examination position.

I was shaking. I was trembling.

Mirth was about.

An aspect of my being, as much as my hair or eye color, had been blatantly exhibited, apparently to see if it might be of interest to masters.

"But what is wrong," I later asked myself, "with being vital, and alive?" The deceits and pretenses of the free woman are not for the slave, who is owned. They are not permitted to her. She is slave.

It had been done gently, but firmly, with the coiled whip. I had been administered the Slaver's Caress!

The men about were muchly pleased. Two slapped their thigh.

"Twenty copper tarsks," said the fellow with the whip, now, again, somewhere before me.

"Done!" said the dealer, pleased. "I will call for the scales."

"Shameless slut," said a feminine voice. There had apparently been a free woman in the throng about, of whose presence, I, in examination position, had been unaware. "I would never react so," she said, apparently to someone with her.

"Nor I," said another feminine voice, indignantly.

"What a disgusting, leaping, meaningless slut she is," said the first woman.

"A slave," sneered the other.

"Yes," said the first.

"They are all the same, in their collars," said the second.

"Yes," said the first.

I think they then took their leave.

"You may break position," said the dealer to me. "Remove yourself from the circle. Go there, to the side, there, and wait. Lie down, in bara."

I then lay on the warm boards, in bara.

"May I be touched, Master?" I asked.

"Be silent," he said.

"Yes, Master," I said.

I recalled the voices of the free women. How contemptuous had been their words, their tones!

"You think you are so lofty, so unmoved, so superior, so immune to everything concealed within your robes," I thought. "But you, exalted creatures, are women, too. Let you be subjected to such a touch. Let men discover whether or not you are alive. I do not think you would leap and cry out other than I."

I lay quietly, waiting.

"You, lofty free women," I thought, "let them take away your robes and veils, burn a mark in your thigh, and fasten a collar on your neck,

and see if you are any different from me! Kneel, and tremble, and lick
and kiss a whip, thrust to your pretty lips, and see if you are any different from me!"

About me, men, and some women, passed. Some men to the side,
who had perhaps lingered after my sale, were engaged in conversation,
and it was impossible that I should not hear, though, I fear, I understood little of what was said.

"You have heard, doubtless," said a man's voice, "of what occurred
in the tavern of Tasdron?"

"No," said another. "What?"

"The tavern was entered by one of the dark caste," said the voice.

"When?" asked a man.

"Six days ago, in the vicinity of the eighteenth Ahn," said the first
man.

"One of the dark caste, here in Victoria?" asked another man.

"Hunting," said the first man.

"I had not heard," said the second man.

"What occurred?" asked a man.

"Four men were slain," said the first man.

"I had not heard," said another.

"Tasdron does not wish the matter noised about," said the first
man.

"Nor would I," said a man. "It is not pleasant to learn that a tavern
has been visited by one of the dark caste."

"How four men slain?" asked a man.

"He of the dark caste was displeased, muchly so," said the first man.

"His quarry eluded him?" said a fellow.

"Apparently," said the first man.

"Why four slain?" asked a fellow, apprehensively.

"He of the dark caste made inquiries," said the first man. "They
proved fruitless. None knew the whereabouts of the quarry."

"And so four were slain?" said a man.

"He of the dark caste was displeased," said the first man.

"So four men were slain," said one of the men.

"Each with a thrust to the heart," said the first man.

"Where is he of the dark caste?" asked a fellow, his voice shaking.

"He is gone," said the first man. "We do not know where."

"He of the dark caste simply withdrew?" said a man.

"Yes," said the first man.

"Undetained?" said a man.

"One does not interfere with one of the dark caste, when he is hunting," said the first man.

"Guardsmen?" inquired one of the men.

"Nor they," said the first man.

"Whom did he seek? Whom did he hunt?" asked a man.

"Let us not speak further of this, not here, not on the wharf," said the first man. "Others approach."

I then heard steps near me.

I tensed, and a new collar, as I lay, was snapped about my throat. The dealer's collar was then removed. Merchant Law recommends that female slaves be kept in their collars.

"You are the property, for the moment," said a voice, "of Raymond of Ti. Who is your master?"

"Raymond of Ti, Master," I said.

I felt slave bracelets snapped about my wrists, my wrists behind my back, as I lay.

"You are not of Victoria, noble Raymond of Ti," said the dealer, who was standing to the side.

"No," he said.

"I gather you are not to be long in Victoria," said the dealer.

"No," said he. "But Victoria is a rich trading place for slaves."

"That is well known," said the dealer.

I had not been given permission to rise.

"For cheap slaves," he said.

"Some, in our markets," said the dealer, "bring prices as splendid as those of other municipalities, Besnit, Ko-ro-ba, Port Kar, Brundisium, even Ar."

"But not so in open wharf markets," said the man.

"Perhaps not," said the dealer.

"Position," said Raymond of Ti.

I then rose, as well as I could, back-braceleted, to a kneeling position. The simple command, "Position," unqualified, is commonly understood to have this import. How one kneels is determined by how one is understood, what sort of slave one is. I knelt with my knees closely together. I was not a pleasure slave. But, of course, any slave, in a sense, is a pleasure slave. She is a slave. I was back on my heels, my back straight, my head up, my hands braceleted behind me.

"You have others?" said the dealer.

"Several," said Raymond of Ti, "housed in the city."

"I gather you will soon be leaving Victoria," said the dealer.

"In the morning," he said. "We will take a ferry across the Vosk, and then, in waiting wagons, hie south and west."

My master then held his coiled whip to my lips, and I bent forward and kissed it, and licked it.

"May I ask your destination?" said the dealer.

"Torcadino," he said.

"Of course," said the dealer.

"Rise," he said to me, "and stand, head down."

A slave, so standing, back-braceleted, is quite attractive. The posture bespeaks submission and helplessness.

"I wish you well," said the dealer.

"I wish you well," said Raymond of Ti, my master, and took his leave.

I hurried after him.

I wore no leash.

But none was necessary.

Indeed, a leash is seldom necessary.

Its primary value is its effect on the slave. There are few things that more profoundly impress her slavery upon a woman than being on a leash. Does this not make it clear to her, and to all who look upon her, a scrutiny of which she is likely to be well aware, that she is a slave?

It is no wonder that former free women, recently enslaved, are often leashed.

So I wore no leash.

But no leash was necessary. I was naked, collared, marked, and back-braceleted. There was nothing to do, and nowhere to run, even had I been tempted, in foolishness or madness, to dart away. Escape was impossible, the culture saw to that, but, too, I realized, a thought that would once have startled me, and the truth of which I would have felt obliged to protest fiercely, I did not want to escape. I had now come to accept myself as what I was, and should be, a slave. I had discovered my identity. I had learned I could find my fulfillment only in being owned, only in being the property of a master.

But does a girl not hope for a given master, to buy her, to put his collar on her, the master of her dreams?

"Oh!" I cried, struck by a free woman's switch, as I hurried past her.

Twice was I hooted at, and twice pinched.

Would my master not defend me against such abuse? But it seemed he did not care to do so. I gathered such things, at least in a common slave, were beneath notice.

After perhaps some thirty minutes he stopped before a heavy wooden door, chained shut. He undid the locks, and swung it open. It was dark within.

"Turn your back to me," he said.

I did so, and he removed the bracelets, and then turned me about, so that I faced him, but inches away.

I very much felt his presence, and, I was sure, he, a man, must feel mine.

"There are stairs," he said, "leading down to the basement. Be careful of the stairs."

"Yes, Master," I said.

He then took me in his arms, suddenly, without warning, and I felt his lips, and the roughness of his beard, and I was kissed, fiercely, with command and authority, as a slave.

I recalled how, on my former world, various young men had asked if they might kiss me, which permission I granted or refused, as the whim took me.

But here he did with me what he wanted, when he wanted.

I was a slave.

Then he thrust me from him.

He looked down at me.

How my body felt him! Would he not do more with me? I was ready, slave ready.

But it seems he was merely trying me, to see how I might do in his arms.

I gathered he had found out.

Perhaps I had been lacking.

"Down the stairs," he said.

I clutched the crude board within the threshold, the board to my left, serving as a banister, and took a step downward, into the darkness.

I heard a voice, plaintive, from below. "May I speak, Master?" it inquired.

"Yes," he called down, into the darkness.

"May we not be clothed?" it asked.

"Wait until you are bought," he called down, into the darkness. "Ask your buyers. Perhaps they will throw you a rag."

"Master!" pleaded the voice.

"You are all pot girls," he said.

"Master!" wailed the voice.

"Where are we to be sold?" begged another voice, arising from the darkness.

"Here and there," he said, "in diverse markets. I have purchased some of you to fill orders."

"For work slaves?" asked a voice.

"Yes," he said.

I heard sobs, and cries of lament, from below.

It was not pleasant, I gathered, to be a work slave.

"Please, no, Master!" wept a voice, from below.

"Be silent," he said.

No sound then emanated from the darkness.

Holding tightly to the banister, half turned, with two hands, I descended the steep stairs, one at a time.

The door closed behind me, above me. All was then in darkness. I heard the chains, the rattle of the placings of the locks.

I felt my way to a wall, to my left, and sat there, my back against the wall, my knees drawn up.

The floor was of wooden planking.

I could not see the others.

"You are the twenty-second," said a girl's voice, not far from me.

"When are we leaving?" inquired another voice.

"I heard tomorrow," I said, "tomorrow morning."

"Where are we going?" asked another voice, in the darkness.

I gathered I was the bearer of news. Did they not know that curiosity was not becoming in a kajira?

"I think," I said, "Torcadino."

"Ah!" said more than one girl.

I knew little more of Torcadino than the name. I had gathered it was south of the river, and overland.

"You have an accent," said a girl's voice.

"So do you," I said, hazarding the remark. To be sure, there was a flavor in her voice that was surely unlike that of the instructresses, at least.

"That is true," laughed another girl, in the darkness.

I would learn later she was from Anango.

For a long time I remembered the imperious, assaultive kiss to which I had been unilaterally subjected.

I had wanted to respond, with a slave's tenderness, hope, eagerness, and gratitude, but I had been given no opportunity to do so.

I was uneasy.

I feared I might be on the brink of slave fires. I tried to think of things as though I might be a free woman, but I was unsuccessful.

"Tell us about yourself," said a voice from the darkness.

"There is nothing to tell," I said.

They need not know I was a barbarian. Doubtless they would find out soon enough.

Barbarians tend to be unpopular with other slaves. They sometimes bring higher prices.

CHAPTER ELEVEN

I leaned against the heavy horizontal pole, chest high, inserted through the large, conical stone. It, like its two similar poles, passed through the stone and emerged on the other side. This produced, given the penetrations, the effect of six poles, against which weight might be pressed, this turning the heavy stone. The miller's man, at intervals, from his ladder, would pour the grain, sa-tarna, the "life daughter," into the opening on the top of the stone, and the stone, when turning, would press down upon it, and grind it, the resultant flour, by means of three descending troughs, being gathered in waiting sacks.

I had not been soon sold from the wharf.

Doubtless that had lowered my price.

As cages were emptied new occupants were procured. The cage to my right that had been emptied earlier now housed a red-headed slave. She was lovely. Her thigh, too, wore the Kef. I did not doubt that men would like her. I had seen her brought in, roped.

"May I speak, Master?" I had petitioned one or another of the two dealer's men, from time to time. It is common for a slave to request permission to speak. Indeed, as she is not a free woman, she is expected to do so. I did not wish to request permission to speak from passers-by, or customers, fearing that this might be displeasing, but, following the example of some of the other girls, I did lodge this humble petition, now and then, with one of the dealer's men. When not busy, they had no objection to conversing with us. They were men, and we were women, and women doubtless selected, at least in part, for their desirability and beauty, and, being men, they, no more than the males of Earth, objected to chatting with desirable and beautiful women, though, in this case, we were slaves, naked, and looking up at them, caged at their feet. Few men of Earth, I supposed, had had such an experience. Had they had such an experience, they might have had, I conjectured, a better sense of their manhood, and the difference between men and women.

How it pleases a man to have a slave at his feet, and how it pleases a slave to be at the feet of a master!

I used such occasions to deepen and broaden my knowledge of Gor, of its castes, customs, terrains and cities, governances, Ubarates, clans, beliefs, plants, fruits and vegetables, trees and flowers, animals, and such. Though I had never seen sleen, tarsks, verr, tharlarion, kaiila, tarns, or such, I did learn something of their nature, habits, and appearances.

I had also had it confirmed that the snakelike visitants that had so frightened and discomfited me in my tenure in the mostly submerged cage were not water snakes, which tend to favor still water, but eels, in all probability Vosk eels, a form of river eel. Such eels, as other eels, are omnivorous, but, free swimming, are accustomed to feed on small fish and plants. They are unlikely to attack human beings, unlike pool eels, unless their nests are threatened. They are found in fresh water, but return, through the delta of the Vosk, to the salt water of vast, turbulent Thassa to spawn. I had also learned that the prodding at the cage, its strikings, twice, by some large body in the dark water, unseen by me, had most likely been a result of the curiosity of a river shark. Such fish, nine-gilled, and slender, sometimes reaching a length of nine to twelve feet, do pose a threat to anything in the water. They were, however, rare in the vicinity of Victoria. They were more common in the delta. Similar fish were found, I was told, in the Cartius and Laurius, the Cartius to the south, the Laurius to the north. Gorean sharks, in their several varieties, of course, are much more common in the waters of Thassa herself, particularly near the shallower banks, where sunlight encourages the growth of plants, and the plants attract several varieties of smaller fish, the parsit and others, on which the sharks feed. The bars of the cage, of course, had protected me from it. That which kept me within had kept it without. The bars of the cage had not been bent, but only prodded, which suggested the fish had been more curious than driven with the frenzy of hunger. One of the dealer's men told of occasions in which a cage had required considerable repair following the onslaught of one or more such fish. In each case, however, the slave, within the battered device, safe within the bars, had escaped harm. Such things, I gathered, presented their greatest danger to captured free women, from enemy cities. Uneasily, I heard recounted occasions, in one venue, or another, of the harrows that might face such women who, being beyond price, are accordingly worthless. At least one has a sense of what a slave will bring. A free woman, stripped and bound, watches the water, and then, when the large, narrow, triangular, dorsal fins of the sharks cleave the water, men lift her, to cast her into the sea; on other occasions, she might, suspended by the wrists, be lowered, bit by bit, into a pit of starving urts who will feed on her, inch by inch; other unpleasant fates involve the fangs of sleen and the wicked hollow thorns of well-rooted, matted, leech plants. In such straits it seemed that the free women often discovered that they were actually slaves, professed themselves such, and begged the collar. Free women of the enemy make lovely slaves, it seems, but what else are they good for? I had learned that it was far safer to be a slave, or a verr or kaiila, than a free woman in the hands of the enemy.

I closed my eyes. I, and the others, were covered with sweat. We welcomed the moments when new grain was poured into the feeding aperture atop the stone. Too, sometimes a pole would snap. This, too, meant a surcease of effort. The stone was large, and heavy. It ground coarsely. There were, about the yard, smaller stones, as well, some of which could be turned by a single girl, kneeling near it. In this way our basic mill produced flour that could be reworked, if one wished, to different varieties of fineness, which would then be priced differently, being addressed to different markets. If we take the three penetrant poles spoken of, and count them as six poles, or spokes, by means of which to turn the stone, there were four girls to each of the six poles, or spokes, so twenty-four of us were used at a time in the work. The mill owner owned some thirty draft slaves, and those not chained in place to their pole, would usually be chained to the side, in the shade, where they might rest. He owned other girls, as well, of course, who had their different employments about the mill, turning the smaller stones, grading and sacking flour, sewing and marking sacks, loading carts, accompanying the drivers, when they made deliveries, and so on. I gathered that those accompanying the drivers, as they were silked, were supposed to be attractive advertisements in their way, for their master's goods. Surely I was familiar with this sort of thing from Earth. What male is not likely to be favorably inclined toward a product that he associates with a beautiful woman? I thought myself obviously superior to them. It seemed to me madness that they should be silked, and I was chained to a pole. For the most part, however, sa-tarna, harvested and threshed, was brought in by peasants, milled, and carried away by peasants. The fee for the milling was in tarsk-bits, but, most commonly, it was taken in kind, a portion of the flour going to the miller, who might then market it as his own. From where we worked I could see the lofty aqueduct by means of which water was brought to Torcadino from the distant Voltai range, hundreds of pasangs away. Once, I had heard, enemy forces had entered the city by means of that aqueduct. The pitch in the aqueduct, supposedly, was less than a hort every twenty pasangs. We, the draft slaves, were camisked. The camisk is a strip of cloth, a brief, narrow rectangle with a circular opening at its center. It is drawn over the head, poncholike, pulled down, and belted with cord, or binding fiber. If possible, it leaves even less of the slave to the imagination than the tunic or ta-teera, the "slave rag." Indeed, I was told that it is outlawed on the streets of some cities. But it was, of course, happily, clothing. Indeed, given our labors, we were perhaps fortunate to be clothed at all. Often, on Gor, I had learned, slaves, and even free workmen engaged in heavy tasks on hot days, might work nude. Male nudity, particularly in the fields, quarries, and such, is not unusual. Little is thought of it. Female nudity, on the other hand, is less common and, if it occurs, it would commonly be limited to slaves, or, one supposes, female captures. Even a free woman is likely to become much more aware of her womanhood, and her difference from men, when she is stripped and bound. The feeling of free women toward tunics and such seems to be ambivalent. They seem to favor them in order to humiliate and degrade the slave, and emphasize the difference between themselves, the free, and the slaves, while, at the same time, they seem to resent the attention and pleasure with which men regard slaves so clad. Surely, in a tunic, it is clear what the slave is for. We were apparently camisked because the gate of the mill yard was usually open in daylight hours, and free women might pass by. Too, sometimes peasant women, accompanying their companions, brought grain to the mill. My two wrists were chained to the pole. I put my head down, upon it. My body ached. "Why are not men, male slaves, or beasts, bosk or tharlarion, used to turn the mill?" I had asked one of my chain sisters. "Male slaves are dangerous," she said. "Few are permitted within a city's walls, save for male silk slaves, the pets of free women, and they make poor draft beasts, and we are cheaper than bosk and tharlarion." I was not popular with the other girls, even more so than is common with "barbarians," I feared, doubtless because of my obvious superiority to them, in both beauty and intelligence. On the other hand, to my amazement, and indignation, I soon realized they did not regard themselves as my inferiors. They seemed to think themselves as beautiful, and as intelligent, as I, and even, in several instances, as more so. I found this incomprehensible. Too, they, though obvious barbarians, natives of this rude, barbarous sphere, had the effrontery to regard me, of Earth, as the barbarian! I saw the miller's man approaching, with his basket of grain, followed by the dark-haired flute girl. He set his ladder against the stone, climbed the ladder, and poured the grain into the cavity within the stone. He then withdrew, setting the ladder aside, and disappeared, with his basket, returning to the receiving house, where grain was brought and weighed, and records kept. The flute girl then climbed to her perch, or platform, on the side, and sat upon it, her legs dangling over the edge. She, too, was camisked, and wore the mill collar. Shortly thereafter the switch slave, a large, strong woman, similarly camisked, arrived, her switch in hand. About her forehead was bound a broad, yellow fillet, from the wool of the bounding hurt. This held back her hair, of course, but its significance, in her case, was considerable. It was a talmit, indicative of rank. She was first girl in the mill yard. The flute girl began to play, and we dug in our feet and pressed our weight against the spokelike poles by means of which the stone was turned. With a heavy, grinding, sound, one we knew well, the heavy, conical stone began to rotate slowly on the thick, flat, circular, platelike stone from which the troughs descended. It was not unusual on this world, incidentally, for many activities to be accompanied by music which, on my former world, would not be likely to be so accompanied. Needless to say, I found this surprising. Warriors might perform martial exercises to music, in the manner of Pyrrhic dances, advancing, withdrawing, wheeling about, and such, brandishing weaponry; athletes might train to music; sa-tarna might be harvested to music; grain might be threshed to music, galleys might be rowed to music, and so on. Similarly, work songs are common in the fields. Warriors might sing battle hymns while moving to engage the enemy. Girls may sing at the looms, and at the potting wheels.

Once, I had heard, the walls of a great city, Ar, defeated in war, had been dismantled, to the music of flute girls.

Doubtless music has many practical applications. It might serve to coordinate activities; it might serve to hearten; to inspirit, and lift hearts; it might be intended to seemingly shorten hours and lighten labors, and so on. The tunes played by our flute girl were not lively, of course, for one does not turn a stone with grace and sprightliness, but were measured to our tread, as we thrust against the poles. Sometimes, when we were resting, leaning on the poles, she would play as she wished. She was quite skilled. I wanted to tear her hair out.

"Ai!" I cried, struck by the switch of the first girl, on the back of the thighs, four times, below the narrow, tiny camisk. "Do not malinger, barbarian," she said. "Feel my switch, you laggard! Others are not to do your work."

I thrust then, again, with a rattle of chains, harder, against the pole. My pole sisters laughed.

I did not dare think of pulling out the hair of the first girl. She was large, and strong. I was afraid of her.

As I made the circuit, in the well-worn circular path, one of four, concentric about the mill, thrusting, I looked again at the flute girl, as I passed, in her camisk, her legs crossed, dangling over the platform. "She has slim ankles," I thought to myself. "They are not unlike mine. What is wrong with slim ankles? Are they not attractive? Would men not bid well for such a girl?" And then I recalled she was only another slave in a mill yard.

Goreans tend to be fond of the arts, at least as they understand them. There are public readings of literary works, recitals of poetry, contests of dancing, musical contests, with various instruments, contests of choral singing, contests of plays, both comedic and dramatic, and so on. The participants in these municipal contests, too, are almost always common citizens, volunteers, for on Gor the common citizen is as likely to be a participant as a spectator. It has not occurred to Goreans that the joys of performance should be limited to a small minority, a professional elite. The arts are too precious for that.

Most flute girls, as those who play the kalika, are slaves, as are most dancers. Most are owned by small companies, from which they may be rented. They are popular at dinners, small parties, banquets, symposiums, and such. They are usually attractive, and are rented for the night. Companies exist, incidentally, for many purposes. For example, there are companies from which you can obtain a cook, or cooks, if you are planning a banquet, companies from which you can rent fine robes, or sandals, jewels for your companion, and so on.

Despite the exalted status of free women, who are equal to men in the holding of a Home Stone, can hold money and property in their own right, may found, organize, and manage businesses, may occupy positions of importance and authority, even to the occupancy of thrones, and who may enter into relationships, or discontinue them, much as they please, the Free Companionship requiring an annual renewal, Gor is essentially a man's world. It is men who carry spears and maintain walls; it is men who encounter the violence of the enemy; it is men who stand, armed and resolute, between the Home Stone and its desecration or destruction; it is men, the masters, who will decide what respect and privileges will be accorded women. They behave so because they are men, and they have never seen fit to relinquish their nature as men, their blood, their natural dominance. Gorean men, for whatever reason, wisely or not, have never chosen to enter into arrangements whereby they might be humiliated, dishonored, reduced, and destroyed. They will not do so. I did not object. I was pleased. A woman, I did not wish to relate to lesser men.

The back of my thighs stung, for a long time.

The day was hot.

I knew that I, a slave, would be kept in a collar. Moreover, an insight I had suppressed on my former world, given its nature, I had come to realize that I belonged in one, and could only be happy in one.

I wanted a master, and yet, too, I feared belonging to one.

I was owned by the miller, of course, as the other girls, but he had never touched me, and had scarcely regarded me. Perhaps, I supposed, he pleasured himself with the "silk girls," those who went about on the cart with the miller's men, attending to their deliveries.

I was miserable, leaning forward, thrusting at the pole.

What could I do?

How vulnerable, how helpless, is the slave!

If I were to improve my lot on this world, I reasoned, I, a slave, had little to hope for from free women. My hope was men. Surely I might, as a free woman might not, and a slave might, be able to influence my situation. I shook the manacles on my wrists in anger. I, despite my beauty and intelligence, my Earth origin, was chained with others, barbarians, to a mill pole.

"Keep thrusting, barbarian," snapped the first girl.

"Yes, Mistress!" I exclaimed. I did not wish to be again switched. She had called me a barbarian! How dared she? But then I thought of the world from which I had come. Was it not, in its way, a barbarian world, stupid, inconsistent, crowded, polluted, thoughtless, greedy, hate-filled, afflicted with envies, resentments, and jealousies, dismal, pathological?

Perhaps it was I, indeed, who, from such a world, was suitably viewed as the barbarian.

I slumped at the pole, suddenly, suspended by my chained wrists.

"Mistress!" cried the girl to my left, alarmed. "The barbarian is ill, she is stricken, she has fainted!" Instantly my chain sisters stopped turning the mill.

I lay, seemingly unconscious in my chains.

The flute girl desisted, and, I gather, leapt from her platform, to rush to my side.

"Poor thing!" said the girl to my left.

"Is she dead?" asked one of those chained behind me.

"I do not think so," said the flute girl, concerned, the flute left behind on the platform.

"What is going on here?" asked one of the miller's men, hurrying to us.

"The barbarian," said the flute girl. "She has collapsed."

"Is she dead?" he asked.

"No," said the flute girl. "I saw her eyelids flutter, weakly."

This small signal, I conjectured, might hearten those about, generating some hope that I might recover.

"Poor kajira," said a girl.

"We might all so collapse," said another girl.

Things were going well, it seemed.

"No more work today," said the miller's man. "Hold her up, that her weight not be on the manacles. Her wrists might be abraded."

I was supported then by the girl to my left.

"Poor barbarian," said another girl.

I smiled, weakly.

"How brave she is," said a girl.

"Yes," said another.

"She is too small, and weak, for this work," said another girl.

"She is not so small or weak," said another girl.

"No more than we," said another.

I did not care much for these two comments.

"If she recovers," said another, "sell her, and find her a gentler, sweeter collar."

I understood what she meant, but collars are much the same. To be sure, some collars are more ornate than others, enameled, even jeweled, and such. And some collars were unpleasant, point collars, punishment collars, and such. Turian collars, I was told, were rounded, and so on.

"Continue to support her," said the miller's man. "I will fetch water, and the key to her manacles."

I was then aware that he had hurried away.

Things, I surmised, were going well.

I opened my eyes, and, to my uneasiness, found myself looking up, into the eyes of the first girl.

"Release her," she snapped to the girl to my left, who was holding me, which command was instantly obeyed. I then gasped, as though in pain, and, momentarily, hung again in the manacles, my body partly on the ground, my wrists up, a foot or so from the pole. Then, as though with great effort, my head down, I struggled to a kneeling position, and knelt behind and below the pole, my wrists raised, on either side of my head, held in the manacles.

"How brave she is," marveled one of my chain sisters.

"Yes," said another, "and she only a barbarian, as well."

"Fraud! Slackard! Inferior actress!" said the first girl.

I fear my eyes opened widely then, in alarm.

"Have mercy on her, noble Mistress," said the flute girl. "Can you not see she is spent? Pity her, lest she perish at the pole!"

"If she perishes at the pole," said the first girl, "it will be my doing!"

The switch then rained down upon my back, and legs, and neck, and I scrambled to my feet, sobbing, seizing the pole.

"Please stop, Mistress!" I begged.

But the switch continued to strike, and I clutched the pole in misery.

"Faker, faker!" said the first girl, and then she desisted in her work. Her arm, I supposed, was sore or weary.

I was shuddering at the pole.

"What occurs?" said the miller's man, returning to the mill, a bota in hand, presumably filled with water.

"Little, Master," said the first girl. "This slacking slave does not even know how to faint."

"She is on her feet," observed the miller's man.

"And eager to work, Master!" said the first girl.

"I was tricked?" said the miller's man.

"It may be so," said the first girl.

"I was tricked!" he said.

"It may be so, Master," said the first girl.

"I do not care to be tricked," he said.

"Many were tricked, Master," she said.

"But not you," he said.

"I know such slaves," she said.

"She has been punished?" he asked.

"I conjecture well enough," said the first girl.

I, clinging to the pole, sobbed, my protesting body raging with pain.

"You will work to dusk," said the miller's man, "and then an extra Ahn." Then he turned to the flute girl. "To your station," he said.

She hurried to her platform, and, a moment later, we heard the flute emit its first notes.

"Pick up the tempo," said the miller's man.

We thrust our weights against the poles.

"Just wait until we get you tonight," said the girl to my left.

"Yes," said a girl behind me.

"Stinking barbarian," said another.

"Be silent," said the first girl.

I lay, chained, in the slave kennel, on my belly.

The first girl was at my side, rubbing ointment into my back, slowly, with firm, circular motions. A small tharlarion-oil lamp was beside her.

"You are a very stupid slave," she said.

"Yes, Mistress," I said.

"Doubtless you thought you were clever," she said.

"It seems I was not," I said.

"It seems," she said, "that the attentions I accorded you were not the only attentions to which you were subjected."

"No, Mistress," I said.

Before we were chained in the kennel I had been well belabored by several of my pole mates.

Slaves often participate in keeping their own order, punishing malefactors.

"That is enough," said the first girl, putting aside the ointment, and wiping her hands.

"Thank you, Mistress," I said. "Mistress is kind."

"I think they are going to let you go," she said.

"Mistress?" I said, frightened.

"Do not be afraid," she said, "not for eels, not for sleen feed. A normal sell, a common sell, somewhere in the city."

"I am to be sold?" I said.

"Yes," she said.

"Why?" I asked.

"They think it may be dangerous to keep you," she said.

"Why?" I asked.

"There were inquiries," she said.

"'Inquiries'?" I asked.

"Yes," she said. "Do you know a man named Kurik, Kurik of Victoria?"

"Yes," I said. "He was my first master."

"You are to be sold tomorrow," she said.

CHAPTER TWELVE

A slave expects to be bought and sold. She is an article of merchandise. I had now come to think of myself as such, it is a strange sense, and realize I was such. My freedom was gone. I had now become a slave. What a total, radical, cataclysmic transformation this wreaks in one's being, in one's self, in one's heart, and understanding. A free woman, I suspect, as she is free, cannot begin to understand the nature and world of the slave. It is a different nature and world. Certainly I, in my freedom, considering such things, had had no comprehension of the collar, and what it would be to wear it. It is a different world, different, profound, and deep, being owned, being vendible. Perhaps the free woman might have some intellectual sense of such matters, verbal, abstract, remote, superficial, or such, or thinks she does, but, I assure you, that intellectual comprehension is quite other than the realization of the reality, that one is, indeed, a slave. It is one thing to hear of the whip, and another to be struck with it; it is one thing to think of chains, and another to have them locked on one's limbs; it is one thing to consider a sale, or even to view one, and another to feel the sawdust beneath your bared feet and hear the bids shouted down from the tiers. What free woman, wise and noble in her freedom, can grasp the consciousness, the fears, the hopes, the helplessnesses, the vulnerabilities, the terrors, the despairs, the desires, the feelings, the joys, the passions, the wholeness, the identity, of the slave? Suppose a woman has been free; then she is a slave. An enormous change then, profound and transformative, takes place in her, in the entirety of her, intellectually, emotionally, and psychologically. She is no longer the same. She is now what she is, a slave, only a slave. I had been free on Earth; now I was a slave, only that. This transformation had now taken place in me. I was a slave. And yet, though I had no voice in the matter, and was helpless to qualify or alter my condition, I had experienced, paradoxically, a sense of rightness, of appropriateness, and freedom. Denied freedom, I was free. At a man's feet, his belonging, chained, I knew a liberation far beyond any I had felt as a free woman. I could now be what I was, and wanted to be, myself, a slave.

CHAPTER THIRTEEN

I, kneeling, with the thick, wooden blade, scraped the grease from the pan. I would then, with white, scouring sand, clean its surface, rinse it with scented water, and dry it with a woolen towel. It was the first of six such pans, placed near me, in a line. I was one of four kitchen slaves, in the house of Lysander, of Market of Semris, he of the caste of Builders. Tyrant of Market of Semris. Common governance on Gor is in terms of Administrators or Ubars. Administrators, in the high cities, are usually appointed by the Council of Castes; to which body, in theory, they are responsible. Ubars are usually generals or war leaders, originally acclaimed by, and empowered by, popular support, most often in periods of crisis. In a sense, I suppose they, too, are tyrants, as there is no legal limit placed on their tenure in office nor are there any obvious provisions for removing them from office, short of, I suppose, assassinations or uprisings. To be sure, they commonly have the support of the people. They select their own successors, often by legally adopting a favored individual. Almost invariably a Ubar is a member of the caste of Warriors. Their power remains in place then, in a sense, not only because of popular support and contentment, but, as well, by means of the backing of the military. I have spoken of Lysander as a tyrant, though he referred to himself, genially, as an Administrator, a humble servant of the people. He was, in effect, a strong man, of considerable economic power, who, by means of a coalition of personal supporters, mercenaries, and the military, controlled the city. I speak of a "tyrant" in the sense that there was no legal limit of a tenure in office involved nor any familiar, established, legal mechanism for removing from office. In a sense the tyrant is, for most practical purposes, a Ubar. To be sure, he does not bear that title. The word 'tyrant', I should mention, carries in itself no negative sense. Many "tyrants" are effective governors and enjoy popular support. The word in Gorean is '*tyrannos*', and some tyrants do not eschew the word. "Hurry," said the kitchen master. "Yes, Master," I said, and bent more vigorously to my task. He was swift with the switch. I was not his favorite. I had often felt it. My hands were reddened, and rough. My hair was tied back, behind my head, with a cord. I and the other girls wore kitchen tunics, brown, brief, ragged, stained. We were low slaves, and were not permitted in the front rooms of the large house. But this bondage was lighter than many in which I had found myself, since my sale in Victoria.

I now cast the scouring sand onto the cooking surface of the pan and reached for the thick, damp, rubbing cloth by means of which it might be put to its purpose. I held the pan firmly down on the flat stone, that it might not slip.

It is not pleasant to be a kitchen slave, a field slave, a mill slave, and such.

I, as other slaves, longed for a private master. What slave would not? Imagine being caressed by a private master, and being in his arms, being his alone. How welcome his collar! How grateful would one be for his chains! Too, one would hope to be the single slave of such a master. Most Goreans, of course, can afford but a single slave, and seldom more than two.

It was interesting to me, from Earth, that there seemed to be little, if any, resentment on Gor for the fact that a rich man might have a thousand slaves and a poor man but one, if that. Indeed, the poor man seems most likely to admire the rich fellow, and wish that he, too, had such good fortune. Indeed, the poor man seems pleased that someone has a thousand slaves, better that than no one, and is inclined to wish that he, too, was so well off. He has never been convinced that the thousand slaves were stolen from him by the rich man, particularly as he never had a thousand slaves to steal. Too, he may share a Home Stone with the rich man, which means he is more likely to view the rich man as a fellow and compatriot than a thief and enemy. Too, the rich man often supports public spectacles and events, such as song dramas, readings, kaissa competitions, civic banquets, and such. Indeed, in harbor cities, rich men, doubtless to their annoyance, are often expected to underwrite the repair of docks, the construction of galleys, and so on.

And so I, scouring the pan, let my thoughts roam about, as might clouds in a clear sky.

How marvelous to be the one slave of one master, particularly if he should be a kind, understanding master, a good master, sensible and thoughtful, who, nonetheless, with his whip, knows how to keep a girl on her knees.

A female slave is never to be allowed to forget that she is a slave. Indeed, she may occasionally be whipped, merely to remind her that she is a slave, only a slave.

"Finish more quickly," said the kitchen master.

"Yes, Master," I said, hastily.

I wondered how long this bondage would last, how long I would serve here, in this house. This may seem an odd thing to wonder about, but, in actuality, it was not.

I see I must explain.

I had been sold in Victoria, from the wharf market, and later, following being ferried across the Vosk and transported in one of four slave wagons south, ankles chained, with five others, to a central bar in the wagon bed, had been again sold, in Torcadino, as a work slave to a mill. From that bondage I had been again sold, to me inexplicably, the first of several sales that saw me vended, usually after only a few weeks, sometimes a few days, out of one city or town, or even village, to another.

I did not understand this.

Had this something to do with me?

Was I somehow different?

If so, how, in what way?

Once, when I was laboring in a field, sickle in hand, with others, harvesting sa-tarna, a great shadow, as of a cloud, raced across the golden grain. I looked up. I heard girls scream, and I saw a sight that I would never forget, what had to be my first tarn, one of the enormous saddlebirds of Gor. Masters with us, peasants, who would bind the sheaves we cut and brought to them, looked up, shading their eyes. "Is it wild?" I asked the girl nearest me. "No," she said, trembling. "It has passed," said another girl. "No," said another. "It is turning!" said another. I saw two of the peasants seize up their bows, large things, at hand even in the field. Many men could not draw such a bow. Arrows were put to the string. The tarn was now no more than fifty feet or so above the grain, approaching rapidly. "Down!" cried a master, "into the grain!" I and the others quickly crouched down, well concealed, for ripened sa-tarna, with its golden, nodding heads, can grow to the chest of a tall man. But then the thing had passed. I had glimpsed the rider, helmeted, seemingly small on his mighty mount. Then the apparition was no more than a dot in the distance, and then it had disappeared. Arrows were removed from the string. We returned to work. Four days later I was sold, in Rarir.

This sort of thing, in my case, had not been unusual.

Oddly, at least to me, I had been not only frequently sold, as I have indicated, but was never sold within the same locale, within the same city, or such, as one would normally expect. I understood nothing of this. If a master tired of me, or needed a stronger girl for heavier labors, for I served commonly as a work slave, why should he not simply hood me and take me to some convenient local market, to be disposed of there? Why did he always solicit a traveling slaver, a passing dealer, the master of a caravan on the brink of departure? The prices I brought, for the most part, were typical, and realistic, and once, thrilling me, most of a silver tarsk, but then, many times, afterward, often to my chagrin or confusion, I would be sold for a pittance, sometimes for little more than being given away. Why must I be so cheaply discarded? Surely masters would not welcome taking a loss on their buy. Indeed, some were merchants, and Goreans, generally, are careful with their coins, often jealously, extremely so. What a worthless, miserable slave, I must be, I sometimes thought. And then I would be purchased for a decent price. Why, I wondered, am I not longer kept, more wanted, for certainly my flanks, as I tried to remain still, standing or lying, had been stroked more than once with interest, in one venue or another. Surely I had noted desire in the eyes of more than one master. But perhaps, I thought, I am not so beautiful, nor so desirable, as I, in my vanity, had conjectured. Yet I did not see myself as that different from others in the same cage, in the same cell, in the same tent, on the same shelf. I had questioned other slaves, but they could make no more of it than I. Sometimes, they had simply turned away from me, uneasily.

Masters vary.

But they are all masters.

In the past few months, since my sale in Victoria, I think the major change that had taken place in me, which muchly transformed me, was the kindling of my slave fires. They had been kindled by masters, as they wished, I given nothing to say about it. Periodically they would rage, and I would become, sometimes to the amusement of masters, cruelly needful, even beggingly so. What can so humble a woman as needing attention so desperately that she must beg for it, and hope that her petitions, often lodged at a master's feet, will be favorably received? How different this seemed from Earth where I, and others, had been sought, and might acquiesce or not, with a kiss or not, as it pleased us, to the importunities of males. But here, on Gor, at least for slaves, whose slave fires raged, the situation was much the reverse.

I had sometimes felt ashamed, crawling to a master on my belly, begging for his touch, until I recalled I was a slave. How helpless we were on Gor! How much here, on Gor, were we at the mercy of men, our masters! How cool and superior to us were the exalted, refined, proud, serene, aloof free women! How they despised us for our needs! But did they not know we were collared? Would they be different, stripped and chained, their slave fires lit, fiercely burning, at a master's feet?

Why should the masters sometimes smile at me, lying before them, on the tiles, my body scarlet, lifted, my eyes piteous?

Why should they find this amusing, when it was they who had made me so? I had had no choice. But this is commonly done with slaves. It improves our price. Men prefer needful slaves.

I had changed much, of course, in many other ways, as well, over the months since Victoria. A girl learns her collar. She becomes more and more a slave. And this, doubtless, in no way I clearly understood, was manifested in my demeanor, my expressions, my movements. Slaves obviously move differently, carry themselves differently, feel differently, speak differently, act differently, from free women. The slave is graceful, deferent, softly spoken, unobtrusive. She is the most female of all women, the most helplessly feminine of all women; she is owned; she is to please. Too, bondage, as is well known, puts a woman at peace with herself. She has come home to her own heart. Too, certainly some of my pricings suggested a discernible increase in my value, however slight or negligible. Yet, despite my understanding of the appropriateness of, and, I confess, my happiness in, my collaring, I remained troubled, and far from content. There is no doubt that the frequency of my sales, which disturbed me, muchly impaired my ease.

It seemed, sometimes, masters wished themselves free of me, and soon. I could not understand this. My body was tanned, and my hair longer. Diet and exercise had shaped me to the interests of men. My Gorean was becoming fluent. I looked well in a tunic. In one sale, I had sold for most of a silver tarsk. I could not help myself, kicking and gasping, on the mat, in the furs. Nor did I wish to help myself. Often I had tied the bondage knot in my hair, and knelt to lick the ankles of a master, or of one of his men.

So my thoughts roved about.

One longs for the master of one's dreams.

If only one could buy such, but it is we who are bought!

The pan, well scoured, I now rinsed with scented water. The senses of Goreans seem much alive, even in small things, and they are likely

to employ color, sound, and scent even where there is no practical purpose to be served in doing so. But, then, what is a practical purpose? Is
the pursuit of beauty, or pleasure, a practical purpose? Perhaps. Perhaps
not. But then, I suppose, there are ends that might be well served even
if there was no practical purpose in doing so. Why not? One supposes
that a scent in a pan of water, the tone of a flute, the color of a simple
thing, like that of a spoon handle or the door of a shed, may serve an
end that is very real, if not practical. One has no objection. Indeed, one
wonders if some things might be demeaned, and less lovely, and less
worthy of regard, had they such a purpose.

I dried the second of the five pans with the towel.

I reached for the third pan.

"Is there a slave in the kitchen whose name is 'Phyllis'?" asked a
voice, from somewhere behind me, at the portal to the kitchen.

I stiffened with apprehension.

I was alarmed.

What had I done?

I had tried to be a good slave. I was docile, and obedient, as most
slaves. It is wise to be so. We do not wish to be punished.

Let free women speculate on how clever and pert, how sprightly,
they might be in the collar, how impudent, even insolent, but they
are not in the collar. Such latitude is permitted by some masters, even
encouraged, but it is a lenience that the slave is not well advised to
abuse. Surely she must understand that it is a permitted lenience,
allowed perhaps because the master finds it interesting or charming,
but that it is a lenience that might be easily replaced, at his will, with
a sterner measure of discipline. The leash may be lengthened, or shortened. It is up to the master. Surely she understands she may at any time
be brought again, quickly enough, to her knees. It is easy to break a
woman to the will of masters. I knew myself, though once of Earth, to
be broken to the will of masters. I did not wish it otherwise.

"Yes," responded the kitchen master.

I feared I had been displeasing, in no way I understood. In the sa-
tarna field, I had once helped myself to a dipper of water from the field
bucket and I had been foot switched, put to my belly, my legs held up
by two slaves, the switch applied to the soles of my bare feet until I
wept with pain and begged for mercy. I had not even understood that
I should have first requested permission to perform so simple an act.
And many masters do not require such a permission. I should have
asked first, of course, for masters differ. If I had been more beautiful,

perhaps I would not have been switched, at all. I had seen other girls help themselves. Perhaps it had to do with my being a barbarian. In any event, any slave knows it is possible to be inadvertently displeasing, and come to rue the indiscretion, no matter how innocent it might have been.

"Phyllis?" asked the voice.

"There," said the kitchen master, doubtless indicating me.

I turned about, and put my head the floor.

Two days ago I had stolen a tospit from the fruit bin, and had been switched for my trouble, a slight, betraying yellow stain having been noted at the corner of my mouth. Surely that was done with. Surely I was not to be punished again, at least not for that. What then had I done? I did not think the kitchen master's favorite, Fina, would have been switched!

I wondered if she gasped and leaped better in his arms than I. I doubted it. There is no accounting for the tastes of masters.

We, kitchen slaves, were all at his disposal. We all responded to him. Certainly I had writhed in his arms, on my chain, pleading, as I succumbed, helpless under his Gorean touch.

But Fina had golden hair, and loved him.

Perhaps that made a difference.

I had now recognized the voice of the fellow who had entered the kitchen. He was Faisal, Lysander's house manager, his bailiff or chamberlain, so to speak.

I had seen him twice before. He rarely came to the kitchen.

"You are Phyllis?" he asked, standing near me.

"Yes, Master," I said, my head down, to the floor.

Though different names had been put on me, from time to time, I was usually named 'Phyllis'.

"You have been chosen to serve, at this evening's supper," he said. "Follow me."

He turned about, and made his way to the portal, without looking back. I rose and looked about. I saw that the kitchen master, and my sister slaves, even Fina, understood no more of this than I.

Certainly I had had no special training, at serving so.

He had disappeared down the hall. I hurried after him.

CHAPTER FOURTEEN

I ladled the grain and vulo soup, seasoned with brown, ground tur-pah, carefully into the bowl.

It would not do to spill it.

Serving slaves, and slaves, in general, were not expected to be clumsy. Clumsiness may be ignored or dismissed in a free woman, but it is not acceptable in a slave. An accident or mistake that will be routinely overlooked in the case of a free woman may, in the case of the slave, bring the whip.

Four served, and there were nine to be served, five men, including my master, Lysander, and four women. I knew none of those served other than my master, and I had scarcely seen him, since having been presented before him, tunicked, after my purchase. He had never so much as touched me.

Being a serving slave in a great house is, by many, viewed as an envied slavery, at least with respect to the lightness of its labors. Surely it is preferable to the fields, the laundries, the mills, bearing water in the mines or quarries, and such. Being a kitchen slave, on the other hand, in a great house is not much different from being a kitchen slave in any large house.

"Enough," said the guest, lifting his finger.

I backed away, head down, as I had been told, and then approached the next guest.

We slaves who served were decorously gowned, though our arms were bare. We wore white, woolen gowns, which descended to our ankles. Our necklines were shallow, and nothing that might distress a free woman. We had washed thoroughly, our bodies and hair, and our hair was bound back, tightly, with fillets of white wool. Our feet were bare.

There was, of course, an obvious difference between us and the free women, other than our serving. We were collared. Too, of course, if one were to investigate, it would be discovered that our left thighs were marked, high, below the hip. We all wore the Kef, the most common slave brand.

The first girl amongst us was Selena, who had been captured on Teletus by raiders from Hunjer, and, with others, sold in Brundisium, where prices seem to run high. Teletus was somewhere to the west, and Hunjer was north, north even, I gathered, of the Vosk. Brundisium, apparently a port, was north, but, as I understood, it was south of the Vosk. I would later learn that both Teletus and Hunjer were islands.

Free Goreans commonly eat at low tables, the men sitting cross-legged, and the women kneeling, their knees closely together within their robes. On the other hand, in certain high houses, and surely in the house of Lysander, often, particularly given the presence of guests, dining couches were employed. It was so this night. On these couches, usually arranged in a square or rectangle, sometimes in a circle or oval, the guests recline and help themselves from the low, narrow tables, these set before the couches. The height of these tables, a bit higher than the common Gorean table, is matched to the surface of the couches, for ease of access. The serving, given the spacing between the couches, may be done from either outside or inside the parallel concentricity, so to speak, of couches and tables. Guests occupying the central position on the couches are, as would be expected, served from the inside, namely, from within the arrangement. In this arrangement the men and women may recline beside one another which, doubtless, in the way of a nice fillip, adds to the informality, stimulation, and delight of the occasion. What male appetite is unlikely to be stirred by the presence of a lovely woman reclining at his side?

As I mentioned, there were nine to be served, five men, including my master, Lysander, and four women. All wore chaplets of flowers, both men and women, which is not uncommon, I learned, in many Gorean cities and towns on festive occasions, holidays, celebrations, companionings, parties, and such. As nearly as I could determine none of the four women were companioned, in a strict sense, to any of the men present, but seemed to have been engaged as professional companions, for the pleasantries of their company and conversation. Such women are not slaves, though they are sometimes, in effect, mistresses. In any event, I knew Lysander was not companioned in the sense of the free companionship, and this seemed to be the case with three of the others, as well, as their charming partners gave no indication of being free companions, either of their partners or of any other, who might not be present. The women, though lavishly and abundantly robed, were not veiled, as presumably they would be on the streets, and of them, though all fair, two, I thought, though free, might be beautiful enough to be slaves, perhaps even "high slaves." The most beautiful seemed to be the dinner companion of Lysander himself. The three other women were paired off with three of the other men. One of the males, a pleasant, handsome fellow, with ringed fingers, in a golden robe, which betokened no caste to my knowledge, was not paired with any of the free women. He was, it seems, an independent, though a congenial, contributor to the evening, chatting, in particular with one or another of the free women who were ensconced beside him. The erudition, and the sparkle, of the conversation of the women tended to confirm my suspicion that they were professional companions. Needless to say, the presence of such women, witty and skilled, much enlivens a dinner. What it costs to hire one for a dinner, I supposed, might frequently suffice to buy a low slave, such as I. Alert to nuances, expressions, and such, I suspected that Lysander's partner might not be averse to a proposal of free companionship. To be sure, such women are seldom taken into the free companionship. It might be added that in many Gorean cities and towns, professional companions are outlawed, their presence being construed as violating sumptuary laws. Indeed, such laws existed in Market of Semris, but it seems they failed to be noted by Lysander, and, I suppose, by other individuals of influence or importance. Laws, it seemed, when inconvenient, might be ignored by the powerful. Laws, as is well known, are not for the mighty. As some concession to propriety, however, that one might not think ill of Lysander and others, it might be noted that women such as those now at the table were, of late, not identified as professional companions but rather as "friends." And what laws would deny to a host a right to entertain his friends in his own home?

As I mentioned, one of the males, the handsome fellow with ringed fingers, he in the golden robe, which betokened no caste to my knowledge, was not paired with one of the free women. In this sense he was alone, though he participated readily and charmingly to Lysander's small event. Perhaps he had been invited late or had appeared unexpectedly and had had no time to either hire, or have hired for him, a companion.

"What of the paga?" I whispered to Selena.

"Wine now," she said, "paga later."

Selena had, in the time at her disposal, coached me in certain niceties of serving, that there was an order to utensils and courses, that one should serve from the left, that there was a way to pour, that free women were to be served first, that one should keep one's head down, and eyes lowered, that one must be quiet, graceful, deferent and unobtrusive, that when one was not serving one was to kneel to the side, head down, that one might be conveniently summoned, and so on. "Watch me, and the others," she said. "I will do so," I said. I was surely muchly uneasy, and was more than eager to attend to, and imitate, genuine serving slaves. "You are not beautiful enough to be a serving slave," she said. "Forgive me, Mistress," I had said. Actually I regarded myself as every bit as attractive as any of them, including herself, even more so, to be perfectly honest. To be sure, such things are best left to men. "You are not trained as a serving slave," she said. "No, Mistress," I said. That was surely true. "Why then," she asked, "have you been sent to the tables?" "I do not know, Mistress," I said. "I do not like it," she said. "If you are clumsy, or spill something, we may all be punished." I lowered my head, and remained silent.

The courses of the meal proceeded apace.

There were only the two soups, four vegetables, and two meats, roast Vosk gull and seasoned, boiled verr, followed by fruit and nuts.

The supper was pleasant and genteel, suitable for a quiet evening with friends. Nothing was boisterous or rowdy. The ka-la-nas were sparkling and mild, not the sort of coarse ka-la-nas commonly diluted in the wine crater, to a proportion agreed upon by guests, which only wild young men would be likely to drink unmixed, hailing one another with frightful jokes and bawdy songs, awaiting the arrival of the dancers and musicians, the drummers, the flute and kalika girls.

We served the ka-la-nas standing, not as I had been instructed in the house of training.

Toward the nineteenth Ahn, an Ahn before midnight, the free women withdrew to their waiting palanquins. The dinner companion of Lysander was reluctant to depart so soon, but was, eventually, gently, conducted to her palanquin by Faisal, Lysander's house manager, he who had fetched me this afternoon, for some reason, from the kitchen. Before she disappeared through the portal of the dining chamber, the second of three such chambers, of varying sizes, one of which was smaller, and the other of which was quite large, and might house two hundred guests, at least, she cast us a dark look. I did not understand this. I was pleased she carried no switch. One fears free women.

"You are a barbarian, are you not?" asked Selena.

"Yes, Mistress," I said.

"And stupid," she said.

"I do not think so, Mistress," I said.

"It is time for paga," she said.

"Mistress?" I said.

"Get your gown off," she snapped.

"But then I will be naked," I protested.

"It is paga time," she said, slipping from her own gown.

"Yes, Mistress," I said.

I gathered that men enjoyed being served by naked slaves. I supposed the men of Earth might merely dream of such things, but, I would learn, if free women were not present, it was commonplace on Gor. What man does not wish to be served by a naked slave? Men, fully clothed, found it pleasant to be served by naked women. Along these lines, when a city falls, the women of the enemy, before their embonding, stripped, often serve at the victory feast of the conquerors, even to the extent of being put rudely to the pleasure of the victors late in the feast. Indeed, whereas a slave would think nothing of this, and expect it, and look forward to its pleasures, it does represent an extraordinary humiliation and disgrace for a Gorean free woman. Afterwards they often beg for the collar for after such usage, irremediably reduced, what are they good for, but to be slaves?

I looked to the side.

On the table, waiting, near the side of the room, were five paga goblets. Also in evidence was the metal paga vessel, with two handles, from which the goblets might be filled. Paga, unlike ka-la-na, is usually not poured at a table. In paga taverns it is dipped from a vat, the goblet itself sometimes used as the dipper, and brought to the table by a paga girl. The girl, if one wishes, commonly comes with the price of the drink. Sometimes a patron will receive paga from three or four girls, before selecting one, if he is so inclined, for thonging and ordering to an alcove, where she, thonged, will await his pleasure. Sometimes, if the patron wishes, one of the proprietor's men will take the girl to the alcove and chain her in place.

"The men will now discuss serious matters," said our first girl, Selena, "the affairs of the day, trade, crops, jurisprudence, markets, ambitions, intrigues, politics, subjects empty-headed free women would find boring. What do they care for but robes, veils, entertainments, perfumes, and gossip?"

"But they would speak so openly before us?" I said.

"Surely," she said. "We are slaves. Might they not speak as frankly before verr and kaiila?"

"My dear Phyllis," said Lysander, Administrator of Market of Semris.

I froze in terror, and went immediately to my knees, my head to the floor. I had been addressed by the high master himself.

"'Yes, Master'," prompted Selena to me, in a whisper.

"Yes, Master," I responded.

"Stand up, my dear," said Lysander, kindly, "there, between the tables, in the center."

"Yes, Master," I said.

"I think this is the one," he said to the fellow in the golden robe, with the many rings on his fingers.

"Quite possibly," said he in the golden robe.

"She is only a work slave," said Lysander.

"I gather that," said the fellow with rings, regarding me.

"But she is rather pretty for a work slave," said Lysander.

I was at that moment very conscious of the collar on my neck, and what it meant.

"I have seen some pleasure slaves," said he in the golden robe, "who were not as attractive."

"Surely you jest," said Lysander.

"Not at all," said he in the golden robe. "Consider her throat, the softness of her shoulders, her forearms, her ankles."

"Her ankles are too slim," said Lysander.

"Many men like them so," said he in the golden robe.

"And you?" said Lysander, smiling.

"I do not object," he said.

"Phyllis," said Lysander, "serve Tullius Quintus, our guest, our associate and dear friend, welcome in our midst, though we share no Home Stone."

Trembling, fearing I might fall, I made my way to the small paga table. My hands shook.

"I will pour," said Selena, apprehensively.

She then poured golden paga from the metal vessel into one of the goblets. I lifted that goblet, holding it in both hands, as one does. I turned about. Selena was filling the other goblets, which would be borne to the tables.

I noted, gratefully, she had not filled my goblet to the brim. I was then less likely to lose any of the golden fluid. It would not do, I perhaps faltering, to have any slip over the rim.

I must be extremely careful.

I would be extremely careful.

I had the sense that I was being watched.

In a moment, from within the rectangle of low, narrow tables, set before the couches, I knelt before Tullius Quintus, he reclining, eyeing me, the table between us.

"Are you frightened?" he asked.

"Yes, Master," I said.

"Do not be frightened," he said.

"No, Master," I said. "Thank you, Master."

"Serve me," he said.

I, head down, pressed the metal goblet into my lower abdomen, feeling it there. I then, not meeting his eyes, touched it to my left breast, and then to my right breast. I then lifted my head and looked at him, over the rim of the goblet. Then, my eyes on him, I kissed the goblet, submissively, as a slave, hoping to please, and then I lowered my head, between my extended arms, and held the goblet to him.

He took the goblet, sipped the beverage, and placed the goblet on the small table. I knelt before him, my head down.

I was relieved.

I had spilled nothing, not a drop.

To be sure, one is careful, and it is very rarely that anything is spilled, or dropped, or broken.

As I have indicated, it does not do for a slave to be clumsy.

I did not think I would be so afraid in the future.

"Look at me," he said.

I did so. He was handsome, and I a slave.

He lifted his hand, his eyes on me.

"Master?" I said.

I watched his hand, uneasily.

Suddenly it swept to his left, and the goblet slid, and fell, and rolled, and clattered, and paga ran on the table, and fell to the floor.

I watched this with horror and dismay.

Selena cried out in misery.

"See what you have done," he said.

"Master!" I said in protest.

"She is not a serving slave!" said Selena. "She is not one of us! She is not trained! She is not skilled! Please, Masters, do not beat the rest of us, for her fault!"

"Be quiet," said Lysander.

"Did you have something to say?" asked Tullius Quintus of me. "Did you wish to object?"

"No, Master," I said.

"You were clumsy, were you not?" he said.

"I did not touch the goblet!" I said.

"Are you accusing a free person of lying?" he asked.

"No, Master!" I said.

"You were clumsy, were you not?" he asked.

"Yes, Master," I said. "Forgive me, Master."

"Surely you know the penalty for lying," he said.

"Master?" I said.

"You saw me strike aside the goblet, did you not?" he said.

"Please be kind to me," I said. "Tell me what to do, or be. I am trying to be pleasing."

"Do you think me cruel?"

"No, Master!" I said.

"You are mistaken," he said.

"Master?" I said.

"Lean more closely," he said.

I did so.

He then struck me across the face, sharply, on the left cheek. It stung. Tears sprang from my eyes.

"Lean more closely again," he said.

I did so, fearing to be again struck.

"You may now lick and kiss the hand that struck you," he said.

I did so, for several moments. I was afraid. I had seldom been so mastered, so dominated. How aware I was then that I was a slave. And I knew, too, I would yield to such a man as the slave I was. I was not a free woman. I wanted him to touch me. I wanted him to take me in his arms and put me to his pleasure, forcefully, as the frightened, eager, meaningless beast I was.

"Kneel back," he said. "Keep your head up."

I knelt back on my heels, my head lifted. My back was straight. The palms of my hands were down, on my thighs. My knees were closely together.

I dared not meet his eyes.

"Look at me," he said.

"Yes, Master," I said.

"You are Phyllis," he said.

"Yes, Master," I said.

"When you were free," he said, "your name was Phyllis Rodgers."

I was startled.

"Yes, Master," I whispered. How would he know that? He must

have, or have had, access to the records of the masters by whom I was first acquired. What could this mean?

"But now," he said, "you are a slave."

"Yes, Master," I said.

"And simply Phyllis," he said.

"If Master pleases," I said. "I have been named variously, but often 'Phyllis'. The name is now, of course, a slave name, put on me by the will of masters."

"You were acquainted," he said, "with an extraordinarily intelligent and beautiful young woman on Earth, your former world, whose name was Paula Prentiss?"

"Yes, Master," I said.

"She is now in a collar," he said.

"Yes, Master," I said.

We both, now, had our collars.

"You are far inferior to her," he said.

"Yes, Master," I said. I felt tears in my eyes.

"This work slave, Phyllis, one of my kitchen slaves, is the one?" asked Lysander.

"Clearly," said Tullius Quintus.

"She is sought?" said Lysander.

"Yes," said Tullius Quintus.

"You know who seeks her?" said Lysander.

"Of course," said Tullius Quintus.

"He of whom you spoke?" asked Lysander.

"Yes," said Tullius Quintus.

"Then," said Lysander, "I do not think it wise to keep her in my house."

"I fear it could be dangerous," said Tullius Quintus.

"They do not buy with copper; they do not buy with silver; they do not buy with gold; they buy with steel," said Lysander.

"I have heard so," said Tullius Quintus.

"And you do not fear to acquire her?" asked Lysander.

"No," said Tullius Quintus. "Her trail will vanish here. Who knows whence the wind blows? The leaf is lifted, flutters, and is gone. Footprints are not left on clouds. No sleen can follow the tarn road."

"I would be afraid," said Lysander.

"I have calculated matters with care," he said. "I have planned well. She will be nowhere, until I wish it."

"She is yours," said Lysander. "She has never been in my house."

CHAPTER FIFTEEN

————————

It was something like the second Ahn, well before dawn.

After the dinner at which I had served, I was not returned to the kitchen, to my housing chain in the pantry, with the other kitchen slaves. Rather I was conducted to the large, velvet-draped, barred-windowed guest chamber allotted to Tullius Quintus, in the southern wing of the house of Lysander, Administrator of Market of Semris. I was put to the foot of the couch, and chained there, by the neck, to a slave ring. I must wait, to discover what would be done with me. It is only favored slaves who are permitted on the surface of a couch, and, even then, they will commonly be fastened to a slave ring, usually by the left ankle, the "chaining ankle." There are few things that better convince a woman of her bondage than being chained. I lay there, waiting, for an Ahn, or better, on the furs, my hands on the chain, close to my neck, run from the collar ring to the slave ring.

The portal opened, and Tullius Quintus, bearing a shallow tharlarion-oil lamp, entered, followed by two of Lysander's men.

I went to the first obeisance position, kneeling, my head down to the furs, my hands, palms down, at the sides of my head.

"Position," said Tullius Quintus.

As I was not a pleasure slave, I knelt with my knees closely together. I kept my head down, humbly.

"Head up," he said.

I lifted my head, but did not dare to meet his eyes.

The chain dangled between my breasts. I felt its weight on my collar ring and its links on my body.

"Bara," said Tullius Quintus.

I went to bara.

I was then bound, hand and foot, my wrists crossed and bound behind me, and my ankles crossed and bound, as well.

This may be conveniently done, as earlier noted, when one is in bara.

I was then relieved of the neck chain. And then one of Lysander's men, in the light of the lamp, above the collar I wore, snapped a new collar about my neck. My former collar, then, that of Lysander of Market of Semris, was removed. There was no moment then when I had not been collared. Both collars were common collars, light, close-fitting, locked in the back. Nothing about either collar would be likely to be noticed, save that their occupant wore them.

"I am Tullius Quintus," said Tullius Quintus. "I am your master."

"Yes, Master," I said.

"Whose slave are you?" he asked.

"I am the slave of Tullius Quintus," I said.

"Of Ar," he said.

"Of Ar," I said. I knew nothing of Ar, save that it was a large city. I did not even know its direction from Market of Semris. I knew very little of Gorean geography. I had no clear idea of the world, or, really, in a sense, where I was, save for some names and vague notions, and few, it seemed, cared to enlighten me.

"Under whose rod of discipline are you?" he asked.

"I am under the rod of discipline of Tullius Quintus, of Ar, my master," I said.

I was aware of some large leather object being unfolded, and shaken out, to the side.

"May I speak?" I asked.

"Yes," said Tullius Quintus.

"Who am I?" I asked.

"The name 'Lita' will do, for the time," he said.

"That is a very common slave name," I said. I had known at least eleven girls in my various slaveries, in the last months, who had borne that name. It is pronounced "Leeta."

"Yes," he said.

"And it is a Gorean name," I said, "not a barbarian name."

"True," he said.

"Then my name will not mark me as a barbarian," I said.

"No," he said.

"I cannot read," I said. "May I know what is on my collar?"

"Of course," he said. "It says, 'I am the slave of Tullius Quintus, of Ar'."

"Then my name will not appear on my collar," I said, "not even the name 'Lita'?"

"No," he said.

"Master," I said.

"You have spoken enough," he said.

"Master?" I said.

A heavy wadding was thrust into my mouth, and fastened in place by four broad leather loops wound tightly about my face, and then tied behind the back of my neck.

I knew I could utter only the tiniest of sounds, or whimpers, and dared not even do so.

"Turn her on her back," said Tullius Quintus.

I then lay at the feet of masters, naked, bound hand and foot, gagged.

"She is pretty," said one of Lysander's men.

"She is only a work slave," said Tullius Quintus.

"Still, pretty," said the man.

"All women look well, so," said Tullius Quintus, "bound, helpless, at one's feet."

"True," said the man.

I was angry. At the supper, had not Tullius Quintus averred that he had seen pleasure slaves who were not so attractive as I? Had he now changed his mind? Too, I had been a slave for months, and had worn, in this time, several collars, and it is well known that in bondage a woman grows more beautiful. As a slave, given attention to cleanliness, appearance, deportment, and such, she has little choice other than to do so. More importantly, one supposes, a number of biological and psychological elements contribute to this matter, having to do with nature, sexual dimorphism, the resolution of ambivalences, fulfillment, self-discovery, and such.

"See her squirm," said one of Lysander's men, amused.

"You cannot free yourself, kajira," said the other.

I knew that was true. I was helpless. My struggles subsided. I had been thonged by a Gorean male.

"Slip her into the slave sack," said Tullius Quintus. "I am eager to be away."

I shook my head negatively, tears in my eyes, mutely pleading. Such a device was unpleasant. Too, such a device was seldom used for slaves, despite its name, for slaves were commonly coffled, chained in wagons, chained to a stirrup, or such. It might be useful, of course, in disciplining slaves, or stealing slaves. But I was not being disciplined, nor was I being stolen. Such a device could be useful, of course, in removing a captured free woman, perhaps one so unwise as to having intruded into a paga tavern, from her own city or town. Perhaps then she might find herself a paga girl elsewhere, given which denouement her presumed curiosity might be well satisfied.

"The information on which I acted," said Tullius Quintus, "may have been available to others, as well. If not, even so, my venture may have been suspected. I may have been followed to this house."

"The grounds, and nearby streets, are deserted," said one of Lysander's men.

"The enemy is not always seen," said Tullius Quintus.

One of the two men shrugged. Is the unseen enemy not the most dangerous?

"What of watchmen?" asked Tullius Quintus.

"There may be a watchman, or so," said one of the men.

I whimpered a little, plaintively, as I was thrust, head first, into the sack. The sack is narrow. One could not turn about within its confines. It was of a size made for women, a common slave sack. It was laced shut, some inches behind my feet.

"Carry her downstairs, to the tunnel portal, and thence to the wagon," said Tullius Quintus. "Then ensconce her, and tie shut the canvas."

Large Gorean houses are often constructed with more in mind than comfort and convenience, luxury or impressiveness; they are often sturdy and defensible, as well. Too, it is not unusual for them to have secret chambers and passages, at least one of which is likely to lead, by means of a tunnel, to another house, or structure, perhaps a quarter of a pasang distant. The burrow of the sleen, for example, has two, sometimes three, openings. In this way an animal might escape a larger, more formidable animal entering its burrow, or, more frequently, utilize the additional opening to withdraw from its lair unnoticed, which may be of advantage in deceiving watchful prey, in surprising an enemy, and so on.

I had not known, until then, that there was a tunnel portal. I did know that a large Gorean house usually had a number of possible entrances and exits, not always obvious.

Somewhere a wagon was to be waiting.

I did not know if the wagon was to be drawn by bosk, tharlarion, or kaiila. The wagons of Raymond of Ti, which had transported me, and others, from the Vosk to Torcadino had been drawn by bosk. They were the first bosk I had seen, broad horned and shaggy. I knew that tharlarion, at least of certain varieties, also served as draft beasts, but I had never, as yet, seen one. I did know something about them, and their varieties, from one or another of the dealer's men in Victoria. I had also heard from them of kaiila. The latter beast, I had gathered, in its varieties, was less likely to be utilized as a draft beast than as a mount. It is apparently less common in the northern hemisphere than in the southern hemisphere. One of the dealer's men, interestingly, had never seen one. Another form of draft beast is the draft slave, male or female. Several males may draw a rubble wagon or a wagon of cut stones in the quarries, or an ore wagon in a mining district, such things. Lighter labors might be assigned to females used as draft slaves. They are often used, for example, to draw the cart of a peddler. Some free women enjoy using harnessed female slaves to draw their carriages, or, chained to their poles, to carry their palanquins.

Little love is lost between free women and kajirae.

I was lifted in the arms of someone, presumably one of Lysander's men, and carried from the room and down the stairs, and, after a time, down another flight of stairs. Later, from the sound of it, a trap was lifted. I felt myself handed downward from one fellow to another. I heard the trap, as I supposed it to be, dropped behind me. At the foot of some more stairs, I was carried on a level for some time, at least for seven or eight minutes. I heard the sandals of the men occasionally scuff pebbles, and, twice, splash a little, as if wading through some shallow expanse of water. Even within the sack I had a sense of coolness, and that the air might be damp and clammy.

"Let us hurry," said Tullius Quintus.

"You will be off well before dawn," said the fellow not carrying me. "Too, the streets for a pasang about are deserted, save perhaps for a watchman."

"The wagon has been concealed," said Tullius Quintus.

"It is in the stable's wagon yard," said the man. "It was brought there yesterday. The walls are high."

"Is it far yet?" asked Tullius Quintus.

"No," said one of the men.

"The tharlarion?" inquired Tullius Quintus.

"From the stable, itself," said the man.

"All is well," said the fellow carrying me.

"Hurry," said Tullius Quintus.

Shortly thereafter the men stopped, and there were more stairs, these ascending, and then, again, I was on a level, and sandals were treading planks and crushing straw. I smelled what must be dung.

Then a door was swung open and it became cooler, chilling the moisture and sweat in the sack, and I was sure they had emerged into the night air. I heard a grunting noise, as of large animals, and, from the conversation in the tunnel, I knew these heavy, bestial sounds must have been emitted from tharlarion. I heard no new voices, either masculine or feminine, so I supposed the grooms must have retired for the night, and the stable slaves, if there were such, would be on their chains until dawn. The slavery of the stable slave is not one hoped for by girls in the presale exposition cages or waiting at the foot of a block, for their turn to be shown to men. Stable slaves often have their heads shaved, for purposes of cleanliness. They are, of course, at the disposal of the grooms.

I heard the unlatching of a wagon gate and then I was lifted and thrust, head first, onto the floor of the wagon bed, near the gate, and the gate was closed. The wagon moved a fraction, as its draw beasts stirred.

"Has a curfew been imposed?" asked Tullius Quintus.

"No," said one of Lysander's men. "It was thought that would arouse suspicion."

"The streets have been cleared, save for an occasional watchman," said the other.

"There may be other wagons about then?" said Tullius Quintus.

"At night," said one of Lysander's men. "By law, heavy drayage is confined to the hours of darkness."

"Surely you are familiar with that, as you are of Ar," said the other fellow.

"Of course," said Tullius Quintus, I thought uneasily.

I had the sense, then, he had climbed to the wagon bench.

"Should another wagon pass this way, we will detain it, on some pretext or another, for a time," said one of Lysander's men.

"My thanks," said Tullius Quintus.

I heard the creaking of what must have been two leaves of a gate, a large gate.

"On!" called Tullius Quintus.

I heard the grunting, and hissing, of one large beast, and then that of another, and the sound of a blow, striking on a massive body, and the wagon lurched forward, and I was shaken on the boards of the wagon bed.

"On, on!" called Tullius Quintus.

I heard another such blow.

A whip is used with bosk or kaiila, but it serves little purpose with tharlarion, given the thickness of their hide, and their comparative lack of responsiveness. In their case a long, supple drive wand, or baton, is normally used, which device may be used either to strike or prod the beast.

The wagon turned, almost immediately, and we were doubtless in the street. I heard metal-rimmed wheels rolling over stones. I knew the sound. The wagons of Raymond of Ti had had wheels rimmed with iron.

We had scarcely made our turn when we, perhaps no more than twenty yards from the gate, from behind us, heard Lysander's men, perhaps rushed out into the street, crying out, "Hold! Hold up your beasts! Hold! Inspection, inspection, in the name of the Administrator!"

Their futile, frustrated cursing then fell behind us.

Tullius Quintus began, desperately, to urge his beasts on, with cries and blows.

The wagon rattled onward.

It took me only moments to realize that something was surely amiss, from the frenzy of Tullius Quintus. Something unexpected, but perhaps feared, must have occurred.

We were being followed!

Our wagon went faster and faster. The domestic tharlarion, both quadrupedalian and bipedalian, differ considerably from most wild tharlarion, most commonly in tractability, stamina, and speed. They are bred, over generations, for such attributes. Even so, the ancient brain lurks within those broad skulls, and ancient instincts, bred for the rivers, swamps, and flood plains, sometimes reassert themselves, and the beasts, as though then strangers to harnesses, reins, and drive wands, become uncontrollable, and, in some cases, dangerous. Most domestic tharlarion are draft beasts, but they also have their applications in sport and war. There are, for example, racing and hunting tharlarion, and tharlarion bred for battle, some of which, ponderous, and armored, can shatter lines and topple siege towers.

We made a sudden turn, and the wagon, veering, was on two wheels, and I was rolled to the side, and then, the vehicle righting itself, we plunged on.

I guessed the metal-rimmed wheels struck sparks in the night, coursing over the cobbles of Market of Semris.

I fought my bonds. I could utter only tiny sounds.

The wagon veered again, and I was rolled to the other side.

"On!" cried Tullius Quintus.

We continued, apace, for several minutes.

"On, on!" cried Tullius Quintus.

I now heard a protestive bellowing from our beasts. I feared that Tullius Quintus, whom I supposed was not a drayman, might drive them to their death. Surely the pounding thunder that had previously marked our pace had become less assured, more erratic. "On!" cried Tullius Quintus. "On!" There were more strikings from the drive wand, now delivered savagely, again and again.

Suddenly, the massive brake was applied, and the wagon, wheels squealing against the pressure, stopped.

"The ferry!" cried a voice. "Are you mad? Come about! Onto the ferry!"

I knew that a waterway, a barge canal, separated east Market of Semris from west Market of Semris, and gathered we had reached that point.

Almost at the same time, I heard a cry from behind. "Hold that wagon! Hold that wagon!"

Instantly Tullius Quintus released the brake and struck the beasts forward, and the wagon, tipping downward, rattled down a slope and struck into the water. The draft tharlarion are quadrupedalian and, as all such animals, willing or not, borne up by their configuration, have no difficulty in negotiating a liquid terrain. As they would walk on land, so they swim in water. Water surged into the wagon bed. Cold water rushed into the sack within which I was confined. I thrashed. Gagged, I could not scream. The gag was tight and sopped. Then the wagon, drawn, swaying and bobbing, was lifted by the water, and sheets of water drained from the wagon bed, and I lay then in no more than two or three inches of water, which quantity would remain in place, the wagon, as any wooden object, displacing water, having found its equilibrium in the medium.

"On, on!" called Tullius Quintus to his beasts.

I heard no evidence of a pursuit, and conjectured that it had been abandoned, or that the pursuing vehicle, rather than risking the water, and the possible confusion or rebellion of its team, would utilize the ferry. If so, Tullius Quintus would have gained an advance of some minutes on he, or those, who followed us. Perhaps this delay, I conjectured, would be acceptable to a pursuer, as the track of a wagon would be difficult to conceal. Tullius Quintus had tharlarion furnished by the stable of Lysander, presumably average beasts. A pursuer, realizing a pursuit would take place, would presumably supply himself with strong, agile beasts, beasts of superior quality, a lighter wagon, and such. I suspected the pursuer was astute, determined, and patient. If an encounter was inevitable, the expenditure of some minutes, spent to eliminate a variety of risks, would be understood as an excellent bargain. If an encounter is assured, it makes little difference whether it takes place now or nearly now.

After some four or five minutes I heard the bluntly clawed feet of the tharlarion scrambling on a bank, tumbling pebbles about, and the wagon, tilted upward, sharply, was dragged from the water. I slid to the back of the wagon bed.

In a moment the wagon was level again.

But Tullius Quintus had halted the vehicle.

The gate of the wagon bed was unlatched, and I was dragged, apparently by the laces on the sack, near my feet, from the wagon bed, and placed on the ground. The laces were then, hurriedly, cut, not untied, and I was drawn from the sack. I lay on the bank of the waterway then, on wet grass, while it was still dark. Tullius Quintus was cutting at the sack, now removed from my body. He cut off the top quarter, or so, of it. He then, by the hair, jerked me to a sitting position, and drew that part of the bag over my head. It fitted, hoodlike, and extended down over my arms, almost to my elbows. I whimpered, but he paid me no attention, not even commanding me to silence. He then seized up the drive wand and smote the tharlarion several times, running beside them, driving them to the right. He then returned, and bent to my ankles, and, with the knife, severed the thongs that had bound them. He then jerked me to my feet, I unable to see, in the improvised hood, by the left arm.

My hands were still tied behind me.

"He will follow the wagon," he said to me.

I had no idea, of course, of whom he might be speaking. But I suspected he, my master, knew.

"He will soon discover the wagon is empty," he said. "But we will have time."

He then began to move rapidly away from the bank, to our left, and then forward. He rushed me beside him, his right hand hard on my left arm, I stumbling, and I would have fallen several times, were it not for his grip.

I was miserable with cold, in the predawn air. My legs began to ache. The coarse grass, knife grass, cut at my ankles.

I whimpered, again, for mercy, that I might be pitied.

I was not a peasant woman, not a large, coarse woman, not a brothel mistress, not a female fighting slave.

For whatever reasons men had seen fit to put me in a collar, it was clearly not for such purposes.

"It is not far now," he said. Shortly thereafter, he began to tread more slowly, more carefully, as though he might be treading amongst stakes. He held me closer to him, tightly, by the arm. Then I felt boards beneath my feet. I was not aware of having entered a dwelling, passing through a portal, or such. I might be on some sort of platform.

"No footprints," said he, "appear on clouds. Not even a sleen can traverse the tarn road."

I understood nothing.

But then I heard a scratching on wood, as though heavy, restless knives were drawn through it.

I sensed something large, and alive, was on the platform with us.

I was conducted to the side.

Something was done before me.

I made a tiny noise, as I was lifted, and then, lowered, placed, sitting, on some heavy wickerwork surface.

My ankles were then, again, crossed, and bound.

A heavy leather belt was fastened about my waist.

The remains of the sack, which had enveloped my head and shoulders, hoodlike, were pulled away and cast aside, through what appeared to be an open, wickerwork gate to my right.

I blinked, and shook my head, my hair loose about me.

I found myself sitting, bound hand and foot, the heavy strap about my waist, holding me in place, in some sort of sturdy basket, its opened wickerwork gate to my right.

I could see little from within the basket other than through the opened gate, the boards outside, but there were numerous, tiny openings between the woven fibers.

I could see the gray sky above me.

Tullius Quintus then inserted his knife, carefully, between the side of my neck and the gag straps, and cut away the gag. I expelled the sodden wadding into his open, waiting hand, which device he then cast aside, as he had the improvised hood, and I looked up at him, confused, and frightened.

"Master!" I exclaimed.

I was cuffed, sharply, the blow jerking my head to the right.

"Forgive me, Master," I said. "May I speak?"

"No," he said, and lashed my face to the left with a second cuff, a sharp, stinging, backhand slap.

"Forgive me, Master," I said, tears in my eyes.

Tullius Quintus then withdrew from the basket.

He, now outside, closed its door, or gate, and tied it shut. Save for looking upward, to the sky, fastened as I was, I could see very little. Ropes were at the corners of this holding device. I did not understand what their role might be. In one corner of my tiny wickerwork prison, the security of which, save for my bonds, seemed dubious, was a ragged blanket. I could not reach it.

As we had stopped, and I had been incarcerated in this small, unlikely wickerwork cell, I gathered that we had eluded our pursuer, or pursuers.

Tullius Quintus, outside, seemed to be looking about. Then he turned, and regarded me, I sitting, below him, bound and tethered. "I am victorious," he said. "All is as planned."

"I beg to speak," I said.

"You are refused permission to speak," he said.

My cheeks still stung, from his earlier ministrations.

Why was I now his? I did not think I had been purchased. Lysander, the Administrator of Market of Semris, had apparently surrendered me to him, and readily. "She has never been in my house," he had said. Surely this sort of transaction, if it were a transaction, was unusual. What slave could anticipate it? It made no sense. What was to be done with me? When a girl is purchased off a shelf, or a block, she will normally have a very clear idea of why she has been purchased, and what will be done with her. Can she not see it in the eager eyes of the brute who has spent his coins on her, and expects to obtain a thousand times his money's worth? But why had I been obtained? Could I truly believe that Tullius Quintus was smitten with my charms, those of a work slave, those of a cheap kitchen slave? And my name had been of importance for some reason, and then it had been quickly changed. I was now "Lita." There were doubtless hundreds, if not thousands, of girls on Gor named 'Lita'. I had encountered several in the past few months. And why was I surreptitiously removed from Market of Semris? I was not a free woman, selected for a collar in some distant town or city, whose abduction might involve considerable risk. And who was it from whom Tullius Quintus fled? How desperate he had been to escape! Whom did he so fear? Who had been our pursuer? Where was that pursuer now? Surely, by now, he was more than aware of my master's ruse, and the falsity of the track on which he had been set. And what was the meaning of my present situation? What temporary prison was this sturdy device in which I found myself? Why the slack corner ropes? What were they for? Were they to tether me further? They were much too large, too coarse and bulky, for that. What was the point of the black strap on my belly? Did my master really think I might easily, bound as I was, hand and foot, climb out, and flee away, from this open-ceilinged cell, this temporary slave-holding device? Its walls were not even metal. It was of mere wicker, even if of sturdy wicker. Too, it was light. Should a holding device not be formed of sterner, weightier stuff?

I then, again, heard the scratching, or drawing, on wood, as though it were being raked by heavy knives.

How clear much of this would have been to me had I been natively Gorean, or even longer on this strange, green, beautiful, fresh, unspoiled, perilous orb!

I looked about, listening intently, straining to see, but I could see nothing but now-manifest threads of morning light glittering amongst the fibers of the wicker walls.

I did not know the whereabouts of my master.

Suddenly, I heard, for the first time, a mighty sound, deafening, but feet away, shrill and sustained, annunciatory, the long, shrieking, readiness cry of an awesome, dangerous, incredible form of life. Doubtless the sound might be familiar to some but it was not to me. It might have rung out in the mountains of Thentis, reflected from peak to peak, causing all who heard it to pause, and tremble, and raise their eyes apprehensively to the sky. My blood froze. For a moment I could neither move nor breathe. Had I seen its source, given its proximity, and understood its meaning, I know not what my response might have been. Can one die of such things? How frightening, and amazing, it would seem to me, later, to understand that men, some rare, few men, dare to share the sky with such things.

But a moment after this startling sound, I heard a human voice, from some yards away. "Hold!" it cried. "Hold! Gold or steel! Hold!"

"Gold!" cried Tullius Quintus, "as and when it pleases me!"

"Sleen!" cried the other voice.

There was suddenly a great crack, as of the smiting of wind, like the crack of sails, like the snapping of a mighty banner, or whip, and the very basket in which I was held shook, and then, suddenly, the ropes were taut, and the basket, as I screamed in fear, thrown back, helpless in my bonds and strap, slid rapidly across the wooden platform, and, a moment later, it seemed to leap from the planks and it swung free, how far above the land I did not know.

Then I screamed, again, for suddenly, with a ripping of fiber, an object, short, narrow, cylindrical, pointed, metal-finned, had burst up through the floor of the basket in which I lay.

It was the first quarrel I had ever seen, and it had introduced itself not more than a foot from my side.

"Kajira," called Tullius Quintus back and down to me, I thought from yards away, "do you live?"

"I live, Master," I called back.

I then heard Tullius Quintus, my master, laugh. "Things proceed," he said, "as I have planned."

I turned to my side.

It was now morning.

I found a narrow aperture in the floor of the container, through which I might peer, and saw the shadow below, of a great winged shape, coursing across the green fields of Gor.

I recalled that footprints are not left on clouds, nor, I gathered, do sleen, a tracking beast, tread the tarn road.

CHAPTER SIXTEEN

I had knelt before him, head down, as was appropriate.

"Beat me," I had said, "if I am not pleasing."

"Lie here, to my side," he had said, "the bara position will do."

I had then lain beside him, in bara.

"Lita," said he.

I had not realized he had risen to his feet. His foot nudged me. I was still in bara.

"Master?" I said.

"You seem lost in reverie," he said.

"Forgive me, Master," I said.

"Position," he said.

I went to position.

My knees, as was customary, were closed.

"What were you thinking of?" he asked.

"Of many things," I said, "of my former world, of friends I knew, of various slaveries, of your mastery."

"Have I been cruel to you?" he asked.

"No, Master," I said, carefully.

"But I have been a master," he said.

"Very much so, Master," I said.

"You are very responsive in your collar," he said.

"I am a slave," I said.

"Would you like to be sold to a woman?" he asked.

"No," I said, "but it will be done with me as Master pleases."

"In the past few months," he said, "I fear your leash has been too short."

"A slave may not question," I said. I understood what he meant, of course, that the discipline imposed upon me might have been excessively severe. That was a judgment with which I could scarcely disagree. In the literal sense, as I have suggested, earlier, I had seldom been leashed, at least publicly. He had usually had me follow him, even in the streets, naked, my wrists bound behind me. This had brought me more than my share of abuse from annoyed free women, many of whom carried switches. Occasionally he would leash me in the house, either fastening me to one ring or another, or having me perform, as the animal I was, on the leash. In the training house I had been taught to perform on a leash, give a master pleasure on a leash, and such. A slave comes to love her leash. On a leash, usually naked, a woman is in little doubt of her slavery. Leashes are usually of chain or leather.

"I have decided," he said, "to give you a tunic."

"It will be as Master pleases," I said.

As I have mentioned, I had once made the mistake of begging clothing too zealously, even that of a slave. "You have not yet earned clothing," I had been informed, and then I had been switched.

I had never been subjected, interestingly, to the Gorean slave lash. I was not eager for the experience.

"You will be less conspicuous in a tunic," he said.

"Yes, Master," I said. In some cities, even camisks and ta-teeras were outlawed on the streets. To be sure, slaves are to be clad as slaves. The usual garb of a slave is a brief tunic.

"And, if I were to keep you housed," he said, "that might provoke even greater curiosity."

I was silent.

"And if I were to house you remotely," he said, "in the countryside, that might arouse even greater interest."

I understood very little of this, if any.

"What is your name?" he asked.

"'Lita'," I said.

"And what is the name of your master?" he asked.

"Tullius Quintus, of Ar," I said. "It is on my collar."

"How does your collar read?" he inquired.

I did not know why he was asking me such things.

Was I to be beaten, if I could not recall? What slave does not know her master? What slave does not know what is on her collar?

"'I am the slave of Tullius Quintus, of Ar'," I said.

"Good," he said.

These questions seemed to me strange.

"In more than one tavern," he said, "and twice in the Plaza of Tarns, I have encountered inquiries pertaining to you."

"Offers to buy?" I asked. Such things were not unknown. It can be flattering, of course, for a girl to know that men might be interested in buying her, in owning her.

"No," he said, "or not usually. Rather there seems to be curiosity as to your antecedents, to the manner of my keeping of you, and such."

"Perhaps they think I am a runaway free woman," I said, "a free lover, concealing herself as a slave?"

"Do not be absurd," he said. "You are clearly a slave. Just as it is impossible for a free woman to impersonate a slave, so it is impossible for a woman, once she has learned her collar, to impersonate a free woman. Her bondage is manifest in every fiber of her body, in her every expression and movement."

"Yes, Master," I said. I had little doubt that I had muchly changed since Earth.

"I do not wish you to appear different, or mysterious," he said.

"I am a barbarian," I said.

"Many notice," he said, "but not all. Your Gorean is excellent."

"Thank you, Master," I said.

"That you are a barbarian does not make you that different," he said. "There are many barbarians. They are cheaply acquired and they sell well. Many are ecstatic, to be rescued from Earth, to be brought to a fresh, untainted, beautiful world, and to find themselves in the collars of true men."

"How, then, am I mysterious?" I asked.

"I do not think you are mysterious, in yourself," he said. "No. I see you much as a presentable, common slave, one nicely vendible amongst others. Indeed, in the past months you have become more appetitious and more lovely, which commonly happens in the collar."

"Am I as attractive as a pleasure slave?" I asked.

"Vain slave," he said.

"Forgive me, Master," I said.

"More attractive than many," he said.

This answer muchly pleased me. I supposed I was vain, but are not all slaves vain, all women vain?

"Surely I am not mysterious," I said.

"It is not that you are mysterious, in yourself," he said, "so much as that some sense me to be mysterious, and this mystery then attaches to you. I think that is it."

"I do not understand," I said.

"I have not been keeping you as a common slave," he said. "And men wonder why. You are naked in public, which suggests I am afraid you may be stolen, or will try to flee. Are you so special? What is different about you? See? And you do not leave the house alone. You do not run errands. You are not visible at the public laundry troughs. You do not consort with other slaves. You have no friends. Why are you not, amongst the porticoes and colonnades, chatting and gossiping with your collar sisters, seeking news, a word dropped in the tiers of the Central Cylinder becoming common knowledge by nightfall, not comparing collars and masters, not complaining about the recent quality of the tunic cloth, not whispering delightedly of the intrigues and doings of free women, and so on."

Much in my bondage was mysterious, and much in my master seemed to me mysterious. For example, I was not at all sure that his Home Stone was truly that of Ar. Months ago he had seemed unaware that heavy traffic on the streets of Ar was prohibited during daylight hours. Also, he had occasionally asked questions, and inquired directions, of passers-by, on the streets and in the squares, the answers to which I would have supposed would be well known to a native of the city. Some of his interlocutors had surely taken him for a guest or visitor. I did not even know his caste, a matter concerning which Goreans are not likely to be reticent. One may be the most easily traced by means of caste, and city, and Home Stone. I did not even know if my master had a Home Stone, and, if so, what Home Stone it might be. And Ar was a large and populous city, one in which, possibly, one individual might not be known to others, and in which an isolated individual might attract little notice, might even, so to speak, vanish from sight. Might not one then, possibly cultivating obscurity, or concerned with secrecy, think of choosing such a concealment? Who, on a beach, would be likely to attend to a single grain of sand? And yet it seemed notice had been taken of such an individual, for those of Ar, following seasons of invasion and occupation, of intrigue and espionage, of treachery and betrayal, of politics, proscriptions, and terror, were more wary than many of those of my former world would have been, of strangers in the streets.

"We will be best concealed, by being least concealed," said Tullius Quintus.

"Then we are mysterious, it seems," I said.

"But must not seem so," he said. "So tomorrow you will be clothed, and allowed to run in the city, and such."

"Do you not fear I will escape?" I said.

"Tunicked," he said, "collared, and branded? Surely you are not serious."

"Forgive me, Master," I said.

"Too," he said, "Ar is walled, gates are guarded, and a slave, unaccompanied, is not permitted outside the walls."

I nodded. Doubtless it was true.

"Moreover," he said, "the world will see to it that you are kept in your collar."

"Yes, Master," I said.

"Do you object?" he asked.

"No, Master," I said.

"Why?" he asked.

"Because I am a slave," I said.

"And wish to be a slave," he said.

"Yes, Master," I whispered, head down.

"I despise you," he said.

"Yes, Master," I said, "but I must be what I am."

On this world I had come to realize that even on Earth I had longed to be a slave, had yearned to be a slave, and now, the matter wholly out of my control, I was on Gor, and whether I wished it or not, I was a belonging, a property, helplessly collared.

"Suppose I am asked my master's caste," I said, "or from whence he derives his coins. How shall I make answer?"

"Say the Builders," he said. "That will do."

I wondered if he might not be of the Builders. As far as I could tell, he had related well to Lysander, who was of that caste. Had he not been an unquestioned, accepted, and welcomed guest at the supper I had helped serve in the house of Lysander, Administrator of Market of Semris? Not all members of a caste, of course, are active in the crafts or professions associated with the caste.

"From whence, should I be asked," I asked, "shall I say my master derives his coins?"

"Say," said he, "he does business, engaging now and then in speculations."

"Yes, Master," I said.

Perhaps then, his caste was that of the Merchants. Surely one particularly associated business with that caste, the risks and hazards of economic venturing, the exciting, harrowing matters of profit and loss, of investment and speculation.

"Master," I said.

"Yes?" he said.

"Am I truly only a work slave, a pot girl, a kettle-and-mat girl?"

"Certainly," he said. "Why do you ask?"

"I fear I have a greater value to you than would be suggested by that," I said.

"Dismiss the thought," said he.

"Am I truly only a copper-tarsk girl?" I asked.

"Certainly," he said. "Look at yourself. Find a pool of still water and examine your reflection. Find a public bronze mirror and, when no free woman is about, regard yourself."

"I thought Master suggested that I might be more attractive than at least some pleasure slaves," I said.

"More attractive than many," he said.

"Perhaps then I am of interest to Master," I said.

"I find you of some interest," he said.

"Of slave interest?" I said.

"Possibly," he said.

"A slave is pleased," I said.

I tried to kneel better in "position." I was back on my heels, my hands, palms down, on my thighs, my back straight, my head up. My knees were closed.

"You look well on your knees," he said.

"Thank you, Master," I said. It thrilled me to be on my knees before a man. I was of the sex that belonged to his sex.

I saw his eyes, and trembled. He regarded me, fiercely. I was before him.

"Split your knees," he said.

"Yes, Master," I said.

"Yes," he said, approvingly, "you look well on your knees."

"Thank you, Master," I said.

My belly began to flame. My thighs were open, before him. He owned me.

"Go to all fours," he said. "Fetch the leash, and bring it to me, in your mouth."

"Yes, Master," I said.

CHAPTER SEVENTEEN

W ho whips you?" she asked.

"Tullius Quintus, of Ar," I said.

Actually he had never whipped me, though I had occasionally felt his switch, and her question was no more than a polite way of inquiring to whom I might belong. Most Gorean slaves are seldom, if ever, whipped. The reason for this is simple. They strive to be pleasing, and, striving so, are found pleasing. Few Goreans would consider gratuitously whipping a slave. That would be as pointless as gratuitously whipping a kaiila, or any other sort of animal. It would be incomprehensible; it would be absurd; it would make no sense. To be sure, the whip is there, and may be used at the master's discretion. The slave well knows she is subject to it. Occasionally she may be whipped, to remind her that she is a slave. That is something she is never to forget.

"My master," she said, "is Camillus, he whose shop is on Emerald."

We were at the Teiban Market.

"My master speculates," I said. "He is doubtless of the Street of Coins."

"You do not know?" she asked.

"Curiosity is not becoming in a kajira," I said.

"My name is Lita," she said.

"Mine, too!" I said.

"Hist!" she whispered. "Let us speed away. A free woman approaches."

We hurried off, going different ways. Free women, I had learned, are not pleased to note slaves in converse. Perhaps they fear that slaves might be dallying, thus possibly neglecting their duties.

Doubtless that is it.

But I think it is really because they hate us, so virulently, and want to humiliate and hurt us, even in small ways, they with all their pride, power, and goods, and we, utterly helpless and powerless, with nothing, not even a rag or collar we can call our own.

Why do they wish to deny us even small pleasures, so important to women, such as those of sweet converse? Do they not themselves frequently indulge in such sweet delights, delights so natural and precious to our sex?

Why should they deny them to us?

Why do they hate us?

Is it our fault that men prefer us, bid on us, and will own us?

In any event, free women neglect few opportunities to remind a slave that she is a slave.

Do they see in us what they might be, and want to be?

How cruel they are to us!

How their switches sting!

I looked back over my shoulder, furtively, frightened.

How vulnerable we were, in our tiny tunics, our single garments, with no nether closure, our bodies so briefly and degradingly bared, before those fierce, looming beings in their resplendent robes and veils!

I no longer saw the free woman. She must have turned aside, or something. I felt a flood of relief. I was not even natively of Gor, and yet I feared them, feared them so. But why should I not? Was I not collared? Was the band of light steel not locked on my neck? Then I recalled that though I was not natively of Gor, I was surely now of Gor, truly and wholly, for I was a Gorean kajira.

Slaves fear free women, terribly. Certainly I feared them, terribly. I, a slave, was so different from them! The men, whose pleasure objects we were, were our only protection from them. How grateful we were. How we strove to please our masters, for so many reasons. It was not simply the fear of their whips, though this fear was genuine, and warranted. We knew that if we were not pleasing, we would be whipped, and as the slaves we were. But rather I think it had more to do with the radical dimorphism of the sexes in our species, divided essentially into the master sex and the slave sex. They gave us the mastering, which we, slaves, so desperately craved, wanted, and needed. What woman does not want her master, what man does not want his slave?

For several days now I had been tunicked, and had, from time to time, sometimes for Ahn at a time, to my joy, been allowed the freedom of the city. Ar, I gathered, was a typical "high city," with its noisy, colorfully garbed, bustling crowds, its affluent quarters and its sorrier districts, some of which were not to be frequented at night; here were places of lofty towers, often linked by graceful, narrow, arching, railless bridges, which I feared to tread, places of glorious fountains, parks, and broad, tree-lined boulevards, and places, too, of mazelike, tiny, crooked streets, and step wells, places of great houses and places of sordid insulae. Here I became acquainted with a splendid civilization, a colorful, intricate, complex civilization, a high, thriving civilization which, as most high civilizations, had a place for slaves, that place in which I found myself. I looked about myself. How glorious was the civilization of Gor! How grateful I was that I had been brought here. How grateful I was that I must have had some appeal to men, however little, that they would permit me to know such a world, in the only way that I, from Earth, was worthy to know it, as a vendible, collared slave. In such a civilization, what could I be but a slave, a humble, joyful, grateful slave?

And then, suddenly, in my joy, I was afraid, terribly afraid, for slavery is not without its terrors. I was not free. I did not own myself, but was owned by another. It would be done with me as others wished. I was a rightless property, a vendible good, a small, soft, collared beast, subject to chains and the whip, who could be bought and sold. I was ownable, and owned. I was a slave.

"Oh!" I cried.

"Clumsy slave!" cried the woman, lifting her switch. There was a swirl of veils and robes, and I flung myself to my knees, my head to the stones.

"Forgive me, Mistress!" I cried.

"My robes are disarranged, my veils are awry!" she screamed.

I shuddered, at her feet.

"Who whips you?" she screamed.

"Tullius Quintus," I exclaimed, "of Ar!"

"We shall see!" she cried. "Kneel up, you disgusting creature!"

I knelt up, and she, bending down, seized my hair and pulled my head back, sharply. I cried out, wincing.

"Who owns you?" she said.

"Tullius Quintus, of Ar," I said.

"Liar!" she cried.

"Mistress?" I said.

"Lying slave!" she cried.

"It is on my collar, noble Mistress!" I wept.

"Liar, liar!" she screamed.

Some men, and one or two women, had gathered about.

"Mistress?" I said.

"So you would deceive a free person?" she cried.

"No, exalted Mistress," I cried.

"Do you think I cannot read?" she said.

"Exalted Mistress?" I said, bewildered.

"You thought I would not look," she said. "But I know the wiles of lying slaves!"

"I do not understand, great Mistress," I said.

"That is not what is on your collar," she said.

"I cannot read!" I said.

The switch struck me across the left upper arm, and then the right upper arm, and tears streamed down my cheeks.

"You should be thrown to sleen," she said.

"Mercy, glorious Mistress," I said. "I thought truly that was what my collar read."

"Liar!" she said. "Do not think to trick a free person. We are a thousand times more clever than a stupid slave."

"I thought my collar read so, truly," I wept.

"Liar, liar!" she said, the switch speaking again, twice.

"You should be boiled alive," she said, "sleen for you, cast you naked and bound amongst ravenous leech plants."

"Please, no, Mistress," I begged.

"Insulting, clumsy, wicked slave!" said the free woman.

"What does my collar read, Mistress?" I begged.

"You know very well, miserable she-tarsk! Remove your tunic. You will rue the Ehn you obstructed my way, and dared to lie to me!"

"Forgive me," exclaimed a man, "but I am much smitten with your beauty!"

I surely did not need such an appraisal at this time, however welcome it might have been at another time, under different circumstances, the free woman standing over me, switch in hand. Might she not be further incensed? And, too, was I not a copper-tarsk girl, a mere copper-tarsk girl?

The free woman spun about, to regard the fellow who had spoken, he in the white and gold of the Merchants, and his robes well draped.

"Forgive me," he said, "but in this wry contretemps your veil slackened, a misfortune for you but a splendid boon to the discerning masculine eye."

"Oh?" said the free woman.

"Forgive me," he said, "but I could not but note, however inadvertently, the loveliness of your features."

She reached to the street veil, but did not hastily fasten it in place.

The glance I had seen of her did not suggest to me that she would be likely to be entered into the plans of roving slavers.

"You will forgive me, will you not?" he asked.

"Perhaps," she said, fastening the veil.

"May I not escort you from this unfortunate place, with its lamentable associations," he said, "bringing you safely to your domicile, after, perhaps, if I might prevail upon your patience, a glass or two of ka-la-na?"

"Very well," she said, as though reluctantly. Then she looked down upon me. "You are contrite, are you not?" she asked.

"Very much so, Mistress," I said.

"And I trust you have been well instructed?" she said.

"Yes, Mistress," I said. "Thank you merciful, kind Mistress."

She then turned about. "One must try to be patient with slaves," she said.

"So true," said the man.

"I fear I am too indulgent, too lenient, with slaves," she said. "It is a weakness of mine."

"What might be a fault in one," he said, "is often a lovely credit or merit in another."

"Do you think so?" she asked.

"Mercy becomes one so beautiful," he said.

"Please forget you glimpsed my face," she said.

"I do not know if I will ever be able to do so," he said.

As they departed, her hand lightly on his arm, he glanced over his shoulder, and smiled.

I did not know him, but I was grateful to him. To whom may a slave look for protection from a free woman if not to a man? Is it not men who put us in collars, and keep us there?

So I retained my tunic, and escaped a belaboring that I feared would have been particularly severe.

My master, whatever his name might be, resided on Venaticus. I must hurry home.

Apparently my collar had been misrepresented to me in Market of Semris, or had been changed in my sleep, my gruel having possibly been affected by the introduction of some sedating substance.

So, again, I realized, my master had had recourse to yet another precaution to make it difficult to follow him. But, I recalled, in his flight from the environs of Market of Semris, he had spoken of "gold," but gold only as and when it pleased him. Too, as I recalled, he engaged, at least occasionally, in speculation.

I did not know in what way I might be involved in these matters.

A man looked down at me. "You had best go," he said. "Free women do not much care for slaves, and particularly not for pleasure slaves."

"Yes, Master," I said. "Thank you, Master." I then leapt up, and sped away. In my hurrying home, I remembered what he had said. He had thought of me, it seems, apparently quite naturally, as a pleasure slave!

Perhaps then I was not a mere copper-tarsk girl, after all.

CHAPTER EIGHTEEN

———————

I do not even know your name!" I cried.

"Position," said he.

Immediately I went to position. As he frowned, I hastened to spread my knees. How helpless and vulnerable does this make a woman feel! What could she be before a man, so positioned? Was the answer to that not clear? And how could such a position not enflame her?

"You will continue to think, and speak, of me as Tullius Quintus, of Ar," he said. "That will be, I conjecture, most convenient."

"That is not the name on my collar!" I said.

"You have learned to read?" he said.

"I have been informed," I said.

"And what is the name?" he asked.

"I do not know," I said. "I was not told."

"It does not matter," he said. "My name is neither Tullius Quintus nor the name on your collar."

"I see," I said.

"But rest assured," he said, "the name on your collar will prove quite sufficient to have you returned to me should you be so unwise as to wander off or stray."

"That is your name in Ar?" I said.

"Yes," he said.

"Surely then I may know it," I said, "as the supposed name of my master."

"Continue to think of me as Tullius Quintus," he said.

"I do not understand," I said.

"I think it is better, at least a little better, that you do not know it, not now," he said.

"Merely that I should be kept in greater ignorance?" I asked.

"Not really," he said. "But there are things in the city, I am sure, that can no more read Gorean than you."

"Things?" I said.

"Yes," he said.

"Thus I could only mislead them," I said, "able only to provide them with a useless name, that of Tullius Quintus."

"Yes," he said.

"But surely there are many about who can read Gorean," I said. "To them the legend on the collar will be clear."

"Doubtless," he said, "but I am most concerned with those who, as yourself, are unlikely to be able to read Gorean."

"Surely they would quickly enlist literate allies, or agents," I said.

"Quite possibly they might already have them at hand," he said. "But, if not, a delay might ensue, which would work to my advantage."

"Permitting escape?" I said.

"Our escape," he said.

"But I know this place," I said.

"And might, under any name, Tullius Quintus or another, lead others to it," he said.

"Yes, Master," I said. "Forgive me, Master."

"And under torture would doubtless do so," he said.

"I fear so, Master," I said.

"If you are accompanied, or watched," he said, "lift the hammer ring, and then strike twice, and then, after a pause, once, again. This signal may be repeated."

"But what if they propose themselves as your friends, or allies?" I said.

"I have no friends, or allies," he said.

"Yes, Master," I said.

"Do not be so concerned," he said. "As Lita, you are unlikely to be known."

"Why should I fear being known?" I asked.

"It is rather I who might fear it," he said.

"I do not think you are of Ar," I said.

"You will continue to respond so, if questioned," he said.

"I do not even know my master's caste," I said.

"Nor need you," he said.

"I am uneasy, Master," I said.

"Much is at stake," he said. "Dark matters are afoot."

"Inform me," I begged.

"Curiosity," he said, "is not becoming in a kajira."

CHAPTER NINETEEN

I lay on my mat, on the floor, at the foot of my master's couch. I drew my blanket more closely about me. I was naked, for slave girls are commonly slept so. I was chained to the couch by the neck. It was late, perhaps the second Ahn. The tiny lamp had long since gone out. The room was totally dark. How strange it seemed, late at night, in the utter darkness, to find myself lying on a floor, as I was, on a different world, at the foot of a man's couch, a couch I dared not ascend, chained to it. Yet how real it was! Had I ever lived so intensely, so explicitly, so fully? I felt the chain. I was in my place, at the foot of a man's couch, on a chain. In my heart I knew it was there that I belonged, at the foot of some man's couch, on some chain. Outside it was pouring. I could well conjecture the light of the door lantern falling on the glistening cobbles, the water, reflecting the light, rushing down the gutters, the water diverted at the intersection by the stepping stones, high enough to protect a woman's robe hems and slippers, spaced widely enough to allow for the passage of wheels. Earlier I had heard men passing by, outside, in the storm, probably fellows returning from some revel. They would have doubtless wrapped their cloaks about them, and drawn them over their heads. Rich men, abroad at night, will commonly be preceded by a lantern bearer and flanked by one or more guards. Arrangements for renting such, a bearer and guards, as with cooks, musicians, dress sandals, dinner robes, sedan chairs, palanquins, and such, if one does not have them in one's own right, are available through a number of enterprises in the city. I lay in the dark, holding the blanket about me, listening to the driving rain. I was not sure why I had awakened. It would be Ahn before I would be unchained and sent to the kitchen, to prepare breakfast for my master, a breakfast in which I, tunicked and kneeling beside him, often partook.

I listened to the driving rain.

I suppressed a whimper. My master had not touched me this night. Certainly he must have noted the simple loop of the bondage knot I had tied in my hair. What master could overlook so simple a thing? This simple loop mutely pleads with the master for his attention. To be sure, there are a thousand ways a girl can signify her needs, and her supplications that her master will condescend to satisfy them, glances, subtle movements, seemingly inadvertent proximities, tiny sounds, kneelings, licking and kissing the feet and ankles, and then raising one's eyes, tear-filled, begging, to the master. How much we are at the mercy of men, once the brutes have, at their inclination, or will, ignited our slave fires, latent in any healthy female. Do free women scorn us for our needs? Do they despise us for our vulnerability, our helplessness? Let them then wear the collar and strive to resist the flames burning in their own bellies! And will they not be successful until, at last, over-come, they crawl to their master, they, too, begging, whimpering, peti-tioning his pity?

I did not know why I had awakened.

Perhaps it was the rain, or the spillage from the gutters to the street below. Then I heard it, or thought I heard it, again.

Was it not a scrape, or a tiny scratching sound?

Surely not.

What could be heard in the storm? The rain would mask out a thousand noises.

I lay awake.

I had heard nothing. One could have heard nothing.

As I lay there, after a time, as it would, the storm gentled; no longer was it some lashing, frenzied assault on the walls and roof; no longer was it beating and savage; it had now become a sustained susurration, and then in time it became less, no more than a soft, quiet, persistent patter. There was now moonlight outside. The yellow moon was no longer obscured by clouds. I could hear the water move in the gutters.

Then I heard it clearly.

Something was outside the house, somehow on the wall, outside, how was it possible, near the barred window?

The house, as I may have mentioned, was on Venaticus. As many of the small houses in this district, it had two floors. We were on the second floor, and the sound came clearly from the wall, outside, near the win-dow. It was a scratching sound, as if some clawed thing were climbing the wall. I listened, frightened. I heard bars grasped, and tested, shaken, quietly. For a moment I could not move. Then I dared not move. I did not know what I might see. Then, slowly, frightened, I forced myself to turn to the window. In the dampness, water dripping at the sill, and the moonlight, from the yellow moon, I saw, framed in the window, outside its bars, a broad, dark shape, or presence. I thought it might be a head but it was surely too broad for a head. I screamed, and it disappeared.

"Ho!" cried Tullius Quintus, leaping from the couch.

Clouds then obscured the moon again, and once more the room was in darkness.

I heard the rain, soft, outside.

How reassuring, and gentle, it seemed.

But something fearful, something large and alive, had been at the window.

In the darkness I heard the snap of a fire maker, and, a moment later, by means of its tiny flame, the tharlarion-oil lamp was alight, and I saw the room about, flickering, yellow, eerie, and empty. Tullius Quintus stood beside the couch. He held the lamp, lifted, in his left hand. In his right hand he held a dagger.

"The window," I said, half pointing, my voice scarcely audible so frightened I was.

He went to the window, and looked out, for a time, down into the street, and then lowered the dagger, and turned back to me.

"It is nothing," he said.

"I saw it," I said, "outside the window, something fearful, something large."

"You were dreaming," he said. "A nightmare."

"I saw it," I repeated, now kneeling, the blanket down, about my thighs.

"There was nothing there," he said. "The night has been foul. Nothing would be abroad in such a storm."

"Master," I protested, weakly.

"The window," he said, "is high above the street. Nothing could be at the window."

"Yet Master took a drawn dagger to the window," I said.

"Go to sleep," he said.

"I was not dreaming," I said.

"The storm," he said, "the height of the window."

"Forgive me, Master," I said, "but I was not dreaming."

He looked down at me.

The lamp light fell upon me, at the foot of his couch.

"I was not dreaming," I said.

"Perhaps not," he said.

"No?" I said.

"No," he said.

"Please enlighten your slave," I begged. "What does it mean?"

"You wish to know?" he said.

"Yes, Master," I said. "Please, Master."

"I think I have made contact," he said. "It is as I have planned."

"I do not understand!" I said.

"You are involved in this," he said.

"Master?" I said.

"Doubtless you think you have value," he said.

"Yes, Master," I said, "forgive me, but perhaps a silver tarsk, perhaps more."

"Vain slut," he said.

"Forgive me, Master," I said.

"But you do have value, shapely barbarian slut," he said, "through no virtue, nor any fault, of your own, value unknown to you."

"Master?" I said.

"—value well beyond what you would bring off a block, as collar-meat."

"I do not understand," I said.

"You are an investment," he said.

"I do not understand," I said.

"I plan to sell you," he said.

"Master will not keep me?" I said.

"No," he said.

"Have I been displeasing?" I asked.

"Not particularly," he said. "You are not hard to look at, and I approve your uncontrollable slave reflexes. Such reflexes improve a girl's price."

I feared I was helpless in a man's arms, in any man's arms.

"But you have more in mind," I said, "than the common things that go into a girl's block price?"

"Yes," he said.

"Master has a buyer in mind?" I asked.

"Of course," he said.

"I have been sold frequently," I said.

"Many feared to keep you," he said.

"Why?" I asked.

"Because of those who seek you," he said.

"Who seeks me?" I asked.

"I think I will soon learn," he said.

"And why am I sought?" I asked.

"I do not know," he said.

"You are not afraid to keep me?" I said.

"One calculates," he said. "One considers profit, one considers risk."

"I understand nothing of this," I said.

"Did I not tell you to go to sleep?" he said.

"Yes, Master," I said.

"Must a command be repeated?" he asked.

"No, Master," I said. The repetition of a command is often cause for discipline.

I then lay down, again, at the foot of the couch, on my chain, and drew my blanket about me.

I was muchly uneasy.

How could I be sold for more than one or two silver tarsks, at best? How could I, one such as I, even a barbarian, have greater value than my likely block price?

How could that be?

I recalled Paula. On Earth I had dismissed her, even pitied her, poor, plain Paula, and considered myself far superior to her in beauty. Then I had heard it said that she was the beauty of our shipment, and had heard it speculated that she might bring as many as five silver pieces, presumably silver tarsks, in a first sale, that she might be marketed on a high block in the Curulean, perhaps even from the Central Block. And what then of me, poor thing that I might be, assessed as a copper-tarsk girl, a pot girl, a kettle-and-mat girl?

What had I to hope for, on this beautiful, perilous world?

How subject we are to our masters! The whip is theirs.

Who would bid more for me than perhaps two silver tarsks?

How could I, a slave, be of more value than that, if that?

I was to be sold.

My master had a buyer in mind.

I did not know who it might be.

And, oddly, I do not think he knew either. One, or those, who sought me, doubtless, but why?

I lay there, warm and dry, wrapped in my blanket, on the floor, on my mat, at the foot of my master's couch, on my chain.

At one time, certainly for me, it would have been a strange feeling, knowing that one can belong to anyone who can buy you. But now, it was no longer a strange feeling. I wore a Gorean slave collar.

I listened to the rain.

I could now see, once more, moonlight at the barred window.

CHAPTER TWENTY

Lita," she said, smiling, and motioning for me to join her in a doorway near the fountain.

"Lita," I said, recognizing her. We both bore the same name. Her master's name, she had informed me, some days past, was Camillus. We had frequently met at the Teiban market, shopping. Her master had a shop on Emerald, which dealt largely with harnessing, harnessing for tharlarion, for kaiila, for slaves. There are many variations, incidentally, in slave harnessing. I think I may have mentioned that slaves often draw small carts, for their masters, commonly peddlers, and that some free women utilize female slaves to draw their carriages. Too female slaves are sometimes harnessed to, or chained to, poles, by means of which they carry their mistress's palanquin. Similarly, male slaves are occasionally used as draft beasts for purposes of heavier haulage. Much harnessing for slaves, of course, is primarily concerned with restraint, for fastening, say, to poles, stanchions, slave rings, and such. There is a particularly rich assortment of restraint harnessings designed for female slaves, most notably display harnessings. Twice I had seen Lita on her leash, attractively, and helplessly, harnessed, preceding he whom I supposed was her master. On her back was a sign which, I supposed, must advertise his goods and shop. Seeing her so, of course, I dared not speak to her. Once she saw me, and smiled. She was rather proud of her harnessing. Certainly it set her off, nicely. Such arrangements usually have, as well, the capacity to keep a slave in place, for example, to fasten her to a stanchion, say, by her tethered wrists behind her back, or to render her, for most practical purposes, incapable of movement, fastening her hand and foot. Such changes are easily brought about with a few simple adjustments, a few snaps or bucklings. In a lovely variation of such harnessing, the slave is knelt, with her hands fastened before her body, close to her waist, by the waist belt, and then, behind her back, by short, stout straps run from the waist belt, and ankle cuffs, she is held on her knees. It might be mentioned in passing, that metal workers have often devised varieties of chain harnessing for slaves, as well. I had never worn such devices, leather or metal, since the house of training. The leather of harnessing comes in various degrees of quality, and is often available, like slave cords, in different colors. Most slaves, of course, are not harnessed. They are more likely, if abroad, and waiting, say, pending the return of a master, to be chained to public rings, these frequently found in public places, supplied by the municipality as a convenience.

I had not seen Lita in days.

She spit a coin or two into the palm of her hand, for she was obviously on an errand of some sort for her master. Goreans, both slave and free, at least the free of the lower castes, sometimes carry coins so. This frees the hands, and it is not obvious that coins are being carried. The upper castes commonly carry coins in a purse or wallet. This provides a public target, of course, for thieves. The usual theft takes place by cutting the strings of the purse or wallet, commonly in a seemingly inadvertent contact or in the press of a throng. Some thieves are trained in this skill from childhood. There is only one city I am aware of in which the caste of thieves is explicitly recognized, which is a port on the Tamber Gulf, bordering Thassa, the sea. Its governance is in the hands of a Council of Captains. It is north of the great port of Brundisium. It is famous for its canals and "Arsenal," which is actually a depot and naval yard. Its name is Port Kar. Few Gorean garments, incidentally, save those of artisans, have pockets, which tend to mar the lines, the fall, of the garment. I did not care, personally, to carry coins in my mouth, and, when shopping for my master, would clutch them tightly in my hand.

"What are you doing here?" she asked. "Surely there is a closer fountain to Venaticus."

"I am wandering about," I said.

"With a bucket?" she asked.

"It will not be heavy," I said. "It is small."

When out of the house, following the night of the storm, I had rearranged the nature of my peregrinations. I even took a different route to the Teiban market. I would vary my comings and goings, both with respect to times and routes. This was less to further acquaint myself with the city, of course, than to evade possible surveillance. I supposed this was rather futile, but it seemed to me, however naive or inept this stratagem might prove, that some such activity might prove to be in my best interest, and, possibly, in that of my master, if anything dangerous might be involved, which possibility, I hoped, of course, was not the case. I remembered, clearly, however, the escape from Market of Semris. This memory did not soothe my apprehensions. Too, if I had some value, of which I was unaware, I knew I might be stolen. Slave theft, as that of kaiila and tharlarion, and such, is not unknown. On the other hand, such would be highly unlikely during daylight hours in any public place, and certainly so in a "high city," such as Ar. It is much less hazardous to buy a slave than steal her. I supposed my apprehensions might be ill-founded, and hoped so, but then, again, I did not know. Precaution then might not be necessary, but, on the other hand, surely no harm would be likely to come from trying to be careful. If an observer failed to note me, I reasoned, he might suppose that I was no longer in the city, for example, that Tullius Quintus had already sold me. Too, by such actions, altering routes, and such, might I not prove a more elusive quarry, if I were a quarry? Frequent changes in itinerary, I trusted, might make me more difficult to trace. I had never asked Lita to read my collar for me. I thought I might be safer, as my master had seemed to think, if I remained in ignorance of its legend.

"I have not seen you since the last passage hand," she said.

"I have been about," I assured her.

"Have you not come far for water?" she asked.

"Not so far," I said.

"I know," she said, conspiratorially, "you have come to see it."

"What?" I said.

"I heard about it, at the laundry troughs," she said. "I wager you did, as well."

"What are you doing in the doorway?" I asked.

"Waiting," she said. "Join me. It is nearly dusk."

"What are you waiting for?" I asked.

"To see it," she said.

"What?" I asked.

"You will see," she said. "It is nearly time."

"What?" I asked. "Is it permitted? We are collared."

"Watch that doorway," she said. "It leads upstairs, to the rooms over the shop of Epicrates, the pottery vender."

"I should fetch water," I said, "and return to the house, surely before the fall of darkness."

We were near the fountain of Aiakos. It is at the intersection of Clive and Emerald. We were on Emerald.

"There!" whispered Lita. "See her?"

"She is lovely," I whispered. "Why is she not veiled? I have seldom seen a woman so beautiful. Surely she is a slave. But she is clad in the Robes of Concealment, save for veils. Would she not be punished for that? The law!"

"That is no slave," whispered Lita. "She is a free woman. But I know not her caste nor Home Stone. I know not from whence she derives."

"She looks about, warily," I said.

"No," said Lita. "Not warily, but idly, merely to survey the street."

"Surely she is a slave," I said. "She is not veiled. But how would she dare risk the wearing of the robes of the free? What of guardsmen?"

"She is not a slave," said Lita. "She is the Lady Bina."

"She is not veiled," I said.

"She may not be Gorean," said Lita.

"How dare she so outrage proprieties?" I said. As much is expected of slaves so, too, much is expected of the free.

"It is not unknown for some women of the lower castes to slacken, or omit, veils," said Lita.

"Her robes do not suggest penury," I said.

"I think she is vain," said Lita. "It pleases her to startle, and arouse, men."

"And," I said, "she may soon find herself on a slaver's rope."

"That is unlikely," said Lita, quietly, backing further into the doorway.

"You have detained me here," I said, "merely to look upon an unveiled free woman?"

"Scarcely," she said.

"Why then?" I asked.

Near us a shopkeeper drew down a screen of boards, closing his shop. I noted two men hurrying away.

"I am uneasy," I said. "I should fetch water, and return to the house."

"Just a moment more," said Lita, watching, intently.

"She lingers by the door," I said. "Does she not understand the danger in which she stands, unveiled, dusk about, the street nearly deserted?"

"I think she is in little danger," said Lita.

"Why?" I said.

"You will see," she said.

"She seems to be waiting," I said.

"Yes," said Lita.

"For what is she waiting?" I asked.

"Her pet," said Lita.

I then saw something large, and dark, in the doorway, hunched down, a shadow, a shape. I could not make it out.

"There is something in the doorway," I said.

It was very still.

"That is what I wanted to show you," she said. "Attend, make no sudden moves."

"I am afraid," I said.

"Be still," she said. "Do not draw attention to us."

"It moved!" I said.

I stifled a cry of alarm.

"It is alive," I said.

"Be still," reiterated Lita.

The Lady Bina had begun to stroll north on Emerald. She would pass us.

As soon as she had begun to move, it had emerged from the doorway, quickly, lightly for so mighty a bulk, crouched down, bent over, looking about, alertly, from one side to the other, eyes bright, its knuckles on the paving stones, following her, a bit behind and to the left.

"What is it?" I whispered.

"I do not know," said Lita. "This is the first time I have seen it."

A fellow, in the gray of the Metal Workers, was approaching, moving south on Emerald.

Gorean traffic generally adheres to the left side of roads, passages, and such. In this way a right-handed person's weapon hand faces the oncoming stranger. In Gorean, as in many languages, the same word is used for both "stranger" and "enemy."

"I wager," said Lita, "that fellow does not know the district."

The thing following the Lady Bina ceased to heel her and moved quickly to her right and placed itself, moving beside her, and a little before her, between her and the approaching fellow who, apparently surprised, and perhaps alarmed, hurried to his left, giving the unusual couple a wide berth. As he passed, the thing near the Lady Bina and somewhat in advance of her, suddenly bared its fangs and growled. The fellow hastened on.

"They approach," I said. "Let us flee."

"We are safe," said Lita. "We are animals. We have value. No man would kill us, no more than other domestic beasts. We would merely be seized and appropriated. Our collars protect us."

"That is not a man," I said.

"Our collars will keep us safe," she said.

"Tell it to larls or sleen," I said.

"Do not be afraid," said Lita. "If we make no sudden moves, I am sure we are in no danger. We will do nothing threatening and will not dash away, perhaps activating a pursuit reflex."

"It is not leashed," I said. "And if it was, that slight woman could not hope to restrain it."

"It is tame, and obedient," said Lita. "It needs no leash."

"Did you not hear it growl?" I said. "Did you not see it bare its fangs?"

"It was merely warning that fellow to keep his distance," said Lita.

"And if he had not?" I asked.

"He gave the fellow fair warning," said Lita. "After that, unless he were deterred by a soft word or gentle gesture from his mistress, I would suppose he would tear him to pieces."

That supposition, it seemed to me, was well warranted, given the size and attitude of the beast, its apparent ferocity, its apparent menace, its seeming readiness to attack.

The unusual couple were now close to us. Lita and I were back in the doorway.

They suddenly stopped, and the beast turned toward us, alertly. The large pointed ears turned toward us, inquisitively. Its demeanor did not seem threatening. It did not growl, it did not bare its fangs.

Perhaps we were safe, protected by our collars.

We both knelt, immediately. We were in the presence of a free person, the Lady Bina.

I realized we were not likely to be attacked. That was a welcome intelligence. Certainly, backed into the doorway, and kneeling, we would have been easy prey for such a thing.

Its eyes, for the briefest moment, met mine, piercingly. I lowered my head, instantly.

"Two pretty kajirae," said the Lady Bina.

Some noises emanated from the beast, strange noises, not altogether like animal noises.

"Come along, shaggy friend," said the Lady Bina, smiling. "We will proceed."

"She speaks to the beast," I thought, "as though it could understand, but then, do not masters and mistresses often address their brutes, however irrationally, as though they might understand? One supposes hunters might hasten sleen on the scent, riders urge on their mounts, drivers encourage their teams. Indeed, did not men and women on my former world occasionally, however irrationally, chat pleasantly to their animals, as though such animals might comprehend their words? Does not such persiflage please the master or mistress, and the beast, as well, welcoming such sounds, however ignorant it might be of the content of such a discourse?"

It was only when they had passed us, moving north on Emerald, that I became very frightened. Surely what I had heard were animal noises, but, in retrospect, there was something very unusual about them. Somehow, they seemed not altogether like animal noises. For example, you may become suddenly aware that a city's time bar has been tolling, apparently without your notice, and then, surprisingly, you realize it has already tolled, say, five times. You heard it without realizing that you were hearing it, and then, later, you recall what you were earlier unaware you were hearing. What had occurred was a bit like this. Noises emanated from the beast, which noises, as I expected, were taken as simple animal noises, and dismissed as such, but, a moment later, as the hair rose on the back of my neck and on my forearms, I no longer heard them as simple animal noises. Without thinking, I must have processed those noises, and, doubtless, substituted phonemes for phonemes, much as one might accommodate oneself to an unusual accent, one which at first seems incomprehensible, but, after a moment, or two, the adjustments made, becomes intelligible.

The couple passed, and Lita and I rose to our feet, looking after them.

"Did you hear it?" I asked Lita, frightened.

"Of course," she said.

"It spoke," I said.

"It made noises," she said.

"Words," I said.

"Do not be silly," she said. "It is a beast. It rumbled, it growled."

"Like a sleen, a larl?" I asked.

"Not like a sleen," she said.

She, Gorean, would doubtless be familiar with sleen. Domesticated sleen are not that unusual.

"Or a larl?" I said.

"I heard larls at the games," she said. "No, not like a larl either. But it is a different sort of beast."

"It spoke," I said.

"It did not speak," she said. "It would have to be rational to speak. It is a beast."

"It spoke," I said.

"What did it say?" she asked.

"The mistress said 'two pretty kajirae'," I said, "and the beast responded, 'but not so lovely as you, dear lady'."

Lita turned white.

"Did it not?" I asked.

"I am afraid," she said. "It is late. Let us hurry to our houses!"

At that point Lita sped away, but I remained, for a time, frightened, in the doorway.

I was sure the thing accompanying the unusual free woman, that slight blond-haired beauty, she who dared to go about unveiled, was a rational organism. It was not a pet. I did not know what it was, but I was sure it was not a pet.

Then I remembered how it had looked at me, so piercingly. Certainly it had not been the look of a human male, a master, that look to which a slave becomes so accustomed, say, that casual, assessing look, from hair to ankles, which undresses her, nor the simple look of a beast, say, curious, hostile, or baleful. It had been a look that seemed, somehow, to be trying to understand my expression. Did it know me? Did I know it? Had we something to do with one another?

I think it had read more than apprehension, or fear, in my countenance, as it might have read in the countenance of Lita.

There must have been more in my expression than I understood. But then it had turned away, tamely following its companion.

Was this only my imagination?

I feared not.

I leaned against the wall of the doorway.

I had heard it speak. I was sure of that. And so, too, upon reflection, apparently, was Lita.

"Can it read my collar?" I wondered.

Why had that question occurred to me? Of course, it had come into my mind because of the words of my master, who had spoken of things, not men, who might not be able to read my collar, no more than I.

And might not that insufficiency buy time?

My master had, the night of the storm, speculated that a contact might have been made.

And I recalled that terrifying night, that in which I had heard bars

gently shaken, quietly being tested, and, then, turning, in the light of
the yellow moon, had seen something in the window, behind the bars,
something large and alive.

Might it not have been something such as I had just seen on Emerald, and which had just seen me?

I did not even pause to fill the small bucket at the fountain of Aiakos. Instead I turned my steps toward Venaticus, rushing through the
half-light.

Again and again, I turned about, fearing I might be followed.

CHAPTER TWENTY-ONE

At the entrance to the house on Venaticus, I turned about, again. The street, as far as I could see, was empty. I saw no indication that I might have been followed.

It was now dark. The dangling lantern by the door was lit.

I was uneasy in its light.

I heard a sound.

It was that of my own breathing, for I had muchly hastened.

I saw nothing.

I was anxious to be inside, and safe.

I was very much afraid from the experience I had had on Emerald, near the fountain of Aiakos.

I had now realized, for the first time, perhaps belatedly, certainly foolishly, that intelligence, rationality, a capacity to calculate and plan, to pursue far goals, might not be limited to my species, but that the dark selections of evolution, in their impersonal, blind processes, without heart, mind, thought, or reason, might endow a variety of life forms with a diversity of attributes and behaviors facilitating survival, doubtless often at the cost of suppressing, eradicating, and feeding on other life forms. Were the beautiful lines of the leaping, fleet tabuk not fashioned by the artistry of the larl, its claws and fangs; did the same blind, nameless gods not balance the swirling school of parsit fish against the strike of the swift-swimming shark; the keenness of the hawk's eye against the tiny urt's immediate flight to cover at the sight of a moving shadow? We find it easy to understand how nature might favor speed, strength, fangs, claws, hoofs, wings, and such in a beast, but why might it not favor, as well, intelligence and cunning, rationality and thought? And what if such attributes might be conjoined with others, such as the tenacity of the sleen, the claws and fangs of the larl?

I must warn my master, that things may not be as before, that danger might be afoot, lurking perhaps nearby, watching, even now, from the darkness.

The beast had not seemed to bear me ill-will, nor its companion, the lovely lady, but who can read what currents of thought might course unseen in dark places, what rivers might flow in the minds of brutes, what might lie behind unreadable eyes?

I seized the hammer ring on the door and lifted it. I then let it fall, twice, against its heavy metal plate. I then waited for a moment, and let it fall once more.

I then stood by the door, waiting.

After a time the door opened, and I slipped inside. A tharlarion-oil lamp hung from the ceiling. I could see the stairs leading upstairs.

"Master," I called, softly.

I heard the door close behind me.

"Master?" I said.

I was seized from behind, a heavy hand over my mouth. I tried to scream, but could not, for the hand over my mouth. It was removed, and I opened my mouth, widely, to scream, but a slave bit was thrust into my mouth and, a moment later, it was snapped shut behind my neck. I whimpered, almost inaudibly. What more can one do in a slave bit? Held as I was, I could not turn to see who held me. I heard a rustle of leather, and a hood was drawn over my head and fastened behind my neck. My wrists, held together behind me, in one hand, were then snapped into slave bracelets. I was then lifted to a man's shoulder and, my head held to the rear, as a slave is often carried, I was carried upstairs.

CHAPTER TWENTY-TWO

At the head of the stairs, he turned right, kicking open the door of the sleeping chamber.

He set me to one side, my back against the wall, by the door. I sat there, my knees drawn up. Where was my master? I twisted my head in the hood, I felt the bit, so tight, in my mouth. I pulled a little at the slave bracelets that confined my hands behind my back.

How foolish it is to do that, but how can one help oneself?

I heard him opening the chests, rummaging through their contents, casting articles about the room. I did not know for what he might be looking. I heard him move my slave mat, kept at the foot of my master's couch, perhaps lifting and turning it over. Surely nothing was concealed within it. He tapped the walls, and floor, here and there. A blade was then rending cushions. At last, I heard him draw the furs from my master's couch, lift and shake them, and then cast them down, to the floor at the end of the couch. I felt one of the furs fall across my foot, and I drew back my foot, quickly.

The room was then still.

I sensed him standing near me, perhaps looking about the room.

I do not think his search, if search it was, had been successful.

Might he not then be angry?

I knew a slave whip hung on its peg, on the far wall.

I suspected this was not a common thief.

Where was my master?

He took my right arm, and drew me away from the wall, and I lay on my side, I thought, across the portal.

He tested the floor, and wall, where I had been sitting, and then, apparently, stood up, once more.

I lay very still.

"It is not here, of course," he said, "no parchment, no small scroll, no slip of paper, no tiny note, coded or not. No street, no domicile. No clue. But I did not expect to find it here. But one looks. One might be dealing with fools. Why should it be here? How could it be here? How would he, one such as he, know what needs to be known?"

I understood nothing of what he said.

"Yes," he said, "I am sure it is as he claimed, so insistently, that he did not know, and, I suspect, another does not know either, as he claimed, but, concealed within the other, hidden within the other, is the key to he who truly knows."

To me this discourse was unintelligible. What was to be known? Who would know it? Who was this "other" who knew nothing? How could one who knew nothing, who suspected nothing, who understood nothing, be the key to what must be known? And what was it that must be known, and why must it be known?

I felt myself lifted in powerful arms, and then, lightly, cast down amongst a plethora of rich furs, at the foot of the couch, those which had been removed from the couch. I was half sunk in the furs, almost lost in them. I had never been permitted to recline on such furs, though I had often cared for them, and arranged them on the surface of my master's couch. Many slaves are limited to their mat; other slaves are used on the furs, but the furs are commonly placed on the floor, at the foot of the master's couch. And some slaves are permitted on the surface of the couch itself, prized slaves, favored slaves, but, even in the case of such a slave, usually the neck, or at least one ankle, commonly the left ankle, is fastened to a slave ring. The slave is not to be confused with a free companion. The free companion, incidentally, as it has been explained to me, to protect her modesty, and make clear the difference between herself and a slave, is touched, if touched, only beneath the covers, she lightly robed, and in a dark room. Too, to preserve her virtue, she is to be dealt with succinctly, this to avoid prolonging any possible embarrassment or humiliation. This is quite different from the slave. The beauty of the slave, regardless of her possible wishes, should she dare to have them, is fully at the disposal of the master. She belongs to the master, and few masters fail, in the light of a love lamp, to relish her least expression, her tiniest movement, her smallest cry. What master would deny himself the wholeness of his property, the sight of her, the feel of her, the grasp of her, the sound of her, the intelligence of her, the emotions of her? Too, although she may be put to use briefly and abruptly, whenever and however the master wishes, as she is a slave, it is not unusual for him to sport with her, to amuse himself with her, to attend to her, intimately and patiently, for Ahn at a time. She is, after all, a slave. It will be done with her as the master might please. Let her moan, and sweat, and beg, in her chains. Doubtless the master will return to her, anon, as he is inclined.

I sensed him standing near me, perhaps regarding me.

"You understand gag signals, do you not?" he inquired.

I made a tiny noise, whimpering once. One such sound means "Yes," and two such sounds signifies "No."

One is taught such things in the pens, or a training house.

"You are a barbarian, are you not?" he said.

I whimpered once.

"It is easy to see why you were picked up for the collar," he said.

I was silent.

"Barbarians are hot," he said. "They sell well. They are grateful to be at the feet of true men."

I would not have dared speak, even had it been possible.

I supposed I was "hot," pathetically, helplessly hot. I had been given no choice. Gorean men had made me so. They like their slaves so. But I did not object. How glorious it was, to be a vital needful woman. How wonderfully liberated we were, so alive and needful, in our collars!

"Why do the foolish men of your dismal orb," he asked, "not tear away the garments of their women, hurl them to their feet, put them in collars, and teach them they are women?"

Hooded and braceleted, I lay supine, deep in the furs, on the floor, at the foot of the couch. The securing of a woman commonly has its effect on both the man and the woman, arousing both. I held myself very still. I tried not to feel. I knew that my slightest movement might precipitate my usage. And I feared that I, even hooded and bitted, to his amusement, would immediately, uncontrollably, spasm in my yielding.

How helpless we are!

How pathetic to be a mere slave, and how glorious!

"Earth woman, slave," he sneered.

I whimpered twice, frightened, weakly.

"True," he said, "you are no longer an Earth woman. You are now only a Gorean slave girl."

I whimpered once.

No longer was I a woman of Earth. I was now only a Gorean slave girl.

"I am sure," he said, "you are she whom I have long sought."

I did not see how this was possible. Why should one seek me, rather than any other possibly comely slave?

"You are Phyllis, are you not?" he asked.

I quickly whimpered twice, frightened. I was not Phyllis, but Lita.

"But your first slave name was 'Phyllis'," he said, "and you have frequently been named 'Phyllis'."

I whimpered once. I had to do this. I did not know what he knew, and I was a slave, and a slave, not being a free woman, is not permitted to lie.

"Good," he said. "You are now Phyllis, once more."

I squirmed in the furs. Then I desisted, quickly, frightened. I think that being named excited me. Such power men have! Was I now, again, "Phyllis," so simply? Why had I moved? Had I wished subconsciously, to arouse him? What, then, did this say about me? Such movements, I knew, those of a helpless slave, even those of a free woman, are likely to have their effect on males. Did he own me? Did he think he owned me? What authority had he to name me?

"Are you Phyllis?" he asked.

I whimpered once. Surely this was the safest thing to do. Too, perhaps I was now, again, Phyllis. How would I know?

"We are going to have a chat," he said. "But first there is something to get over, something that will make clear to you the nature of our relationship."

I sensed him crouch beside me.

"It is important that we understand one another," he said.

I tried to shrink deeper in the furs.

I could not see in the hood. I could not speak.

The tunic was torn away.

I felt my ankles grasped, each seized in a strong hand. My legs were then widely parted.

"Prepare yourself for being used as what you are, a slave," he said.

Frightened, I whimpered, once.

CHAPTER TWENTY-THREE

————————

I was knelt on the floor, at the foot of the couch, facing the couch. He was behind me. The hood was unbuckled, and lifted away. "You are not to look back," he said. I blinked against the light, little as it was, from the lamp. I blinked, again, and shook my head, loosening my hair. It must have been two or three Ahn before dawn. The locking bands of the slave bit were then unsnapped, from behind my neck, and the device was removed from my mouth.

How good it was to be rid of that effective, stern impediment, which renders a slave so helpless. How helpless a woman is when she cannot speak. How a girl's slavery is impressed upon her, when she may not speak. Men do not always care to hear a woman speak, and, if she is a slave, she may be silenced, and perfectly silenced, by as little as a word, a frown. Consider the tumult within her when she desires to speak, and is not permitted to do so. She is, of course, a mere slave. How different with the free woman, who may speak if, and when, and in whatever manner she might wish.

I did not speak, of course. I had not been addressed. Too, I feared to request permission to speak. I did not know the name, the nature, the disposition, the intent, the caste, the Home Stone, anything about my captor. I did not know where my Master might be, nor if he were still my master.

"You are a hot one, as many barbarians," he said, "you pathetic, miserable, neck-ringed tarsk."

I knelt, naked, facing the couch, my hands braceleted behind my back, he behind me.

"You respond helplessly," he said. "It seems you cannot help yourself."

"No," I said. My slave fires had been ignited.

"I think we will get along very well," he said.

"May I speak?" I asked.

"Later, perhaps," he said. "Now you will listen to me, and answer whatever questions may be put to you."

"Yes, Master," I said.

"You look well," he said, "kneeling as you are, naked, your hands braceleted behind you."

"Thank you, Master," I said.

"Still," he said, "I think you should kneel properly."

"'Properly'?" I said.

"Spread your knees," he said.

"That is the position of the pleasure slave," I said.

"Not every pleasure slave is a gold-tarsk beauty," he said. "Assume the position."

"Yes, Master," I said.

I was now, I gathered, a pleasure slave. How far I was, from the receptionist's desk, from the office, from the firm, from the building, from my former world!

"According to records," he said, "to which I was made privy, albeit somewhat reluctantly, you were, on the slave world, named Phyllis Rodgers."

"On the world, Earth, yes, Master," I said.

"Your first master," he said, "was Kurik, of Victoria, of the caste of Slavers."

"Yes, Master," I said.

"He rid himself of you," he said.

"I was sold," I said.

"Doubtless you bear him ill will," he said.

"No, Master," I said. "I think I displeased him on my former world, and this contributed to his decision to bring me to the markets of Gor. In any event, he saw me as a slave, and evaluated me accordingly. At that time, I knew nothing of masters and slaves, nor that he was a master, and I a slave."

"He was scouting you?"

"I think so," I said.

"And you did not treat him well?"

"I did not know that he was a master, and I was a slave," I said.

"And you think your small contretemps brought you to the collar?"

"I suspect so," I said.

"Nonsense," he said. "You are clearly choice collar-meat. Even had you been the most pleasant and least offensive of prospects, you would have been destined to feel the sawdust of the slave block beneath your bared feet and hear the screams of excited, bidding men."

"Yes, Master," I said.

I thought of my friend, Paula.

"That you might have been a bit annoying, or unpleasant," he said, "would do no more than add a welcome piquant touch to the act of marking you down for shipment. Men enjoy seeing such women naked, and at their feet, in the chains of slaves."

"Any woman," I said, "Master."

"Of course," he said. "It is where you belong."

"Yes, Master," I said.

"How you must hate Kurik of Victoria," he said.

"No, Master," I said.

"He brought you to the collar," he said.

"Yes, Master," I said.

"You would rejoice to see him come to ruin," he said.

"No, Master," I said. I recalled being in his arms, and crying out my love for him.

"I do not understand," he said.

"I belong in the collar," I said. "On my former world I was not in a collar, and though I knew, somehow, I belonged in a collar, I would have denied that I belonged in one. On Gor I am in a collar, know that I belong in one, and admit, and rejoice, in the fact, that I belong in one, and that I am in one."

"You are a slave."

"Yes, Master."

"It is hard to understand your former world," he said. "Are not women women, and men men?"

"Doubtless," I said, "but it is not to be admitted."

"Why?" he asked.

"I do not know," I said.

"It is hard to understand the betrayal of nature, and the denial of blood," he said.

"There are those who profit from the misery and deprivation of others," I said. "Causing pain to the many can be a path to power for the few."

"Surely there are some who see through this pathology," he said.

"Doubtless," I said, "but it can be hazardous to notice such things, and even more hazardous to speak of them."

"I gather then," he said, "if you are candid with me, which I trust you are, you do not hate, abominate, and loathe Kurik of Victoria."

"No, Master," I said.

"He sold you."

"I gather I was a poor slave, that he did not want me."

"Do you think you could recognize Kurik, of Victoria, should you see him again?"

"Assuredly, Master," I said.

"I suspected," he said, "that you hated Kurik of Victoria, and thus that I could most easily have my will with you did I pretend enmity to that noble, prized fellow, that most fortunate fellow, whom I gladly seek."

"I do not understand," I said.

"That you would recognize him, and, in your hatred, would zealously seek him out, and report to me your success, that I might proceed with my mission."

"I do not hate him," I said.

"Excellent," he said. "My work is then lighter, and more agreeable, given the welcome discarding of the burden of prevarication."

"Master?" I said.

"Now," he said, "I may manifest the benignity of my quest."

"I know nothing of this," I said, looking at the foot of the couch. "I am only a slave."

"You do not bear Kurik of Victoria ill will?" he asked.

"No, Master," I said.

"Would you like to see him profit, wax important, and come into great wealth?" he asked.

"I would be pleased," I said, "if I might, in some small way, further such an end."

"You would do your best to contribute to the welfare and good fortune of Kurik of Victoria?" he asked.

"Yes, Master," I said, uneasily.

"Your wrists look well, braceleted," he said.

"Thank you, Master," I said.

"I act on behalf of my principal," he said. "He seeks Kurik of Victoria, to tender him position, riches, and power."

"Kurik of Victoria is then most fortunate," I said.

"On behalf of my principal, it is incumbent upon me to contact Kurik of Victoria."

"Master does not know him?" I asked.

"I have never, to my knowledge, seen him," he said.

"Surely he may be traced through the caste of Slavers," I said.

"There are elements in the caste of Slavers," he said, "bands that are secret, that proceed covertly, even having recourse to vehicles forbidden by the laws of Priest-Kings."

"I know nothing of Priest-Kings," I said.

"Indeed," he said, "it is rumored that certain elements of the Slavers, and others, have dealings with the enemies of Priest-Kings."

"I am ignorant of such things," I whispered.

"You do not think you were brought to Gor in a wagon or cart, surely," he said.

"No, Master," I said.

"Such vehicles, which tread the skies themselves, are forbidden to the men of Gor by the denizens of the Sardar, the Priest-Kings," he said.

"I know little of such things," I said. I did not even know if there were Priest-Kings.

"My charge," he said, "is to make contact with Kurik of Victoria, to see that he receives what he deserves."

"And I could identify him for you," I said.

"Yes," he said. "I have little more to go on than a description, which might fit a thousand men."

"Surely," I said, "there must be many who could do this as well as I."

"Doubtless," he said. "Who are they, where are they, how may I find them?"

"I am only a slave," I said.

"So much the better," he said. "I need a human sleen, who can be owned, and controlled, and leashed, so to speak, who can abet my work for months, if necessary, who fears not to be pleasing, who can be disposed of instantly. A slave is ideal for my purposes."

"There are many slaves," I said.

"Slaves can be difficult to trace through the markets," he said. "Consider the difficulty I have had in locating just one, you. He brought you to the collar. He was your first master. Who would better serve my benign purpose?"

"Your purpose is benign?" I said.

"Of course," he said.

"May I inquire the name of your principal," I said, "the source of the projected emoluments, and the deserts you plan to bestow on my former master, the noble Kurik of Victoria?"

"*Ela*," he said, "such matters are confidential."

"Curiosity," I said, "is not becoming in a kajira."

"I fear so," he said.

"And if I should be reluctant?" I asked.

"You will not be," he said, "for you wish the best for our dear Kurik of Victoria."

"But, even so," I said.

"You will obey, of course," he said, "regardless, and, in your service, you will strive to be as diligent, efficient, and pleasing as possible, for you are not a free woman, but what you are, a fearful, collared beast, a slave."

"What," I asked, "if I should fail?"

"Then," he said, "I will cut your throat."

A silence ensued.

"Does my master, Tullius Quintus, live?" I asked.

"That is not his name," he said.

"There is another name on my collar," I said.

"Neither would that be his name," he said. "He is Arnold, a renegade from Harfax, a vagrant who haunted the wharves of Brundisium. It was there that he acquired information pertinent to the interests of my principal."

"It had to do with Kurik of Victoria?" I said.

"With some venture in which he was involved," he said.

"A venture?" I said.

"Kurik of Victoria," he said, "is the key to the venture, and you are the key to Kurik of Victoria."

"My master," I said, "he whom I knew as Tullius Quintus, of Ar, I fear, wished to sell me to some bidder, that I might be used to locate Kurik of Victoria."

"He realized you were sought," he said, "relentlessly, and, accordingly, anticipated that matters of moment were afoot, and, if he held you, he might realize from some source a handsome profit, one well beyond your likely market value."

"I see," I said.

"He trolled," he said, "casting his lines about, a word here, a word there, in the taverns, in the markets, words that would be meaningless to most, stray sounds, but telling to he who might have an ear for the name 'Phyllis', for the name 'Kurik of Victoria'."

"It was you who sought me," I said.

"Yes," he said, "and perhaps others."

"Many, it seemed, feared to keep me," I said.

"It is dangerous to hold a slave," he said, "who would be purchased with steel."

"My master," I said, "wanted gold."

"And would conceal you until this gold was forthcoming," he said.

"He courted danger," I said.

"He gambled," he said, "neither wisely nor well."

"Did he know you sought me?" I asked.

"He suspected one such as I would do so," he said, "but hoped nonetheless to purse gold before letting you go."

"Were you once in Market of Semris?" I asked.

"Possibly," he said.

"So I was purchased?" I said, shuddering, keeping my eyes forward.

"Yes, kajira," he said.

"With gold?" I said.

"With steel," he said.

"Does he live?" I asked.

"I was not paid to kill him, so he lives," he said.

"I do not see how I can help you," I said. "I can recognize Kurik of Victoria, surely, but I have no idea as to his whereabouts. I gather he is not in Victoria. Might he not be in a hundred cities, a thousand towns or villages?"

"He is in Brundisium, now, or will be shortly," he said. "I am sure of it. My sources inform me that it is to Kurik of Victoria, in Brundisium, that the package is to be delivered, Brundisium, a great port, familiar with exotic cargos, unusual birds, mighty serpents, surprising beasts, a port where such cargos are not likely to elicit undue attention. It must be intercepted."

"From whence derives this cargo," I asked, "that is to appear in Brundisium?" Brundisium was Gor's greatest port on the continent. Once, I had heard, a large fleet, an invasion fleet, made landfall there, from the island Ubarates of Cos and Tyros. I knew little about such matters.

"Have you heard of dark wars, of secret wars, wars challenging the reign of Priest-Kings themselves, wars for viable spheres, for Gor itself? Have you heard of Kurii, of Steel Worlds?"

"No, Master," I said.

"The cargo," he said, "derives from a Steel World."

"A Steel World?" I said.

"A spherical, enclosed world, one of several concealed within the Sea of Stones," he said.

This made little sense to me.

"What cargo?" I asked.

"A gift," he said, "but a gift we intend to acquire, a gift for which we have our own purpose."

"And you will discover, and obtain, this gift through the offices of Kurik of Victoria?"

"Yes," he said.

"To whom your principal is to accord position, riches, and power."

"Yes," he said.

"Your principal is generous," I said. "Kurik of Victoria is fortunate."

"And thus your cooperation," he said, "given your hope to do well by Kurik of Victoria, is well assured."

"Am I yours?" I asked.

"Yes," he said.

"I was purchased with steel," I said.

"Yes," he said.

"May I inquire the name of my master?" I asked.

"Tyrtaios," he said.

"May I look upon my master?" I asked.

I heard him rise, behind me, and then he came about, and stood near me. I lifted my head, and looked upward.

"What is wrong?" he said.

"Nothing, Master," I whispered.

"You are frightened," he said.

"Forgive me, Master," I said.

"It is well for a slave to fear her master," he said.

"Yes, Master," I said.

"For she is subject to his whip," he said.

"Yes, Master," I said, putting down my head.

I had seen this man before, this large-handed, lean, hard man, on the wharf at Victoria, from my cage, he passing by, feral, wary and taciturn, men withdrawing from his path. He had inquired of my dealer the location of the tavern of Tasdron. To be sure, he was now dressed differently, rather nondescriptively, in a tan, pocketed work tunic. He wore, as well, a wide, double-buckled belt, from which a dagger, in its sheath, was suspended, and ankle-high, cord-laced street sandals. About his throat was a laborer's brown sweat scarf, which might be raised about the face, to protect one from dust, or conceal the features. When I had seen him before, that morning in Victoria, he had been clad differently, more somberly, in a sable tunic, a cape, high, black, bootlike sandals. He had been armed, a short sword in its scabbard slung from the left shoulder, rather than across the body. In his left arm, cradled, had been a black helmet. In his appearance there had been a particular oddity that I recalled well. I took it to be a caste mark, or festive design. In black, painted or inked in place, small and delicate, on his forehead, was the image of an unsheathed dagger. Certainly now there was no sign of such a design or device on his forehead.

Four men, I recalled, had been killed in the tavern of Tasdron.

Perhaps they had displeased this man. Perhaps they had been uncooperative.

"You are trembling," he said.

"Forgive me, Master," I said.

He reached down, amidst the furs on which I knelt, and lifted up the collar and chain, it fastened to the slave ring set in the foot of the couch.

"Master?" I said.

The collar was snapped about my throat. I was thus fastened to the couch.

"You may recline," he said.

I lay on my side, as I had been trained, my knees drawn up, my toes pointed, to shape the calves.

"The flight to Brundisium is long," he said. "We depart tonight, after dark."

"After dark?" I said.

"Yes," he said.

"That will be several Ahn," I said. "It is not yet dawn."

"I am sure we will find ways to pass the time," he said.

"Yes, Master," I said.

CHAPTER TWENTY-FOUR

You need not look," said Tyrtaios, lounging on the supper couch, on one elbow, looking to the circle of sand about which were arranged the tables. I was kneeling beside the couch. There was a chain on my neck; it was fastened to a ring fixed in the stone floor.

Several days ago, my master and I had left Ar. I suspect he had disguised himself in yet another fashion. Certainly a common laborer would not be likely to be able to hire a tarn rider and tarn, and tarn basket, for a journey as far as Brundisium. I do not know how he had then attired himself in Ar, nor what identity he might have assumed, though one supposes it might have been of the Merchants, the richest caste. I would not be recognized either, for, in our peregrination afoot to the tarn cot, I had been placed in a body hood, in which, indeed, I would spend much of the journey. The body hood is somewhat reminiscent of the common slave sack, if it were half its size, and open at the bottom. It slips over the head, and comes down to the waist. It is fastened on the slave my means of a heavy belt that is anchored in the back, and drawn up snugly between the slave's legs, and then buckled shut in front. In this arrangement the slave cannot see, as she is hooded, and she is helpless, as her arms are confined. She can walk, of course, and there is a leash ring on the hood, so that she may be leashed and led by the leash, should her master wish to do so. Normally she is freed of the body hood to be fed and watered, and such, but there is a laced flap near the mouth, that may be opened, and laced shut, if one wishes, through which she may be fed and watered. Happily I was not gagged, or put into a slave bit. That was not necessary, of course, for I was not given permission to speak. I had been silenced, as it is said, by the master's will. On the journey itself, my master wore nondescript garments, suggestive of no caste in particular. Our rider, or driver, he on tarnback, proved discreet. That I was given to him for his pleasure several times perhaps contributed to his discretion. Some tarns, incidentally, bearing tarn baskets, are controlled from the basket itself. Indeed, as I understand it, this is the more common arrangement.

Happily, I was later given a standing permission to speak, though I seldom dared to use it. I muchly feared my master, Tyrtaios, whom I little understood. Such a standing permission is commonly granted to slaves. Needless to say, it may be rescinded or granted anew, as the master might wish.

I do not know where, for the body hood, in the vicinity of Brundisium, that the tarn rider brought his immense, broad-winged beast to earth, but I think it must have been near the coast, probably south of the port, as we had come from Ar, for I heard gulls and smelled Thassa, the sea. I was knelt on the wood of the platform. I heard coins shaken from a wallet. Shortly thereafter I heard the ascent of the dangling mounting ladder, the sound of restless talons on wood, and the snap of wings. I could sense the rush of the stirred, smitten air about me, tearing at the hood. Then it was quiet.

"Up, girl," I was told, and I struggled to my feet.

I then heard the click of the leash lock, it secured about the leading ring on my hood.

"The wagon," he said, "will be closed."

"Then may I not, master," I asked, "be relieved of the hood?"

"No," he said.

The hood would be removed only when we reached our destination, and we were within the walls, within the walls of what place I did not know.

The wagon ride, it was a fee wagon, took more than an Ahn. I sat, hooded, on the wood, my back against the side of the wagon bed. The road, rutted and pitted, was better graded as it neared the city, and, later, within the city, the metal-rimmed wheels would rattle over cobble stones. My master sat on the wagon bench, beside the driver. He conversed with him, pleasantly, which, I guessed, was an aspect of his disguise. Putting my head back, in the hood, I could feel canvas behind my head. Had I not been hooded, as I was alone in the wagon, I think I could not have resisted trying to peep beneath the canvas, to see where we might be. After the better part of the Ahn, we had doubtless entered one of the gates of Brundisium, as I then heard the cries of vendors, the rolling of wheels, the snorting of draft beasts, the sounds of men, music, a kalika, from somewhere. I also heard the sound of a lash. The street perhaps led past a shelf market. I myself had never felt the slave lash, even in the house of training. I was no stranger, however, to the admonitions of the supple switch. It was sufficiently unpleasant, and I would do my best to escape its attentions.

"We disembark," called my master back to me.

I was lifted from the wagon and set on flat stones. The driver received his coin, and the wagon rolled away.

My master then exerted a bit of pressure on the leash ring, and I followed him. We walked for seven or eight Ehn. Surely the wagon could have approached our destination more closely, but, it seems, it had not, or did not. It was only later that I realized that my master may not have cared to have the driver know our destination, nor the nature of the fellow with whom he had so pleasantly shared the wagon bench. Indeed, perhaps the driver would not have cared to approach our destination.

"We are here," said my master.

I heard a rattle of chains and the striking of some heavy object, wooden, I think descending, on stones. Then, too, I heard the noises of more chains and the creaking of iron, and a ratcheting sound. Oddly, the normal noises of the city seemed subdued, or absent, in this locale. I followed on the leash. I heard words spoken, but could not make them out.

Later I was unhooded.

The room was muchly barren, save for some kennels at one wall. They were empty. I, on all fours, was entered into one of these kennels, and the gate was padlocked shut.

"You will be given a new tunic and a new collar," he said.

He then left.

I lay down, curled, in the kennel.

I think I must have slept, but I awakened rather abruptly. I strained my hearing. Far off I thought I heard the sounds of men, shouts, and the striking of metal on metal, often quick, and sharp, and sometimes so rapidly I could not distinguish the sounds. Then I was tired, and again slept.

After a time there was a tapping on the kennel gate, and I rose to my knees, and put my head down, to the floor of the kennel, the palms of my hands beside my head, in first obeisance position.

"Emerge," said my master, opening the gate, "and remain on all fours, head down."

He carried a bit of cloth, a tiny scrap of black silk, and something wrapped within the silk. He put these things down, behind me, and he stood, too, a bit behind me and to the side. Accordingly, I could not well follow what he was doing.

Then a circlet was placed about my neck. I heard the snap, and realized I wore a new collar.

My original collar was still on my neck.

"Arnold of Harfax," he said, "kindly delivered to me, upon my request, the key to your collar."

My earlier collar was then removed, and cast aside. I heard it clatter on the stones. He then adjusted the new collar, which I could not see. It fitted nicely, closely. Such collars cannot be slipped.

He then came about, before me.

"Stand up, kajira," he said, "and strip."

I swiftly removed the tunic, and handed it to him. As one receives clothing, if one receives it, at the hand of the master, so, too, commonly, one returns it to the hand of the master. It is thus clear that clothing, if it is permitted, is at the discretion of the master.

I was then regarded, in my new collar.

I put my head down. It seems I had not lost my shyness from Earth. Yet, too, such a posture, betokening humility, and deference, is suitable for a slave.

But I had noted, furtively, his regard, before lowering my head. I do not think he was displeased.

Might I not, I wondered, on this world, have become more beautiful? How a woman changes in the collar! How she becomes so much more a woman, her natural being, in her rightful place.

What alternative has she?

But I wanted no alternative, not with such men. And I was pleased that I would be granted none.

How, at last, one can be what one is, oneself!

"Here," he said.

He had reached down and picked up the bit of black silk, from the floor of the chamber.

He tossed it against my body, and I clutched it.

"Put it on, Phyllis," he said.

I looked at him.

"Yes," he said. "We will keep that name, at least for the time."

As the slave is an animal, she may be named as the master pleases, as any other animal.

"Yes, Master," I said.

"What is your name, slave?" he said.

"'Phyllis, Master," I said, well apprised of the name that had been put on me.

I was Phyllis.

It was the will of the master.

I looked down at the tiny bit of silk in my hands.

"What is it?" I asked.

"A tunic," he said. "Put it on. I would see it on you."

I slipped it over my head, and tried to pull down the hems at the side.

"It is short, so little, almost nothing, such fine silk," I said. "It is diaphanous. I can be seen through it."

"We like our girls so clad," he said, "when we permit them clothing."

I did not know who "we" were. I did not understand where I was. Surely the common slave tunic, often of rep-cloth, was short enough, and well identified its occupant as a slave. At least it was usually of rep-cloth, or of some other cloth, such as the wool of the bounding hurt, and, even when of silk, it was seldom diaphanous. One could well imagine the reaction of free women to that! In the latter aspect, diaphanous, it was rather like the yellow or red dancing silk in which the tavern dancers swirled amidst their veils, their shimmering jewelries, often to the sparkle of finger cymbals.

"Outside this house, most often," he said, "you will wear a different tunic, and a different collar."

"I am pleased," I said, "but why, Master, a different collar?"

"Naive barbarian," he said.

"I do not know what my collar looks like," I said, "nor what is on it, if anything."

"Follow me," he said.

I followed him from the room, to a nearby room, down a lamp-lit hall. In this room there was a mirror, and I regarded myself in it.

How revealed I was in that tunic!

"You will be found acceptable," he said. "Indeed, you will fit in nicely."

"It is a strange collar," I said. "What is on it?"

The light of the lamp reflected from the collar.

"It is a black-enameled collar," he said. "There is nothing on it. The collar is enough. It would be recognized, and you would be returned to this house by guardsmen or others, and left bound, helpless, by the drawbridge and gate."

"There would be no reward for my return?"

"To return you would be less hazardous than failing to do so," he said.

"Surely at least some copper tarsks," I said, "perhaps a silver tarsk, perhaps, for a better slave, a piece of gold?"

"Some pay in copper," he said. "Some pay in silver, some in gold. Some pay in steel."

"When I awakened, in the kennel," I said, "I thought I heard the shouts of men, the ringing, far off, of metal on metal."

"You did," he said. "It was the sound of men engaged in the practice of arms."

"There are warriors here," I said, "guardsmen?"

"In a way," he said.

"What house is this?" I asked. "Where am I?"

"You are in the Black Court of Brundisium," he said.

"I do not understand," I said.

"It is not necessary that you do," he said.

CHAPTER TWENTY-FIVE

Y ou need not look," said Tyrtaios, lounging on the supper couch, on one elbow, looking to the circle of sand about which were arranged the tables. I was kneeling beside the couch. There was a chain on my neck; it was fastened to a ring fixed in the stone floor.

Two men, stripped to the loins, dagger in hand, were cautiously circling one another on the sand.

I wore a black tunic, and a black collar.

Two slaves, similarly clad and collared, but free of impediments, both exquisite, were serving the tables. Their hair was long. The hair of slaves is often long. Much can be done with it, in the furs, to please masters. Some dozen or so men, in black dinner robes, were reclining on the supper couches; some attending to the circle of sand, others differently occupied, chatting, sipping ka-la-na, sampling assorted viands proffered by the serving slaves.

The men at the tables, those attentive, those bemused, those bored, those testing and savoring beverages and dishes, wore dark chaplets upon their brow, these woven from somber dark leaves, muchly different from the tangles of aromatic blossoms worn by many Goreans at festive suppers. There was little of brightness or color in this place. It was muchly different from the bold and striking colors that, in bold display, characterize so many Gorean rooms, halls, and domiciles.

"It is dark, Master," I whispered.

He had spoken to me.

"There is the lamp," he said.

"So little light, for so large a place?" I said.

"Darkness is not to be feared," he said. "Let others fear it. For he who is at ease in the darkness, in the dusk, in the stillness before the dawn, who is patient, who waits, it is a friend, a shield, an abetment to one's work. Who knows what lurks in the darkness, what might emerge from the night? Too, skills and strengths honed in, and augmented under, adverse conditions prepare one well for the tests of the common day. Why do you think runners train in heavy sand, and hurlers of the stone use stones twice in weight to those they will cast in the games? Why do you think that some, in training beasts, tharlarion, tarns, and slaves, weight saddles, and such things?"

"This is a place of police," I said, "a barrack of soldiers?"

A fellow at a nearby table laughed, a short, unpleasant sound.

"Many warriors," I said, "wear the scarlet of their caste."

"That is true," said Tyrtaios. "I have stained my blade with the blood of several."

"It is dangerous to deal with them," said a fellow at a table.

"Openly, to be sure," said another fellow, peeling the rind from a larma.

"Better a flighted quarrel in the darkness, a tethered tarn at hand, awaiting one's departure," said another.

"I favor the poisoned Anango dart," said another.

"I favor," said Tyrtaios, "the confrontation, the sword."

"*Ela*, dear fellow," said a man, "I fear the codes of your betrayed caste yet linger."

"Rather," said Tyrtaios, "one is unwilling to allow certain skills to languish."

There was a sudden cry of pain, short, and ugly, from the sand, and I looked about, wildly, suddenly, startled, back to the sand, and then turned away, and put down my head, covering my eyes with my hands.

"Light the torches, the lamps," said a fellow from a table across the sand. He wore the somber robes and dark chaplet of the others but seemed more dour, more formidable, more terrible, surely in a way the others did not. I had seen him enter the room, and the others, including my master, Tyrtaios, had stood, acknowledging his presence, and did not resume their positions until he had taken his place on his couch, a higher couch than the others. I gathered his presence was not usual in this place, but that he was a guest of sorts, perhaps a visitor to these precincts. In entering, he had passed closely to me, so closely that his somber robe had touched me, and I had drawn back, chilled. He stopped, stood near me, and looked down at me. I looked away, quickly, putting my head down. His skin seemed unusual, grayish, his eyes were as unexpressive as glass. He was a large man, and moved easily. The head, a large head, had moved a little, gently swaying, as he had entered, scanning the room. It reminded me, oddly, of the movement of another form of life, the movement of the head of a snake.

Before he had taken his position, one of the men had said, "We are honored that you appear in our court."

"We are honored," had then said the others, including my master. Shortly after that the two men with daggers had entered the circle of sand. Both had bowed to the strange figure, and then withdrawn to opposite sides of the circle of sand.

Slaves, the two who were serving the supper, and some others, similarly lovely, similarly long-haired, similarly clad and collared, hastened to kindle torches and lamps, and, shortly, the room was well lit.

The body of one of the two men who had trod the now-reddened sand was dragged away.

The other approached the high couch and knelt before it, head down.

"Bring him a robe, a supper robe, and a chaplet," said he on the high couch.

Slaves soon adorned the man.

"Come, join me on the high couch," invited he on the high couch.

This invitation was greeted with a murmur of surprise by several of those assembled. I gathered that this sort of recognition was unusual in this place.

The fellow from the sand, startled, awed, and elated, had soon ascended the high couch, to join the dark figure reclining there, as though enthroned.

"Give me the dagger," said the imposing figure on the high couch.

The dagger was instantly surrendered to him.

He of the high couch then reached to the head of the fellow and, by the hair, pulled him to the knife, which was thrust through the supper robe, to the heart.

"You were clumsy," said he of the high couch.

The eyes of the fellow were wide, and then empty, and he expired without a sound, and was thrust from the supper table to the sand. I saw the blood, the staining of the rent garment, the dark chaplet fallen to the sand. The body was removed.

"Master," I whispered, in horror, to Tyrtaios.

"The kill is to be clean," said Tyrtaios. "We are not butchers."

"I had thought he would have reached the fourth step," said a man.

"No," said another.

"Master," I said.

"Yes?" he said.

"This place," I said, "is the Black Court of Brundisium."

"Yes," he said.

"But what," I asked, "is the Black Court of Brundisium?"

"You are, indeed, a naive barbarian," he said.

"Please, Master," I said.

"It is little different from other black courts," he said.

"Master," I begged, looking up, the chain on my neck.

"This is a chapter house," he said, "of the black caste, the caste of Assassins."

CHAPTER TWENTY-SIX

———————————

It may be useful to speak briefly of the nature of a black court.

As you have doubtless surmised, there is, and remains, much on this unusual, perilous, lovely world of which I am unaware, or, at least, too little informed.

A black court, I gather, is named for the color of the caste of Assassins, which is black. The caste is sometimes spoken of, when men dare to speak of it, as the black caste, or the sable caste. In many Gorean cities it is unwelcome, even outlawed. For example, it is outlawed in Ar and in Market of Semris. Its outlawry in Ar, I gather, followed an unsuccessful attempt by an army led by Pa-Kur, a high Assassin, to seize that great city, the largest, richest, and most populous in Gor's northern hemisphere. The city, it seems, was in disarray, and its Ubar challenged, following the temporary loss of its Home Stone, purloined by an unidentified tarnsman during the revels of the Planting Feast. Supposedly instrumental in the defeat of Pa-Kur and the restoration of the Ubar of the city to power was a figure known in the songs as Tarl of Bristol, which figure, as many such figures recounted in such songs, is presumably legendary. The hostile army, in some of the scrolls, is spoken of as the Horde of Pa-Kur, which disparaging epithet occurs in common parlance, doubtless reflecting the truism that history is likely to reflect the views of the victors. The outlawry of the caste of Assassins in Market of Semris may have been an independent act, or may have followed the example of Ar. In any event, it seems that "black courts" exist in a number of cities, though surely not all, either openly, as in Brundisium, or, one supposes, sometimes, where outlawed, secretly.

The existence of a "black caste," on a world such as Gor, is not as surprising, inexplicable, or unconscionable, as it might seem. Indeed, it is highly likely that, long ago, in the beginning, the caste was formed to supply a need, or perform a role within society that was perceived as being not only fully justified, but desirable. On Gor there are no, or few, "nations" in the sense that one of my former world would be likely to think of as nations. Similarly there is no international law. Law, for most practical purposes, reaches no further than the swords of a given polity. The common Gorean polity is the town, village, or city, and whatever territory about the polity to which it can extend its hegemony. In this sense, polities may appear on maps but not borders. The territory controlled by a polity is likely, historically, to wax and wane with the fortunes of the polity. The nearest things to nations would seem to be the large island Ubarates, such as Tyros and Cos, where the sea forms natural barriers, or borders, so to speak, but even there power seems centered in particular cities, such as Kasra and Jad. A saying I have heard seems germane here, "the laws of Cos march with the spears of Cos." Two further aspects of the Gorean way might also be considered, first, the suspicion and hostility obtaining amongst diverse polities, which militates against cooperation and assistance, and the limits of Gorean law, even within a polity, as Goreans tend to be radically independent and likely to resent the intrusion of others, even a polity, into what are regarded as their own concerns or affairs. For example, vendettas occasionally take place amongst families, in which the polity, and others, respecting the wishes of the participants, decline to intervene.

Given such considerations, and the consequent difficulty, frequently recognized, of obtaining justice, satisfaction, or vengeance, as the case may be, one can well understand the existence of an order of men, itinerant, independent, dedicated, armed, and skilled, for hire. Such men may, for example, pursue a fugitive from city to city with impunity, regardless of caste, warfare, and Home Stone. Few will interfere with the hunting Assassin, sable-clad, dagger on brow, passing amongst them, going quietly about his work. Similarly, few would challenge the wind, or the dark sky from which lightning might strike.

Some Assassins are particular in accepting their commissions, but, clearly, others are not. One might accept a handful of copper tarsks to do justice, at least as he understands it, whereas another, for a purse of gold, might kill an administrator, murder a business rival, or eliminate a competitive legatee. Some rich men pay local black courts not to accept commissions against them.

There seems little doubt that over the years the black courts became less scrupulous in the commissions they accepted. The original image of the elite mercenary, hired to do good and carry right into otherwise inaccessible precincts, supplying a needed service not otherwise available, became transformed into that of the contemporary black caste, an order of skilled, dangerous men particular about little else but their fees.

It might be noted, in passing, that the black caste is jealous of what it regards as its prerogatives. It will seek out and kill other hired killers. It does not favor competition, and wishes to maintain, in effect, its monopoly in that area. It might also be noted, again in passing, that the black caste, as a matter of policy, does not concern itself with members who might be slain while about their work. There is no notion of vengeance or seeking retribution involved. It might be regretted that a fee is lost, but nothing else. One who is slain in his work is regarded as having failed, and, in virtue of this, is denied any further consideration. It will, on the other hand, hunt an individual who might, in its view, have gratuitously slain one of its members.

In my time in the black court I occasionally witnessed the admission of clients who sought the services of the "dark sword." Other clients, by means of messengers, may request a discreet interview with a representative of the caste, in which fees might be negotiated and arrangements made. As is understandable, certain individuals would not wish to be noticed entering the precincts of the court. Slaves were not privy to such interviews, either within or outside the court.

As I suppose is clear, the caste of Assassins is not a typical caste. For example, there were no free women in the black court. Companionship is forbidden to members of the caste. Membership, as with the Warriors, with which caste the Assassins are often compared, is not earned by birth, but by deeds. In the case of the dark caste, however, there is no devotion to the codes of honor, which might spare a disabled foe, which might temper victory, say, with the recognition of opposed valor, no generous companionship of the blade, no brothers in arms. Friendship is frowned upon. Emotion is eschewed. Such things are alleged to weaken the will, to soften resolve, to stay the hand the fraction of an Ihn that might compromise the strike. The Assassin is to be much alone. Like the forest panther, he is commonly a solitary hunter. He is to have no associations, connections, interests, or entanglements that might distract, compromise, or impair his capacity to discharge the requirements of his office, the fulfillment of his commission. His life belongs to the caste. His allegiance is to be undivided. He is to devote himself to his skills, and to his tools, the dagger, the quarrel, the wire noose, the dart, the brewing of poisons, to deception, patience, disguise, and ruthlessness. One applies, one trains, one strives, and one is either accepted or rejected, and the rejected have commonly perished in trials of arms.

The black caste is generally feared, and loathed.

Who then would seek admission to such a despised caste?

Perhaps the feared, and loathed.

But, too, in some, is there not an attraction to dark power, and the gratification of inspiring apprehension?

But admission is not easily purchased. Few are permitted to compete, and of those who are permitted to compete, few live to don the sable tunic. It is not easy to climb the nine steps of blood.

There is no place in the caste, incidentally, for the inept and dull, for thugs, vandals, and bullies, for the naively, simplistically brutal, for the petty, or the merely cruel and greedy, for the refuse of a city's gutters, for those regarded as the unworthy. Few survive to carry the "dark sword."

Doubtless there are reasons why one, perhaps despairing and ruined, might seek entrance into dreaded precincts.

Amongst applicants might be found the dishonored and failed, the disappointed and abandoned, the despised and hated, the hopeless and resigned, the mocked and ridiculed, ones who have fled from Home Stones, who have repudiated codes, perhaps fugitives who seek a sanctuary behind dark walls, possibly seekers of thrills, possibly mercenaries intent on bartering steel for gold, without compunction, perhaps those seeking approval for their pathological instincts that, suitably exercised, will be condoned, even celebrated.

It is hard to say.

Much in the black court is secret. If they have codes, I do not know what they would be, saving perhaps a relentless fidelity to a commission. For example, slaves were not permitted to witness training, not that I would have cared to do so, certainly following the killing I had seen at the banquet, nor attend instructions, even while serving, addressed to the candidates. I have seen the plates of weapons and devices borne to the training chambers, the daggers, the balanced throwing knives, the easily concealed hook knife, the swords, the darts, the loops of wire, the chain garrotes, and, in particular, the crossbow and quarrel, the favored striking weapon of the caste, which may be easily concealed beneath a cloak, and in whose guide a quarrel may wait for Ahn, like the ost, before it strikes.

I was some days in the black court.

My master, for I was not owned by the court, frequently occupied himself in the city, I think in the vicinity of the wharves, presumably waiting for, or searching for, the mysterious shipment that was supposed to arrive at Brundisium, claimedly deriving from a "steel world." I had no idea what might be the contents of this shipment, or its importance, or what it might have to do with me, or with my first master, Kurik, of Victoria.

In the meantime I was kept busy in the court, cleaning, scrubbing, laundering, assisting in the kitchen, and serving at the common meals. The first girl was stern, but fair. She played no favorites. That I was a barbarian did not adversely affect my treatment, as it might easily have done in many situations. I was grateful to her. The slaves are at the disposal of the men, as one would expect, but I, as a private slave, a status envied by my collar-sisters, was reserved to my master. On the other hand, he made little use of me, apparently busying himself, in various disguises, conducting inquiries in the city, attempting to garner useful gossip, or intelligence, at various taverns, and so on. Accordingly, most nights I lay in my kennel, untouched, and, I confess, as a slave, deprived, and miserable. We need the touch of our masters. Men have made us so. We are no longer ours, but theirs.

I will recount an anecdote, or two, which, in their way, might shed some light on the nature of a black court. First, let it be understood that the edifice that houses the black court is not large, but it does have a formidable, menacing aspect. It is like a small fortress in the city, with high, dark walls, with a moat, a drawbridge, and a portcullis, a heavy, vertically barred, reinforced gate that may be raised or lowered by means of a windlass. The court's position is isolated, in a sense, as, even within the city, it occupies an area of unplanted ground on all sides. This area is several yards in width, and, as it is open, it affords no cover to any who might approach the court, and its moat.

"You two," said the first girl, "go to the salt market, at the east gate, to the vendor, Porus, and return with a stone of salt."

"As we are, in the black collar?" asked the other girl.

"I will have it so," said the first girl. "Here is the sack. When it is filled, have its contents weighed carefully."

"Porus switched you, yesterday, did he not?" asked the other girl, amused.

"Perhaps," said the first girl.

"Come along," said the other girl.

I had no idea, of course, of the best route to the east gate.

"Why am I coming along?" I asked her.

"Someone must carry the salt," she said.

"Why not you?" I asked.

"I am not a barbarian," she said.

"I see," I said.

This was the first time, since my arrival at the black court, that I had been allowed outside the court.

I did not think of escape, of course, as I was collared. Tunicked, collared, and marked, there is no escape for the Gorean slave girl. The best she might hope for would be to fall into the hands of a new master, who would know she has fled a former master. How heavy then would be her chains, how cruel the stroke of the lash! Too, the recovered slave girl risks at least a severe beating, but perhaps, as well, a hamstringing, or being disposed of, perhaps being fed to sleen, or being cast, naked and bound, amongst writhing, ravenous leech plants. But I did not even wish to escape, for I had found myself on this perilous, beautiful world. I had learned something on Gor, of which I had been unaware, or, better, not completely or fully aware, on my former world, that I belonged in a slave collar. How thrilled I was to be so reduced, so shamed, so owned! I dare not speak for other women, being a mere slave, but, for me, it was right. I wanted the collar, and belonged in it, and was in it. I loved that it was on my neck, closed and locked. It was there. I could not remove it. I did not wish to remove it. I was a slave.

Let other women scorn me, if they wish.

I loved being a slave.

How glorious to be a property, helpless, and owned by men!

How free I was!

I was a slave.

"Have you money?" I asked.

I had not seen the first girl hand her any money. Too, as far as I could tell, she had no coin, or coins, in her mouth, nor clutched in her hand.

"No," she said.

"I do not understand," I said.

"Do not concern yourself," she said.

We continued on for a time. I held the empty sack, four times folded. We turned onto a large street.

"Beware," I whispered, "a free woman approaches." She walked regally, and carried a switch.

"Keep your eyes down," my companion whispered. "Do not make eye contact. You do not see her. She does not see you."

"Let us go to the side of the street, and kneel, head down," I said. I had no wish to feel a switch.

"Now look up," she said, a moment later, merrily.

I did so.

"She is gone," I said, looking about. "The free woman is gone."

"Not really," said my companion. "She merely went to the other side of the street."

"Why?" I asked.

"We wear the black tunic, the black collar," she laughed.

As we continued on our way, even men tended to avoid us. We did receive, as some passed us by, closely, dark looks, and we noted sneers of contempt, but no one seemed interested in interacting with us, neither free men nor free women.

"The men do not seem to regard us with appetition, frankly and appraisingly," I said, puzzled. Certainly this was muchly different from my former experiences on open streets, as in Ar, and was muchly different from the common experiences of slave girls on open streets. One of the pleasures of being a Gorean male, I had gathered, was the inspective perusal of frequently encountered kajirae, in markets, in the plazas, on the boulevards and in lesser thoroughfares, kajirae running errands, chained to public slave rings, conveniently located, awaiting the return of masters, and so on. Do not such slaves dress up a city? Indeed, when visiting dignitaries are about, citizens are encouraged to set their girls, attractively tunicked, wandering about the city, that a suitable impression may be conveyed to the visitors. Surely these lovely slaves contribute, like parks and well-designed, colorful buildings, to the beauty of a city. Indeed, the number and quality of slave girls is taken as evidence of a city's taste, success, power, wealth, and prowess in warfare. Some of the girls so displayed may even have been obtained from the dignitary's own city. But that matters not, for, once collared, a slave is a slave.

"No," said my companion. "They are uneasy with the black court, and many fear it."

"I do not like being ignored," I said.

"Vain slave," she said.

What slave is not pleased to be the object of interest and regard, to know that she is looked upon and desired, that she stirs and heats the blood of men, that they would like to have her at their slave ring?

"Surely we are not sent forth commonly as we are now," I said.

"Not at all," she said, turning left.

I recalled there was nothing on my collar, but that it would be recognized, for its black enamel, and that I would be returned to the court. I would be left, helplessly bound, by the court, presumably at the edge of the moat, before the then-raised drawbridge. Apparently no reward would be expected, or proffered. On the other hand, court slaves, when sent forth from the court, were commonly tunicked nondescriptly and opaquely, and put in a collar that did bear a legend. That legend, I was informed, would return me to an address unlikely to be recognized as having anything to do with the black court, from which address I would then be, in due time, returned to the court.

"Why now?" I asked.

"Our first girl," she said, "was not pleased to have been switched by Porus, the salt merchant."

"We are seldom pleased to be switched," I said.

"He is not even a desirable master," she said.

"Oh," I said.

"It is not far," she said.

The salt in the local markets is obtained from the sea. Large pans are set forth with a thin film of sea water, which, as it evaporates, leaves the salt behind, which is then scraped together, and sent to the markets of the city.

"We are here," she said.

The fellow looked up, quickly, shrewdly, from amongst the kegs of salt, amidst which he sat, and turned white.

"Tal, noble Master," said my companion, kneeling. "We would like a stone of salt."

I knelt, too.

"That is four tarsk-bits," he said, cautiously.

"It is to be weighed out, carefully," said my companion.

"Four tarsk-bits," he said.

"Give the noble master the sack, that he may weigh out the salt," said my companion.

I made to hand the sack to the fellow who was, I gathered, Porus, but he thrust it away.

"Four tarsk-bits," he said.

My companion then rose and I, decidedly uneasy, for we had not been given permission to rise, rose to my feet, as well. I knew nothing else to do.

"Come, Phyllis," she said. "There is nothing for us to do now but return to the court, and inform the masters that Porus, the salt merchant, he who deals near the east gate, declined to weigh salt for us."

She then backed away, a step or two, as did I, and turned to leave. We had scarcely gone three steps when Porus called out to us, "Wait, sweet kajirae," he said, "I did but jest."

Shortly thereafter we left his impromptu place of business, amongst the kegs, I bearing a bulging bag of salt, one which, we noted, bore well over a stone's weight of the sparkling mineral, sometimes called the diamond of the sea.

"The first girl will be pleased," said my companion. "Her switching cost him four tarsk-bits."

"She was not recognized as being of the court," I said.

"Of course not," she said. "Even free women are unlikely to strike a girl in the black tunic."

"Surely," I said, "those of the black caste, as others, purchase goods."

"Commonly," she said, "but when they are in the dark habiliments, it is not unknown for merchants, and others, unrequested, to force goods upon them, as gifts."

We continued on.

"The salt is growing heavy," I said.

"It is not far now," she said, "no more than a pasang."

As my master continued his watch, or prolonged his inquiries, I was occasionally allowed out of the court, usually to fetch water from the stone steps under the Cloth Maker's Bridge, which, with other bridges, spanned the Lena, one of the two streams that flowed through the city and debouched into Thassa. The other was the Dacia, to the south. Although I never saw them I also understood that at various points about the city there were large underground cisterns, designed to supply water for months in case of a siege, in which case it was supposed that the Lena and Dacia would be dammed, diverted, or fouled, and the harbor blockaded.

In a typical tunic and my neck encircled with a common collar, bearing its legend, I was soon reassured as to certain particulars. Any doubts I might have hitherto been tempted to entertain with respect to my possible attractions or the gusto and lust of the men of Brundisium were dispelled. As with many slaves, particularly when unattended, I was frequently exposed to the rowdy gauntlet of male regard. Such attentions, coupled with the very clear knowledge that one is a property, and may be bought and sold, gives one a sense of self very different from that likely to be entertained by the free woman, protected by her robes and dignity. Often I must retie my tunic, and often, as I was held, it was lifted, to ascertain my brand. Sometimes bets are made on such things. My master, when he chained me to the ring in his quarters, was often amused at the marks on my body. And sometimes when I was seized, I must struggle, squirming, to resist the passion welling up within me. They were a man's arms. But moments and I might have begged use. But then I would be released, and turned, and, with a stinging, humiliating slap below the small of the back, sped on my way. "A helpless, hot one," laughed a man. "Two tarsk-bits!" called another, "No, three," cried another, as I fled away. How I longed for a private master, a normal master, at whose feet I might kneel, whom I might serve humbly, heatedly, passionately, in the way of the slave! Too, in a common tunic and collar, I found myself more than once berated and twice switched by free women. I was once leaned toward a wall, the palms of my hands on the wall, to keep my balance, and switched across the back of the thighs. It was not my fault if I may have fallen favorably beneath the gaze of her free companion! That was not my doing! I had not even been aware of his regard. In the case of the other, we were drawing water, and I had not noticed her waiting. "Are you mad?" she asked. "Do you expect me to dip my flask behind the bucket of a filthy slave, where she has sullied the water?" I was then liberally switched until I was crying, and, I think, her arm grew tired. And then, my body stinging, she had me dip her own flask, and then proffer it to her, as though I might have been a woman's slave, her own serving slave. She then spat on me, and left. I did not tell her I was housed in the black court, nor was I permitted to do so.

Then one morning my kennel was unlocked, and I was summoned forth. He wore a tunic that gave no hint of his caste. In his hand were various objects, three of which I recognized, and two whose purpose was uncertain to me. The three I was familiar with were a common tunic and collar, such as the slaves would most often wear outside the court, and a belly chain with attached bracelets. The other two, the purpose of which I was uncertain, were a wooden rod terminating in a collar, and what seemed to be a dark, narrow, bandage.

"I am informed," he said, "that the shipment has been transmitted. It may now be in Brundisium. That is possible. If so, it is presumably on one of the wharves or in one of the wharf warehouses. Its intended recipient, whom I understand is in Brundisium, he to whose care it will be consigned, will lead us to it."

"He to whose care it is to be consigned?" I said.

"Yes," he said.

"Kurik, of Victoria?" I said.

"Of course," he said.

"You do not know him," I said.

"It does not matter," he said. "You will indicate him for me."

"That you will tender him riches, and such?" I said.

"You are an intelligent woman," he said. "You are now familiar with the black court, and my caste. Surely that transparent subterfuge, that ruse of fond benignity, is no longer viable."

"No," I said. "It is no longer viable, not since the black court."

"Surely one of the dark caste would be a strange agent for one to choose," he said, "to deliver to another prestige, power, glory, honor, and wealth, such things."

"Yes, Master," I said.

"More likely one to deliver the intrusion of steel," he said.

"The shipment emanates from a steel world?" I said. I recall he had told me this before, even in Ar.

"Yes," he said, "that of Lord Arcesilaus, Twelfth Face of the Nameless One."

"I understand little of this," I said.

"You need not do so," he said.

"Curiosity is not becoming in a kajira," I said.

"Precisely," he said.

"How are you to deal with Kurik of Victoria?" I asked.

"You will locate him for me," he said. "He will then, unwittingly, lead us to the shipment. That done, the shipment discovered, I will dispose of him. Having done so, I will obtain his credentials and assume his identity. I, and others, who choose not to appear publicly, will then see that the shipment itself is diverted to our principal, who will put it to his own purpose."

"I bear Kurik of Victoria no ill will," I said.

"You need not," he said. "It is only necessary that you identify him for me."

"But what," I asked, "if I am unable to do so?"

"You will be unable to help yourself," he said.

CHAPTER TWENTY-SEVEN

My legs ached.

It was the fourth day of our search.

We were now in the vicinity of the southern wharves, or piers.

The wharves of Brundisium curl about its harbor. The greater wharves are the central and northern wharves. That is also where the larger warehouses are found. The lesser wharves, or piers, are the southern wharves or piers, where they are divided by the Dacia, as it feeds into Thassa. The southern piers, I had been told, are farther from the oversight of the harbor authority. I suspect, however, that the comparatively lax standards of inspection and monitoring, if such is the case, have less to do with the danger or remoteness of the district than with the surreptitious movement of silver between parties, some of whom were rumored to be high personages in the harbor authority itself. Be this as it may, the southern piers were supposedly a haven for unauthorized, unlicensed vessels, those lacking recognition by the authority, those somehow not appearing in the carefully kept registration lists.

I preceded my master.

Many are the markets of Gor, and some are supplied by contraband merchandise, of dubious origins, and evasive of taxes and harbor fees, such as rogue silver from the mines of Tharna, to be exported to Cos and Tyros, and the Farther Islands, even to the World's End; the beans from which Black Wine is brewed, so carefully guarded by those of Thentis, famed for its tarn flocks, to be shipped as far south as Schendi, as far north as Torvaldsland; purple, dyed cloth from Tabor; dates from the Tahari; hides from the Barrens; ivory from the massive, aquatic brutes of the Ice Seas; and coffles of stolen slaves, sometimes with their brands altered.

"I am sore, I am weary," I said. "May we not pause, may we not rest, Master?"

"Do you wish to be denied speech?" he asked.

"No, Master," I said.

"On," he said.

"Yes, Master," I said.

I moved forward once more. At least the street would soon begin to lead downward toward the wharves. I could see the masts of galleys, round ships, in the distance. The masts of round ships, or cargo ships, are commonly fixed. Those of war galleys, the long ships or knife ships, are commonly raised and lowered, depending on wind, and battle conditions. Both forms of ship, usually lateen-rigged, make use of a variety of sails, depending on the wind, ranging from the billowing fair-weather sail to the narrow, tightly rigged storm sail, suitable for running before blasting wind. Both forms of ship, too, are usually double helmed. The northern long ship, or "dragon ship," on the other hand, seldom seen this far south, has a fixed mast and a fixed, square sail, and is single-ruddered, the steering board, or starboard, on the right side.

I continued to move forward, the guide stick at the back of my neck.

I was determined not to reveal the identity of Kurik of Victoria to my master. That, I supposed, would be easy enough to do. I need only refuse to recognize him. I trusted he would not make himself known to me. Surely, if he were engaged in some sensitive, dangerous mission, he would be wary. Would he not be aware that others might seek to compromise or frustrate his intentions? Too, he might not even recognize me. Was I not only another slave? What was different about me, different from thousands of others? And what if he should recognize me? My very appearance in Brundisium might suggest danger to him. I would hope so. What was I doing here? Could it be a simple coincidence? That did not seem likely. What I did not understand was why my master had said I would be unable to help myself, why he thought that I could not help but identify Kurik of Victoria. Surely I need only pretend I had not recognized him. I hoped, but did not hope, that Kurik of Victoria was not even in Brundisium. Were he not here he would be safe, at least for a time, from the steel of my master, Tyrtaios, he of the dark caste. But, too, my heart ached for the sight of him, his proud, splendid form, his easy carriage, the narrowness of his waist, the strength of his arms, the width of his chest, the breadth of his shoulders, his frank, piercing gaze before which, now, I feared I could not remain standing, even had I desired to do so. Were he not in danger, I would have cast myself to my belly before him, and kissed and licked his feet and ankles, begging forgiveness for not having been sufficiently pleasing. I recalled I had, in Victoria, cried out my love for him, a slave's love for her master. Then he had rid himself of me.

Should I not have hated him? But I wanted his collar, his lash on my flesh, showing he owned me.

We passed two seeming ruffians, sitting at the side of the street, cross-legged. Both perused me, and my master. One was whittling on a stick. I did not care for their gaze.

"I think we may be in danger, Master," I said.

"No," he said. "It is they who are in danger."

Surely we seemed a vulnerable pair.

I wore a brief, yellow tunic, which would be likely to catch the eye of any we might pass. Thus, as we might be looked upon, so, too, those who looked upon us could be looked upon, as well, their faces raised, their features revealed. I wore, too, a locked belly chain, tight on my waist. The lock was at my waist. My hands, then, were held behind my back, fastened in the attached bracelets. If the chain is locked in the back, then one's hands are fastened before one, at one's waist. I now understood better, though, as it later became clear, did not understand well enough, the purpose of the collar-and-stick arrangement that had puzzled me that morning, four days ago, in the black court. I was to be taken as a "guide slave." The collar is locked about one's neck, and the stick, rigid, and more than a yard long, is held by the individual supposedly being guided. My master followed me, as though a bit uncertainly, the dark, narrow bandage wrapped about his face, over his eyes. He would appear to the casual observer one who was blind, being led by his guide slave. On the other hand, as he had demonstrated in the court, the bandage was a prepared, magician's bandage, and one could see through it quite easily. Despite its apparent opacity, wearing it, one could move about naturally, and swiftly, well aware of one's environment. In it one could thread one's way amongst obstacles, note subtleties in one's milieu, see small things, even read a scroll.

"Hold," he said.

I stopped, instantly.

"It would not do," he said, "for me to turn about, but you may turn about, in the guide collar, as though you had been addressed. In doing so, without being obvious, see if the two fellows we passed, to the left, the one whittling the stick, are following us."

"I fear so," I said, in misery.

"Unfortunate," he said.

"We must abandon our disguise," I said, "and flee."

"Where?" he said.

"Down the street is a tavern," I said. "We could take refuge there."

"That is the Sea Sleen," he said.

"They would not attack us in the tavern," I said.

"Could they not wait until we emerged?" he asked.

"Let us abandon our disguise," I said. "Hire men to convey us safely to the vicinity of the court."

"I think it likely," he said, "that by now Kurik of Victoria is in Brundisium. Too, the shipment is almost certain to be in the vicinity of the wharves or warehouses. We have, without fortune, prowled the northern and central wharves, and will do so again, and time and time again, if necessary. Surely it seemed likely the shipment would be delivered to such precincts, safer precincts. But now I am not sure. The southern wharves are rife with smugglers, their vessels, their goods. Perhaps here, though the shipment might be less safe, in theory, it might be safer, in fact, might be more easily concealed, might be less likely to be noticed. And if Kurik of Victoria wishes to conceal his presence, as he may well wish to do, where better than in the district of the lower wharves."

I could hear water lapping against the pilings of a pier, some yards away.

"They are closer, Master," I said. "Discard your disguise, hasten to the tavern!"

"Do not be absurd," he said.

"I am shackled," I said. "You are unarmed."

"Perhaps not," he said.

"Plans often fail to come to fruition," I said. "Let us flee."

Tyrtaios straightened up, as though he had detected some unexpected movement. He lifted one hand, and turned, as though quizzically, to face the two men, now but two or three yards away.

"Who is there?" he asked me.

"Two citizens," I said, "two noble masters."

"Two friends," said one of the men.

"Calm your slave," said the other. "Have her put aside her fears."

"There is nothing to fear, Phyllis," said Tyrtaios. "These men are friends."

"Assuredly," said one of the men.

"You seem strangers here," said the other, kindly.

"Where are we?" asked Tyrtaios, his head lifted, looking blankly about.

"On the Pier Road," said one of the men, "north of the Dacia, not far from the pier of Critias."

"I fear we are lost," said Tyrtaios, as though dismayed.

"We feared distress," said one of the men. "May we be of assistance?"

"I trust this district is safe," said Tyrtaios.

"*Ela*," said one of the men. "I fear it is less safe than one might wish."

"True," said the other, regretfully. "Particularly after dark," he added.

"Is it dark?" asked Tyrtaios.

"Yes," said the other.

It was not yet dark, but the fellow who had been whittling on the stick held his knife to my throat.

"My purse is heavy," said Tyrtaios. "Might you direct us to the refuge of an inn?"

"We would be pleased to do so," said one of the men.

"Surely you will accept some gratuity for your trouble," said Tyrtaios, looking off toward nowhere.

"Not at all," said the fellow with the knife, regarding me.

"I insist," said Tyrtaios.

"No," said one of the men. "It is we who insist. The pleasure of being of service is more than ample pay."

"What noble masters," said Tyrtaios, wonderingly.

"That way," said one of the men, indicating a dark passage.

"What inn have you in mind?" asked Tyrtaios.

It was easy to see that the fellows had not anticipated this question. Then one said, quickly, "the inn of Eteocles." I supposed there was no such inn, or, if so, that it was unlikely to be in this area.

"Do they house slaves?" inquired Tyrtaios.

"I am sure they can find her a cage, and blanket, in the basement," said the fellow with the knife.

"We must ascertain that," said the other. "Go, inquire. I shall wait here with the slave. It is only some paces away."

The other fellow then, he without the knife, approached me, put his hand over my mouth, and held me, tightly, in place. In his grip and in the belly chain I was helpless.

I watched the other fellow then, he with the knife, he who had threatened me, take Tyrtaios by the arm, gently, helpfully, and begin to conduct him down the dark passage.

"Do not struggle, kajira," said the other, now my captor.

I looked wildly about, as I could. The guide stick, attached to the collar, dangled behind me. It moved. I could feel it, against my back.

Surely someone might see!

I saw no one.

"Steady, kajira," I was warned.

I could scarcely move.

"Do not be concerned," he said. "At least four ships depart this very night. We can put you in thongs and a slave bit, sell you, and you will be on your way to the Farther Islands by the Twentieth Ahn. To be sure, there will be time for us to pleasure ourselves with you first."

We waited for some Ehn.

"I do not understand," he said.

After a bit, he put me to the pavement and, with a short thong, lashed my ankles together, closely.

"Remain silent," he said, "or I will return and cut your throat."

I saw him disappear into the dark passage.

I did not lie there long on the pavement before a figure, his eyes bandaged, seemed to emerge, hesitantly, from the darkness.

He reconnoitered, and apparently noted that the street was deserted, and then moved easily to me, and slashed apart the thong on my ankles.

But then a mariner staggered from the Sea Sleen.

At that point the demeanor of my master changed, and he became again hesitant, and uncertain, as though lost in a darkness. He rose up, and I did. He then reached about, and then apparently managed at last to grasp the guide stick, and, once again, it was perpendicular to my neck.

"I think," he said, "that the shipment may be about, and Kurik of Victoria, as well, here amongst the southern piers. Where better could it be concealed? Where better might he move unnoticed? We must thus examine this area more carefully, more thoroughly. But our presence, if we are to linger about, must have some vindication, some justification or pretext. Tomorrow then my guise will be that of a blind beggar, depending on his guide slave. We shall now return to the court."

"What of the two men?" I asked.

"They will not bother us anymore," he said.

"Master was unarmed," I said.

"The hook knife is easily concealed," he said.

CHAPTER TWENTY-EIGHT

The tarsk-bit struck into the metal cup slung about my neck.

"Thank you, kind Master," said Tyrtaios.

The guide stick, with its attached collar, buckled under my chin, was tight against the back of my neck.

I felt it press me forward.

I again wore the brief, yellow tunic, and the belly chain, its brace-lets once more confining my hands behind my back.

"Twenty copper tarsks for your slave!" laughed a man.

"Is she truly so ugly?" asked Tyrtaios, the dark bandage swathing his eyes, seemingly surprised, even dismayed.

"A she-tarsk would bring more on the block," laughed another fellow.

"*Ela*!" cried Tyrtaios. "I paid a silver tarsk for her. I was told she was beautiful!"

"Fool!" called a man.

"Unsighted dupe!" called another.

"Be gentle," said another fellow. "You see he cannot see. The slave is comely enough."

"Indeed," said another. "I have seen worse in the taverns."

"Twenty-one copper tarsks then!" called out the fellow who had bellowed forth the supposed offer of twenty tarsks but a moment ago.

"But I need her, to show me my way!" laughed Tyrtaios, seemingly joining in the sport.

"Buy a sleen!" suggested a man.

"But I cannot afford a sleen," cried Tyrtaios, as though in distress.

There was more laughter.

Miserable, I felt tears running down my cheeks, to and beneath the curved rods of the device fastened on me, the bit drawn back between my teeth.

I did not care to be demeaned, or humiliated, but then what did it matter? I was a slave.

Had Tyrtaios been truly blind, and had bought me, unable to ascertain the quality of his purchase, he might, indeed, have been duped. Had he been truly blind he might have been in anguish then, not so much for having a plain or homely slave, for such might guide one as well as a high-block beauty, but for having been misled and cheated, a possibility not lightly regarded by most Goreans. Indeed, a merchant who misrepresents his goods may have his business burned and his stock confiscated, may even be denied bread, fire, and salt, and be driven naked from the city.

I did not know my worth, of course. Indeed, how does a woman know what she is worth until she is sold? But I thought I would now sell for at least a silver tarsk in most markets. Indeed, Arnold, of Harfax, if that was his name, he whom I continued to think of as Tullius Quintus, of Ar, had twice been offered that for me, on the streets in Ar.

I did not hope, of course, that I could bring as much as a trained sleen. But then a trained sleen will sell for more than most slaves, just as a tarn will commonly sell for more than several sleen.

"Let us share a round of paga!" called a fellow.

There was assent to this.

Another tarsk-bit was placed in the cup about my neck.

"Thank you, Master," called Tyrtaios.

The coin had been dropped into the cup by the fellow who had made the supposed bids of twenty and twenty-one copper tarsks for me. I supposed he was seeing fit to pay for the pleasure of his sport.

"To the right, down that street," said Tyrtaios.

The bit was back, deeply, between my teeth.

I turned right, responsive to the stick.

"Here," said Tyrtaios, "we shall try our fortune. What, and whom, we seek, I am sure is in this district, somewhere. May this path prove propitious."

We had soon entered into that street.

It bore no signs, but that is common in many Gorean cities. It is not that the streets lack names, only that the names are not likely to be known by strangers. One may inquire, of course. The situation is occasionally complicated by the fact that a street may have more than one name, depending on your informant, and, sometimes, it will change its name, depending on your location, a street having, say, one name closer to the piers, and another name closer to the markets. In Ar, street maps, at least public street maps, are forbidden, largely as a military precaution. The map, as I understand it, precise and reliable, studied behind closed doors, is amongst the subtlest and most potent vehicles of war. Campaigns are conducted, wars are fought, on its quiet surface. It is before the trumpet; it precedes the drum and the cadenced tread of marching men.

"The street is dingy," said Tyrtaios. "The gutters are unkempt and foul. The insulae are squat, dirty, and odorous. Excellent. Quite suitable for an unnoted residence. The piers are near, too. Excellent. Who knows what, at hand, baled and crated, might prove of interest? On these stones we shall try our fortune. Too, it is near the tenth Ahn. The bar will soon ring. Men will be about the street. I can smell the cook shops, fresh bread, and sausages. Perhaps, at last, here, we shall detect our elusive Kurik of Victoria, and be led by him, unwittingly, to our prize."

Another coin was deposited in my cup.

"Thank you, Master," called Tyrtaios, feigning gratitude.

I had not been put in the bit before.

Did Tyrtaios fear I might call out to Kurik of Victoria, to warn him of his danger? Surely not. I need only pretend that I had not seen him.

That would be simple enough.

But why then had I been placed in the bit?

The tenth Ahn is the noon hour.

I could smell the fresh hot bread, so different from the bread to which I had been accustomed on my former world, baked, marshaled forth, aligned, wrapped, shipped, and stored, long removed from the ovens of its birth, long departed from the pinnacle of its taste, its perfection. I feared many on my former world had never tasted fresh bread, which seemed a sadness. How little they knew of what bread might be. The common Gorean loaf, so to speak, is flat and circular. It may be larger or smaller. It is commonly divided into four, if smaller, or eight, if larger, wedgelike pieces, these pieces sold separately. Odors, too, emanated from the crackling pans, plates, and griddles of the cook shops. Soup, usually thick, sometimes with suls, as in sullage, but commonly comprised of other vegetables and noodles, would be ladled into wooden bowls. And there would be, too, behind the counter, in baskets, grapes, tospits, larmas, nuts, and olives, and, in blocks, cheeses, and, in its amphorae to be lifted from its racks, cheap ka-la-na.

The street was now relatively crowded.

The bar for the tenth Ahn sounded.

Another coin was placed in the cup.

"May the Priest-Kings look upon you with favor," called out Tyrtaios. Then I felt the rigid guide stick, fastened to the close-buckled collar, tight against my neck. Any movement I might make would then be conveyed back through the stick, to the hand of Tyrtaios.

"Be watchful," said he, "slave girl."

I whimpered, once. How helpless one is, bitted, and braceleted.

We were passing one of the cook shops, on the left, open, little more than a hole in the wall, set into the ground floor of an insula, as are many shops.

A tall man was standing outside the shop.

As we approached, he turned.

I started.

This involuntary motion was conveyed instantly through the guide stick to the hand of Tyrtaios.

I tried to continue on, as though nothing had occurred, but I could not move against the collar, for Tyrtaios had stopped. This held me in place.

"So," said Tyrtaios, pleasantly, "that is Kurik of Victoria."

I whimpered twice, and then twice, again, desperately, piteously.

"You lie most lamely," said he. "I shall not even bother lashing you. Indeed, you have done well to betray your former master."

I whimpered again, twice, desperately.

"I am in a good mood," he said. "But do not press the matter. Do not court the lash."

I was silent. Tears formed in my eyes.

"Yes," said Tyrtaios. "He matches the description perfectly. Excellent. You have done well, kajira."

To my misery I saw Kurik of Victoria approaching us.

Did he recognize me?

It seemed not.

I was, after all, only another slave.

"Is someone approaching?" asked Tyrtaios, as though he might not be certain of the matter.

I whimpered, once.

I tried to stand still. I now knew my slightest tremor, perhaps not even visible, would be conveyed back to Tyrtaios, through the stick. I had been unable to help myself, as he had said. I could not have helped but react to the sight of Kurik of Victoria, my first master. That Tyrtaios had anticipated. My clever plans, that I might refrain from disclosing the proximity of Kurik of Victoria, did I see him, had been unfounded. It was rather like the magician who, by muscle reading, by a held arm, may force an unwilling accomplice to lead him to the location of a concealed object. My eyes were filled with tears. I fear my expression was one of fear, protest, and agony, as I tried to warn Kurik of Victoria of his danger.

But he approached, easily, smiling.

He stopped but a foot from me.

Tyrtaios could not see my expression. He could detect, through the stick, little more, I suppose, than my subtle agitation, which I was trying to subdue. But he could see the expression of Kurik of Victoria, which conveyed naught but interest, and perhaps concern.

"You pause, sad Master," said Kurik of Victoria.

"I fear I know not which way to turn," said Tyrtaios.

"You are on the street of Crates, near the food shop of Bion," said Kurik, of Victoria.

"It is as I suspected," said Tyrtaios. "My slave has made the wrong turn."

"She seems distressed," said Kurik.

"Of course," said Tyrtaios. "She fears a beating."

Kurik, with his thumb, wiped the tears from my cheek. I tried not to press my face against his hand. Could he not see my misery, my fear?

"She is pretty," said Kurik. "It would seem a shame to beat her."

"Is she truly pretty?" asked Tyrtaios, as though interested.

"For a pot girl," said Kurik, "for a kettle-and-mat girl."

I was sure then he recognized me!

I was thrilled that he might recognize me, even bitted, but, too, what was I doing here? Would his suspicions not be aroused? Might not he be sought? What likelihood was there that this encounter would be utterly fortuitous?

"I am sure," said Kurik, "her misadventure was unintended. Let us not hurry to strip and bind her, and apply the lash to her fair skin."

"I will merely withhold her evening gruel," said Tyrtaios.

"Merciful Master," said Kurik.

He then reached into his wallet.

"Why is she bitted?" he asked.

"Yesterday evening she was displeasing," said Tyrtaios, regretfully.

"Perhaps then," said Kurik, "we should give her a taste of the lash."

I feared I turned white.

Kurik then took out a copper tarsk, and dropped it into my cup.

"Master," exclaimed Tyrtaios, "beware. I fear you have inadvertently deposited a full tarsk in the cup!"

"How do you know?" asked Kurik.

"The weight, the sound, Master," said Tyrtaios.

"Remarkable," said Kurik.

"Retrieve it, I beg of you," said Tyrtaios.

"It shall remain where it is," said Kurik, magnanimously.

"May I inquire the name of so thoughtful and generous a master?" asked Tyrtaios.

"Of course," said Kurik, "I am Tenrik, of Siba."

"Noble Master," said Tyrtaios.

"Where did you buy your slave?" asked Kurik.

"In the market of Eamon, here in Brundisium," said Tyrtaios. "She is a barbarian."

"Barbarians make good slave girls," said Kurik.

"I am told so," said Tyrtaios.

"Take this one," said Kurik. "Wherever she might be first seen, and however she might be dressed, one could see, at a single glance, that she should be a slave girl, indeed, that she is a slave girl."

"I am pleased to hear it," said Tyrtaios.

On Gor I was a slave girl. And on Gor what else could one such as I be? And I did not wish to be other than I was, a slave. I suspected I had been bred, through a thousand generations, to wear a master's collar. Had I known on Earth what I had learned on Gor, I would have knelt and begged a collar.

But there were few masters, I feared, on my former world.

Who amongst them knows what a woman is, what she wants, and what are her needs?

"I wish you well, kind Master," said Tyrtaios.

"I, too, wish you well, gentle Master," said Kurik, turning away.

No sooner had Kurik vanished than I was pulled about by the stick and collar, and hastened, half dragged, back up the street.

"What a fool," said Tyrtaios, delightedly, contemptuously, tearing the wrapped bandage from his face. I tried to keep up with him, half running, he now leading, the stick in his left hand, held behind him. "He did not even recognize you. My disguise was perfection. How could things proceed more smoothly? And consider the absurdity of the name, 'Tenrik', obviously reminiscent of his real name, 'Kurik'! Could he not do better than that? And he alleges to be of Siba, he, of Victoria! Siba is another of the towns on the Vosk, like Victoria. Why could he not, at least, have pretended to be from somewhere else, away from the Vosk, Corcyrus, Helmutsport, Besnit, Bazi, Tor, anywhere apart from Victoria? What a fool, a fool!"

I fell, weeping, and, by the collar and stick, it turned on my neck, was yanked to my feet.

"He will be known as Tenrik of Siba," said Tyrtaios. "I know his district. He will be known, here and there, by that name, surely at least by description, in some insula, at a cook shop, somewhere. I must not allow the trail to fade. I need now only maintain contact. The package, or shipment, may have already arrived. Or will soon arrive. This contingency, needing to make contact with the shipment, will keep him in place. It is at, or should come to, a southern pier, or warehouse. I am sure of that. He is here. I follow him, he leads me to the material, I dispose of him, acquiring his identity or credentials, and then claim the goods for myself, thence to be presented to my principal. All proceeds well."

I could do little more than whimper, for the bit.

"You would have warned him, I sensed that," said Tyrtaios.

I whimpered desperately, twice.

"Lying slave," he said. "I suppose I should kill you, say, bind you, and cast you to the harbor sharks, but a dead slave is worthless. You have been of use. I am grateful. You have identified Kurik of Victoria for me. Too, you should be worth most of a silver tarsk, perhaps more."

We were now on the higher streets.

"Still," said Tyrtaios. "You tried to warn the quarry. It is not your fault he was too stupid to understand. And you lied."

I whimpered, but not in response to signals, rather from misery. I did not attempt to deceive him further.

"Here!" said Tyrtaios, stopping by a public slave ring, one with its chain, collar, and key.

I was drawn rudely to the ring, by the arm.

"Kneel here," he said, "lying slut."

I knelt. He removed the stick and collar from my neck and cast it aside. "We no longer need this," he said. "It has served its purpose." I was still, of course, bitted, and braceleted. He then took the cup on its cord from about my neck and poured the coins into his wallet. "A coin is a coin," he said. "Small emoluments are not to be neglected, however humble their origin. And we would not wish the modest proceeds of our work to be made away with, would we, while you wait here, so patiently?" Then he flung the cup away, it rolling and clattering on the stones. The ring collar was then snapped about my throat. The ring itself was about a yard high. The chain, running between the ring and the collar, was about a foot in length. He then removed the key from its hook by the ring. The key is numbered, and the number matches the number on the plate to which the ring is attached. He put the key in his wallet.

"I will ascertain, as I can," he said, "his place of residence, and then, by arrangements, employ others to observe him. Copper tarsks, in that district, will be sufficient for such a purpose. I will frequently be in contact with these others. Indeed, I will take up quarters from which it will be convenient to keep our friend under surveillance. He will not recognize me for I have removed the bandage that muchly concealed my face. Was it not like a mask? When he moves to the piers or warehouses I shall be nearby."

I shook my head, protestingly, pleadingly. The chain shook, rattling on the ring.

"I shall return for you shortly, or surely before morning," he said. "You will be returned to the court. My work may take a day or two, or perhaps more. During that time we are unlikely to see one another."

I whimpered, helplessly.

I squirmed.

"Trust," he said, "that my mission is successful, for if Kurik of Victoria should survive, and learn you betrayed him, as you did, and very nicely, it would not be well to fall into his hands."

I looked up at him.

"Not at all," he said. He then turned about and retraced his steps, once more downward, toward the pier district.

I wept.

I had betrayed Kurik of Victoria.

CHAPTER TWENTY-NINE

I leaned against the wall to which, by the ring, I was chained. I was on my knees, as I had been placed. My knees were sore, from the stones. I could not lie down, given the collar, and the length of the ring chain. I was high above the pier district. This, I take it, was fortunate. Men had occasionally glanced at me, as they passed, but I was neither accosted nor molested. It was not unusual, of course, to see a slave chained at a public ring. That is what such rings are for. I was grateful I had not been secured closer to the piers. Bitted and back-braceleted, and slave, would one not prove delicious sport for the disorderly and unruly? Happily no free women passed the ring. A slave, I lived in terror of free women. It would be difficult to make clear to those unfamiliar with the culture the animosity with which the slave is viewed by the free woman. Occasionally they will gratuitously, and fiercely, beat an unattended slave fastened at a public ring. They are pleased to take out their hatred and rage on a helpless, vulnerable slave. She is made to stand proxy for a thousand collar sisters hitherto resented and loathed. I had often looked up, above my head, to the hook on the wall where the collar key had hung. Its number, as noted, corresponded to the number on the plate to which the ring was fastened. I had seen my master, Tyrtaios, of the black caste, deposit it in his wallet. I had not noted the number, nor, as I was illiterate, could I have read it, had I noted it. On the other hand, I knew it was likely to be one in a sequence, given that it was numbered. Most slave rings, of course, as far as I know, are not numbered, even in Brundisium. I had never, for example, seen one in Ar that bore a number, and such rings, in Ar, are quite common, particularly in commercial districts.

Eventually night fell.

I remained alone, at the ring.

The sky was overcast, but occasionally the light of the white moon, the clouds parted, broke through, illuminating the street and adjoining buildings.

Then it was dark, again.

I heard the bar for the eighteenth Ahn.

From what my master had said, I might not be fetched before morning.

I grew hungry, and I was cold.

Two men were approaching. One carried a lantern. I kept my head down. The light fell on me. Then they moved away. They were guardsmen.

Later I heard the bar for the nineteenth Ahn.

Shortly thereafter I heard more footsteps, these climbing, coming from the pier district.

My senses sprang alert. I was afraid. I peered into the darkness.

Bitted, I could do no more than whimper.

I could not see the form in the darkness, but I knew it was there.

I whimpered, again.

"Face away," he said.

I turned away.

"Nadu," he snapped, and I assumed position, as well as I could, being back braceleted. I knelt back on my heels, my body tall, my back straight, my head up, my knees spread. I could not place the palms of my hands down on my thighs, for the restraints.

"You respond nicely," he said. "I see you have had some training."

I whimpered, muchly distressed.

"Head down," he said.

I lowered my head, humbly.

I felt hands at the back of my neck, and the bit snaps were released, and the bit was pressed forward, and then pulled from my mouth.

It was glorious to be free of that detestable impediment! It seemed I could still feel the metal back between my teeth, the pressure at the sides of my mouth.

The device was then, apparently, thrust into a satchel, or pouch, probably suspended across the body.

"I did not mean to betray you!" I whispered.

I could not but recognize the voice of my first master, Kurik, of Victoria.

"Did you request permission to speak?" he inquired.

"Forgive me, Master!" I said. "May I speak? I supplicate you! I plead to speak!"

"If you wish," he said.

"Beware!" I said. "My master is not blind. The bandage he wore is a hoax! His sight is as keen as that of the tarn! He is as dangerous as the larl in rutting time. He hunts you. He is of the black caste!"

"I thought," said he, "the black caste might be involved. They prove to be excellent agents, well worth their pay."

"Master!" I protested.

"Surely one must admire them," he said.

"He is armed," I said. "He is dangerous! He follows you, to discern some object, an object to which he expects to be led. Then he intends to slay you, secure your authorization or credential, and thus obtain the object."

"What object?" he asked.

"I do not know," I said.

"A bold plan," he said, "one worthy of the black caste—or others."

"He may return, momentarily," I said. "Flee! Make away!"

"You expect his return, I take it, anon?" he said.

"At any moment," I said. "Do not dally! Flee! Make away! He is a killer. He knows you!"

"How could he know me?" asked Kurik.

"From before, from information, from descriptions, somehow," I said.

"But not by sight," he said.

"No," I said, "not until today."

"I see," he said.

"I identified you," I said.

"I see," he said.

"I was tricked," I said. "I could not help myself!"

"The guide stick," he said.

"He seeks you," I said. "He intends you harm, death. Do not loiter here! Run! He is of the dark caste! You are hunted! Neither dismiss nor ignore this threat! You are not dealing with an ordinary man! He is of the dark caste! He is one who has ascended the nine steps of blood."

He was crouching near me, behind me. He reached about me, and unhooked the belly belt. The two lengths of open chain then fell behind me.

"Master!" I wept. "Run, I beg of you!"

I felt a small key inserted into one of my bracelets, and then the other. My wrists were freed.

I rubbed my wrists, bewildered.

"How is it you have the key to the bracelets?" I said.

The belly chain and the bracelets were then deposited, as had been the slave bit, in some sack, or container, which proved to be an across-the-body satchel.

I had not been given permission to turn about.

At that moment the clouds parted, again, and the light of the white moon fell on the stones before me.

"Master?" I said.

I felt a key thrust into the collar lock, and, a moment later, the collar, opened, fell back against the wall, dangling from the ring. A bit later Kurik stood, and replaced the key on its hook.

"You have the key to the lock," I said, frightened.

"The number," he said, "made it easy to locate you."

"You killed my master, Tyrtaios!" I said.

"So that is his name," he said.

"You know it?" I said.

"Only now," he said.

"You slew him," I said.

"I am not an Assassin," he said.

"He will resume his hunt," I said.

"It is not he whom I fear," he said. "It is the others."

"What others?" I said.

"The beasts," he said.

"What beasts?" I said.

"Are you hungry?" he asked. "Cold?"

"Yes, Master," I said.

"Then," he said, "we shall patronize some tavern, until the nineteenth Ahn, tomorrow evening."

"I do not understand," I said.

"The 'object', as you called it," he said, "is to be received at the twentieth Ahn tomorrow, at the house of Flavius Minor, and is to be claimed precisely at the first Ahn."

"Precisely?" I said.

"That is the credential," he said.

"No paper, no document, no divided coin, no ostrakon?" I said.

"Such might be stolen," he said.

"Then," I said, "how could Tyrtaios, my master, assume your identity?"

"It would be difficult to do, would it not?" he said.

"Master is wise," I said.

"Or those in whose cause I labor," he said.

"You will take me to a tavern?" I said.

"Surely you do not think I am going to leave you here, do you, behind me, to inform on me, to be interrogated," he said.

"I would not inform on you," I said.

"Perhaps you have never heard a slave girl shriek," he said, "the splinters beneath her nails."

"I have never been in a tavern," I said.

"You may find the experience instructive," he said.

"Might I not flee from the tavern, and betray you?" I asked.

"I do not think you could manage that," he said.

"I do not understand," I said.

"It is a Gorean tavern," he said.

CHAPTER THIRTY

He thrust me through the small opening, and then turned to buckle shut the leather curtain.

He then turned, and, sitting cross-legged, faced me. I knelt. Slaves are not permitted to sit cross-legged. Too, he was a free male. It was appropriate then that I, a slave, should kneel, and be in a position of suitable subservience and submission, before a free person. The enclosure was not large, but it was large enough, and high-ceilinged enough, for a full-grown man to stand upright within it, and, if he wished, wield a whip. It was lit by a single tharlarion-oil lamp, set in a niche, to the left of the opening, as one would enter, now to my right. There were cushions about. The floor was carpeted with deep, lush furs. The floor itself, where I could see it, was of dark, varnished wood.

"What manner of place is this?" I asked.

"Get your clothes off," he said, "completely."

"One garment I cannot remove," I said. "It is locked on my neck."

"Appropriately so," he said.

I slipped from the tunic, and was then before him, clad only in my collar.

I had dared to be impertinent. I knelt before him, insolently, naked. I was angry. He was not claiming me. Again I was nothing to him. He was merely holding me, that I might not compromise his plans, that I might not reveal a time, a place, an identity. Had he not once told me I would not be kept, had he not sold me, had he not rid himself of me? Now it seemed he must keep me, for a time.

How unfortunate for him!

Poor, inconvenienced master!

I was furious, but, too, I knew I was at his mercy, completely. There was a collar on my neck.

We had entered the tavern but shortly before. At the door he had put his hand in my hair and bent me over, holding my head at his right hip. Then, I in leading position, he had entered the tavern, I stumbling helplessly beside him, so conducted, my hands on his wrist. I glimpsed the low tables, the hanging lamps, the fellows at the tables, cross-legged, conversing, drinking, gaming. Two were playing kaissa, which game I recognized, but did not understand. Beside the table a slave lay, bound, hand and foot. She was doubtless a paga girl. I saw other paga girls about, bearing goblets, replenishing goblets at the vat, serving paga, fetching viands. How sensuous they were, I thought. Doubtless they were purchased with such things in mind. How could a man keep his hands from them? Too, they were cheap; they would go with the price of a drink. I saw two of these regard me, curiously. How dared they? Did they think I was being brought to the tavern as a new paga girl? Did they think I was to be put in so tiny and thin a tunic, to be so helplessly, so shamelessly, displayed before a master's patrons? But then I realized I could be sold to such an establishment, for just such a purpose. Then I, too, would be a paga girl! How far I was from my former world, the office, my well-chosen, fashionable garments!

Kurik then went to the proprietor's counter, where he released me, and I knelt beside him. A paga girl, carrying a tray, regarded me. No, I was not a paga girl. I pretended I did not notice. Meanwhile, Kurik, by means of a coin or two, was making certain arrangements.

I was not clear on the nature of these arrangements.

He then turned about, and leaning his back against the counter, his elbows on it, looked about the dimly lit, but well-occupied, tavern.

I saw, centrally, a circle of sand, which, I supposed, was dancing sand. There were cushions to the side, probably for musicians. The accompaniment for a dancer can vary considerably, from as little as a single flute, often the case with a street dancer, to several individuals and a variety of instruments. A typical group would consist of a czehar player, usually the leader, one or two flautists, one or two players of the kalika, and a taborist.

It was clear to me that Kurik, to my annoyance, while waiting for his specifications, whatever they might have been, to be effectuated, was considering the paga girls, two or three of whom were only too well aware of his regard, and little loath, I fear, to bring him paga.

"Master," I said, "at the far table two men play kaissa. Why is a slave lying beside them, on the floor, bound?"

I was curious, but, too, I thought it not amiss to distract him from his observations and, doubtless, speculations.

"She is for the winner," he said. "The loser will pay the proprietor for her use."

He then returned his attention to the subject matter of his former purview.

Need they move like that, I wondered. Could they not take a more circuitous, a more remote route, to the paga vat?

Shortly thereafter the arrangements, whatever they might have been, seemed to have been completed. In any event, Kurik then indicated an opening in the wall, one of several such, and I, at his gesture, approached it. It was then, as I hesitated, that he had thrust me through the opening, and then turned to buckle shut the leather curtain.

He had then turned, again, and, sitting cross-legged, had faced me, and I had knelt.

I was now before him, kneeling, unclothed, slave naked, namely, naked as a slave is naked, naked, but collared.

I could see the leather curtain behind him, buckled shut.

I looked about, uneasily. Here and there, mostly fixed to rings, were collars, chains, and shackles. To one side, at hand, I saw strips of cloth, by means of which one might be bound, or from which might be fashioned gags and blindfolds. I saw, too, on their pegs, a long, supple switch and a whip, a slave whip, with its five broad blades.

The only light was from the small tharlarion-oil lamp.

My knees were half buried in the furs on which I knelt.

"What manner of place is this?" I asked, again.

"An alcove," he said.

"I have heard of such places," I said.

"You are now in one," he said.

"To such a place as this paga girls are brought?" I said.

"Yes," he said.

"To be put to use," I said, "for the sport and pleasure of masters."

"Yes," he said.

"I am not a paga girl," I said, angrily.

"You will do," he said.

"Surely I am not to be put to use," I said, indignantly.

"We shall see," he said.

"Oh?" I said.

"Do not look disappointed," he said.

I turned away, angrily.

"As I recall, from Victoria," he said, "you had the incipiency of collar readiness. By now, doubtless, slave fires have been kindled in your small, shapely belly."

"I cannot help what men have made me," I said.

"Amusing," he said.

"'Amusing'?" I said.

"Yes," he said.

"A slave is pleased," I said, bitterly, "that she has amused Master."

"You are now a slave of your needs, wholly so, as men wish their slaves to be," he said.

"I see," I said, angrily. How true that was! How helpless I was! What choice had I been given? They do with us what they please, they make us what they want!

"But it is not just that," he said. "It is the whole thing, all of it."

"Oh?" I said.

"Yes," he said, "surely, from what I knew of you, and your personality and character, on your former world, you should not be surprised that I find it amusing to see you as you are now, kneeling before me, naked, a collared, Gorean slave girl."

"It was you who brought me to the collar!" I charged.

"Where you belonged," he said.

"Beware of Tyrtaios, of the black caste!" I said.

"I shall be," he said.

"I may escape," I said. "I may inform on you. I may betray you, as I did before!"

"You could not help yourself," he said. "It was the trick of the guide stick. You did not wish to betray me. That was clear. Your agonized expression informed me of as much."

"Perhaps I would now enjoy betraying you," I said.

"You are not now likely to receive the opportunity to do so," he said.

"I see," I said.

He glanced to the side, to the dangling whip.

I was uneasy.

"You are going to hold me," I said, "until the nineteenth Ahn, tomorrow?"

"Or have you held," he said, "on a chain somewhere."

"You are not going to keep me," I said.

"Who would want you?" he said.

"I see," I said, angrily.

"To be sure," he said, "it would be judicious to keep you until we have made our visit to the house of Flavius Minor."

"Perhaps I would cry out," I said.

"There is the slave bit," he said.

"I do not wish to be bitted," I said.

"One could scarcely blame you for that," he said. "Still, a woman looks well in a slave bit."

"I am missing from the slave ring," I said. "Guardsmen may be alerted."

"The yellow tunic," he said, "is too striking, surely too easy to recognize. We shall have to find you another, shorter, but less conspicuous, as a tunic."

"Surely," I said, "the yellow tunic is short enough."

"Not for my taste," he said. "Also, you have excellent legs."

"Surely I would be more conspicuous," I said.

"But not for the tunic," he said. "Guardsmen will be looking for a yellow tunic. One sight of you, and they may be distracted from thoughts of a tunic."

"Apparently I have some value," I said.

"Far more now," he said, "than when you were on your former world, clad in its cumbersome, barbarous garments. They do not know how to clothe a slave."

"I have a collar," I said.

"What does it say?" he asked.

"I do not know," I said. "I cannot read."

"You have not been taught," he said.

"No," I said.

"Good," he said. "I want you illiterate."

"So I am even more a slave!" I said.

"Of course," he said. "Was the collar never read to you?"

"No," I said. "But its legend is deceptive. It would have me returned to one address, not obviously connected to the black court, from which address I would then be remanded to the black court."

"Clever," he said. "But no matter. Collars may be easily changed."

"I cannot do so," I said.

"No," he said.

"This tavern," I said, "is not the Sea Sleen."

"No," he said. "Obviously not. This is a larger, better tavern, more respectably situated, the Tavern of the Slave Whip. I expect that your Tyrtaios, and his colleagues, would not expect me to conceal myself in a public tavern, and surely not in one as prominent as this. Thus, they are not likely to look for me here."

"Doubtless Master thinks himself clever," I said.

"Apparently you think me stupid," he said.

"Master?" I said, uneasily.

"On the street," he said, "when you had inadvertently identified me for your Tyrtaios, you tried, by your expressions, to warn me of my danger."

"Yes, Master," I said.

"Thus," he said, "you thought me so stupid as not to be aware of my danger."

"I did not think you were aware," I said.

"And thus thought me stupid," he said. "Did you not realize that I would instantly be aware of the anomaly of a former possession of mine suddenly appearing in Brundisium, who might be used in identifying me, and did you think I would be unaware that your supposedly blind master had the body of a human panther, and limbs and hands shaped by the practice of arms, limbs and hands that might have been expected in an arena fighter, a warrior—or Assassin?"

"Apparently Master thinks me stupid," I said.

"Naive, ignorant, unreflective, not thinking, perhaps," he said, "but not stupid. We do not bring stupid women to Gor. What would they be good for? Who would buy them? They do not sell well. We want something worthwhile, stripped on the block. We look for women who are highly intelligent, and highly sexed, women who are healthy and vital, women with profound physical and emotional needs, women who desire to be women, desire to submit and surrender, who long for the collar, who desire to love and serve, who find themselves and their fulfillment in their subjugation, who understand and become themselves only in a man's chains."

"And perhaps beauty is a consideration?" I said.

"Certainly," he said. "They are to be marketed."

"I am not stupid," I said.

"I trust not," he said.

"I am not stupid," I said, again, angrily.

"And it is my hope that neither am I," he said.

"May I speak frankly?" I asked.

"Yes," he said, "of course. At least until I forbid you to speak."

"Speaking of stupidity," I said.

"Or of naivety, or of a lack of reflection," he suggested.

"Yes," I said.

"Continue," he said.

"Tyrtaios, of the black caste," I said, "regards you as a fool."

"Good," said Kurik, of Victoria.

"'Good'?" I said.

"Yes," he said.

"He thinks you were unaware of your danger," I said.

"Excellent," he said.

"He mocks you, that you chose the name 'Tenrik of Siba' as a concealing name," I said, "for it is foolishly and clearly close to that of 'Kurik', and he finds it pathetically inept that you should have claimed to be from Siba, for that is merely another town on the Vosk, as is your true town, Victoria, thinks that you should have chosen a more judicious name and claimed to come from a farther place, one remote from the great Vosk."

"That such inferences be drawn was my hope," he said. "One strives to be underestimated by one's enemy."

At that point, a girl's voice spoke softly, from the other side of the buckled-shut leather curtain. "Provender, and drink, Master," she said.

Kurik turned to the curtain, but remained a bit to the side. "Speak," he said.

"Victoria is the ruby of the Vosk," she said.

He then unbuckled the curtain, and took from the girl, a paga girl, a large tray, containing two bowls, a trencher, and a bottle. This he placed on the floor of the alcove, while the girl, her head lowered, backed away. He then rebuckled the leather curtain. I gathered that this business had been included amongst the arrangements he had made with the proprietor.

"As I recall," he said, "you were very much hungry."

"Very much so," I said, "Master."

Of the two bowls on the tray, one contained gruel, and the other, I conjectured, water. I did not know the contents of the bottle, but, I supposed, it would contain either ka-la-na or paga, most likely paga. As it was bottled, it was presumably not vat paga, but some selection from a more reserved, or private, stock, doubtless more expensive. The contents of the trencher still steamed. It was amply laden, with strips of roast bosk, suls hot with butter, a salad of tur-pah and nuts, slices of tospit, and two large wedges of fresh bread. Naturally I regarded these treasures with unfeigned interest. To the side were a flat spatulalike spoon, and a pointed stick, a northern analog to the Turian eating, or dining, prong.

"It seems," I said, "Master dines well."

He looked at me, narrowly.

He broke off a piece of the bread and held it out to me. I leaned forward, eagerly, and stretched out my hands, but then, wary, I drew back, quickly.

He smiled.

I looked at him, angrily.

"I dare not feed," I said. "Master has not yet fed or begun to feed."

"See," he said, "you are not stupid, or not altogether stupid."

"Thank you," I said, "Master."

"You look well in a collar," he said.

"I am pleased that Master is pleased," I said.

What a monster he was! It had been a test. I dared not conjecture what might have occurred had I failed such a test, so simple a test! He was a monster, and I was in his power, and I knew that I could not resist his touch, even had I been permitted to attempt to do so.

"I see I have again amused Master," I said.

"You are insolent," he said. "That is not permitted."

"I am from Earth," I said.

"Earth is now behind you," he said. "You are now of Gor."

"Yes, Master," I said.

That was true.

"A Gorean animal," he said.

"Master?" I said.

"A slave," he said.

"Yes, Master," I said.

In Gorean law the slave is an animal. I was a domestic animal, a slave.

"You were worthless on Earth," he said, "utterly worthless, but now, here at least, you have some value, a modicum of value, the pittance that would take you off a slave block."

"May I partake of the contents of the trencher?" I asked.

"You are presumptuous," he said.

I regarded the heaped trencher, avidly. "Surely there is more there than Master requires," I said.

"Can it be," he said, "that after months on Gor, you still do not know what you are?"

I knew well what I was, and wanted to be. But, as much as I knew I was a slave, and wanted to be such, as much as I was helplessly drawn to this Gorean brute, as much as I wanted to belong to him, as much as I wanted to be his property, as much as a brush, a buckle, a comb, a sandal, I was furious with him, as well. Had he not claimed I was not worth keeping, had he not sold me, had he not rid himself of me?

Looking at me, he put the bit of bread he had pretended to offer me in his mouth, and finished it.

"I am very hungry," I said. "And Master has begun to feed."

"But has not yet finished," he said.

I knelt back, and waited, for several Ehn, until Kurik had finished with the contents of the trencher. He then finished his dinner with several swigs from the bottle, the contents of which proved to be, judging by the apparent fire of its taste, and the apparently satisfactory burning in his mouth, some special paga. He then recorked the bottle, put it aside, and looked at me.

"Master is finished," I said, archly.

He rose up, went to the wall to my right, as I knelt, and removed the slave whip from its peg.

He shook out the five broad blades. It is designed to punish, and terribly, but not to mark. One does not wish to lower the value of merchandise.

"I merely observed that Master was finished," I said, frightened.

He looked down at me, both hands on the handle of the whip. I had never felt the Gorean slave whip, even in training, and had no wish to do so, certainly not now, and in this situation.

"Forgive me, Master," I said. As is well-known what is said, however innocent the words might seem in themselves, may be said in a way, or a tone, or with an expression, that transforms and parts the veil of benignity, that moves it to the side, and conveys a message of quite dissimilar import.

He replaced the whip on its peg, to my relief, and then sat down, cross-legged, before the leather curtain, his back to it, the tray at hand.

"Approach, slave," he said.

I crawled to him on all fours.

"You are hungry?" he said.

"Yes, Master," I said.

He then took me by the hair, and forced my head down, holding it over the bowl of gruel, now little more than cold mush.

"Please, no," I whispered.

My face was then thrust down into the bowl, deeply. I shut my eyes, the gruel was all about my face, to my ears and hair. I could not breathe. I feared I might drown, so held.

"Feed, slave," he said.

I moved my head, as I could, to clear mush to the sides, to open up crevices and passages into which air might penetrate, and began to bite and swill at the mush, desperately, filling my mouth, and struggling to swallow down great gluts, as best I could, again and again. Then he wiped the inside of the bowl with my face, and bade me, with my tongue, to waste no gruel. Then, still holding me by the hair, he thrust my head down into the other bowl, that of water, and, my hands on the floor, on either side of the bowl, I drank, lapping the water, as I could, being shown the beast, and slave, that I was.

After a time, he released my hair, and sat back, watching me, while I continued to drink.

When I had drunk my fill, I lifted my head from the bowl.

"Position," he said.

He then, as I knelt, reached to a cloth to the side, of the sort that might serve diversely, as a bond, as a gag, as a blindfold, and dampened the cloth in the bit of water remaining in the bowl, and then, as I kept the palms of my hands down, on my thighs, in position, he gently dabbed my face dry and clean, removing the water and the residue of gruel.

Despite the rudeness, and the commanding brutality, of Kurik, of Victoria, in the manner in which it had occurred, I had been fed and watered. I was grateful that this had been done. I felt stronger, and refreshed.

Then the realities of my situation once again became evident, acutely so. I knelt before this brute, alone with him, in a Gorean alcove, wholly in his power, stark naked, a collar on my neck, his to do with as he wished, a slave.

"What are you going to do with me?" I asked.

"What I wish," he said.

"Of course," I said.

How alive my body was! How I wanted him to touch me!

"I am considering the matter," he said. "What do you suggest?"

"It is for Master to decide," I said.

I realized, suddenly, that I had turned my hands on my thighs, so that the palms were no longer down on my thighs, but up, displaying the small expanse of the nerve-ready, sensitive, vulnerable tissue of the palms to the master. It is a slave's begging gesture. Quickly, reddening, shamed, I turned the palms of my hands down, again, quickly, on my thighs. I trusted he had not noticed this inadvertent self-betrayal of my needs. He smiled. He had seen! I hated him! Before him, before this master, I had betrayed my slave needs!

"What do you think I will do with you?" he asked.

"I am a slave," I said.

"I am aware of that," he said.

I regarded him.

I wanted to loop the bondage knot in my hair, but I did not dare remove my hands from my thighs. As I was right handed, I would commonly put the knot at my right shoulder.

"Do you beg for attention," he asked.

"Do not make me beg," I said.

"You seem ready," he said.

"Do not make me beg," I said.

There, before him, kneeling on the furs, in the half-lit alcove, in the soft, warm light of the small tharlarion-oil lamp, a collar on my neck, which I could not remove, I knew the ecstasy of being wholly dominated by a male. I rejoiced in my sex. Can men, I wondered, understand such desire? I had never felt so ready, so intensely female.

At that moment there was, from beyond the leather curtain, the sudden skirl of a flute, the swift strumming of a kalika, and the pounding of the tabor.

"A dancer!" he said, pleased. "The Slave Whip is a proper, fine tavern. It can buy the best!"

"Master!" I said.

But he seized my wrists and forced me back, against the wall, at the back of the alcove. A moment later manacles were snapped on my wrists, and my wrists were fastened back, to the wall, on either side of my body. Then my ankles were seized, and I was pulled forward, and was supine, and then my ankles, in his grip, were parted, widely, and shackled to rings on the floor. I reared half up, in protest. I jerked futilely at the chains. I could not bring my hands before my body, nor could I close my legs.

"Now," he said, turning about, reaching for the curtain straps, "I will see what a real woman is like."

"Master," I begged. "Please, Master!"

But he had unbuckled the curtain, departed, and yanked it shut behind him. I caught the briefest glimpse of tanned legs in the sand, each ankle ringed with slave bells, and a swirling skirt of scarlet dancing silk. I heard the jangle of jewelry, and the sudden, bright flash of finger cymbals. I heard men crying out, and pounding paga goblets on the tables.

I wept in misery, pulling against the chains, twisting and turning, and then, my desperate efforts mocked by obdurate, clasping steel, I lay back in the furs, in helpless frustration, a slave, chained in place.

It seemed forever that the slave danced, but it was doubtless no more at a time than a handful of Ehn, perhaps no more than three or four. Four times the music stopped, and I waited for the return of Kurik, of Victoria, but it would begin again, perhaps with another slave, certainly with another tempo, another mood, another exhibition of how marvelously beautiful and desirable a human female can be, another exhibition of why they should be possessed, owned, collared, and mastered.

I rehearsed a hundred greetings, criticisms, comments, witty remarks, and clever observations, for when I should be rejoined by Kurik, of Victoria, that he might realize how little his absence concerned me, that his neglect of me was scarcely noticed, if at all, and perhaps had even been welcomed, surely that I had not been perturbed, that his callous abandonment of me had caused me no distress, that to it, and to such things, and to him, I was completely indifferent.

Eventually he reentered the alcove, and, turning about, rebuckled shut the leather curtain. Then again he sat opposite me, cross-legged.

He looked at me.

I pulled a little at the chains. I could not bring my hands before my body. I could not close my legs, for they were widely separated.

He regarded the helpless expanse of slave spread before him.

"I beg attention," I said. "I beg attention, Master."

Many times then, that evening, the next morning, and the next afternoon, did Kurik of Victoria pleasure himself with me.

The first time, when my limbs were still chained apart, and I could not bring my arms before my body nor close my legs, he drove me wild, bit by bit, touch by touch, with expectation, with passion, and need. Then, as I writhed in the chains, and lifted my body piteously to him, that he would allow me the succession of explosions the foundations for which, and the readiness for which, he had so patiently and skillfully prepared, to whose brink he had brought me, he desisted in his work.

I regarded him, eyes wide, aghast, disbelievingly. "Master!" I cried, in misery. "Please, Master!"

He sat back, regarding me in the chains.

I shook them, helplessly, pulling against them. "Please!" I wept. "Please!"

He reviewed me, amused, satisfied.

"Relief!" I begged. "It needs but a touch, a touch! Please! Relief, relief, Master!"

"Perhaps you remember the office," he said, "on the dismal, polluted, spoiled world of Earth, when you were short with me."

"Mercy, have mercy, Master!" I cried. "Have mercy on a poor, miserable, meaningless slave!"

"Perhaps you beg?" he inquired.

"I beg!" I cried. "I beg! I beg!"

He then bestowed upon me a single, deft touch.

"Yes, oh, yes, yes!" I wept, gratefully, yielding as the slave I had been made, as the slave I was.

On Gor, Ahn may be spent in making love, mornings, nights, evenings, and afternoons. Many are the arts of love, harsh and gentle, fierce and tender, commanding and solicitous, and love's artists are patient and talented. Kurik of Victoria knew well the handling of helpless slaves, their caressing and owning, their grasping and stroking, their conquest and fulfillment. There was his breath, his tongue, his touch. He could play the body of a slave, producing a rapture of sensations, much as the master of the czehar or kalika can play his lovely instrument, drawing forth its laughter and tears, its moans and cries, its pensive contemplations, its incitements and ardors, its valleys and mountains, its depths and its ecstasies.

Never was I off a chain, though commonly it was only a shackle on my left ankle. Did he fear I would attempt to escape him? It would have required chains to draw me from his side. I strove to please him, and in many ways, many of which were conventionally forbidden to the free woman, for they were regarded as incompatible with her status and dignity, for I had been much instructed in the house of my training. Even those who are not expected to be pleasure slaves, even pot girls, and kettle-and-mat girls, must know how to please a master, and as the slave they are. Domestic tasks, too, I had been instructed in, to some extent, cooking, cleaning, sewing, and such, tasks that I would once, as a free woman, have regarded as beneath me, for a slave is many things to a master, tasks that I now loved as they would help me, in their humble way, to better serve a master, but there is no doubt that the central point of my training, its predominant emphasis, had been oriented to the central purpose of the slave, which is to please the master, and as the slave she is.

More than once I had seized the slave whip, kissed it, and licked it, and, kneeling, proffered it to Kurik of Victoria. "Whip me," I had begged. "Whip me! I want to be whipped!" "Do not be absurd," he had laughed, and pulled me to him. It seemed strange to me that I, who muchly feared the whip, would implore this man to use it on me. Interestingly, the Gorean master seldom uses a whip on a slave, even when supplicated to do so. The power of the whip is primarily in its presence, and in its readiness to be used, not in its actual employment. If a slave must be frequently whipped, she must be a very poor slave. She is then less likely to be whipped than sold. Why then had I begged this man to beat me? I suspect, upon reflection, puzzling on this anomaly, that this act convinces the slave that she is truly owned, is truly under the whip, that she is truly a slave, and of this man. This reassures her, heartens her, and pleases her. To be sure, one does not wish too much of this. The slave is not stupid. Convinced of her slavery, she is then likely to go contentedly about her business, that of loving and serving her master. To be sure, sometimes a slave is whipped to remind her that she is a slave. After a lashing, she is no longer in any doubt about that.

I fear that I many times cried out my love for Kurik of Victoria. I wept in his arms, his. At last he cuffed me to silence. "The love of a slave is worthless," he said. "She is merely to be dominated, owned, ravished, mastered, and put to one's pleasure as the worthless, meaningless beast she is. She is bought, and collared, an article of property. Do not dare speak of love!" "Yes, my Master!" I cried. "Own me, as the worthless, meaningless beast I am!" He then struck me, again. "Do not use the words 'my Master' to me," he said, angrily. "Forgive me, Master," I begged. The slave addresses all free men as 'Master', and all free women as 'Mistress', but she uses the words 'my Master' only to her actual master, her owner. "Perhaps," I thought, "the love of a slave is worthless, but what love can begin to compare with the love of a slave for her master? What greater, deeper, more profound love can a woman have than that of a humble, abased, collared slave for her master?"

He looked away.

I had seen anger in his eyes, but, too, so briefly, for a moment, I thought I had seen apprehension. He could not fear me, as I was a mere slave. Who then could he fear, but himself? I recalled how, long ago, in Victoria, when I was new to my collar, I had cried out my love for him, and had been soon, I thought abruptly, inexplicably, sold. One is not to care for a slave. Did not all know that? Might one not be mocked for such a weakness? Would that not call forth laughter in the taverns and exercise yards? How that would lessen a man in his own eyes! How then could he respect himself? Did he fear some concession or compromise that might diminish or tarnish his cherished, mighty self-esteem? But could a master not care a little for a slave? Why not? Might he not feel as much for a kaiila or pet sleen? I was afraid, for I wanted to belong to him. I must try to conceal my love for him, but it is not easy for a slave to conceal her love. She is the most open and helpless of all women. How is she to control her expressions, her lips, her tiny movements, her eyes? It is as difficult for her to conceal her feelings as it is her body. Her emotions are as public to view as her lineaments.

"Forgive me, Master," I said, again, and then, again, he reached for me, and I was drawn again into his arms.

I did not wish to be discarded, as might easily be done with me. How easy it is to sell a slave, or give her away! I must obey. I must be pleasing. Too, I did not wish to be again cuffed. Next time the slave whip might be used on me!

"Oh!" I cried, softly.

"You need a man's hands on your body, slave," he said, "possessive and commanding."

"I have been made so," I said.

"Good," he said.

"I want to be so," I said.

"You are so," he said.

"Yes, Master," I said.

"Slave," he sneered.

"Yes, Master," I said.

Then I cried out, helpless in the throes of an ecstasy, that to which he had seen fit to subject me.

Toward noon of the next day, the day on which he was to venture to the House of Flavius Minor, a tool was brought, and my collar was changed. I was told it read, "I am the property of Tenrik of Siba." I dared not ask him if it were his intention to keep me. I did know that the name on the collar was not his real name. After our evening meal, in which he permitted me some meat, he said, "We must have a new tunic for you." I nodded. It would not do to keep the bright yellow tunic I had worn at the slave ring, that which I had worn when posing as a guide slave for Tyrtaios, of the Black Court. It was too conspicuous, and guardsmen might well have been instructed to watch for a slave so clad.

"Wear this," he said, tossing me a handful of cloth.

"It is so tiny," I said, "and it is damp, and warm."

"We took it off the body of one of the paga girls," he said. "Put it on."

"Master!" I protested.

"Do not be concerned," he said, "the girl has been given a new, clean tunic, freshly pressed."

"I am not a paga girl," I said.

"I need only give you to the proprietor," he said, "and you will be a paga girl."

"I do not wish to wear my chain in a tavern," I said.

"You will wear your chain wherever men wish," he said.

I slipped into the tunic, for I did not wish to risk a command being repeated.

"Now," he said, looking at me, as one might look at a paga slave, "you are indistinguishable from a paga girl."

"Certainly not," I said.

"Prettier than some, not so pretty as others," he said.

"We are to leave," I said, "in the neighborhood of the nineteenth Ahn?"

"Yes," he said. "I think that will do, well enough."

"The delivery, the package, the object, or such," I said, "is to be received at the twentieth Ahn, and is to be claimed at the first Ahn."

"Exactly at the first Ahn," he said.

"I am to accompany you," I said.

"I think that is safest," he said. "Torture easily loosens a slave's tongue."

"I wish to accompany you," I said.

"The decision is mine," he said.

"Of course," I said. "Is the House of Flavius Minor far?"

"Not too far," he said. "It is amongst the houses on the southern piers."

"How is it," I asked, "that we depart the Slave Whip at the nineteenth Ahn and claim the object at the first Ahn? That is two Ahn, and surely more than is required to reach the house of Flavius Minor, be it at the southern piers."

"We will bide a suitable interval," he said, "at the House of Anesidemus."

"May I ask," I asked, "what manner of house is the House of Anesidemus?"

"Certainly," he said. "It is a slave market."

CHAPTER THIRTY-ONE

She is so beautiful!" I exclaimed.

"She will do," said Kurik of Victoria.

I knelt beside him, at his knee, as he sat in the tiers, savoring the sales of women, below.

"See this one," called the auctioneer, turning the beauty before the buyers, with deft touches of his whip, "see this olive skinned, green eyed beauty, with long, glossy, night-black hair, recently imported, with many others, from the World's End. Think of her at your slave ring, leaping helplessly in your arms! Train her in slave dance. Chain her outside your place of business. Would she not bring in customers? Buy her to rent her out. Buy her on speculation! If she is proud, humble her. If she is displeasing, whip her."

I heard bids called from the floor.

"Sixty copper tarsks!" I heard.

"Eighty!"

"Eighty-five!"

"Surely she is worth more, Master," I said. I had seldom seen a more beautiful woman.

"This is a cheap market," said Kurik of Victoria. "Men do not have much to spend here."

"Surely that is not a cheap-market girl," I said.

"I think not," he said. "I have seen worse marketed from the central block of the Curulean."

"I do not understand," I said.

"Nor do I," said Kurik. "It is an anomaly. Perhaps she muchly displeased someone, and he wished her sold beneath her value, to humiliate or punish her, assuring himself that she would find herself the property of a rude, lowly, impatient master, that she would be worked hard, and wear her chain in a hovel. Perhaps someone wanted her sold inconspicuously and cheaply, for some reason. Perhaps the matter was sensitive, in some way. Perhaps she was of high caste, and had enemies, and her seller chose to dispose of her, to lessen the risk of having her fall into the hands of enemies."

"A merciful vendor," I said.

"If so," he said, "she should strive to be a humble, inconspicuous, and perfect slave."

"We all hope to be pleasing," I said. "We are all collared."

"But perhaps she was of high caste, and known, and her seller did not want her to be purchased by a friend, and freed," said Kurik.

"I think there is little danger of that," I said.

"No," he said. "Once the collar is on them they are slaves."

"Who would free a slave girl?" I laughed.

"I see you now know something of Gor," he said.

"I have learned much in the collar," I said.

"Only a fool would free a slave girl," he said. "They are better as slaves. One wants them as slaves."

"Yes," I said, delighted, at his knee.

"The slave bow," said the auctioneer, seizing the slave by the hair and bending her backward so that the joy of her figure was displayed for the buyers.

"Ninety copper tarsks!" I heard.

"Ninety-two!" called another, not far from where we were in the tiers, about two-thirds of the distance between the raised, torch-lit block, and the last row, against the back wall.

"Straighten up," ordered the auctioneer. "Hands behind the back of your neck, turn. Good. Enough. You may now lower your hands. The buyers have seen what you look like, so posed. Is she not lovely, Masters? Now, kneel, address the masters. Beg to be purchased!"

The whip snapped.

The slave fell to her knees, and extended her hands, piteously, to the buyers. "Buy me, please, buy me, Masters!" she begged.

There was laughter.

In the alcove, earlier, when I had learned that the house of Anesidemus was a slave market, I had, distraught, in misery, cast myself to my belly before Kurik of Victoria, who was sitting, cross-legged, his back to the leather curtain. I lifted my head, tears in my eyes. "Keep me!" I begged. "Do not sell me!"

"I have no intention of selling you," he said.

"But, the slave market!" I said.

"I enjoy seeing women sold," he said.

"You do not intend to sell me?" I said.

"No," he said.

"Master!" I wept, gratefully.

"At least not immediately," he said. "You are privy to matters concerning which discretion is imperative."

I was silent, on my belly.

"Too," he said, "you juice well."

"Own me," I said. "Your collar, I beg your collar, your real collar, your true collar, not that on me now, not some false collar, not some dissembling collar, not one of duplicity and subterfuge! I want to wear the true collar of my master! Put slave claim on me!"

"You would be mine?" he said.

"Yes!" I said.

"You would follow me?"

"I would follow you!" I said.

"Heeling me, appropriately?" he said.

"Yes, Master," I said.

This expression, in this context, of course, was symbolic. To "heel appropriately" signified that one's submission would be utter and uncompromised.

"If you follow me, you will follow in my chains," he said.

"Yes, yes," I said, "Master!"

This expression, too, of course, was used metaphorically. To "follow in a man's chains" is a way of alluding to the categorical and absolute nature of the bondage to which the slave would be subjected. The stoutest chains of her servitude would be legal, social, psychological, and cultural. To be sure, it is not unknown for a girl to follow her master in chains, literally. She is, after all, a slave.

I was begging Kurik of Victoria to own me.

To be sure, when a master decides to own a girl what she wishes is no longer of interest or importance. He will then see to it that she will be a helpless, total slave. It is the way of Gor.

He looked at me.

"I put slave claim on you," he said.

I then lay before him, in the furs. I remember feeling the shackle, and chain, on my left ankle. And I think I then, overcome, lost consciousness in the furs.

Sometime later I regained consciousness.

My master was putting his across-the-body satchel in order.

"It must be nearly the nineteenth Ahn," I said.

"Yes," he said.

"We will soon leave," I said.

"Yes," he said, "in a bit."

"Surely I am not to wear this tiny thing, this partly torn rag," I said, "this soiled paga tunic, outside the tavern, openly, publicly, in the streets?"

"You will do so," he said. "And you will find yourself well regarded."

"Masters, it seems," I said, "enjoy displaying their properties."

"Yes," he said, "it is one of the many pleasures of the mastery."

"I have one silver tarsk ten!" called the auctioneer. "That is too little, far too little, for such a beauty. Who will bid more? See her in your chains, kneeling at your slave ring! Who will bid more?"

"A silver tarsk ten is too much for a slave!" called a fellow from the darkness of the tiers.

"He would think," said Kurik of Victoria, "sixty or seventy copper tarsks would be too much."

"Many," said a fellow, near us, "go for no more than thirty or forty in this market."

"I do not doubt it," said Kurik of Victoria, my master.

I was now his property, I belonged to him, as might a sandal or a pet sleen. I was overjoyed to belong to such a man. What woman would not wish to be owned by such a man? I must strive to be such a good slave to him! I must please him so! And his touch! How could a woman not in a collar experience such ecstasy? He must not sell me! He must not sell me! I must strive to please him so! "Do not sell me, Master," I thought. "Do not sell me!"

"Well, Adraste, mediocre slave," said the auctioneer to his charge, the merchandise being vended at the moment, "it seems we can get no more for you than a silver tarsk ten."

He loosened the blades of the slave whip.

"Forgive me, Master!" she pleaded.

"Is the slave vital?" called a man from the tiers.

"Is she alive?" called another.

"Stand upright, Adraste," said the auctioneer. "Clasp your hands together, behind your neck. Part your feet a little."

"Master?" she said.

"Now," he said. "Good."

"What manner of name is 'Adraste', Master?" I asked.

"Cosian," he said. "But she could be from anywhere. We name them as we wish."

"She was imported from the World's End, it was said," I said.

"Perhaps," he said. "But she is not native to the World's End. The slaves native to the World's End have their special sort of beauty."

"Doubtless many of them are now entering the markets," I said.

"Yes," he said, "and doubtless, similarly, many slaves native to the continent and the islands are now being shipped west, to the World's End."

"Dear Masters," called the auctioneer, "I had originally thought this slave an unusual buy, an excellent buy, but your bids have convinced me of my error. Clearly, as determined by the hesitancy and reluctance, the indifference, of your bids, she is, as I now recognize, *ela*, merely another mediocre slave."

There was laughter from the tiers.

In this market, I had gathered, a bid of a silver tarsk, or more, was an excellent bid.

The slave stood on the block, stripped, as women are sold, her feet in the sawdust, her body illuminated in the torchlight, her hands clasped behind the back of her neck, her feet slightly parted.

The auctioneer had drifted behind her.

"Should the auctioneer not close the sale?" I asked.

"Shortly," said Kurik, of Victoria.

A shriek rang out in the auditorium.

"Master!" I cried.

"You have never been sold from a block, have you?" asked Kurik.

"No," I said.

"It is the Slaver's Caress," he said.

The woman had cried out, wildly, startled, disbelievingly, protestingly, dismayed at what had been done to her, how she had been unexpectedly, callously forced to betray herself.

Raucous male laughter, in gales, greeted her response.

"No, no!" she cried.

"Get your hands together, behind the back of your neck!" warned the auctioneer.

"Please do not show me so before the men!" she begged.

"Apparently she is not used to being sold," said Kurik.

The whip flashed twice and the woman cried out with pain, and threw herself to the auctioneer's feet, pressing her lips upon them.

How I feared then what must be the kiss of the Gorean slave whip!

"On your feet," said the auctioneer, "stand, hands clasped behind your neck, feet spread, as before, no, more widely!"

The woman, sobbing, obeyed.

Then she cried out, again, helplessly.

"Do we not have a juicy pudding here?" inquired the auctioneer.

There was more laughter.

"She was, I wager," said a fellow, "once of high caste, so lofty and regal she was, but now she is revealed as only another tasta!"

"They are all tastas," said another.

"Yes," agreed another.

Little love was lost between the higher castes and the lower castes. Indeed, it is one of the occasional pleasures of a lower-caste male to obtain a slave who was once of a high caste, usually one who has been captured from another city, a prize in one of the many skirmishes, wars, and raids that characterize the municipalities of Gor. One can then well imagine how the woman is treated by one she would have, perhaps only days or weeks ago, regarded as a social inferior, one beneath her attention, once she is a slave. She is then made well aware of her bondage. How then, a slave, once such a high woman, she must strive to please her lowly master!

How ready the whip is to instruct such!

"A hot little vulo!" called a fellow in the second tier.

"Please, not again, Master!" sobbed the woman.

"Remain standing, as you are," said the auctioneer.

"Aii!" she cried.

"She objects," said Kurik, "the little fool. Does she think she is free? Does she not know there is a collar on her neck?"

"How she is shamed before the men!" I said. "Perhaps she was once of significant station, of high caste!"

"Why should one be shamed, to have been demonstrated to be alive, healthy, vital, and well?" asked Kurik.

"Still!" I protested.

"She is in a collar," he said. "Do you think you would respond otherwise?"

"I fear not," I whispered.

Well did I remember that I, long ago, on a wharf in Victoria, had been subjected to the Slaver's Caress. How I had leaped, startled! How I had, unexpectedly, unmistakably, revealed myself as appropriately collared!

"Surely, Masters," called the auctioneer to the crowd, "you have seen enough!"

Bids stormed forth from the tiers.

The woman sold for a silver tarsk fifty, which, I gather, was a splendid price for such a market.

"The slut is yours," said the auctioneer, thrusting the woman down the steps of the block to his left where an attendant seized her and threw her to the feet of her new master, counting out his coins at the pay table. The block is commonly ascended by means of the stairs on the auctioneer's right, and descended, as in this case, by means of the stairs to his left, as he would face the auditorium.

"Poor woman," I said.

"Not at all," said Kurik. "Do not concern yourself with her. She is a slave, a beast, as are you."

"Yes, Master," I said, kneeling beside him.

"What do you think you would bring?" he asked.

"Very little, I fear," I said. Indeed, if such a woman did not bring a full two silver tarsks, what might I expect, a partially trained barbarian?

"It is a low market, of course," he said.

"I hope Master is not contemplating selling me," I said.

"After tonight," he said, "it would not matter, one way or another."

Tonight his imminent business was to be concluded at the house of Flavius Minor, perhaps within the Ahn.

I strove, disconcerted, to hold back tears.

"Please do not sell me," I said.

"Where did you get the paga girl?" asked a fellow nearby. He had doubtless conjectured thusly, given my tunic.

"At the Slave Whip," said Kurik, my master.

"Cheap?" asked the fellow.

"Yes," said Kurik, of Victoria.

"I will give you twenty copper tarsks for her," said the fellow.

"I would hope for a tarsk-bit or two more," said Kurik.

Doubtless I am vain, but what woman, free or slave, is not? I was quite angry. Twice in Ar, on the streets, a whole silver tarsk had been offered for me, and I thought I might, in a decent market, go for even more. Surely I had seen the eyes of masters on me, a slave is aware of such things, surely as much as a free woman with a slackened veil or an exposed ankle, when we, I heeling my master, had approached the market, when we had entered the market, when we had climbed the tiers and found our place, even as I knelt beside my master during the sales.

"Put me up for sale," I said, angrily. "I am not so cheap! I am beautiful, very beautiful! I will show you I am worth more!"

Kurik laughed.

"Perhaps I will do so," he said.

"No!" I cried. "Do not sell me! Please do not sell me!"

How vulnerable are slaves! How easy it is to hood and bind one, and lead her, on her leash, to a market!

"Not until at least the second Ahn," he said.

Another girl had now been conducted to the height of the block, a short, sweetly thighed blonde. I no longer saw she who had been sold for a silver tarsk fifty. Doubtless she had been back-braceleted and leashed, and, possibly hooded, led away. How helpless we are, the goods of masters!

"It must be past the twentieth Ahn," said Kurik. "We must be away."

"Yes, Master," I said.

We then left our place, descended the stairs, and took our leave of the house of Anesidemus.

CHAPTER THIRTY-TWO

It was now well past the twentieth Ahn.

I took it that my master well knew the location of the house of Flavius Minor. Surely he would endeavor to be at the house by the first Ahn.

The "southern piers," as the district is spoken of, is lonely at night. There were few, if any, guardsmen about. There were rumors, I recalled, as to why this area was less supervised or patrolled. It scarcely seemed a part of the harbor authority's jurisdiction. In Brundisium, as in many cities, much may depend on where one is, and the time of day or night. The southern piers, as we shall speak of them, were now muchly deserted. Surely the clamor and bustle of the day was absent. The walkway from which the piers extended was heavily planked and broad, several yards in width, the piers and water on the one side and the maze of warehouses, and shops, separated by alleys, on the other, leading up to the higher districts. The many crates, barrels, boxes, bales, and such piled about the walkway and piers during the day were no longer in evidence, having been stowed on the ships or shut away in the warehouses. Unprotected objects, as is well known, if deemed of value, may find themselves relocated during the hours of darkness. *Ela*, they are wont to vanish. This absence of the usual diurnal clutter, such a massive jumble of goods, attendant on these obvious mercantile precautions, made the walkway and piers, of course, seem even more spacious, lonely, and frightening. On the other hand, my master, I am sure, welcomed such an arrangement, particularly this night. In any event, we stayed near the center of the walkway, away from the buildings and shadows. In such a way it is not easy for one to be approached, unnoticed. There were several galleys moored in the area, at the piers, and at the edge of the walkway itself. On the knife ships the masts were down; on the round ships no canvas was slung to the yards. The ships, the long ships, or knife ships, and the round ships, the freighters and

coasters, seemed dark in the night, and disquieting, like quiet, watching, lurking things. On some of the ships, the knife ships, canvas was
stretched between the bulwarks, to shield the deck. Sometimes mariners sleep beneath such canvas. Occasionally we saw a lantern, usually
at the stern. One could hear the water lapping against the pilings, and
hear the occasional creak of ropes and timber, vessels pulling against
their moorings. It was windy and cloudy. A rope would dip beneath the
water, and then, as the ship rocked, and moved, it might lift, taut and
dripping. Occasionally one saw, in the light of the moons, the shimmering droplets, shed from the tautened rope, fall to the water. A rain,
scarcely noticeable, was falling. The paga tunic, now damp, afforded
little comfort. Two of the three moons were in the sky, occasionally
visible through the clouds, the white and yellow moons. The smallest
moon could not be detected, and it was not always easy to note, even
under better conditions. The smallest moon is called the Prison Moon,
but this name made little sense to me. How could a tiny moon, or any
moon, be a prison? Perhaps it was called that because it seemed prison-
like, small, remote, forbidding, cold, and desolate.

I was little more than a pace behind my master. I suspect I clung
about him more closely than propriety would suggest for a suitable
heeling distance, but I was uneasy. Thankfully he did not warn me
away. He seemed tense, and vigilant. This did not decrease my apprehension. A slave, as other animals, I suppose, is likely to be quite sensitive to the emotional states and moods of her master. Sometimes her
life might depend on that. Had he not feared a slave's looseness of
tongue or her defection, I might have been left to the comfort of some
kennel or cage, or to the security of a chain and ring, nicely sheltered,
wrapped in an ample, pleasant blanket, warm and dry. But had I been
given a choice, and who gives a slave a choice, I would have chosen
to be with him. I had been in the arms of Kurik of Victoria. I was his
slave. I did not wish to languish for him, fearing for him, suffering in
his absence. I was his. I wanted to be with him.

"That is the house of Flavius Minor," said Kurik, pointing to a large,
dark warehouse. It must have been seventy yards wide, and it extended
back into the darkness, perhaps as far. The front of the building was
some ten yards in height, suggesting that the building contained levels. Its huge gate had two leaves, and, were it opened, it would easily accommodate the passage of a double-harness tharlarion wagon.
Within this larger gate, in the right leaf of the gate, as one would face
the building, there was a smaller opening, a door, by means of which

individuals might come and go. Near this door, to the side, on the right, as one would face the building, on the wall of the building, was a small, lidded tharlarion-oil lamp. This illuminated a flat sign under the lamp on which there was some lettering that, I supposed, identified the structure. When we approached the building more closely, I noted that there was a small, sliding panel in this door, which, if opened, would allow someone within the building to peer outward without opening the door. During the day I supposed that the larger door, the two-leaved gate, would be open, allowing access to and from the interior of the large structure. But it would not be so at night. The lamp on the wall was so situated that the would-be visitor, or whosoever might seek admittance, by means of the door, would be illuminated in its light.

Kurik hesitated some yards before the small door, and looked about.

"All seems quiet," he said.

"And lonely," I said.

"We may not be alone," he said.

"I see no one," I said.

"Nor I," he said.

"It must be nearly time," I said, "for the ringing of the first Ahn."

"No," he said, "not yet."

"What is the nature of the package, the delivery, its contents?" I asked.

"It is a gift," he said.

"For whom?" I asked.

"You need not know that," he said.

"Doubtless the package is of value," I said.

"Perhaps," he said. "Its origin is far away, a steel world."

He then approached the door within the right leaf of the closed gate. He looked about, again. I think he was uneasy to stand within the compass of the lamp, as small as this compass was.

Kurik rapped lightly on the door, and then stepped to the side, into the shadows.

We waited.

"Perhaps Master should knock more loudly," I said.

"Perhaps you should be bitted," he said.

"Forgive me, Master," I said. I had no desire to be fastened again in that horrid device. A girl, bitted, is in no doubt she is a slave.

"A light knock is more than adequate," he said. "One or more will be within, listening. They will have been alerted to expect a claimant."

The small, narrow, rectangular panel slid back.

"Stand in the light," said a voice.

Kurik stepped into the light.

"What do you want?" said the voice.

"A package has been delivered," said Kurik, "perhaps recently. I come to claim it."

"Many packages are delivered," said the man. "Return in the morning. Bring your claiming disk."

"I have no claiming disk," said Kurik.

"How then can you claim the package?" asked the voice, narrowly.

"As the package for which there is no claiming disk," said Kurik.

"From whence is this package?" asked the voice.

"From far away," said Kurik.

"From farther than Torvaldsland, from farther than Schendi?" said the voice.

"Yes," said Kurik.

"Perhaps," said the voice.

"You are expecting me," said Kurik.

"We are expecting someone," said the voice.

"Admit me," said Kurik.

"Surely, Master," said the voice.

The panel slid shut, and the door opened partly, and Kurik slipped through.

"Not the slave," said the voice. "Chain her outside, there is a ring."

"And risk having her cry out?" asked Kurik.

"True," said the voice, "there must be no noise, nothing to attract attention, nothing to stir curiosity. Better to bring her within then, where, if she dares to murmur, her throat can be cut."

I was not pleased, nor was I reassured, in any way, to hear such a remark.

Quickly I entered, and hid myself, as I could, behind my master.

A lantern was lifted, by a second man within.

He regarded my master, carefully, saying nothing. He then turned to me and I, illuminated and before a free person, knelt, my head down.

"A paga girl," he said, he with the lantern.

I stiffened, angrily. How dare he think of me as a paga girl!

"Yes," said my master.

I dared not cry out.

But, surely, I thought, if my master can assume some guise, why not I? But why, I asked myself, that of a paga girl? Did my master so think of me? Did he think of me as no more than a paga girl, if that?

Who could look at me, and think I was a mere paga girl? But then I realized that any master, even my master, Kurik of Victoria, might sell me so, and then I would be no more than another paga girl.

"I like paga girls," said the fellow with the lantern. "They are hot on the end of their chain."

"So is any slave," said my master.

"They had better be," laughed he with the lantern.

It was not our fault what men had done to us! Too, I hoped my master would soon touch me. How alive, and needful, I was on Gor, helpless in my collar.

"It is not a badly curved slave," said the first fellow, he who had peered through the sliding panel.

"She will do," said Kurik.

"Where did you get her?" asked the second fellow.

"At the Slave Whip," said my master.

"Cheap?" he was asked.

"Of course," he said.

I did not think such an asseveration was necessary to support our imposture.

"Follow me," said the man with the lantern, turning, and beginning to make his way deeper into the interior of the warehouse.

I rose, unbidden, and followed the men.

The space we traversed through the center of the warehouse was muchly open, but there were many boxes, crates, and such, stacked about the walls.

"The crate to be surrendered without a claiming ticket?" said he with the lantern, leading the way.

"That is my understanding," said Kurik.

One could not see a great deal in the light of the lantern, for the shadows about us, and above us, to the sides, but even a small light, in a darkness, may seem surprisingly bright. It would have hurt my eyes to look directly at it. I could sense darknesses about us, and above us, and sensed, on the sides, and at the back, two tiered, interior balconies, presumably leading to rooms beyond. The first balcony level could be reached by a ramp, and ladders. A similar arrangement, I supposed, characterized the second, higher balcony, beginning from the level of the first. The roof over the central area of the house was lost in shadows. To the side, against a wall, on the ground level, I saw two carts, and detected another on the first balcony. There was also, on the first balcony, and, I supposed, also on the second, though it was difficult to tell, a projecting beam, from which descended an apparatus of ropes and counterweights.

The tread of the three men, the heels of their high-laced, bootlike sandals, marked our passage in the gloom.

I was barefoot.

I had not been given sandals.

We envied those who were permitted sandals.

"It is there," said the fellow who had admitted us, pointing to a large crate, against the back wall. The fellow with the lantern stood to the side, the lantern lifted.

"It is large," said Kurik. "I did not know it was so large."

"Claim it," said he who had admitted us, moving a bit to the other side.

"I would not stand so close to us, Phyllis," said my master.

I then knelt, somewhat puzzled, uneasily, to the side.

I did not understand my master's instruction, but it is not necessary that I do so. It is enough for a domestic beast to obey. The domestic beast does not hesitate, or question. She obeys.

The switch and whip are not pleasant.

"It has no markings," said Kurik, peering at the crate.

"Nor has it a claiming ticket," said he who had admitted us.

"You are sure it is the one?" asked Kurik.

"It is the one," said he who had admitted us.

"Good," said Kurik.

"Claim it," said he who had admitted us.

"No," said Kurik.

"'No'?" asked the man.

"No," said Kurik.

"It has been delivered," said he who had admitted us. "It is here. That is it. Claim it."

"I decline," said Kurik.

"I do not understand," said the man.

"I decline," repeated Kurik.

"Do not try our patience, nor waste our time," said the fellow. "If you want it, claim it. The transaction may be done in an instant."

"Doubtless," said Kurik.

"The house is closed," said the man. "Claim it, or not. Do you wish to be put out? If you do not wish to claim it now, return in the morning."

"I would not be able to do so," said Kurik.

"Why not?" asked the fellow.

"I would not be alive in the morning," said Kurik.

"I do not understand," said he who had admitted us.

"I suspect you understand quite well," said Kurik. "If you do not, seek for enlightenment from the fellows on the first balcony, doubtless employees of the house, who have crossbows trained on me."

"You are observant," said he who had admitted us.

"Not really," said Kurik. "Rather, I conjecture."

"Oh?" said he who had admitted us.

"Why else," asked Kurik, "would you and your friend have so subtly separated yourself from me, and from what better vantage point might one fire than from the first balcony?"

"And you conjecture more than one?" said he who had admitted us.

"One might miss," said Kurik. "To be sure, if one knows his business, one would not be likely to miss at this distance."

"And crossbows?" asked he who had admitted us.

"It is the ready weapon, the patient weapon," said Kurik.

"Perhaps you know the signal upon which your conjectured bowmen will fire?"

"*Ela*," said Kurik, "I do not."

"Perhaps you are in danger," said he who had admitted us.

"It is quite possible," said Kurik.

I looked up to the first balcony, and now detected darknesses behind the rail.

"I doubt," said he who had admitted us, "you are the intended recipient of the package."

"I commend your skepticism," said Kurik. "It does you credit."

"The intended recipient," he said, "would by now have claimed the package."

"I see," said Kurik.

"The matter is one of import, which brooks no delay," he said. "Yet you dally. Clearly then you are not the intended recipient of the package, he for whom we have been instructed to wait. So, claim the package now, friend, or I will issue the signal and, in the instant, you will have two quarrels in your back."

"Now?" said Kurik.

"Yes," said he who had admitted us.

"It would not be wise," said Kurik.

"Oh?" asked he who had admitted us.

"No," said Kurik.

Then a single, long, reverberating note rang out in the night, wrought by a mighty hammer having struck against a large, hollow, suspended metal cylinder, mounted somewhere in the center of the city, which note would be audible from the outer walls to the southern piers.

"That is the bar for the first Ahn, is it not?" said Kurik.

"It is," said he who had admitted us.

"I claim the package," said Kurik

"It is yours," said he who had admitted us.

CHAPTER THIRTY-THREE

—————

W hat is this thing?" he cried.

"It is alive," said the man. "Beware!"

The two fellows who had been stationed on the first balcony, summoned, had disarmed their weapons and joined us on the floor of the house of Flavius Minor. They had then, with tools, addressed themselves to the opening of the large crate, to which no claiming disk was to be pertinent. Board after board was pried free, to the wrenching of wood and the squeak of dislodged nails, and then, finally, freed, the panel fronting the crate was pulled away.

"What is this thing?" one had cried.

"It is alive," had said the other. "Beware!"

"What is it?" cried he who had admitted us.

"I do not know," said the first man.

It was hard to see within the opened crate, but something was inside, a dark shape, crouched within, at the back, in the corner to the right.

"Restore the panel, close the crate," whispered he who had admitted us.

"No," said Kurik.

"Arm your bows," said he who had admitted us to the two who had now, warily, drawn back from the crate.

Feet were thrust into the weapon's stirrup, the cable seized, and the metal leaves were drawn back, and the device was cocked. I heard two quarrels slipped into the guide. The weapons were then raised and leveled.

"Steady," said Kurik. "Do not fire."

"Bring the lantern closer, lift it, illuminate the interior of the crate," said he who had admitted us.

"Ai!" cried one of the two bowmen.

"Steady," said Kurik.

I held back a cry of alarm, for it seemed, for a moment, in the light of the lantern, that two bright, sudden, feral disks of copper blazed forth from the darkness. Then there was a whimper, and a hairy limb was raised and I could no longer see the creature's eyes. The thing was huddled in the corner of the crate, its head down.

"Draw back the lantern," said Kurik. "Do not hurt it. Do not frighten it."

"It is a beast, a large, live beast," said the fellow with the lantern. The lantern light moved about, as his hand was unsteady.

"Not so large," said Kurik.

"A beast!" said the fellow.

"Much like a beast," said Kurik.

"Is it dangerous?" asked he who had admitted us.

"Possibly," said Kurik.

"Let us kill it," said one of the men with a crossbow.

"No," said Kurik.

"It is a Kur," said he who had admitted us. "I once saw one. I have never forgotten it. It is a Kur."

"What is a Kur?" asked he with the lantern.

"It is small for a Kur," said Kurik.

"It is large enough," said the second man with a crossbow.

"Remove your finger from the trigger of your bow," said Kurik. "Do not release the quarrel. Let it rest. There must be no chance misfire."

The creature in the crate lifted its head from the shelter of its arm. Again glowed the eyes like burnished copper.

I shuddered.

"A quarrel to the heart," said the first fellow with a bow.

"Do not fire," said Kurik. "This thing has value."

At that point the creature, looking up, eyes flashing, opened its jaws, angrily.

"Aii," muttered the man with the bow.

"No," said Kurik. He gently pushed the loaded bow to the side.

There was no mistaking the fangs, bared, white, curved, long, in that bestial maw. "It is wild," said the fellow with a lantern.

"If it were wild," said Kurik, "it would not be here."

"It is a Kur," said he who had admitted us.

"Like a Kur," said Kurik.

"It is small for a male Kur," said he who had admitted us. "It is a female Kur."

"I am familiar with females of the Kurii," said Kurik. "It is not a Kur female."

At that point, emanating from the beast in the crate, was a stream of what, initially, I took for simple bestial noises, rude, guttural, snarling sounds, growls, and rumblings. I was reminded of what noises might be emitted by beasts of my own world, large cats, lions, lords of the African veldt, tigers, sleek and silent-footed, moving like shadows, lords in the Asian jungles, and yet these noises, alarming me, had about them an unusual modulation, an articulation, a subtlety, a delicacy, an exactness, and precision, that eerily suggested a form of speech. If a panther could speak, would it not speak thusly?

"That is Kur," said he who had admitted us.

"Yes," said Kurik. "It is Kur."

"So it is a Kur," said he who had admitted us.

"Or like a Kur," said my master.

"I wish I had a translator," said he who had admitted us.

"What is a translator?" asked the man with the lantern.

"This beast," said Kurik, "has been transmitted from afar, for a particular purpose. It seems highly unlikely that it would have been committed to those who could not communicate with it, and with whom it could not communicate."

"So?" said he who had admitted us.

"Kurii," said Kurik, "are a dangerous, rational, technologically advanced species. They are intelligent, and cunning."

"And glorious and powerful," said he who had admitted us, looking about.

I glanced about the darkness.

"If you wish," said Kurik.

"Continue," said he who had admitted us.

"And this beast," said Kurik, "if it is not Kur, is assuredly Kurlike."

"Granted," said he who had admitted us.

"Thus," said Kurik, "I do not think our hirsute friends, considering the presumed importance of this business, would be so negligent or stupid as to omit instructions, or forget to provide a translator."

"I see!" said he who had admitted us. Then he turned to the beast, it crouching back in the crate. He glared at it. "Speak Gorean," he said.

Once again a stream of sound, whose phonemes, if it were a form of speech, seemed unfamiliar, and unintelligible, emanated from the throat of the creature.

Once before, in Ar, I had heard something similar, but heavier, more explosive, more frightening.

"It cannot speak Gorean," said he who had admitted us.

"Let us kill it, before it attacks us," said one of the men with an armed crossbow.

The creature shrank back in the crate.

"It is frightened," I thought. "It understands."

"Perhaps," said Kurik, "it is speaking Gorean."

"Absurd," said he who had admitted us. "A larl, a sleen, could do as well."

"It is a different throat, a different vocal apparatus," said Kurik. "Could you speak Kur, any dialect of Kur?"

"I could not make such noises," said he who had admitted us. "Where is the device, the translator?"

"One, I suspect," said Kurik, "was not deemed necessary."

"A tragic omission," said he who had admitted us.

"May I speak, Masters?" I asked.

"No," said he who had admitted us. And then he turned to Kurik. "Your slave is presumptuous," he said. "Is she so poorly trained? I fear so. Beat her, cuff her, or, if you wish, I shall have the five-stranded disciplinary device brought, and put to a richly deserved use."

"No," said Kurik, looking down at me. "Speak," he said.

"I heard something, long ago, in Ar," I said. "It was something like this."

"Continue," said Kurik.

"It seemed unintelligible to me," I said. "It was so different. I would not understand it. I refused to do so. I would not try. I resisted it. I dismissed it. Yet, moments later, I trembled, frightened, for I realized I had understood it. It is much like struggling to understand a Cosian accent, and then, somehow, suddenly, it is understood. It is a matter of subtle adjustments, of transposing sounds, of substituting one sound for another."

"Absurd," said he who had admitted us.

"I am sure the beast understands Gorean," I said. "Did you not note its reaction when it thought itself threatened?"

"It understood the weapon," said he who had admitted us. "Perhaps it had seen such a thing, discharged, a kill made with such a thing. It might easily have understood the menace in the tone. Any beast could do as much."

"May I, Master," I asked, "attempt to communicate with the thing?"

"Do not permit her to waste our time," said the fellow with the lantern.

"Would you prefer, instead, to engage the beast in discourse?" asked Kurik.

"No," said he with the lantern. "It cannot be done."

"The beast, I am sure," said Kurik, "is female. It seems Kurlike, but it is very different from a Kur female. By now a Kur female might have torn open our throats."

The other fellows drew back, a bit.

"It, I am sure, is a female," said Kurik, "and the slave is a female, the most female of females, one in a collar. Perhaps there is some affinity there. Too, the slave, if she may be credited, has had some experience that might prove relevant."

"If she is not lying," said he who had admitted us.

"Slaves seldom lie," said Kurik. "They are not free women. The free woman may lie with impunity, but not the slave. For the slave, the penalties are too severe."

"Perhaps," said he who had admitted us, "the slave is merely mistaken, possibly deluded."

"Perhaps," said Kurik.

"Let her try," said he with the lantern. "She may be beaten if unsuccessful."

"This slave," said Kurik, "is a barbarian, brought to our markets from the slave world. And yet, you will note, her Gorean is quite passable."

"It had better be," laughed one of the fellows with a bow.

"The switch and whip have seen to it," said the second fellow with a bow.

Well was I familiar with the switch. But I had never been whipped, had never had the Gorean slave lash applied to my body, for my improvement or instruction.

"Things are not so easily explained," said Kurik. "It is well known that women, interestingly, have a surprising facility for the acquisition of languages."

"So?" said he who had admitted us.

"Why would this be?" asked Kurik. "Surely this is not some vast, inexplicable, overwhelming coincidence."

"What might explain it?" asked he with the lantern.

"Consider women," said Kurik, "small, slight, lovely, desirable, an exciting and ideal form of wealth. Are not such creatures esteemed trading goods, suitable plunder, desiderated loot, sought for, and fought for? While men are slain, are they not stripped and led away on their neck ropes? Will they survive, or perish? Surely those who, first, and best, learn the languages of their masters will, on the whole, be most pleasing and survive most frequently. Thus, over millennia, in thousands of venues, the female with suitable linguistic aptitudes entwined within her hereditary coils will tend to be favored by the stern choices of a harsh world. And these linguistic aptitudes, favoring survival, like beauty and appetition, like the graceful fleetness of the tabuk, the hearing of the larl, the tracking capacity of the sleen, are transmissible. And thus women are born for masters."

"The beast can speak Kur," said he who had admitted us.

"Undoubtedly," said Kurik.

"We heard it speak Kur," said he who had admitted us.

"I am not sure," said Kurik.

"But surely not Gorean," said he who had admitted us.

"That remains to be seen," said Kurik.

"If I can understand her, if it is a her," I said, "surely you may, as well, Masters."

"We might learn to do so," said Kurik. "Proceed."

With trepidation, the men watching, I rose to my feet, went to the opening of the crate, and knelt down.

I looked into the recesses of the crate, at the crouching life form near its back. It was breathing quickly. I could hear its breath. I could see it in the lifted light of the lantern.

I had learned it was too small to be a male Kur, and, for all I knew, it might be smaller, even, than the female Kur. It was, on the other hand, considerably larger than I. I conjectured it to approximate, or exceed, the height of the men, large men, behind me. To be sure, it was crouching down, apprehensively.

"I will speak to you," I said. "If you understand me, touch your right paw to the floor of the container."

"Ai!" cried two of the men.

"She understands Gorean!" said Kurik.

"It could be a coincidence," said he who had admitted us.

"Possibly," said Kurik.

"Please touch the floor of the container twice with your right paw," I said, slowly.

"She knows Gorean," said Kurik.

"But we do not know Kur," said he with the lantern.

"Can you speak Gorean?" I asked.

There was a tiny sound, from back in the crate.

"That noise was meaningless," said he who had admitted us.

"If you can speak Gorean," I said, "please touch the floor of the container twice with your right paw."

"The beast lies," said he who had admitted us.

"Perhaps not," said Kurik.

"It is hard for us to understand your Gorean," I said, slowly. "Perhaps it is hard for you to understand our Gorean. I will speak slowly and carefully and I hope you will do the same. I think then, after a time, we may understand one another well enough, and may then speak more easily. Please speak to me, and I will try to understand."

I felt sorry for the beast which, I was sure, was frightened, and disconcerted. How strange it must be for it to find itself as it was, on a foreign world, alone, queried by strangers, threatened by weapons. Then, for a time, some Ehn, it uttered its noises, slowly, and patiently. I strained to interpret these emanations, conjecturing, hazarding possibilities, making little or nothing of them.

"I have failed, Masters," I said.

"No, you have not," it said.

"Ai!" I cried.

"What is it?" demanded Kurik.

"I understood!" I said, trembling.

Doubtless it is difficult to understand how it is that one does not understand and then one understands, and one knows not how, or exactly when, this remarkable transition occurs. What is difficult, and perhaps impossible, is suddenly at one's disposal, and, seemingly, familiar and even trivial. Some adjustments are doubtless made of which one is not aware. How complicated is the brain, and mysterious its secret courses and routes! Yet the phenomenon is not without precedent. One can make nothing of a gesture language and then, suddenly, it is intelligible. One does not understand a mode of speech, or an accent, and then, suddenly, one does. It is the language one knows but it was seemingly distorted, concealed, or transformed, and then, as though the curtain was swept aside or the key suddenly revealed, all that which a moment ago defied comprehension is suddenly made manifest, simple, even embarrassingly so.

"I do not understand," said he who had admitted us.

"Continue," said Kurik.

"Long ago, in Ar, I had had a similar experience, on Emerald, in the vicinity of the fountain of Aiakos," I said.

"The intelligence of slaves is quick," said the fellow with the lantern.

"Of some slaves," said Kurik.

"That makes it more pleasant," said the fellow with the lantern, "to subdue, own, and master them."

"You do not think we bring them to Gor simply for their beauty, do you?" asked Kurik.

"I suppose not," he said.

"Stupid slaves do not sell well," said Kurik. "Who would want to own them?"

"True," said he with the lantern.

"The intelligent woman," said Kurik, "makes the best slave. She is more in touch with her feelings and needs. She is least a stranger to herself. She most quickly understands what it is to be in a collar, one she cannot remove, which is locked on her neck. She has longed to submit herself to a master. She is the first to come to her knees, where she knows she belongs."

In the following, I shall proceed largely as if these exchanges occurred between the beast and myself, or between others and the beast, facilitated by my mediation. In actuality, of course, particularly in the beginning, I must translate continually, and later, often, from the beast's Gorean into a more easily intelligible Gorean, one rendered in familiar phonemes, that the masters might at all times be fully cognizant of what was transpiring. Later, the men, in particular my master, began to fathom the discourse of the beast.

"What are you?" I asked.

"I do not know," it said.

"Surely you know."

"No."

"You have heard others," I said. "You have been explained to yourself."

"No," it said.

"Are you a female?" I asked.

"I do not know," it said. "What is a female?"

"You have come from a steel world," I said.

"From far away," it said.

"Let me address her," said Kurik. "She will understand my Gorean. You may translate her responses." He then spoke to the beast slowly, more slowly, I suspect, than was necessary. "Do you understand Kur?" he asked.

"Yes," it said. "It is the language of the great ones."

"Can you speak it?" he asked.

"Yes," it said, "but poorly. My throat is deformed. I was born awry, twisted, and imperfect."

"Are you Kur?" he asked.

"I am other than the splendid ones," it said.

"You are much like a Kur," said Kurik.

"I am unworthy to be so," it said.

"It is a beast," said he who had admitted us.

"Yes," it said.

"Are you a beast?" I asked. Surely the thing was beastlike.

"Yes, I am a beast," it said.

"What else?" I asked.

"A monster, ill-begotten, and ill-constituted," it said.

"Amongst the Kurii," said Kurik, "there are three, or, if you like, four sexes, the dominants, the females, the wombs, and the nondominants. A nondominant may, in certain circumstances, become a dominant. This emergence is sometimes fearful to behold. The wombs are sensate, but sessile, and irrational."

"I do not understand," I said.

"The seeded Kur female, after conceiving," said Kurik, "deposits the fertilized egg in one of the living wombs, usually housed in remote areas, often in caves or tunnels. There it comes to term and, unaided, frees itself, or dies, and is ejected. It lives for a time off the tissue and blood of the womb, but it is normally collected and taken to a nursery before the womb perishes. If the womb heals, it may accept another egg."

"This is hard to understand," I said.

"The Kur female is dangerous and appetitious," said Kurik. "In this way she is not slowed, or burdened, by carrying young. I do not know if this is a portion of the biological heritage of the Kur species, or if it was introduced technologically, by medical intervention, at some point in the development of the species."

"Then there is nothing like the family," I said.

"There are analogs," said Kurik. "Records are kept of bloodlines."

"This creature then, in the crate," I said, "came so to be?"

"I do not think so," said Kurik. "I do not think this thing, small, and different, could have bitten, clawed, and torn its way out of one of the Kur wombs."

"How then is it brought about?" I asked.

"I think," said Kurik, "it was delivered from a human womb."

"Surely not," I said.

"It had a mother," said Kurik.

"But look at it," I said.

"Its father, or fathers, for seeds may be mixed, and fused, was Kur," he said.

"It could not be," I whispered, frightened.

"An advanced biological and medical technology was doubtless involved," said Kurik.

"Surely, Master, that is impossible," I said.

"It is not impossible," he said. "I know of another case."

"Kill me," begged the creature in the crate.

"No," said Kurik.

"You are far from a steel world," I said. "You are on a world called 'Gor'. Do you know for what purpose you were brought to Gor?"

"No," it said.

"You are a female," said Kurik.

"What is a female?" it asked.

"It does not know why it was brought to Gor," I said.

"No," said Kurik.

"Surely someone must know why it was brought to Gor," I said.

"Someone does," he said.

"Who?" I asked.

"One known to you," he said.

"Who?" I asked.

"I," said Kurik.

"You know?" I said.

"Yes," he said. "I know."

"Master has explained little to his slave," I said.

"That is because she is a slave," he said. "Perhaps later, if you are sufficiently pleasing, and writhe well, I may choose to assuage your curiosity."

"Master sports with his slave," I said. "Master well knows that I cannot bargain. Even the suspicion that I might wish to do so could bring me a beating."

"True," he said.

"And Master well knows," I said, "that the whip guarantees that I will strive earnestly to be pleasing, and that, at his least touch, I cannot help but writhe spasmodically, helplessly, beggingly, in his arms."

"True," he said, "and I find it quite amusing, particularly given our first encounter, that on this world you are not only a defenseless, rightless, abject slave, but that you are helplessly collar hot."

"Of course," I said. "I am now the property of masters. I can be bought and sold. I am a slave."

"As you should be," he said.

"Yes, Master," I whispered, a slave.

Kurik then turned to the huddled beast in the crate.

"Why, Beast," he said, "do you think so little of yourself? Why do you regard yourself as a monster, as a thing ill-begotten, and ill-constituted?"

"Look at me," it said, and the bitterness of its response was clear, even in its rude approximations to the phonemes of Gorean, even in that rude, issuant conjunction of vocables scarcely distinguishable from those of a simple beast. "Consider my voice, how unnatural it is, how distorted! I cannot enunciate Kur well. I cannot enunciate Gorean well. Kurii mock me. Humans draw back, baffled, and repelled."

"The slave," said Kurik, "a mere slave, understands you, and I am beginning to understand you. Even amongst the Kurii, whom you call the splendid ones, few can speak Gorean. Most avail themselves of mechanical devices, translators. You are thus superior to them. You can do what they cannot. And there are many steel worlds inhabited by Kurii, and, I assure you, the Kur of some of these worlds is barbaric, even unintelligible, to those of other such worlds. Dare they openly mock one another? I think not. Would it not mean a challenge to the rings? And I suspect you speak Kur ably enough, for they mock you. Thus they understand you. Surely they need no translator, a device for deciphering alien speech, to understand you. Thus, you speak both intelligible Kur and intelligible Gorean."

"My voice is hideous, strange," it said.

"It is merely different," said Kurik, "wholly suitable for, and appropriate to, a differing form of life."

"See my eyes," it said. "They are the wrong shape."

"Not wrong," said Kurik. "Different."

I did not think them so much different from those of a human.

"They are the wrong color," it said.

"I cannot see the color, as you are in the darkness of the crate," said Kurik.

"They do not speak of the night, as should those of the prowling hunter, nor of the darkness of the corridors of caves, but of the day, of the sky."

"Perhaps you are a creature of the day, as many others," said Kurik. "What graceful tabuk, in its sunlit glade, would envy the sleen its burrow?"

"Do not mock me," it said. "I will show you my horrors. Prepare to be dismayed. Be strong. Brace yourself. I will show you how misshapen I am, how grotesque, twisted, and malformed."

"Do so," said Kurik. "I welcome the intelligence."

I shuddered, for the creature shuffled forward, claws scraping on the wooden floor of the crate.

Then it was at the entrance to the crate, illuminated in the light of the lifted lantern.

Its eyes, I saw, were gray, or blue. It was hard to tell.

"Look!" it exclaimed, thrusting forth its paws, the digits widely spread.

"So?" said Kurik.

I was unaware of what might be awry, if anything. I had no idea what I had been expected to note, from which I might have been expected to recoil, frightened, or sickened. I was apprehensive, however, for I feared the beast might emerge from the container.

"Behold, cringe!" it said, this time more forcefully. And then it raised its paws once more, thrusting them yet more forward, and then it made a miserable, half choking noise. It was much like a sob. I did not understand this. One can tell, of course, when an animal is agitated, or disturbed, and that was surely now the case. Its eyes were bright, glistening, in the lantern light. It seemed they were indeed blue, or gray, or, more likely, some blend of such colorings. I feared it was in pain. It trembled, as though shaken with some feral emotion, doubtless naturally enough, given such a dreadful form of life. As it had emerged more into the light, I could now see that the fur at the sides of its face was wet, as though it had suffered from the coursing of small rivulets of fluid.

Surely such a thing could not cry.

It was a beast.

"I do not understand," I whispered to my master. "What is it we are supposed to see, what unwelcome sight?"

"Five digits," he said, "not six."

"I do not understand," I said.

"The paws of Kurii," he said, "are massive, and six digited, powerful, like cables, almost like tentacles."

Then he turned to the creature, who had now turned about and retreated into the recesses of the crate. She, for I shall now so refer to her, at least frequently, was turned away from us, crouched down, her shoulders shaking.

"Most humans," said Kurik to the beast, "have five digits on each appendage. It seldom occurs to one to bemoan this fact."

"I am not human," she said.

"No," said Kurik, "you are not human."

"I am not Kur," she said.

"No," said Kurik.

"What am I?" she asked.

"Part Kur, part human," said Kurik.

"So not Kur, so not human," she said.

"True," said Kurik.

"I am a monster," she said.

"Not at all," said Kurik. "It is true that you are not human, and it is true that you are not Kur. But you are not failing to be what you are. You are exactly what you are, and were intended to be. You are a new form of life. You are merely different."

"Different?" she said.

"Precisely," said Kurik. "And some might find you beautiful."

"'Beautiful'?" she said, turning about, lifting her head.

"Yes," said Kurik.

"I might be found beautiful?" she said.

"Yes," said Kurik.

"By whom?" she asked.

"By one like you, or one much like you. One of your own species, so to speak. Indeed, you were doubtless formed with just such a thought in mind."

"I do not understand," she said.

"You are a female," said Kurik.

"I do not understand," she said.

"Are you sure it is a female, really a female?" I asked.

"Of course," he said. "Consider the softness, the lesser size, the contours of the body. She is too small for an adult Kur female. Her body is not straight and hard. The Kur female does not suckle young. When they are taken from the external, rooted womb they have already fed on blood and flesh, that of the womb from which they have torn their way free."

"I do not understand," she said.

"What is your name?" he asked.

A sound emanated from the beast, she, or it, lurking in the back of the crate.

"What did she say?" asked Kurik.

"I have no idea," I said.

"Of course," said Kurik. "That is her name in Kur."

"What is your name in Gorean?" he asked her.

"I have no name in Gorean," she said.

"What is the meaning of your name in Kur?" he asked.

"It has no meaning," she said. "It is letters, and numbers."

"So perhaps experiments, or projects, are so identified," said Kurik. I feared so.

"Surely then the beast is unnatural, a monstrosity," I whispered, in horror, in little more than a breath, an utterance intended only for the ears of my master, and scarcely for his.

"Yes," said the beast.

I shrank back. I had not taken the beast's hearing to be so keen.

"Not at all," said Kurik. "All is within nature. There is not a hair in that pelt, not a corpuscle in that body, that is not natural. In nature there are many colors, and from many colors one can paint many pictures, some of which are beautiful."

"The thing is ugly," said he who had admitted us. "What shall we call it?"

"We will give her a barbarian name," said Kurik.

"Good," said the fellow who had admitted us. "Let it be so demeaned."

"A name from a barbarian world," said Kurik, "one I think not unfitting."

"What?" asked he who had admitted us.

"'Eve'," said Kurik, my master.

I shuddered.

"As she is the first of her kind," said Kurik.

"I do not understand," said he who had admitted us.

"It is not necessary that you do," said Kurik.

I thought 'Eve' a lovely name. How dreadful then that this monstrosity should be so designated!

"I do not like to have this thing here," said he who had admitted us. "I do not understand what is going on. The business is strange. I suspect there may be danger."

"You have been paid well," said Kurik.

"And how many golden tarns will one accept for one's life?" said he who had admitted us.

Kurik turned to the beast. "Your name," he said, "is 'Eve'. That will do for now. Later, if you wish, as you are free, a free person, you may choose another."

"I am a person?" she said.

"Of course," said Kurik.

Then he turned to me. "What is wrong?" he asked.

I was angry. That simple beast, a mere beast, a thing that was crated, was free, a person, and I was not! It was on my neck, not hers, that there was a collar! But, of course, I was a mere woman of Earth, an object, a suitable property for the men of this world!

"Nothing, Master," I said.

"Put your head down, as you are kneeling," he said, "and press your right cheek against my thigh."

I did so, and I knew I was where I belonged, at my master's feet.

"I am afraid," said he who had admitted us.

"Dismantle the crate," said Kurik.

"It will be done," said he who had admitted us.

"It was never here," said Kurik. "There is no record, no claiming ticket."

"No record, no claiming ticket," said he who had admitted us.

"Nothing," said Kurik.

"I would this business were done," said he who had admitted us.

"Be content," said Kurik. "We will make away, and soon, long before light."

"I fear the second bar will ring any moment," said he who had admitted us.

"Bring a blanket, or cloak," said Kurik.

"Fetch something, a crate cover, or such," said he who had admitted us, addressing one of the two fellows with him, one of those who had pried open the crate, which fellow then sped away.

Kurik then turned to the beast.

"You will accompany me unquestioningly," he said. "You will obey me in all particulars, as would a slave. Your life and our lives may depend on this. I know your purpose, that for which you were contrived. When we are safe, and far away, I shall explain all to you."

The beast lifted its head, quizzically.

"There was a plan, long ago, a plan of war and deceit," he said. "You were to be a component in that plan. Accordingly you were thought of, and planned, years before your formation. But the plan proved unfeasible. It fell into ruination. There was anger, much disappointment. Later, there was civil war. On the scales of power were heaped the steel of weapons. Mighty heroes fought and died on both sides. Seed fought seed, corridors raged with fire. Then the cries were done; the flames extinguished."

"The second bar!" said the fellow with the lantern.

"Yes," said Kurik.

"You must trust me," said Kurik to the beast. "I shall explain all."

"Hurry," said he who had admitted us, looking about, even to the higher levels, and to the shadows and darknesses in the rafters above us.

"What did she say?" asked Kurik.

"She asked," I said, "if she should be afraid."

"Do not be afraid," said Kurik to the beast.

"She asks," I said, "why we hasten, why we seek to leave before light."

"I cannot tell her that," said Kurik.

"She presses the question," I said to Kurik.

Kurik turned to the beast. "To disguise your hideousness," he said.

"I understand," said the beast.

"Surely that is not true, Master," I said.

"It is something she will understand," said Kurik.

At that moment one of the two fellows who had opened the crate, he who had been sent to fetch a blanket, or such, returned, bearing a sizable scrap of canvas. It was probably from sail cloth. It was large enough to stretch over the bed of a peddler's cart.

Kurik took the cloth and flung it at the beast. "Cover yourself," he said, "that your ugliness not offend those who might chance to look upon you."

Bending down she picked up the canvas, with two paws, and prepared to put it about her shoulders.

"She is crying," I said. "I am sure she is crying."

"No," said Kurik. "It is a simple beast."

"Before you were kind to her," I said. "Now you are otherwise. I do not understand."

"Hurry," he said to the beast. "Hurry."

But the beast did not move.

"What is wrong?" asked Kurik.

Her head was lifted.

"What is wrong?" asked Kurik.

The beast was unmoving, the head lifted.

"Master," I whispered, "I think she hears something, something that we do not hear."

"I hear nothing," said Kurik.

"Nor I, Master," I said.

"It is nothing," said Kurik.

At that moment I heard a horrifying roar, husky, piercing, claimant and enunciatory, as if a larl might speak, or a storm possess a throat, a sound I shall never forget, and a huge form dropped down from the rafters, struck the flooring, and then crouched in place, surveying us. The light of the lantern was reflected from two large eyes, as though the doors of a furnace might have been flung open. The jaws opened, and I glimpsed fangs. The body was bent over, like a mountain of fur, and its mighty legs were coiled beneath it. These mighty appendages, I gathered, had cushioned the shock of its descent. With what force it might spring forward! I could not move. Almost at the same time I heard a shriek of dismay from the beast in the crate, and was aware, a moment later, of two other large, hirsute forms descending, forms in the darkness, away from the lantern, one leaping from the first level to the flooring, and the second swinging down from the second level to the first, and then swinging lightly to the floor. The arms of these creatures were long. Were they to stand upright, if such were permitted by their structure, the arms might have reached to their knees. These things were fearful, and, in a terrible way, they were graceful. I feared, further, that these things, whatever they might be, were intent, rational, and purposive. The two sprung from the balconies approached. They shuffled, bent over. I heard claws moving on the wooden flooring. The first continued to regard us, not moving. I saw, now, three belts, one at the waist, two running from the shoulders to the hips, crossed the bodies of these three beasts. I heard the jangle of accoutrements. On the left wrist of the nearest beast there were two metal rings.

At the time I did not know the terrifying meaning of these rings.

Leadership amongst these forms of life is not easily purchased.

"It is too late," said Kurik, facing the beasts, drawing a dagger from his belt. "We have been betrayed from the steel world."

A fierce burst of sound emanated from the first beast, it which had dropped from the darkness of the rafters, and his two confederates approached more closely.

A howl of misery escaped he who had admitted us, and he, and his fellows, fled to the sides, disappearing into the darkness. The lantern, cast down, rolled on the floor, feet away.

"Stay back!" said Kurik, brandishing his dagger. "Go! Beware! Interfere not! We labor in the cause of Arcesilaus, Twelfth Face of the Nameless One, Theocrat of the World!"

I understood nothing of this.

"Away!" said Kurik, waving his arm, dagger in hand, in what was clearly a violent, desperate, shunning, warning, gesture.

The meaning of such a gesture was easy to read.

The three beasts, now illuminated from the side by the fallen lantern, it inert but still burning, to our left, the flame oddly vertical, the lamp horizontal, shuffled a pace closer.

"They have no translators," said Kurik. Then he called back, over his shoulder. "Warn them away!" he said.

"What did she say?" he demanded.

"They will not be warned," I said.

"Our task," cried Kurik, "is set by Lord Arcesilaus!"

"She says," I said, "these are not the minions of Lord Arcesilaus."

"I feared so," said Kurik, "seekers of vengeance and renewed war, partisans of a more fearsome lord, adherents of a throne unforgotten and never surrendered."

The lead beast suddenly sprang forward, and was precipitately upon us, far more quickly than I might have deemed possible, and, with a contemptuous sweep of its mighty paw, struck Kurik to the side, into the darkness. I doubted consciousness could endure such a blow. I myself was seized by another of the beasts and flung rudely to the other side, a dozen yards away, skidding and rolling, into a line of boxes.

I lay there, half in shock. I could not move. I knew I must be abraded. My right shoulder and side seemed afire. I lay beside a box, against it, fighting for breath. My consciousness was oddly disrupted. The pain I felt seemed as though it might be the affliction of another. I struggled to comprehend the horror of what had occurred, not what I had felt but what I had seen. I had witnessed, for the first time, what must be Kurii. How terrible, and fearsome, seemed that form of life! What could stand against such things? Might not such things rule worlds? My comprehension, and the horror of it, seemed far more grievous than the impact I had sustained. That was easily comprehensible, a simple matter of an explicable, fierce collision of forces. But that life forms such as I had just seen might exist was other than this; it was devastatingly disconcerting. One's position in a chain of life, one's place in a complacent universe, is suddenly challenged. My view of the world was shaken. What an unwelcome revelation to the verr to learn that sleen exist, to the tabuk that it shares its world with the larl! I feared I might lose consciousness. I knew not if bones were broken. I seemed unable to rise. The tunic of the paga girl, I would later learn, was half torn from me.

I did hear, emanating from the large, dark crate, from within that deep, opened, splintered housing, noises from its occupant, the pathetic beast we had interrogated. She had apparently withdrawn into its recesses, as though they might afford her shelter. She was frightened. Doubtless she was speaking in Kur. I could make out nothing. The noises could be read, however, as those of any animal, whether speeched or not. They were noises of petition, of protest, of pleading, of fear.

Suddenly I hated the thing.

It was her presence, I gathered, to which we owed the intrusion of the three hideous visitants.

I raised my head, and, in the dim, flickering light of the awry lantern, saw one of the beasts scramble into the crate and, a moment later, emerge, dragging forth its occupant.

No longer then did I hate the innocent, ugly, helpless thing.

I feared for her life.

Had they come to kill her, for some reason? Did she pose some incomprehensible threat to a form of life? It seemed not. What could such monsters fear from that slighter, far-less-imposing monster? Surely she was not a form of life that one might wish to exterminate before it could multiply, as one might, with a stone, sufficiently apprised and motivated, crush the egg of the first ost, as the verr might choose to destroy, if possible, the first small sleen, or the tabuk thrust its single horn, if possible, into the heart of the first small larl? Might this be an assassination of sorts? But I did not think so. What sort of blow might be struck here? Surely that surprising beast we had interrogated did not constitute a threat to a family, a party, a state?

But who knew?

Perhaps.

To me she seemed large, and formidable.

To them she was nothing.

I feared then, again, they would kill her.

But they struck her, those terrible, mighty things, until she whimpered and cringed, and then they hooded and bundled her in the very sheet of canvas in which Kurik had expected to conceal her, to take her through the streets of Brundisium in the night. This sheeting was then bound about her, so that she was helpless within it. Startled, I recalled I had occasionally seen slave girls rendered similarly helpless. Then I saw a leash put about her neck, over the hooding sheet, its leather in the grasp of one of the monsters. She was then theirs. She was now silent, hooded, bound, and on the leash, fearing perhaps to be further struck.

I understood little, if anything, of what had occurred.

She had not been killed.

Not her death then, but her acquisition, it seemed, had been the object of the dreadful intrusion.

But what could they want of her?

Of what value could she be to them, or to anyone?

How could she, or it, such a thing, figure in the plans of rational beasts?

Then I realized, shaken, that she might be a female, as Kurik had said. Might this not be relevant then, somehow? Surely there are better things to do with a female than kill her. Is it not true? One does not kill the female animal. One keeps it. One owns it. One collars it. One masters it. It is not to be slain but enjoyed. The subdued, mastered female is to be worked, and used for pleasure. Free, the woman is a bother and a source of pain. Collared, she is what nature designed her to be, a thing of joy, a possession, an object from which the most inordinate of pleasures may be derived, a slave.

We are women.

It is on our throats that the leash collar will be fastened.

And who does not wish to be on her master's leash?

One of the beasts led the hood-blind, bound, tethered female by the leash toward the door in the large gate fronting the house of Flavius Minor. Another thrust her forward with a broad paw against her back, through the door. I saw no signs of the employees of the house, he who had admitted us, he who had borne the lantern, and their two cohorts. They had fled at the first appearance of the beasts. I did not know where my master was. I assumed he lay somewhere, perhaps amongst the bales, barrels, and crates about the walls. I supposed him unconscious, so grievous was the blow to which he had been subjected. How had he dared to place himself, armed with naught but that sliver of a knife, between a Kur and its quarry?

The largest Kur, it whom I took to be their leader, it with the two rings on its left wrist, to whom the others had seemingly deferred, stood near the fallen lantern, and looked about.

I lay as quietly as I could.

That massive head was facing me. I could see its two large, pointed ears lift from the sides of its head, broaden, and, seemingly cupped, incline toward me.

I had the sickening feeling, even yards away, that it could hear me breathing.

Then it reached down and snatched up the lantern.

"No!" I cried, leaping to my feet.

But the lantern was dashed to the floor, where it shattered in a spat-tering rainbow of glass and oil, and, a moment later, a hungry torrent of fire, raging, ever enlarging, began its bright feeding, racing across the boards of the floor of the house.

"No!" I cried again, as the large beast began to cast boxes and wired bales, most of rep cloth, on the flames.

His two cohorts had left the building.

I began to cough. My eyes stung.

The beast was wild in its work.

Then it paused, the flames about, and its nostrils flared. It fixed its gaze on a barrel, one amongst several, hurried to it, and broke it open, splintering its lid with a blow of its paw. I smelled tharlarion oil. I watched, in horror, as the beast spread this oil like a fuse about the floor, and into the midst of crates and bales, which fuse, a moment later, took fire, and, ignited, coursed its way like a swift, burning snake through the stored wealth it would claim as its tinder.

I put my hand before my face. I could feel the heat of the flames.

The beast leaped and spun about, and stomped, and turned again, and put its head back, and roared, lifting its paws to the rafters. Then it spun about, again, and again. I think it was dancing, drunk in the wanton joy of destruction.

Then it looked at me, eyes like golden fire, through the flames. I saw the long, dark tongue dart forth and then back between those mighty jaws. It opened its cavernous maw and I saw the fangs red in the firelight. It took a step toward me.

I screamed in fear.

Then, oddly, it crouched down, and, eyes toward me, backed rap-idly away, snarling, and then it turned and slipped through the still-open portal in the large gate and disappeared into the night.

A sheet of flame then obscured the area.

"It is important to let it live," said Kurik, my master. "Much may depend on that, the life of Eve, the opportunity to confute their intentions."

"Master!" I coughed.

He lowered the crossbow from the leveled position. Doubtless its presence had dissuaded the beast from approaching me more closely. In its jaws a head might be torn from a body. The quarrel, at close range, can sink two horts into a solid beam. The weapon was surely one of the two that had been borne by the cohorts of he who had admitted us.

"There is a rear entrance," said Kurik, slinging the bow over his shoulder, seizing me by the arm. "I have ascertained it."

He then began, I coughing and stumbling in his grip, to hasten toward the back of the building.

Flames roared behind us.

In a moment we were in the cool of the night, behind the house of Flavius Minor. Through the open door in the back of the building we could see the fire raging inside.

"In a matter of Ihn," he said, "the alarms will sound, and a hundred men will be about. We must make away."

"They are terrible things," I said.

"They are Kurii," he said.

"Master has saved the life of his slave," I said.

"Possibly, possibly not," he said. "Our friend may have thought the better of approaching you more closely, the barrier of fire, the risk of remaining longer in the house."

"It feared your weapon!" I said.

"That is possible," he said.

"Master is hurt," I said.

"No," he said.

The left side of his head was bloody.

"Let me bathe and bind your wound," I said.

"Hurry," he said, drawing me with him, hurrying down the alley behind the building. "We must not be discovered here."

"Did you see the thing?" I stammered, shaken, half dragged at his side, stumbling in his grip. "It was glad, joyful, wheeling about, dancing, wreaking pointless, unnecessary destruction."

"Sometimes one makes a festival of fire," said Kurik. "Is voracious flame not stimulating? Does it not excite and stimulate, does it not, in all its brightness and heat, speak of violence and power, does it not rage as it wishes, go whithersoever it will, devour as it chooses, destroy what it pleases without heart, qualm, or conscience?"

"Let us proceed more slowly, Master," I begged.

"The house would have been burned in any case," said Kurik. "Evidence must perish. No sign is to remain of what took place there. All traces were to be covered. No trail would lead to the house, no trail from the house."

We had turned right, in the alley, and were making our way between buildings onto a street, that which we had originally descended, leading toward the wharves, where we turned left.

Some men were hurrying by, toward the wharves.

A bar had begun to ring, and the ringing was taken up by others, elsewhere in the city.

"What is going on?" a fellow inquired, pausing.

"I think a fire, at the wharves," said Kurik.

The fellow who had inquired cast me an appraising look, as though I might have been exposed for my sale, and then hurried on.

I then realized that the scanty paga tunic, so brief and humiliating, in which my master had chosen to place me, consulting me not, for I was a slave, had been half torn away. Also, I again became aware, then, again, from the discomfort, of the abrasions on my right shoulder, and side, sustained in the house of Flavius Minor.

Two more men hurried past.

The street was steep, descending to the wharves.

We climbed.

We crossed the street, to the far side, and turned, to look back.

"There," said Kurik, pointing.

I could see the surprising brightness in the sky, against the night. I had no doubt that by now the roof might be afire. Even this high, and this far removed from the fire, we could smell smoke.

"There are fire brigades," said Kurik. "It is not likely the flames will spread beyond the house of Flavius Minor. It has been a century since the Great Fire, which wiped out most of the southern piers."

I was pleased that we had desisted in our progress. I gasped for breath. I felt now the night was cool. I tried to hold the shreds of the tunic about me.

"The animals, the beasts," I said, "how fearsome they are, such terrible things."

"It is said," said Kurik, "that one, unarmed, could kill a sleen."

I shuddered.

"But it is said, as well," said Kurik, "that one would be no match for a larl."

"I am afraid," I said.

"They are neither invulnerable nor invincible," said Kurik. "They are no more immune to the thrust of a spear, the flight of the cable-sprung quarrel, the greeting of the long shaft of the peasant bow, the stab and slash of steel, than other forms of life."

"But if they derive from metal worlds," I said, "such bespeaking sophisticated technologies, surely greater weapons and more fearsome power is at their disposal."

"Doubtless," said Kurik, "but they would do well to refrain from availing themselves, at least openly, of such advantages on this world."

"Why?" I asked.

"You need not inquire," he said.

"Curiosity is not becoming in a kajira," I said.

"I have heard so," he said.

"I beg to know," I said.

"What is not becoming in a kajira?" he asked.

"Curiosity," I said.

"Be silent," he said.

"I would know," I said.

"If you were not well bared," he said, "I would cuff you."

"But I am well bared," I said.

"I think you could do with a taste of the whip," he said.

"No," I said, instantly kneeling at his feet. "Please do not whip me, Master! I beg not to be whipped! Be lenient, be kind, Master! I beg it!" I muchly feared the whip, to which, as a slave, I was subject. "Rather let me strive to make amends," I said.

I pressed my lips to his bootlike sandals, and then looked up at him, frightened.

He was looking down upon me.

"Let me strive to placate you," I said.

"In the way of the female slave?" he said.

"Yes, Master," I said.

"You look well on your knees, half naked," he said.

"It is my hope to please, Master," I said.

"You are a slave," he said.

"Yes, Master," I said.

"And you are a bold, and stupid slave," he said.

"Master?" I said.

"You cried out twice in the house of Flavius Minor, protesting the Kur's enflaming of the house. This not only recalled to it your existence, and that you were conscious and might act, but marked your very position. You even screamed, once. Such an exclamation might trigger an attack. Not unoften, it might do so. Could you not sense your jeopardy? It is even likely you were within the beast's critical charging distance, within that perimeter within which the least movement can precipitate a charge. It is the same with a sleen or larl."

I put my head down.

"But your flanks, slave girl," he said "are not without interest."

"I am pleased, if Master is pleased," I whispered.

What had I with which to please him but my body, my needs, and, I fear, the love of a helpless slave?

"Perhaps," he said, "you would bring a full silver tarsk on the block."

"I would hope to bring my seller coin," I said. Indeed, if I did not, I knew I might be beaten.

"You did well in the house of Flavius Minor," he said, "in the questioning of the female thing, whom we choose to call 'Eve'. For some Ehn I, and I am sure the others, could not decipher her Gorean. Only toward the end of her interrogation, shortly before our hirsute friends appeared, did I begin to fathom her analogs to the sounds of Gorean. I admire your intelligence."

"Thank you, Master," I said.

"To be sure," he said. "We pick our slaves, in part, for their high intelligence. Such women, subdued, and mastered, fastened in their collars, subject to our whips, are exactly what we wish to own, wholly and uncompromisingly own."

"Doubtless," I said, "highly intelligent women make the best slaves."

"Yes," he said, "and I wish that you were half as intelligent as your Earth chain sister, Paula."

"Oh?" I said.

"She was a gem," said Kurik. "Gloriously bodied, extremely intelligent, with utterly helpless and profound slave needs."

"I see," I said.

I had always thought Paula rather plain. She did not dress smartly. She read books. She was unfamiliar with the proper magazines.

"I did well, I trust," I said, "in interpreting the Gorean of the crated beast."

"Quite well," he said. "I was proud to have you in my collar."

"Perhaps then," I said, "I should be freed?"

"Why?" he asked.

"In gratitude for my services," I said.

"Do not be a fool," he said. "Your services, and more, are owned to me, as you are my slave. Too, as you should understand by now, unless you are quite stupid, more so than I feared, your intelligence is relished and makes you much more pleasant to own."

"I see," I said.

"Do you wish to be free?"

"No," I said.

"Why?" he asked.

"Because, on this world," I said, "I have learned that I am, and should be, a slave."

"Excellent," he said. "And you have learned, as well, I trust, that that is all you are, and no more."

"Yes, Master," I said.

He pointed to his bootlike sandals, and I put my head down, my hair falling about his feet, and, tenderly and gratefully, permitted to do so, began to lick and kiss his feet, those of my master. How far I was from the office, and another world!

"Enough," he said, after a time.

I lifted my head. I could still taste the leather of the sandals.

"It is cool," he said. "We must get you indoors. We must get you somewhere, for warmth, and such."

"Master is injured," I said.

The side of his head was caked with blood. It had been raked with the clawed paw of the foremost of the three beasts. Had he not been pulling away from the impending blow it might have broken his neck. As it was, it had sent him reeling yards from the opened crate, into the darkness to the side.

"It is nothing," he said.

"I gather that the plans of Master, whatever they might have been," I said, "have come to naught."

"The attempt to interfere was anticipated," he said.

"Clearly your plans have been ruined," I said.

"Thwarted," he said, "not ruined."

"Master?" I said.

"Adjustments must now be made," he said. "Factions do contest. The intentions of one faction, obviously, became clear to those of another faction, which then acted, but, in turn, it is not difficult to fathom the likely intentions of the interfering faction. Thus, all is not lost."

"Seek care," I said. "Your wound must be bathed, treated, and dressed."

"You shiver," he said. "I must get you to shelter."

CHAPTER THIRTY-FOUR

Keep your hands, palms down, on your thighs," he said.

He had earlier treated the rawness on my right shoulder and side, attending to it with a soothing lotion.

He had been firm and gentle.

We were in an alcove, of the Slave Whip, one other than that we had hitherto occupied. To be sure, it was similarly lit, with the small tharlarion-oil lamp in its niche, and was similarly equipped, the chains, the straps, the materials for gags and blindfolds, the switch, a coiled whip, on its peg, various articles in the presence of which a slave would be in no doubt that she was a slave.

In his hand was a goblet.

Into it he had poured wine.

Surely it was not for me.

I was a slave.

"Master?" I said.

He put his hand in my hair and pulled my head back, so I gazed on the low, rounded roof of the alcove.

"Get your mouth open," he said.

His hand was tight in my hair.

"Wider," he said.

I complied.

"This will warm you," he said. He then, slowly, a bit at a time, gave me to drink. Gratefully I imbibed the fluid, a wine, a ruby wine, how it purred in one's mouth and throat, like a soft, stirring, liquid flame. Only once before, in the storage facility on Earth, shortly before my shipment to Gor, had I tasted such a beverage. Again, it far exceeded, in bouquet and flavor, any wine with which I had been familiar on Earth.

"Ka-la-na," I whispered.

He drew away the goblet. "Cheap, of course," he said.

"Master is kind," I said.

"Do you wish to be whipped?" he asked.

"No, Master," I said.

He then finished the contents of the goblet, and set it aside.

"I tasted such a wine once before," I said, "on Earth."

"The barbarian world," he said.

"Yes, Master," I said.

"This, however," he said, "contains no tassa powder."

"A slave is grateful," I said.

The alcove was warm. The shreds of the paga tunic had been discarded. I was naked, as slaves are commonly kept in alcoves.

"To all fours," he said.

I went to all fours.

He reached to the side, and picked up a chain and collar. He clasped the collar about my neck, and snapped it shut. The far end of the chain was fastened to a ring, in the wall.

I was then chained by the neck to the wall.

He then sat down, cross-legged, and pointed to the fur-strewn floor, near him, to his left. I then lay where he had indicated. I lay on my right aside. My face was near his left knee.

"May I speak?" I asked.

"Surely," he said.

"Master is injured," I said. "He must seek refuge, and rest."

"There is no time," he said.

One of the attendants in the Slave Whip had washed the lacerations at the side of his head, applied an antiseptic, and affixed a bandage. Kurik had refused the entreaties of the tavern master to summon a member of the green caste. I suspected this had primarily to do with matters of security. Presumably he thought it best that the fewer who knew of his presence here the better it would be. The discretion of the tavern master and his attendants was seemingly deemed sufficient. I suspected, as well, that a coin or two, perhaps of gold, had added to his confidence in their discretion. To be sure, attendants in paga taverns were not without experience in dressing wounds and keeping to their own affairs.

My master and I had fed earlier, as we had before, the drink and victuals brought discreetly to the alcove itself.

"You look well on a chain, Phyllis," he said.

I touched the collar, lightly. "Phyllis is a slave," I said.

"Every woman," he said, "looks well on a chain."

"We belong on them," I said.

"It is true," he said.

Were we not the slave sex? Did we not belong at the feet of masters? I had learned that on Gor, to my fear, my fulfillment, and joy.

How wonderful it is, and reassuring, to be a man's possession, to belong to a man, wholly.

I wondered if free women could understand the slave's feelings, her desires, her sense of rightfulness, her heat, her passion, her longing to be owned.

Perhaps only if they were put in a collar.

What a joy it is to have a master!

"You are different from what I remember from the barbarian world," he said.

"I am now a slave," I said.

"Now," he said, "you are nearly beautiful."

"Oh?" I said.

"Yes," he said.

"Some have thought me beautiful," I said.

"Here?" he said. "On Gor?"

"Yes," I said.

It was a common joke, amongst the men of Gor, that the men of Earth thought some women beautiful merely because they had seen no better, as though, say, Gorean women might be superior to those of Earth. How this arrogance had angered me! How absurd it was! The women of Earth and those of Gor were of identical stock. From whence did they think came the humans of Gor, and their own ancestors, if not from the precincts of Earth at one time or another! And what of some Gorean beauties, slave-clad and in their collars, to whom they might point as excellent examples of their claim, the superiority of Gorean beauties to those of Earth? Upon inquiry they might learn that those very beauties had been brought from Earth to be sold on Gor! If there were differences, negative differences, between the women of Earth, at least those still on Earth, and Gorean women, it seemed clear that these differences might be attributed to the diverse social and psychological pathologies found on Earth, inimical to the genetic heritages of human nature, which sanctioned and inculcated, strove to deny womanhood to women and manhood to men.

"Yes," he said, musingly. "Perhaps you are beautiful."

I kissed his left knee, softly, and put my head down again, my right cheek on the furs.

I gathered I had much changed on Gor, a collared slave. I had become soft, and graceful, and yielding and surrendered, and needful, terribly needful. I had become myself, reduced to my essentials. On this world I had been stripped of pretense and convention. On this world I had become what I was, and no more, a female animal, suitable for owning.

"Master could have been killed," I said.

"I was not," he said.

"Flee," I said. "Seek safety, elsewhere."

"No," he said.

"I understand so little of these things," I said.

"Dark games are afoot," he said.

"Withdraw from them," I said.

"What is life without its games?" he said.

"Surely these games are not yours," I said.

"I choose my games," he said.

"And you find zest in this, excitement?" I said.

"Surely," he said. "What games can compare to those of blood and steel?"

"Those of flowers, and love," I said.

"They are often intertwined," he said.

"I do not understand," I said.

"I will speak to you, briefly," he said. "There are forms of life, abundant and diverse, on untold worlds, worlds beyond numbering, those that eat and those that are eaten, those that kill and those that are killed, those that rule and those that are ruled. Let us suppose there was once a lovely world on which the factions of a fierce form of life, technologically gifted, and ruthless, unchecked, disrupted, poisoned, and sterilized a world, perhaps shattering it, perhaps inadvertently, ignorantly, forcing it from its very orbit, into its star, to be consumed in fire, or away, into a frozen desert of airless darkness. Some remnants of this destroyed world, one might suppose, survived, in enclosed metal rafts, so to speak, in artificial satellites, perhaps mixed with the debris of their former world, or perhaps, rather, fled far from their original star, seeking a new world to replace the one ruined, one does not know. But suppose then the remnants of the destroyed world discovered new worlds, one lovely, as lovely as was their former world, and another, one seemingly engaged in the same dismal, menacing process of climbing to the same harrowing, technological summit, polluted with the same territorialities and hatreds that had led to the destruction of their

former world. Either of these new worlds might be suitable for conquest, and colonization, obviously, but surely the lovelier world might
be preferred."

"Doubtless," I said.

"But suppose," said Kurik, "that it was discovered that the lovelier
world was not as innocent and vulnerable as had been conjectured. Suppose, rather, it was the world of a considerably different form of life,
a mysterious, powerful form of life, about which we know little, that
within its caves and dens, so to speak, quiescent until aroused, armed
and wary, lurked beasts between whose paws worlds might be crushed."

"I am afraid," I said.

"These latter beasts," he said, "of which I conjecture, are much
like gods, content unto themselves, with little interest in the politics
and vicissitudes of mundane matters, and certainly not those of other
species. Still, despite their passivity and aloofness, their singular lack
of imperialism and aggression, they will protect the integrity of their
habitat to the death."

"They are Priest-Kings," I said. "I have heard of them."

"They have enacted laws, weapon laws, communication laws, and
such," said Kurik, "that are enforced with severity, that no other form of
life, Kur or human, or other, may reduce, sicken, or ruin their world."

"Why do not the Kurii," I asked, "if they are so ambitious, violent,
and powerful, if this world is not yet available to them, seize Earth?"

"Priest-Kings," said Kurik, "shelter Earth. Who would place at the
disposal of an enemy the resources of a planet, who would grant them
an island, a platform, from which, in time, to launch a great attack, a
mighty armada, against them?"

"How is it," I asked, "that Priest-Kings have permitted humans on
their world?"

"Gods," said Kurik, "have their curiosities, their hobbies, their passions, and interests. Gor has been stocked with thousands of life forms
from throughout the galaxy. Humans were brought to Gor with many
other forms of life. Surely humans are an interesting form of life."

"And Priest-Kings," I said, "condone humans, and even Kurii, on
Gor?"

"Provided the laws are kept," said Kurik.

"I was not brought to Gor by Priest-Kings," I said.

"No," he said, "you and others, in a sense, are contraband."

"The ship was a Kur ship?" I said.

"Yes, modified," said Kurik.

"Then you are in league with Kurii," I said.

"With some," he said, "not others. There are factions amongst Kurii."

"Your name!" I said.

"Of course," he said.

"Why should you be allowed a ship?" I asked.

"Men serve Priest-kings, men serve Kurii," said Kurik. "Men may move easily amongst humans on Earth, and easily amongst humans on Gor. Thus, in various ways, they may be found of value to both Priest-Kings and Kurii, and on both Earth and Gor. For example, certain commodities are scarce on the steel worlds. Thus, it is in the interest of the Kurii to enlist men to obtain them on Earth, and convey them to the steel world, copper, for example. Thus ships are furnished."

"But why are women brought to Gor?" I asked.

"To wear collars and give pleasure to masters," he said.

"Doubtless we are a part of your pay," I said.

"A very pleasant part," he said. "We are slavers. Surely you do not begrudge us our business, such a pleasant business."

"I am glad I was brought to Gor," I said.

"It does not matter one way or another," he said.

"Of course," I said. "I am a slave."

"Kurii may war not only upon other forms of life," he said, "but, as you would suppose, given the destruction of their world, on Kurii, as well."

"There are factions," I said.

"Even within the same steel world," he said. "Now I will tell you a story. Accept, first, if you will, that both Priest-Kings and Kurii have uses for humans."

"You have made that clear," I said.

"And that humans, suitably armed, can be as dangerous as any other aggressive, stupid, self-seeking territorial form of life, similarly armed."

"That is doubtless true," I said.

"And that there are few humans on the steel worlds, but many on Gor."

"Surely there are many on Gor," I said.

"But few, compared to Earth," he said.

"It seems so," I said.

"But yet many," he said, "at least in areas with which you are likely to be acquainted."

"Let it be as Master speaks," I said. I still knew so little of this world.

"To be sure," he said, "much of Gor, to humans, if not to Kurii or Priest-Kings, is *terra incognita*."

"I did not know," I said.

"A paradox obtains," he said.

"Master?" I said.

"Gor, as you probably know," he said, "is smaller than the Earth. Surely you noted the difference in gravity, a difference to which you are now accustomed, one that you now accept, and no longer notice."

"I remember," I said.

"But what you may not know," he said, "is that Gor has more land surface than Earth. She has her turbulent, mighty Thassa, but she has no second, vast sea, like that you speak of as the Pacific."

"I know of Thassa," I said, "and of lesser lakes or seas, but none that are comparable to Thassa."

"So," he said, "humans are many on Gor, at least in places, but few, it seems, given the wealth of land, muchly unexplored, at their disposal."

"Gor is thinly populated," I said.

"It would have occurred to Kurii, would it not," he said, "to recruit to their purposes not only particular agents, and scattered, small groups, but larger portions of the human population of Gor?"

"I would suppose so," I said.

"Yet," he said, "the very sight of a Kur militates against the success of such a scheme."

"They are frightening, horrifying things," I said. "They inspire fear. Their very sight repels humans. They would not be trusted."

"It would be a foolish tarsk or tabuk," he said, "that would ally itself with a larl."

"Surely," I said.

"So a plan was formed," he said, "to produce a form of life to bridge that chasm of mistrust and terror, to produce a form of life more acceptable to humans, one that might enlist the aid of thousands of humans, suitably armed, to rise against and overthrow Priest-Kings, thus unwittingly to do the work of concealed Kur masters."

"And what, later, of such humans?" I asked.

"It would be a foolish tarsk or tabuk," he said, "that would ally itself with a larl."

"I see," I said.

"But the project failed," he said. "The monstrous creature thus formed, though part human, was no more acceptable to humans than a full-blooded Kur that had eaten and torn its way free from a sessile, tunnel womb."

"But what, Master," I asked, "has this to do with the hideous, crated creature taken from the house of Flavius Minor?"

"Later, in the same steel world," he said, "that in which this unnatural experiment, so grievously unsuccessful, was consummated, internal strife arose. Kur fought Kur. The tides of war ebbed and flowed. Deceit reigned. Terror stalked. The day rang with steel. The night was filled with blood and fire. Heroes clashed. And then the war was done. The ashes cooled, the blades were cleaned. Upon the throne, surveying his metal domain, crouched a new ruler, Lord Arcesilaus, High Kur, the Twelfth Face of the Nameless One, Theocrat of the World, that world."

"I understand nothing of this," I said. "Has this to do aught with the creature seized in the house of Flavius Minor, she carried away into the night?"

"One of the mighty heroes who labored in the cause of Lord Arcesilaus," he said, "was the outcome of the aforementioned hideous experiment. Following the war, he emigrated to Gor, with a human female, one known from the steel world, that she might be accompanied, protected, and sheltered."

"They were companions?" I said.

"Not in the sense you might think," he said. "To him she was more in the nature of a dear, wayward pet, for whom he cared."

"Surely she does not regard herself as such," I said.

"I would suppose not," he said.

"But the beast from the crate?" I pressed.

"When the first monster was conceived and delivered," he said, "and sanguine hopes flourished, a mate for it was planned, the more to make it seem human, the more to endear it to men, the better that it might carry out its tasks, but with the debacle attendant on the failure of the first project, the second project, that of the mate, was abandoned."

"I gather" I said, "interest was renewed, the matter was rethought."

"Clearly," he said, "but now with a very different end in view."

"I do not understand," I said.

"What a misery and loneliness to be the first and last of its kind," he said.

"Master?" I said.

"The monster, and others, had served well in the war, that which had brought Lord Arcesilaus to the throne. Some Kurii, as some men, believe in fittingness. Do not speak of gratitude, but of fittingness. In Torvaldsland, jarls give rings and places at table, some above the salt. In the Barrens, are there not prize hides and belts of beads? Do not Ubars bestow women, land, and power?"

"I do not know," I said.

"She is a reward, a reward for the emigrated monster, now on Gor, to be delivered to him," he said, "she whom we find so repulsive."

"Oh, yes, Master!" I said. "I recall! Tyrtaios, your enemy, he of the Assassins, spoke of a gift!"

"What did you say?" he said, sharply, angrily.

"He spoke—of a gift," I stammered, frightened.

"Who?" he demanded.

"Tyrtaios, Master," I said, "he of the Assassins!"

Kurik of Victoria rose up and removed the switch from the wall.

"Master?" I said.

"On your belly," said he, "slave."

He then applied the switch to me, methodically, administering ten strokes, spaced from the back of my neck to my ankles.

The back of my body stung. My eyes burst with tears.

"Master?" I begged. *Ela*, how stupid I was!

"Who?" he demanded.

"Tyrtaios," I wept. "No, no, please!"

Then ten more strokes were laid upon me.

My cheeks, and the furs, ran with tears. My head was down. I clutched the furs tightly.

"Who?" he asked, again.

"Master Tyrtaios!" I blurted out. "Master Tyrtaios."

He then replaced the switch on the wall, and resumed his place, sitting, cross-legged, near me.

"But he is your mortal enemy, Master!" I said. "I fear so. He might well seek you out, and kill you."

"But he is also a free man," he said.

"Yes, Master," I said. "Forgive me, Master." How stupid I had been! One of the first things of which the new slave is apprised is the deference owed to the free. A slave, if she speaks the name of the free, is expected to do so with the respect to which the free, being free, are entitled. It is offensive to speak of them as though they might be only another slave.

"May I speak?" I asked.

"Yes," he said.

"Master Tyrtaios spoke of her, the beast, as a gift, as you suggested, but a gift others intended to acquire, to use for purposes of their own."

"Of course," he said. "But for what purpose?"

"Master Tyrtaios did not say," I said.

"The matter cannot be a simple one of vengeance, or spite," he said. "If all that was wished was to deprive the monster of a companion, a mate, or slave, or such, she could have been summarily killed in the house of Flavius Minor, perhaps even on the steel world, he being informed, of course, of what was done. Surely that would have done, nicely."

"Yes, Master," I said. My back still stung. It was as though it had been lacerated with fire. From each stroke, pain, like a ripple in boiling water, spread about my back.

"But, clearly," he said, musingly, "this purpose, it will have to do with the monster."

I supposed this so.

"The thing was made," I said, "to be the companion, or mate, of the monster."

"That is my understanding," he said.

"And you were to deliver the thing to the monster?" I said.

"That was the intention of the faction of Lord Arcesilaus," he said.

"Am I to speak of Mistress Eve?" I asked.

"That is not necessary," he said, "as she is not human, but merely another beast."

"But you said she was free, a free person," I said.

"At least not a slave," he said.

"What if," I asked, "if she is a person, if she is free, she does not wish to companion herself with the monster?"

"Then," said he, "as she is a female, she may simply be collared, and owned."

"I see," I said.

"So we have 'Eve'," I said. "And what is the name of the other?"

"The names of Kurii, and such," he said, "cannot be rendered in the sounds of Gorean, or, I suppose, in any human language."

"Surely some provision must be made for dealing with them in Gorean," I said.

"Names are chosen," he said, "either by the animal itself, or by others. He whom you spoke of as 'the other' chose his own name, which is Grendel, Lord Grendel."

"That is the name of a monster, a hideous monster," I whispered.

"He chose it for himself," he said.

"I see," I said.

For a moment, Kurik of Victoria seemed unsteady.

"Master?" I said. "Your wound!" Some blood had seeped through the bandage that had been affixed by the tavern master's man.

"The purpose obviously has to do with the monster, with Lord Grendel," he said.

"Allow me to call for an attendant," I said.

"Therefore, our next step is clear," he said.

"Allow me to summon an attendant," I said.

"No," he said.

"You must hide, and rest," I said. "Master Tyrtaios, and doubtless others, the beasts and others, know you. You have done all you could do. Now, desist, and, in some days, when you have recovered your strength, return to Victoria."

"In the morning," he said, "we leave for Ar."

He then lay down, and was asleep. I covered him over with one of the furs. I then lay beside him, on my chain, my head at his thigh.

CHAPTER THIRTY-FIVE

Paula!" I cried.

"Phyllis!" she cried.

We embraced, weeping, in the shaded street bordering the market of Cestias, in Ar. It was not that far from the Plaza of Tarns. From where we were we could see the Central Cylinder towering toward the sky.

We wore tunics, collars.

How appropriate it was! We were slaves.

"Come to the side, lest free women pass," she said, delightedly, but anxiously, looking about.

We hurried, to the side, and withdrew into a doorway. There we again embraced, and began to cry.

"I never thought to see you again," I said.

"Nor I you, dear Phyllis!" she exclaimed, crying. "How beautiful you are!"

"As a slave!" I laughed.

"Of course," she laughed. "We are women! We are most beautiful as slaves!"

I did not gainsay her. I am sure Paula had known that long before I had, perhaps even when we had been on our former world, and had been, as it was there understood, free women. How far we had been from "free women," as that condition is understood on Gor!

"Who whips you?" she asked.

I thought for a moment, hesitating.

"Surely you know who whips you?" laughed Paula.

"Tenrik, of Siba," I said. "Who whips you?"

I had never been whipped, though my master, Kurik of Victoria, never hesitated to use the switch on me when I had been stupid, slow to respond, or in any other way the least bit displeasing. I well knew myself under discipline. I would have it no other way. A woman, I was thrilled to be subject to a man's discipline. I wished, desperately, to be pleasing to my master. The question, incidentally, is little more than a ritual. It is merely a slave's way of inquiring concerning the master of another slave, or a free person's way of inquiring of a slave the name of her master. The question, in effect, inquires as to whose whip one is subject, namely, who owns one.

"Decius Albus," she said, "trade advisor to the Ubar."

"To the Ubar?" I said.

"Marlenus, Marlenus of Ar," she said.

"You are owned by so high a personage?" I said.

"So are many," she said. "He may not even know he owns me."

"I do not understand," I said.

A tear clouded her eye. "I am a display slave," she said, "one kept largely for show."

"Surely you know," I said, "what it is to be at his feet, to have your embonded body helpless in his imperious grasp, that of a master?"

"*Ela*," she said, sadly. "Let us speak of other matters."

"Where were you sold?" I asked.

"In Ar," she said. "I was transported immediately to Ar."

I had heard that prices were highest in Ar.

"In what selling house were you vended?" I asked.

"The Curulean," she said. I had heard of this house.

"What block?" I asked.

"The Central Block," she said. "Why do you ask?"

"I do not know," I said. "I was curious."

"Your tunic is short," she said. "It seems you, too, belong to a master who enjoys displaying a slave."

"Or humiliating her," I said, smiling.

"The two matters are wholly compatible," she laughed.

"It seems so," I said.

"I always thought you had exquisite legs," she said.

"Fit for a slave block," I said. Paula's legs seemed well-formed but sturdier than mine. Surely her ankles were thicker.

"As is the whole of you, lovely Phyllis," she said, admiringly.

I smiled.

I could not help that I was beautiful, of course. And, to be sure, I did not object to being so. I felt sorry for Paula, plain, simple Paula. How then, I asked myself, could she be a display slave? I wondered what she had cost.

"Your tunic," I said, "is more modest than mine." Surely its greater length, not that it was so much greater, was to conceal more of her legs.

"Tastes differ," she said. "My master's slave dressers favor a subtle discreetness, speculating slyly that it is more reserved, more provocative."

"The cloth appears rich," I said.

"I am told it is a Turian silk," she said.

"Its draping, with its smooth folds, muchly flatters your body," I said.

"I fear it is the same body, however it is garmented," she said. "I would much prefer the simplicity of your own garment."

My tunic, I knew, left little to the imagination. I was grateful that Paula had not called attention to the fact that it was of simple rep cloth.

"You have a lovely collar," I said. "I wager it was expensive."

My collar was indistinguishable from thousands of others, a quite common collar.

"I do not know," she said. "All the display slaves have similar collars."

"Your master must be rich," I said.

"I fear so," she said. "I have heard his chamber slaves and dancers are sometimes put in jeweled collars."

"Like expensive sleen," I said.

"But more silken, and caressable, than sleen, I conjecture," she laughed. I wondered again what she had cost.

"You have sandals," I said.

I was barefoot.

"All the house's slaves are sandaled," she said. "I think the master wishes to display his wealth."

"What a vain monster," I said.

"Except for those who work in the kitchen and gardens, of course," she said, "or are being punished."

"Of course," I said, annoyed.

"Your master is of Siba," she said. "That is somewhere on the Vosk. What brings him to Ar?"

"Business," I said.

"May I inquire as to what business?" she asked.

"Pottery, securing recipes for glazing," I said. I knew this was not true, but I did not clearly understand what his business might be, and this account was the one furnished to me by my master, which account I was to proffer in the event that any condign inquiries might arise.

Why, I asked myself, had Paula been shipped so promptly to Ar? Indeed, perhaps she had been sold but once. Was that not unusual? Why had she been vended in the Curulean, and from the Central Block, and why was she a display slave?

"It must be nice," said Paula, "to know the arms of a master."

"We have little to say about such things," I said.

"Do you buck and kick, and writhe, and squirm, and gasp and moan, and whimper and beg well?" she asked.

"Paula!" I protested.

"Do you?" she asked.

"Yes!" I said, angrily.

"I thought, once collared, you would," she said.

"What choice have I?" I asked. "He is a Gorean master! I am in his hands! He does with me what he wishes! I am helpless. He excites me as he pleases. I cannot help myself."

"Do not be so defensive," she laughed. "Do not be so indignant, so righteous. We are women. We are born slaves."

"Oh?" I said.

"You need not deny it now," she said. "You are not now on Earth."

"I see," I said.

"Would you want it otherwise?" she asked.

"No!" I said. "I have never before known such feelings, such emotions, such helplessnesses, such sensations, such global raptures, physical and psychological, such a being owned, such yieldings and such beggings!"

She embraced me. Tears were in her eyes. "I envy you, lovely Phyllis," she said.

"I must see you again," I said. "Where are you kenneled, where are you chained?"

This, again, was a ritual matter, a slave's way of asking, so to speak, for an address.

"In the house of Decius Albus," she said, "off the Plaza of Tarns."

"So close to the Central Cylinder?" I said.

"My master," she said, "is trade advisor to the Ubar."

"Of course," I said.

"And where is your cage?" she asked.

"We are renting on Emerald," I said, "not far from the fountain of Aiakos."

"I fear it grows late," said Paula, looking about. "I must be away."

"I, too," I said.

"Dear Phyllis," she said.

"Dear Paula," I said.

"We must meet again," she said. "Let it be, when we can, sometime, near the fountain of Aiakos."

"What did you sell for?" I asked.

"What difference does it make, dear sweet Phyllis?" she said.

"No difference," I said, "but I am curious."

"I am not nearly so beautiful as you," she said.

"Nonsense," I said. "You are quite nice."

"How kind you are," she said. "I know little of such things."

"It has been conjectured," I said, "that I might bring as much as two silver tarsks."

This may not have been true, but I wished to impress Paula. I, at least, had conjectured that I might bring that much.

"That is a splendid price," she said. "The bidders, those sweet monsters, are no fools."

"It was only conjectured," I said. "I never actually sold for that price."

"Still," she said.

"Two coins," I said, "and of silver!"

"*Ela*," she smiled, "I sold but for a single coin."

"A silver tarsk is an excellent price," I said.

"Indeed it is," she said.

A shadow fell across us.

We turned about, frightened.

"Loitering slaves!" cried a woman's voice.

Instantly we went to our knees.

"Slothful slaves!" she exclaimed.

"Forgive us, Mistress," said Paula.

"Barbarian!" cried the woman.

"Yes, Mistress," said Paula.

"And the other, too, I do not doubt," she said.

"Yes, Mistress," said Paula.

"Of course," she said. "What slave of Gorean birth would permit herself to consort with a barbarian?"

I was uneasy, as the woman carried a switch. It is not unusual for a Gorean free woman to do so. I recalled the free woman from the wharf in Victoria. She, too, had carried a switch.

"How dare you neglect your duties, your tasks, how dare you dally?" she asked.

"We just met," said Paula. "We knew one another, from before."

"From the barbarian world!" said the woman.

"Yes, Mistress," said Paula.

"Now you are where you belong," she said, "on Gor, in collars!"

"Yes, Mistress," said Paula.

"Hiding in a doorway," she exclaimed, "hoping to avoid detection! I should bind you, hand and foot, and leave you for the rounds of guardsmen!"

A slave is not permitted to resist her securing. She can be bound helplessly, by any free person.

"Please do not do so, Mistress," said Paula.

"Shirkers," she said, "idlers, malingerers!"

"Forgive us, Mistress," begged Paula.

The free woman then, enraged, lifted her switch.

"Keep your hands on your thighs!" she said.

"Yes, Mistress!" said Paula.

Then, as we put down our heads to protect our face and eyes, she began to lash at us with that supple leather wand. We were struck, at the back of the neck, and across the shoulders and arms. "Now, up, go, slothful slaves!" she cried. We sprang up, eager to escape her blows but the pursuing switch, hastening in our wake, struck each of us at least twice across the back of the thighs as we fled.

Surely we should have been more watchful!

So distracted we had been that we had not noticed the approach of a free woman.

Hot tears burned in my eyes and my body stung, but, as I ran from the street at the side of the market of Cestias, toward Emerald, I was joyful. I was weeping, and laughing. Dear sweet, plain Paula! I had never thought to see her again! Then we had met! In my joy, I was weeping. How wonderful, how amazing! I was so grateful. We had been reunited, if only briefly. I did not know if I would ever see her again, but surely I was hopeful. She was in Ar! And I knew the fountain of Aiakos. It was at the intersection of Clive and Emerald. I knew it, even from before, from Venaticus. Indeed, it was from that very fountain that I drew water.

I was pleased to learn that she had sold for only one coin.

If my master had thought so highly of her, it would do no harm for me, inadvertently, to mention that.

CHAPTER THIRTY-SIX

That is interesting," said Kurik of Victoria.

"I thought you would be interested," I said. "I had never thought to see her again."

"I would not have thought so, either," he said.

"I recall you so speculated," I said, as I cleared the dishes of our simple repast.

"And Ar," he said, "is so large a city, and we are here so briefly."

"You do remember her, do you not?" I said.

"Of course," he said. "Who could forget such a beauty?"

"'Such a beauty'?" I said.

"Of course," he said.

"I know something you do not know," I said, lightly.

"You doubtless know many things I do not know," he said.

"She was sent to Ar shortly after arriving on this world," I said, "and sold in the Curulean, from the Central Block."

"I am not surprised," he said.

"It has been speculated," I said, "that I might bring two silver tarsks at auction."

He need not know that the speculation was mine. What did that matter? Surely I thought I was worth at least two silver tarsks, and perhaps more. Why not? Had I not been lovely even on Earth? And I was now in a Gorean collar! Too, had I not seen men regard me, as though I might be a two-tarsk girl?

"It is easy to speculate," he said.

"Perhaps Master concurs," I ventured.

"Perhaps," he said, "in some auction, where slaves are scarce."

"Am I not worth two silver tarsks?" I asked.

"You might bring that," he said, "in one market or another, where slave raids are infrequent, and the walls of cities have held."

"Please, Master," I said, plaintively.

"Very well," he said. "I conceive it possible that you might go for two silver tarsks."

"Well," I said, "Paula, with whom you were so impressed, went for but a single coin."

I waited, for his response.

"I am not surprised," he said.

"I thought you might be," I said.

"Not at all," he said. "You mentioned that she was a display slave of Decius Albus."

"Yes," I said.

"The trade advisor to the Ubar?"

"Yes," I said.

"Then I am not surprised," he said, "for the wealth and taste of Decius Albus, high counselor to the Ubar, trade advisor to the Ubar, are well known in Ar, as is the quality of his display slaves. He never pays less than eight silver tarsks for a slave. If your Paula sold for a single coin it would have been a gold tarsk, or a gold tarn, probably a gold tarsk. A gold tarsk is usually valued at ten silver tarsks, and a gold tarn, in today's market, might well purchase two draft tarns, a racing tarn or a war tarn."

"Oh," I said.

"She herself suggested a rendezvous at the fountain of Aiakos?" he said.

"Yes," I said, "Master."

"Not you?"

"No," I said.

"That is far," he said, "from the market of Cestias, from the Central Cylinder, from the Plaza of Tarns."

"Yes," I said.

"But not far from Emerald," he said.

"No," I said.

"You are a little fool," he said, "but I would grant you that your flanks are not without interest."

"Master?" I said.

"Did you not think it strange that a display slave should be loose in the streets of Ar, not on a chain following a borne palanquin, not reclining on flower petals or luxurious furs, on the steps before a curule chair, not shut within a pleasure garden?"

"I did not think of it," I said.

"Be careful of the dishes," he said. "Do not drop any. I do not wish to switch you now. I must think."

"Our meeting," I said, "was not a coincidence?"

"Do not be absurd," he said.

"I know Paula," I said. "She was as surprised as I."

"Why do you think she suggested the fountain of Aiakos?" he asked.

"I mentioned it first," I said. "And it is a well-known fountain. It is much frequented. It is a familiar meeting place. Even free persons have trysts in its vicinity."

"That is possible," he said. "Too, as she is doubtless highly intelligent, she may have wished a rendezvous in a popular place where two slaves might attract little attention, and, more importantly, one far from the Central Cylinder and the Plaza of Tarns, where she might be recognized."

"I am sure that is it," I said.

"And it is on Emerald," he said.

"Yes," I said.

"Near the housing of Lord Grendel," he said.

"She did not know that," I said.

"Are you sure?" he asked.

"No," I said.

"Why was she loose on the streets?" he asked.

"I do not know," I said.

"She is a slave," he said. "She was instructed, or manipulated."

"It was all a coincidence," I said.

"I do not think so," he said. "I am sure she was released, with the speculation of such an encounter, perhaps even commanded, on some pretext, to make her way to the market."

"It was surely a coincidence," I said.

"Do not be concerned," he said. "It is quite possible that she is as innocent as you."

"As I?" I said.

"Why do you think I ordered you, for three days now, to frequent the central portions of the city, the Central Cylinder, the Plaza of Tarns, the market of Cestias, and such?"

"That I might become more familiar with the city," I said.

"To allow a contact to be made," he said, "which contact now, obviously, has been made."

"I do not understand," I said.

"As Tyrtaios used you to locate me," he said, "so might another, and as easily."

"To do you harm?" I said, frightened.

"Perhaps to do me assistance," he said.

"I was well manipulated," I said.

"You are a slave," he said.

"We are pieces on a kaissa board," I said.

"And pieces," he said, "of little value."

"I see," I said.

"But still," he said, "you might bring two silver tarsks. It is hard to know."

I began to attend to the washing of the dishes, in the washing pan.

"Stop crying," he said. "I must think."

"Forgive me, Master," I sobbed.

"Perhaps I will caress you later," he said.

"Master may do with me as he wishes," I said. "I am his slave."

"We came quickly to Ar," he said. "The enemy, the three Kurii, carrying the captive female, Eve, must proceed more slowly, and more judiciously. They would not wish their presence to be broadly known. It would stir notice, interest, and, doubtless, alarm. And they must house their captive. I conjecture then they have not yet contacted Lord Grendel."

"For what purpose would they contact Lord Grendel?" I asked.

"They must have some purpose, some dark purpose," he said. "But what it may be is not clear to me."

"You suspect they have confederates in Ar?" I said.

"Of course," he said. "And I suspect, further, that word of the doings in the house of Flavius Minor has already reached Ar, perhaps even the steel world of Lord Arcesilaus."

"From the fire," I said, "from the fled men of the house of Flavius Minor?"

"Borne, perhaps, if not otherwise," he said, "by a single tarnsman."

"Master Tyrtaios?" I said.

"Possibly," he said.

I placed the last dish in the wooden drying rack.

"From your encounter this afternoon," he said, "it is clear Decius Albus is somehow involved in this matter."

"He is in league with Kurii?" I said.

"Clearly," he said, "but with what faction, that of Lord Arcesilaus, or Lord Agamemnon?"

"Lord Agamemnon?" I said.

"Yes," he said.

"That is the name," I said, "of a Greek king."

"An Argive king," said Kurik, my master, "a name chosen doubtless with something in mind."

"It is not his true name," I said.

"Of course not," he said. "We could not pronounce his true name, no more than we could pronounce the true name of Lord Arcesilaus, or Lord Grendel, or the Kur name of Eve."

"Should we not attempt to contact Lord Grendel?"

"We do not have the female," he said. "What credential might we proffer? Why should he believe what we might say?"

"It might be dangerous?" I said.

"Yes," he said, "he might tear off our heads."

"What are we to do now?" I asked.

"Nothing now," he said.

"'Nothing now'?" I said.

"No," he said, "but tomorrow, as though nothing had occurred, you will resume your customary duties."

"My customary duties?" I said.

"Yes," he said, "such as drawing water at the fountain of Aiakos."

"They would contact you through me?" I said.

"I think so," he said. "Slaves are often used for such purposes. Recourse to an intermediary is likely to be judicious. A slave is less likely to attract attention, or be suspected. Too, he who has made contact through your Paula may not know my location."

"Why would they wish to contact you?" I said.

"If our friend, Decius Albus, is of the faction of Lord Arcesilaus," he said, "doubtless to welcome me to Ar, to offer me instruction, and abet my cause."

"And if he is not of the faction of Lord Arcesilaus?" I said.

"Then," said he, "doubtless to assure himself that I will not interfere with certain plans."

"How might he assure himself of that?" I asked.

"How do you think?" he said.

"I see," I said, shuddering.

"Tomorrow," he said, "as though nothing had happened, fetch water at the fountain of Aiakos."

"Master will not withdraw from the dark games?" I said.

"No," he said.

"I am afraid," I said.

"That is acceptable," he said. "You will not be switched for that."

"Flee, withdraw!" I begged.

"Do not be foolish," he said.

"Please!" I begged.

"No," he said.

"Please, Master!" I said.

"Are you importunate?" he asked.

"I trust not," I said.

"For that you can be switched," he said.

"Yes, Master," I said.

"The matter is then closed," he said.

"I cannot prevail upon you?" I said.

"No," he said.

"Please," I wept.

"Beware," he said.

"Yes, Master," I wept, lowering my head. He had spoken. My will was nothing. He was master. I was slave.

I feared I had displeased him.

"Master," I said.

"Yes," he said.

"I would be caressed," I whispered.

"You beg attention?" he said.

"Yes, Master," I said.

"Spread the slave mat on the floor," he said.

This took but a moment. I then knelt beside it, head down, waiting.

"Prepare yourself for being used as what you are, a slave," he said.

"Yes, Master," I said.

CHAPTER THIRTY-SEVEN

I put down the wooden pail, which I had just filled.

"What is wrong?" asked Paula. "Dear Phyllis, there is something wrong!"

"No," I said.

"Here, to the side," said Paula, concerned.

"No," I said. "I must return, soon, to my master."

"Surely there is time," said Paula.

"How promptly this rendezvous takes place," I said.

"Surely you do not object," she said.

"We met but yesterday," I said.

"To my joy," she said.

"I did not expect our rendezvous to occur so soon," I said.

"Surely you are as pleased to see me, as I you," said Paula.

"It seems you are free of your house again, so soon," I said.

"Are you angry, are you frightened?" asked Paula, troubled.

"No," I said. "I thought you a display slave."

"I have served so," she said.

"I am surprised that a display slave could so easily slip her chains," I said.

"A girl does not slip her chains," she said. "You are well aware of that. Have you not worn them, felt their weight, felt them clasp your limbs, your throat, so obdurately? Do you think you could slip them? What is wrong with you this morning?"

"Why are you here?" I asked.

"To see you, dear Phyllis," she said.

"You are far from the house of Decius Albus," I said.

"I have a coin," she said. "I was sent to the Teiban market, to buy tur-pah."

"May I see the coin?" I said.

"Surely," she said, holding out her hand, opened, in the palm of which lay a copper tarsk-bit, "but why?"

"You are far from the Teiban market," I said.

"Yes," she said, "and at considerable risk to myself, to see you, to keep our rendezvous."

"I see," I said. Of course, I thought. Decius Albus would see to it that she had a coin, to add credence to her story.

"Are you angry?" she asked. "Have I somehow offended you?"

"How is it that you are free in the city, to wander about?" I said.

"Many slaves are free in the city," she said, "as you are."

"I am not a display slave," I said. "I am not a prize slave. I did not sell for a golden tarsk, or tarn!"

"I did not tell you that!" she said.

"It is common knowledge," I said, "that Decius Albus will not buy a cheap slave, any who might go appropriately for less than eight silver tarsks."

"It was only a golden tarsk," she said. "The bidding must have been irrational. The agent of Master Decius was doubtless inattentive or incompetent. You are far more beautiful than I."

"If you are so valuable, such a beauty," I said, "why are you loose, marketing?"

"For weeks," she said, "I pleaded to be a common slave, to serve in the house, in the kitchen, outside in the garden, anywhere, but free from the misery and sadness of the display chain."

"And your pleas," I said, "were acceded to, I take it, but recently."

"Yes," she said. "Only three days ago."

"I see," I said.

"But I am still a display slave," she said. "My new service, that of a house slave, is yet on probation, to see if I might prove satisfactory as a house slave."

"I am sure you will do so, splendidly," I said.

"That is my hope," she said.

"What were you doing yesterday, at the market of Cestias?" I asked.

"It is the season for tospits," she said. "I was sent there to assess their quality, for this early in the season."

"And we met by chance?" I said.

"Surely," she said. "What is wrong with you, Phyllis? Do you not believe me? How could it be otherwise? Do not be inexplicably bitter. Do you suspect something? Do not! I am your friend, even from Earth. Let us not be rancorous. Let us, rather, rejoice, as yesterday. How marvelous to be reunited, to see one another again! What joy! We were so happy yesterday! Have I done something wrong? Tell me, tell me, I beg of you, dear Phyllis."

"No," I said. "You have done nothing wrong. Of course not. How could that be?"

"You are changed today," she said. "It is not my fault I sold for a golden tarsk. Do not be angry! Do not hate me! You are far more beautiful than I! I am the first to insist on that. Surely it was a mistake."

"Men have eyes," I said.

Tears were running down Paula's cheeks.

"Doubtless you serve your master well," I said.

"We must," she said, puzzled.

"I congratulate you on escaping the collar of a display slave," I said.

"I have not yet escaped it," she said. "I may be returned to the chain. Why are you angry?"

"I am not angry," I said.

"It is not my fault I sold for a golden tarsk," she said.

"Of what interest could that be to anyone?" I asked.

"Hopefully of no interest, to anyone," she said.

"Doubtless you performed well on the block," I said.

"The auctioneer had a whip," she said.

"I expect, in any event," I said, "you would have done your best to influence buyers."

"Yes," she said, "as would you, lovely Phyllis. We are not free women. We are slaves. We want masters. We need masters."

"Of course," I said.

"Let the whip snap," she said, "and you would writhe, and beg, as desperately and piteously as any other vended property, as any other toy offered for the sport of masters."

"Perhaps," I said. Certainly I knew I would strive to excite the interest of Kurik of Victoria. And then, too, I sensed how my needs might build up within me, now that my slave fires had been kindled, so much so that I would hasten to lick and kiss the feet of any Gorean master, and perhaps even a man of Earth, though I doubted they would know what to do with a slave at their feet.

"I do not understand you this morning," she said. "We were so happy yesterday! I have risked much coming here, this morning, away from the Teiban market."

"Perhaps," I said, "you have a message for me?"

"Only," she said, "that I am your friend, that I hold you in affection, that I care for you, that you are dear to me, that you are so dear to me!"

"Do you wish to know where I am caged?" I asked.

"Only if you care to tell me," she said. "What is wrong with you?"

"Perhaps you would like to accompany me to my domicile?" I said.

"There is no time," she said. "I may be beaten now. I have dallied overlong. I may be returned to the display chain!"

"Do not let me detain you," I said.

"Phyllis!" she said.

"I must return to my master," I said, and turned from her.

"Phyllis!" she cried.

I lifted the bucket, which was heavy, and began to make my way from the fountain, but, of course, not toward my master's temporary rental on Emerald. I must take care that I not be followed.

"Phyllis!" she called after me, once more, plaintively, her voice now well back of me.

I continued on my way, paying her no attention. I did turn about once, after a bit, however, and, to my satisfaction, saw her in the distance, turned away, making her way from the fountain. She was not following me. She was hurrying, perhaps fearing to be late in her return to the house of Decius Albus. Something in her carriage, or gait, hastening, yet uncertain, unsteady, suggested she was miserable, or distraught. Perhaps she was upset that her rendezvous had not been as successful as she might have hoped. Perhaps she would be beaten in the house, when she returned. I hoped not, however, for she had been my friend.

I continued to take a circuitous route to my master's rental. The water was heavy.

In one way I was pleased at the morning's business, but, in another way, frightened. I was pleased that I had not given away the location of my master's domicile, and was eluding any possible pursuit, but, in another way, I was frightened as I had been given no message to convey to my master, for it seemed clear, then, that Decius Albus, whose business Paula was discharging, was no ally of my master. I took him then to be of the party of Lord Agamemnon, and, perhaps, privy to the plot my master supposed was being contrived against Lord Grendel.

I continued on.

I stopped frequently, for the pail seemed to grow ever more heavy. By now, had I proceeded directly, I would have been at my master's rental.

My arms ached.

I stopped, again.

"You have put too much water in the pail, kajira," said a male voice, concerned.

Instantly I fell to my knees, head down, but, a moment later, looking up, embarrassed, rose to my feet.

"You are obviously too slight for a draft slave," he said. "You
should carry less water, or use a yoke, with two lesser buckets, or each
half-filled."

"I have no yoke," I said.

"You must have a cruel master," he said, "to burden so fair a slave
so grievously."

I smiled.

"He is strict," I said, "but not unkind."

"One so lovely as you," he said, "should not be so cruelly laden."

I fear I blushed. In a slave tunic the exposed portions of one's body,
which in a slave tunic are considerable, color.

"What a beautiful smile," he said. "You must have brought a very
high price."

I put my head down.

Yes, I thought, or, at least, I should have brought a higher price
than I commonly did. Surely I was worth at least two silver tarsks,
perhaps even three!

"I have not seen you about," he said.

"Only recently," I said, "has my master come to Ar."

"I am sorry for you," he said, "that you should be so mistreated."

"I am only a slave," I said, softly, head down, demurely.

"Our masters can be cruel," he said.

"Yes," I agreed.

He was a handsome fellow, in his tunic and collar, bronzed, with
fine thighs, and strong arms. He was dark-haired and brown-eyed. It
was a bright day, and the street was public. I did not think he would
take me by the arm and force me into a doorway, or alley. How like a
gentleman he seemed! How gentle, and concerned, he was. How different from a master! Was he not like a man of Earth? Too, it could be
dangerous for him to do so, to handle or seize me, or force me to his
pleasure, for we belong to the free. Trysts between slaves are clandestine, and fraught with peril. We may be bred, of course, but such cross-
ings are wholly at the discretion of the masters. Such fine handsome
slaves, of course, are not unoften noticed by free women, who may
even buy them. On the other hand, in the law of Ar, and several other
cities, the free woman who pleasures herself with a male slave risks her
own enslavement, and becoming the property of the slave's master.

"What is your name?" he asked.

"'Phyllis', I said. "What is yours?"

"Drusus," he said.

"You are barbarian, are you not?" he asked.

"I fear so," I said. "But, I beg you, despise me not!"

"I would not do so," he said. "Barbarians are marvelous. I am fond of them. They sell well. And many of them, such as you, are every bit as beautiful, as desirable, and exciting, as a native-born Gorean kajira."

I looked down, pleased, flustered. I fear I blushed once more.

"But you are cruelly overburdened," he said.

"Mayhap," I said, "a little."

"Clearly," he said, "you are exhausted, you are grievously fatigued."

"My arms are a little tired," I said.

"Surely your body aches," he said.

"A little," I said.

"I am strong," he said. "For me the bucket is light. Permit me to carry it for you. For me it is nothing."

He reached down and lifted the bucket, and, in one hand, raised it up and down, easily, three or four times, beside him.

"See?" he said.

"You are strong," I said.

"Permit me to help you," he said.

"You are very kind," I said.

"Please," he said.

"If you wish," I said. "It is not far to my master's domicile. But you must not permit him to see you."

"We will be careful," he said.

CHAPTER THIRTY-EIGHT

A nd there was no message?" asked Kurik.

"No," I said.

"Decius Albus then," he said, "is in league with Lord Agamemnon."

"I fear so," I said.

"You were not followed?" he said.

"No, master," I said. "But is it not possible that my meeting yesterday with the slave, Paula, was indeed, as it seemed, a coincidence?"

"No," he said.

"It is possible," I said.

"No," he said.

"I detected nothing in Paula's behavior or mien, today or yesterday, that suggested otherwise," I said. I was upset, in retrospect, with the manner in which I had treated Paula. We had been friends. We had been so happy, or surely had seemed so, yesterday, encountering one another again. I feared I had hurt her.

"The slave," said Kurik, "is extremely intelligent. She may be a fine actress. But, too, she may be an unwitting dupe in the plans of Decius Albus. That is possible."

"As I, in your plans?" I said.

"Precisely," he said.

"If there was no message," he said, "then the purpose of the rendezvous, in the plans of Decius Albus, was to locate me in Ar."

"Which plan failed, signally," I said.

"No," he said. "You would have been followed. I am certain of that."

"I was not followed," I said. "I returned by a devious route, complex and tortuous, and frequently looked about and behind me. No one followed me. I am sure of that."

"No," he said. "If there was no message, Decius Albus would

be in league with Lord Agamemnon, and he would have had you
followed, that I might be discovered. I counted on that, and have
prepared."

"But I was not followed," I said.

"You must have been," he said.

"Master is mistaken," I said.

"Tell me everything that occurred," he said, "no matter how seemingly unimportant or trivial, following your departure from the fountain of Aiakos."

"I can think of little, or nothing, nothing of importance," I said.

"I see you are hesitant, and troubled," he said. "Perhaps a few
strokes of the whip might stir your memory."

"Nothing of importance, Master," I said.

"And what then, of unimportance?" he asked.

"My arms were tired," I said. "The pail was heavy. The journey was
much further than usual, my body ached, a kindly kajirus helped me,
carrying the pail for much of the distance."

Kurik, my master, slapped his thigh in amusement, and broke out
laughing.

"Master?" I said.

"I see," he said, "as you said, you were not followed."

"No, Master," I said.

"Rather," said he, "you were accompanied."

"Master?" I said.

"The slave," he said, "if he were a slave, was an agent of Decius
Albus, and you led him to my doorstep!"

"He was kind," I said. "He was solicitous, he was helpful."

"How naive you are," he laughed. "You were in a collar, and he was
a man. Do you think men do not know what to do with slaves, and
how to treat them? He will probably dream of you tonight, perhaps
well whipped, fearful, chained at his feet."

"But was he not a slave?" I said, in dismay.

"He might have been, he might not have been," said Kurik. "But
surely it was intended he would seem a slave. Did I not tell you how
useful slaves can be, how they tend to be less suspected?"

"Forgive me, Master!" I wept, in horror. "Do not kill me!"

"Why should I kill you?" he laughed. "I might, in a good market,
get two silver tarsks for you."

I lay on the floor, weeping, covering my head with my hands.

"I expected," he said, "if there was no message, we might soon expect a visit from our friends."

"Forgive me, Master," I wept.

"It will not occur until dark," he said. "What have you planned for supper?"

CHAPTER THIRTY-NINE

Fire!" whispered Kurik, shaking me.

I awakened suddenly, abruptly, jarred to a sense of peril.

I had not intended to sleep.

Kurik's hand prevented me from springing to my feet.

I conjectured it must be the second or third Ahn. I could smell smoke.

"You thought there would be an intruder, or intruders, did you not?" he said.

"Yes," I whispered.

"It would be a bold fellow to climb the stairs in the dark, knife in hand, when he might be expected, would it not?" he said.

I, released, rose to my feet, and hurried to the portal, at the head of the stairs.

"Do not go downstairs," he said.

"We must escape!" I said, turning about.

"They will be waiting," he said.

"The back way!" I said.

"Would you not have that covered, as well?" he asked.

"Master!" I cried.

"Scream," he suggested.

But no sound escaped me. "I cannot," I whispered. I was too frightened to scream. I could not make myself scream.

"Very well," he said, "Perhaps later."

"We must depart the building!" I said.

"Into the night," he said, "framed in a doorway, the fire behind us?"

"We cannot remain here," I said. "If we remain here, we will perish in the fire."

"Clearly," he said.

"Please, Master!" I said.

The boards of the flooring were hot. I could hear the fire raging on the bottom floor. My eyes began to sting. I coughed. Smoke was now ascending the stairwell. I shut the door at the head of the stairs. I could see fire through some of the cracks in the flooring. As I was barefoot, it was painful to stand on the boards. I ran to the wall to my right, and put my hands against it. The wall, too, was hot. I could see smoke curling up through the opening at the bottom of the door at the head of the stairs. I was sure the stairs were aflame. We could not well then descend to the ground floor and attempt to avail ourselves of the rear exit to the building, even if we had wished to do so.

"We cannot remain here!" I wept.

"Perhaps we will not do so," he said.

"Master, Master!" I cried, in misery, coughing.

"I think we might now signal our distress, and assure our friends that we are well aware of our plight."

"Master?" I said.

"Surely we would not want them to think we were ignorant of our peril," he said.

"Master!" I wept.

"That should please them," he said.

"We must flee the building," I said.

"And rush through flames to the points of waiting knives, to the greeting of flighted quarrels?"

"Surely we do not want to be burned alive!" I said.

"Certainly not," he said.

"The flames, the flames!" I said.

"They reflect nicely on the metal of your collar," he said.

"The building is afire!" I said.

"Perhaps, now," he said, "you might scream a bit."

"Master?" I said.

"Surely we owe them some satisfaction," he said. "What if they fear we might have left the building?"

I saw no hope, now, save in some frantic rushing forth, attempting to descend the flaming stairs and bolt into the night and into whatever might be there, if anything, waiting for us.

"Steady," he said.

I feared that Kurik of Victoria, seemingly so calm, seemingly so oblivious of the danger, was now deranged, or mad.

"Steady," he said.

I stood, uncertain, dismayed, in the center of the room. Smoke was about. The floor grew ever more heated!

I coughed.

I was seized by a sudden panic.

I waited! He decided nothing! He gave no command!

How frightful that he should be so inert!

I was wild with terror.

"Steady," said he, "kajira."

"Master!" I cried, and I ran to the door at the top of the stairs, and seized the handle, which was hot, and threw open the door, and then staggered back, shielding my face with my arms as a burst of flame and smoke roared into the room. Kurik of Victoria, a step behind me, flung shut the door and drew me back into the room. I was coughing and sobbing. He then stood behind me, holding me by the arms. I could not move. I threw back my head and, sobbing, screamed, piercingly, again and again.

"Excellent," he said. "That will do, nicely."

He then swept me up, into his arms, and, shortly thereafter, climbing the narrow stairs leading up, from the kitchen, we had reached the roof.

I could see buildings about, and, in the distance, several of the lofty towers of Ar, lights in many of the narrow windows, not wide enough to admit the passage of a body, and several of the narrow, graceful, lamp-lit bridges that, like delicate traceries, at various levels, linked the towers. I could even see, across the city, the beacon fires of the Central Cylinder. Tarnsmen come and go, during the day and night.

"Forgive me, Master," I sobbed, in his arms, "I ran."

"No forgiveness is necessary," he said. "One expects a frightened animal to run from fire."

"And I am an animal?" I said.

"Of course," he said. "You are a slave."

"Might not even a free woman have run?" I said.

"Quite possibly," he said. "A free woman is only a slave inappropriately clad."

"I was afraid," I said. "I could not help myself! I screamed!"

"I intended that you do so," he said. "And you did so quite nicely."

"I see," I said.

"You may be far less bright and beautiful than your friend, Paula," he said, "but I doubt that even she could improve on your screaming."

"A slave is pleased, if her master is pleased," I said.

"There is no need to be bitter," he said.

"May I recall to Master," I said, "that the building is afire. I fear Master has done no more than postpone the inevitable."

"It certainly seems that way," he said.

"Perhaps Master might put me down now," I suggested.

"It is pleasant to hold you in my arms," he said.

"My feet cannot reach the ground," I said. "I have no leverage. I am helpless."

"Very pleasant," he said. "But perhaps I should limit your gruel, to reduce your weight by two or three minna, and trim your curves a bit, to bring you a little closer to what, for you, would be ideal block measurements."

"Please, Master," I said, "put your slave down."

"You are aware, of course," he said, "that many masters enjoy keeping their slaves to their ideal block weight and block measurements, so they will look well in their tunics."

"Yes, Master," I said. "I am aware of that."

"Only free women," he said, "are allowed to be gross, slovenly, and fat."

"Doubtless that changes," I said, "when they are collared."

"Of course," he said. "They must then become lovely, obedient, and exquisitely feminine."

"The building is afire," I said.

"You wish to be put down?" he asked.

"Yes," I said.

"First," he said, "snuggle closer to me, lift your head, lick and kiss my neck, and then press your lips to mine, kissing, as a slave."

"'As a slave'?" I said.

"Of course," he said.

I complied.

"Please, Master," I wept, "do not become excited."

"Your tunic has slipped up a bit," he said.

"I cannot help it, as I am carried," I said.

"As I have often thought," he said, "your flanks are not without interest."

"A slave is pleased, if her master is pleased," I said.

"I thought that would be so," he said, "even in the office, on Earth, when you dared to conceal them from me."

"It was my lapse, Master," I said.

"It is unimportant," he said. "I can now look upon them when, and as, I please."

There was a crash from within the building.

"The second floor has collapsed!" I said.

"Yes," he said.

"May I be put down?" I asked.

"Surely," he said.

It would not do to tell my master, but, in his arms, I began to tremble with need. In pleasing another, one not unoften pleases oneself; in arousing another, one often arouses oneself.

I wondered if masters realized what effect they had on slaves.

We are so different from men!

It is little wonder we treasure our bondage, our helplessness, and collars.

I think a beam fell, below, for there was a crash.

"The roof may collapse any moment," I said.

"I fear you are right," he said.

"I am certain of it," I said.

He then lowered me to the floor of the roof, and went himself to the side. He then turned back, to face me. "By now," he said, "I expect our friends will suppose us perished in the flames."

I did not respond. His surmise seemed not unjustified.

"But," he said, "given the fire, the hot ash, the dangers of collapsing wood, it will take some time for them to make their way into the building."

"I wish you well, Master," I said, sobbing.

"Where are you going?" he asked.

"Master?" I asked.

"You may precede me, or follow me," he said.

"I do not understand," I said.

"You cannot see it from where you are," he said, "but I have fixed a narrow beam in the outside wall, which leads up to the adjacent roof."

"Master!" I cried, rushing to the wall, then crying out with fear as I almost plunged from the roof to the alley below.

"Where is it?" I asked, drawing back, sick with fear.

"There," he said, pointing over the edge of the wall, to his right.

"I see it," I said.

It seemed less a beam than a narrow, springy rod.

"That will not hold my weight," I said, "let alone yours."

"Nonsense," he said, "it is tem wood. In the south it is used for lances, it can bend almost double before snapping."

"I cannot walk on that," I said. "It is too narrow." I was sure it was little more than an inch in width, if that.

"It weighs little," said Kurik, "and can be handled easily with one hand, as might be a rod."

"It is black," I said, "it is hard to see, it is night!"

"All tem wood is black," he said.

He then, carefully, put one foot on the narrow wood. It was supple. I saw it bend a little beneath the press of his foot.

Meanwhile the fire roared ever more fiercely. I could see flames at the front of the house, where the original blaze must have been set, to seal off the front entrance. The floor of the roof was hot. I heard not only a crackling of flame, nearby, but a snapping sound, almost beneath my feet.

"Carry me!" I begged.

"I thought you wanted to be put down," he said.

"No, no!" I said.

"A slave is commonly carried over the right shoulder, if one is right-handed," he said, "but I think that might unbalance me, and the paving stones of the alley are hard, and, I fear, rather far below."

"You carried me forward upstairs," I said.

"That is a pleasant way to carry a woman," he said. "It is often used with naked free women, captured but not yet collared, which preserves their dignity as they are not yet slaves, but also, upon occasion, with slaves whom one wishes to relish in one's arms."

"But if I am carried so," I said, "how can you see the pole?"

"One looks ahead, to the destination," he said. "Too, one feels it with one's feet."

"I am afraid," I said.

He then approached me, and lifted me in his arms, and I clung to him, and shut my eyes, fiercely.

I heard the roar of the flames behind me.

I cried out, for the pole dipped down, unexpectedly, given our weight, but, after a few terrifying moments, Kurik had trod the pole upward to the higher roof, across the way. On the new roof, he put me down, and I collapsed, shuddering, unable to stand, to the floor of the roof. He then freed the pole, and pulled it up, and over, onto the roof, so that it could not be seen from below.

"What will we do, where will we go?" I asked.

"While our friends are scouting the ashes," he said, "we shall descend, into this building, and, shortly, exit from its back entrance."

"Master has essayed the practicality of this?" I said.

"Certainly," he said. "We will then go to the new rental I arranged, as I anticipated the possibility that a change in lodging might prove advisable."

"And you made these arrangements," I said, "when I was familiarizing myself, so to speak, with the city."

"Of course," he said.

"How shall we proceed?" I asked.

"You felt well in my arms," he said.

We could hear men in the street below, for a throng had gathered. "It is a tragedy," we heard. "The building is done," said a voice. "Why was the alarm not given sooner?" asked a voice. "The blaze was not discovered in time," said another. "There was no opportunity to extinguish the flames," said another voice. "I trust no one was hurt," said another voice. "We do not know," said another. "Perhaps the building was unoccupied," said another. "Let us hope so," said another. "How did the fire begin?" asked another. "That is not known," said another.

At this point there was a cry of awe, and alarm, from the throng, for, with a great crash, the roof of the building we had just abandoned collapsed, and a torrent of smoke, sparks, and flame roared upward.

I could not see the features of my master, but only a dark form, a silhouette, behind which the flames raged.

I sensed I was being regarded.

He was immobile.

I was uneasy.

"Let us flee," I said.

"Be patient," he said. "The fire continues to burn, fiercely. Our friends will still be about, and doubtless watching, doubtless in both front and back. Our departure is best postponed until they are otherwise occupied, until they begin their examination, thrusting about in the ashes, in the smoking debris."

"We are to wait," I said.

"Yes," he said.

"I cannot well see Master," I said, "the fire, behind him."

"I can see you, quite well," he said.

"It seems Master Decius Albus is in league with the faction of Lord Agamemnon," I said. "It seems we are without allies in Ar. We know neither the location of, nor the plans of, the three Kurii encountered in the house of Flavius Minor in Brundisium. We do not know the location of the hideous beast, Eve. We do not know what is occurring. We dare not approach Lord Grendel. We are fortunate to be alive. There is nothing more to be done. All is lost. Let us flee!"

"No," he said.

"What are we to do?" I asked.

"You," he said, "are to kneel there, facing away from me."

"I cannot then see Master," I said.

"It is not necessary that you see me," he said.

"All is lost," I said. "What are we to do? I beg to know!"

"I have plans," he said. "It is not necessary that you be privy to them."

"I beg to know!" I said.

"Curiosity," he said, "is not becoming in a kajira."

"I am not to be told?" I said.

"No," he said.

"Please, Master!" I begged.

"Now," he said, "put your head to the floor, as you are kneeling, and clasp your hands together, behind the back of your neck."

How vulnerable are slaves!

"Who is Master?" he asked.

"Master is Master," I said.

How owned we are!

Yet who would have it otherwise?

"Ohh!" I cried, grasped and mastered.

CHAPTER FORTY

W hat do you want?" demanded the large, gross woman glaring down upon me.

I had knelt, of course, as she was free.

A small pouch, on a string, was slung about my neck, over my collar.

I did not dare meet her eyes. I was very much afraid of free women. I well remembered the free woman, slender, possibly lovely, veiled and robed, on the wharf in Victoria, who had, in her rage, at some conjectured insult, screaming, lashed the bars of my cage, for better than an Ehn, while I shrank back within it. I had made the grievous error of appealing to her as though she might be concerned for a slave. I had even, ignorantly, so haplessly, addressed her as "sister."

"Well?" she demanded.

The shop of the potter, Epicrates, like most Gorean shops, was open to the street during the day and would be closed at night, usually by means of heavy, folded wooden screens, secured with chains or rods. I could see he whom I took to be Epicrates in the back of the shop, who had looked up from his wheel. Shelves lined the walls of the shop, laden with an assemblage of diverse platters, craters, bowls, dishes, pitchers, and vessels. There were several other larger vessels, amphorae, and such, stacked, inverted, in the corners of the shop, and toward its rear. In the back I could also see the portal that, probably, led to the living quarters of Epicrates and his companion.

"Forgive me, Mistress," I said. "I am Phyllis. Forgive my unworthiness, and that I should dare to speak, unaddressed by one who is free, but I am on my master's business."

The large woman was not clad in the robes of concealment, and was not veiled. She wore a work himation, of Cosian cut, with bare arms. Certain Cosian fashions and manners had tended to linger, even following the withdrawal of the occupation forces of the Cosian alliance.

More to the point, perhaps, was the utility and comfort of such garments, and their popularity, which antedated the troubles in Ar, in particular, the occupation of the Cosian alliance and the tyranny of the false Ubara, Talena, brought to an end by the uprising that restored the current Ubar, a man named Marlenus, to the throne of the city. The whereabouts of Talena were unknown. A reward had been posted for her capture and return to the city, ten thousand gold tarn disks, of double weight, a sum that might buy cities and fertile, well-harbored islands. It is difficult to move about, and work, of course, in the cumbersome Robes of Concealment. Lower-caste women not unoften reserved such regalia for festivals and holidays.

"And what is your master's business?" demanded the large woman. Her hands were moist from kneading clay. In one corner of the shop there was an oven in which, I supposed, materials might be treated, might be fired and glazed. It was open now, and not in use.

He whom I took to be Epicrates was watching us.

"You know of him, I am sure," I said, as I had been coached, "he is the master potter, Tenrik of Siba, famed throughout the caste of potters, well known from Skjern to Turia. Do you know of him?"

"Of course," said the woman. "Who of the caste of potters does not know of Tenrik of Siba?"

This response alarmed me. I hoped there was not, by some coincidence, a well-known potter, Tenrik of Siba.

"You are fortunate, girl," she said, "to belong to so famous a fellow."

"Yes," I said, "a slave rejoices."

At this point he whom I took to be Epicrates rose to his feet, as though curious, and came to the front of the shop, where I knelt.

"Return to the wheel," she said to the fellow. "There is nothing to see here. Do not dally about. It is only a slave. Return to the wheel."

He did not move, but, instead, regarded me.

"You need not look upon this slave," said the woman. "She is nothing, merely another common, worthless kajira. Have you never seen enough of the legs and arms, and curves, of these shameless, vendible, collared beasts? I shall inquire into this business."

He stepped back a pace, but did not return to the wheel, on which was fastened a vessel, half-formed.

"Surely you are the Lady Delia," I said to the large woman. Kurik of Victoria, of course, had made certain inquiries.

"I am Lady Delia," she said.

"I was sure of it," I said, "for my master informed me that I might recognize you, might you be less than fully veiled, instantly, by your incredible beauty."

"Oh?" she said.

"Yes, lovely Mistress," I said.

"Well," she said, "I am a free woman."

"And surely amongst the fairest of such," I said. Free women commonly regard themselves as far more beautiful than slaves, but, if that is the case, I wondered, why are they not all in collars? Perhaps men did not want them that much. If one were truly beautiful, might she not be seized and collared? What man, honestly, does not want a beautiful woman at his feet, in his collar?

And, from the woman's point of view, how exciting to belong to a man, and be his rightless, helpless slave!

"Delineate, girl," said the Lady Delia, "your master's interests."

"Is Master," I said, to he whom I took to be Epicrates, "Master Epicrates, Master Potter of Ar?"

"That is he," said Lady Delia.

"Look at my shop," he said. "Does it appear to be the shop of a master potter? Where is the yard, the dozen ovens, the jars of pigments and glazes, the slaves and apprentices at their wheels?"

"He will not trust work to menials," said Lady Delia.

To be sure, I had no illusions as to the standing of Epicrates in his field. He was, by all accounts, a fine potter, and an honest one, but his work, as far as I knew, had never been singled out in the city, nor, say, had it been displayed in, let alone won prizes in, the exhibitions held in the great Sardar fairs. One might mention, in passing, that Goreans commonly view pottery as an art, and, in many cases, as a fine art, as much so as sculpture and painting. There are few things as beautiful as a well-formed, well-painted, well-glazed vase. Indeed, some vase artists are as well-known as artists who work in fresco, or in gold, wood, or canvas. Indeed, several artists work in more than one medium. To be sure, the Goreans do not dissociate utility and beauty, in artifacts no more than in slaves. A spoon or paddle may be well carved; a door frame or chest may be a work of art. Art may be lavished on rooms and buildings, on bedding and clothing, on the saddle or harness of a kaiila, even on cuisine, in its preparation and display. But I saw little evidence in the shop of Epicrates, despite its pleasantness and attractiveness, of the higher reaches and glory of the potter's art. I saw no vessel there for which might be exchanged a dozen slaves or a tarn.

"We even rent out our second floor," said Epicrates.

"Times are hard, too, in Siba," I said.

"Speak your business, girl," said Lady Delia.

"*Ela*, Mistress," I said, "it has to do with the subtleties and mysteries of glazes, and the exchanges of mixtures, in varying proportions, and my master forbids me to speak to anyone but the great Epicrates, Master Potter of Ar, and to he alone."

"I am his companion," said the Lady Delia.

"I am helpless, Mistress," I said, "my master has spoken."

This pretext was not in the least far-fetched. There are, in many crafts, trade secrets, which are zealously guarded. Whereas most Gorean cities share in, and respect, Merchant Law, the only common law binding scattered, and often hostile, communities, there are no provisions in such law for securing protections against one party's appropriation of another party's methods, processes, formulas, techniques, devices, or such.

"My master has placed something in the pouch about my neck," I said.

"Doubtless his proposal or petition," said Lady Delia.

"I fear it must have something to do with his proposal or petition," I said.

"Why does he not come himself?" she asked, belligerently.

"He wishes, first, for the way to be cleared," I said.

"Beware," said Lady Delia to her companion, Epicrates, "he wishes to steal your secrets."

"No, Mistress," I said. "He wishes an exchange that would be found mutually satisfactory, mutually profitable."

"Ah," said Lady Delia. "I see now why he did not come himself. His proposal is so contrived as to assure him an untoward advantage, and he fears, doubtlessly justifiably, that he would be scorned, and beaten from the shop."

I did not think it likely that Epicrates, who seemed a gentle, pleasant-enough fellow, would be likely to set upon and beat anyone, let alone a visitor, and fellow caste member, to his shop.

"I do not think so, Mistress," I said. "I think he was reluctant to present himself directly and brashly before such a renowned master of his craft, as Master Epicrates."

"Perhaps, dear Delia," said Epicrates to his companion, "you might withdraw."

She cast me an angry, suspicious glance, turned about, and went to the portal leading, I assumed, to their private quarters. There, wiping her hands on her himation, she turned about, again. "Beware!" she advised Epicrates. She then disappeared within the portal.

"Now," said Epicrates, smiling, looking down on me, "what is all this about?"

"Master?" I said.

"I have never heard of a potter, let alone a master potter, named 'Tenrik of Siba'," he said. "I doubt there is such a fellow. Also, I am not a master potter, and I am no authority on pigments and glazes, at least no more than most in my caste."

I remembered last night, when our former dwelling place had been set afire, and we had made our escape. Before we had descended into the interior of the building that we had reached by means of the narrow tem-wood bridge, and while the fire was still raging, and while we were waiting for it to subside, when, we anticipated, those of the faction of Lord Agamemnon would proceed to investigate the smoldering debris, to determine the success of their assignment, I had been put to use, as a slave. Later, I had lain beside him, gratefully, my lips pressed to this thigh.

I felt his hand, roughly, but affectionately, in my hair, as one might hold an animal. "You are well subjugated," he said. "Yes, Master," I had whispered, kissing his thigh. How subdued, and well subjugated I was! I was owned. He was my master! How his I was. I would have it no other way. I had no choice but to yield the submission I was born to yield, and had longed to yield. I feared only he might tire of me, and sell me. How vulnerable, and yet loving, I felt. I wanted so to be a slave, and the slave of such a man. I was happy. What terror there is in the collar, what joy there is in the collar! I loved him, but dared not tell him. He was my master.

"I had hoped," he had said, musingly, "for the assistance of adherents in Ar, for that, given the contact made by the slave, Paula, of Decius Albus, but clearly he is our foe. No other contacts were made. We must now proceed alone. We know nothing, as yet, of the Kurii from Brundisium, nor of their prisoner. They may not, as yet, have put their plan into effect. In any event, we will have to make contact with Lord Grendel."

"Let us give up the matter," I said.

"No," he said, "we must essay the matter."

"The fire burns but yards away," I said. "It seems clear that desperate, unscrupulous men are about."

"Undoubtedly," he said.

"Withdraw," I said. "Abandon these terrible games."

"Never," he said. "Can you not sense the exhilaration of the play?"

"Men are mad," I said.

"A larl is a larl," he said, "a man is a man."

"Do not mix in these things," I said. "There are Kurii, and there is even Lord Grendel himself."

"Lord Grendel is to be contacted," he said.

"Might not danger attend such an effort?" I said.

"That is quite possible," he said. "Lord Grendel is part Kur, and the Kur tends to be violent, short-tempered, and unpredictable, easily provoked, easily excited to attack. They are very dangerous, even to one another."

"Do not approach Lord Grendel," I urged.

"I will not do so," he said.

"Good," I said.

"You will do so," he said.

"I?" I said.

I was not cheered to receive this intelligence.

"Yes," he said. "You are a woman, and a slave. Even a Kur knows the value of a woman, and a slave. Where a man might be summarily bitten to death and eaten, a woman would be seized and bartered for food or coin. Where a blade or quarrel might await a man only a new pen or chain awaits a woman, or at least one who is a slave. A free woman might be slain, mayhap, for she is free, but who would destroy a domestic beast, a kaiila, or a domestic beast as vital, as silken and soft, as helplessly inflammable, as a kajira?"

"Yes, Master," I whispered.

"Too," he said, "a slave is less likely to be suspected."

"Yes, Master," I said.

"You did not even suspect a slave, if he were a slave," he said.

"No, Master," I said.

"You will go to the pottery shop of Epicrates," he had said. "It is on Emerald. His companion is the Lady Delia. The upper floor of the building is occupied by a free woman, whose name is Bina. With her you will find Lord Grendel."

"Yes, Master," I had said. I recalled the shop, and the woman, and the beast, for I, long ago, had seen these things. I had not known, of course, that the beast, so large, agile, and wary, was Lord Grendel.

"So," said Epicrates, kindly, "what is this all about, lovely kajira?"

"I may not touch the pouch, on its string, about my neck," I said, "but Master may open it."

At least Kurik of Victoria had not braceleted my hands behind my back, before sending me on his errand. I would not, on any account, however, have touched, let alone opened, the pouch, for I had been forbidden to do so. Sometimes a stain is put on the pouch and, if the girl dares to touch, or open it, the residue of this stain, which may last for days, will betray her. She is then likely to be subjected, and well, to the attentions of the slave whip. Back-braceleted slaves are often used for conveying messages, transferring coins, and such. Too, it is not that unusual for unattended slaves to be back-braceleted. In this way they are much less likely to seize up a tospit or small larma from a vendor's cart. If apprehended, of course, she may expect a generous switching. As their arms are pinned back, this arrangement does tend to accentuate their figure. When back-braceleted, incidentally, a girl is more likely to be subjected to the attentions of passing masters met on the streets, being lip-raped and fondled. Whereas this is frowned upon in theory the girl is, it must be remembered, only a slave. On the other hand, a back-braceleted slave is less likely to be stopped and switched by a free woman. I suppose that is because she is obviously so helpless. Free women, on the other hand, might not realize how attractive a back-braceleted slave can be.

"Please, Master," I said, "that which is in the pouch is for you."

Epicrates reached down and lifted the loop of string, with its pouch, over my head.

I saw it dangle before me.

I watched him open the pouch.

"There is nothing here," he said, "no note, no letter, no proposal, only a silver tarsk."

"It is for you, Master," I said.

A potter such as Epicrates, as many in the lower castes, would usually deal in tarsk-bits, or copper tarsks. Indeed, much transaction amongst the lower castes was done in terms of barter. A member of some of the lower castes might seldom see a silver tarsk. Even amongst the lower orders of the high castes some of the Builders and Scribes might see a year's wages in terms of a handful of silver tarsks.

"I do not understand," said Epicrates. "I am not an Assassin, I have no secrets to sell. I do not wish to sell the shop."

"To rent from you," I said, "a lovely lady, and another, her fearsome pet or creature. My master asks only that you, who will be known to them, who are presumably in no danger from them, and will not fear them, intercede on his behalf, and permit me, on his behalf, to speak with them."

"The lady," said he, "is a strange, imperious little thing, whose Home Stone I do not know, but her pet, though large, is pleasant, sweet, and gentle. My companion helped her learn to read, if you can imagine that. She is not a slave, but could not even read Gorean. They had a slave, but not now. They pay their rent on time."

"I am instructed to assure you, by my master," I said, "that the silver tarsk is yours, and agreeably so, whether you approach the couple on his behalf, or not."

"Your master is generous, quite generous," he said. "Your accent is barbarian. I wonder if you know the value of a silver tarsk. Possibly you have never seen one hitherto. In any event, you needed only ask. No tarsk is necessary. I would be pleased to inquire on behalf of your master."

"A slave is grateful," I said.

"What is going on?" inquired Lady Delia, thrusting her head through the portal leading, I supposed, to their living quarters.

"It is a petition from the master potter, Tenrik of Siba," he said, "he whom you well know by reputation, that I refrain from marketing my purple-and-white craters in the Vosk markets for at least one year."

"The sleen!" she cried. "He wants to duplicate your work, and flood the river markets with his own cheap trash while you sit like a dolt at your wheel, doing nothing!"

"I fear so," said Epicrates.

"How much did he give you?" she asked.

"A silver tarsk," said Epicrates, lifting the coin.

"Demand two, five!" she said.

"I wonder how he heard of my purple-and-white craters," said Epicrates.

"Spies," she said. "Give me the coin!"

Epicrates surrendered the coin and Lady Delia examined it, carefully.

"I have never sold anything in the Vosk markets," he said. "I have no intention of doing so. They are far away. The goods might never reach there. I do not think I could afford the shipping. Roads are precarious."

"Tenrik of Siba does not know that," she said.

"Perhaps not," said Epicrates, thoughtfully.

"It seems silver," she said.

"Take it to the Street of Coins," he said. "See if they will give you a hundred Brundisium copper-tarsks for it."

"A single silver tarsk is not enough," said the Lady Delia. "Demand ten silver tarsks, a gold tarsk!"

"*Ela*, dear companion," he said. "I have already accepted the arrangement."

"For but a single silver tarsk?" she asked.

"I fear so," he said.

"I shudder," she said, "to think what it is for a shrewd woman like myself, one of acumen, one with hard business sense, to be companioned to so simple, naive, innocent, and gullible a fellow as you."

"Yet we have renewed the companionship forty times," he said.

"Someone must look out for you," she said.

Epicrates then replaced the empty pouch on its string about my neck.

"I am off to the Street of Coins," said Lady Delia.

"There is more clay to be kneaded," said Epicrates.

"It can wait," she said, hastening out into the street.

"Should you not veil yourself?" he called after her.

But she was already well down the street.

"Master?" I said.

"I cannot return the coin to you now," he said. "You see the difficulties. I am sorry."

"The coin is yours," I said.

"Wait here, a bit," he said. "The tenants upstairs are congenial, and affable, if unusual, and they are both home. They seldom go out until evening. I will return in a moment."

"Thank you, Master," I said.

A short while later, Epicrates returned. He seemed slightly troubled.

"May I ask, Master," I said, "how the matter went?"

"Well enough, it seems," he said. "But they seemed surprised, uncertain, and circumspect. I have not hitherto seen them so. Perhaps it is because they have so few visitors. Surely they were not expecting this business, this new business. I know little about them, really. I am unsure of their background and antecedents. I do not think they are of Ar. I do not know the source of their coins. Too, they know no Tenrik, of Siba."

"Were they alarmed?" I asked.

"Rather, puzzled, I think," he said.

The nature of their response suggested to me that they were, as least as of yet, unaware of anything that might have to do with the recent events in Brundisium.

"May I go upstairs now?" I asked.

"No," he said. "You are to return at the eighth Ahn tomorrow."

"My master did not anticipate a delay," I said, distressed.

"They may wish to think, to talk," he said, "to inquire, to consult, to prepare."

"My master," I said, "I am sure, will not welcome the delay."

"I am sorry," he said.

"Time may be crucial," I said. I feared this might be true.

"You are not the first to seek such an audience," he said.

"There is another?" I said.

"Yes," he said, "and that perhaps accounts for their puzzlement, their possible apprehension."

"When is this first audience to take place?" I asked.

"It is scheduled for the seventh Ahn tomorrow."

"An Ahn before mine," I said.

"Yes," he said.

"A coin was rendered?" I asked.

"No," he said. "But, as with your master, the party, or her principal, seemed reluctant to approach our tenants abruptly, to approach them unexpectedly, or uninvited. They, no more than your master, it seems, understood the lady's pet to be as harmless and placid as it is. To be sure, it has a fierce, dangerous mien."

"This earlier interview was also arranged by a slave?" I asked.

"Yes," he said.

"Might you describe her?" I asked.

"Like yourself," he said, "she has brown hair and brown eyes."

"Anything else?" I asked.

"Well," he said, "she was very beautiful, even for a kajira."

CHAPTER FORTY-ONE

The seventh bar had rung. I had heard it even before I had slipped from my master's new rental on Hermadius. From Hermadius I had gone to Clive, and, after a few blocks, turned south, from Clive, at the Fountain of Aiakos, onto Emerald. It was now near the eighth Ahn.

"I fear," had said Kurik, my master, "we will not make the first contact with Lord Grendel. That is unfortunate. In this way he will not be warned. He will not have had time to reflect, will not have had time to prepare. He will be taken unawares. Who knows what his mood may be once he is contacted by the agents of Kurii."

"Perhaps I should have rushed up the stairs, despite Master Epicrates, and intruded upon Lord Grendel," I said.

"So precipitously?" he smiled.

"Perhaps," I said.

"I think not," he said. "Even your collar might not protect you from so indiscreet and rash an act. As the ancient joke has it, many a track leads into the den of the larl but few lead out."

"Master Epicrates assured me that Lord Grendel is a gentle creature," I said.

"So, too, is the larl," said Kurik, "until it is hungry, or needful, or surprised or annoyed, or suspects its territory is transgressed."

"Master Epicrates seemed clear on the matter," I said.

"Lord Grendel knows Epicrates," said Kurik. "He does not know you, or whom you might represent."

"Could I not go earlier," I asked, "before the seventh Ahn?"

"No," he said. "The matter has been arranged. The time was set. One does not tamper with the plans of the larl. We shall make the best of it."

"What could the Kurii want with Lord Grendel?" I asked.

"We do not know," said Kurik. "But when you arrive, at the Eighth Ahn, Lord Grendel might know."

"I fear so," I said.

"If the eyes blaze, the breathing quickens, the paws tremble, the claws extrude, the ears lie back against the head, the jaws open, and the fangs are moist, do not dally, but withdraw, politely, and respectfully, with all expedition."

"Master?" I said.

"There is always a moment, however fleeting, before the Kur charges," he said.

"I trust Master jests," I said.

"If you read the signs aright," he said, "there will be no danger, even were you a male."

"I shall withdraw promptly," I said.

"I recommend it," he said. "A more auspicious meeting time may be arranged later."

"Yes, Master," I said, uncertainly.

"Do not be concerned," he said. "Your sex will protect you. That is doubtless why the Kurii are making their own contact by means of another kajira. Just do not make any sudden moves, and, if you sense impending danger, a readiness to attack, withdraw."

"Master Epicrates informs me that his tenant, whom we know as Lord Grendel, is harmless."

"Lord Grendel is part Kur," said Kurik.

"I shall leave shortly after the seventh Ahn, in the morning," I had said.

"Beware of being followed," he said.

"I shall be careful," I said.

"Beware of anyone," he said, "even one who might seem innocuous."

"I understand," I said.

I remembered the strong, handsome fellow, with long, powerful arms, a kajirus, or one seemingly a kajirus. His name, I recalled, or what he had proffered as his name, had been 'Drusus'. A woman who is a slave is not likely to forget such a fellow. Were he not in a collar, and clad kajir, it would have been easy to think of him owning slaves. How women might tremble when he entered the slave quarters, carrying his whip!

The seventh bar had rung. I had heard it even before I had slipped from my master's new rental on Hermadius. From Hermadius I had gone to Clive, and, after a few blocks, turned south, from Clive, at the Fountain of Aiakos, onto Emerald. It was now near the eighth Ahn.

I looked about myself.

As nearly as I could determine, I had not been followed. Certainly I had seen none about in my journey whom I deemed suspicious, nor did I see any about now, here in the vicinity of the shop of Epicrates, who seemed other than what one might expect at such an Ahn on such a street. No one seemed to pause, or linger. No one seemed to feign, perhaps too studiously, a lack of interest in a mere kajira, one doubtless bound on some trivial errand for her master. I think my master's new rental was unknown to those who might be his foes. Those who had set the fire, and perhaps waited outside to strike us, if we fled the building, would by now have determined, presumably to their chagrin, that no charred bodies lay amongst the debris. I thought it even possible that they might have reported to their superiors that their mission had been successfully completed, or, more likely, more judiciously, that we had not been in the building. I supposed that a fellow might think carefully before he chose to acknowledge that he had failed to carry out a task set to him by creatures such as I had seen in Brundisium, in the house of Flavius Minor.

I had crossed the street, to be less conspicuous when I had passed the shop of Epicrates, which was now open, the wooden screen folded back and secured. I did see Epicrates at his wheel. I did not see the Lady Delia. The screen may have been folded back and the shop opened as early as the Fifth Ahn, for the shops of craftsmen commonly open early, and commonly close in the late afternoon, which economy conserves on candles and lamp oil. Breakfast and lunch, by the craftsmen, are often taken in the shop itself. The markets commonly keep similar hours, produce brought in early from the fields. On the other hand, there are many avenues and boulevards in Ar where more aristocratic or expensive tastes may be satisfied, for example, those for Tharnan silver and Turian silk, even carved jade from the World's End. In such districts it was not unusual to note the veiled palanquins and upholstered sedan chairs of women of the higher castes.

I had come early.

I had stationed myself in such a way that I could see the stairwell at the side of the shop of Epicrates, which would lead upstairs to the dwelling quarters on the second floor. I was curious to see who might, if anyone, descend those stairs. Indeed, I had come early with just this in mind. I had also taken care to position myself in such a way that I could not be seen from the shop itself unless one went to its fronting and surveyed the street.

I had been waiting for some time.

I felt the ringing of the bar for the eighth Ahn must be imminent.

I sensed a movement to my left, turned my head, and immediately knelt, humbly, submissively, head down, for it was a free woman. I kept my head down, waiting for her to pass. But, to my dismay, she stopped, before me.

"Mistress?" I said, keeping my head down. One must be careful of meeting the eyes of free persons, particularly free women, lest one be deemed insolent.

"Look up," she said.

I raised my head.

Her raiment was unusual for this district, for it was of shimmering white and yellow, colors of the Merchants. She wore golden sandals. Her veil was yellow, and the hooding of her robes was white. She carried a small yellow parasol, which was opened against the late-morning sun. Such parasols are occasionally carried by women of fashion, largely as an accessory. From the utilitarian point of view they have less to do with sheltering the bit of a woman's face that might be unveiled as to keep much of the robes of concealment shaded, this lessening the build-up of heat within the raiment. Interesting, as well, the parasol, in its opening and closing, in its lifting and lowering, its playful twirling, its coy movements, its modest interventions, revelations, and such, often functions, rather as a fan, as a flirtation device, hinting, teasing, promising, refusing, suggesting, denying, and so on. Indeed, its use, as that of the fan, may convey boredom, invitation, mystery, impatience, annoyance, rage, and so on. In the case of some free women, too, the parasol may have another attribute, one more sinister, an attribute of which I was not aware at the time.

I did note the switch that, like many free women, she carried at her belt.

"Do I not know you?" she asked.

"I trust not, Mistress," I said.

It is easy for the veiled to regard the unveiled, less easy, by far, for the unveiled to regard the veiled.

"What are you doing here?" she asked.

"Waiting for my master," I said.

"Why are you not chained to a ring?" she asked.

"I do not know, Mistress," I said.

"You should be chained to a ring!" she said.

"Yes, Mistress," I said.

In many public places, particularly in the high cities, provided as a public convenience, there are slave rings to which a slave might be fastened while her master busies himself elsewhere. Indeed, in many public buildings slaves are not allowed, no more than other domestic animals.

"One should keep meaningless sluts, she-urts like you, on a chain," she said. "How else to keep you from roving about, gossiping, lapping water from the fountains, perhaps even from the higher levels, from stealing from carts and stalls?"

"Forgive me, Mistress," I whispered. I did not dare meet her eyes. I feared I knew her.

She turned away, and continued on, but, a moment later, she turned about, again, and abruptly.

"The wharf!" she said, suddenly. "Victoria!"

"Forgive me, Mistress!" I said. "I have not now, unaddressed, dared to speak to you. I have not accosted you."

"So," she said, "am I not your sister?"

"No, no, Mistress!" I said, hastily, plaintively. "That cannot be! You are free. I am a beast, a slave! I was ignorant before, stupid, a fool! Forgive me! I am kajira, only kajira! I am unworthy to tie your sandals, unworthy to perfume and garland your couch, unworthy even to cast petals in your path!"

"And a barbarian, too!" she said.

"Yes, a barbarian, too!" I said. "Forgive me, Mistress!"

She then, to my relief, turned away, and departed, continuing down the street.

I then rose, again, to my feet, shaken, miserable.

I saw a figure hurrying down the stairs across the way. It was not a man. It was a slave, a slave! I ran toward her, and, as she, not seeing me, was hurrying away, to my left, I ran after her, and called out, "Paula!"

She did not stop.

I seized her by the arm, and turned her about. "Paula!" I said.

She was white-faced, trembling. I thought her legs might give way beneath her. I had never seen her so frightened.

I steadied her, my hands on her arms.

"Phyllis!" she said, eyes wide.

"What is wrong?" I said.

"What I have seen!" she said. "It is hideous, dangerous, terrible! I did not know such things could exist! I saw only the woman at first. How wise she was! She lashed my ankles together so that I could not rise. Then it entered the room, and I screamed, and tried to rise, and run, but, my ankles tied, I fell. I tried to crawl to the door, the stairs, but the woman blocked my way, and ordered me to position, facing the monstrous thing!"

Clearly Paula had never seen a Kur before, or anything Kurlike. I had, of course, months ago, seen the beast, whom I had later learned was Lord Grendel, on Emerald, when I was in the company of Lita, my friend, the slave of Camillus, the Leather Worker. At that time I, too, was to be known, at least publicly, by the name 'Lita'. It is, as I have indicated, a common slave name.

"What are you doing here?" I demanded.

"I was to deliver a message to a personage named Grendel, Lord Grendel," she said, "but I never saw him, only the woman, who is seemingly free, and her gigantic beast."

I removed my hands from her arms. She stood, unsteadily, still shaken.

"The beast," I said, "is Lord Grendel."

"No," she said, "it is a beast."

"Lord Grendel," I said.

"It never spoke," she said.

"It listened," I said. "It could understand you. And, in its way, it can speak. You might not understand its speech."

"No," she said. "It is a simple beast."

"The human is a beast, too," I said. "Rational life is not confined to a single vessel, or form. What we term 'beasts' might, clearly, not expect to find rational life in our form, which might be unfamiliar to them. The commonality for rationality is not determined by shape and size, by fur or skin, by hands or claws, but by cunning, by thought, by planning, by awareness."

"I am afraid," she said, trembling.

"Be afraid," I said.

"What are you doing here?" she asked.

"What message did you deliver to the woman, the beast?" I asked.

"I dare not say," she said. "The slave master might kill me."

"Speak!" I demanded.

"No!" she said. "What are you doing here?"

"What slave master?" I said.

"The slave master in the house of Decius Albus," she said, "he who is in charge of the slaves of Decius Albus."

"Tell me!" I demanded.

"No," she said, shaking her head, fearfully.

"You fear this slave master," I said.

"He is slave master," she said.

"It must be pleasant to be slave master in a house such as that of Decius Albus," I said.

"It is a great house," she said.

"Doubtless he has access to all the slaves in the house," I said.

"Not to the high slaves, the preferred slaves," she said. "They are reserved for the master, Decius Albus."

"But to such as you?" I said.

"Yes," she said. "I am helpless in his arms. I yield to him, helplessly."

"You must," I said, "you are a slave."

"There is more," she said. "I yield to him wholly, helplessly. He permits no reservations nor could I attempt any, even if I wished."

"You are a slave," I said.

"We are both slaves," she said. "We are no longer on Earth, trying to live its lies. Here we are women. Here we are domestic animals, animals who belong to men."

"What message did you give?" I asked.

"What are you doing here?" she asked.

"Speak!" I said.

"No," she said. "No!"

"What," I asked, "is the name of this slave master, before whom you kneel in such fear?"

"'Drusus'," she said.

"'Drusus'!" I said.

"Yes!" she said.

At that moment the eighth Ahn began to ring.

I turned about, and, in that moment, Paula spun about, wildly, and began to run down the street.

I hesitated to follow her. I looked to the stairwell leading up to the second floor of the building in which Epicrates had his shop. I wished to reach the second floor before the last of the eight bars had rung.

I was startled to see the free woman, she clad in shimmering white and yellow, she with the parasol, she whose acquaintance I had briefly and unpleasantly made long ago on a wharf in Victoria.

She was hurrying after Paula.

Then I turned to the stairwell.

I did not wish to be late.

The third of the eight bars had already sounded.

CHAPTER FORTY-TWO

"Kneel here," said the Lady Bina, "and cross your ankles."

I felt my crossed ankles tied together with a silken cord.

"May I speak openly, frankly, and freely, Mistress?" I asked.

"Certainly," she said. "We are very permissive here. But if we do not care for what you say, you will be whipped."

"Yes, Mistress," I said.

"For you are a slave," she said.

"Yes, Mistress," I said.

I looked to the door in the apartment, which led, I supposed, to the kitchen. Nothing was framed in that portal.

But I knew what must be within that room.

"What does your master call you?" inquired the Lady Bina.

"'Phyllis'," I said.

"Who is your master?" inquired the Lady Bina.

I hesitated.

"Tenrik of Siba," I said.

"Very well," smiled the Lady Bina, "that will do—for now."

"I understand I am your second visitor this morning," I said.

"That is true," said the Lady Bina. Then she added, "I receive few visitors."

"I would speak," I said, "on behalf of my master."

"Do so," said the Lady Bina.

"His message, forgive me, Mistress," I said, "is for Lord Grendel."

"Lord Grendel?" she said. "I do not understand. I know no Lord Grendel. There is no Lord Grendel here."

"For your pet, your beast, Mistress," I said.

"I see," she said.

"Lord Grendel," I said.

"You are the second this morning," she said.

"Please, Mistress," I said.

"Very well," she said. She then turned to the side, toward the kitchen. "You have heard, sweet friend," she called.

I heard a scratching, I supposed, of claws moving on the wood of the kitchen floor, and then there was silence, but I saw the shadow of something large, but crouched, moving, on the jamb of the door. I supposed the claws had been retracted. I closed my eyes, briefly. I was far better prepared, of course, than poor Paula had been, for I had seen this thing before, and, in the house of Flavius Minor in Brundisium, had seen similar things, full-blooded Kurii. Still I was frightened. I was very much aware, for an instant, of the cords fastening my ankles together. Perhaps, I wondered, that was more necessary than I had realized. Then that mighty form, broad, and hirsute, ears lifted, was in the doorway of the kitchen.

Now it crouched in the room, in front of the entrance to the kitchen, and regarded me.

"Do not be frightened," said the Lady Bina. "He can dismember an adult sleen and bite the heads from men, but his temper is commonly equable. I am sure you will find him understanding, sweet, and gentle. He is rarely violent and seldom kills. Twice I saw him spare assailants. He has never fed on a human kill. If you do not anger, annoy, or displease him in any way, you have little to fear. I am sure you will like him." Then she turned to the beast. "It seems, dear friend," she said, "that your disguise, as a mere guard brute, dumb and servile, has been twice penetrated in a single morning."

The beast, not moving, continued to regard me.

I was not greatly soothed by the reassurances that had been tendered by the Lady Bina.

I hoped he had understood her.

Certainly he could not regard me, a half-naked, ankle-roped kajira, as any threat to him, or to his mistress, or colleague.

I felt very small, very helpless.

As my ankles were tied, I could not rise to my feet.

I was sure I was well within the "critical charging distance" of which Kurik, my master, had spoken.

A swift wrenching of those mighty jaws, I was sure, could tear an arm from my body.

"Are you uneasy?" asked the Lady Bina.

"A little, Mistress," I said.

"Do not be," she said.

"Yes, Mistress," I said.

"Proceed," she said.

But how I might speak, I thought, might much depend on what had transpired before I had been admitted into their presence.

"May I ask," I said, "what was the import of the message delivered by my predecessor, who lately exited the building?"

"What a pretty thing she was," said the Lady Bina. "I wager she would bring at least five silver tarsks on the block."

"Perhaps," I said, annoyed. "But, Mistress, her message?"

"Doubtless," said the Lady Bina, "it is the same as yours, entrusted to two couriers, lest one be too confused, frightened, or distraught to deliver it properly, or comprehensibly. My friend's appearance is sometimes found disconcerting."

"I do not think it will be the same message," I said. "May I inquire its nature?"

"Later, perhaps," said the Lady Bina. "First, we would hear your message."

"May I ask from whom was my predecessor's message?" I asked.

"As you know of Lord Grendel," she said, "I see no harm in responding. It was from Lord Arcesilaus."

"No, Mistress," I said, "I doubt very much that it was from Lord Arcesilaus."

"I do not understand," she said.

The ears of the beast, already turned toward me, lifted a little more, and, subtly, I thought, widened.

Its mien was alert, too alert, I feared.

I thought of the energy latent in that mighty form.

I was frightened.

How swiftly it might have sprung forward!

My ankles were tied.

"Speak," said the Lady Bina.

I then told them of the supposed gratitude of a supposed Lord Arcesilaus, seemingly a Kur, spoken of as the Twelfth Face of the Nameless One, entitled "Theocrat of the World," or, at least, I supposed, of one world, a particular steel world, a gratitude that was to find expression in a gift, a gift to be delivered to Lord Grendel in recognition for his services, which services, it seemed, had assisted in bringing about an alteration of the power structure of that world, one to the advantage of Lord Arcesilaus. This gift was to be transmitted to Brundisium, a well-known port on the coast of continental Gor, where it was to be received by my master, Tenrik of Siba, who, in turn, would conduct it safely to Ar, where it was to be presented to Lord Grendel.

"What is the nature of this gift?" inquired Lady Bina.

"In its contrivance," I said, "I understand it to be something like Lord Grendel himself, an adjustment of, a treatment of, and an intertwining of, hereditary coils, in such a way as to produce a new form of life, a fusion of components, both human and Kur, to be implanted not in a rooted womb but a human womb, and then brought to term, and delivered, as though it might be a wholly human child."

At this point there was a menacing growl from the beast crouched before the doorway to the kitchen.

"Should I continue?" I asked the Lady Bina. I was not sure it was wise to do so. Too, I was not sure the beast could understand me.

"By all means," said Lady Bina.

"It is my understanding," I said, "that factions exist, some of which may be inimical to the interests of Lord Arcesilaus."

"Yes," said the Lady Bina, "and certainly any faction loyal to that of the supplanted Lord Agamemnon, but there is little to be feared from him now as, I believe, he is currently without a body."

"You mean he is dead?" I said.

"Not at all," she said, and declined to explain this, apparently feeling a matter so obvious needed no explanation.

"The gift was delivered to the house of Flavius Minor in the port city of Brundisium," I said, "and was claimed by my master, Tenrik of Siba, as planned, but intruders, three beasts, intervened. The gift was seized by these beasts and spirited away, we know not where nor for what reason."

"These intruders," said the Lady Bina, "were doubtless Kurii. You should not speak of Kurii, the high ones, as beasts."

"Forgive me, Mistress," I said.

"Kurii," she said, "are not beasts. Sleen and tarsks are beasts, slaves, such as you, are beasts, Lord Grendel, who is not full Kur, fond as I am of him, is a beast, but Kurii, the august ones, the noble ones, the high ones, are not beasts."

"Yes, Mistress," I said.

"Do you understand?" she said.

"Yes, Mistress," I said.

"Why would Lord Arcesilaus wish to give some malformed monstrosity to Lord Grendel?" she asked.

"He doubtless thought Lord Grendel would be pleased," I said.

"Interesting," she said. "I wonder why."

"I am sure no insult was intended," I said.

"I would suppose not," she said.

"I am told," I said, "the gift was female, a female."

"What would be the point of that?" she asked.

"Perhaps," I said, "Lord Arcesilaus thought Lord Grendel would be pleased."

"To be given a monster?" she said. "Lord Grendel regards himself with misery, with loathing and horror. He avoids mirrors, and reflective surfaces, will not look into pools of still water. And Lord Arcesilaus would send him a mirror of his own misshapen form, a reminder of what is most repellant and repulsive to him, himself? Look at him! See the eyes, the paws!"

"Surely he is much like a Kur, Mistress," I said. I was not sure I could distinguish him from a Kur, a "high one."

"A counterfeit," said Lady Bina. "It would be less abhorrent if he were not so close to a high one. Better to be an honest copper tarsk than a copper tarsk painted silver or gold, one pretending to be silver or gold."

"I am sure Lord Grendel pretends nothing," I said.

"No," she said. "It is his body that pretends."

"Mistress informed a slave that the first message, that borne by my predecessor, another mere kajira, was conveyed on behalf of Lord Arcesilaus, a claim concerning which I dared to express doubt. The foundation for my skepticism will now be understood."

"Very much so," said the Lady Bina.

"May I now inquire the nature of the earlier message?" I asked.

"I do not see why not," she said. "A meeting was proposed, in which a message from Lord Arcesilaus to Lord Grendel was to be delivered, one pertaining to worlds."

"And what credentials were borne by my predecessor," I asked, "she who bore this message, certifying its authenticity, that its source was Lord Arcesilaus?"

"None," said the Lady Bina.

"I see," I said.

"And what credentials do you bear?" she inquired.

"None," I said.

"I see," she said.

"I would not attend such a meeting," I said. "I fear for the life of Lord Grendel."

"It is no wonder you are in a collar," she said. "It is no wonder you are a man's plaything. You are so stupid."

"Forgive me, Mistress," I said, "but I am not stupid. I am quite intelligent."

"Perhaps, then," said the Lady Bina, "you are merely unaccustomed to wandering in the byways of intrigue."

"I fear so, Mistress," I said.

What man would not wish to lock his collar on a highly intelligent woman, just as on a highly intelligent sleen or kaiila? We make the best collar meat! Too, it seemed clear that the average slave was far more intelligent than the average free woman, for a very simple reason. Slavers selected with high intelligence in mind, as well as beauty and passion. It is well known that high intelligence improves the price of slaves, and, similarly, of course, ignitable passions, which place us so much at the mercy of our masters. And how thrilling, and fulfilling, it is for us to find ourselves in our place in nature!

"If enemies wished to kill Lord Grendel," she said, "it would be easy for them to attempt to do so, in a hundred places, at a hundred times. Clearly their intent, if what you suggest should be true, is to make use of Lord Grendel, for one purpose or another."

"Yes, Mistress," I said.

"But for what purpose?" she asked.

"I do not know, Mistress," I said.

"And how, I wonder," she asked, "might they think to influence Lord Grendel, to encourage him to accede to their wishes?"

"By means of the female, Mistress," I said.

"Absurd," she said. "By your own testimony the female is a contrivance, a biological artifact, a monster, and is doubtless, in her own way, as hideous, as gross and repulsive, as my dear friend, Lord Grendel, himself. It is preposterous to suppose she could produce any effect in him other than loathing and dismay. Should these supposed enemies think otherwise they are as naive, and as unaccustomed to the byways of intrigue, as I suggested, as an ankle-roped slave. Surely Lord Grendel, a creature of sensibility and taste, would be more likely, in disgust and rage, to destroy such an affront to nature than spare it. He does not even regard his own image in reflective surfaces. The existence of such a thing is a veritable reproach to him. Who would dare to confront him with so painful a mockery? Would it not be most merciful to put such a horror out of its misery? Should it not beg to be terminated? What kindly fellow would deny it such a mercy? Should it not dash itself to pieces?"

The beast crouched before the doorway to the kitchen had not moved.

"Nonetheless, Mistress," I said, "I am sure it is on Gor, was delivered with benign intent, and was seized with some end in view."

"The other messenger," said the Lady Bina, "mentioned nothing of this sort."

"Slaves," I said, "are seldom made privy to the plans of masters and mistresses."

"Poor Lord Grendel," she said, "how hard this must be for him."

"A meeting was proposed," I said.

"To which we have acceded," she said. "The time and place have been arranged."

"Beware," I said.

"I do not think there is danger," she said. "The message was from Lord Arcesilaus, with whom we are on excellent terms."

"It was not from him, Mistress," I said.

"Your story," she said, "is clearly a fabrication. What is unclear is its motive."

"I dare not lie, Mistress," I said. "I am a slave!"

"You were ordered by your master to lie," she said.

"No, Mistress!" I said.

"It is plausible that Lord Arcesilaus might wish to communicate with Lord Grendel," she said. "Plans abound, dark winds scurry about, secrets are in the streets. The most likely faction opposed to Lord Arcesilaus would be that of the deposed Lord Agamemnon, but his faction is inert as of late, indeed, perhaps dissolved, and, to the best of our knowledge, Lord Agamemnon, lacking a body, is little to be feared. Your story is absurd. Why would Lord Arcesilaus duplicate the experimental debacle that resulted in the formation of Lord Grendel? And if someone did, it would not be sent to Gor, and proffered as a present. More likely, if only to avoid offense, it would be sequestered in some remote corner of a steel world. How insulting it would be to even let Lord Grendel know that such a monstrosity might exist. No, your story is grossly false, patently so, but what is not clear is what you or your master might have in mind. What is your purpose?"

"I have spoken the truth, Mistress," I said.

"I do not believe you," she said.

"Forgive me, Mistress," I said. "If Mistress will untie my ankles, I will return to my master."

The Lady Bina put back her head, and laughed, I thought rather merrily.

"Mistress?" I asked, uneasily.

"Surely you do not think this matter is so expeditiously settled," she said, "that you are now going to leap up and rush off to your master, that you will be allowed to slip away with impunity?"

"I do not understand," I said.

"You will remain here," she said.

"Surely not," I said.

"You will not escape," she said.

"'Escape'?" I asked. "I do not understand," I said.

"You will accompany Lord Grendel to the meeting, where your lie will be confounded and exposed, and thence you may be used for sleen feed," she said.

I attempted, wildly, irrationally, in sudden panic, to spring to my feet, but, my ankles bound, I fell heavily to the flooring, before the door.

"You see, dear Grendel," she said, "binding a slave's ankles is an excellent way to control her."

I turned about, sitting, my ankles now before me, and reached to undo the cords. Did I not know I had not been given permission to do so? Did I not know I was now a Gorean slave girl?

"Are you going to run away?" she asked.

"Please, Mistress!" I wept, quickly removing my hands from the cords.

The Lady Bina seized me by the ankles and drew me across the floor, to the wall. There was a slave ring there, anchored in the floor. I glimpsed a collar and chain.

"Mistress!" I protested.

"On your belly, worthless, lying slut, worthless beast," said the Lady Bina, "and put your wrists behind your back."

There were two decisive snaps and my wrists were fastened behind me, in slave bracelets.

"Please, no, Mistress!" I wept.

But then the collar was snapped about my neck, and by this, and its chain, I was fastened to the slave ring near the wall.

I was still on my belly.

"You look well as a chained slut," she said. "Indeed, do not they all?"

"Please free me!" I begged.

"Surely, as a slave," she said, "you are used to being on a chain, being helpless in bracelets, and such."

"Let me go," I begged.

"Surely you suspect you will remain here, my dear," said the Lady

Bina, "until you are so privileged as to be taken to a certain rendezvous, in the neighborhood of the Twentieth Ahn, at which time you will be turned over to an agent of Lord Arcesilaus."

I moaned.

"I understand your apprehension," she said. "Too, do not expect that your sex, your collar, and your beauty, such as it is, will protect you at such a meeting. You are not one of their own females, a high female, of Kur blood. As a lying, displeasing slave you may well be cast naked to leech plants or fed to sleen, or, more mercifully, perhaps, to save time, be simply, swiftly, bitten to death."

"I am a poor slave," I said. "I know nothing of these things."

The Lady Bina then undid the knots of the cords wound about my ankles, and put the cords to the side.

"While waiting," she said, "perhaps you would care for a handful of slave pellets or a bowl of slave gruel?"

"Mercy, Mistress," I said.

"It seems not," she said, and turned away.

The floor was hard.

I turned on my side, and pulled futilely at the encirclements, fastened so snugly on my wrists.

"Please, Mistress!" I begged.

"Were you given permission to speak?" she asked.

"No, Mistress," I said.

"Be silent," she said.

"Yes, Mistress," I said.

I felt the weight of the chain, dangling from the collar ring. I pulled again, at the bracelets.

"You will be blindfolded, of course," said the Lady Bina. "That will give them the option of sparing you, should they be so inclined. One supposes you might be worth something, off a slave block. In any event, you will learn what is to be done with you."

"Thank you, Mistress," I whispered.

I looked to the large beast, across the room, still crouched before the doorway. It was looking at me. I quickly lowered my head. One must be careful of looking into the eyes of the free.

I hoped I might be spared.

CHAPTER FORTY-THREE

I heard the rubbing of stone on metal, long, firm, rhythmic, smooth strokes.

I sat in the wagon, my back against the side of the wagon box, my legs drawn up. My wrists were still confined behind my back in the slave bracelets. I could feel the stones of the street as the wagon rumbled forward. I was blindfolded. The leash had been put on me before the blindfolding, in the apartment of the Lady Bina and Lord Grendel. The Lady Bina had remained in the apartment. I had been carried downstairs, and hoisted onto the wagon bed. I had heard canvas being drawn, so I supposed the wagon was a closed wagon.

"Can you understand me?" asked the beast.

I hesitated a moment, and then said, "Yes, Master."

I had understood him long ago, when I, with Lita, had watched him pass with she whom I now knew as the Lady Bina. Her name had been subsequently made clear to me by my master, and that he was a Lord Grendel. Too, I was now more alert to, and familiar with, the transformations or qualifications of Gorean phonemes that might occur with such a form of life given my interactions with the beast, Eve, in Brundisium.

"Good," he said. "The translator will not be needed."

The wagon was being drawn by a draft tharlarion. I could tell this from the sound of claws on the stones. I supposed it to be a small one, as such is the case with most fee wagons within the city.

I continued to hear the rubbing of the stone on metal.

I did not know the driver. It was, doubtless, a pay wagon, or fee wagon, such as might be hired about the city. The Lady Bina, I gathered, had arranged the conveyance, probably engaging the first that came to hand. I suspected it would be exited before we approached the rendezvous point.

"You are Phyllis?" he asked.

"A slave is named as masters please," I said.

"So, what is your name?" he asked.

"Phyllis, Master," I said.

"You should be more prompt, slave," he said.

"Forgive me, Master," I said.

"I suspect," he said, "you may have told the truth."

"I did!" I said, eagerly. "I did, Master!"

"The Lady Bina," he said, "is suspicious, and impetuous, and thinks little of slave girls."

"She is free," I said.

"I have often thought," he said, "that she should best be stripped and collared herself."

"But she is free!" I said.

"Were you not once free, somewhere?" he asked.

"Once," I said, "—legally." Surely I had been legally free on Earth, but I had learned, on Gor, that even on Earth I had been a slave, a slave in the profoundest of senses, a natural slave, a bred slave, born to be fittingly collared. It was only that, on Earth, I had not met masters. On Gor there was no dearth of masters. How differently I viewed the men of Gor from how I had viewed those of Earth! How weak, help-less, moved, and thrilled, I felt, as a woman, to be amongst such men. Perhaps even the free women of Gor experienced such feelings. Were they not, too, women? But then they were not owned.

"She would look well on her knees, in a collar," he said.

"It is where we belong, Master," I said.

"Her origin," he said, "was a steel world. She was once the pet, a grooming pet, of Lord Arcesilaus."

"I do not understand," I said.

"Kurii, not unoften," he said, "keep human females as pets. Their bodies can warm feet; their fine, small teeth are excellent for grooming, for ridding pelts of parasites."

"I did not know," I said.

"Most are not taught to speak, but only to recognize simple com-mands in Kur, much as a sleen might learn to respond to certain vocaliza-tions in Gorean. Without speech, what is a human but another beast?"

"She spoke well," I said.

"She is highly intelligent," he said. "She learned much Gorean on the steel world, from some who could speak the language. Lady Delia, the companion of Epicrates, taught her to read Gorean. In many respects she is untutored and naive. She knows little of Gorean cul-ture. She holds herself in high regard, deeming herself, as many lovely women, the fairest woman on Gor. Indeed, she once sent a slave to propose her companionship to Marlenus of Ar, that she would become thereby the Ubara of Ar. The poor slave, unfortunately, was much ridiculed, and well beaten. The Lady Bina found this rebuff of her suit surprising, and somewhat annoying. It took days for the slave to recover. In some respects she is imminently practical, and, in others, oblivious of practicalities which, to a normal person, suitably acculturated, would seem patent, practicalities of Home Stone, of family, of caste, of station, of power, and such. She is not, really, either moral or immoral. Similarly one would not expect a sleen, or a pet urt, to be either moral or immoral. They are merely what they are."

"Master is different," I speculated.

"Perhaps," he said. "I have wondered, I have thought, I have had friends, I have felt the voice, the call, of honor."

"How is it," I asked, "that Master is on this world?"

"You looked upon me," he said. "You have seen how hideous I am, neither Kur nor human, naught but a monstrosity. How could I endure to remain amongst the mighty and beautiful? Better to hide on this world, pretending to no higher office than that of a pet, or guard brute."

"But the Lady Bina," I said.

"She is ambitious, as well as beautiful," he said. "She, however naively, intends to acquire fame, wealth, and power on Gor, an open world, one with many humans, through the weapons of her intelligence and beauty. Gor lies before her, a world to conquer, a jewel to possess. If you were she, would you not have hurried to Gor?"

"How is it that she was brought to Gor?"

"By my request, for her sake, to Lord Arcesilaus, whom I once served in a time of dark troubles."

"This is hard for me to understand," I said. "How is it that you are with the Lady Bina?"

"Unbeknownst to herself," he said, "she needs counsel and protection. Who would watch out for her on this world, if not I? Who would protect herself from herself, if not I? Too, she is not a wicked thing, or not intentionally so, perhaps only, occasionally, accidentally so. Too, we are fond of one another. Surely a human can be fond of a brute, just as a brute may be fond of a human."

"Surely there is more," I said.

"Perhaps," he said. "I am part human, and the human part of me surely sees how lovely she is, and, in a way, how helpless she is. She is a treasure, remote, and yet at hand."

"You care for her," I said.

"You looked at me," he said.

"Even so," I said.

"But not in the way you may think," he said.

"I suppose not," I said.

"I had a human mother," he said.

"I understand so," I said, shuddering.

I heard the stone continuing to move on the metal.

"Is she still alive?" I asked.

"No," he said. "I killed her."

"Surely not," I said.

"She saw me," he said, "what she had produced, what was taken from her body, and she killed herself."

"You did not kill her," I said.

"As much as if my hand had been on the knife," he said.

"No," I said. "You are innocent, wholly so. You are in no way responsible. Do not think such thoughts. Forgive me, Master, but you are mistaken. She took her own life. I do not think it likely she held you. I do not think she nursed you. I do not think she knew you."

"Who would care to know a monster?" he asked.

How could I respond to that?

"One," he said, "once did, on the steel world, in the time of the tribulations, in the time of dark troubles, a member of the scarlet caste."

I was silent.

The stone continued to move on the metal, and I suddenly realized the meaning of the sound. The blade of a weapon, apparently a large and heavy weapon, was being sharpened.

"By now," he said, "we are outside the city, on the Viktel Aria, moving north."

"I do not know, Master," I said.

"We will soon halt the wagon, and proceed on foot," he said.

"Yes, Master," I said.

"There will be a guide," he said.

"Perhaps he will wish to blindfold you," I said.

"Doubtless," he said.

"He will then do so," I said.

"No," he said.

"Why not?" I asked.

"Because he will not wish to die," he said.

CHAPTER FORTY-FOUR

A light rain had begun to fall.

We had left the wagon some Ehn ago.

I followed, blindfolded, my wrists pinioned behind me in slave bracelets, on my leash. I did not know in whose hand, or grip, it might be. How is one to know, as a blindfolded slave? I followed, responsive to the slight pressure on the leash ring, as I must, as what I was, a tethered, leashed beast.

As the rain fell, I could feel the thin, scant, damp rep-cloth against my skin. I would be much revealed, for whoever might care to look upon me. How vulnerable we are! How helpless we are! We are owned. Yet I would not have had it differently. I now knew myself a rightful slave, the fitting property of men. I was content and overjoyed to be a slave. It was what I was! Soon the blindfold became sopped.

We continued on.

I did not know how many might be about. Surely there were at least two, Lord Grendel and the guide, who had not spoken.

I later conjectured we had left the wagon some fifteen Ehn ago. I did not know if the driver had been instructed to wait or not. Most likely that detail would have been arranged by the Lady Bina, who would have engaged the wagon. I supposed the driver had been instructed to wait. We must be some pasangs from the city. I was not sure that the driver even knew the nature of his passengers, perhaps only a slave and a beast, if that. The driver, of course, even if waiting, could be sped away, dismissed by a word from another, informed that his services, following an alleged change in plans, would no longer be needed.

I was barefoot. I was not a high slave, or a favored slave. The ground was soft. Occasionally I made my way through puddles. Cold water splashed about my calves. Once I slipped and fell, and then, the leash taut, I rose to my feet, and hurried on, obedient to the tether.

It was not much later that we stopped.

The hair on the back of my neck rose as I heard an exchange in Kur, between Lord Grendel and two others.

Apparently no translator had been activated.

"We are stopped," said Lord Grendel to me.

"Forgive me, Master," I said, and knelt instantly in the mud. How stupid I had been! Did I not know that I, a slave, was in the presence of the free? For that I could be switched, even whipped. Goreans do not accept laxity, let alone insolence, in a slave.

"Head down," said Lord Grendel.

I lowered my head.

I feared I might be punished.

But the high ones and Lord Grendel continued to speak amongst themselves, in Kur.

I was not important.

Then the leash was shaken once, and I rose to my feet. An Ehn or so later, we halted again, and I heard a heavy portal being opened. Conducted within I felt tiles beneath my feet. The portal was then closed behind us and, I gathered, from the sound, barred.

As we had stopped again, I knelt.

"Welcome," said a voice in Gorean. "Welcome to one of the houses of Decius Albus, loyal ally of Lord Arcesilaus, Twelfth Face of the Nameless One, Theocrat of the World."

I was sure I had heard the voice before.

Interestingly, almost simultaneously, softly, I heard mechanically produced phonemes in Kur. The sounds were subtle, to me little more than a susurration. To the hearing of a Kur, or Lord Grendel, however, I had little doubt that they were clearly audible. In the dark history of the high ones I gathered that evolution, in virtue of whatever considerations, had tended to favor keenness of hearing. On the other hand, when a Kur utterance was registered by such a device, its emanation in Gorean was clearly accessible to the human ear. I would later learn that the volume on such machines, in either Kur or Gorean, could be regulated by means of a dial. In what follows, unless otherwise specified, I shall report utterances, and interchanges, in Gorean, that for purposes of simplicity and clarity. If no translator was present, of course, the average human would find Kur unintelligible, as much so as the snarling of a sleen or the growling of a larl. Similarly most Kurii would find Gorean unintelligible. These differences would occasionally be relevant to this account.

I could not immediately place the voice that had spoken in Gorean.

I was sure I had heard it somewhere, not as I heard it now, but otherwise, perhaps in a disguise, perhaps in gentler, kinder, more understanding, more solicitous tones, not as I had just heard it now, in a host's forward salutation, expressed in warm tones, blunt, sturdy, and forceful. What I had heard before might even have been the voice, polite and diffident, of a male of Earth, reduced and trained, but what I had just heard, pleasant, assured, forthright, and direct, was the voice of a Gorean, and, I feared, a master. The voice was clear and manly; in it there was no apology for strength and manhood; such a voice carries a natural authority; perhaps it is best listened to when one is on one's knees.

"Dear Lord Grendel," continued the voice, "let this occasion be one of conviviality, celebratory of friendship and collaboration."

"There is a message for me," said Lord Grendel, "from Lord Arcesilaus?"

"Indeed," said the voice.

"May I receive the message now?" asked Lord Grendel.

"Shortly," said the voice, "but Lord Arcesilaus wishes it to be appropriately delivered."

"I do not understand," said Lord Grendel.

"We crave your patience," said the voice.

"I await your pleasure," said Lord Grendel.

"We shall begin with a light collation," said the voice, "following which, suitably set forth, suitably framed, so to speak, we will make known to you the will of Lord Arcesilaus."

"Be it so," said Lord Grendel.

"Now," said the voice, "you will be conducted to a small, pleasant chamber, wherein you may remove the stains and soilings consequent upon your journey, for, as I hear, the weather is foul and the terrain unpleasant, and you may then refresh and repose yourself until invited forth."

"My hosts are kind," said Lord Grendel.

I felt the leash gently shaken, once, and rose to my feet. I then followed, over tiles, making one turn or another, for two or three Ehn, until, I gathered, we had been ushered into a chamber. I heard the door close, and I knelt.

"May I speak?" I asked.

I heard the click that, I gathered, deactivated a translator. What we said, then, in Gorean, would be unintelligible to most Kurii, should they be listening.

"Surely," said Lord Grendel.

"I am afraid," I said.

"There is much to fear," said Lord Grendel.

"These are not allies of Lord Arcesilaus," I said.

"Clearly not," said Lord Grendel.

"You believe me?" I said.

"I believed you from the beginning," he said.

"A slave is pleased," I said.

"Too," he said, "they gave no sign, one to which I would have supplied the countersign."

"I fear for your life," I said.

"If they wished to kill me," he said, "it could have been done by
now. It is not my life they want, but my claws, my intelligence, my
knowledge, my connections, my relationships, my honor."

"They wish to recruit you to their purposes," I said.

"Obviously," he said.

"Decius Albus," I said, "whose house this is, is amongst the richest
men in Ar."

"What is a man, or Kur, whose honor is lost?" he said.

I felt the breath of the beast on my shoulder.

"Do not be afraid," he said.

I felt the bracelets removed from my wrists. He then relieved me
of the leash, and, lastly, the blindfold. This is the order in which such
things are commonly done. Is the leash not suitable for a slave? Does it
not help her to keep in mind that she is a beast? And how helpless, and
vulnerable, and in ignorance, is a blindfolded, or hooded, slave! Is it
not suitable then that that bond would be the last removed? I blinked
against the lamplight. One lamp hung from the ceiling; two others
were in wall niches. There was a small, wheeled brazier on the floor,
which warmed the room. There were chests in the room, too, and a
curule chair, and a couch. There was a slave ring anchored in the foot
of the couch. On one wall, on its peg, common in a Gorean bedding
chamber, I saw, dangling, the five-stranded slave whip. About the neck
of Lord Grendel, on a light chain of red and yellow enameled links,
hung a small, metallic device, about the size of a man's fist, which I
assumed was a translator. Against one wall, apparently brought into the
house, and now into the room, doubtless brought from the wagon, was
a formidable implement. Its haft was easily five or six feet in length,
and it had a large, single, double-edged blade. I had never seen such
a thing before. It was a Kur ax. Such a thing, I would learn, could, in

a single blow, fell small trees and shatter walls. It not infrequently figured, I was given to understand, in the "games of the rings," whatever
they might be. As light and terrifying as such a thing might be in the
grasp of a Kur, I was sure, did I dare to touch it, I would have found it
difficult to lift, let alone employ. To be sure, I would not have dared to
touch it, for a slave might be slain for so much as touching a weapon
without permission.

"You are muddy, and filthy," said the beast. "Go to the basin to the
side, crouch therein, and clean yourself."

I slipped from the tunic, went to the large, shallow basin, and stepped
into it. There was some six inches of water in the basin. Modesty is not
permitted to us, no more than to a she-verr or she-tarsk. Yet we are sometimes sensitive to such things. If we were not, perhaps men would not
so enjoy having us naked before them. Surely nudity, and the collar, well
remind us that we are slaves. Yet, too, there can be an exquisite joy in
being naked, perhaps, too, because it reminds us that we are slaves, and
we rejoice to find ourselves the exposed properties of our masters. How I
pitied free women! What a joy to be collared, to know ourselves subject
to being bought and sold, to be owned! I wonder if free women can
know such a joy. But, too, what did my nudity matter to such a beast?
But then I recalled he was part human, and doubtless had something of
an eye for female beauty, such as that of the Lady Bina.

"May I not, when presentable," I asked, "wash, comb, and brush
the fur of Master?"

"No," he said. "You are ignorant. You would do it poorly. You do
not even have the training of a Kur pet."

"No, Master," I said.

"Hurry," he said.

"Yes, Master," I said, and began to bathe. The Gorean bath can be
a pleasure, and a delight, prolonged and refreshing, but there seemed
little time now to relish such simple pleasures. Part of the training of a
slave girl, incidentally, is the bathing of a male.

Lord Grendel applied himself meanwhile to his grooming, and, a
bit later, began to rummage through the chests in the room. From one
of the chests he drew forth a long, flowing, red, silken robe, which he
hung about his shoulders. He then, with a flourish of the robe, turned
to face me.

"Master looks splendid," I said.

He then removed from the chest a large metal mirror, of polished
bronze, with an ornate back, and regarded himself in the reflective surface.

"Master?" I said.

He then snarled, and cast the mirror from him, and it struck against the wall. The stone was gouged where it struck.

"Yet, splendid," I insisted.

He then put back his head, and I feared he was going to howl in rage, and frustration, but he controlled himself.

Then he regarded me.

I was frightened.

"Forgive me, Master," I said. "But you are large, and strong, and the robe is surely a fine one."

"Let it cover a monstrosity," he said.

"Surely Master is much like a high one," I said.

A menacing growl issued from the beast, and I shivered, standing in the water.

"Forgive me, Master," I said, "if I have displeased Master."

"You are not to be blamed," he said. "It is only that you are ignorant. You look, but you do not understand on what it is you look. You look, and you do not see ugliness and horror. Doubtless you mean well."

"What of a larl?" I said. "Surely a larl is similarly impressive." I had been informed about larls, but I had never seen one. It was reputedly the largest, most dangerous land predator on Gor.

"A larl is a beast!" he said.

"Forgive me, Master," I said.

"But, *ela*," he said, "I, too, am a beast, naught but a beast!"

I did not feel I could honestly gainsay that.

"I find Master impressive, and mighty," I said.

"I have killed," he said. "I could demand rings."

I did not understand this.

He gestured, curtly, to the floor, to the side, where my tunic lay, near the brazier.

I stepped, dripping, from the basin.

"We must wait," he said.

"Yes, Master," I said.

I knelt near the brazier, warming myself, and wiped water from my body.

After perhaps a quarter of an Ahn there was a knock at the portal.

Something was said in Kur, to which Lord Grendel responded, also in Kur.

The door then opened and a Kur was framed in the threshold. A sound of surprise, and pleasure, I thought, escaped Lord Grendel. This seemed to please the hideous creature framed in the doorway, for it lifted its head, and drew back its lips from its fangs. The thing looked at me, and I, kneeling, put down my head, quickly. It then said something in Kur, to which Lord Grendel responded in Kur. It then bent down, and whisked my tunic from the floor, and cast it into the brazier where, for a moment, it smoked, and then, a bit later, the dampness steamed away, and the cloth dry, the tunic disappeared in a bit of flame. The high one then turned about and withdrew.

"Master?" I said, plaintively.

"She will wait in the hall," he said.

"'She'?" I said.

"Yes," he said. "Have you ever seen a more beautiful Kur female?"

"It was a female?" I said.

"Of course," he said, "and one incredibly beautiful."

"Oh," I said.

"It seems our hosts will stop at little, if anything, to get their way," he said.

"Is Master tempted?" I said.

"Who would not be?" he asked.

"Surely she could tear an arm from the socket or bite off a foot," I said.

"Of course," he said. "Such attributes much enhance the loveliness of a Kur female."

"I see," I said.

I knew little of Kurii, but I knew something of men, and women, and competition, and war, and politics. Women, slave and free, often figured in the plans of men, as instruments, as enticements, as bribes, as prizes. I supposed something of the sort might obtain amongst Kurii, as well.

"She burned my tunic," I said.

"It was soiled," he said.

"Even so," I said.

"It would not have been permitted to you anyway," he said.

"How so?" I said.

"As long as you are here," he said, "you are to aid in the serving. Some of the guests will be human males."

"I see," I said.

Many human males, though perhaps not those of Earth, enjoyed being served by naked, collared slaves. This was alleged to improve the appetite. Does this practice not add a sauce to any dish? Consider the slave kneeling, proffering the dish, hoping the master will be pleased. If free women were to be present, of course, it was common for slaves to be decorously clothed, even to the ankles. The rationale of this is easy to see. Suppose a young free woman was present. Might not then the imagination of male diners stray inevitably to thoughts of how she might appear, similarly serving?

"We must not keep our hosts waiting," said Lord Grendel.

"No, Master," I said.

CHAPTER FORTY-FIVE

Y ou have not tasted the tospits in black syrup, have you?" inquired the reclining, garlanded male.

"No, Master," I said, kneeling, offering the plate to him.

"Open your mouth," he said, "and stick out your tongue."

How pleased I was that I had not, even in the kitchen, thrust so much as a finger into the syrup and licked it.

I did not wish to be whipped.

He thrust a food prong into the bowl, lifted forth a drenched tospit slice, and, nibbling, savored it.

"Excellent," he said.

"A slave is pleased," I said.

He then thrust the prong once more into the bowl, secured some three or four more slices, and slid them onto his plate, which was already laden with parsley, steamed rice, fried verr, and roast bosk.

I was very hungry.

With a gesture I was dismissed, and I rose, and backed away.

No food had yet been given to the animals.

The room was large, and long, with a high ceiling. It was lit with torches. The walls and ceiling, as nearly as I could tell in the light, were covered with scenes suggesting tranquility and prosperity, scenes of fishing, herding, and agriculture, scenes of flocks and herds, scenes of sowing and harvesting, scenes suggesting, too, caravans, fairs, and markets. I recalled the post of Decius Albus in the administration of the city. There were several supper couches, with their narrow tables, aligned, facing one another, in two long lines, these two lines parallel to the walls, and oriented toward the end of the room, where there was a high dais. There was a serving aisle between the couches and tables. The supper, which had been earlier characterized as a light collation, proved more in the nature of a small feast. Eleven slaves, including myself, were serving. There were perhaps forty men present, and, on a high dais, at the end of the room, crouching, facing the diners, six Kurii, including the she-Kur that had so impressed Lord Grendel. Lord Grendel, whom I might easily have mistaken for a Kur, was in a place of honor. The she-Kur was crouched on his left. I supposed he could feel her presence. I had no doubt it had been seen to that she was well groomed. Perhaps, too, she was perfumed. A difference in her harnessing and accoutrements had been called to my attention by Lord Grendel before we had entered the room, and this made it easier for me to distinguish her from the male Kurii about. At Lord Grendel's right was a Kur whom I recognized from Brundisium, largely because of the two metal rings on his massive, left wrist. I did not know if the other two Kurii from Brundisium were present or not. It is difficult, particularly at first, to tell one Kur from another. Indeed, I might easily have taken the she-Kur for a male. The she-Kur tends, statistically, to be slighter than the male, and narrower in her frame. The Kur fertilized egg, at an early stage, is deposited in one of the "rooted wombs," where it is brought to term, or, better, comes to term, as it feeds and tears its way from the womb.

"To the noble Lord Grendel!" called a large, handsome, long-armed, reclining, red-robed fellow at one of the two tables closest to the dais, lifting a wine goblet toward the dais.

"Lord Grendel!" said several others, lifting their goblets.

The Kurii on the dais, too, lifted their goblets, and Lord Grendel modestly inclined his head, briefly, acknowledging this attention. The she-Kur at his left held her own goblet to his lips.

This seemed to have been done in a most sensual, even seductive, manner.

The long-armed, red-robed fellow who had first lifted his cup to Lord Grendel, initiating this gesture of recognition and esteem, signaling out and honoring him, was the same as he who had first cordially saluted him upon his entrance into this house, apparently one of several owned by Decius Albus. Decius Albus himself, as far as I could tell, was not present. Perhaps that was because of the nature of the occasion. How could the master of the house, if present, not be in the highest place? But only Kurii, the "high ones," so to speak, occupied the dais, except, of course, for Lord Grendel. Perhaps they, these "high ones," did not care to share the dais with representatives of what they might regard as an inferior species. I knew little of these things. In any event, Decius Albus was not, as far as I could tell, present. Perhaps he would not have cared to sit at one of the low tables, in his own house.

I, now no longer blindfolded, had recognized the red-robed fellow instantly upon entering the serving chamber. But now he was not disguised, not collared, not clad in a humble tunic, that of a kajirus, a male slave. He was now garlanded, and clothed in the robes of a free person, and apparently one of high station. It was he who had identified himself as 'Drusus' and had so thoughtfully and solicitously carried my burden of water to the very entrance of my master's rental on Hermadius. Unwittingly, foolishly, I had betrayed my master's whereabouts, leading a foe to his very doorstep. Even when I had been blindfolded, and had recently entered into this house, the voice had sounded familiar, and, despite the accents of a free man, I had thought I might have recognized it. Then there had been no doubt when I saw him, following my entrance into the dining chamber, or feasting room, heeling Lord Grendel. And he had looked upon me, as well, as I was, stripped and collared, smiled, and returned to his conversation with a fellow to his left. I had no doubt that he had recognized me, his dupe, she whom he had so easily and effectively deceived, she whom he had so easily tricked into serving his own purpose. Lord Grendel was conducted to the high dais, and I was set about my duties by the first girl.

There were no free women present.

Perhaps that was why we served as we did, clad only in our collars.

I had little doubt that the handsome, red-robed fellow was important, and stood high in the service of Decius Albus. He had greeted Lord Grendel upon Lord Grendel's admission into the house; he was on the right side of the room, on the couch nearest the dais; and he had first lifted his goblet to him, during the feast, a prerogative of the feast host. I hated him for how he had fooled me! I wondered what it would be to be in his arms, submitting to him as I would have to do, as a slave, as though I could have helped myself! I was no longer my own person, not that I wished to be. That had ended when I was collared.

"Stop staring at the handsome master," hissed the first girl. "He is not for you! See what he has chained behind his couch! That is the sort of slave he can command! Why would such a man want one such as you? Now, serve, serve, lazy slut!"

"Yes, Mistress!" I said, and hurried again, amongst the tables.

I was very hungry.

"Napkin!" called a fellow. He had just rinsed his hands in a hand bowl. He now had his hands lifted from the bowl, water falling from them. A slave rushed to him, on whose hair he dried his hands. In conversation, he paid her no attention.

"Wine!" called another fellow, and a lovely red-headed slave hurried to him, with her pitcher, and replenished his goblet. She, rather as the other, was not even looked upon. He had merely extended his goblet. She backed away, head down.

I had made it a point not to go near the first couch.

I did not think that I could endure the humiliation and embarrassment should I find myself looked upon by him. It was not so much that I was a naked slave, as that I would be a naked slave before him, she of whom he had so cleverly and thoroughly made a fool.

My serving dish was shortly empty, and I knew I should withdraw to the kitchen, either to have it layered with more syrupped tospit slices, or supplied with another provender, perhaps rice, white, or brown, or red or purple, from Cos, or a plate of cheeses, from local dairies, served with warmed bread, or prepared after the fashion of Ti, rolled in honeyed tur-pah leaves.

"But what slave," I wondered, "is chained behind the couch of handsome, mighty Drusus, so important here, he not now in a collar and tunic, not now imposing on a naive slave, but in fine supper raiment, and so near the dais?"

"I would see such a slave," I thought.

I determined the first girl was not watching, and made my way about the tables, so that I might be behind the couches on the right, those nearest the dais.

"Paula!" I said.

"Phyllis!" she whispered, eyes wide, moving in the chain, locked about her throat, by means of which she was fastened to the back of the couch of Drusus.

I knelt down, to be more on a level with her. How naturally, how unthinkingly, I knelt!

"What are you doing here?" I asked.

"I am put where masters will put me," she smiled.

"Who whips you?" I asked.

"I am the slave of Decius Albus, of Ar," she said. "With more than four hundred others!"

"I do not think he is here," I said.

"I think not," she said.

"I am naked," I said.

She was not, but clad in an ample, silken tunic, white. To be sure, I could see much of her. It was a slave tunic. It seemed she had a fine collar, probably a dress collar.

"Are not the others?" she asked.

"Can you not see?" I said.

"No," she said. "The back of the couch is high, my chain is short. I cannot look over the couch."

"Oh," I said.

"Kajirae," she said, "commonly so serve."

"It seems you do not," I said.

"I begged to serve," she said. "I would do so! I was not permitted, not so privileged."

"I am barefoot," I said.

"I did not ask for sandals," she said. "They were forced upon me."

The sandals were golden, with purple straps.

"It seems you are a high slave," I said.

"Do not be angry, Phyllis," she said. "You are far more attractive than I."

"It seems many masters do not agree," I said.

"I cannot account for the judgments of men," she said. "I am only a woman, helpless, and a slave."

"You delivered a message in Ar," I said. "I saw you."

"Yes," she said, "pertaining to a meeting. But I was terribly frightened. There was a gigantic beast in the place."

"There was no point in being frightened," I said. "It was only a Kur, or something much like a Kur."

"I had never seen such a thing," she said.

"I had," I said.

"You are so brave, Phyllis," she said.

"I suppose, a little," I said. "Do you know there are intrigues afoot, that we are pawns in a game we do not understand?"

"I am only a slave," she said. "I obey. I must do what I am told."

"There is a war," I said. "I fear we are on opposite sides."

"If we are pawns," she said, "who moves us?"

"I do not know," I said.

"The pawn," she said, "does not understand the game. It does not even know the hand that moves it."

"True," I said.

"And then," she said, "understanding nothing, it may find itself swept from the board."

"I fear so," I said.

"Let it not separate us," she said. "We were friends on Earth. Let us be friends here, on Gor, in our collars."

"I never sold for a golden tarsk," I said.

"Forgive me," she said.

"Perhaps we will compete for masters," I said.

"I do not think my master, Decius Albus, even knows I exist," she said.

"You are chained behind the couch of Drusus of Ar, of the service of Decius Albus," I said.

"I long to be at his feet, his slave," she said. "The first time I saw him he so excited me that I almost swooned. I did not know such a man could exist, and I, a slave, whom he might buy! I was giddy with desire. Even now my knees are weak in his presence, and I desire to cover his feet and legs with the petitioning kisses of a female slave! How thankful I am to be in a collar, where one such as I rightfully belongs!"

"Why has he not stripped you and put you to serving?" I asked.

"I do not know," she said. "I am not special. I wish to serve, as the others, as a meaningless, naked slave."

"You have a fine collar," I said. "You are gowned, and sandaled."

"Surely a slave tunic is not a gown," she smiled.

"It seems," I said, "he has looked upon you with favor."

"Before him," she said, "I oil, and beg to please!"

"Perhaps you enjoy his caresses," I said.

"I live for them," she said.

"Perhaps he puts you to use," I said, "slave use."

"Frequently," she said. "It is what I am for. I am a slave. And what ecstasy can compare to that of the mastered, ravished slave? I love it! I love it!"

"Oh!" I cried, suddenly, stung sharply across the calves by the first girl's switch.

"Oh!" cried Paula, startled, in sympathy. We had not noted the arrival of the first girl.

"Lazy girl!" said the first girl. "To the kitchen, the kitchen!"

"Yes, Mistress," I cried, and leapt up, and hurried toward the kitchen, running, trying to escape the repeated, stinging blows of the angry, pursuing first girl.

"Oh, Phyllis!" cried Paula, miserably, behind me.

The collation, or feast, was drawing to its close.

Steaming black wine, with its trays of sugars and creams, one of which I bore, and liqueurs, some apparently from as far away as Turia, were being served.

Black wine is expensive.

The plants from which its seeds are obtained apparently grow favorably, perhaps even most favorably, on the slopes of the Thentis Mountains, an area under the jurisdiction of the mountain city of Thentis. The trade in black wine is closely controlled by the so-called "vintners" of Thentis. For example, it is forbidden to take viable black-wine seeds or plants from the vicinity of Thentis. And, as one would suppose, the sale of the roasted seeds from which the black wine is brewed is carefully supervised and regulated. Doubtless some smuggling occurs. Where such plants are found, illegitimately planted, at least from the point of view of the Thentis "vintners," they are uprooted and destroyed. Similarly, smugglers, if apprehended, are often dealt with harshly, by impalement, or servitude in the mines, quarries, or galleys. This policing is commonly done by representatives of the "vintners" of Thentis, but it is sometimes hired out to the caste of Assassins, which constitutes the nearest thing to an international police force on Gor, a force subject neither to the constraints of walls, borders, or Home Stones. Most public eating establishments cannot afford to serve black wine. There are several cases where a female slave has been exchanged for a cup of the beverage. Needless to say, the serving of this beverage at our small collation, or feast, was an indication of the formidable wealth, and widely ranging connections, of Decius Albus, trade advisor to the Ubar of Ar, a man named Marlenus. Whereas the plants from which the seeds, or beans, for black wine are brewed may have been native to Gor, I rather suspected that their world of origin might have lain far away, perhaps on another world.

Then, after a time, the tiny vessels of black wine, and the liqueurs, were put aside.

There was a stirring on the dais, and I gathered that the supper was at its end, or nearly so.

I was hungry, very hungry. And so, too, I supposed, were the other slaves.

"The slaves have not been fed!" called Drusus, addressing the diners, from the first couch. "Shall we feed them?"

"It is agreed!" responded several of those present.

I was pleased that there were no free women present. Men are fond of slaves. If there were free women present, the decision as to the feeding of the slaves would have been left to them, in deference to their status, which is far higher than that of free women on my former world, Earth, sometimes referred to by Goreans privy to the second knowledge as the Slave World. In such a case the slaves are often sent to their chains hungry. The kajira is vulnerable, helpless and rightless, an animal, and is commonly despised and hated by free women. Accordingly, she looks to men, often piteously and desperately, for protection.

Sometimes a master will feed a slave at table, by hand. Sometimes she may feed with him, from her plate or bowl, kneeling beside the small, low table, where he sits, cross-legged. His is always, of course, the first bite. Sometimes food is cast to the floor, and she, on all fours, not permitted to use her hands, will feed upon it. Sometimes, if there are several slaves present, it may be cast to the floor and the slaves, permitted to use their hands, will scramble for it.

I saw the first girl, with her basket of scraps, look to the feast host, Drusus.

I readied myself.

"Napkin!" called Drusus, summoning me to him. Miserable, I hastened to him, and knelt, and put my body across the table, my head down, and he locked his two hands, tightly, in my hair. His hands were not damp. There was no hand bowl at his immediate disposal.

"Feed the animals!" he called cheerily to the first girl, and she, with a wide, sweeping motion, scattered the scraps between the tables.

"Please, Master," I begged. "I am very hungry!"

He did not loosen his grip. I heard the girls scrambling behind me, fighting for the scraps.

There was laughter from the men at the tables.

"I presume you recognize me," he said.

"Yes, Master," I said. "Please let me go. I am very hungry."

"Not every slave," he said, "has a free man carry water for her."

"Forgive me, Master," I said. "I did not know you were free."

"You led us promptly to the concealment of Kurik of Victoria."

"Yes, Master," I said.

"You were a well-curved little dupe," he said.

"I was well tricked by Master," I said.

"It was all I could do," he said, "to refrain from fondling you."

"A male slave may not touch a female slave without permission," I said.

"But I was not a male slave," he said.

"No, Master," I said, trying to move my head a little. Then I stopped, for it hurt.

"I heard you behind the couch," he said, "conversing with the slave, Paula."

"We knew one another, Master," I said.

"Even from the Slave World?" he said.

"Yes, Master," I said.

"You were friends?"

"Yes, Master."

"On the Slave World?"

"Yes, Master."

"It must be interesting," he said, "for you to see one another as you are now, on Gor, in slave collars."

"We are slaves," I said.

I heard the girls behind me, fighting for scraps.

"She is lovely, is she not?" he asked.

"Yes, Master," I said.

"Exquisitely lovely," he said.

"Yes, Master," I said. On Earth, I had thought Paula rather plain. How could it have been that she had allegedly sold for a golden tarsk?

"And she juices well, and is helpless, and hot on her chain," he said.

"She is a slave," I said.

"And you, barbarian," he said, "do you juice well, and are you helpless, and hot, on your chain?"

"We are slaves," I said.

"Of course," he said.

"Yes," I thought, "and let those smug women of my former world, so proud of their superiority to sex, and their vaunted indifference to men, find themselves naked and in collars, at the feet of Gorean males! Let them see how long then they can prolong their poses of inertness and frigidity. Let their slave fires be lit and they will crawl and beg as needfully, as piteously, as we!"

"I cannot help myself," I said.

"You are not permitted to help yourself," he said.

"No, Master," I said.

"And would you wish to help yourself?" he asked.

"No, Master," I said.

"Why not?" he asked.

"I am a slave," I said.

What free woman, I wondered, can even begin to understand the ecstasies of the female slave?

"Up, kajirae," called the first girl, from somewhere behind me. "Haste, through the kitchen! You have but ten Ehn to relieve yourselves, wash, and crawl to your cages!"

Drusus, of the service of Decius Albus, then released me, and I backed away, on my knees.

"The food is gone," I said.

"Perhaps you should not have addressed yourself to the slave, Paula, without permission," he said.

"Forgive me, Master," I said.

"I think Lord Grendel awaits you," he said, gesturing toward the dais. Lord Grendel stood there, looking toward us, with four or five of the Kurii, one of which, I thought, was the female Kur, from the harnessing, and one, I was sure, was he who had been the leader of the three intruders in Brundisium. I recognized him from the rings on his left wrist.

I rose to my feet, and turned toward the dais.

"Kajira," called Drusus.

I turned, and he threw me a strip of roast bosk, which I caught against my body. "Thank you, Master!" I cried, tears in my eyes, and turned, and hurried toward the dais, thrusting the meat in my mouth, tearing at it with fingers and teeth. Soon I was following Lord Grendel through a portal that led away from the feasting hall, down a long corridor. Following so, I fed on the meat, ravenously. When finished with it, I rubbed my finger on my body where the flung meat had struck, for there was a stain of grease there. I wiped this, as I could, from my body, and licked it from my finger.

CHAPTER FORTY-SIX

Fed now, I heeled Lord Grendel closely and with a sprightly step. The corridor was long. It lacked the light, the decor, of the first corridor we had trodden, in being conducted to the washing-and-robing chamber, and certainly it was a far cry from the light, and spaciousness, and the mosaics and paintings, of the feasting hall. As we continued on, it seemed to descend somewhat, but not all that noticeably, and to become ever more gloomy. It was lit by small lamps, which, as we continued on, seemed to be more and more widely separated.

After a time the lamps were so infrequently ensconced that the corridor was almost dark.

But the Kurii, and Lord Grendel, proceeded on as surely as before. Then it occurred to me that their night vision might be far more acute than that of the normal human, and more akin to that of the larl or sleen. The sleen in the wild tends to be nocturnal. Perhaps, I thought, Kurii, given their fangs and claws, their seeming night vision, and, as my master had averred, their keenness of hearing, were originally night hunters. This conjecture, as it later proved, was unjustified, or, at least, partially so. The primitive Kur, rather like the cat of Earth, was scarcely less dangerous at night than during the day.

Occasionally Lord Grendel and the Kurii, five in number, conversed amongst themselves, in Kur. As none of this was picked up in Gorean I supposed the translators were deactivated.

"Master," I whispered, "it is hard for me to see."

"Cling," he said, "to my fur."

"Perhaps I should have been left behind," I said.

"I did not think that would have been wise," he said.

"Why not?" I asked.

I sensed that with Lord Grendel I had a standing permission to speak. Many slaves are given such a standing permission by their masters. It is a permission, of course, that, at a word or gesture, may be instantly revoked.

"I feared," he said, "you might be eaten."

I then clung more closely to him.

I had fed. I did not wish to be the feeding of others.

"Our brethren," he said, "commonly like to make their own kills. The blood and meat is fresher."

"Oh," I said.

"You may be a slave," he said, "but your collar will not protect you from our friends."

"Yes, Master," I said.

I smelled perfume. That was from the she-Kur. She sped along, partly on her knuckles, on the right of Lord Grendel.

To me she was hideous.

To him, I gathered, she was an incredibly beautiful she-Kur, one that might, plausibly, with promised favors, sway a beast not immune to her charms.

"I am going to activate the translator," said Lord Grendel. "If I should perish, and you survive, I wish you to have some understanding of what may transpire. This may be important to others."

I heard the click, and, almost at the same time, an issuance in Kur, from the leader of the Kurii, the beast with two rings on the left wrist, which, produced in Gorean, was straightforward, "Why did you do that?"

"It was my will," said Lord Grendel.

"Be it so then, noble lord," said the leader. Shortly thereafter I learned that his name, that of the leader, in Gorean, was 'Surtak'. The name of the she-Kur, or what served for her name in Gorean, was 'Lyris'. I also learned that the fuller name of Drusus, who apparently stood high in the house of Decius Albus, was 'Drusus Andronicus'.

"The portal is here," I heard.

I could see nothing.

I clung to the fur of Lord Grendel.

Then I saw a crack of light, vertical, and then it became a shaft of light, and, as the portal was opened, I saw a room beyond, severe, and plain, and, for the most part, empty. There was a stone block in the center of the room, a cube of a yard square, and, on this block, within a meshwork of wire, was a metallic box.

"Tal, noble Grendel," said a voice, as the issuant Kur was translated into Gorean. I saw no speaker. The Kur vocables, as I soon determined,

emanated from the box, through which, I supposed, they were transmitted from some remote location. The speaker, I supposed, might be
anywhere, in the next room, or even pasangs away.

"You!" said Lord Grendel. The utterance, in Kur, was startled,
shaken, but its reproduction in Gorean, with its single, flat, unemo-
tional, metallic syllable, conveyed nothing of Lord Grendel's surprise,
dismay, or agitation.

"Do not attempt to rush forward and seize the cabinet," said Surtak. "The wire mesh is stoutly charged."

"I had supposed so," said Lord Grendel.

"A touch would be instant death," said Surtak.

"I understand," said Lord Grendel.

"My dear friend," came from the box, or cabinet, "we have had our
differences. But I am prepared to forgive you."

"Lord Agamemnon is most gracious," said Lord Grendel.

"I retain cohorts on my world, seized by the usurper, Arcesilaus, he
who in blasphemy dares to term himself a Face of the Nameless One,
he boldly aspiring to the title 'Theocrat of the World'."

"It was supposed so, great lord," said Lord Grendel.

"And on other worlds, of prowling steel, as well," said the voice
from the box, "and on Gor, too, green Gor, Gor of flowing grass and
bright skies, secretly ensconced, both high ones and humans. My minions are many and well placed. I can unite worlds, and use worlds to
seize worlds."

"You were mightiest of the Kurii," said Lord Grendel.

"I am mightiest of the Kurii," came from the box.

I had first heard of Lord Agamemnon from Kurik, my master, and
then, later, in the apartment of the Lady Bina and Lord Grendel.

I knelt.

No one was paying me any attention, but, as I understood myself
amongst the free, I thought it best to do so.

Lapses in slaves are seldom overlooked by Gorean masters. Discipline helps us keep well in mind that we are slaves, that our necks are
locked in the collars of our masters. Even the most beloved of slaves is
seldom permitted to forget she is a slave, and only a slave.

"But it seems, great lord," said Lord Grendel, "however far flung
your interests, deep your plans, and plentiful your allies, that you lack
even a body."

"I have a thousand bodies," came from the box, "amongst which I
am free to choose."

The utterance in Kur seemed tinged with impatience, or anger, but the metallic tones of the translator were judiciously noncommittal.

"*Ela*," said Lord Grendel, "I fear your enemies do not suspect that."

I could not understand why Lord Grendel seemed to address himself to that inert, wire-enclosed cabinet on the stone cube as if it might be a conscious being, or the habitat of a conscious being. This seemed terribly odd to me. It was rather as if one, on my former world, were to address himself seriously to a device, say, a radio, rather than utilize it as mere means by which to communicate with the unseen individual, perhaps far away, whose voice was conveyed by means of the contrivance. And why, too, should it, a mere device, merit so apparently fearsome an electronic defense?

"How kind you are to shelter a grooming pet," said the box.

"The Lady Bina," said Lord Grendel, "is a free woman."

"Had you remained on the world, amongst the river of stones," said the box, "you would have stood high, and been held in esteem."

"Better," said Lord Grendel, "that I, shamed and malformed, not remain to give offense on a Kur world. Better that I should conceal the horror of my body here, far from the dismay of high ones."

"And perhaps you had in mind, as well, the interests and ambitions of the grooming pet."

"The Lady Bina," said Lord Grendel. And then he added, "Perhaps."

"You must be nearly destitute," said the box.

"A jewel or two remains," said Lord Grendel.

"Do you expect to dig suls?" asked the box. "Do you think peasants will share fields with you?"

Lord Grendel remained silent.

"Do you wish to reduce the Lady Bina to begging in the streets?"

"No," said Lord Grendel.

"Or to seek employment in a brothel?"

"No," said Lord Grendel.

"I have long been fond of you," said the device.

"I am gratified," said Lord Grendel.

"Perhaps," said the voice, "you would enjoy status, position, power, and riches."

"As the noble lord knows," said Lord Grendel, "I have Kur blood."

"And does it remain unstirred at the proximity of beauty?" asked the box.

Lyris, the she-Kur, made a tiny, soft sound.

"It does not remain unstirred," said Lord Grendel.

"Consider graceful Lyris," said the box. "Have we not chosen well?"

"Eminently well," said Lord Grendel.

"You may have her," said the box.

"She is not a slave," said Lord Grendel.

"I command her," said the box.

"She is not a slave," said Lord Grendel, again.

"It would be simple enough to strip her of her harnessing, put her in a collar, and throw her to your feet," said the box, "and then she would be no more than the naked, meaningless, collared little beast beside you."

Lyris hissed in fury, and darted backward, snarling. But two Kurii, growling, stood between her and the door.

How, I wondered, would a remote speaker even know I was in the room? Perhaps there was a camera somewhere, to which the absent speaker had access. There were, I had noticed, a number of orbs, panels, and lights, sometimes flickering and flashing, on the cabinet. Perhaps one of them was a camera, or something related to a camera.

"Of what use might a monstrosity such as I be to a great one?" asked Lord Grendel.

"Much," said the box, or he who spoke through it. "You are known on my world, stolen by Arcesilaus and his brigands. You would have access to their thoughts and plans. Armaments and ammunitions, materiel, ships, resources, could be discovered, and recorded, or sabotaged. Your prestige might ease the recruitment of agents. Those who waver might incline to follow one such as you, so fearsome and well known. Who could forget your triumphs in the arena? Would you not care to be one of the founders and leaders of a splendid new order? On Gor, on this world, you are known to the bandit and pirate, Tarl Cabot, and doubtless others, and might, in our interest, well exploit and utilize the bonds of friendship and trust. No one would suspect you. You have contacts and connections, here and elsewhere, which might prove of great value to me. To many you are renowned, a hero. Consider your prestige, the weight of your words, of even a carefully dropped hint or suggestion here or there. Join us. Join me. You will have gold, and power, and Lyris, surely amongst the most beautiful of all Kur shes, for whom a thousand brothers would dare the rings."

Lyris spun away from the blocked portal, and regarded Lord Grendel, shuddering.

"The great lord," said Lord Grendel, "offers much. Be it known I am keenly aware of the dignity he is willing to confer upon me. I am humbled by his estimation of my possible value to his cause, surely exaggerated, and I am overwhelmed by the remarkable generosity with which he is prepared to reward one who would doubtless prove an unworthy servitor."

"I will accept your oath," came from the box.

"I am a monstrosity, and a horror," said Lord Grendel. "But in all the hapless ugliness and misery of my being there is an unseen richness that I do not choose to betray or surrender. It does not appear in the mirror and it is not visible to others, but it, in its way, redeems me in my own sight. With it I am myself; without it, there would be only the truth of the mirror, that of the beast."

"And what is this thing I do not see?" inquired the box.

"It is called 'Honor'," said Lord Grendel. "I decline your kind offer. Now kill me."

"Take him to the next room," came from the box.

"You are horrifying, and ugly!" screamed Lyris. "I no longer need maintain my pose, no longer need play my hateful role. I detest you! It sickens me to be near you, the voice, the eyes, the malformed hands!"

Lord Grendel was then ushered into a new room, one behind the box, protected within its mesh shield, by Surtak, and two of the others. I sprang up, and accompanied them, fearing to be left alone. Lyris and the other Kur remained behind, with the box, or cabinet.

"Where is the killing ax," asked Lord Grendel, "or is that too quick?"

"Please wait," said Surtak.

Surtak disappeared behind a panel. The other two Kurii remained with us.

Lord Grendel switched off the translator.

"Master," I said.

"It seems, I am not to be killed," he said, "at least not now."

"You are more valuable to them alive," I said.

"I do not understand," he said.

"There are many springs and engines, and levers," I said, "by means of which great weights may be moved."

"Lord Agamemnon is shrewd and deep," he said. "I am now afraid."

"I think I know what it is, Master," I said.

"What?" he asked.

At that moment Surtak emerged from behind the panel and thrust forth the hideous she-beast, Eve, stolen from the house of Flavius Minor in Brundisium.

"It is the gift of Lord Arcesilaus," I said, "delivered to Brundisium, to be claimed by my master, Kurik, of Victoria, and brought to Ar, to be given to you. It was stolen. It, like yourself, is part Kur. Lord Arcesilaus, as I understand it, thought you would be pleased."

Surtak thrust Eve more to the center of the room, and stepped back.

Lord Grendel stared at the beast for a time, and then walked slowly about it, and then returned to stand beside me, as he had before. Eve was shuddering.

Lord Grendel touched the translator slung about his neck, activating it. I was not sure why he did this. Apparently he wished me to have some understanding of what might occur.

"What is it?" asked Lord Grendel of Surtak.

"A she," said Surtak, "made for you, intended as a gift for you, by the pretender, Arcesilaus."

"How is it here?" asked Lord Grendel.

"We brought it here for you," said Surtak. "There is only one such thing. Shall we kill it?"

"Do you think I want it?" asked Lord Grendel. "It is a monster. Who would want such a thing? See how ugly it is, the eyes, and the hands."

Though I could not gainsay his appraisal, I thought it needed not be so bluntly expressed. Eve, I knew, could follow both Kur and Gorean. I saw a tear run down her face, wet in the fur.

"Kill me!" she cried.

"It is not worth killing," snarled Lord Grendel.

"There is only one of her," said Surtak. "She is much like you. She was engineered for you. In her, as in yourself, there are many biological subtleties. She is yours, for your oath."

Lord Grendel made a contemptuous, snorting noise.

"Surely you prize her, and want her," said Surtak, puzzled.

"You would seek to buy my oath with such a thing?" said Lord Grendel. "You must be mad."

"Do you not want her, more than anything?" asked Surtak, puzzled.

"No," said Lord Grendel. "Keep it for the scullery, or to amuse high ones."

"Shall we kill it?" asked Surtak. "Surely you would give your oath rather than have it die. It is like you, made for you. Do you not find it unique, inestimably precious?"

I saw fangs, suddenly, curved and white, at the side of the jaw of

Lord Grendel. The lip was drawn back, about the fangs. Lord Grendel snarled, and then there was, again, that raucous noise, snorting and ugly, which I took to be a Kur laugh, a derisive laugh.

"I do not understand," said Surtak.

"Do not insult me so grievously," said Lord Grendel. "I cannot abide my own image in the mirror, and you would confront me with a living mirror, that I be reminded of my own misery, of my own appearance, which I regard with loathing and self-disgust."

The she-beast, shaken, was now clearly sobbing. It was much like the crying of a human female. I could not understand the sternness, the lack of feeling, on the part of Lord Grendel, who had hitherto shown even me, a slave, consideration and kindness.

"You do not want it?" asked Surtak.

"I should kill it myself," said Lord Grendel, "to rid the world of such a creature." He then turned away from Eve, who was sobbing, and faced the door. "You may kill me now, if you wish," he said.

"Go the robing chamber," said Surtak. "Take up your ax. You are free to leave."

For a moment Lord Grendel, clearly bewildered, did not, or could not, move.

"Come, Master," I urged.

Later we emerged from the house. The rain had stopped. The ground, of course, was still wet.

"We shall return to the wagon," said Lord Grendel.

"Let us hurry," I said. I was eager to be away from the house.

"Lord Agamemnon," he said, "is deep, and shrewd. I do not understand."

"Master was cruel to the she-beast," I said. "We call her 'Eve'."

"'Eve'?" he said.

"Yes," I said.

"Do not call her a beast," said Lord Grendel.

"It is not her fault," I said, "that she is so ugly."

"Are you mad?" he said. "She is the most beautiful creature I ever saw. One would kill for her."

"But what of the she-Kur, Lyris?" I said.

"Compared to Eve," he said, "she is nothing, no more than a tarsk."

"Oh," I said.

"The wagon is this way," he said.

"There is one thing I do not understand, Master," I said.

"Why we were released?" he said.

"Besides that," I said.

"What?" he asked.

"There were many humans at the feast," I said, "such as Master Drusus, humans doubtless in league with the house of Decius Albus, and the Kurii of Lord Agamemnon. But there is another, one I am sure would now be in Ar, but whom I did not see."

"Who is that?" he asked.

"An Assassin closely involved in these matters," I said, "one named 'Tyrtaios'."

"You are sure?" he said.

"Very much so," I said.

"Of course!" he said. "It is clear now! I am a fool, a fool!"

"Master?" I said.

"The Lady Bina!" he cried, "the Lady Bina!"

Lord Grendel then, uttering a cry of rage, and misery, ax in hand, hurried away. I strove to follow him, hastening, splashing, through the puddles and mud. He did not stop at the wagon, but rushed past it, hurrying toward the road. He did not wish to wait upon the ponderous tread of the draft tharlarion. I did not know what to do, and stopped, distraught, gasping for breath, at the side of the wagon. The driver, in the darkness, stood on the wagon bench. I could not see him well. To my surprise, cradled in his arms, he carried a crossbow, a quarrel in the guide. He was looking back, toward the house of Decius Albus.

"Are you followed?" he asked.

"Master!" I cried, in astonishment. Then I said, "No, I do not think so."

Kurik of Victoria, for a time, continued to survey our back trail.

"Master," I said, kneeling in the mud.

"I do not think you were followed," he said.

"I do not think so, Master," I said.

He then placed the weapon on the wagon bench, and descended, lightly, to stand beside me.

"Where is your tunic?" he said.

"Master Grendel," I said, "fears for the Lady Bina. He hurries toward the city. Tyrtaios, the Assassin, may be about. I have seen the she-monster, Eve. I saw he who tricked me in the guise of a slave. He is a free man, Drusus Andronicus, in the service of Decius Albus!"

"Where is your tunic?" he said.

"It was taken by a she-beast," I said, "and burned. I, with other slaves, served at a feast. We served as men are often pleased to have us serve, served stripped."

"The night has become chilly," he said. "Stand."

He gently placed his jacket about my shoulders. I clutched it about me. It fell to my thighs.

"Thank you, Master," I said, wonderingly, for his act suggested concern, or consideration, for a slave. Are we not mere objects and beasts, to be bought and sold, to be put to work, or ravished for our owner's pleasure? I was grateful for the warmth.

"You are not unattractive," he said. "We must not invite predation on the streets."

"I see," I said.

He regarded me, in the light of the white moon, as a free man commonly regards a slave.

"This jacket, I fear," I said, "conceals little of a slave."

"But more than a slave tunic," he said.

"Yes, Master," I said.

The slave tunic is designed not only to mark a woman as a slave, and distinguish her dramatically and unmistakably from a free woman, but to enforce upon its occupant the understanding that she is a slave and only a slave. It is also designed, of course, not only to display the woman as a slave, as a commodity and a domestic animal, but to enhance her beauty, as well. It might also be noted that such a garment, like the camisk and the ta-teera, can stimulate and arouse desire. Certainly it has that effect on men, and, if it must be known, it has that effect on the woman, as well. Certainly, in such garments, we know what we are for.

"Am I truly attractive, Master?" I asked.

"Certainly," he said. "You might bring as much as twenty copper tarsks in a good market."

"I see," I said.

He then lifted me to the wagon bench.

"I am to sit beside you?" I asked.

"Are you a free woman?" he asked.

"I will kneel below the bench," I said.

"Precisely," he said.

He then sat upon the bench.

"This is a pay wagon," I smiled. "I fear I have no way to pay my fare."

"Do not concern yourself," he said. "As you are my personal property, you would pay a fare no more than a belt, or sandal."

"As I have no coin," I said, "it is fortunate that I am your property."

"If you were not," he said, "a fare would nonetheless be collected."

"But I have no coin," I said.

"Do not fear," he said. "You would pay the fare."

"How so?" I said. "How could it be paid?"

"You would pay, and amply," he said.

"How?" I asked. "How would I pay for it?"

"In the manner of the female slave," he said.

"Oh," I said.

"With your body," he said.

"I see," I said.

"The driver would see to it," he said.

"I understand," I said.

He then snapped the reins of the tharlarion and, with a jangle of harness, the wagon lurched forward.

"It seems Master rented a pay wagon, and lingered in the vicinity of the shop of Epicrates," I said.

"Who suspects a pay wagon?" he said.

"Did you anticipate that the Lady Bina would wish to engage a pay wagon?" I asked.

"I did not know," he said. "When you did not return, it seemed clear that something must soon ensue."

"In its way, it provided a good concealment," I said.

"Surely better than loitering about," he said.

"Doubtless she thought it fortunate that a pay wagon might be so easily come by."

"Perhaps," he said. "I myself would have thought the business a bit too convenient. Yet, to be sure, it is not unusual for pay wagons to be about, waiting for fares, and such."

I pulled the jacket somewhat more closely about me. It was warm. "I think Master may care for his slave," I said.

"Do you wish to be whipped?" he said.

"No, Master!" I said.

"Have you ever been whipped?" he asked.

"I have been switched," I said, "many times, but I have never been whipped, not with the five-stranded slave lash."

"Do you wish to feel it?" he asked.

"No, Master!" I said.

"Normally, in a girl's training," he said, "she is whipped at least once, so that she may understand what it is to be whipped."

"Oh," I said.

"After that," he said, "she redoubles her efforts to become a diligent pupil."

"I hope to be pleasing to my master," I said.

"To any master," he said.

"Yes, Master," I said, "I am a slave."

We rode on, and, after a bit, reached the Viktel Aria. There was no sign of Lord Grendel.

"Are you cold?" he asked.

"No, Master," I said.

I was shuddering, but not with cold. It was difficult to cope with what I had seen, and now knew.

"Tell me, in some detail," he said, "all that occurred, from the time you left Hermadius this morning until you returned, tonight, to the wagon."

I recounted, as I could, the events of the day, and, as he also demanded, my responses to these events, and my thoughts pertaining to them. In a way he was merciless, but I was more than pleased to unburden myself of my fears and surmises. He was attentive to me, and, as far as I could tell, relished my discourse. Masters are well aware that a slave has a rich inner life, replete with thoughts and feelings. Accordingly, as she is their belonging, they wish to know everything about her. Who does not wish to understand their belongings? It is, after all, the whole slave that is owned. They enjoy listening to their slave, who is commonly intelligent and perceptive, sensitive, and much alive. And, in the end, of course, they may simply snap their whip, so to speak, and put her back on her knees.

So I knelt beside him, and put my cheek down, on his knee. I wanted to cry out my love for him, for my master, but I dared not do so, lest I be whipped, and sold. How vulnerable and helpless we are, in our collars! How warm, rewarding, and glorious to be a slave, and how fearful!

We are owned.

We have masters.

"It is much as I thought," he said. "The forces of Agamemnon wished to use the she-monster, Eve, to bend Lord Grendel to their will, that he would yield either to obtain her as a treasure, or, as she was much like him, and unique, and intended for him, was a center of consciousness, and such, would yield to prevent her destruction. But he seems to have handled the matter well, concealing feelings of amity and attraction, even desire, while professing loathing and disinterest. That he was not then killed immediately, to at least deprive Lord Arcesilaus of a valuable friend and ally, demonstrated that this possibility, a lack of cooperation in the matter of Eve, had been anticipated and prepared for. Thus, one supposes, given the possible failure of one plan, a second plan was already in place, and simultaneously in motion, an additional move in this game of dark kaissa, the acquisition of the Lady Bina. There would be no doubt of her importance, and his concern for her welfare. Too, of course, Lord Grendel, lured away, would not be present to defend her. As you report the assessment of Lord Grendel, Agamemnon was indeed shrewd and deep."

"I saw nothing of Agamemnon, Lord Agamemnon," I said. "He was not present. He may have been pasangs away. He communicated through a device."

"No," said Kurik. "He was present."

"I did not see him," I said.

"In a sense, you did," he said.

"I do not understand," I said.

"The cabinet," he said.

"Master?" I said.

"It houses a living brain," he said, "vital and mighty."

I was silent.

"Agamemnon," he said, "may have lost his natural body centuries ago."

"The cabinet is his body," I said.

"In a sense," he said, "but it may be ensconced in larger bodies, or devices, sometimes formidable and terrifying."

"He said," I said, "that he had a thousand bodies, amongst which he was free to choose."

"I doubt that," said Kurik. "If he had had even one, I am sure it would have been present, if only to awe Lord Grendel. Such bodies are not easily obtained. They require subtle design, complex components, and demanding tooling. They are the products of a sophisticated technology. The power and resources of Agamemnon have been much reduced. On this world, he is, in a sense, an exile and outcaste, one far removed from the world that had been his own. Too, such devices might be deemed to contravene the technology laws of Priest-Kings, in which case their construction and employment might be attended with great danger."

"He is then little to be feared," I said.

"On the contrary," he said. "He has minions on this world, Kur and human, and, on his former world, Kurii secretly loyal to him. Furthermore, he has contact with other steel worlds. The Kur dream is to possess Gor, and Agamemnon is a respected tactician and strategist in various campaigns that have that object in view. Even Lord Arcesilaus, whom he regards as an enemy and usurper, might enleague himself in such projects. It is not unthinkable. He, too, after all, is Kur. Steel worlds might well unite to seize a world, after which they can dispute it amongst themselves, as Kurii are wont to do, amongst crumbling, melting mountains and rivers running with blood."

"We approach the walls of Ar," I said.

"By now," he said, "I suspect the Lady Bina is a prisoner in the palace of Decius Albus."

"What will Lord Grendel do?" I asked.

"I do not know," he said. "I suggest we ask him."

CHAPTER FORTY-SEVEN

W e will be contacted," said Lord Grendel.

"Surely the Lady Bina is held in the palace of Decius Albus," said Kurik.

"That is likely," said Lord Grendel, "but we do not know that."

"In any event," said Kurik, "without an army we could not storm the palace."

"I could go alone," said Lord Grendel.

"No," said Kurik, "too many quarrels and swords would lie between you and the throat of Decius Albus."

"And there is the beauty, Eve," said Lord Grendel.

"You find her of interest?" said Kurik.

"Who could not?" asked Lord Grendel.

"Of course," said Kurik.

Lord Grendel crouched on the floor of the apartment, above the shop of Epicrates. Before him lay the great ax. I was sure it might, with a single blow, delivered with the strength of a Kur, fell a small tree or shatter a wall. Occasionally he would grasp the ax, arms trembling, and lift it a hort from the floor, eyeing the door leading downstairs to the street. I had the sense that he was ready to kill. Kurik sat cross-legged, in the Gorean fashion, near him, and I knelt, unobtrusively, to the side.

"I will go, alone," said Lord Grendel.

"And kill ten, and fail," said Kurik. "We must wait."

"We will be contacted," said Lord Grendel, a noise that, even in Gorean, conveyed feral menace.

"Certainly," said Kurik.

"Why have we not been contacted?" snarled Lord Grendel.

"Be patient, great lord," said Kurik.

"I do not understand," said Lord Grendel.

"It is a device, doubtless," said Kurik, "to increase your apprehension, to multiply your speculations and fears, to make you more ready to succumb to their wishes."

"It is a torture," said Lord Grendel.

"One you impose upon yourself," said Kurik.

"Of irons and tongs," said Lord Grendel, "I prefer those you can weigh and see. More dreadful are the irons and tongs of the night."

"The most pointless of pains," said Kurik, "are those one inflicts upon oneself."

"Why have we not heard?" asked Lord Grendel. "It has been four days!"

"I am sure the Lady Bina is quite well, and not now in danger," said Kurik. "Agamemnon needs her, to command your oath. Indeed, Epicrates informed us that she left of her own free will, in good spirits, escorted by an officer of the Taurentian Guard, doubtless the Assassin, Tyrtaios, in disguise."

"She is so naive, so trusting, so ambitious, so unaware of the world," said Lord Grendel.

I recalled that she had once been a grooming pet on a steel world, no more than an animal, apparently not even taught to speak. What, then, can one expect of such a thing, entered into a complex, stratified, perilous culture?

"And beautiful?" said Kurik.

"Yes," said Lord Grendel.

"But uncritical, and muchly uninformed," said Kurik.

"She once sent a slave, who returned muchly belabored, to the Central Cylinder, to propose her as companion to Marlenus, Ubar of Ar, that she might become Ubara."

"Fortunately she was free," said Kurik. "Otherwise she might have found herself added to the stock in the Ubar's pleasure garden, or given as a gift to some foreign ambassador."

"And what of Eve?" said Lord Grendel, agonized.

"We do not know," said Kurik.

"Would that I had Surtak, and others, within the compass of my ax!" said Lord Grendel.

"Patience, noble lord," said Kurik.

"I do not rejoice in titles," said Lord Grendel. "We are enleagued. Therefore, speak me as 'Grendel', a suitable name for me, a monster. You could not pronounce my true name."

"As you wish, Grendel, my friend," said Kurik.

CHAPTER FORTY-EIGHT

Cross her ankles, and bind them," said Kurik, my master. I recalled that I, earlier, had been treated similarly.

The precaution is doubtless judicious.

So bound, a girl cannot leap to her feet and run.

She was terribly frightened.

She knelt, trembling, before Lord Grendel and Kurik, my master. I was pleased to see her fear. But why should she be afraid? Had she not seen Lord Grendel before? Was she such a coward? She knelt with her knees pressed closely together. It was the position of the tower slave. At a word she would have had to spread her knees before them, in the position of the pleasure slave.

We are slaves.

Men are our masters.

I crossed her ankles, and looped the cord three times about them, and yanked the knots tight, much tighter than was necessary.

She regarded me, startled, reproachfully, not understanding.

How dared she protest or object?

Surely she understood that, in this situation, I was her superior. I was to her as first girl.

"Try leaping to your feet now," I thought, "you thing that men seem to prize so highly."

It was a day later, in the afternoon.

The large, pointed ears of Lord Grendel had suddenly lifted, and he had looked up. "Someone is on the stairs," he had said. "Small, not heavy, hesitant, perhaps unwilling, perhaps frightened."

"A slave," had said Kurik.

At that point there was a knock at the door.

"We are contacted," had said Lord Grendel.

I rose to my feet, and regarded her. I then withdrew to the side, and knelt.

How lovely she was in her collar. But are not all women attractive in collars? How little we had envisaged such things on Earth! But we were now on Gor, both of us, belongings, owned by masters.

How furious I was with Paula. Was she truly such a jewel, so desirable, so soft, in her tunic and collar? How could it be that she had sold for a golden tarsk? How could it be that some men found her, or claimed to find her, she, plain Paula, more desirable than I? How could a master, one such as Drusus Andronicus, a powerful, handsome fellow, find her of such value? How could she have interested a man such as him? Could I not, if I wished, despite his estimation of her, despite her love for him, take him away from her? What she did, could I not do better, more deliciously?

Could I not conquer with a smile, a turn of my body, in its tunic?

Could I not wrench the heart of Drusus Andronicus, and put him, though free, in my collar?

Surely I could do so.

Surely a slave, despite the collar on her neck, the brand on her thigh, is not without power.

I had had such power, even on Earth, which I had occasionally exercised, as it might amuse me.

And was it not accentuated, and enhanced, exponentially, on Gor?

To be sure, in the end, it was men who held the whip.

"Identify yourself, and your errand," said Kurik.

I gathered that my master, Kurik, of Victoria, would muchly conduct this small colloquy. She might well have difficulty in following the vocalizations of Lord Grendel. I wondered if she even realized he was no simple beast, that he was a rational creature, and perhaps one of formidable intellect.

How stupid she was!

Too, she was our foe, or a tool of our foes.

"I am Paula, Master," she said, "slave of Decius Albus, of Ar. On his behalf, through his agent, the noble Drusus Andronicus, of Ar, I am commanded to address one understood as Lord Grendel."

I suddenly realized that Paula assumed either that Kurik of Victoria, whom she had presumably never seen, was Lord Grendel, or an agent of Lord Grendel. Her attention to Kurik, and her relative indifference to Lord Grendel, made this clear. She had, quite possibly, before her first visit to the apartment of the Lady Bina, never seen a Kur or anything Kurlike. Her consternation and terror, evinced after her first encounter with Lord Grendel, suggested this was the case.

Presumably she still saw Lord Grendel as no more than a dangerous, possibly unpredictable, form of guard animal.

"Speak, slave," said Kurik.

Paula squirmed a little, frightened, her ankles bound.

"Try to get up and run," I thought to myself, "golden-tarsk girl! Your opaque, silken tunic, and your sandals, will avail you nothing now. You are no more now than another tethered slave."

"I have the honor, as I understand it," said Paula, regarding Kurik, "of addressing Lord Grendel."

Kurik smiled.

"My speech, as I understand it," said Paula, "will be at least delivered to one known as Lord Grendel."

Kurik smiled once more.

"I am only a slave," she said. "I must do as I am told."

"Speak," said Kurik.

"My master," she said, "Decius Albus, of Ar, Trade Advisor to the Ubar, welcomes Lord Grendel to the city. He regrets only that he was not earlier informed of his presence. Master Decius understands that Lord Grendel stands high in the estimation of a Lord Arcesilaus, magistrate of a remote city, and hopes that his presence here might lead to arrangements of mutual profit. With this end in view, Master Decius invites the presence of Lord Grendel, or his agent, to a meeting at the tenth Ahn tomorrow, in his home, the House of a Hundred Corridors."

"And how, slave, do you understand this?" inquired Kurik.

"I am only a slave," she said.

"Speak," he said.

"I speculate," she said, "given the office of my master, that of trade advisor to the Ubar, that he is interested in the possibility of establishing trade relations between Ar and the city of the Lord Arcesilaus."

"What city is that?" asked Kurik.

"I do not know," she said. "We are told little. We are slaves."

"Perhaps your master is interested in an exchange of valuables," said Kurik.

"One supposes so, Master," she said.

"Tell your master he will be attended upon at the tenth Ahn tomorrow," said Kurik.

"Yes, Master," she said. "You know the House of a Hundred Corridors?"

"Yes," said Kurik. "Free yourself, and leave."

"Yes, Master," she said, gratefully.

I watched Paula turn about, and, sitting, bring her feet before her, and address herself to the cords on her ankles. It was not easy for her to free herself, but, after a bit, she had managed to do so. She did not look at me, but kept her eyes averted. She then rose, bowed her head, and backed to the door, where she turned, and began to descend the steps. She did so uncertainly, perhaps from having been tied, or perhaps from the trauma of the small, recently concluded conference.

"One tells a slave little," said Lord Grendel.

"We are slaves," I said.

"Follow her," said Kurik. "See who is about. See if she is accompanied."

I darted from the room, and hurried down the stairs. But Paula was not far. She was at the bottom of the stairs, leaning against the wall, gasping for breath. She was trembling, and shaken. Her head was back, against the wall. She looked at me.

"You must be very brave," she said. "How can you be calm, in proximity to that gigantic, fearsome beast?"

She did not mention how I had dealt with her, in the matter of the loops of cord.

"I fear," I said, "I may have tied you too tightly."

"You were commanded," she said.

"Would you have tied me so?" I asked.

"No," she said. "But I would have tied you well. You would have been absolutely helpless."

That is how masters tie slave girls, not cruelly, but perfectly. One does not tie to hurt, which is stupid and gratuitous, one would not even tie a beast so, but to secure, with perfection. The best ties have their psychological dimension. Pain is to be avoided. It is unnecessary, and distractive. What is important is that the girl understands perfectly that she is controlled, that she is absolutely helpless, that she is fully at the mercy of another. That is what it is to be tied as a slave girl.

"Are you alone?" I asked, looking out, toward the street.

"No," she said.

I drew back within the doorway.

"There is a free woman," I said, "in merchant garb, with a parasol. I have seen her before."

"She is of the house of Decius Albus," she said, "the city house, the House of a Hundred Corridors. She is free. She stands high in the house. I think she may be the confidante of Decius Albus himself. She thinks little of slaves. Beware of her!"

"I see she carries a switch," I said.

"Many free women do," she said, "a symbol of their superiority, and authority. I have felt it many times."

"What is her name?" I asked.

"I do not know," she said.

"She is just 'Mistress'," I said.

"As any free woman," she said.

"She is with you?" I said.

"She accompanies me," she said. "She conducts me, she sets me about my errands, she waits for me, she herds me back to the house."

"It seems she does not trust you," I said.

"What free woman trusts a female slave?" she asked. "Fear them. They are free. They hate us."

"Doubtless she is lively with her switch," I said. I had reason to suppose that, from long ago, from a wharf on the Vosk.

"As many free women," she said, "and we are so helpless!"

"Only she is about?" I asked.

"No, another, as well," she said, "Drusus Andronicus, servitor to Decius Albus."

"I do not see him," I said.

"Sometimes he does not care to be seen," she said.

I regarded this intelligence with some apprehension.

"He is of the Assassins?" I said.

"No," she said, "of the scarlet caste, the Warriors."

I recalled the supper, the banquet. He had had her chained behind his couch, where she was near, but could see little. "He may have some interest in you," I said.

"I hope so!" she said. "He keeps me often with him. He permits me to sandal him, and remove his sandals. He permits me to bathe him. He often puts me to slave use. When he is about, he will not permit the free woman to switch me."

"You are his slave," I said, archly, skeptically.

"In heart," she said, "but not in law. I am the slave of Decius Albus. And I do not think Decius Albus even knows I exist. I was purchased by an agent. Were it not for my collar, he might not even know he owns me."

"'In heart'?" I said.

"I love him, Drusus Andronicus," she said.

"Have you told him?" I asked.

"No!" she said. "I do not wish to be whipped, and sold."

"You are daring, indeed," I said, "to love one not your master. Consider the risks attendant upon so grievous an indiscretion."

"I am well aware of the dangers," she said.

"Put thoughts of Drusus Andronicus from your mind," I said.

"I cannot," she said.

"You are the slave of Decius Albus," I said.

"Decius Albus knows few of his slaves, and has little interest in them," she said. "Drusus Andronicus is powerful in the house. It is his whip that is muchly feared in the pens. And, to my dismay, he can have his pick of most of the slaves, many of whom are far more beautiful than I, and some of whom, I fear, dear Phyllis, are even as beautiful as you. On a whim, should I prove in the least displeasing, or even if I were not displeasing, he could have me hooded and taken to a market. No, I am a slave, and dare not confess my love for him, even were he my master. It must be enough that I am beside myself, helpless, and uncontrollable, a slave, in his arms."

How could it be, I wondered, that Paula, plain Paula, could interest a master such as Drusus Andronicus? He had scarcely looked upon me, when I had served, naked, with other slaves. Surely I was far more attractive than she.

I looked out, from the doorway.

"The woman," I said, "she in the white and gold, with the parasol, is waiting."

"Are you so anxious to speed me on my way?" she asked.

"I do not wish you to be found displeasing," I said.

"What free woman does not find a slave girl displeasing?" she said.

"The day is cool, the woman is veiled, the sky is cloudy," I said. "Why does she carry a parasol?"

"I do not know," said Paula.

"I should return to my master, upstairs," I said. Certainly I had gathered the intelligence I had been dispatched to obtain; the messenger of Decius Albus was not alone; two others were about, who might be watched for in the future, a free woman, in Merchant colors, who stood high in the house of Decius Albus, in charge of whom was the slave, and, somewhere, as I understood it, a male, the powerful and formidable agent of Decius Albus, Drusus Andronicus. Given the presence of such attendants it seemed clear that the delivery of Paula's message was to be understood as more than the discharge of a simple errand.

Paula regarded me. "Do you like me?" she asked.

"Of course," I said.

"You are dear to me, very dear," she said.

I was silent.

"I am your friend," she said.

"Of course," I said.

"You are my friend, are you not, Phyllis?" she asked.

"Certainly," I said. "Why do you ask such a question?"

"I wish you well," she said.

She then turned away, to hurry from the doorway, to put herself in the keeping of the free woman, she with the parasol, whose mien, I feared, now suggested impatience.

"Good-bye," I said to her, in English.

CHAPTER FORTY-NINE

And that, dear Grendel, my friend," said Kurik of Victoria, "is what transpired in the House of a Hundred Corridors."

The strokes on the great bar, signaling the tenth Ahn, were still ringing when Kurik of Victoria and I, I heeling him, were ushered into an audience chamber in the House of a Hundred Corridors.

The building was large, but I doubted that it contained one hundred corridors.

"Welcome!" called a large, coarse-featured man in white and gold, rising from his curule chair on its dais, and hurrying down to embrace Kurik of Victoria, warmly. "Welcome, welcome, Lord Grendel," he said. He then drew back, smiling, and gestured to a lacquered table below the dais, which was round, and circled by six curule chairs, of identical fashioning. Accordingly there would be no obvious distinction of rank amongst those who might sit about the table. I took this personage, affable and pleasant, to be Decius Albus himself. But surely he knew that Kurik of Victoria was not Lord Grendel. Might not the presence of the actual Lord Grendel have startled, perhaps even horrified, those present?

I attended to my surroundings.

The room was large, and it was occupied by several individuals, differing much amongst themselves. There must have been between forty or fifty present. Most were in the colors of the Merchants as might be expected. I supposed they represented various interests, or perhaps various facets, of the economy and administration. I was sure that more individuals were present than might be directly concerned in trade. I saw two of the individuals present were in the green of the Physicians, and one was in the yellow of the Builders. Some four or five present were clearly of the scarlet caste. I supposed them guards. Clearly they were armed, their scabbarding presumably hosting that short, wicked blade known as the gladius. Whereas most of those present were clad in variations of the Merchant colors, the next group most prominent, or abundant, was the Scribes. I recognized them from their blue robing. Some were standing, their scribe kits slung over their shoulders. These kits were rectangular, shallow boxes snapped shut or tied closed with blue ribbon. They contained pens, ink, and sheets of rence paper. When opened and turned, the lid provided a writing surface. I had seen occasional scribes on the streets, at given corners, where they, for their fee, usually in tarsk-bits, would read or transcribe letters. Many Goreans of the lower castes could not read and write. Interestingly, some Goreans of the upper castes, notably the Warriors, prided themselves on their lack of "letters," regarding reading and writing as scribes' work and beneath their dignity. I think few of them would have regarded the "pen" as "mightier than the sword." Their pen, so to speak, was the sword, and their ink, blood. Certainly in any contest of the pen against the sword, one supposes it might be judicious to wager on the sword. It tends to be longer and sharper, and often dictates what the pen will write. Four members of the scribes were seated at a table to the side, their papers before them. I saw no members of the lower castes present. Commonly, popularly, there are five high castes, the Warriors, which claims sword right to the status, and who would deny that right to armed men, the Physicians, Builders, Scribes, and Initiates. Of the five "high castes," I saw no representative of the Initiates. They regard themselves as the highest of the high castes, presumably in virtue of their claimed relationship, a very privileged relationship, apparently, to the Priest-Kings, the "gods" of Gor. I do not know whether Priest-Kings exist or not, or, if they do, if they are aware of the existence of the Initiates. Initiates are easily recognized by their shaven heads and white robes. They maintain temples and conduct services. They bravely stand between the power, mystery, and formidableness of Priest-Kings and ordinary people, on whose behalf they will intercede, for a fee, with the Priest-Kings themselves. If one wishes good fortune and success for oneself or one's enterprises, or woe, even disaster, to one's enemies and their projects, or such, one need only contact Initiates, whose fees are, I gather, commensurate with the amount of good fortune, or woe, or such, desired. The projects need not be mighty, of course. Whether one is interested in the success of a supper, a happy outcome at the tarn races, or merely wishes to melt the heart of some aloof free woman, or such, the Initiates, humble in their holiness and concern, earnest and sympathetic, stand ready to take action, notifying the Priest-Kings of the matter and, if all goes well, securing a favorable result for the petitioner. If all does not go well, perhaps there might be some flaw or fault in the petitioner. Too, even in the best of cases, it must be admitted that the will of the Priest-Kings is sometimes inscrutable, even to Initiates. The awesomeness of the caste of Initiates is further enhanced by the fact that they refrain from sex, devote themselves to mathematical studies, and eschew meat and beans. Some Initiates dabble in signs, omens, and such, the formations of clouds, the flights of birds, the eating habits of sacred fowl, the livers of sacrificial animals, and so on, but that work, which commonly pays less well, is usually surrendered to augurs, haruspices, and such. In any event, there were no Initiates present. Perhaps this was because only relatively unimportant matters, mundane matters, were at hand. Initiates do sometimes have, however, a certain political power in various municipalities, largely in virtue of their influence on the lower castes, in virtue of their hints, warnings, demands, exhortations, denunciations, and so on. It seems they have occasionally toppled Ubars. In any event, whatever one thinks of Initiates, many of them, particularly in the larger, urban temples, make a good living at their business. Many individuals, particularly in the lower castes, need, or think they need, their Initiates, which view, it seems, is encouraged by the Initiates.

"Behold Lord Grendel," said Decius Albus to the gathered assembly, indicating Kurik of Victoria, "ambassador and plenipotentiary of the great Ubar, Lord Arcesilaus, of rich Mytilene, amongst the Farther Islands, well beyond Cos and Tyros, come to establish ties of friendship and commerce between that great ubarate and our own glorious Ar."

Those present smiled, and, lightly, struck their left shoulders, softly, repeatedly, in Gorean applause.

As far as I knew, there was no ubarate, Mytilene, amongst the Farther Islands, or elsewhere. On the other hand, much of Gor was terra incognita, and who would be likely, I gathered, to challenge the confident assertion of an individual as prominent and powerful, and as presumably well informed, as Decius Albus.

Kurik, who must have been somewhat puzzled by this attention, and its nature, smiled, and raised his hand, briefly, acknowledging this introduction.

At that point, the throng in the room gathered about Kurik and Decius Albus, and Decius Albus began to introduce them, or most of them, one after the other, to Kurik, and all were exchanging hand clasps, hand to wrist, in the Gorean fashion, which grip is more secure than the hand-to-hand clasp, with which I was familiar from my former world. On my former world, as I later learned, however, that grip is also known, the hand-to-wrist grip, but primarily amongst mariners.

I was the only woman in the room, and I knelt to the side, unnoticed. Indeed, who notices a slave when the business of men is afoot? Lord Grendel had wished me to accompany my master to the meeting, presumably to have an additional and independent witness to the proceedings, for the sake of a fuller account, as one person might notice or remember things not noticed, or remembered, by another person. Too, a slave might notice things that might escape the notice of a free person. Slaves are commonly perceptive, and aware. They tend to be muchly aware of their environment, small movements, subtle tones of voice, shades of expressions, and such. That is much in the interests of a girl. It goes with the collar. I suppose, too, it was appropriate that Kurik, my master, in such a situation, be attended by at least one slave.

I have spoken of the five high castes, as they are usually understood, the Warriors, Physicians, Builders, Scribes, and Initiates. On the other hand, obviously the Merchants is an extremely important caste. It controls much of the wealth on this world. Merchants, with their connections amongst houses in diverse cities, sometimes at war with one another, with their vouchers, notes, seals, stamps, letters of credit, and such, have created a subtle, almost invisible, but very real, commercial world. Merchant routes link cities. Merchant Law, instituted at, and revised in, the Sardar Fairs, is the only common body of law on Gor. Accordingly, many amongst the Merchants regard their caste as a high caste, and, it seems, with good reason. Surely gold is no more to be ignored than humbler metals, even if they be of edged steel. One might also note, in passing, that controversy may attend such things. For example, some regard the caste of Slavers as a subcaste of the Merchants, and others regard it as an independent caste. My master, Kurik of Victoria, thinks of it as an independent caste, judiciously or not. He seems to prize autonomy and independence. My own view is that it is a form of merchantry, and that its difference from other forms of merchantry is merely in the nature of the goods with which the merchants deal. Ubars wisely refrain from making rulings upon such things. As I may have indicated before, considerable differences may exist within a given caste. For example, a given merchant, such as Mintar, of Ar, may be the master of a thousand enterprises and another may be an itinerant peddler; and one scribe may be a city's most esteemed jurist, selling his advice for gold, while another ekes out a living on some street in the

Metellan district, reading and writing letters for tarsk-bits at the behest of the illiterate. One of the most interesting castes is that of the Players, who live by means of a board game called 'Kaissa'. In most cases, they will sell a game for a tarsk-bit, but, in certain cases, certain Players, such as Scormus, of Ar, or Centius, of Cos, may receive as much as a golden tarn for a single game. The best players are entitled to set their boards on the highest bridges. Membership in the caste is not determined by birth, but, as with the Warriors, by skill. Most Players do not make much of a living, but they have seen, I gather, as many have not, the beauty of the game. Important matches are often wagered on, and, sometimes, take place at the Sardar Fairs. The Sardar Fairs, so to speak, are treaty grounds, where lethal enemies may sit side by side, observing the great boards, where the match movements are posted. At the times of important matches, even the roads to the Fairs, within a circuit of a hundred pasangs, are deemed treaty grounds.

I am not sure I understand Goreans.

Some things in their thinking seem to me paradoxical, though not all Goreans, of course, are the same. Goreans, on the whole, seem to care for nature, for trees and green grass, for flowing brooks, and the blue sky, and, at the same time, seem to think little of the harsh selections of war, of long marches, of the clash of arms, of besieging, sacking, and burning cities. Men, being beasts, can be zestful for such things. Doubtless they are different from us. Yet I would not wish them otherwise. Who would wish a man other than a master, one to whom one must succumb? It is in the arms of such that we belong. Such activities, while admittedly hazardous, may, when successful, have their rewards, gold, for example, and women. I was told of an incident along these lines, the seeming paradoxicality of matters, that took place in a winter campaign, unusual for Goreans, as the favored time of war, as that of most sports, is the warmer weather. Indeed, most campaigns begin in the spring, and may continue through the summer and early fall. One advantage of extending a campaign to the early fall is that, at that time, the enemy's sa-tarna is ready for harvest. In any event, the winter, in the year in question, apparently set in early, and unexpectedly, and with ferocity. A blizzard, with its bitter cold, fierce winds, and blinding snow enveloped the two armies, not only postponing hostilities, but rendering the most tentative efforts at reconnaissance impractical. Dispatched scouts might be disoriented and lost in the storm, and freeze, or even, under the conditions, might wander, distraught and aimless, into the enemy camp itself. In any event, as the account goes, these warring armies were not the only creatures discomfited by the sudden, unexpected cruelty of the weather. Thousands of tiny defts, a small, flocking, gray, migratory bird, undistinguished in its plumage and not noted for its song, on their way to the shores of the Cartius, had been caught in the storm, as well, and, paralyzed with cold, with wings coated with ice, unable to continue their journey, had fallen to the snow-covered ground, littering the no-man's-land between the two armies, the projected field of battle. This became clear on the morning after the third day of the storm when the weather suddenly cleared, and, to the surprise of the potential combatants, a dreadful landscape was revealed, dark with the tiny bodies of stricken, half-frozen birds, partly buried in the snow. In short, the truce standards were raised, and hundreds of men, from each army, came onto the field, gathered up the birds in their helmets and the basins of their shields, and returned to their respective camps, where the birds were nursed, being warmed and fed, and, two days later, on a common signal, between the two armies, were lofted into the air, where they rose above the field, circled it three times, and then resumed their journey. After that, the truce standards were returned to their racks, and, the next day, the battle was joined, one that was fought with unusual ferocity.

"Ho!" cried Decius Albus, jovially, lifting his hand, and separating himself from the group about Kurik. "We have welcomed noble Grendel, of far Mytilene. We have introduced him to colleagues and compatriots, to representatives of diverse castes, herein publicizing his presence and the nature of his charge. His appearance here, as his purpose, is now well accounted for, as the lists will show. An official invitation was authorized and issued; it has been acknowledged, and, obviously, accepted. The records will show this. Now, dear colleagues, and friends, it is time for the subtler aspects of our meeting to begin, in which we must attempt to establish how fair Mytilene and glorious Ar may prove to be mutually beneficial to one another. Clearly the nature of these discussions, as you all recognize, must, for the present, remain confidential. Accordingly, I wish you all well, and thank you for your attendance."

"The matter," asked a fellow, in the white and gold, "should be mentioned to the Ubar?"

"Of course," said Decius Albus. "We have no secrets from great Marlenus, our beloved Ubar. Naturally he will be kept informed of all proposed arrangements in a suitably prepared memorandum, long before we consider drafting a formal document, one to be submitted for his review, signature, and seal."

"Yes, noble Albus," said the man, bowing and withdrawing.

It took but a few moments for the throng to depart, and then Decius Albus, Kurik, and myself were alone.

"I see," said Kurik, "you must concern yourself with spies."

"Yes, *ela*," said Decius Albus. "I may be watched. Careful attention, I fear, is devoted to whom I see, and, indeed, to whom I fail to see."

"I see," said Kurik.

"I think not," said Decius Albus. "I have in mind economic matters. Many merchant houses keep spies, to appraise themselves of the investments, plans, and ventures of competitors. Many a fortune has been made by the utilization of information not yet publicly available. Even now I expect several of our friends are hastening to locate Mytilene, that they may investigate hitherto unnoted opportunities."

"I expect they will encounter some difficulty in doing so," said Kurik.

"They will be frustrated," said Decius Albus, "but they will merely suspect that Mytilene is a code name on which we had agreed, to conceal the identity of an actual city. I represent business interests in this city, some even close to the throne, that prefer to be first to the feast."

"As the larl?" said Kurik.

"Of course," said Decius Albus.

"Deception, it seems," said Kurik, "has its role in business as well as in war."

"Business is war," said Decius Albus.

"I meant, of course," said Kurik, "other sorts of spies."

"Oh, yes," said Decius Albus. "Those we kill."

"Clearly I am here in the interests of my principal," said Kurik.

"Understood, of course," said Decius Albus, affably. "Am I to address you as Tenrik of Siba, or Kurik, of Victoria?"

"'Tenrik' will do," said my master.

"You have a pretty slave," said Decius Albus.

"There are thousands better," said my master, which remark seemed to me unnecessary. Surely the remark of Decius Albus might have been responded to more simply, as with a polite acknowledgement.

"To the business at hand," said Decius Albus.

"By all means," said Kurik.

Decius Albus then turned about, and clapped his hands, twice, and a portal opened behind the dais, and three individuals entered the room, two men and a woman, a free woman, and approached the round table, that appointed with identical chairs.

"Drusus Andronicus," announced Decius Albus, "agent and advisor, loyal and reliable servitor, swordsman, warrior. I think he may be known to your brand slut."

"That is my understanding," said Kurik. "Tal, noble Andronicus."

Drusus looked to Decius Albus.

"Tenrik of Siba," said Decius Albus.

"Tal," said Drusus, bowing.

I kept my head down. I did not care to meet the eyes of the man who had made such a fool of me.

Decius Albus then turned to the second man who had entered. He was robed in white and gold.

"Meet Marcellus, of Ar, Dealer in Fabrics and Furs," said Decius Albus, to Kurik.

"This Marcellus," said Kurik, "is mistaken in his robing. He should be clad in a more somber hue."

"That is not always wise," said Decius Albus.

"At least," said Kurik, "he does not have the dagger fixed upon his brow."

"Not now," said he who had been introduced as Marcellus of Ar, almost a hiss.

"Such as he," said Kurik, "like the vart, is a creature of the night."

"But admire the fine robes, surely, the shimmering white, the gloss of the gold," said Decius Albus, smiling.

"True colors," said Kurik, "are those that clothe the heart."

"I gather you may have met," said Decius Albus.

"Tyrtaios," said Kurik, "one of my few acquaintances from the black caste."

"I see," said Decius Albus.

"I gather you may not have been fully informed," said Kurik, "of all that occurred in Brundisium."

"Perhaps not," said Decius Albus.

"I fear that our friend Tyrtaios would have disappointed you," said Kurik, "in being outwitted, in being discommoded, in being struck unconscious, in being bound, in failing to fulfill his charge, in botching his mission."

"I was not aware of all this," said Decius Albus.

"I suspected you might have been provided with a different account of the proceedings," said Kurik.

"Somewhat," said Decius Albus.

The hand of Tyrtaios slipped within his robes, where I glimpsed a sheath fastened athwart the left shoulder. His hand was on the hilt of the housed dagger. He removed his hand from the hilt, responding, however reluctantly, to a slight, dismissive, admonitory gesture from Decius Albus.

"I trust he refused to accept his fee," said Kurik.

"But, happily," said Decius Albus, "things seem to have turned out well, even splendidly."

"Due to the independent action of others," said Kurik.

"Perhaps we shall meet, anon," said Tyrtaios, to Kurik.

"I am sure you look forward more eagerly than I to such a pleasure," said Kurik.

"Come now," said Decius Albus. "We are all friends here." He then turned to the free woman who had accompanied Drusus and Tyrtaios into the room. She, too, as Tyrtaios, wore white and gold. She was blond, and unveiled. I knew her well, from a wharf in Victoria, from a street in Ar. I looked up at her, as a slave looks upon a free woman, with awe, trepidation, and fear, but also with a slave's speculation, and appraisal. Is she truly so great, and important? What would she bring, stripped, on the block? Would she be worth bidding on? The particular nature of these speculations may be most germane to slaves, whose chains and collars have well accustomed them to thinking of themselves as properties and merchandise, and other members of their sex, as well, but I suspect similar speculations are not unknown to men. What free man, looking upon a free woman of possible interest, does not, in his imagination, consider her as a slave, how she might look, barefoot in a tunic, a collar on her neck? Does he not idly ponder how she might look, bellied and bound before him? Does he not wonder, sometimes, what might be the feel of her small tongue, licking his feet? What free woman, one of possible interest, has not, in the imagination of a thousand men, been a thousand times undressed and put upon a block? After all, even in the glory of her freedom, she is a woman, and a member of the slave sex. "May I present my lovely colleague, the noble Lady Alexina, of the House of Portia, in Victoria?"

"I am delighted, but puzzled," said Kurik, bowing.

"Puzzled?" asked Decius Albus.

"I do not believe I am known to the noble lady, or she to me, and yet she, though certainly to my gratification, chooses to appear before me, a stranger, unveiled," said Kurik.

The Lady Alexina smiled.

She was rather lovely.

I hated her.

"Not a stranger," said Decius Albus. "We are all friends here."

Free women, of course, play games with their veils, with their adjustings and slackenings, and raisings, and lowerings, much as might be done with fans, or even a parasol. Too, to my interest, and amusement, I fear, the Lady Alexina carried, even here, indoors, within the House of a Hundred Corridors, that parasol I had seen her carry first on a street in Ar. Was the sun so bright in this room? Did she fear a sudden torrent of rain might fall from the ceiling, from which a parasol, even so improbable a defense, might serve to protect her?

"Tenrik, of Siba," said Decius Albus.

"I am delighted," said the Lady Alexina. I saw the switch was still fastened at her belt.

"The House of Portia is well known for its jewelries," said Kurik.

"I am flattered that you are familiar with the house," said the Lady Alexina, I thought somewhat apprehensively.

"Moderately so," said Kurik. "I have sold more than one display slave to the Lady Portia," said Kurik.

"And they were lovely indeed," she said.

"Does the Lady Portia still ship from the wharf of Terence?" he asked.

"Less frequently now," she said.

"It is a famous house," said Kurik to Decius Albus. "It is one of the few houses this far north where one can hope to obtain jewelries fashioned in the shops of Schendi and Turia."

"We import work from a hundred cities," she said.

"This is all very interesting," said Decius Albus, "but let us attend to business."

"By all means," said Kurik.

The free persons then took seats about the round table, and I knelt near my master, a bit behind him and to the left.

"I see Lord Grendel did not come himself," said Decius Albus.

"Are you surprised?" asked Kurik.

About the table were six curule chairs, five of which would be occupied, those by Decius Albus; Drusus Andronicus; Tyrtaios; Kurik of Victoria, my master; and the Lady Alexina. The sixth chair, I gathered, was intended to be largely honorary, representing a place for the absent Lord Grendel. Surely it was too small for such a beast to crouch within it.

"No," said Decius Albus.

"Nor in attendance," said Kurik, "are certain allies of yours."

"Are you surprised?" asked Decius Albus.

"No," said Kurik.

"Our friends might attract attention in the streets," said Decius Albus. "Too, our friends commonly have short tempers, and I think we might do better without them. Certainly, we need no ring challenges in the house."

I did not understand this remark.

"No," said Kurik.

"Are you authorized to negotiate?" asked Decius Albus.

"No," said Kurik, "merely to convey proposed arrangements to Lord Grendel, and return to you his responses."

"That is what I supposed," said Decius Albus. "You are well aware, I trust, that the Lady Bina, whom we suppose to be of interest to Lord Grendel, is in our power."

"I intend no impugning of your honor," said Kurik, "but my principal, understandably, might wish to be assured on that point."

Tyrtaios made an angry noise.

"And wisely," said Decius Albus. "Lady Alexina," he said.

The Lady Alexina drew forth, from within her robes, a veil, a house veil, I think, and handed it to Kurik, who put it in his pouch.

"Lord Grendel," said Decius Albus, "will doubtless recognize the veil, and, I suspect, will by scent, as well, verify its authenticity."

"I am sure of it," said Kurik.

"The terms of my principal—," said Decius Albus.

"Lord Agamemnon," said Kurik.

"Quite," said Decius Albus, "are simple—we will return the Lady Bina to the care of your principal, Lord Grendel, well and unharmed, in exchange for his oath, that he will be a loyal and active servitor to Lord Agamemnon, obedient and zealous in his service."

"And if he refuses to give his oath?" asked Kurik.

"Then the Lady Bina will suffer the consequences," said Decius Albus.

"Torture?" asked Kurik.

"More likely, she would be run for our friends," said the Lady Alexina. "They enjoy such sport, taking prey in flight, and then feeding."

"Lord Grendel fought against Lord Agamemnon," said Kurik.

"An indiscretion that will be overlooked," said Decius Albus.

"What if he should give his oath, and then betray it?" asked Kurik.

"He will not," said Decius Albus, "he is Kur, or much like a Kur."

"Honor is stupid," said Tyrtaios, "but it is a useful device for con-
trolling and manipulating fools."

"Too," said the Lady Alexina, "the Lady Bina remains vulnerable.
Acquired once, she may be acquired again."

"I shall convey your proposal to Lord Grendel," said Kurik, beginning to rise.

"No, tarry, be here a bit, a moment," said Decius Albus, placing his
hand gently on Kurik's arm.

Kurik resumed his seat.

"I am distressed," said Decius Albus, drawing back his hand, as
though in disappointment. "You do not seem pleased."

"Forgive me, noble Albus," said Kurik, "but I find little here in
which to rejoice."

"You are a realist," said Decius Albus. "I am a realist. One does
what one can, in what conditions obtain. The world is as it is. You may
like it or not. It does not care. You may be happy or not. It is up to you.
It is more pleasant to be happy. Let us all be friends."

"Dally, handsome Tenrik, noble citizen of Siba," said the Lady
Alexina, gracefully placing her dropped veil over her left shoulder, "an
exquisite ka-la-na, from the terraces of Cos, waits to be served."

Kurik inclined his head, politely.

"From the terraces of Naxos, on Cos," she said.

"Ah!" said Kurik, lifting his head.

I gathered this beverage might be of some special interest.

They looked into one another's eyes. Free persons may do this with
impunity.

She dared to place her small hand on his.

I hated her. I hated her!

How could I compete with her, half-naked, in a tunic, collared, on
my knees?

"A single bottle," said Decius Albus, "may cost as much as a golden
tarsk."

Drusus Andronicus, who had remained discreetly silent, then rose
to his feet, and clapped his hands together, sharply, twice.

The portal behind the dais then opened again, and a slave entered,
bearing a tray, on which were five, and only five, small glasses, and a
small decanter of some ruby beverage, which, I gathered, must be that
to which the Lady Alexina had alluded.

That there were only five glasses on the tray suggested that either
Lord Grendel's presence had not been expected, from the beginning,

or that the number of free persons to be served had been discreetly ascertained, perhaps by means of a viewing panel. Had I known more of Gor, a more frightful interpretation might have occurred to me. It is extremely dangerous to serve paga, or ka-la-na, or other such beverages, to a Kur. Would one, say, give paga to a larl or sleen?

"Paula!" I thought to myself.

She was sandaled, even indoors. The sandals had golden straps. Her collar was a fine one, close about her neck. Her tunic was of yellow silk, brief, low-cut, and slashed at both hips. There was no doubt it garbed a slave. Her dark hair was knotted at the back of her neck. When such a knot is undone by a master, and the hair, loosened, falls about her shoulders, the slave is in little doubt that she will soon serve to slake, and well slake, her master's lusts, and as the obedient, comely beast she is.

She, head down, placed the tray on the table, at the empty place. I do not think she had seen me, kneeling, near my master.

Clearly Decius Albus was perusing the slave.

I supposed that Paula might not be all that plain, really, all things considered. Certainly some men had seemed to find her of interest.

"I do not recall this girl," he said. "Perhaps I have not seen her before. She is lovely enough to be a display slave."

I did not care for the notion of a display slave. What slave does not wish to be the single slave of one master?

"She has been a display slave," said Drusus Andronicus. "She is now in the common bondage of a house slave."

"How long have we owned her?" inquired Decius Albus.

"Since the Curulean sales of En'Kara," said Drusus.

The En'Kara sales are associated with the time of the vernal equinox on Gor, which, too, is when the Goreans, rather as nature, begin their new year. The Curulean is the major auction house in Ar. It is regarded as a great honor for a girl to be sold in the Curulean, even from a minor block. I recalled that Paula had been marketed from the central block. I was not, however, in the least bit, jealous of her in this respect. Men may do as they wish with us. We are slaves. The harvesters of slaves on Earth, as I understand it, often coordinate their operations with the Gorean calendar. For example, spring tends to be an attractive time to buy livestock, including slaves. Accordingly, the actual acquisitions of earlier-selected merchandise are often timed to allow for transportation and training prior to a given, projected sale, at one time or another, in one market or another. A girl, in the view of the slavers, becomes a slave when she is placed on a harvesting list. Her actual acquisition may not take place for months. Thus, interestingly, from this point of view, a girl may be a slave and not know she is a slave. Perhaps you are such a girl. Then she finds herself naked in a Gorean pen, with chains on her fair limbs. Should she remain in doubt, the collar, and her brand, will make the matter clear.

"What do we call her?" asked Decius Albus.

"'Paula'," said Drusus Andronicus.

"A barbarian name," said Decius Albus.

"She is barbarian, noble Albus," said Drusus.

Paula, humbly, head down, placed the first tiny glass before Decius Albus, who was her master.

"Next, dear," said Decius Albus, "our noble guest, Tenrik of Siba."

The Lady Alexina drew back, angrily. She held the shaft of her parasol in two hands. Her knuckles were white.

"Forgive me, lady," said Decius Albus, "he is our honored guest."

"Of course," smiled the Lady Alexina.

As a free woman, she had expected to receive precedence, after the master. And what slave girl would dare not serve her master first?

Paula put one of the small glasses before my master. She saw me, I think then for the first time. Her hand shook. The glass touched the table twice, rather than once, gently.

"Careful," whispered Drusus.

How shaken Paula seemed, to see me here.

"Yes," I thought. "It is I, on my knees, while you are standing."

"What is wrong, Paula?" asked Drusus.

"She is surprised," said Kurik. "These two knew one another on the Slave World. They were brought here in the same lot."

"What a difference," said Decius Albus.

I did not care for this observation.

Paula then placed the third glass before the Lady Alexina.

"Her tunic is a bit short, is it not?" inquired the Lady Alexina.

I was pleased that she was as exposed as she was. I had rather resented the modest tunic she had worn in the streets. She was a slave. Let her be exposed as one, as others! To be sure, she was now in the house. Perhaps she should have been grateful to have been permitted clothing. Then I scorned myself. We were slaves, not free women. How excited and pleased we were to be slaves, free to rejoice in our attractiveness, free to revel in our beauty and its power, well aware of its effect on ourselves and others, no longer permitted, lest we be whipped, the curbs and checks, the ten thousand constraints and inhibitions, of the free woman. The collar freed us, giving us no choice but to be ourselves, slaves. Then I remembered that a free woman was present.

"Forgive us, fine lady," said Decius Albus, "but our guest, the esteemed Tenrik of Siba, is male."

"I fail to understand," said the Lady Alexina, clutching the parasol, so anomalous an accoutrement under the circumstances, "what men can see in slaves. What useless, worthless things they are."

"They do have their purposes," said Decius Albus.

"Undoubtedly," she said.

Paula glanced at Drusus, who indicated that Tyrtaios would be the next before whom a glass would be placed. After this, she placed the last glass before Drusus, as though he might have been her master, which behavior, happily, was not noted by Decius Albus.

In any event, Paula, happily, was not subjected to the attentions of the Gorean slave lash.

Paula then, in the same order in which she had placed the glasses, filled each, something like a third full.

How precious then, I thought, must be the beverage!

"I shall not propose a toast," said Decius Albus, "as I am unsure we share a common sentiment, but let us drink, as might friends."

My master swirled the tiny ruby lake enclosed within its crystal shores, observed it, and then took its scent, as though it might have been a tiny bouquet of dinas. He then barely touched it to his lips.

"How is it?" inquired Decius Albus.

"I have heard of the ka-la-na of Naxos," said Kurik. "This is the first time I have tasted it."

"I trust you find it satisfactory," said Decius Albus.

"It is exquisite," said Kurik.

"I once, in Venna," said Decius Albus, "exchanged five girls for a bottle."

"A bargain," said Kurik.

I rather doubted that. Still, who is to say what slave girls are worth? Men, of course.

"Drink again," said Decius Albus. "One would not ruin a ka-la-na of this rarity by mixing it with poison. Too, we need you to convey our offer to Lord Grendel."

"My thinking, exactly," said Kurik.

"Join with us," said Decius Albus, "and you may swill the ka-la-na of Naxos with the same abandon as vat paga."

"That," said Kurik, "would be desecration, like uprooting flowers."

"True," smiled Decius Albus, "but it would be a desecration well within your means."

"There is another slave here," said the Lady Alexina. "I would be served a second glass, by that slave."

"I am sure she is not a trained serving slave," said Decius Albus, "and she belongs to our guest."

"I would be served by her," said the Lady Alexina.

"Surely not," said Decius Albus.

"It is quite all right," said Kurik. "I am more than pleased. Phyllis, be about it. Serve the noble mistress."

I rose to my feet, and saw that Paula, now kneeling near Drusus, was frightened. I was muchly unsettled by this. Why should she be frightened? I glanced at the Lady Alexina, and then, swiftly, lowered my head. What I had seen there, in her eyes, was not reassuring. It had not been difficult to detect the interest of the Lady Alexina in my master. Perhaps Paula, too, had noticed that, glances, subtle movements, proximities. Too, free women and slave girls, as is well known, are rivals. The free woman has her freedom, her place in society, her influence, her connections, her resources, her position and power, all that she can offer a man, while the slave has little more than her helplessness, her collar, and her needs. The advantages are clearly with the free woman. It is she who holds the whip. And yet men will seek the slave, worthless as she is, to have her at their feet. I was apprehensive. Certainly I knew I was not a trained serving slave. I had been taught, as any slave will be taught, something of the serving of ka-la-na or paga to men, but I muchly doubted that the same protocols would be appropriate in the serving of a free woman. Indeed, even the hint of such might, I supposed, bring the switch or lash. Then I remembered Paula. She had served the Lady Alexina, and then, as the Lady Alexina was present, a free woman, had served the men, similarly. I would then, to the best of my ability, do as she did. Stand, wait for the nod, and then pour, deferentially, and carefully, very carefully, and then step back, head down, lest one's eyes meet those of a free person, in particular those of a free woman.

"Fill my glass, girl," said the Lady Alexina, "to the brim, the brim, exactly, and do not spill a drop."

"Beware the parasol," whispered my master.

I did not understand this. Did he fear she would strike me with it, with a much more apt tool, her switch, at hand?

I lifted the decanter, gracefully, as had Paula, and went to the place of the Lady Alexina, where I waited, standing. Her eyes glowed, with anticipation. She nodded, curtly.

I began to pour.

"To the brim," she said, "so that not another drop might be added, and let none run over the edge, not a drop, nor the part of a drop."

I held the decanter with both hands, and, in misery, poured with great care. Then the fluid was held in the tiny glass by naught but surface tension. I could even note the swelling of the fluid slightly above the level of the glass.

I then stepped back, shuddering, head down.

"Nicely done, girl," said Decius Albus.

I heard a small, inadvertent sigh of relief escape Paula, which, to her consternation, brought a frown from Drusus Andronicus.

"Not so nicely done, noble Albus," said the Lady Alexina. "The slave may now lift the glass to my lips."

Paula, at a nod from Drusus, leapt to her feet and took the decanter from me, for the wine swirled within it, placing it on the tray, which was in the empty place at the table.

"Do not fear, pretty slave," said the Lady Alexina. "Take the glass in both hands and lift it carefully. I will steady your hands."

"*Ela*, Phyllis," said Kurik. "Consider the Ahn. We must convey the proposal of the noble Albus to our principal, Lord Grendel."

"Yes, Master," I said, gratefully.

"Lift the glass," said the Lady Alexina, coldly.

"Attend me," said Kurik.

I hurried to his side, and knelt at his thigh. I put my cheek against his thigh, frightened. I was still shuddering. Obviously the command of the master takes precedence over the command of one not the master, even though it be that of a free woman.

"I thank you, noble Albus," said Kurik. "I have muchly enjoyed the gracious and generous hospitality of your house. You are a most estimable host. Too, you have given me the opportunity to see my friend once more, noble Tyrtaios, of the Merchants, as I understand it, whom I had not seen since Brundisium. For that, who would not be grateful? Too, what free man would not rejoice to meet so charming a woman as the lovely Lady Alexina? Compared to these delights, even those of the ka-la-na of Naxos must be overlooked."

"Surely the pleasure here is that of the house," said Decius Albus. "We shall look forward to hearing from you, and trust that the response of Lord Grendel to our proposal will be favorable."

"How could it not be?" said Kurik.

He then turned about to leave the room. We had gone but a step or two when we heard a cry of rage from the Lady Alexina, and the shattering of glass in our wake. Turning about, we saw her standing, enraged, behind the table, looking after us. She had apparently seized the glass and cast it after us. There was wine on her robes, and on the table, and on the floor, amidst a litter of sparkling crystal.

"It is a shame to waste a fine ka-la-na," said Kurik, regretfully.

I hurried after him, and, shortly, we were in the street.

"Why," I asked, "did Mistress Alexina wish to have me beaten?"

"First," he said, "you are a slave, second, you are my slave."

"She is a very beautiful lady," I said.

"I would like to see her naked and in chains," he said.

"Master!" I protested.

"A woman when free is worthless," he said. "Once enslaved, she is worth something. Then you can put a value on her."

"I am glad I did not feel her switch or whip," I said.

"If that were all," he said, "I would have let her jostle your arm. An occasional slap of a switch or a blow of the whip is good for a slave. It reminds them that they are slaves. What I feared was the parasol."

"A parasol," I said, "is nothing. It is innocent."

"Not all parasols are the same," he said.

"Why would one such as she, a high woman of the Merchants, of a jewelry house in Victoria, be here, enleagued with Decius Albus?"

"She is not of Victoria, nor of the house of Portia," said Kurik. "She knows little, or nothing, of Victoria, or the house of Portia. The house of Portia does not use display slaves to exhibit their merchandise. They regard that as demeaning to the merchandise, and to free women. Furthermore, the house of Portia does not import finished work, set pieces, and such, but only the appropriate materials, silver, gold, pearls, stones, and such. These materials are then worked up in the house's own shops. The house is very particular about that. Too, the house of Portia would find it difficult to ship from the wharf of Terence in Victoria, as there is no such wharf."

"She is then a mercenary, of sorts," I said.

"Doubtless," said Kurik. "A lovely free woman, with all the powers of a free woman, and those of a lovely free woman, can be of great use in a thousand enterprises."

"Her antecedents, then," I said, "are immaterial."

"Yes," said Kurik, "but it is quite possible she is actually of the

Merchants. I would not be surprised. Some members of that lofty caste are not particular with respect to which mine it is from which they extract their gold."

We continued on.

"What is wrong, Master?" I asked.

"I fear the game is theirs," said Kurik. "Lord Grendel must deliver his oath, or sacrifice the Lady Bina."

"The game is lost, then," I said.

"I fear so," he said.

"And that, dear Grendel, my friend," said Kurik of Victoria, "is what transpired in the House of a Hundred Corridors."

"They have designed the game, and chosen the pieces," said Lord Grendel. "I do not think we can win their game."

"What, then, are we to do?" asked Kurik.

"Begin another game," said Lord Grendel.

CHAPTER FIFTY

Snarling, enraged, Lyris flung her body against the bars, as though she would press her body between them. Then she seized the bars, and shook them, savagely. But they held. The structure was stout. She howled in frustration. She then suddenly thrust her right forelimb between the bars, claws out, like hooks, and I leaped back, with a cry of fear, away from the bars. To be sure, I had judged the distance earlier, and would not, by any means, have placed myself within her reach. Still, it was terrifying, to see the wildness in her eyes, the glistening saliva at her fangs, the outstretched limb with its clawed tentaclelike digits scratching in the air, reaching for me, hearing that horrid bestial noise, half shriek and snarl, of rage and hatred.

Lord Grendel, crouching in the Kur fashion, was nearby. He kept his eyes on Lyris. His translator, on its chain, was slung about his neck.

A flood of angry sound hissed through the lips of Lyris, she glaring out at us from behind the bars. I took it that that sound was half in articulate Kur, which I was able to at least recognize as Kur, and half, perhaps, in nothing that could even be understood as intelligible discourse, but might better be interpreted as no more than shrieks and cries, a frightful ventilation of frustration and fury.

"What is she saying?" I asked.

"She is displeased," said Lord Grendel.

"I had suspected that," I said.

His translator had not been activated. Perhaps it was just as well.

"Does she understand Gorean?" I asked.

"No," he said.

This was not unusual, of course, as few Kurii do. They rely on translators of various sorts.

Lord Grendel then said something to the prisoner.

In response to this her cries, angry and protestive, sputtering and menacing, shrill and violent, were muchly augmented.

"What did you say to her?" I asked.

"I asked her to make less noise," he said.

"Perhaps she thinks she can be heard above, outside," I said.

"Do not insult her," he said. "She is Kur. She will realize she would not be placed in a situation where her cries might be heard."

I did not think, given the depth of the lowest basement, and the floors above, a battle trumpet could have been heard outside, far above, on the street. Kurik, my master, had arranged the terms of the rental, and the discretion of the landlord. The cage, large and thickly barred, would have held a larl.

"I gather," I said to Lord Grendel, "she has threatened us, elaborated in detail upon a variety of lengthy and elaborate tortures, assured us of a prompt, fearsome reprisal, and such."

"Something along those lines," said Lord Grendel. "I thought it best not to have the translator activated."

I was not reassured by the receipt of this intelligence.

Then Lord Grendel addressed himself again, but briefly, as before, to Lyris.

She drew back in the cage, snarling.

"What did you say to her?" I asked.

"I suggested, if she wishes to free herself, that she should chew through the bars," he said.

"She cannot do that," I said.

"I thought it would not hurt to remind her of that," he said.

"I see," I said.

I was well reminded of my collar.

There are many ways to bring a woman to heel. There are ropes and chains, cords and laces, switches and whips. Clothing may be supervised, and determined. How can a woman dressed as a slave not come to understand that she is a slave? What is done on the outside will have its inevitable effect on the inside. Truth can be denied only so long. Too, of course, clothing may be denied, even in the streets and plazas. Food may be controlled. A scrap of meat, cast to the floor, may become a banquet, a candy a treasure. There are many ways in which a slave will learn she is a slave, and only a slave. The best, of course, is to kindle her slave fires, mercilessly, if it should please one, to the point that she will crawl to one on her belly, in tears, and need, begging to be touched. She then well knows she is in her collar, and would not have it otherwise.

"Behold, Master," I said. "Her behavior has suddenly changed. She has become tractable, and docile."

"Perhaps," said Lord Grendel, "she has taken my meaning."

Certainly something of a transformation had taken place in the attitudes and demeanor of the prisoner.

Lyris had now crawled to the front of the cage, and a soft, ululating sound escaped her lips, and she then lay on her left side, her legs drawn up a bit, near the bars. She began to whimper. And then she began to make soft sounds, in Kur. Her eyes were fixed on Lord Grendel.

"Yes," said Lord Grendel, "she is indeed beautiful."

"Is that what she is saying?" I asked. The translator was not on.

"Scarcely," said Lord Grendel.

I was not sure I understood the meaning of Lyris' behavior. But it was muchly different from her earlier hostility and manifest belligerence.

"Turn on the translator, Master," I suggested.

But he made no move to do so.

"Surely you understand her," I said.

"Who would not?" he asked.

He approached the bars.

"Beware, Master," I said.

"She will not attack now," he said. "If she did, I would bite off her hand."

"I am uneasy," I said. Certainly her attitude, for a Kur, seemed unusual. I had never seen a Kur behave so, even on the dais, at the supper, when she had lifted the cup to the lips of Lord Grendel.

She twisted her body, softly. Her nostrils widened, her ears were half lifted, inclined vulnerably toward Lord Grendel, very different from when, in her rage, they had been flat, and back, against the sides of her head. Her breathing was deep, and regular. A strange, small noise escaped her. She expressed herself in Kur, and then there was again, twice, that small noise.

"Yes," said Lord Grendel. "She is one of the most beautiful female Kurii I have ever seen."

"I do not understand her behavior," I said. "I do not understand what she is doing."

"Surely you suspect," said Grendel.

"It seems almost sensuous," I said.

"I suspect," said Lord Grendel, "that a thousand Kurii on a dozen steel worlds would kill to have lovely Lyris so before them."

"I see," I said.

"I had not realized I was so handsome a fellow," he said, "that so beautiful a female could be so taken with me, and at the first glimpse.

How poor Lyris has suffered, trying to conceal her mighty, forbidden passion for me from Surtak and the others. Only now she dares to express it."

"I see," I said.

"Brave Lyris," he said.

"What is she doing?" I asked.

"She is petitioning seeding," he said.

"Oh," I said.

"She wishes to be released, that she may serve my pleasure."

"Beware, Master," I said.

"Why?" said he. "She is Kur. She professes herself mine, and, indeed, from long ago, that she has long been smitten with helpless love for me, even, secretly, from the steel world of Agamemnon."

"Please, Master," I said. "Do not approach the bars more closely."

But Lord Grendel, despite my warning, did so. He even reached between the bars, and touched her flank. She made again that soft, now-unmistakable sound, and, her eyes upon him, tenderly, she rolled to her back, and lifted her body to him.

Lord Grendel then held to the bars, and, with one mighty foot, with this leverage, disdainfully, violently, thrust Lyris feet away, rolling across the floor of the cage.

He then, glaring at the startled, disconcerted Lyris, snapped on his translator, surely for my benefit.

"You worthless, deceitful she-urt," he said, "I am mindful to relieve you of your harnessing. You would look better without it. So you would serve my pleasure, would you? Splendid! How generous! But know this, worthless she-urt, and know it well. If I choose, I will put you to my pleasure, again and again, if and when I wish. You should have been seized after the war, as were many others, adherents of Agamemnon, deprived of their harnessing and put in collars, to belong to, and serve, the victors."

I expected Lyris to leap to her feet snarling, and rush to the bars, but she withdrew, going to the back of the cage. She crouched there, watching Lord Grendel. She whimpered, once.

"Be silent," said Lord Grendel.

Lyris was then silent.

She seemed shaken, awed.

Lord Grendel had well surmised that the Kurii associated with Decius Albus would be quartered away from the city, probably in the house off the Viktel Aria, where the supper had been held. This surmise had proved correct. Moreover, as Lord Grendel had further anticipated, the security at the facility would be negligible, or non-existent. The house was not known to be tenanted, and it was, in any event, remote and strong. The resident Kurii had no reason to expect discovery or intrusion. Indeed, given the complacency of Kurii, and their contempt for humans, they had not even seen fit to post guards, a laxity that was doubtless remedied by now. In short, Lord Grendel, with the strength and agility of a Kur, undetected, had had little difficulty in gaining access to the premises. Once within, he had soon located the room allocated to Lyris. There he had seized her and, as she awakened, wildly, and might have cried out, he had thrust a wad of ground meat into her mouth, stifling any possibility of a scream. He had then clapped his hand over her mouth, so that she was unable to expel the meat, and, with his other hand, covered her nostrils, preventing the ingress of air. This was reminiscent of a common way in which slave wine is administered to a slave, to preclude conception, as the breeding of a slave is, naturally, at the discretion of her masters. In short, Lyris was given the choice of engorging the meat, which was feasible for a Kur, if not a human, or suffocating. Predictably, after a certain amount of time, she swallowed the meat. It was then only necessary to hold her mouth closed for a bit, until the tassa powder, with which the meat was liberally laced, should take effect. I had assisted Lord Grendel in his preparations and the amount of tassa powder used might have sedated four or five free women. A drink with a stranger is often the last thing a free woman remembers until she awakens, naked and chained, in a slave wagon. In the case of Lyris, she awakened in her harnessing, but in a harnessing now devoid of accoutrements and weapons, in the stout cage.

"Surtak," said Lord Grendel, "is much taken with the sleek and delicious beauty of Lyris. He hopes to be her seed provider. Yet she has been reluctant to accept, and has even been scornful of, his overtures. He will be more than willing to effect an exchange, Eve for Lyris. If it were not for seeming to be demeaning to Eve, the true beauty, I could doubtless suggest that a sizable quantity of gold be added to the scales."

"Your proposal will be conveyed to the House of a Hundred Corridors by my master," I said, "and Surtak, and his cohorts, will be soon apprised of the situation, but I do not see how this will effect a favorable resolution in the matter of the Lady Bina, a matter both Decius Albus and Lord Agamemnon are likely to regard as far more important."

"True," said Lord Grendel. "That is a different matter."

"We do not even know the location of the Lady Bina," I said.

"But we know of one who does," said Lord Grendel.

"Decius Albus," I said, "Tyrtaios, perhaps even Drusus Andronicus."

"I am thinking of another," he said.

"The Lady Alexina?" I said.

"By whose presence we expect to be shortly graced," he said.

"I do not understand," I said.

"She should be here shortly," said Lord Grendel.

"Surely not," I said.

"It is my understanding," he said, "that the Lady Alexina was less than subtle in the House of a Hundred Corridors, in indicating her interest in your master."

"My master spoke to you of this?" I asked. Men, I supposed, the vain, pompous braggarts, might enjoy regaling disinterested bystanders with such details.

"Only insofar as might be useful in pursuing our interests," he said.

"She was as subtle as an obese, blundering tarsk sow," I said.

"Please," said Lord Grendel, "by report, the Lady Alexina is neither obese nor clumsy, nor likely to be confused with a tarsk sow. Indeed, I gather from your master that she is quite lovely."

"Perhaps, for a free woman," I said.

"In any event," said Lord Grendel, "it was arranged that a message be delivered this morning to the Lady Alexina. The purport of this message, to make matters short, was that your master was muchly taken with her charms, but, at the time, in that company, thought it unwise to express himself, but now, unable to rid himself of a vision of such loveliness, wished her to have a rendezvous with him in the Park of Demetrius, near the Fountain of Veminiums."

"I see," I said.

"Unfortunately," said Lord Grendel, "the Park of Demetrius is some distance from the House of a Hundred Corridors."

"I know little of Ar," I said.

"Thus," he said, "when the Lady Alexina slips discreetly away from the House of a Hundred Corridors, she will presumably wish to engage transportation to the park."

"Very well," I said, cautiously.

"She will have the good fortune," he said, "of finding a pay wagon at hand, driven by a bearded, cloaked driver, a closed wagon."

"I see," I said.

"And thus," he said, "I expect her here shortly."

At that point there was a scuffling on the stairs, and, turning, I saw a small, roped, bundled, face-swathed figure, her arm in the grip of a bearded figure, descending the stairs. Instantly I knelt. It was my master. He, Kurik of Victoria, released the arm of his captive, thrust back his hood, and drew away the false beard with which he had concealed his countenance. That he cast aside. He then removed from his belt that bright yellow parasol that had been so common a feature of the Lady Alexina's ensemble, and discarded it, as well. The Lady Alexina, his captive, her sleeved arms roped, her wrists pulled back, under the ropes, and bound behind her, stood where she had been placed. There was a small noise from within the swathing of hood and veils that completely covered her head. From the sound, it seemed clear that, beneath those concealing amplitudes of cloth, she had been gagged.

"It seems matters proceed apace," said Lord Grendel.

The Lady Alexina twisted her head from side to side, angrily; she stamped her small sandaled foot.

"Let us undo the veils and hooding about her mouth," said Lord Grendel.

Kurik moved some of the cloth upward, and worked the gag from her mouth. She remained, of course, unable to see.

"Release me," she cried, "foul brigands! You do not know whom you have discomfited! I am Alexina, from the House of a Hundred Corridors, colleague of the mighty Decius Albus! You have judged unwisely, my fine fellows! Do not think you can hold one so important as I for ransom! Consider your error! Tremble! Lose no time! Hasten! Return me to the House of a Hundred Corridors!"

At a gesture from Lord Grendel, Kurik drew away the hood and veils that had obscured her vision.

"You!" she exclaimed, seeing Kurik, my master.

"I have rearranged the time and place of our rendezvous," said Kurik.

Suddenly, seeing Lord Grendel, she screamed in fear.

Kurik held her in place, her arm again in his grasp.

"What is that?" she cried, shuddering, aghast.

"A friend," said Kurik.

I gathered that the Lady Alexina had never seen a Kur before, or anything similar to a Kur. She had not been at the supper in the house off the Viktel Aria. Too, Kurii were not likely to be in attendance at the House of a Hundred Corridors. Presumably, then, she would have supposed, in her involvement in the intrigues of Decius Albus, that

Lord Agamemnon and Lord Grendel were men, and that the entire matter was one dealing merely with differences between competitive human factions.

"And the other?" gasped the Lady Alexina, her eyes wide, regarding Lyris, who had now come forward in the cage, indeed, to just behind the bars.

"Kur," said Kurik, simply.

The eyes of Lyris blazed, and her jaws parted, revealing fangs, and she snarled. I surmised that Lyris, for whatever reason, was not well disposed toward the Lady Alexina. In this respect, we shared a view.

"It is an animal, a hideous animal!" exclaimed the Lady Alexina. I deemed it fortunate that the translator of Lord Grendel was not activated. Still, even a larl or sleen might have understood something of the Lady Alexina's revulsion.

"No more an animal than you," said Lord Grendel, "and she is remarkably beautiful, even for a Kur."

The Lady Alexina turned angrily, reproachfully, to face Kurik. "I am a free woman," she said. "Yet you had the effrontery to touch me, to seize me, to subdue me!"

"Forgive me, lady," said Kurik.

"You tied my ankles together," she said, "as might have been the ankles of a slave!"

"Surely, Lady Alexina," I thought, "the ankles of a free woman tie quite as nicely as those of a slave, and doubtless her small wrists, as well."

"I could not stand," said the Lady Alexina, "you bound me, you used my clothing to blindfold me, your leather bands denied me speech! You placed me, helpless, on the floor of the wagon bed, on the floor!"

"Forgive me, Lady," said Kurik, "had I thought, I would have provided cushioning."

"Where is my parasol?" she inquired.

"There," said Kurik, indicating where it lay, to the side.

I wondered if the Lady Alexina might be mad. If I were in her position, I did not think I would be muchly concerned with the location of that humble accessory.

"Unbind me," she said, "and give it to me."

"Perhaps later," said Kurik.

"I know why you have abducted me," she said to Kurik. "You represent the interests of your employer, Lord Grendel."

"True," said Kurik.

"Where is Lord Grendel?" she asked.

"Not far," said Kurik.

"Very well," she said. "Proceed with the business. I am here. Make the arrangements. Exchange me for your precious Lady Bina."

"I fear, noble lady," said Kurik, "that you far overestimate your importance."

"I do not understand," she said. "I am the favorite of Decius Albus, his ally, agent, and confidante. He would give anything to obtain my safe return."

"With a brand on your thigh, and a collar on your neck?" asked Kurik.

"Of course not," she said, uncertainly. "I would then be worthless."

"Not at all," said Kurik. "You might be worth a silver tarsk or two."

"Sleen!" she hissed.

I supposed it was just as well that she was bound, else she might have, as she could, being a woman, attacked Kurik. A free Gorean male is highly unlikely to strike a free woman, unless as a prelude to reducing her to slavery. As a result, a free woman, given the privileges of her liberty, usually feels free to abuse a free male, verbally or corporally, much as she might wish. The matter is very much different with a slave, of course. The merest suggestion, on her part, of a quick word or an impatient shrug, or gesture, may bring her the lash.

"What do you think, Phyllis?" asked Kurik.

"Must I speak truthfully, Master?" I asked.

"Certainly," he said.

"She is not beautiful enough to be a slave," I said.

"Collared she-urt!" screamed the Lady Alexina.

Kurik laughed, and I thought that there was movement about the jaws of Lord Grendel himself, what I took to be an indication of mirth. I found these reactions annoying.

"I fear," said Kurik, "that Phyllis, as a slave, does not hold free women in high esteem."

"Oh, no, no, Master!" I protested. "I hold free women in the highest esteem!"

Certainly it seemed I should make that clear.

"To speak objectively, Phyllis," said Kurik, "the Lady Alexina is a very lovely woman, and, I expect, given her coloring, which is rarer than yours, would be likely to sell for more than you."

"Oh," I said.

"It is well known," said the Lady Alexina, coldly, "that free women are a thousand times more beautiful than slaves."

"Then," said Kurik, "if you were to be enslaved, you would be a thousand times less beautiful?"

Lady Alexina did not respond to that question.

"Most slaves," said Kurik, "were once free women."

"Perhaps," said the Lady Alexina, angrily.

"Most men," said Kurik, "regard slaves as a thousand times more beautiful than free women, for then, on their knees, soft, vulnerable, owned, stripped and collared, they are in their place, and wholly women."

"Be that as it may," said the Lady Alexina, "I do not have a brand on my thigh or a collar on my neck. I am a free woman and I am price-less. Further, as noted, I am the favorite of Decius Albus, and am his ally, agent, and confidante. He will give anything to have me back."

"I doubt," said Kurik, "that you are the favorite of Decius Albus. He may have a favorite, or several favorites, but they will be slaves. Men prefer them as favorites. And he can always hire himself another ally, another agent, and confidante."

The Lady Alexina, with an angry movement of her head, freed herself of her hood and veils. "Behold," she said, "my long, fine hair, as gold as ripe sa-tarna, my eyes, blue as the sky, or the veminiums of Anango!"

"Excellent," said Kurik.

I did not think all that was so fine. Most women had dark hair, and a great many, I suspected most, like Paula and myself, dark eyes.

"And my figure," she said, proudly, straightening her body.

Free women tended to have slovenly posture. That was not permit-ted, of course, in a slave.

"That is difficult to say," said Kurik, "as your robes obstruct my vision."

"Sleen!" she said, again.

The difficulty in question was not encountered, of course, in most of the garments in which a slave would be likely to be placed.

"Exchange me for the Lady Bina," said the Lady Alexina.

"We have no intention of doing so," said Kurik. "The Lady Bina is worth far more to Lord Agamemnon and the noble Decius Albus than a replaceable hireling."

"I do not understand then," she said, apprehensively. "Why have I been abducted, why have I been brought here? What do you want of me?"

"Information," said Kurik.

"I know nothing," she said.

"I find that doubtful," said Kurik.

"What do you wish to know?" she asked.

"The location of the Lady Bina," he said.

"I do not know her location," she said.

"That is unfortunate," said Kurik.

"I am a free woman," she said.

"Granted," said Kurik.

"Untie me," she said.

Kurik, taking the Lady Alexina by the arm, conducted her to the side, to the wall, rather opposite the cage in which Lyris was confined. Lyris, having crept forward, near the bars, even unfamiliar with Gorean, must have had some sense of what was transpiring. Certainly she knew Lord Grendel and had been present at the interview in the house of Decius Albus near the Viktel Aria. Similarly, she would doubtless have been aware of the concurrent plan to abduct the Lady Bina, and, later, would have learned of its success. And the prisoner in the basement, here and under these circumstances, could scarcely be the Lady Bina. The party of Lord Grendel, then, must have acquired the captive with the end in view of deriving some value from her apprehension.

"Why have you placed me here, by the wall, across from that hideous, caged creature?" she asked.

No translator was required to make clear the Lady Alexina's disapproval, or revulsion. Lyris, glaring through the bars, growled. I gathered she was extremely displeased. She, I supposed, was well aware of her own indubitable attractions, surely as a female Kur, and would not easily countenance the scorn of an animal she might well despise as human, and far inferior to herself, both in beauty and power. Surely the Lady Alexina was small, scarcely pelted, and lacked both fangs and claws. It was unlikely she could tear away the head of a tabuk with her teeth.

Lyris growled, again.

I found this satisfying, as I, too, did not care for the Lady Alexina.

"What is wrong with that dreadful thing?" asked the Lady Alexina.

"I think she is hungry," said Kurik.

"It is carnivorous?" asked the Lady Alexina.

"Yes," said Kurik.

"I trust that the cage is strong," said the Lady Alexina.

"The bars are stout," said Kurik.

"I trust that she cannot squeeze between them," said the Lady Alexina.

"Nor could you," said Kurik.

"Why have you placed me here, as I am?" asked the Lady Alexina.

"Because of the slave ring, and shackle," said Kurik. He then crouched down, lifted the shackle on its chain, the chain running to the slave ring, and snapped it shut about the left ankle of the Lady Alexina.

Her body stiffened.

I supposed this was the first time the Lady Alexina had found herself on a chain.

If a single chain is on a slave, it is most commonly put on the left ankle. But, too, slaves are not uncommonly chained by the neck. Being on a chain has its psychological effect on a woman. On Gor, where, given her branding, garbing, and collaring, and the culture, there is no escape for a slave girl, they are still commonly chained, that they may the more know themselves slaves, and the property of their masters. How we can writhe and plead in our chains!

"You have chained me, like a slave," she said.

"Yes, I have," said Kurik.

"I am not a slave," she said.

"Perhaps we will sell you," said Kurik.

"If you do," she said, "I will be purchased by Decius Albus, and instantly freed."

"If the collar is put on you," said Kurik, "it will stay on. Only a fool frees a slave girl. Do you not think your noble Decius Albus has given some thought to how you would look, chained at his couch ring?"

"You would not dare enslave me," she said.

"Surely you think you are beautiful," he said.

"Yes," she said.

"Well," said he, "the throat of a woman is much more beautiful when encircled with the collar of a slave."

"I see," she said.

"Similarly," he said, "the beauty of her thigh is muchly enhanced when imprinted with the slave mark."

"Untie me," she said.

"Certainly," he said, and he then, carefully, relieved her of her bonds.

"Now," she said, shaking her small ankle, "remove this hateful shackle."

"I think it will stay for a time," he said. "We would not wish you to run away."

"Have your slave bring me my parasol," she said. "I am fond of it. It comforts me."

"Perhaps shortly," said Kurik.

I found the Lady Alexina's interest in that artifact incomprehensible.

"Where is the Lady Bina?" asked Kurik.

"I do not know," she said.

Kurik stepped back from the Lady Alexina, and regarded her.

"Well?" she asked.

"Remove your clothing, completely," he said.

"I am a free woman," she said, drawing back, against the wall.

"Completely," said Kurik.

"I have no serving slave at hand," she said. "How can you expect me to disrobe? I am no peasant. I am of the high merchants. Consider the intricacy of the fastenings."

"I am not going to put my hands into those folds and draperies," he said, "nor am I going to risk a slave."

I did not understand this.

"You need not fear," she said. "I have no recourse to the concealed needles. Such are perilous, even to the occupant of the garment."

"I thought not," said Kurik.

"Reconsider your suggestion," she said.

"I do not wish to have my patience challenged," said Kurik.

"Please," she said.

"If your words are true," he said, "you have nothing to fear."

"The fastenings," she protested.

"Tear them loose, strip," he said.

"I am a free woman!" she cried.

"Phyllis," said Kurik, "upstairs, in my things, you will find a slave whip. Fetch it."

"Yes, Master," I said.

"No, no! Not the slave whip!" said the Lady Alexina.

She seemed familiar with that tool. I doubted that she had ever felt it. Certainly I had not felt it. It had not been used on me even in my training, to let me know what it might do to me. But I did not doubt that the Lady Alexina, as is not uncommon with women of her sort, had used it, and liberally, on her slaves. In any event, it was clear she did not wish to feel it, even through her robes.

"Hold," said Kurik.

"Yes, Master," I said, and returned to his side, where I knelt.

Kurik then surveyed his fair captive.

"Please, no!" she said.

"You will now remove your clothing, completely," said Kurik.

She regarded him, wildly.

"Off with it, all of it," he said, "every thread, every stitch."

"Please, no!" she wept.

"Now," he said, "instantly."

Angrily, with hot, bitter tears, the Lady Alexina tore at the robes, frenziedly, ripping loose hooks, and fastenings, and then she stood before him, the bulky, cumbersome robes of concealment beside her, discarded.

Kurik then gathered up the robes, the hoodings and veils, and put them to one side, and then returned, to gaze upon the Lady Alexina.

The Lady Alexina looked to her robes, where they lay. Given the length of her chain she could not reach them.

Then she straightened her body, angrily, and looked into the eyes of Kurik. I was uneasy. No slave would have dared to look into the eyes of a man so.

"Marvel," she said, acidly. "My robes no longer obstruct your vision."

"One," said Kurik, "perhaps two—two silver tarsks."

"Monster!" she cried.

Certainly her lineaments might now be ascertained as easily as might be those of a slave.

I was uneasy. Did he not know she was a free woman?

"Off your feet," he said to her.

Angrily she lowered herself to the floor.

To be a woman unclothed before a clothed male has its decided effect on the woman; similarly, to be an unclothed woman, not permitted to stand, placed, reduced and controlled, before the male, at his feet, as might be a slave, increases her sense of helplessness, exposure, and vulnerability, and her recognition of her now-undeniable femaleness.

Kurik then regarded the Lady Alexina, clad only in her shackle.

"Now, Phyllis," he said, "fetch the whip."

"Surely not, Master," I said.

The Lady Alexina paled with fear.

"Now," he said.

"Yes, Master," I said, and hurried to the stairs.

I trusted he would not strike her. She was bared. Too, she was a free woman. One does not whip a free woman. On the other hand, the Lady Alexina had not appeared to be convinced of that.

In a matter of an Ehn or two I had returned to the basement, and, kneeling, head down, with both hands, lifted the whip to Kurik, my master.

Kurik then turned to the Lady Alexina.

"Where is the Lady Bina?"

"I do not know!" she said.

"You know," he said.

"No!" she cried, looking up at him.

"Perhaps now," he said, "now that you are stripped, you would particularly appreciate the return of your parasol."

"Surely," she said, "if only to better conceal myself from your unabashed perusal."

Kurik then, to my relief, folded the blades of the whip about the handle, clipped them closed, and hooked the handle at his belt.

I could now understand the current value of the lovely parasol, formerly so fetching an element in the ensemble of the Lady Alexina. Her desire now made sense to me, particularly as she was free. Opened, she could, in effect, conceal herself behind it.

Kurik then went to the parasol, which was closed, and, interestingly, grasped it at its closed end, rather than at the small, narrow, trimmed handle. As it was closed, the ribs, or spines, of the parasol were above and about the handle. He then, suddenly, jabbed it toward the Lady Alexina, and she shrieked, and drew back. He then snapped it open and, twirling it, leaned toward her. There was a rattle of chain. She had now shrunk back, flattening herself against the wall. She had turned white, and her features trembled with terror. "Take it away! Take it away!" she cried.

"Very well," said Kurik and he returned the parasol to where it had earlier lain.

Clearly the Lady Alexina, for some reason, feared the parasol. I could not understand her fear. To me, of course, it seemed harmless. Perhaps she was afraid, abnormally so, for some reason, that Kurik might strike her with it.

"Where is the Lady Bina?" asked Kurik.

"I do not know," she said, sullenly.

Kurik's hand went thoughtfully, speculatively, to the butt of the whip, hooked at his belt.

"Lash me," she said. "I will never speak!"

"All free women should be lashed, and made slaves," said Kurik. "It would be good for them. It would teach them they are women."

I was sure that Kurik would never strike a free woman. Few male Goreans would do so. To be sure, the free woman would have no guarantee of that. Gorean masters, on the whole, incidentally, seldom apply the lash, even to their slaves. There is seldom any point in doing so. The slave attempts to be pleasing, honestly and fervently, to the best of her ability. It would be absurd then to do her hurt. She is a prized possession, a treasure, lovely and desirable; she is the most delicious thing a male can own. Let him rejoice in his slave. There she is, at his feet, curled, exquisitely desirable, needful, hoping for a smile, or a caress. She longs not for a whipping, but for her possession, her being owned, her ravishing. She is her master's possession and plaything, and would have it no other way. She longs for discipline; she desires to be taken in hand, and subdued. She desires to yield the surrender that, in any case, she knows would be taken from her. She longs to be mastered. So work her, and well, and enjoy her, and never let her forget she is a female, and, in a collar, a slave. It is enough that the whip is there, and she knows, if it is appropriate, it will be used on her. This is very different from the case of the free woman. The free woman and the slave sense they are competitors, rivals. Thus, free women can be very cruel to slaves. Slaves commonly hope they will not be purchased by a woman.

"I will never speak!" she cried. "Starve me! Put water outside my reach! I will never speak!"

"We do not have time for such things," said Kurik.

His face was unreadable. This frightened me.

"I will not speak!" she cried.

"You are my prisoner," he said. "Though you are a free woman, you are naked, on a chain, as might be a slave."

"So?" she said.

"Perhaps then," he said, "as a free woman, you would like to earn your keep."

"'My keep'?" she asked.

"Being kept alive," he said.

"You do not frighten me," she said.

"Remember," he said, "you are a free woman. You are not a slave, not a domestic animal, protected by her collar, not a property, a loot, which would merely change hands. You are a free woman."

"You would do well to spare me," she said.

"Why?" he asked.

"The vengeance of Decius Albus," she said.

"By tomorrow," said Kurik, "Decius Albus will realize you are in our hands, and will discard you, a tool that is no longer useful, and, unfortunately, will change the location of the Lady Bina."

"If you slay me," she said, "I will never reveal the location of the Lady Bina!"

"And if you do not," he said, "of what use are you to us?"

"Collar me," she said.

"You would look well in one," he said, "but what woman would not?"

The Lady Alexina rose to her knees, and extended her hands, piteously, to Kurik, my master.

"You look well on your knees," he said. "Split them."

"Please, no!" she said.

"Now," he said. "And now, back on your heels, place your hands, palms down, on your thighs. Get your back straight, get your head up."

Then the Lady Alexina, though free, was before him, in nadu, the position of a Gorean pleasure slave.

"Put the iron to my thigh," she begged. "Mark me! Put me in the degrading, scandalous scrap of cloth, fit only for a slave!"

"No," he said. "I deny you the protection of a collar. For my purposes it is important that you be free."

"What are you going to do?" she asked.

Kurik then turned to me. "Has Lyris been fed?" he asked.

"No," I said.

"Then she must be quite hungry," he said.

"I do not know," I said, "but surely sooner or later."

"Who is Lyris?" asked the Lady Alexina.

"Look to the cage," said Kurik, as he bent down and disengaged the shackle on the fair ankle of the Lady Alexina.

"No!" she said.

At the same time, Lord Grendel, who had maintained until now a discreet silence in the presence of the Lady Alexina, presumably that she might think of him as no more than a simple guard beast, one of an unusual nature, went to the cage and said something, in Kur, to Lyris, who, snarling, withdrew, going to the back of the cage. Lord Grendel then freed and held open the gate of the cage.

"No, no!" cried the Lady Alexina, held by the arm, being dragged by Kurik to the cage. She was then thrust within and Lord Grendel closed the gate, fastening it shut with the heavy chain and padlock.

The Lady Alexina cast a wild look at Lyris, snarling in the back of the cage, and turned, and pressed herself piteously against the bars of the gate, extending her small hands through them.

"Mercy!" she cried. "Let me out! Let me out!"

"Well, pretty Lyris," called Kurik to Lyris, "here is your meal." Lyris, of course, would find Gorean unintelligible, but the meaning of the words was not lost on the Lady Alexina, who, doubtless, having seen Lord Grendel work the opening and closing of the gate, now realized he was no simple guard beast. Too, for all she knew, if Gorean might be at the disposal of one beast, it might be at the disposal of another, as well. And, if Kurik's words were no more than the cheerful prattling of a man to a beast, such as a pet sleen, there was still little in that possibility from which to gather reassurance or consolation. "Note, Lyris," called Kurik to Lyris pleasantly, "your supper has been nicely prepared. You will not have to bite, and chew, and tear, through cloth."

"Let me out!" screamed the Lady Alexina, reaching through the bars toward Kurik.

"You are free," Kurik reminded her.

"Collar me!" she cried. "I beg the collar, I beg it!"

"It is denied to you," said Kurik, "be wished well, free woman."

"Mercy!" she begged.

Kurik turned away.

"When does it feed?" she screamed.

"I do not know," said Kurik, "but it will feed, sooner or later."

Kurik and Lord Grendel then, followed by me, left the basement. I was much disturbed.

On the upper floor, I threw myself to my knees before my master, and wept. "Please, Master," I begged, "do not resign her, even though she be an enemy and free, to so horrible a death!"

"Do not be concerned," said Lord Grendel, "I informed Lyris that if she so much as touches the Lady Alexina, I will kill her."

I collapsed to the floor, in relief.

Shortly thereafter we heard piteous screams from the basement. "I will speak! I will speak! I will speak!"

CHAPTER FIFTY-ONE

Crossed spears barred our way.

Kurik flourished the ribbon of yellow paper, embossed with the red seal of Decius Albus. As we had supposed, the Lady Bina was being held in the House of a Hundred Corridors. This had been confirmed by the Lady Alexina, beside herself with hysteria, in Lyris' cage. More importantly, she had revealed the secret location of the Lady Bina's quarters within the palace. Kurik's pretext for gaining admittance to the palace was twofold, first, supposedly to guarantee the current safety and well-being of the Lady Bina, for Lord Grendel, and, second, to make clear to Decius Albus, who would convey the information to Surtak and his cohorts, that Lyris was in our custody and would be returned, safely and unharmed, for Eve. We anticipated little opposition to this proposal. The case with the Lady Bina was quite otherwise. She was brought from her hiding place, cell, or quarters, to a court chamber near the front of the palace. There, unseen ourselves, by means of a secret panel, we observed her, sitting, being shown varieties of rich cloths by slaves, from amongst which cloths she might choose, for the measuring and sewing of robes. It seemed she was pleased with everything shown. She seemed intent, and in good spirits, and did not seem aware she was in any sense a prisoner. She was then, after a time, her business seemingly concluded, conducted away, to be returned to her secret location in the palace, which secret location was now known to us, thanks to the intelligence afforded by the Lady Alexina, who had been only too pleased to be removed from Lyris' cage and returned to her shackle, fastened at the slave ring.

The spears were pulled away, and Kurik and I proceeded down the hall. The embossed pass had been removed from the pouch of the Lady Alexina, which pass allowed her free movement in the palace.

We continued down the hall.

"It should not be far now," said Kurik.

I felt exceedingly uneasy, for several reasons. First, I was preceding my master. On a street, unless on a leash, being exhibited, this can bring the lash. Furthermore, we were in the House of a Hundred Corridors, clearly under false pretenses. Lastly, and perhaps most frighteningly, I was clad in garments that had been taken from the Lady Alexina. We had repaired the damage to her robes, the rent hooks, and such, as best we could. I was well veiled, and I had the parasol, which I used in such a way as to give a casual onlooker very little opportunity to look closely upon me. I often looked down, or away, to the side, that the color of my eyes not be noticed. Decius Albus, Drusus, Tyrtaios, and some others, doubtless, would be aware of the coloring of the Lady Alexina, but many guards, we hoped, would not. They could, however, recognize the meaningfulness of the pass.

"We are on the third level, in the Corridor of Turia," said Kurik. "The Renata Chamber must be near."

"I hope so, Master," I said.

The corridor was long.

"If the Lady Alexina lied," said Kurik, "we will return and feed her to Lyris."

"I am sure she is aware of that," I said.

"Are you all right?" asked Kurik.

"Yes, Master," I said.

"Your step is uncertain, you are trembling," he said.

"Forgive me, Master," I said.

"You do not walk like a free woman," he said.

"I am not a free woman," I said.

"Nor are you much of an actress," he said.

"I am in a collar," I said. "Perhaps Master might have removed it."

"Do not be foolish," he said. "You belong in a collar, and I want you in a collar. Collars are not removed from slave girls until a new collar has been affixed."

"Surely sometimes it is done," I said. "Masters have little to fear. We cannot take off our brands."

"Are you a clever slave?" he asked.

"I do not know if I am clever," I said, "but I am highly intelligent. Else I fear I would be of little interest to Master."

I knew that men, the beasts, Gorean men, at least, loved to have their collars on intelligent women. Were they not the prizes? Did they not bring the highest prices? The three major criteria for selection by Gorean slavers were beauty, intelligence, and passion, helpless passion, slave passion, a woman's slave needs. And it was in the most intelligent women, commonly, that these needs were the deepest and the most profound, the most irresistible, and intense. How, once we were collared, these put us at the mercy of our masters, at whose mercy we soon begged to be!

"How do you like the Robes of Concealment?" he asked.

"It can be death to a slave who is not a serving slave to touch them," I said, "and it can be death to any slave who dares to wear them."

"How do you like them?" he asked.

"I do not like them," I said. "They are heavy, bulky, and cumbersome, the folds, layers, and draperies. Were free women not free women, I might almost feel sorry for them."

"But consider such robings," he said. "They are beautiful, are they not?"

"Yes," I said, "they are commonly very beautiful."

"They are concealing," he said. "Few raiders, without independent information, from the baths, or such, would care to risk their lives to seize such a woman, one who might, when unveiled, dismay a male tarsk. Slaves, thus, distract attention from free women, and are more likely to be carried off. This provides a measure of protection for their glorious and noble free sisters. Too, free women are likely to be more closely guarded. Too, of course, they like the contrast between themselves and slaves to be clearly marked. Too, hating slaves, they enjoy exhibiting and humiliating them, almost denying them clothing."

"Men do not seem to object," I said.

"That is true," he said.

"Nor do I," I said.

"You are a slave," he said.

"Yes, Master," I said.

In the beginning, many new slaves, just out of the pens, or shortly after feeling the capture loops, are terrified to be viewed in the garments in which they will now be placed, tunics that make their new status, that they are only slaves, clear to all, let alone camisks or ta-teeras. Sometimes they must be whipped into the streets. But later, reveling in the freedom of their collars, and having no choice but to move as what they are, women, and slaves, they, now perfect and real, having found their identity, and rejoicing in it, brazen in the recognition of their uniqueness, their specialness, and desirability, move with a naturalness befitting the lovely, graceful animals they now are, move with pride and joy, save in the presence of free women, of course, whom they muchly, and justifiably, fear.

"Tunics are more comfortable," I said. "It is easier to move in them."

"I would suppose so," said Kurik. "It is not that much different from being naked."

"We are naked, often enough," I said.

"Try to walk more like a free woman," he said.

"It is nice to have sandals," I said.

"Enjoy them while you can," he said.

"Yes, Master," I said.

"I trust guards will not observe you attentively," he said.

"Why?" I asked. "My eye color?"

"They probably will not do so, as you are with me," he said. "With me, they are likely to take you for what you seem. They are unlikely to be attentive, to be suspicious."

"I do not understand," I said.

"After even a rudimentary slave training," he said, "a woman is transformed, often in ways she does not even understand. She is different. She speaks like a slave. She thinks like a slave. She moves like a slave. She is a slave. Sometimes a slave, usually a new slave, foolishly thinking escape might be possible, dons the garments of a free woman, and hopes to pass herself off as a free woman. She may even have obtained the key to her collar, and removed it. But her movements, her walk, her carriage, her small gestures, induce suspicion, for they seem reminiscent not of a free woman, but a slave. She is detained, to her misery, by guardsmen. Free women are brought in and she is stripped. The brand is then revealed. Her first punishment is at the hands of the free women. It is not pleasant. She is then remanded to the authorities, and returned to her master."

"I see," I said.

"Too, of course," he said, "she may be investigated by means of her Home Stone, her family, her friends, her connections, her doings, her address, and so on."

"Each Gorean," I said, "has his place in society."

"Yes," he said, "and each slave girl hers."

"And where is that?" I asked.

"At the feet of her master," he said.

I felt warm, and grateful, and needful. What a wonderful gift was my bondage! I had come to realize that I had longed for it, even on Earth. Now, on Gor, I was in my collar!

"Stay on your feet," he said. "Do not kneel. Do not press against me."

"Yes, Master," I wept.

I longed to lie at his feet, naked, lifting my body to him, begging for the attentions to which a master frequently subjects a slave.

"If others are about," he said, "I would not use the word 'Master'."

"Yes, Master," I whispered.

"There is a guard," he said. "That must be the Renata Chamber."

"Tal," said Kurik. "The Lady Alexina calls upon the Lady Bina."

I gathered this was not an unfamiliar business from the guard's point of view. Quite possibly the Lady Alexina had frequently called upon the Lady Bina. That would make sense, I supposed, that one free woman would attend upon another. Kurik had not even displayed the pass that had brought him this far. He was not challenged, possibly because of my presence, I taken to be the Lady Alexina, possibly because of the assurance with which he presented himself, possibly because the guard was accustomed to seeing the Lady Alexina accompanied in the halls of the palace by one associate or another.

We were admitted into the Renata Room.

The door, which was ornate and heavy, was closed behind us. The room was large, bright, light, and airy. The walls were painted with rich colors, which was often the case in a Gorean dwelling. The room was richly appointed. There was nothing about it that suggested a cell, or an incarceration of any sort.

"Tal, dear Alexina," said the Lady Bina, pleasantly, approaching us. Her veils were lowered. I had the sense that she thought little of displaying her features. Her origins, I had been given to understand, were not Gorean. She was quite beautiful and, I did not doubt, was well aware of that fact. "What news from the Central Cylinder?" she asked. "Has the date been determined? Have the preparations for the Ceremony of Companionship been completed? Poor Marlenus. How he must chafe at these delays. He must be patient and brave. I trust you bring good news. I plan to remember you well, dear friend, for all your efforts, your comfort and counsel, when I am Ubara."

I knelt, which muchly puzzled the Lady Bina.

"Do not kneel, Alexina," she said. "I shall not expect that of you, my friend, even when I am Ubara."

"She is not the Lady Alexina," said Kurik. "She is a slave, my slave. Her name is 'Phyllis'. You know her from the house of Epicrates. I am Kurik, of Victoria, ally to Lord Arcesilaus, friend to your protector, Lord Grendel. You, noble lady, are in grave danger."

"You are the driver of the pay wagon," she said. She had engaged him, when arranging the transportation of Lord Grendel, and a slave, to the late-evening meeting at the house of Decius Albus, off the Viktel Aria, purportedly to make contact with a representative or representatives of Lord Arcesilaus.

"A ruse," he said, "to pursue a purpose."

"Does it seem to you that I am in danger?" asked the Lady Bina.

"I assure you, you are in dreadful danger, terrible danger," said Kurik.

"I am to be Ubara of Ar," she said.

"The Ubar," said Kurik, "has never seen you."

"Secretly," she said, "or my beauty was described to him."

"He does not even know you exist," said Kurik.

"Nonsense," said the Lady Bina. "He even sent an officer of the Taurentians to inform me of his suit, of the projected honor, and fetch me to this palace, while a thousand details were attended to."

"It was no Taurentian," said Kurik. "It was an Assassin, a member of the Black Caste, in the uniform of a Taurentian, Tyrtaios, by name."

"I do not understand," she said.

"You have been deceived, misled," said Kurik. "You are a hostage, who could be lightly sacrificed."

"I have been treated well here," she said.

"Of course," said Kurik. "Why should you not be?"

"Only a few Ehn ago, I ordered robing," she said.

"We were permitted to witness that," he said, "from a concealed vantage point."

"That was part of the deception?" she said.

"Of course," said Kurik.

"I am a prisoner?" she said.

"Surely, consider the guard, outside," said Kurik.

"He is there for my protection," she said.

"To prevent your escape," said Kurik.

"Slave," said Lady Bina, "brush back your hood, sweep aside your veils."

I did so.

"Am I in danger?" she asked.

"Yes, Mistress," I said.

"And slaves may not lie," said Kurik.

"They may be instructed to do so," she said.

"I will speak briefly, and plainly," said Kurik. "Lord Agamemnon still lives. He is active and dangerous. His cohorts are loyal and determined. He wishes to recruit Grendel to his service, as spy and tool, as

Grendel is respected, trusted, and well known to the faction of Lord Arcesilaus, which Lord Agamemnon wishes to supplant. If Grendel does not give his oath, your life is forfeit."

"Surely not," she said.

"Dear Lady," said Kurik, "I have no doubt that your intelligence is high, extremely so, but the data at its disposal, on which it must rely, is egregiously sparse, and bears little relation to the intrigues and complexities of this world. You are, forgive me, noble Lady, incredibly innocent and naïve. Your antecedents almost guarantee that. You are recently from a steel world, and you know little or nothing of this world, its customs, habits, and politics. You do not even have a Home Stone. How could you then expect, in a state such as Ar, rich and populous, to so simply ascend a throne? You lack family relations, connections, position, and power. Your ambition is unjustified, your hopes unfounded. If Marlenus knew of you, and truly desired you, would he not have confronted you in person, urging his suit with fervor?"

"But I am beautiful, am I not?" she asked.

"Very much so," he said, "but so, too, are thousands of others, a thousand times more plausibly poised to realize such an ambition."

"How am I to know what is true?" she asked.

"You can wait here to die," he said, "and then the matter will be clear."

"I am confused," she said. "I do not know what to do."

"We will try to get you out of the palace," he said. "Then you will be safe, at least for a time. If Marlenus attempts to search for you, and recover you, with all the resources of the state, then you will know his suit is genuine. If he does not, then you will know I speak the truth. Accompanying us, you have nothing to lose; remaining here, your life is in jeopardy, unless Lord Grendel delivers his oath to Lord Agamemnon."

"He must not," said the Lady Bina.

"Come with us," said Kurik.

"How can we leave the palace?" she asked.

"You will be hooded, and veiled, and dressed in the garments of the Lady Alexina. Accordingly, your progress from the palace should not be impeded."

"What of the guard?" asked the Lady Bina.

"I shall inconvenience the guard," said Kurik.

"What of the slave?" asked the Lady Bina.

"She is a slave," said Kurik. He then turned to me. "Remove your garments, to the tunic," he said, "and then assist the Lady Bina to assume her disguise."

"Yes, Master," I said.

Shortly thereafter the Lady Bina was in the garments of the Lady Alexina, even to the grasp of the parasol, and I, now bared to tunic and collar, as was appropriate, was now again on my knees, for I was in the presence of the free.

"May I speak?" I asked.

"Of course," he said.

"I understand that I am to be left here," I said. "That is obvious."

"Oh?" he said.

"Naturally I am uneasy," I said.

"I would think so," he said.

"My collar will protect me, I take it," I said, "as I am a slave, a mere beast. I will merely be newly acquired, differently owned?"

"Commonly," he said, "that would be the case. Who would slay a tharlarion or kaiila?"

"I do not wish to be differently owned," I said.

"Oh?" he said.

"It is not only my body that is yours," I said, "but my heart. You own the whole of me. It is the whole of me that is yours."

"I do not understand," he said, "speak clearly."

I looked up at him, with fear. It is hard to be at the feet of a man, owned, in his collar, mastered, his, and not be overwhelmed with the heat and rush of blood, the desires, hopes, and needs of one's sex. One knows oneself his property, his belonging. They are such magnificent, virile brutes, and one rejoices before them, at their feet, a succumbed slave. He dominates, we are dominated. He commands, and we, hoping to be found pleasing, hasten to obey. In our collars, we are returned to nature.

"I love you," I said.

I cried out with misery, as he seized my hair, and yanked me to my feet, and cuffed me, twice, and I tasted blood in my mouth, and he threw me angrily to his feet, and I put my head down over his feet, my hair over them, my forehead pressed against them. "Forgive me, Master," I said.

"Are you ready, Lady Bina?" inquired Kurik.

"Yes," she said.

"Then," said Kurik, "we shall call the guard."

He stepped back from me.

"The slave is not uncomely," said the Lady Bina.

"There are thousands better," he said.

"If, as you say," said the Lady Bina, "Kurii are involved in this, I do not think her collar will protect her. I know Kurii. There will be much rage and frustration. Some feed on humans. What would her collar be to them? What would her comeliness be to them? They will want satisfaction, retaliation, even blind, meaningless vengeance. She would be run for sport in the feeding lanes, she would be torn to pieces."

"I agree," said Kurik.

"Let her don the garments I discarded," said the Lady Bina, "and we shall attempt to effect our departure together."

"Our scheme would shortly come to ruination," said Kurik, "for you would not be allowed to leave the palace."

"If your claims are true, your story true," she said.

"They are," said Kurik, "and it is."

"Then," said the Lady Bina, "you have included the slave in your plans."

"Yes," said Kurik.

"She is a part of your plan," said the Lady Bina.

"Certainly," said Kurik.

"So she is condemned," said the Lady Bina, "to the fangs of Kurii, or perhaps to the tortures of the house of Decius Albus?"

"Not at all," said Kurik. "That is not my plan."

I looked up, quickly.

"On your feet, Phyllis," he said.

I sprang up.

"Recently," said Kurik, "at the behest of Decius Albus, I, in the guise of a merchant envoy from a mythical city, Mytilene, was introduced in, and entertained in, the Commerce Court, one of the receiving courts of the palace, and there, in that guise, met numerous officiaries, administrators, dignitaries, guests, clerks, and such, most having one thing or another to do with the commerce of Ar. The slave accompanied me, and, on the way to, and from, the receiving chamber, we passed numerous guards. And guards, as you know, as other men, are attentive to the carriage, features, and limbs of slaves."

"Yes, men are beasts," said the Lady Bina. "Please, continue."

"Phyllis," he said, "a barbarian, may not even be aware of how she was seen, and how she might be recalled."

I thought I was much more aware of that sort of thing than he suspected. I did not think it took long on Gor for a woman, collared and tunicked, to realize how men looked upon her. Who could mistake those bold, appraising glances, those frank, zestful inspections, which well reminded a girl she was a purchasable object. Here, at least in the case of a slave, there was nothing furtive, sly, quick, apologetic, or clandestine in those male looks, no more than to regard a dog or horse on my former world. Similarly, on Gor, the excitements and glories of biology, even in the case of free women, have never been denounced as shameful nor treated as crimes, inviting the intervention of guardsmen. Rather they are welcomed and celebrated.

"It is natural," said Kurik, "for a guard, or a man, looking upon a slave, to ponder how she might look, stripped, and helpless, chained at his slave ring."

"And you expect," said the Lady Bina, "that the guards will recall the slave, doubtless even associating her with you?"

"Certainly," he said, "they will not think twice about it."

"Go on," she said.

"Recently," he said, "when we attended the supposed trade meeting in the receiving chamber, we entered through the east gate of the palace. The guards should remember us there, or, at least, the slave. Men tend to remember slaves. This afternoon, however, we entered through the west gate of the palace, I and the supposed Lady Alexina."

"Where, may I ask," inquired the Lady Bina, "is the Lady Alexina?"

"Where it is quite appropriate for her to be," said Kurik, "chained, naked, in a basement."

"I see," said the Lady Bina.

"Now," said Kurik, "we will exit though the east gate of the palace, the supposed Lady Alexina, myself, and the slave. The guards at the east gate will assume that we had entered through the west gate and are now merely exiting by means of the east gate. They will think nothing of the Lady Alexina, I, and a slave, leaving by means of the east gate. Thus, there will be no question as to where the additional person, in this case, a slave, came from."

"What of the guard?" asked the Lady Bina.

"This lamp stand should do nicely," said Kurik, lifting, and hefting, the sturdy artifact. "And, I think, those drape pulls should do nicely for bonds, and, surely, there is enough veiling, and such, about to serve as a gag."

Shortly thereafter the Lady Bina summoned the guard into the room, while Kurik remained to the side, rather behind the door, as it would open. The guard became aware of Kurik's presence at about the same time that Kurik employed the lamp stand.

Seven or eight Ehn later Kurik, the Lady Bina, in the robes of the Lady Alexina, and I were ready to exit the Renata Chamber.

I could still taste the blood in my mouth, from the cuffing I had received. What a fool I had been! Did I not know that I was a slave? Did I not know that there was a collar on my neck, a brand on my thigh? Did I not know that slaves were worthless animals, that we were to be demeaned, scorned, exploited, worked, and ravished, that our purpose was to serve our masters and see to it that they received from us, at any moment they might desire, the most inordinate pleasures derivable from the body of a slave?

"May I speak?" I begged.

"Yes," said he.

I fell to my knees before him, Kurik, of Victoria, my master. I, though a slave, had dared to speak my heart to him.

"The beast is crying," said the Lady Bina.

I was muchly distraught.

I looked up.

"I fear," I said, "your slave has been displeasing. She begs the forgiveness of her master. She is contrite."

"It is acceptable for a slave to love her master," said Kurik. "What does it matter, one way or another? She is only a beast, an animal, a slave."

"But not to tell him so?" I said.

"It can bring the lash," he said.

"Then," I said, "the slave is so helpless, that her love burns so in her heart, but she dare not cry out her love for her master?"

"I wonder," said he, "if you would bring as much as a silver tarsk and, say, a half, in the market."

"Master!" I wept.

"Perhaps as much as two," he mused.

"Master, Master!" I wept.

"But I think," he said, "more soberly, upon reflection, you would probably go for a single silver tarsk. Yes, I think you would be a single-silver-tarsk girl, if that. You are, after all, a barbarian."

"Please do not sell me!" I begged.

How helpless we are as slaves, as properties!

"You would sweat, and leap, in any man's arms," he said.

"I am a slave," I said.

"Would you wish to be otherwise?" he asked.

"No, Master," I said.

"Why?" he said.

"Because I am a slave," I said. How vital I now was. How I loved my collar! Only after my collaring had I begun to live.

"We must be on our way," said the Lady Bina.

"Please do not sell me!" I begged.

"We shall see," he said.

Could he care for me, I wondered, wildly, if only a little? Then I chastised myself for so naive and absurd a thought.

Knew I so little of Gor?

What man would be fool enough to care for a slave? How he would be mocked by his peers! Would he not be the butt of many a merry jest? Chagrined he might, for a time, avoid the gymnasium, the baths, the gaming tables, the tarn races, the song dramas. Consider the dinners, the jokes, the gestures, the laughter! How amusing would be the very thought itself, a master, caring for a slave!

I looked up at him.

I saw in his eyes how he looked at me, a slave, at his feet.

"I beg to be kept," I said.

How far I was from the office on my former world!

"Perhaps," he said. "Your flanks are not without interest."

"A slave is pleased," I whispered.

He and the Lady Bina then exited the Renata Chamber. In the hall, he turned about, to regard me. "Heel," he said.

We then proceeded down the hall, I a bit behind, and on the left.

CHAPTER FIFTY-TWO

Please, Master, mercy!" I cried.

I was well stretched, standing on my toes; my wrists were bound tightly together, and drawn up, high over my head; I was naked; the rope that bound my wrists together was run through the ring fastened in the ceiling, and then brought down, diagonally, to the side, and tied about another ring in the wall, across the room.

"Forgive me, Master," I wept. "Please forgive me!"

"Who begs mercy?" he asked.

"Phyllis," I said, "Phyllis, the slave of Kurik of Victoria!"

He came about, and stood before me. I watched him unclip the blades of the slave whip.

I regarded this action with much uneasiness.

He lifted the whip before me, the blades dangling. "What is this?" he asked.

"A whip, a whip!" I said.

"What sort of whip?" he asked.

"A slave whip!" I wept.

"And what is it for?" he asked.

"The whipping of slaves," I said.

"And what are you?" he asked.

"A slave," I said, "Master."

I trusted he would not strike me.

"Mercy, Master!" I said.

I had meant no harm. Surely he must understand that! Surely the matter was trivial. I had only been angry, and jealous. I had not expected that matters would turn out as they had. Who could have expected that? I had merely wished to satisfy myself, to exert my powers, and revel in them, those of a slave. I had only wished to prove something to myself, to interest the fellow, to arouse him, and prove to myself that I could make him desire me, surely more than plain Paula, whom I would easily outdo, and then I, satisfied, the point made, having demonstrated my equivalence to, if not superiority to, Paula, I might scamper back to my master, leaving the fellow excited, stranded, abandoned, needful, abashed, miserable, distraught, and unfulfilled. Surely I had done that sort of thing, in a way, frequently enough, on my former world, long before I had the power of the collar and tunic, the actuality of the female slave, whose mere appearance and movements can drive a male mad with passion. Surely Drusus Andronicus was a handsome, powerful, attractive male. Surely he might figure in the dreams of a thousand slaves in their chains, but he was not my master. I had no particular interest in him. Indeed, in a way, I had a matter to settle with him, as he had once made a fool of me, when he had donned the disguise of a male slave, and tricked me into revealing the domicile of my master. How could I forget that? How could I forgive that? I was still angry. Though I had no doubt I would writhe helplessly in his arms, as might any slave, the matter had had little, if anything, to do with him, and a great deal, indeed, everything, to do with Paula. I had always regarded Paula, sweet, understanding, kindly, shy, unadorned Paula, plain Paula, with her books, and such, as far inferior to myself. Yet, on this world, incredibly enough, many men seemed to regard her as being more beautiful and desirable than I, even far more so. How they praised her, and stood back, marveling, their eyes alit with desire. How could this be? Was I not a thousand times more interesting and attractive than Paula? Surely there was no comparison. Indeed, on our former world, Paula had seemed appreciative, even grateful, that I, informed, attractive, and chic, would let her be my friend. I did not mind doing so, of course, you must understand. I liked, and do like, Paula, and very much. Who could not be fond of so simple, earnest, honest, sweet, and devoted a creature? Where I had often sensed that others were critical of me, or jealous of me, or did not like me, Paula was always steadfast in her respect and affection. Indeed, I think Paula was my only true friend. In any event, I could understand the interest of men in me. That had been clear enough on my former world. Was I not the sort of woman they had been taught to prefer, well-dressed, clever, attractive, and witty? I could well understand how slavers might select me, how I could be brought to Gor, put in a collar, and sold. But I could not understand that in the case of Paula. Yet, incredibly enough, we had been handcuffed together and brought to Gor together. And many of these men, these intelligent, powerful, virile brutes, these men who carried the blood of masters in their veins, seemed to prefer Paula! It was she they wanted at their feet! Indeed, Paula had sold for a golden tarsk, had been bought from the central block of the great Curulean auction house itself. On the other hand, I had gathered that two silver tarsks might be a good price for me, indeed, a splendid price for me! I suppose I was jealous of Paula. I did not care for our roles to be reversed. Was she truly such a "collared Ubara," and I little more, if that, than a pot girl, or a kettle-and-mat girl? To be sure, few pot girls or kettle-and-mat girls would go for, say, two silver tarsks! In any event, following the abduction of Lyris and, far more importantly, the extraction of the Lady Bina from the House of a Hundred Corridors, consternation, and fury, must have reigned in the enemy's camp. I doubted that Kurii brooked frustration with equanimity. The savagery, and rage, of such beasts was a most fearful prospect to consider. Lord Agamemnon, if he were truly about, a living brain, unbodied, might howl through the speakers of his sophisticated ensconcement. Surtak might be ready to bite and tear his way through a hundred men. Decius Albus, from whose house, or palace, the Lady Bina had been removed, might be sick with terror. Surely one does not lightly disappoint or displease Kurii. Surely he would be desperate to placate his mighty allies, to remedy matters to whatever extent possible, to redeem the plausibility of his house, to reassert the sturdiness of his allegiance and the value and reliability of his service. Yet we had heard little of late. Matters had been muchly calm. Perhaps Kurii had, by now, having no option, resigned themselves to their defeat. Perhaps, on the other hand, this calm boded a gathering storm. A surface may seem placid, concealing currents, roiling below. Lord Grendel had repudiated the game of Lord Agamemnon, and substituted his own. But somewhere a new game might be in progress, with moves and pieces yet unnoticed. Lady Bina, in any event, as there was no sign of public concern or agitation at her removal from the House of a Hundred Corridors, as exhortations, alarms, proclamations, offers of rewards for her return or information leading to her return, and such, were not being broadcast throughout the city and countryside, as there was no hue from the public criers or letterings in red on the public boards, as the city was not swarming with soldiers and guardsmen searching for her, had come to reconcile herself, however, reluctantly, to the fact that her presence in the House of a Hundred Corridors had not been a benevolent sequestration prior to an eminent companionship but a detention, and one of a possibly dark import. The first sign of some

contact between the factions of Lord Agamemnon and Lord Arcesilaus had occurred this morning, when Drusus Andronicus, on behalf
of Surtak, had called on Lord Grendel to arrange for the return of
Lyris, accepting, as was not surprising, Lord Grendel's proposal of an
even exchange. Doubtless, from the point of view of Surtak, such an
exchange was an indication of simple madness or an incredible lack of
perception on the part of Lord Grendel, to return Lyris, an unusually
beautiful Kur female, I had gathered, for a monstrosity, part human
and part Kur, Eve. Surely Lord Grendel, as I well knew, was well aware
of the charms of Lyris, and yet, as I recalled, he had asserted that she
was nothing, no more than a tarsk, compared to Eve.

"No, my dear Drusus," had said Kurik, "the Lady Bina is not here."

Drusus had called at the apartment above the shop of Epicrates,
where Lord Grendel, ax at hand, saw fit to be found.

"She is elsewhere," continued Kurik, "where, we trust, she is safe."

I supposed this was at the house, in the basement of which Lyris
was still encaged, she, a high one, as though she might be no more
than a slave.

"Noble Tenrik," had said Drusus, "we are not so obtuse as to suppose that the lovely Bina would be on these premises."

I smiled at Drusus, that he might be aware that I, at least, appre-
ciated the cleverness of his remark, the subtle barb. My approval did
not seem noticed by him, but I supposed the point, nonetheless, had
been taken. I knelt a bit closer to him than would be the normal distance. Usually a slave remains to the side, to be unobtrusive, and yet
in attendance.

"I come for another purpose altogether," said Drusus. "I bring
words from Surtak, colleague of Decius Albus, to Lord Grendel."

Lord Grendel was crouched near Kurik, at his left, a little behind
him. His eyes were much on Drusus.

"Does Lord Grendel follow Gorean?" asked Drusus.

"Yes," said Kurik, "no translator will be necessary."

"He speaks it, as well?" inquired Drusus.

"Yes," said Kurik, "but you might find it difficult, at first, to understand him, so he has asked me to speak for him, to interpret his Gorean
for you, and so on."

"I can understand him, Master," I said. Then I put my head down.
"Forgive me, Master," I said. I had not been asked to speak, nor had I
requested permission to speak. However, I had not thought it amiss to
let Drusus be aware that I possessed this skill, one that he might well

lack. It would not hurt for him to know I was rather special, and gifted, as well as beautiful.

Neither Drusus, Kurik, nor Lord Grendel paid me any attention.

I fear I reddened.

But who would notice?

"My principal, in this business, Surtak, high Kur," said Drusus, "informs Lord Grendel that his terms, expressed in the proposal recently tendered to Decius Albus, by Tenrik of Siba, in the House of a Hundred Corridors, are accepted."

"Splendid," said my master. "Now we must arrange sensitive matters, such as the time, place, and conditions of the exchange."

"Surely," said Drusus.

"Phyllis," said Kurik, "fetch ka-la-na."

"Yes, Master," I said, rising easily and gracefully, as a slave does. I then, with a glance at Drusus, and a smile, went toward the chest, for glasses, and a bottle.

"I should inquire," said Drusus, "after the Lady Alexina. Decius Albus is no longer interested in her, save perhaps to put her in a collar and sell her, but Surtak is interested in her."

"Why?" asked Kurik.

"She is a duped, failed operative," said Drusus.

"For what, then, would he want her?" asked Kurik.

"For sport, for running her in the feeding trough," said Drusus.

The lid of the chest up, I, kneeling before the chest, started, the glasses I was holding touching one another. Nothing broke.

"What is wrong, Phyllis?" asked Kurik.

"Nothing, Master," I said.

"They bet on such things," said Drusus. "Surtak wishes the Lady Alexina to be turned over to him."

"We shall take the matter under consideration," said Kurik.

I then placed the glasses and bottle on the small, low table at the side of the room. Kurik and Drusus took their places, sitting cross-legged, at the table, and Lord Grendel crouched near it. I, kneeling beside it, then began to fill the glasses.

"No," said Drusus, "the master, first the master."

I had already begun my campaign to interest and arouse Drusus Andronicus.

"Forgive me, Master," I said, and filled the glass of Kurik. I then, head down, slowly, very slowly, lingering in the service, filled the glass of Drusus Andronicus.

"She is a barbarian," said Kurik.

Did he really think I knew no better?

I put a bit of ka-la-na in Lord Grendel's glass, in whose paw, or hand, the glass almost disappeared. Lord Grendel was almost twice the size of the men. He seldom drank. I think this had something to do with his Kur blood. Might it not be dangerous to give ka-la-na or paga to a larl?

"I am fond of a barbarian," said Drusus, "a hot, shapely slut whom I put to frequent, ruthless use. She juices at the snapping of my fingers and crawls to my feet, whimpering, begging, like a she-sleen in heat. I hope one day to buy her. Her name is 'Paula'."

"Do you know," asked Kurik, "that she and my Phyllis are acquainted, that they knew one another on the Slave World, that they were brought to Gor on the same chain, so to speak?"

"What a difference," laughed Drusus, "that beauty and this, forgive me, pot girl."

"Now, now, dear Drusus," said Kurik, "Phyllis is scarcely a pot girl. She might bring nearly two tarsks."

"Paula went for a golden tarsk," said Drusus.

"And a steal, at that," said Kurik, unnecessarily in my view.

"I think so," said Drusus, whose opinion, as far as I could see, was not required on the matter.

"There is much to be said for pot girls and kettle-and-mat girls," said Kurik. "They frequently make the best of slaves."

"And," said Drusus, "often enough one man's pot girl is another man's preferred slave, and sometimes one man's preferred slave is no more than another man's pot girl."

"It is all very mysterious," said Kurik.

"Did you know, Phyllis," asked Drusus, "that Paula has often spoken of you, that she is concerned for you, that she has never forgotten you, that she wants you to be happy, that she hopes you will find yourself owned by one who will master you to the last corpuscle in your body, that you will find yourself in the collar of your dreams?"

"No," I said, "I did not know that."

He sipped the ka-la-na.

"You talk to her?" I asked.

"Of course," he said, "frequently, and at length."

"She is a slave," I said.

"It is the whole woman," he said, "who is owned."

"She is attractive?" I asked.

"Very much so," he said.

Something in me was very angry that Paula would be concerned for me. Was this not another thing to hold against her? Was she so superior that she would wish me well! How concerned, how solicitous, how condescending! Did she think I was pitiful? How dared she speak of me to a master? Was I not a thousand times the woman, a thousand times the beauty she was? Was this not recognized, even by Paula? And so Drusus Andronicus regarded her as attractive, did he? We shall see about that! He will see how attractive she is when compared to a truly attractive woman, a true beauty!

"Perhaps, Master," I said to Drusus Andronicus, "dear Paula is below, or nearby, in the street, waiting, chained to a ring. I might then visit with her. I would be so happy to see her."

"*Ela*," said he, "kajira. She is not about. Uncertain as to the outcome of this meeting, whose prospects now seem bright, I left her behind, in the house of Decius Albus, in the House of a Hundred Corridors."

"Oh," I said, as though disappointed.

But this response much pleased me. I had hoped it would be so. The last thing I wanted was for Paula to be about.

The men, and Lord Grendel, then, affably and civilly, began to discuss a number of arrangements that might appertain to the projected exchange of two captives, Lyris, a Kur female, and Eve, whose nature or status seemed less clear.

Soon Drusus was ready to make his departure.

"May I accompany Master Drusus to the street," I asked my master, "that I may inquire after my friend, Paula?"

"Yes," he said, readily enough. Surely he had no reason to suspect that my request might be less than disingenuous.

Past the stairs, on the street, I knelt before Drusus.

"Paula is well, kajira," said Drusus. "Perhaps she wishes the collar on her neck was other than that of Decius Albus."

"Perhaps she would like to be in the collar of Master Drusus," I said.

"Perhaps," he said.

"Master Drusus finds her attractive?" I said.

"Yes," he said, "certainly."

"Am I not attractive, as well?" I asked.

"You are not badly curved," he said. "I find it easy to believe some men might find you of interest. You and Paula both seem to have been bred to wear a collar and tunic, but then I suppose you both were, as you are both women."

"Perhaps Master finds me of interest," I said, putting my head to his thigh.

"Were I, passing on a street, to find you chained on a slave shelf," he said, "it is true that I might look twice."

"I find Master handsome and strong," I said. "Does he not feel Phyllis near him?"

"I am not unaware of your proximity," he said.

"Is Paula truly so attractive?" I whispered.

"Yes," he said.

"Is Phyllis, too, attractive?" I asked.

"Yes," he said.

"Does Paula please Master?" I asked.

"Very much so," he said.

"Let Phyllis please you more," I whispered.

"Bara!" he said, sharply.

Instantly, not even thinking, reflexively, I went to bara. I felt my ankles crossed and tied together. I could not then rise. I was in consternation. My wrists were crossed, and bound together, behind my back. "Master!" I protested. He then lifted and turned me, placing me, seated, against the wall of the building, near the foot of the stairs. I sat there, looking up at him, my knees drawn up a bit, my wrists bound behind me, my ankles tied together. "Please let me go," I said. "Please untie me! Free me, I beg you, Master! I meant no harm! Do not let my master find me like this!"

Drusus then drew my tunic down at the left shoulder, and, with a marking stick removed from his pouch, firmly pressing in the lettering, inscribed something on my left shoulder. "Please, come back," I begged. "Please free me!" But I could see nothing then but his back, as he strode angrily away.

"Please, Master, mercy!" I had cried.

I was well stretched, standing on my toes; my wrists were bound tightly together, and drawn up, high over my head; I was naked; the rope that bound my wrists together was run through the ring fastened in the ceiling, and then brought down, diagonally, to the side, and tied about another ring in the wall, across the room.

"Forgive me, Master," I had wept. "Please forgive me!"

"What a petty, worthless slut you are," he said, shaking out the blades of the whip.

"Forgive me," I begged.

"Do you think," said he, "I was not aware of your clumsy,

transparent attempts to interest our guest, to intrude your presence upon him, the proximity, in violation of customary distance, the smiling, the glances, the movements, the way of pouring the wine, your solicitation to accompany him to the street, on the pretext of learning more about a friend, and such?"

How helpless I was, tied as I was!

"I meant no harm," I said. "Master Drusus is fine, and handsome, but I have no interest in him. I have no desire for his collar. Yours is the touch for which I long, Master!"

"You wished to interest Drusus Andronicus," he said.

"Yes," I said, "but not as you think!"

"You failed," he said.

"Yes, Master," I said.

"I can well imagine it," he said, "the words, the protestations, the pleadings, the movements, the soft looks, the earnest words! Doubtless you put yourself at his feet, closely, as well."

"Yes, Master," I said.

I had pressed my cheek against his thigh. We are taught many ways to excite and please a master, ways that, when sincerely tendered, have their effect on ourselves, as well. This, of course, had not been the case with Drusus Andronicus as my intentions had had nothing to do with him but only with my own vanity. My performance had been feigned, my words empty, my actions lies.

"But all was for naught," he said.

"Yes, Master," I wept.

"You failed to interest him," he said.

"Yes," I said.

"But you tried," he said.

"Yes, Master," I said.

"Do you know what was written on your shoulder?" he asked.

"No, Master!" I said. My body was beginning to ache, as I was stretched.

"It was a simple message," he said. "It was merely the word 'No', and then his signature. You were a rejected slave."

"The matter," I wept, "had nothing to do with Master Drusus. It had to do with my jealousy of Paula. I wanted to prove that I could do what she could do, that I could interest he whom she had interested. It was to be my vengeance on Paula for her being so preferred to me, my vengeance on her for having sold for a golden tarsk, for having been sold at the Curulean, from the central block!"

"You would try to seize the affections of he for whom she, your friend, might care?"

"I did not want his affections," I said. "I only wanted to arouse him and then reject him."

"And thus prove yourself superior to her, by winning and then lightly discarding a prize for which she, herself, might scarcely dare hope?"

"Too, Master Drusus once tricked me, made me seem a fool. Might I not then hope to discomfit him, if only a little?" I wept.

Kurik then, the blades of the whip loose, suddenly rent the air, with a blazing hiss, but a few inches from me.

I shrieked with fear, startled, dangling in the ropes.

Kurik of Victoria regarded me. I trusted he would not strike me.

"You have not been pleasing, Phyllis," he said.

I regarded him.

"Forgive me!" I cried.

His eyes were hard.

"No, no!" I cried.

I was then lashed.

Afterward, freed of the ropes, I lay, sobbing, shaking, below the whipping ring. My body was afire. I had been switched, now and then, occasionally, but I had never before, even in my training, been subjected to the attentions of the slave lash.

"Do not fear, worthless slut," he said. "It will not mark you. It will not reduce your value. You will be marketed the same as before, only now there will be a difference. You will know what it is to have felt the slave lash."

How I had twisted in the ropes, dangling, crying out, scarcely comprehending the pain. Let those who have never felt the lash scoff at it, or speculate how they would brave it. What fools they are! They have never felt it!

"Forgive me, Master," I wept.

I think he had returned the whip, the blades clipped, to his belt.

"Please do not sell me," I begged.

"Why should I not sell you?" he asked.

"Because I am your slave," I said. "I want to be your slave. I want to please you, so much! I want desperately to be found pleasing by you! I am in your collar! You are my master!" I dared not cry out my love for him. I did not want to be cuffed, or kicked, or put again under the lash! How unworthy I was, a woman of Earth, a barbarian, even to be the despised slave of such a male!

"You were not pleasing," he said.

"Forgive me, Master," I said.

As I lay at his feet, lashed, sobbing, my skin aflame, my greatest pain, by far, was my remorse, my bitter shame and grief, that he had seen fit to beat me. I had not been found pleasing. The depth, the globality, the poignancy of this misery is perhaps comprehensible only to a woman who has been a man's slave.

"Do you know why you were beaten?" he asked.

"I attempted to interest another master," I said.

"What a fool you are," he said. "Do you think I do not know the nature of slave girls, how they relish being looked upon, how conscious they are of their attractions, how they love it that a scarcely garbed flank is viewed with interest, that one observes the sensitivity and delicacy of their features, speculates on what would be the touch of their lips, or hair, marvels at the provocativeness of a shoulder, a forearm, the delicious curve where hip meets waist, the madness of their ankles and calves, the joys of their bosoms, the loveliness of a waist, the sweet width of their love cradles, the excitements of their throats, locked in their collars. Why do you think we buy and own them! And do you not think they do not well know why they are bought and owned? They love being the fullest, the most complete, and most perfect of women."

"I do not understand," I whispered.

"A master," he said, "might even, as a matter of hospitality, put you to the feet of a guest, have you report to a friend, and so on."

Somehow I suspected he would not do so.

"I can understand," he said, "how a slave might find another master attractive. Bondage causes a woman to see a great many men as attractive. Are they not possible masters? It illuminates the opposite sex in a way no other condition can."

"Yes, Master," I said. Certainly, as a slave, a woman sees men much differently from a free woman. I knew this from my own case. In a tunic and collar one was in no doubt as to what one was, and the radical centrality of sex to what it is to be human.

"Much depends on the slave and master," he said. "If one has no particular interest in a slave, and she is no more than another plate or goblet, another vase or brush, and she desires another master, and he is interested in her, one might give her to him, or, better, sell her to him. Indeed, one might enjoy making him pay more than she is worth. That is amusing. Would you like me to give you to Drusus Andronicus, or sell you to him?"

"No, no, Master!" I said.

"Or take you to a market, and get rid of you there?"

"No, Master!" I said.

"To be sure," he said, "there are proprieties to be observed. It would be fully appropriate for you to be lashed for what you did. One cannot have slaves going about like free women."

"No, Master," I said.

"Perhaps you think that is why you were beaten," he said.

"Surely, Master," I said.

"Not at all," he said. "It was clear to me that you had no interest in Master Drusus and he none in you, other, of course, than the materially obvious facts that you would see him as an attractive male, which I suppose he is, and that he would see you as not without interest, which you are not without."

"It all had to do with Paula," I said.

"Of course," he said. "That is clear."

"And I was still whipped?" I said.

"Of course," he said. "I had not known until then what a vain, petty, worthless slut you were. Paula is your friend. She feels for you, is concerned for you. Why then should you wish to outdo her, to demean and hurt her, and, in a sense, steal from her? Drusus Andronicus may be fond of her, and she may care for him, and you, supposedly her friend, to assuage your jealously, to soothe your wounded vanity, would gratuitously intrude yourself between them? What if Drusus Andronicus had succumbed to your fraudulent overtures? What then of Paula, who cares for you, of Paula, your friend?"

"I did not think of her," I said.

"You thought only of yourself," he said, "and your pride."

"Yes, Master," I said.

"Had you many friends on the Slave World?" he asked.

"I was popular, very popular," I said.

"Had you many friends?" he asked.

"No," I said. "Many sought my company, and flattered me. But I do not know what they felt, or said, behind my back. I think they did not really like me. One senses such things."

"Perhaps," said he, "they were jealous, of your looks, your taste, your charm, your popularity?"

"I do not know," I said. "But I think they did not really like me."

"Perhaps you were not all that likable?" he said.

"I wanted to be liked," I said.

"So, how many friends had you?" he asked.

"Only one, truly," I said.

"Paula?"

"Yes," I said. "She was my friend—my only friend."

"And now," he said, "you have lost her."

"No!" I said. "No, Master!"

"How could it not be so?" he asked.

"Surely Master Drusus would not tell Paula!" I said.

"He will, surely," he said.

"No," I wept, "no!"

"He will not let her live on in ignorance, misinformed and deluded," he said. "One she thought her friend proved herself not to be so. She must learn of this, and will learn of it."

"No, no," I said.

"You no longer have a friend," he said.

"No!" I said.

"You have lost her," he said.

"No," I said, "no, no!"

I lay beneath the whipping ring, sobbing. I had not realized until then how grievously I had betrayed Paula, and might have injured her. I had not realized until then how much she had meant to me, and for so long, how understanding, devoted, and precious she was, how important she had been in my life. I shook with tears, miserable and desolate, empty and lost. How fortunate I had been, one such as I, so light and frivolous, so smug and pretentious, so trivial and unworthy, to be befriended by one such as she, so deep and loving. I had not felt for her, nor accorded her, the appreciation she deserved. I had taken her for granted. I had treated her as little more than a mirror in whose reflection I might admire myself. I had pitied her, and treated her with condescension, the only true friend I had ever known, forgiving and uncritical, selfless, sweetly affectionate, patient with my vanity, tolerant of my superficiality, caring for me as I was, not expecting me to change, not wanting me to be different.

I shook with sobs.

She had been near, and little noted. She had been a treasure, ignored or scorned. I had looked at her and not seen her.

She had been my friend.

And now I had lost her.

"Master!" I wept. But he had turned his back, and walked away. I looked after him, agonized. Had I lost my master, as well? "Master," I called after him, "am I not to be chained to your slave ring?" But he made no response. Later that night I crawled to the foot of his couch, and lay down, beneath the slave ring.

He was on the couch, asleep.

I was very quiet, that I not disturb him.

CHAPTER FIFTY-THREE

There," said Kurik, pointing.

"Yes," said Lord Grendel. "I see."

The high cities of Gor are, for the most part, within the pomeriums, or legal boundaries, of the cities, tower cities. These towers, often in their clusters, cylindrical and rearing, loom well over the walls of the city. They may be seen from many pasangs away. Pomeriums, as noted, are the legal boundaries of a city. The lines of the pomerium are often not identical with the lines of a city's walls. Sometimes the pomerium extends beyond a city's walls, and, sometimes, it is within the walls, and the same pomerium might be partly within the walls and partly outside. The pomerium and the walls are, so to speak, independent of one another. The pomerium will commonly antedate the walls. Many pomeriums are ancient. They may be established in various ways. Some are related to a plowed line, often attributed to a legendary figure; others might be determined, given the auspices, by a given number of hides that are cut into exceedingly narrow strips, these strips later being joined to form a cord, the cord then used to circumscribe a given area. A surprisingly large area may be enclosed in this fashion. Still, again, the pomerium may date back to a territorial claim, usually backed by war, in which the pomerium line is scratched in the earth by the point of a sword or the tip of a spear. The same sword or spear may be used generations later, to fix the pomerium of a colony city, as Ar's Station to Ar herself. It may be clearly seen that the city walls and the pomerium may not be identical. The location of walls, for example, as well as their height and nature, as one would expect with military architecture, is heavily influenced by a consideration of the resources to be protected, their extent and nature, and the topographical features of the land. Too, walls may be extended and enlarged, or rebuilt. Sometimes, partial and scattered, there are the remains of abandoned walls within the city itself, as in the Metellan district, one of the older districts in Ar.

Such remnants may be preserved, as part of the city's history. Most of the stone from earlier walls, however, naturally enough, is incorporated in the newer walls. It might be mentioned, in passing, that the pomerium, as one would expect, given its legal status, is often attended by certain social and legal restrictions. For example, in some cities, a victorious general is not permitted to bring armed troops within the pomerium. Accordingly, the nature of triumphs, accorded to victorious commanders, triumphs celebrating successful campaigns, the acquisition of loot, the capture of prisoners and slaves, and such, might range from parades through the city in full panoply, displaying spoils, chains of slaves, and such, to processions in which the general and his troops appear unarmed and in civilian dress, to the music of bands, followed, to be sure, by wagons and carts of treasure, often drawn by naked, chained slaves, formerly women of the enemy. Each of the towers in a city is, in essence, a fortified keep, furnished with water and supplies. Thus, if walls should be breached, a city's population may withdraw into a number of stout, defensive strongholds. The cylindricality of the towers reduces the number of direct strikes by catapult stones, and maximizes the amount of living space in proportion to the exterior walls. These towers, which are almost always brightly colored, as Goreans are fond of bright colors, inside and outside, in both private and public buildings, in fountains and walls, and so on, are often joined, as well, at different levels, by narrow, graceful, colorful, arching, railless bridges. These bridges allow communication and movement amongst the cylinders, facilitating, in case of need, the passage of supplies and reinforcements, and, given their narrowness, may be easily defended, and, if it is thought judicious, may be broken, denying entrance to intruders.

"How many in the approaching party?" asked Kurik.

"There should be only two," said Lord Grendel.

It was not easy to see, this early, and for the wisps of fog swirling about the bridge.

The curvature of the bridge, too, was not helpful.

Lord Grendel straightened his body. When he did this he was some eight to nine feet in height.

He was intent. He peered ahead. His ears were delicately cupped, and, lifted, inclined forward.

I could see little. I could hear nothing.

It was chilly this early.

I was sick with fear at the height, narrowness, and arching curvature of the bridge. Most Goreans, of course, at least those of the "high cities," are familiar with such bridges, and think nothing of availing themselves of their convenience. They no more fear utilizing them than the average person of my former world would fear utilizing a common sidewalk. Who, leaving a house, would be afraid of going out and falling off a sidewalk? Yet, I think it could be understood that if that sidewalk were some hundred or more yards above ground the entire complexion of the matter would be altered. In any event, I was very frightened. It was all I could do to refrain from going to my hands and knees and crawling. Indeed, had I been alone, I would undoubtedly have done so. Indeed, had I been alone, I do not think I would have been where I was. The Goreans have a saying, "Let those who fear the high bridges not walk them." This bit of folk wisdom is one to which I subscribe, most heartily. Much, of course, depends on what one is used to. Even so, even Goreans recognize that it is not likely to be much in one's best interests to negotiate the high bridges while in desperate need of sleep or profoundly drunk.

Lord Grendel's nostrils widened, in that wide, dark, flattish muzzle. "Two," he said, "one Kur, Surtak, one human."

"Tyrtaios?" said Kurik.

"No," said Lord Grendel, "Drusus Andronicus."

I realized this determination might have been made by scent.

"Then it is as it should be," said Kurik.

I did not think that Lord Grendel had ever encountered Tyrtaios. He may have encountered his scent, about the apartment, and stairwell, in the house of Epicrates, when he had returned from the remote house of Decius Albus, off the Viktel Aria. He had, of course, met Master Drusus in the apartment, yesterday morning. Speculating that Lord Grendel might have determined the nature of the individuals perhaps a hundred paces ahead on the bridge, in the near darkness, made me decidedly uneasy. If he could manage such a thing, I did not doubt but what a Kur could, as well.

"Eve, in the care of a slave, is there?" asked Kurik.

"Yes," said Lord Grendel.

"It all goes as agreed," said Kurik.

"Yes," said Lord Grendel.

"I fear deceit, treachery," said Kurik.

"I do not think so," said Lord Grendel. "Surtak has honor, and he wants Lyris."

"The exchange will be effected, as planned?" asked Kurik.

"I think so," said Lord Grendel.

"And then?" asked Kurik.

"And then I am not sure," said Lord Grendel.

Lord Grendel, in one hand, or paw, grasped his great ax. Kurik had with him a crossbow, and a cylinder of quarrels.

These were to be left behind, on the bridge, of course. Weapons were not to be present at the exchange.

It was yesterday morning that Drusus Andronicus, coming to the apartment above the shop of Epicrates, had brought to Lord Grendel word of Surtak's acceptance of his proposal, that of an even exchange of prisoners, Lyris for Eve, Eve for Lyris. That was also the morning of my attempt to seduce Drusus Andronicus. About an Ahn afterward Kurik had come downstairs and found me as Drusus Andronicus had left me, sitting against the wall, bound hand and foot, the laconic message inscribed on my left shoulder. He had not seemed surprised. He wiped away the message, and untied me. I then followed him upstairs. He said nothing to me until after supper, when he stripped me, bound my wrists together, and stretched me, beneath the whipping ring.

It was now dawn.

"They approach," said Kurik.

"Yes," said Lord Grendel.

This particular bridge, the Sleen's Back, was little frequented, and arched between two towers in the Claudian district, which is in the northeast section of the city. The Claudian district, like the Metellan district, is one of the older, and shabbier districts in Ar.

The time arranged for the meeting was today, at this time, at dawn. A bridge seemed an appropriate venue for the exchange as, in such a location, one could easily determine the nature and numbers of either party, and an ambush, a sudden rush from a doorway, an emergence from brush, or concealed pits, or such, would be impractical. The Sleen's Back Bridge in the Claudian district was selected largely because of its obscurity. In such a location, certainly at such an Ahn, the appearance of two small parties, each with its supposed guard beast, would not be likely to produce the same stir as would be likely to be the case, even at such an Ahn, on a better-known, more frequented bridge, such as the Cloud Bridge or the Bridge of the Five Markets.

"They have stopped," said Kurik.

"To disarm," said Lord Grendel.

"They approach, again," said Kurik, "slowly."

"They are cautious," said Lord Grendel.

"They have stopped, again," said Kurik.

"It is now our turn to advance," said Lord Grendel.

He placed his ax on the bridge, and Kurik put his crossbow, and the cylinder of quarrels, some five quarrels, beside it.

I heard a rustle of chain behind me. I also felt a slight draw on the chain I held in my hand, it stretching back, behind me.

Our party consisted of two persons, and a slave, as would theirs. The principals were Surtak and Lord Grendel. One human would accompany Surtak, presumably to report back to Decius Albus, and Lord Grendel, in turn, in balance, would be seconded by a human, as well. Apparently Drusus Andronicus had been selected either by Surtak or Decius Albus, most likely Decius Albus, for the choice might be immaterial to Surtak, and Lord Grendel, of course, selected his colleague and ally, my master, Kurik, of Victoria. It had been further agreed that each party would be accompanied by a single slave. The slave would be utilized to conduct the prisoner, relieving the free persons of this task, and be available for any sundry task that might be appropriate for her, fetching, carrying, keeping watch, running a message, or such.

Lord Grendel was now advancing toward the obscure figures ahead, on the bridge.

I could now see, over the curve of the bridge, in the dim light, a Kur, and a human male, who, I feared, would be Drusus Andronicus. I did not know if I could face him. I was even more frightened that he might have Paula with him. How could I face her? I could not even dare meeting her eyes, given what she must now know, the miserable, stupid, petty, pointless thing I had tried to do. She must now despise and scorn me. Did I not know how dear Drusus Andronicus was to her, how she rejoiced at his feet? How could I, supposedly her friend, have done what I had done? With what contempt and amusement, with what disgust and loathing, she must now view me, and with such terrible justification!

"Follow us," said Kurik.

"Please, Mistress," I said to Lyris.

I knew she did not comprehend Gorean, but I trusted she could understand my reluctance, my deference, my trepidation, my unwillingness to hold the chain leash attached to her metal collar. Lyris might be slight, and lovely, to a male Kur but, to me, she was a large, dangerous animal. I moved the leash a little, to let her know we should proceed. "Please, Mistress," I said. I dared not give it the peremptory draw that well reminds a slave that she is leashed, and will be conducted where, when, and as, her master might wish.

The leash was of chain, of course, that Lyris, with one bite, with one snap of those jaws, might not part it.

Her ankles were shackled, and her wrists were fastened closely before her body, manacled together and held in place by a chain encircling her waist. Lord Grendel had also informed her that if she should attack either Kurik or myself, her fangs and claws would be extracted. He had had his translator activated when issuing this warning, presumably that any anxiety we might feel would be to some extent assuaged. I cannot speak for my master, but this assurance did not much reduce my own anxiety. If I should lose an arm or leg, or have my head torn off, I would not expect to be greatly comforted by the thought that Lyris might later regret her hasty act. It was my impression that the behavior of Kurii might be difficult to anticipate, at least for humans, as that of many other aggressive, predatory animals. How did I know what the dark selections of nature might have favored in the history of the Kur species? Indeed, it is not clear that it is rational to be rational in all situations. Might not the pause to reflect prove upon occasion to be a lethal error, the undoing of a combatant, a hesitation that might prove mortal in its consequences? The time when fangs lunge for the throat is not a time for reflection. It is a time for reflexive defense. Sometimes he who acts first is also he who acts last, as the other at that point is unable to act at all, lying in his own blood. In any event, it was clear to me that Kurii might, prompted by a sudden frustration or rage, act without reflection. Indeed, I had some reason to fear the temper of Lord Grendel himself. In his veins coursed Kur blood.

I followed Lord Grendel and Kurik, and then, of course, with a rustle of chain, the chain to her metal collar in my hand, I was followed by Lyris.

Lord Grendel's translator was turned off.

He and Kurik could communicate in Gorean, and one translator, Surtak's translator, would be activated, else he could not communicate with his human confederate, whom I now understood was Drusus Andronicus. Two translators, concurrently activated, might interfere with one another, with overlapping emissions. Eve could understand Gorean, and, of course, was fluent in Kur.

In a few Ihn, the two groups halted, on that high, chill, narrow walkway, and, in the dim light, through the tatters of fog, regarded one another.

Surtak and Lord Grendel addressed one another in Kur. I followed the conversation via Surtak's translator, which, I supposed, had been activated for the benefit of Drusus Andronicus.

To my dismay I saw Paula behind Surtak and Master Drusus. In her hand was the heavy leather leash by means of which she led Eve. Eve's ankles were not shackled or hobbled, but her arms were bound to her sides by several loops of coarse rope. I did not look at Paula, for I feared to meet her eyes. I kept my head down. I felt miserable and cold.

"Your word, as I hear, has been granted," said Surtak to Lord Grendel.

"It has been," said Lord Grendel.

"I spoke it so," said Master Drusus.

"You are here," said Surtak.

"I am here," said Lord Grendel.

"The conditions are satisfactory?" asked Surtak.

"My word was granted," said Lord Grendel. This utterance was reproduced with the same neutrality as any other issuing from the translator, but even I could detect the exasperation or regret in Kur.

The explosive, sardonic snorting of Surtak, I took it, was an expression of irrepressible Kur mirth.

Lord Grendel looked aside, angrily. I saw Eve shudder in her ropes.

"You might have asked ten tarns of gold," said Surtak, "of double weight."

"*Ela*," said Lord Grendel, "I did not know Lyris was so precious to you."

A pleased sound escaped Lyris.

"I do not understand why you would want this malformed creature behind me," said Surtak. "Surely she is not to be used for sleen feed. Perhaps you want her to carry swill to tarsks. Perhaps you want to sell her to a carnival, to be exhibited as the freak she is."

I heard Eve sob.

"She was sent to me from Lord Arcesilaus," said Lord Grendel. "Who could say why? I abide his will. Perhaps he did not want her on his world, who would, and did not know what to do with her."

"So he sent her to you to be disposed of," said Surtak.

"To be dealt with as I wished," said Lord Grendel.

"So the matter has to do with the usurper, Lord Arcesilaus," said Surtak. "I suspected it so. You wish, however unwillingly, to accommodate yourself to his vagrant whims."

"Lord Arcesilaus is no usurper," said Lord Grendel. "He is, by right of war, the Twelfth Face of the Nameless One, Theocrat of the Metal World."

"Do not fear him," said Surtak. "There is a place for you, even as you are, ill-constituted and malformed, in the rightful government, lurking in exile, to be soon restored. Indeed, I think you are out of favor with the usurper. Why else would he send you such a monstrosity, except in the way of mockery, to confront you with a living reproach and insult, reminding you of your own distortionate, manifold imperfections?"

Eve was shaken, weeping.

"Let us conclude the matter," said Lord Grendel, an utterance that, in Kur, was tinged with impatience and embarrassment.

Lifting my head I saw Paula, tears in her eyes, attempting to comfort Eve. "How like Paula," I thought. Her arms were partly about that shaggy body. I, too, of course, felt sorry for Eve. Who would not? But I do not think I would have dared to touch her, or would have wanted to touch her. She was too different, too hideous. In some laboratory a mistake had been made, an experiment had turned out badly, and a sentient creature had been twisted awry. How could one help but regard Eve askance, and yet I could understand, and well, what it was to want to be wanted, to want to be cared for, not to be rejected, or shunned. What a simple pleasure it is, I thought, just to look into a mirror, and not to want to cry out in pain, or weep.

Lord Grendel was relieving Lyris of the collar, the leash, and the metal impediments that had rendered her, even so formidable a beast, tractable and manageable. Meanwhile, Drusus Andronicus had thrust Paula aside, and was similarly relieving Eve of her restraints. He placed the leash, collar, and ropes in a large sack, which he wore at his left hip, slung from a strap over his right shoulder. Lyris rose up to her full height, snarling, and I backed away, frightened, against my master, who, to my misery, thrust me from him. The attitude of Lyris toward Lord Grendel, interestingly, was quite different. She made a soft, whimpering sound, but he gestured she should proceed toward the other group. Then, her demeanor changed again, abruptly, and she bared her fangs at Lord Grendel, and snarled and hissed, and he snarled back at her, and she turned about, angrily, and rushed to stand with Surtak and Drusus Andronicus, from which point, facing us, she, again, snarled and hissed. She drew herself up, then, with pride. Why should she not? Was she not beautiful, and had not Surtak, high Kur, been willing to spend the untold amount of ten tarns of gold, and of double weight, a sum that might ransom a Ubar's daughter, for her return?

Lord Grendel, angrily, disgustedly, motioned that Eve should join our group. "Hurry, loathsome creature," he snarled, "bring your sorry self here, taking it from the view of a high Kur, the noble Surtak, servitor of mighty Lord Agamemnon. Hurry. Do not continue to offend his sight!"

Eve obediently, crouched over, shamed, hurried to join us, her head down, the fur about her muzzle wet with tears.

Paula seemed stricken that Eve should be so addressed, with such cruelty. I myself did not understand the apparent contempt and hostility with which Lord Grendel apparently saw fit to abuse Eve, who, surely, was not responsible for what she was, for the failure or negligence of some scientists or technicians on some remote steel world.

Indeed, earlier I had thought he had found her at least tolerable.

We were then preparing to leave the place of our rendezvous.

"Let us return to the house of Decius Albus," we heard Lyris say, the words in Kur picked up by, and transmitted by, Surtak's translator. "I do not care to remain longer here, in the company of monsters."

"We shall shortly do so," said Surtak. It was not difficult to detect something menacing in the utterance, in Kur.

We turned about, curious.

"What is wrong?" said Lyris.

"Much, and nothing," said Surtak.

"I do not understand," said Lyris.

"You are a stupid little fool," said Surtak.

Lyris, I supposed, might be small compared to a male Kur, but, to me, of course, she was large and formidable.

"Beware how you speak to me!" said Lyris.

"You are unworthy of your harnessing," said Surtak. "You are an embarrassment. That your abduction did not disorder our plans was no fault of yours. It might have done so. It is one thing for the Lady Bina to be expeditiously removed from the House of a Hundred Corridors under the very nose of the fool, Decius Albus, and quite another for a Kur female, fully grown and supposedly intelligent, to be seized and carried away as easily as a human slaver or raider might hood and gag a human female, carrying her off to a well-deserved collar and brand."

"Do not dare speak to me so!" cried Lyris.

"Surely you know the fate of many Kur females, females of the party of Lord Agamemnon, following the victory of the usurper, Lord Arcesilaus?"

"What has that to do with me?" she said.

"They will remain as they are," said Surtak.

"I do not understand," she said.

"We can learn something from humans," said Surtak.

"Beware," said Lyris, "I might be displeased."

"You beware," said Surtak, "lest I find you displeasing."

"Sleen!" she said. "Stop! Stop! What are you doing?"

"You will not need these things any longer," he said.

"No, stop!" she cried.

"You see, my dear Kurik," said Lord Grendel, "she does look better without her harnessing."

"If you say so," said Kurik.

Deprived of her harnessing, I supposed Lyris must seem reduced, vulnerable, exposed, naked, in a sense, though, from my point of view, of course, she seemed little different from before. A female Kur without harnessing is without status. Other female Kurii look down upon her. Male Kurii, on the other hand, may then look upon her differently, and with a new, and aggressive, interest.

Surtak then seized Lyris, and threw her to his feet, and then held out his hand, or paw, to Drusus Andronicus, who removed an opened, metal object from the large sack at his left hip.

"No!" cried Lyris, struggling, her hands, or paws, trying to tear the encircling metal collar from about her neck.

"It is on you," said Surtak. "Remain at my feet, where you belong."

"Please, no!" she said.

"You have rejected and scorned me for the last time," said Surtak. "Now you will have to hope to please me."

"Release me!" she cried. "You would have paid ten tarns of gold, of double weight, to free me!"

"I would have paid that much, and more," he said, "to have you where you are now, in my collar."

"Take this hideous thing off my neck!" she cried.

"It is actually quite attractive on you," he said. "It enhances your loveliness. It makes you a thousand times more beautiful."

"Return my harnessing!" she cried.

"Kur slaves are not permitted harnessing," he said.

"'Slaves'!" she cried.

"Free males are to be addressed as 'Master'," he said, "and free females as 'Mistress'."

"Free me!" she cried.

"As our human friends have it," he said, "only a fool frees a slave girl."

"Let me go!" she cried.

"Do not become tiresome," he said.

"Free me! Free me!" she cried.

"Beware," he said, "lest you be found displeasing."

"Let me go!" she cried.

"Have you requested permission to speak?" he asked.

"I am not a slave!" she cried. "Take this thing off my neck! Return my harnessing!"

Angrily Surtak jerked Lyris to her feet and, holding her, forced her, struggling, to the side of the bridge.

Then she was very still, not daring to move, held at the edge.

Paula screamed, "No!"

"Be silent," said Drusus Andronicus, sharply, and, seizing Paula by the hair, thrust her to his feet.

I closed my eyes.

It made me ill, to even think of looking over the edge, to the street far below.

Lyris was uttering terrified, rushing, howling, piteous sounds in Kur. The transmissions from Surtak's translator were jumbled, and crowded together, almost like static, as the machine tried to isolate and sort out Kur, and produce comprehensible Gorean. Even so, there was little similarity between the placid output of the translator, however hesitant and disjointed, and the marked agitation and terror registered in the original Kur.

"Mercy, have mercy!" cried Lyris. "I beg mercy! Mercy! I beg mercy! Please, Master! I beg mercy, Master! Master!"

Surtak then drew Lyris back from the edge, and she collapsed to the floor of the bridge, shuddering.

"Your name," he said, "is 'Lyris'."

"Yes, Master," she said.

"What is your name?" he asked.

"'Lyris', Master," she said.

Surtak then turned to Lord Grendel. "Now each of us has his worthless she." He said.

"I wish you well," said Lord Grendel.

"I wish you well," said Surtak, and turned about, and took his leave.

I saw Paula at the feet of Drusus Andronicus. She thrust her cheek to his thigh, and held his leg.

How right she was there, at his feet!

How fulfilled she was to be a well-mastered slave!

How profound were her slave needs!

And on Gor, freed of the walls and fences, of the hobbles and lacerating wires, the closures and stern barriers, the prescriptions and prohibitions, the confinements and cruelties, of my former world, I, too, now liberated, now enslaved, had found the self I had been denied on Earth, a self I had been ordered not to recognize. If one hungers, why should one not eat; if one thirsts, why should one not drink; if one has slave needs, why should one not satisfy them, at the feet of a master?

Drusus Andronicus gently pushed Paula from him, and turned to follow Surtak. She, still kneeling, lifted her head and looked at me, and before I, frightened, and distraught, could look away, I saw her smile. She seemed clearly happy to see me, however briefly. I had read the light of affection in her eyes. She had now leaped up, to hurry behind Drusus Andronicus.

I sobbed with joy.

As I had anticipated, Drusus Andronicus had not informed her of my contemptible indiscretion, my petty attempt to interest and ensnare him. Why should he have informed her? My master had been wrong. Paula knew nothing of what I had done. She would never learn. Things would be as before, save that I now cared for her a thousand times more than in the past. I had not lost my friend. I had found her. She would never learn what I had done. My heart flooded with relief, with gladness, with my love for her.

I saw Lyris, trembling, following Surtak, Master Drusus, and Paula.

"Phyllis," said Kurik, "prepare to heel."

"Yes, Master," I said, and hurried to kneel near him, at his side.

Eve was nearby, crouched down, weeping. I did not know why Lord Grendel had spoken to her so cruelly, so abusively. Surely she needed no additions to her other miseries and pains. To see herself, to think of herself, put a whip to her heart. Did she not suffer enough, being herself?

"Do not cry, Eve," I whispered to her.

But my words, if heard, were not heeded.

Lord Grendel was looking after the retreating party. At his feet, looped, seemingly discarded, was the chaining, the manacles, shackles, collar, and such, that had restrained Lyris.

"They will have their weapons in a moment," said Kurik.

"No matter," said Lord Grendel. "Surtak has honor, and now he has Lyris, as well, and as he has always wanted her."

"Would he have cast her from the bridge?" asked Kurik.

"Surely," said Lord Grendel. "He is Kur."

"May I speak, Master?" I asked Kurik.

"Yes," he said, looking after the withdrawing party.

"Phyllis displeased Master," I said.

"Yes," he said, "and your back, belly, and legs should remind you of that."

"They do," I said.

"Good," he said.

"Does Master care for Phyllis?" I asked.

"Not particularly," he said.

"Would you," I asked, "in such a situation, as that between Master Surtak and Lyris, have cast me from the bridge?"

"No," he said.

"Then perhaps Master cares for Phyllis, a little," I said.

"Of what use is a crushed, lifeless slave?" he asked. "I would not cast you from the bridge. I would sell you, for a handful of tarsk-bits, or whatever you are worth." He then spoke to Lord Grendel. "They have their weapons by now," he said. "And continue on their way."

"Of course," said Lord Grendel.

"Then we are safe," said Kurik.

"I do not think so," said Lord Grendel. His head was back, and his nostrils were wide.

"What do you smell?" asked Kurik.

"Kurii," said Lord Grendel.

CHAPTER FIFTY-FOUR

W hat do you smell?" had asked Kurik.

"Kurii," had said Lord Grendel.

"Let us hasten to our weapons," said Kurik.

"It is no use," said Lord Grendel. "They will have been upon them shortly after we abandoned them."

"We are betrayed," said Kurik, bitterly.

"Not really," said Lord Grendel. "The rendezvous was fairly met, and the exchange conducted as agreed."

"So this exhibits the honor of Surtak," said Kurik.

"I do not see Surtak in this matter," said Lord Grendel. "I see Lord Agamemnon."

"Failing to win your oath by gifts and power, or by intimidation, threats, and guile," said Kurik, "he would respond to your resistance with steel."

"Do not think poorly of Lord Agamemnon," said Grendel. "It is not his way to endure misfortune with equanimity."

"He would make an example, it seems," said Kurik, "of those who would brook his will."

"Influence can be brought to bear in many ways," said Lord Grendel.

"Doubtless," said Kurik.

"He was the Eleventh Face of the Nameless One," said Lord Grendel.

"We must withdraw," said Kurik.

"Do not be foolish, dear friend," said Lord Grendel. "If the way forward, toward our weapons, is blocked, the way back will be closed, as well. We are trapped on the bridge."

"Phyllis," said Kurik, "stay behind me, as you can. If there are men in this, it will be no more than a change of collar for you."

"I do not want a change of collar!" I said.

"Be silent," he said. "You are a slave. You are a beast, nothing. Understand that. It will be done with you as masters please."

"Yes, Master," I wept.

"I do not think there will be men in this," said Lord Grendel.

"With the bow," said Kurik, "I could charge them a high price for my life."

"A bridge, in a high city," said Lord Grendel, "is not a bad place to die. One feels the wind. One sees the towers, the clouds, the sky."

"What of Eve?" asked Kurik.

"Poor Eve," said Lord Grendel.

He then approached the beast, Eve, and gently, very tenderly, put his paw on her shoulder. "Forgive me, Beautiful Thing," he said to her. "I spoke brutally to you, to convince Surtak that you were nothing to me, that he would not think of utilizing you in some way to influence me, as Lord Agamemnon tried to do with a free woman, she called 'Bina', whom I protect and care for, as one might care for, and protect, an amoral, innocent, naive, wanton child. Know, lovely creature, that you are the dearest, most beautiful thing I have ever seen in my life. You are a thousand times more beautiful than Lyris, the most beautiful Kur female I have ever seen. In seeing you I am reconciled to myself."

Eve regarded him, wide-eyed. "My eyes," she said, "my hands, my voice."

"Your eyes," he said, "are beautiful, the gray, tinged with blue, the sky awakening in the early morning. Your hands are lovely. What matters it if you have five fingers and not six? Five is natural for you, as for many fine forms of life. Cannot five fingers hold, grasp, caress, and touch as well as six? Your voice is soft, and not harsh; it can utter Kur, and make human sounds, as well. It can do both. How many humans can speak in Kur, how many Kurii in the tongues of the humans?"

"I am a monster," she said.

"You have been told so," he said, "but you are not. You are merely different, as I am different. We bring two bloods together and, in doing so, become a new blood, strong, fine, and wondrous."

"I am not ugly, I am not terrible?" she asked.

"No," he said. "You are not ugly, you are not terrible. You are beautiful, you are fine."

"I am afraid to see myself as I am," she said.

"I see you as you are," he said, "beautiful, and fine."

"It cannot be," she said.

"It is," he said. "The mighty tarn soars in the sky, putting clouds beneath its wings. The larl rules the mountains and forests. Do not judge the tarn by the larl, or the larl by the tarn. The tarn is not a failed larl, nor the larl a tarn gone awry. Each is different. Each is magnificent, and right. You are not life gone wrong, but life born anew."

Eve began to sob in his arms.

"Grendel," said Kurik, "I can see, behind us, approaching on the bridge, Kurii."

Lord Grendel rose up then to his full height, and looked back. In that moment there was something awesome, mighty, and fearfully Kurlike in his mien. "Yes," he said, "six."

"The two groups will trap us between them," said Kurik, "those by our weapons, and those approaching."

"Scarcely," said Lord Grendel.

"I do not understand," said Kurik.

"Do not fear, little Phyllis," said Lord Grendel, looking down, towering over me. "If your collar is changed, it will be because your master decides to rid himself of you, to give you away or sell you, as is his right."

I did not respond, but feared some disorder, occasioned by the hopelessness of our situation, had unsettled the mind of Lord Grendel. It was true, of course, that my master could do with me as he pleased. He was master. I was slave. On this world I was what I should be, and should have been, as well, on my former world, had it been naturally and rightfully ordered, property.

"We are lost," said Kurik.

"Not at all," said Lord Grendel.

"I do not understand," said Kurik.

"You see the Kurii behind us," said Lord Grendel. "It will take them some time to reach this point."

"Doubtless," said Kurik, looking back.

"You know, I assume," said Lord Grendel, "that Kurii possess impressive weaponry."

"Of course," said Kurik.

"Gases, explosive substances, rays, and such."

"I suppose so," said Kurik. "I know little of it."

"One such weapon," said Lord Grendel, "could, in a matter of two or three Ihn, turn this bridge, and the cylinders it connects, into plunging, falling, air-scalding molten metal and stone."

"I know little of such things," said Kurik.

"But such things, surely, for the most part," said Lord Grendel, "are on the steel worlds, or carried in the ships of the steel worlds."

"The Kurii behind us grow nearer," said Kurik.

"Did you know," asked Lord Grendel, "that such devices still figure in wars amongst the steel worlds?"

"No," said my master, looking back. "I did not know that wars might exist amongst the steel worlds."

"Old habits," said Lord Grendel, "are hard to break. I think sometimes the only thing that maintains the peace, such as it is, amongst the steel worlds, is the hope to obtain Gor."

I had come to gather that the Kurii, those whose orbiting domiciles, far off, were concealed in the River of Stones, whatever that might be, coveted Gor.

"And what stands between the Kurii and Gor?" inquired Lord Grendel.

"The Priest-Kings," said Kurik.

"And that is why," said Lord Grendel, "we are going to live."

"I do not understand," said Kurik. He then looked back, again, uneasily. "Those approaching, I conjecture," he said, "are some one hundred paces distant."

"Few Kurii, on Gor," said Lord Grendel, "will risk the bearing of a forbidden weapon. The laws of the Priest-Kings are strict. Their enforcement is merciless. Doubtless their surveillance, limited as to resources and interest, is incomplete and sporadic, but it exists. There have been several well-documented instances of the Flame Death. No, Kurii on Gor are very much aware, even more so than humans I suspect, of the Weapon and Technology Laws of the Priest-Kings and the hazards of contravening them. Many humans do not believe in the existence of Priest-Kings, supposing them to be no more than an invention of Initiates, to deprive the simple and trusting of their coins, but no Kur doubts their existence. Their evidence is irrefutable, destroyed fleets and devastated landing forces."

"Those behind," said Kurik, grimly, "are within fifty paces and approach in confident leisure."

"Surely, dear Kurik," said Lord Grendel, "you have been following what I have been saying."

"I could not avoid it," said Kurik.

"The purport," said Lord Grendel, "is that the armament of our friends, those before us, and those behind us, is unlikely to be in violation of the laws of the Priest-Kings. It is almost certain to fall within the perimeters of permissible weaponry, knives, swords, pikes, spears, staffs, axes, and such, and most likely axes, for Kurii, like the men of Torvaldsland, are fond of the ax."

"As are you," said Kurik, continuing to look back.

Lord Grendel had left his ax behind when he had advanced to meet Surtak's party, to effect the exchange. Kurik, too, had left his weapons behind.

"In twenty paces," said Kurik, "those behind will have reached this point."

"And they will find it empty," said Lord Grendel.

"How so?" asked Kurik.

I dared not look over the edge.

"We will first engage those before us," said Lord Grendel, "for it is there our weapons lie."

"They are armed," said Kurik. "We will be unable to reach our weapons. We will be cut down. We have no weapons."

"But we do have a weapon," said Lord Grendel, "a most fearsome weapon, one that I, in their place, would not care to encounter, particularly on this narrow field of battle."

I saw no ax, no staff, no club, not even a knife, in the grasp of Lord Grendel. Again I feared our predicament might have disordered his mind.

"You will please follow behind me," said Lord Grendel to Kurik, "and, if possible, retrieve your bow. It may deter those behind. And you, dear, beautiful Eve, and you, Phyllis, pretty collared barbarian, follow us, and wish us well."

"And where, dear friend, is your weapon?" asked Kurik.

"We will approach them at great speed, violent speed," said Lord Grendel, "and beware the compass of my weapon, the spinning hurricane I will hold in my hands. Should it strike you you would be swept a hundred feet from the bridge."

"Ai!" said Kurik, softly.

Lord Grendel reached down to the floor of the bridge and lifted up the heavy linkage of the chain that had lain, looped, seemingly discarded, at his feet. As it had held Lyris, it might, as well, have held a dozen male Kurii. I now realized that it had not been simply cast aside, as I had thought, but, in its looping, had been fashioned into a long, heavy cordage of iron, like a mountain's necklace, a necklace set with stones of iron, shackles, manacles, and the collar. This length he doubled, so that two strands hung together.

"You feared treachery," said Kurik.

"I know Lord Agamemnon," said Lord Grendel.

He then, with a wild cry, which I feared was a war cry of Kurii, the great chain spinning about, hissing in the air, almost invisible, a blur in the morning sky, rushed upon his startled foes.

CHAPTER FIFTY-FIVE

The great cry that had rent the morning air, as Lord Grendel had rushed upon his foes, terrified me, in its sudden, unexpected, thunderous loudness, in its nearness, in its might and bestiality. For a moment afterwards it seemed I could hear nothing, as though lightning had struck near me, shattering a roof or tree, so frightening and deafening had been the sound. Too, I could not move, surely for an Ihn or two, for the moment in which I heard that cry, so close, and wild, I was shocked, paralyzed, immobile, frozen in place, despite the obvious need to hurry in his wake. Would not such a cry, as the roar of the larl, startle and momentarily immobilize a quarry, or foe, allowing for the rapid, unchallenged advance, the strike or pounce, of the predator, the assailant? I suspected it was an ancient cry, such as might well have antedated the working of metals, a cry that might have first been heard on a far world, one perhaps now destroyed or sterile, a cry that might have rung out in primitive, brutal combat, in small, isolated wars, fought between small groups with sharpened poles and stakes, with clubs and cast rocks.

I was almost pulled off my feet as Eve swept by and seized me, half dragging me behind Lord Grendel and Kurik. I heard bestial cries, too, from behind us, and a scratching of claws on the bridge's surface. Surely those behind us had now expedited their pace! The Kur is not only larger and more agile than a human but it can, for a short distance, outrun a human. It tends, however, unless trained, to have less stamina than a human. When not encumbered it falls to all fours and races on its feet and the knuckles of its forelimbs. It is, for short distances, capable of remarkable bursts of speed. Those about now, however, were armed, with axes, and thus could not use all their limbs in their running. The weight of the axes, too, and the great hafts, must militate against speed. Too, those behind had been climbing the arch of the bridge, a climb that would, I supposed, take its toll of wind and muscle. It is likely that humans, or their predecessors, after the loss of the forests, were pack hunters, who might pursue and harry a prey for pasangs, until it collapsed, exhausted, and the pack would close in for the kill. Much was doubtless learned from the wolf, with which species, and its scions, humans would form their bond of thousands of years.

The great chain, in its air-lacerating hiss, like a hurtling flail, an almost invisible scythe, each link an ax, struck two Kurii from the bridge, plunging, twisting, through the air, howling, to the street far below, and the four others fell back upon themselves, jumbled, half-fallen, impeding one another, and the chain lashed down on them, again and again, like fierce, black lightning and limbs were broken, and a head crushed. I was barely aware of Kurik, on hands and knees, crawling toward the weapons he and Lord Grendel had left on the bridge before advancing to the rendezvous. It was over these that the Kurii had taken their stand. Lord Grendel spun about. "Down!" cried Eve, and pulled me to the surface of the bridge. Lord Grendel, the chain dangling in his grasp, was regarding the Kurii who had been approaching from behind. They were now within five or six yards of us. Lord Grendel snarled. The chain hung easily in his grasp. He was breathing heavily. Clearly the pursuers had taken caution from what they could make of what had just occurred on the bridge. Their hith-erto rapid pace had been arrested, abruptly. Lord Grendel turned back, seemingly to see the three remaining of the six who had held the bridge before us. Eve cried out in dismay but I think, truly, that Lord Gren-del's apparent lapse of attention to those who had been behind us was not what it had seemed, given his swift turn, which preceded Eve's out-cry, to face the Kur scrambling forward, from those behind, ax raised. The charging Kur was struck fully on the side of the neck by that storm of chain, and I screamed for the headless body, blood pumped by that mighty heart showering into the air, staggered toward us, two, and then three, steps, paws outstretched, and then fell before Lord Grendel, who swept the trunk through the blood with one huge, clawed foot, to the edge of the bridge, and then tumbled it over the edge. He then turned about, again, quickly, but of the three only one seemed a likely foe. One was clearly crippled, and must support his body with one foot, and his paws, his right leg useless, and another's arm flopped uselessly at his side. Neither had his ax. "I will watch!" called Kurik, who had now retrieved his bow, had drawn the cable, and fitted a quarrel to the guide. The bolt of such a weapon, whether metal or wood, well-lodged, can fell a Kur as easily as a man. The leader of the six who had followed us, now five, lowered his ax, and called out, in Kur. A brief exchange took place in Kur. "What is going on?" I asked Eve. "Leave is asked to pause, to negotiate," said Eve. "Wait," she said. "Grendel requests that the minion of Lord Agamemnon activate his translator, that his ally, the human, Kurik, may be apprised of what occurs." I shortly thereafter saw the hand, or paw, of the Kur move to the translator. "It is only a human," came from the translator. "But," responded Lord Grendel, "it is a human armed, and a human armed is a human who must be reckoned with." "As you wish," came from the Kur's translator. "Speak," said Lord Grendel. "I am authorized," said the Kur, "to accept your oath, on behalf of Lord Agamemnon. Put down your weapon, advance unarmed, and swear." "And then perish beneath five axes," said Lord Grendel. "No," said the other. "Surely not." "Lord Agamemnon is generous," said Lord Grendel. "As always," said the Kur. "Were such an offer authentic," said Lord Grendel, "it would have been tendered at the time of the exchange, by the officer, Surtak." "We are six," said the Kur, "five here, one behind you. You are one." "Before," said Lord Grendel, "you were twelve." "If you care for those with you," said the Kur, "the two humans, and the monster, surrender." "I do care for them," said Lord Grendel, "and thus I decline to surrender." "Then," said the Kur, "you leave me no choice." "You are mistaken," said Lord Grendel, "it is you who leave me no choice." "I do not understand," said the Kur. With a wild cry Lord Grendel, the chain aflight, was upon the Kurii. Eve clutched me, and looked away, and I buried my head in her fur. I heard cries of pain, and war, both ahead of us and behind us. There had been five Kurii behind us, those who had been approaching, but when I dared to look, the bridge was clear of bodies, save for one inert body, which I saw Lord Grendel, snarling, thrust from the bridge. "I am afraid of him," said Eve. "He is Kur, Kur." I rose to my feet. Kurik was standing, his bow discharged. "Master?" I asked. He faced three bodies, two were severed asunder, and the third lay on its back, just the metal fins of a quarrel visible in his chest. "The crippled two, I think," said Kurik, "were ordered to attack, but either refused to do so, or were unable to do so. The third then put them to the ax." "It is the Kur way," said Eve, shuddering. "Kurii have no place in their dens for the old, the weak, the ill, the useless." "Well done," said Lord Grendel, coming up behind us. "One is unlikely to miss at this range," said Kurik. Lord Grendel then approached Eve, who shrank back. He touched her with great tenderness. "Are you all right?" he asked. "You are Kur," she said. "I saw." "I am Grendel," he said. "You are Eve. We are what we are."

"I am afraid of you," said Eve.

"I would die for you," he said.

"I am still afraid of you," she said.

"Would you prefer for me to pretend to be what I am not?" he asked.

"No," she said, "but I am still afraid."

Lord Grendel then, the chain in its two loops, in one hand, or paw, went to the three bodies left on the bridge.

One after another he thrust them from the bridge.

"Would Master similarly die for Phyllis?" I asked.

"Do not be ridiculous," he said. "Phyllis is a slave. One would be better advised to die for an urt."

"Perhaps Master cares for Phyllis, a little," I said.

"I shall try to make it as little as possible," he said.

"Then a little?" I said.

"No," he said. "I have rethought the matter. Not even a little."

"I see," I said. I recalled he had put me behind him, before advancing, shielding me, averring that I would only be subjected to a change of collar, at least if men were to be amongst the pursuers.

"Phyllis is worthless," he said. "That was clear even on the Slave World."

"Yet," I said, "it seems Phyllis was not without interest to Master, even on the Slave World."

"Perhaps Phyllis would like to be lashed again," he said.

"No, Master," I said.

"But Phyllis, as others of her sort, has her uses," he said.

"Perhaps Phyllis then," I said, "as others of her sort, may hope to be soon put to one or more of her uses."

"We shall see," he said.

"The way is clear," said Lord Grendel, calling to us. "Let us be on our way."

CHAPTER FIFTY-SIX

T he matter has come to hiatus," said Drusus Andronicus.

"Our good will was evidenced by the return of the prisoner, the Lady Alexina, to Decius Albus," said Kurik.

"And ours," said Drusus Andronicus, "by the sparing of the house of Epicrates, and the cessation, however temporary, of hostilities."

"You come in the name of truce," said Kurik.

"That is my understanding," said Master Drusus.

"Perhaps you can clarify matters," said Kurik.

"As I can," said Master Drusus. "I am not privy to the secret councils of Decius Albus and the—others."

I suspected Master Drusus might have said 'beasts' but refrained, as Lord Grendel and Eve were present. We were in the apartment over the shop of Epicrates. Master Drusus sat cross-legged, in converse with Kurik and Lord Grendel. The Lady Bina, well robed, but unveiled, for she did not much care for veils, apparently suspecting they obscured her beauty, although, of course, some veils, in their way, suggest, and even enhance, beauty, knelt modestly near Lord Grendel, her knees closely together, as those of a free woman, and Eve, in lovely harnessing, in four colors, crouched close by his side, one of her hands, or paws, touching his fur. I had poured the wine, serving my master first, which is to be done unless one is instructed otherwise, and then the guest, Drusus Andronicus, and then the Lady Bina. Lord Grendel and Eve, the Lady Eve, I supposed, though she did not care for that form of address, declined to drink. Lord Grendel seldom drank, and only then in small portions. This may well have been wise. I think he feared to drink, being aware apparently of the powerful and possibly dangerous effect alcohol might have in his form of life, or that of a Kur, and Eve followed his lead. I made it a point, as was proper, not to meet the eyes of the guest, and I made certain I poured his wine no differently than I had the wine of the others. This manner of serving is common.

The girl does not know, of course, whether or not she will be made available to the guest. That is at the discretion of the master. If a guest is to stay overnight in a large house, he is almost certain to be offered a slave for the night, of which convenience he is expected to avail himself. At an inn, of course, there is a charge for the slave, as for the food, as for the bed, or mat. In a small house an overnight guest may, as a gesture of courtesy or hospitality, be offered the use of a slave, but he will commonly, while expressing his appreciation of his host's generosity, politely decline to accept the offer. This is less because he might have his own slave, or slaves, in attendance, and more because he is well aware that the master's offer is likely to be little more than an exercise in etiquette, a mere concession to social proprieties. Many Gorean masters, of a single slave, or a small number of slaves, prefer to reserve the pleasures of their properties to themselves. It is my impression that many Gorean masters, despite professions to the contrary, tend to be covetous, possessive, and jealous where their slaves are concerned. They want them all to themselves, even to the sword and knife. Perhaps this is selfish, perhaps it is something else altogether. Few free women comprehend how much a slave may be desired, how much she may be wanted. Strange how a fine, strong man can be so fond of a mere collared animal. How they want to keep their collars on them! How they want to own them! What joy is theirs, having their slave at their feet! But even were Drusus Andronicus staying the night, I suspected my master might not offer me to him, even were this to constitute an obvious infringement of the canons of hospitality. To be sure, if I were offered to a guest, and the guest accepted the offer, or if I were ordered to serve a guest, I would have to obey. I must do so. I was marked and collared. I was a slave. When not serving, I knelt back, unobtrusively. I even knelt farther away than custom would prescribe. Drusus Andronicus, doubtless in view of the innocuous nature, the prosaic sociality, of this meeting, had brought a slave with him, who knelt unobtrusively, to be sure, but a bit closer to him than I would have supposed customary, Paula. She smiled at me, from time to time. I loved her. How pleased I was that she knew nothing of my attempt to seduce Drusus Andronicus. Yet I was troubled, as well, for I knew of it, and I felt guilty, and terribly ashamed. But at least she had no idea of what I had done. The collar on her neck, of course, was that of Decius Albus. I suspected she would have preferred the collar of another.

"What brings about this hiatus?" inquired Kurik.

"Practicality, I gather," said Drusus Andronicus. "Surtak does not wish to risk more minions. Twelve died in the business of the Sleen's Back Bridge. Decius Albus does not wish to commit several men to an attack that might occasion attention in Ar, and lead the Ubar to inquire into the nature of the matter. What has Decius Albus to do with beasts, if I may use the expression, or beasts with the state of Ar? Might not the disclosure of certain secrets invite banishment, a denial of bread, salt, and fire, if not impalement? And we expect you will find the proposal of a hiatus congenial, for your associates are vulnerable, the Lady Bina, and perhaps others."

"Can you understand my Gorean?" inquired Lord Grendel, who had not spoken until now.

"I shall try," said Drusus Andronicus. "And I am sure others will be of assistance, if needed."

"I will now speculate," said Lord Grendel, "on the motivation of what you speak of as the 'hiatus'."

"Please do so," said Drusus Andronicus. "Your speculations may be more sound than mine, more honest than the explanations delivered to me."

"I acknowledge the vulnerability of my associates," said Lord Grendel. "That is granted. On the other hand, Gor is large, a world, much of it unknown, and what is concealed, while perhaps vulnerable, is in little danger if it cannot be located."

"To live in hiding, fearing each footstep, each shadow," said Drusus Andronicus, "is scarcely pleasant."

"I have acknowledged the vulnerability of my associates," said Lord Grendel, "but I beg to submit that vulnerabilities are scarcely restricted to my associates. For example, with a single bite I could now tear the head from your body."

"No!" cried Paula.

"Be silent!" snapped Drusus Andronicus.

"Yes, Master," she whispered.

Eve shrank back, away from Lord Grendel.

"But I have no intention of doing so," he said, "at the moment."

"I am pleased to be in receipt of that intelligence," said Drusus Andronicus.

"Besides," said Kurik, "we have sipped wine together, here, at this table, this afternoon."

It was true that the free humans had done so. Lord Grendel and Eve, as noted earlier, had refrained. As suggested, their abstinence, under the circumstances, was not intended to be, nor was it regarded as, a slight.

"That is true," said Drusus Andronicus. "It would be an egregious breach of hospitality."

"Also," said Lord Grendel, "I can move in the night, with stealth, in dark pathways, across roofs. I can tear a door off its hinges."

"I shall inform Decius Albus," said Drusus Andronicus.

"One might die now, and another then, and another later, and so on," said Lord Grendel.

"I understand," said Drusus Andronicus.

"Too," said Lord Grendel, "I need not abide by the code of the Assassin, to make no kill from which I cannot slip away in safety. I can be careless of my life, and thus, sufficiently motivated, might kill several, publicly, before I could be brought down."

"I understand," said Drusus Andronicus.

"I can understand the possible reluctance of Decius Albus to invest several men in an effort that might prove difficult to explain, if not scandalous. On the other hand, he could use one, or two, and that would attract little attention. It could always be ascribed to a misadventure of independent thieves, with no obvious link to the house of Albus."

"As I understand it," said Drusus Andronicus, "something of that sort was attempted, on Emerald."

"Unsuccessfully," said Kurik.

"One could always try again," said Lord Grendel.

"Of course," said Drusus Andronicus.

"So now," said Lord Grendel, "let me explain to you the nature of your 'hiatus'."

"Please," said Drusus Andronicus.

"Lord Agamemnon has withdrawn," he said. "Else there would be no hiatus. I do not know where he has gone, nor why, but I suspect. He troubled himself here to obtain a recruitment he thought might be profitable. He is now through with the business. Something more important has emerged. I think he was in Ar, waiting for word, which has now been received. So he has withdrawn. He is no longer in Ar. The hiatus is presumably brought about by Surtak, who bears me little, if any, ill will."

"You killed several of his minions," said Drusus Andronicus. "The Sleen's Back Bridge."

"You know little of the ways of the Kur," said Lord Grendel. "Surtak has stood in the rings. It was a good fight."

"You think he is your friend?" asked Drusus Andronicus.

"As enemies can be friends," said Lord Grendel. "You are of the Scarlet Caste, are you not?"

"I am," said Drusus Andronicus.

"I know one of the Scarlet Caste," said Lord Grendel. "He would understand such words."

"I did not think such things obtained amongst beasts," said Drusus Andronicus.

"From the point of view of the High Ones, the Kurii," said Lord Grendel, "it is such as you who are the beasts."

"Forgive me," said Drusus Andronicus.

"I speculate as follows," said Lord Grendel. "Were Lord Agamemnon in Ar, there would be no hiatus. I know him. From the proposal of the hiatus, we may infer he is no longer in Ar. But what would take him from Ar? What might lead him to abandon Ar, an ideal center for clandestine operations, a repository of gold and diverse resources, and a fortress of relative safety, given the houses of Decius Albus, and the protection of his power in Ar, to accept the risks of travel and discovery? I think I know. I fear I know. And the hiatus, as I see it, is a proposal of Surtak, who, in the absence of Lord Agamemnon, sees little profit in pursuing projects of dubious importance or value."

"It may be so," said Drusus Andronicus.

"But," said Lord Grendel, "you are scarcely here to inform us of what is already obvious, that a cessation of hostilities has taken place, and that a truce of sorts is in effect. Have we not already met, and without bloodshed, representatives of Decius Albus? Have we not already released the Lady Alexina, and seen to her safe return to the House of a Hundred Corridors?"

"It is as you say," said Drusus Andronicus, "and, beyond this, let it be known that the noble Decius Albus, grateful for the return of his protégé, the lovely Lady Alexina, salutes you, and wishes you well."

"All then is at peace," said Kurik. "The war is done."

Eve, happily, crept a bit closer to Lord Grendel.

"Please convey to the noble Albus," said Kurik, "that his salutation is accepted, that it is returned, and that his kind wishes are reciprocated, most heartily."

"I shall do so," said Drusus Andronicus.

"Our meeting is now at an end," said Lord Grendel.

"Not quite," said Drusus Andronicus.

"I did not think so," said Lord Grendel.

"I bear word, a message," said Drusus Andronicus.

"That is the true purpose of your visit here," said Lord Grendel.

"I fear so," said Master Drusus.

"Word from the noble Decius Albus," said Lord Grendel.

"No," said Master Drusus, "from another."

"Who?" asked Kurik.

"From he known as 'Surtak'," said Master Drusus.

"Of course," said Lord Grendel, and he quietly uttered, in Kur, the true name of he whom I knew only as Surtak, apparently an officer, quite possibly a high officer, in the service of Lord Agamemnon.

"Surtak, officer of Lord Agamemnon," said Drusus Andronicus, "proposes a feast of amity, a banquet in which pledges of peace and friendship may be formally exchanged, this occasion to recognize and seal the current truce. This feast is to take place four days from this day, at the fourteenth Ahn, at the house of Decius Albus, that which is a pasang from the Viktel Aria, which house is known to you."

"It is known to us," said Lord Grendel.

"I shall convey to the noble Albus," said Drusus Andronicus, "that you thank him for his invitation but, due to pressing matters, must decline to accept."

"Not at all," said Lord Grendel. "Inform him that we are delighted to accept."

"Surely not," said Master Drusus.

"But surely so," said Lord Grendel.

"I wish you well," said Drusus Andronicus, rising.

"We wish you well," said Lord Grendel.

Drusus Andronicus then turned about, went to the stairs, and descended to the street.

Paula leapt up, smiled, gave me a quick kiss, and followed him down the stairs.

I looked about.

I was decidedly uneasy.

"You cannot be serious," said the Lady Bina to Lord Grendel. Eve whispered something to Lord Grendel, in Kur. I could not understand her meaning, but the monitory and concerned aspect of her communication was evident.

"May I speak?" I asked. I was anxious to convey my misgivings, that such an invitation had been accepted.

"No," said my master, and I, disconcerted and miserable, forbidden to speak, was reminded that I was a slave.

"Grendel?" asked Kurik.

"Surtak," said Lord Grendel, "has honor."

"Are you sure?" said Kurik.

"He has stood in the rings," said Lord Grendel. "I am confident. Such an invitation would not be extended if not in good faith. We need fear nothing from such an invitation tendered by Surtak."

"You are familiar with the saying, I take it," said Kurik, "that many a track leads into the den of the larl but few lead out."

"Yes," said Lord Grendel, "but let me add to the saying, that those tracks that lead out may be awash with the blood of the larl."

"I advise, most strenuously, that we decline the invitation," said Kurik.

"It is accepted," said Lord Grendel.

"Why?" asked Kurik.

"Surtak has honor," said Lord Grendel. "He is not Lord Agamemnon. Lord Agamemnon would propose a truce, or amnesty, and then slaughter those who would be so foolish as to avail themselves of it. He is honorable only when it suits his convenience. Lord Agamemnon sees honor only as a weapon by means of which to control, deceive, trick, and manipulate others. I do not read Surtak as Lord Agamemnon. He is not Lord Agamemnon."

"Perhaps Lord Agamemnon is about," said Kurik.

"I do not think so," said Lord Grendel.

"Why?" asked Kurik.

"The hiatus," said Lord Grendel.

"You said," said Kurik, "you feared you knew why Lord Agamemnon had withdrawn, why he was no longer in Ar."

"Yes," said Lord Grendel. "But I may be wrong. I want to be wrong. Let us hope that I am wrong."

"What is it you fear?" asked Kurik. "You seem harrowed by your suspicions."

"I dare not speak," said Lord Grendel. "The prospect is too fearful."

"I do not understand," said Kurik.

"It is a frightful, terrible thing," said Lord Grendel.

"What?" asked Kurik.

"I think it best not to speak of it," said Lord Grendel.

"I do not think it was wise, dear Grendel," said the Lady Bina, "to have accepted the invitation."

"We had no choice, dear lady," said Lord Grendel. "The matter must be finished somehow. We are vulnerable. We do not wish to live in hiding, in fear. In peace all are victors, in war, only one, if that. One must have this business done, one way or another."

"And it will be done, one way or another?" said Kurik.

"Yes," said Lord Grendel, "near the fourteenth Ahn, four days from now, a pasang or so from the Viktel Aria."

"You place great confidence in the honor of Surtak," said Kurik.

"I do," said Lord Grendel.

"Then what is there to fear?" asked Kurik.

"Only that the invitation did not come from Surtak," said Lord Grendel.

CHAPTER FIFTY-SEVEN

W elcome, noble friends," called out Decius Albus, hurrying forward, under the shading latticework through which the afternoon sun stroked the laden tables with a melody of light and shade. Certain streets in Ar, in certain districts, are similarly sheltered from the sun, though with vines clinging to the latticework, and then, usually, here and there, there are stands of fruits and vegetables lining the walls. I was familiar with one such street, the Street of Dinas, near the theater of Elbar, for I had shopped there. Frequently assignations take place in such streets, which, in their way, constitute lovely, extended bowers, half lit even in the noonday sun. Some, such as the Street of Dinas, are fragrant with flowers.

"Noble Albus," said Lord Grendel, in intelligible Gorean.

"Noble Albus," said my master.

By one of the tables, heaped with viands and blossoms, I beheld a Kur, in festive harness. It quickly turned away.

I was tunicked, and well scrubbed, brushed, and combed. I stood, lithe, supple, and graceful. I was not a free woman. I was collared. On Gor, as I had not on Earth, I had discovered the joy of being honestly and freely what I was. How different we were from men, and how wonderful! And how marvelous and wonderful were men, so different from us! How they were, unreduced and uncrippled, our rightful owners, our masters! I had not become a true woman until I had been put in a man's collar. I could almost pity free women. How little they had, how much they missed! The tunic was brief, even for a slave tunic, for my master liked me in such tunics. After all, I was an animal, so why should I not be displayed as one? Why should he not, if he wished, display an animal he owned? Were the men of Earth not proud of their dogs?

"Help yourselves from the tables," said Decius Albus. "Eat well, drink freely."

"Where is the noble Surtak?" inquired Lord Grendel.

"He is detained," said Decius Albus. "He will be here shortly. In the meantime, feast, enjoy yourselves. Here and there you will note, placed on the ground, near or below the tables, bowls of slave gruel, and slaves may join the feast, feeding there, feeding, of course, as slaves."

"The noble Albus is most thoughtful," said my master.

"I must now attend to my other guests," said Decius Albus.

"Surely," said Kurik.

"Entertainment will be afforded later," said Decius Albus.

"We shall look forward to it," said Kurik.

There were several men about the tables, under the latticework. I recognized some of the men, from the Commerce Court, one of several receiving chambers, I had gathered, in that palace known as the House of a Hundred Corridors, when my master had been introduced under the name of Tenrik of Siba, a representative of a Lord Grendel, a trade envoy from Mytilene, a supposed city located somewhere in the Farther Islands. What rendered me more apprehensive was the positioning of several guards, clearly armed, with spear and sword, about the fringes of the sheltered area. The day was hot, one of those days in which a free woman, if not for modesty, might envy a slave her tunic. The house itself could be seen in the distance.

"Surtak should be here," said Lord Grendel.

"He is not," said Kurik, looking about.

I was hobbled.

This had been done shortly after we had descended from the closed wagon, closed to conceal the presence of Lord Grendel, which wagon Kurik had rented to carry us to the feast.

"Hold!" had called a guard, the leader of some five guards. "Descend, to be conducted to the feast." From the wagon, we could see what must be the feasting area, an open, sideless, shaded, temporary structure, hung with banners, ribbons, and garlands, ahead and to the left. The house was beyond that, and to the right. "No weapons are permitted at the feast," we were informed. "Of course," had said Kurik. We had then descended from the wagon. Neither he nor Lord Grendel, given the nature of the event, had come armed. Two of the guards then examined the wagon, determining that it was empty. "Your wagon will be placed with the others," we were told, "and your beast will be stalled and fed."

"It seems we are not the only guests," said Kurik.

"The slave is to be hobbled," said he who seemed to be first amongst the guards.

"Why?" asked Kurik.

"She is a slave," said the guard.

"We are outside the walls of Ar," said another.

"She might helplessly run in terror, at the sight of some of our guests," said another.

"I see," said Kurik.

The clasps were put on my ankles, the bar between. All of these answers, I supposed, had their point. One needs no justification for binding, roping, chaining, hobbling, or in any other way restraining a slave. She is a slave. Such things convince her of her bondage, and deepen her sense of being owned, of being a helpless property. These things make her a better slave, and more wholly a slave. It is part of what it is to be a slave. Too, of course, it excites men to see her so, and excites the slave in being so, knowing herself vulnerable and helpless, at the mercy of a master. With respect to the walls of Ar, those walls not only preclude the convenient entry of an intruder but lock within, and protect, valuables, amongst which are slaves. The same wall that keeps an intruder without keeps a slave within. For example, unescorted slaves are not allowed to exit the city. Whereas, given the collaring, clothing, and marking of a girl, the closely knit nature of the society, the acceptance and approval of bondage in the culture, and the culture's unquestioned support of, and enforcement of, the rigors of the institution of bondage, there is no escape for the Gorean slave girl, escapes are occasionally attempted, either from ignorance or desperation. The best that might be hoped for would be to fall into the chains of a different master who, realizing she was a runaway, would be likely to be far more cruel to her than her former master. Indeed, there are even fugitive brands, and it is not in the best interest of a girl to have one put in her body. Thus, outside the walls, where escape might seem more likely to the uninformed or naive, it is not unusual for a girl to be hobbled, chained to a wagon, or such. Thirdly, most Gorean slave girls have never seen a Kur, and do not even know they exist. Thus, it is quite possible that the first sight of such a creature might precipitate flight, as from a larl or sleen. Hobbling, obviously, militates against a girl's acting freely from some hysterical response. I recalled that the Lady Bina had made certain that Paula's ankles had been bound before she was given her first glimpse of Lord Grendel. I recalled how shaken she had been following that occasion.

"Would that I had even a knife," had said Kurik.

"No," had said Lord Grendel, softly. "Even so small a thing might insult our host, Surtak."

"It is a risk I would be prepared to take," said Kurik.

"More than one Ubar has been slain by a knife thrust at a feast," said Lord Grendel, "the knife sometimes wielded even by a slave. Why else do you think that slaves at such a feast are to serve with two hands on a goblet, or platter, their hands thusly in plain sight?"

"I find it hard to believe that a slave would strike such a blow," said Kurik.

"To be sure," said Lord Grendel, "it is usually a free woman masquerading as a slave, expecting to be spirited away once the blow is struck."

"Amidst feasters, and guards?" asked Kurik.

"If her blow is successful, she dies, of course, following lengthy tortures. If it is not successful, she becomes the slave of the Ubar."

"You will please follow me, to the feast," said one of the guards.

"Master!" I said, plaintively.

It is easy to stand gracefully, and such, in hobbles, but it is not at all easy to move in them. One can move only in short, awkward steps, and the slightest miscalculation, or haste, may plunge one to the ground. But one can move, of course. Thus, in a night camp, even a hobbled girl is likely to be chained to a tree, or, by the neck, to the foot of her master.

"Master," I breathed, delighted, swept into his arms. I was not even put over his left shoulder, my head to the rear, as a slave is usually carried. In this way she is reminded she is property, and cannot see toward what she is being borne.

"Master carries me as though I might be free," I said.

"Scarcely," he said, "you are tunicked, and this way you are closer to me, and I can see more of you."

I put my head back, against his shoulder.

"You are heavier," he said. "I think I shall cut down on your gruel."

"It is the hobbles!" I said.

In a short time we had come to the feasting area, under the latticework, and I had been restored to my feet, and Decius Albus had approached us, to welcome us to the feast.

"Surtak should be here," had said Lord Grendel.

"He is not," had said Kurik, looking about.

"I sense we are being observed," said Lord Grendel.

"It is not unlikely," said Kurik.

"Doubtless Surtak will appear shortly," said Lord Grendel.

"Doubtless," said Kurik.

"Behave in a natural manner," said Lord Grendel. "Smile. Be at ease. Take food and drink only from what is publicly available, and from locations where you see others doing so. Decline whatever might be offered to you."

"Decius Albus spoke of entertainment," said Kurik.

"You are Gorean," said Lord Grendel. "What do you conjecture?"

"If it were night, indoors," said Kurik, "I would suppose any number of things, depending on the house, music, the kalika and czehar, the aulus and tabor, acrobats, jugglers, flute girls, eaters of fire, the reading of poetry, the chanting of histories, professional tellers of stories, the singing and dancing of slaves, many things."

"And if it is outdoors, and day?" inquired Lord Grendel.

"I do not know," said Kurik.

"I would think contests, games," said Lord Grendel.

"I fear so," said Kurik.

"Have you noticed something unusual here?" asked Lord Grendel.

"Only what is not seen," said Kurik.

"Precisely," said Lord Grendel. "Although the occasion is putatively festive, and the banqueting bower is open, and easily accessible, there are no slaves about."

"We are outside the walls of Ar," said Kurik.

"Even hobbled slaves," said Lord Grendel. "Besides, country slaves, the slaves of villas, of country houses, the slaves of peasants, are seldom restrained, except at night."

"By the tables, sometimes below the tables," said Kurik, "there are bowls of gruel."

"But no slaves," said Lord Grendel.

"Then," said Kurik, "the slaves have been removed."

"Or were never here," said Lord Grendel, "the bowls intended to suggest otherwise."

"I am uneasy," said Kurik.

My master was jostled, as a fellow in the yellow of the Builders made his way by. "How clumsy I was," said the fellow. "Please, forgive me."

"It did not occur," said Kurik, smiling. Kurik then spoke softly to Lord Grendel. "He determined," he said to Lord Grendel, "that I was not armed."

"We must not arouse suspicion," said Lord Grendel.

"Do not neglect the black wine, flavored with Turian sugars," said a fellow in merchant robes, nearby.

He poured himself a tiny cup of the beverage. Black wine tends to be expensive. Its presence at the feast in more than one vessel bespoke the affluence of Decius Albus. Some Goreans have never tasted the beverage.

"I approve your slave," said the fellow with the cup of black wine. "Is she not hungry?"

"I would expect," said Kurik, "that by now she is quite hungry."

"You have her in the presence of food, and yet deny her permission to eat," said the fellow. "Excellent. You keep her under strict discipline. I do the same with my sleen. Keeping a slave under strict discipline makes her more responsive, more helpless in her chains, more pleading for the least caress."

"It escaped my mind," said Kurik. "I forgot. It has been some time now. Thank you for calling the matter to my attention."

"You suppose her to be quite hungry?" said the fellow.

"Yes, by now," said Kurik.

"She does not ask to be fed?" he asked.

"She knows better than that," said Kurik.

"The whip?" he said.

"Of course," said Kurik. He then turned his head to me. "You may feed, Phyllis," he said.

"Thank you, Master," I said.

"Appropriately," he said.

"Yes, Master," I said.

I went to all fours, put down my head, and began to feed. I must not, of course, use my hands. There are a thousand ways in which a girl's knowledge of her bondage may be forced into every cell of her body. A girl's food bowl and water bowl are often kept on the floor of the kitchen, in a corner, sometimes in the vicinity of the master's couch. Many a girl has fed so, the master standing over her, with his whip. Later, he may not even be present, or he might be to one side, scarcely noticing, perhaps reading.

"How charming a collar slut looks while thusly feeding," said the fellow.

"Indeed," said Kurik.

How far I was, I again thought, from the office on my former world!

Few young women, I supposed, expected to be carried to another world, and made a slave. And then they find themselves on the auction block, their bare feet in the sawdust, a collar on their neck, under the light of torches, being bid upon!

Kurik, of course, seldom forgot, or neglected, my feeding. I did know enough, of course, not to ask to be fed. The typical Gorean master takes excellent care of his slave. He sees to it that she is sheltered and well rested, and has a nutritious diet. He may occasionally limit her food, in the interests of her health and beauty. More annoyingly, he may impose exercises upon her, usually to reduce a bit of weight or improve a curve. All in all, vital and flourishing, she is usually in far better condition than the typical free woman who, lacking a master, is likely to gain weight, grow careless, and become slovenly. When a free woman is captured and stripped, it is usually obvious what must be done to make her more worthy of the honor of a slave block. Too, it must be remembered that the slave is a possession, and that men tend to be concerned with, proud of, and, I suspect, despite their usual protestations, fond of their possessions. Too, obviously an investment is involved.

"Finish it all, Phyllis," said Kurik.

"Yes, Master," I said.

I was hungry.

I fed well.

Generally I did not feed much differently from my master, and would partake of the same foods, which I, of course, had prepared. Strictly, rather as I must have permission to speak, so, too, I must have permission to clothe myself, to feed, and so on. On the other hand, in many domiciles, nothing onerous is involved in such matters, as, with respect to a variety of such activities, a standing permission is in place. I almost always fed myself, save when it pleased him, or amused him, to put me to all fours, at an animal dish, the use of my hands denied to me, or would choose, I kneeling, or sometimes lying, to feed me by hand. I was even permitted, commonly, the use of a spoon. One matter in which an explicit permission is usually required is when a slave would leave the domicile. In requesting this permission, the slave will be expected to make clear the point of her trip and her anticipated time of return. With respect to food, the master, of course, as a matter of propriety, begins the meal. An exception to this might be when the master suspects the slave may have poisoned the food. She will then be forced to eat first. Slaves are denied access to poisons, as to more common weapons. But an enemy may plant a girl in an enemy household, supply the poison, and so on. The most exotic form of this sort of thing is the poison girl who, over months or years, is rendered immune to a poison, but whose bite is lethal. There are, of course, a variety of ways in which a toxin may be administered, for example, by means of a fang tooth, a poison ring, and so on. A simple method is to introduce an ost into the intended victim's sleeping furs.

The fellow who had poured the cup of black wine was now gone.

We then heard an abysmal howl some yards to the right, outside the bower. I froze in place. Surely it was a noise emanating from some dreadful, horrifying beast. But there could be no larl here, no forest panther, so close to Ar! And there were armed guards about, and it did not seem they were engaged. Surely I heard no cries of alarm, no orders to deploy and attack. The source of that howl, then, must have been deemed acceptable, perhaps unobjectionable, even innocuous. I kept my head down.

"Look," said Kurik. "The Kur!"

"I see it," said Lord Grendel.

"It stumbles, and reels," said Kurik.

"Yes," said Lord Grendel.

"What is wrong with it?" asked Kurik.

"This bodes not well," said Lord Grendel.

"Has it gone mad?" asked Kurik.

"In a sense, yes," said Lord Grendel. "It is drunk."

"'Drunk'?" said Kurik, incredulously.

"Yes," said Lord Grendel. "Decius Albus is a fool. He knows nothing of Kurii. Such a splendid host, so eager to please his guests! How he would pander to the High Ones! He would pour oil, explosive dust, on fire!"

"I do not understand," said Kurik.

"This is no sipping of ka-la-na," said Lord Grendel. "The fool! He has put paga before Kurii!"

"That is some sort of mistake?" said Kurik.

"The blood of the Kur is dark and deep," said Lord Grendel. "There are ancient gates behind which lurk ancient things, things best shut away, things best left unstirred. Paga opens such gates."

"There is danger?" said Kurik.

"Great danger," said Lord Grendel.

"How could Surtak permit this?" asked Kurik.

"Surtak would not," said Lord Grendel. "In this I see the hand, and ignorance, of Decius Albus."

"It is coming this way," said Kurik. "Men withdraw!"

"Get up, Phyllis," snapped Kurik, and I rose to my feet, wiping gruel from my face with the back of my right hand.

I saw the reeling Kur, no longer howling, enter the festive structure, look about, and then leap up, seizing the latticework of the bower, and then falling back to the ground amidst a confetti of flat, narrow boards that could not have begun to hold his weight. The guests, most of them, had now drawn back in such a way as to have the tables between themselves and the Kur. Then the Kur, angrily, suddenly, overturned one of the tables, spilling wine, cakes, and fruit, but it made no effort to more closely approach the guests, who had shrunk back even further. Indeed, some had fled the bower. We were still on the same side of the tables as the Kur, and it turned about, and regarded us.

"Prepare to run," said Kurik.

"I cannot!" I said.

"As you can, little fool," he said.

He then placed himself between me and the beast.

"Do not be afraid," said Lord Grendel. "If necessary, I will kill it."

The Kur approached a bit toward us, and growled.

Lord Grendel snarled back, and then uttered something in Kur, fiercely, that I could not understand, as his translator was deactivated. The Kur blinked, and then, growling, stumbled away.

"It declines to have its throat torn out," said Lord Grendel.

"How many Kurii are there about?" asked Kurik.

"I do not think there are many," said Lord Grendel, "perhaps ten, perhaps fifteen. Lord Agamemnon, following the revolution, is severely limited as to cohorts, and it is difficult to bring Kurii into populated areas, to conceal them there, and so on."

"Happily, only one was drunk," said Kurik.

"Our delightful host," said Lord Grendel, "would scarcely serve paga to but one guest."

"Then there are others," said Kurik.

"Doubtless," said Lord Grendel.

"Where?" asked Kurik.

"I suspect, in the place of entertainment," said Lord Grendel.

"What are we to do?" asked Kurik.

"You, and your lovely collar girl, Phyllis," said Lord Grendel, "will continue to enjoy the sumptuous provender so generously provided in this festive structure, and make my excuses to any who might inquire."

"And you, what are you to do?" asked Kurik.

"I intend to find Surtak, or his body," said Lord Grendel.

CHAPTER FIFTY-EIGHT

H ave you dined well?" inquired Decius Albus.

"Very well," said Kurik, finishing a small pastry.

Behind Decius Albus were an officer and eight guards.

"And I trust your girl enjoyed her gruel," said Master Albus.

"As you can see, noble Albus," said Kurik, "the bowl has been licked clean."

No one, it will be noted, had asked me about the matter. There are, of course, many variations where slave gruel is concerned, ranging from bland mush to exotic mixtures that might tempt a free woman, were it not for the name. Needless to say, such mixtures were occasionally sold, and for a good price, to free women under different names. I had not, incidentally, thought the gruel of any particular note, but it was good enough, not that I had anything to say about such matters. Certainly I had been hungry, and that is often a great help, that serving to elevate one's assessments. That the bowl was licked clean was to be expected. Slaves are not to waste food.

Upon the arrival of Decius Albus and his small retinue, I had immediately knelt.

"Where is the esteemed Lord Grendel?" asked Master Albus, looking about.

"He was here a moment ago," said Kurik. "Doubtless he will be back shortly."

Neither Decius Albus nor my master paid me any attention. I did sense I was being assessed by one of the guards. I had learned that the curves of a woman's body, at least if they were of sufficient interest to masters, were often referred to as slave curves. I wondered if free women sometimes, before the mirror, in the privacy of their boudoir, regarded themselves, and wondered if their curves were slave curves, and, if they were, what this might mean. Surely humans are not exempt from the selections of nature. Does nature not, in its thoughtless processes, in its blind, dark game, favor the organ sensitive to light, the organ sensitive to sound, the capacity to discriminate tastes and odors, the capacity to grasp, to feel, to think? Does it not, without thought or heart, fashion the wings of the tarn, the fleetness of the leaping tabuk, the stealth of the sleen, the claws and fangs of the larl? It casts its dice, on the board it cannot see, and there are consequences, unexpected and unforeseen, but real, very real. Nature favors victory, and the storms of sex. It favors men and women, and a kind of man, and a kind of woman. Would it not favor the man who would prize, seize, own, and master a woman, and the woman who would thrive joyfully at his feet, prized, seized, owned, and mastered? What man does not long for his slave, what woman does not long for her master? So I think there is a sense to the expression 'slave curves'. Are they not slave curves, in a more literal sense than is often understood? Have we not been bred to find our joy in bondage, in loving and belonging; have we not been bred to be slaves?

"I am disappointed," said Decius Albus. "I had hoped, personally, to conduct the noble Lord Grendel and his colleague, Tenrik of Siba, to the entertainment."

"After which, formal pledges of peace are to be exchanged," said Kurik.

"Of course," said Decius Albus.

"I hope that your disappointment will not last long," said Kurik.

"I do not think it will," said Master Albus. He then turned to the officer beside him. "Take four men," he said, "locate Lord Grendel, and escort him to the entertainment."

The officer and four of his men then departed, making their way toward the house.

"Ah, see," said Decius Albus, sympathetically. "Tenrik's poor slave is hobbled."

"It was done when we left the wagon," said Kurik.

"I apologize," said Decius Albus. "It is a matter of routine precaution when dealing with visiting slaves. It discourages wandering about." He then turned to one of the remaining guards. "Let us relieve this poor love beast of the cruel impediments fastened so closely about her ankles."

With a sound of metal, the guard lifted me to my feet. It is difficult to rise to one's feet when hobbled, and, without a display pole, extremely difficult to do so gracefully.

I expected then to be directly relieved of the device but Decius Albus was looking at my ankles.

"Her ankles are rather slim, are they not?" he asked.

"She is a barbarian," said Kurik. "On the Slave World, one does not object to such ankles. Indeed, they are approved."

"Interesting," said Decius Albus.

"They shackle nicely," said Kurik.

"Even as other ankles," said Decius Albus.

"Of course," said Kurik.

I then expected to be relieved of the hobbles, but, to my surprise, my wrists were drawn behind me, and braceleted. I was then leashed.

"I do not think she is going to run away," said Kurik.

"I do not think so, either," said Decius Albus.

"I did not know she was to be hobbled, or braceleted and leashed," said Kurik.

"Oh?" said Decius Albus.

"Phyllis," said my master, "if it should prove feasible, later, you might locate our wagon. I may have forgotten something."

"Yes, Master," I said. I had no idea what he was talking about, as the wagon had been empty when we had left it. Indeed, guards had checked the wagon, and determined that it was empty, quite empty.

"Take off the hobbles," said Decius Albus.

The guard then, with a key, addressed himself to the hobbles.

I pulled at the bracelets a little. Though one knows one is held perfectly, helplessly, how can one resist doing that? My leash was in the hand of another guard, its end knotted about his fist.

Braceleted and leashed, is one not well aware that one is a property, an animal, a slave?

Then the hobbles were off, and cast on one of the tables, amidst the residue of the feast.

"Now, Phyllis," said Decius Albus, "were you free of the leash and bracelets, you might leap about much as you might please, darting here and there."

I did not understand him.

My master seemed troubled.

"Now," said Decius Albus, "let us proceed to the entertainment."

"By all means," said Kurik.

CHAPTER FIFTY-NINE

It was hard to see, for the lack of light. I heard whimpering about me, small sounds of questioning, of fear. "Why are we here?" asked a woman's voice, doubtless that of a slave, for the free and the slave would scarcely be kept together. We were somewhere within the house of Decius Albus. I had been hastened into the house, braceleted and leashed, through a side entrance, shortly before the festive bower in which the banquet had been served had been attacked by some four or five rampaging, apparently drunken Kurii. Behind me I had heard the tearing of wood, the clatter of vessels flung from overturned tables, the howling of the beasts. The guards, too, I think, were frightened. I hooked my fingers in the stout mesh. Some forty of us were penned in the enclosure. To my left there was another enclosure, in which were penned several bleating verr. Ahead I could see two cracks of light, indicating, I supposed, doors. It seemed a natural light under the doors. Beyond the doors then, I supposed, one would be outside. Perhaps there would be a garden outside, or the fields, the Viktel Aria beyond. Each pen had a shoot, each shoot leading toward one of the doors.

I was unclothed, save for my collar, and I had little doubt but what the others in the enclosure, in the darkness, were similarly served, their raiment limited to a metal slave band locked on their neck. Nudity is not that uncommon with slaves. They are, after all, animals. And whereas an animal may be clothed, it need not be. As it has no rights, it has no right to anything, including clothing. It does not even own its own collar. The master owns it. The slave wears it.

"Bind him," had said Decius Albus, and three of the four guards remaining with Decius Albus had set upon my master, who struggled wildly, until his arms were pinned back by two of the guards, one to each arm, and the other, standing close to him, struck him a sudden, heavy blow to the body, following which he was cast to the ground, struggling to breathe. His wrists were tied behind him and his arms were roped to his sides. He was then yanked to his feet, still struggling to get air into his lungs. He was held upright by two of the guards. Otherwise I did not know if he could stand. When the guards had lunged toward Kurik, grappling with him, I, dismayed, had cried out "Master!" and, not thinking, had tried to run, but I was, of course, caught up short by the leash, and then the guard in whose charge I was, with a motion of his foot, swept my feet from beneath me and I was put to my belly, and the free end of the leash was pulled back, under my body, and my ankles were seized, crossed, and thrust up, and forward, and then pressed down, behind me, and bound together with the free end of the leash. I then lay there on the ground, prone, beside the table, my wrists braceleted behind me, my ankles pulled up behind me, high, crossed, tightly bound.

"Ah, my dear Tenrik, of Siba, or whatever might be your name, as though it mattered," said Decius Albus, "it seems we are now ready to be off to the entertainment. I trust you will enjoy yourself, perhaps so much so that you will consent to participate." The eyes of Kurik of Victoria seemed glazed. I did not think he could speak. Decius Albus then turned about, in good humor. He was looking off, beyond the uprights of the open bower, toward the house. "Bring our friend along," he said. "Noble Albus," said the guard who stood near me, he who had held my leash, and then discomfited me, "what of the slave?" "Put her with the others," had said Master Albus. "To be done with as the others?" had asked the guard. "Yes," had said Decius Albus. "Of course."

I blinked suddenly, and drew back, my eyes half shut. The door to the left had been thrown open and bright sunlight enflamed the doorway, and I heard the sound of men outside, and there was a sound of cheering, and an eager howling of Kurii, and two gates were flung up, one at the near end of the verr pen, to my left, separating it from its chute, and that at the far end of the chute, leading toward the opened doorway, and now, from behind, entering the chamber, I heard the shouts of men, and I saw one, far to the left, outside the verr pen, carrying a pointed stick, and then other men, with sticks, had entered the pen, from behind, and were herding the verr out the chute, through the doorway, into the light outside.

I understood nothing of what was occurring.

Surely this had nothing to do with the entertainment to which Decius Albus had alluded. The verr, the domestic verr, is a placid, contented, gregarious, grazing beast, raised for meat. Flocks of verr might figure in bucolic pageants or dramas dealing with the romances of shepherds and shepherdesses. What other contribution to an entertainment might be expected of verr? What else could be their role? Too, these were familiar verr, not the related beast, the larger, belligerent, territorial mountain verr I had heard of, horned and agile, which are dangerous to approach, particularly on precipitous slopes. To observe a flock of verr might be soothing, but I saw little in it that would be likely to be denominated amusing or enjoyable, a spectacle, or such.

But I did not know, at that time, much about the feeding habits of Kurii. The Kur, in its variations, of course, is essentially a carnivore. I have little doubt that it stood at the top of the food chain on its former world, a world about which we know little, other than that it was destroyed or rendered unviable. Some Kurii, even today, are strictly carnivorous. Most, on the other hand, can ingest and retain a larger spectrum of substances. There are, interestingly, very few strict or pure carnivores. Most animals known as carnivores do not, or need not, restrict their diet to meat. Natural selection in what one might think of as "food deserts" would see to that. There are, of course, preferences, and the ancient hunt can lurk in the genes. The Kur doubtless favors meat, and fresh meat, and many prefer it hot and saturated with blood, torn from the living animal. Too, for many it seems there is a pleasure, a zest, in making one's own kill. That, for many, seems to add a sauce to the repast.

I crowded to the front of the pen, until I was pressed against the gate at the front of the pen, that which closed off the pen from its chute, the chute that led to the second door, now closed. I was desperate to look, as I could, through the opened portal, that of the first door, leading outside, that through which the verr had been driven. I saw nothing but some ground, and grass, and then the door was flung shut, and we were, rather as before, muchly in darkness.

I had detected, however, in that moment, a slight smell of smoke.

I would later learn that the drunken Kurii, leaping about, reveling in their carnival of destruction, had set fire to the lovely, shaded bower that had sheltered the riches of the afternoon banquet.

"What is going on?" begged a woman, beside me.

"I do not know, I do not know!" I said.

Who knew what lay beyond the two closed doors?

Who knew, then, even the meaning of that bit of smoke?

I did know that some four or five Kurii, like wild beasts, seemingly out of their senses, had entered the bower about the same time that I had been hurried from it, toward the house. There had been one earlier, too, which Lord Grendel had warned away. That one, if Lord Grendel had been correct, had been drunk. Those appearing later, I supposed, might have been drunk, as well. Perhaps the first one had returned, bringing others with him. I did not know. Kurii looked much alike to me, as I supposed they would to any human.

The Kur, at its best, is a form of life that tends to be impatient, dangerous, unpredictable, and violent. Its restraints of rationality and prudence are tenuous in the best of times. It was fearful to contemplate what its behavior might be in the absence of such restraints, as modest and precarious as they might be.

Although I was unsure at the moment, I deemed it likely, following the surmise of my master, that Decius Albus, wisely or not, by design or in ignorance, eager to appease and impress the Kurii, would have been generous in the distribution of paga. How could he have given it to some, and not others? And what Kur, unacquainted with the beverage, curious, jubilant, in holiday mood, would refuse to accept a gift made so freely available, by so trustworthy and generous a host and ally? And so, in many cases, the amber swirl of liquid fire, for the first time, would course through new countries, new bodies, large, dark, dangerous bodies, hitherto untouched by such flames, racing where it had never burned before. Who, knowingly, would give paga to a larl? Who, knowingly, would break through the thin crust concealing a seething volcano? Lord Grendel had spoken of ancient gates, behind which lurk ancient things, things best shut away, things best left unstirred. Who knows, I wondered, what waits, restless, behind those gates? Do not such gates make possible civilization, intelligence, and thought? Perhaps, in the case of the Kur, those gates had not been opened for a thousand years. Paga, I feared, as had Lord Grendel, opens such gates.

I heard, frightened, crowded with the others, in the darkness, from outside, from the other side of the doors, the penetrating blast of a festive trumpet and a cry of eagerness, of anticipation, from a crowd, and, mixed therein, the wild roars and howls of excited Kurii.

"What is going on?" cried a woman.

"I do not know!" I said.

"I know the trumpet!" cried a woman.

"Yes!" cried another.

"Yes," said another, "it is the trumpet!"

"What trumpet?" I asked.

"Such trumpets announce the games," said one of us, in the darkness.

"What games?" I asked.

"Arena games!" said another.

Almost at the same time we heard a frenzied bleating outside, and the shrill noises of terrified verr. This continued for a short time, and then there would be a silence, and then, in a bit, the silence would be shattered, again, by a brief, tortured, bleating, terrified, noise.

"What are they doing?" asked a woman.

"They are running verr, pursuing them, seizing them, and feeding," said a woman. "I saw it in the house, once, when the beasts were alone. Now it is in the open, public!"

"Surely no arena trumpet would be sounded for such a thing," said a woman.

"Something different must be going on," said another.

"I saw it at the house, too," said another, "a different time. It can be a blood sport. They take pleasure in it. There is the thrill of the chase, the apprehension of the quarry, the kill, the relishing of the hot, living, bloody meat of victory. There are wagers made. Which beast will first seize which animal? How quickly can a given animal be seized? Who of two beasts will retain most of the animal?"

We heard another horrifying bleating from outside.

"Another kill," said the first woman who had referred to the matter, from the house.

"I hear the howling of the beasts," said a woman. "I do not now hear much cheering from the men."

"They did not know what to expect," said a woman. "Now they do."

Surely there did now seem less enthusiasm from the men outside.

"No matter," said the second woman who had seen Kur feeding, in the house. "The party is not for the men. It is for the beasts. It is their party, their joy, their festival."

How tense, I thought, and how precarious, must be the relationship between Kurii and humans.

"What are we here for?" asked a woman, "penned in the darkness?"

"You heard the trumpet," said another. "It is an arena trumpet. There are games. We are prizes. It is common in arena sports, in the killing games, the beast fights, in the tarn races, the races of kaiila and tharlarion, as in the contests of dramas, of choral song, of music, and poetry, to include kajirae amongst the winnings, amongst the spoils of victory. What do men care more for than power, gold, silver, and women?"

"True," said another woman.

"So, there is nothing to fear," said another woman. "We will merely have new collars, new chains."

"If our new masters do not want us, they will sell us," said another.

"Yes," said another.

"If we are prizes," said one of the women in the darkness, "why have we not been displayed?"

I knew little of such matters, but I gathered that it was customary to publicly display at least some of the goods that might accrue to a victor, perhaps a vessel of silver, a buckle, pin, or armlet of gold, a fine kaiila, a lovely kajira.

"The master has arranged this festival for the beasts," said a woman. "It is their festival. Of what interest could we be to the beasts?"

At that point there was a noise in the chamber behind us, and, when we looked back, we saw, moving toward us in the darkness, a number of glowing objects, some red, some white. The pen was opened in the back, and some of the glowing objects apparently entered the pen, and, at the same time, before us, the gate leading from the pen to the chute was flung upward.

"Into the chute!" we heard.

We crowded into the chute, frightened, pressed closely together. There were men behind us, and the glowing objects. We could not retreat. I heard a scream of pain. Then, suddenly, the door at the end of the chute, leading outside, was thrown open. I shut my eyes, briefly, against the light. I heard another scream of pain from somewhere behind me.

We could hardly move, so much we were crowded, so closely we were pressed together.

"Out! Move! Move, sluts! Move, two-legged animals! Move, branded, shapely beasts! Move, marked collar trash! Move! Move!"

I heard another scream of pain behind me. I could not hold my place, I was thrust forward.

"Please, Master," I heard, "do not touch me again with the hot iron!"

Some of the irons, held in the heavily gloved hands of the men, had glowed redly, dully, and others had been white with heat.

I heard another cry of pain.

We were being driven from the chute by hot irons.

I was pressed forward. I almost lost my footing. Then I cried out with fear, for one of the men was outside the chute, to the side, close, carrying one of the glowing irons. I could feel the heat a yard away.

I pressed forward, thrusting those ahead of me forward, and being forced forward by those behind me.

And then, suddenly, I was outside the chute, and door, and, a moment or two later, the door was shut, and I stood on the grass, locked outside, as the others, and looked about myself.

CHAPTER SIXTY

I was not the only kajira who screamed in fear and misery.

To our left, as we emerged from the chute, and into the light, we saw a small set of tiers, on these tiers, bright with festive regalia, mostly in the colors of the upper castes, but subdued, and restless, were perhaps two hundred men, doubtless mostly those who had been at the feast. I supposed they would be unarmed, as had been my master and Lord Grendel. I saw no women. Also, on the tiers, mixed in with the men, crouching, I saw several Kurii, in bright harnessing. There were also several Kurii, also in bright harnessing, on the ground, before, and to the sides of the tiers. Lord Grendel's conjecture to the effect that the numbers of Kurii in the vicinity might be some fifteen, presumably at most, had proved woefully conservative. I was not sure of the numbers but I would have hazarded that the number might more closely approximate some forty Kurii, say, twenty in the stands, and twenty on the ground. The scene of the entertainment, as it had been spoken of, was not an arena or a theater, but it was, in effect, a closed area, closed on one side by the tiers, to my left, and, on another side, that behind me, by the house of Decius Albus. The other two sides, that before me, and to my right, were closed with armed guards, of which there might have been seventy or eighty. These wore the livery of the House of a Hundred Corridors. In the center of the tiers, to my left, there was what, garlanded and ribboned, I supposed, might count as a box, or reserved area, in which were three men and two Kurii. I did not know this at the time, as I found Kurii difficult to distinguish from one another, as perhaps they did humans, but the two Kurii there were the two Kurii who had been colleagues of Surtak, and had assisted in the raid in Brundisium, which had succeeded in capturing Eve, she apparently intended by Lord Arcesilaus as a gift for Lord Grendel. In the center of the three men in the box, not surprisingly, was the true host of the festivities, large-bodied and coarse-featured, in white and gold robes, Decius Albus, trade advisor to the Ubar, Marlenus, and master of the House of a Hundred Corridors. On his right was Drusus Andronicus, long-armed, handsome, and stalwart, in suitable scarlet, betokening his caste, who stood high in the house, and, on his left, clad openly, brazenly, unapologetically, in the hues of the night, was Tyrtaios, of the caste whose members acknowledge no Home Stone, the caste of Assassins. I saw a great vat at the foot of the tiers, on their left, as I faced it. Near the vat, on a bench, there were several large, figured, ceramic bowls, each with two handles, some with black figures on a white background, and some with black figures on a red background. I saw a Kur thrust one of these bowls, with two paws, or hands, into the vat, and raise it, spilling fluid, to his mouth, and he quaffed the contents, apparently entirely, his head back, and then he howled, and reeled away. In the stands, too, I saw, here and there, such vessels in the grasp of one Kur or another. I saw two Kurii before the stands, and one to the side, sprawled on the ground, sleeping, or sense-less. One had a broken bowl near it. I saw no sign that the two Kurii in the box with Decius Albus had shared in the conviviality, the signs of which were so obvious amongst their cohorts. Decius Albus seemed expansive, pleasant, jovial, and communicative, almost obsequious, in addressing himself, via their translators, to the two crouching, hirsute guests with whom he shared the honor of his box. From his appearance and deportment, I suspected that he himself had not proved immune to the charms of the vat. Neither Drusus Andronicus nor Tyrtaios, on the other hand, appeared to have shared in that amiable brew, that "gift of the Life Daughter," tawny, high-growing, flowing-in-the-wind sa-tarna, so readily available about. One was of the Warriors, one was of the Assassins. Neither will drink freely, when unaware of what might be at their elbow.

When we had rushed forth, crowded together, fearing the irons, it had taken us but a moment to register, and react to, the carnage into which we had been introduced. The grass here and there had been soaked with blood, and parts of verr, organs and limbs, skin and heads, were scattered about the field. Half-eaten bodies lay about. One Kur regarded us, a trembling, bleeding verr hanging from its jaws. I fear I was not the only kajira who screamed in fear and misery.

At the height of the tiers, on a separate platform, raised above the last tier, there was a helmeted fellow in the garb of the House of a Hundred Corridors, who stood near a stand on which there was fixed a large trumpet.

It was that trumpet, I supposed, that had emitted the blast that had initiated the games, if one might so refer to them.

I saw, on the field, rather toward the house, not far from where we had entered the field, chained to a stake, by hands, body, and legs, my master, Kurik of Victoria.

Distraught, miserable, sobbing, I ran to him. I shook the chains, and pulled at them, but I could not undo the locks.

"Why are you not kneeling?" he inquired. "Surely you know you are in the presence of a free person."

I ran about, before him.

"Surely you know that can be cause for discipline," he said.

"Master!" I wailed, in misery, putting my head to his chest.

"For discipline," he said.

"Master, Master!" I wept.

"Do you think you are a free woman?" he said.

"No, Master!" I said. I flung myself to my knees before him. "Forgive me, Master!" I said.

"You look well there," he said. "You always looked well there."

"It is where I belong," I wept.

"And others," he said.

"No!" I said. "I, only I!"

"Many have knelt there," he said.

"I love you!" I cried.

"A slave's love is worthless," he said.

"No!" I said. "The love of a slave is the fullest, the deepest, the most helpless of all loves! No love can compare with the love of a slave!"

"Do you wish to be cuffed?" he asked.

"Forgive me, Master," I said, "but I think I am in little danger of that at the moment."

"I often thought you might prove to be a perceptive slave," he said. "One is always pleased to encounter intelligence in a beast, particularly in one whose flanks are of interest."

"What can I do?" I begged, suddenly, looking up at him.

"I do not know," he said. "If something should occur to you, let me know."

"Please, Master," I said. "Do not be frivolous with your slave."

"How can one better approach the Cities of Dust," he said, "than with a light step and a laugh on one's lips?"

"I shall plead on your behalf," I said. "I shall plead with Master Albus."

"Do not be absurd," he said. "That would avail nothing."

"Nonetheless!" I said.

"That would make the victory theirs," he said.

"Surely it is already theirs," I said.

"No," he said. "How I die is mine."

"I shall plead," I said, and made to rise.

"You have not been given permission to rise," he said.

Frightened, I sank back to my knees.

"Master!" I wept.

"Do not demean me," he said, and in such a voice that I trembled.

"Forgive me," I said.

"Poor Phyllis," he said. "You know so little of this world and its ways."

"There is Lord Grendel," I said.

"There is nothing he can do," he said. "Let us hope he can make it away, safely."

"I do not understand all this," I said. "What is going on? Where is Surtak? Why was the hiatus terminated? What has Master Albus to gain by this madness?"

"Much," he said. "He wishes to redeem himself in the eyes of the Kurii. In the absence of Lord Agamemnon, he wishes to achieve the coup left undone, the recruitment or demise of Lord Grendel, a feat by which he would hope to regain the approbation of Lord Agamemnon. Accordingly, he took it upon himself to end the hiatus. To do this he must supplant Surtak, by which victory he would hope to clear the way for his scheme, and win prestige and power amongst such disaffected Kurii as hope to profit from the reduction or fall of Surtak."

I reached wildly, foolishly, to the chains at his legs, and tried to pull them loose.

"Poor Phyllis," he said. "Do not concern yourself with me. Be done with fearing for me. If you would fear, fear for yourself. Look about you. Your collar, such a lovely shield from men, who would own you, will not protect you here. Decius Albus is desperate to please his dark allies. Do you think they care for kajirae? Consider the verr, and their remains. That is only a prelude, to whet the appetites of the beasts. Who knows how long it has been since they have fed in the ways they most wish to feed, and feed to their fill, on abundant, living, bloody meat, either on a steel world or here, on verdant Gor? You and the others, I fear, have been brought forth for Kur feeding, and Kur sport, as much as the eviscerated, shredded verr."

I shuddered. The other kajirae were huddled together, near the door through which they had been herded into the fearful open. How forlorn they looked, small, frightened, and lost. Some knelt, others held to one another.

"I should have left you on your former world," he said.

"No, Master," I said. "On this world I have been collared, I have served, I have lived."

"I wish you well," he said.

"No, no!" I cried. "Tal, tal, greetings, always greetings!"

"I fear the trumpet is to be blown," he said.

"Master!" I wept.

"Wait!" he said. "The noble Decius Albus must have his moment! He rises, if unsteadily."

Turning about, toward the stands, I saw Master Albus get to his feet. He was assisted by Drusus Andronicus.

"Paga!" he called to a soldier, who hurried to fetch him a goblet of the fiery, amber brew.

Shortly thereafter, the vessel in his hand, he called out, "To glorious Ar," and then drank. "To Glorious Ar," said the men in the stands, and soldiers about. He then called out, "May she soon have a Ubar worthy of her throne, worthy of her glory!"

"Yes, yes!" called some in the stands, but most paused, and exchanged glances.

"He speaks dangerously," said Kurik. "I did not know his ambition soared so high. It would startle tarns."

"I fear he is drunk," I said.

"Paga loosens the tongue, and opens doors best guarded," said Kurik.

Decius Albus quaffed once more.

"And now," called Decius Albus, swaying in the box, then steadied by Drusus Andronicus, "let us salute our revered and mighty allies, our friends from afar, whom we honor with these games."

Master Albus then quaffed once more.

"I fear he knows little of the games of Kurii," said Kurik, "the dark games of the rings."

I recalled that Surtak had had, on his left wrist, two rings. I had gathered that such rings must be earned, but I knew little about the matter.

"I have noted," called out Decius Albus, waving the goblet about, "that some of you, my dear friends of Ar, administrators and magistrates, companions and colleagues, have witnessed the pleasures of our friends with but subdued enthusiasm. Understand then that these games are in their honor, and not ours. They are on their behalf, and not ours. Different cities, different worlds, different customs. Do not begrudge our friends their pleasures, no more than we would wish them to begrudge us ours. Be patient, and try to see things as others see them. What would entitle you to impress your prejudices on others?"

"The sword!" cried out Kurik, angrily.

"Master!" I said, fearfully. "Be silent!"

"Did the prisoner speak?" called Master Albus, trying to focus his eyes.

He was assured of that, apparently by Drusus Andronicus.

I moaned, for the five occupants of the box, Master Albus, Drusus Andronicus, Tyrtaios, and two Kurii were making their way down the tiers, to approach us. With them were some soldiers, and two or three other Kurii, apparently curious.

"Do not run, stay on your knees," said Kurik.

"Yes, Master," I said.

Decius Albus then stood before us. He retained the goblet, but it was, I think, empty. "You spoke of the sword," said Decius Albus. "It is easy to speak of the sword when one is in chains."

"Make it more difficult," said Kurik. "Free me, and put one in my hands."

"The bow is your weapon," said Master Albus.

"A knife will do," said Kurik, "or a pointed stick."

"I thought," said Master Albus, "to have you witness the slaughter of the beasts, four-legged and two-legged, and then have you eaten to death, prolonging it as long as possible, eaten bit by bit, bite by bite, by our noble allies, the High Ones, but, as you have seen, some members of our audience seem reluctant to participate in the festivities, even vicariously."

"Perhaps they will object," said Kurik.

"They are not soldiers, they are not armed," said Master Albus.

"Spare the kajirae," said Kurik.

"That would disappoint our noble friends," said Decius Albus. "They are looking forward to the hunt."

"It is not a hunt," said Kurik. "It is the slaughter of penned verr."

"In deference to the sympathies of the crowd," said Decius Albus, "I am prepared to be merciful."

"'Merciful'?" said Kurik.

"To you," said Decius Albus.

"I do not understand," said Kurik.

Master Albus turned to Tyrtaios. "Kill him," he said.

"No!" I cried. "No, Master!"

"I kill for pay," said Tyrtaios.

"Will a tarsk-bit be sufficient?" asked Decius Albus.

"I am not a novice," said Tyrtaios.

"Two, then," said Decius Albus.

"Let us return to the box, noble Albus," said Drusus Andronicus, supporting Decius Albus, who might otherwise have fallen.

Tyrtaios had turned away.

"A golden tarn then," called Decius Albus, the words slurring.

Tyrtaios turned back.

Surely a Ubar might have been attacked for such a fee.

"You have had much paga, noble Albus," said Drusus Andronicus. "Let us return to the box, and you may rest, think, collect yourself, and be at ease."

"A golden tarn!" roared Decius Albus.

"Ho, noble Tyrtaios," said Kurik. "The fee is good, and the risk is slight. Do not hesitate. What have you to fear? Your target is stationary, and cannot resist!"

"A golden tarn," repeated Decius Albus, slowly, separating the words.

"I am a high Assassin," said Tyrtaios, turning angrily toward Decius Albus. "I have trained for years. I have ascended the Nine Steps of Blood. I do not slaughter a tethered tarsk. I am not a butcher. Kill him yourself. Do not be afraid. A child, or slave, could manage the matter!"

"Noble friend!" protested Decius Albus, turning white. Two of the soldiers present grasped their spears more firmly.

"Do not be offended, noble colleague of the Dark Caste," said Drusus Andronicus. "Hold. Do not draw your sword. Be at peace. He is not himself. It is the paga that speaks, not the noble Albus."

Tyrtaios gestured toward Kurik. "Unchain him," he said. "Put a sword in his hand."

"Surely not," said Master Albus.

"I am an indifferent swordsman," said Kurik. "You have nothing to fear. I am no match for an Assassin, or warrior."

"It would be something for the crowd," said Drusus Andronicus to Decius Albus. "It is not much pleased with what has ensued thus far. What is amusing in the slaughtering of verr? Surely it is entitled to a kill it can understand, an arena kill, as in the Stadium of Blades."

"—Yes, very well," said Decius Albus, leaning on Drusus Andronicus. "Let him be unchained, and armed."

"And," said Drusus Andronicus, "as the Kurii have had their sport
with the verr, let us return the kajirae to their kennels and chains."

"No, no," said Decius Albus. "Our dark friends must not be disappointed. This day is theirs. I need this day for them. It is important."

"You are afraid of them?" said Drusus Andronicus.

"Of course," said Decius Albus. "Are you not afraid, also?"

"Of course," said Drusus Andronicus.

"It could mean our lives," said Decius Albus.

"I understand," said Drusus Andronicus.

Of the Kurii about, only the two who had descended from the box
had translators, and neither device was activated.

I deemed this fortunate.

Decius Albus was then conducted across the small, bloody field,
and assisted in climbing to his box, and, shortly thereafter, he sank
into the curule chair at its center. I was not sure he was still conscious.
Drusus Andronicus was seated at his side, and the two Kurii who had
accompanied Surtak in Brundisium, and apparently now held posts of
high station, had returned to their places in the box, as well.

A soldier approached, with keys to the padlocks that secured the
chains of Kurik of Victoria.

"I am not a good swordsman," said Kurik to Tyrtaios.

"I take it, that is your first thrust," said Tyrtaios.

"Not at all," said Kurik, as the chains were being removed.

"It would not matter much if you were an excellent swordsman,
or not," said Tyrtaios. "It might take a moment longer, another parry,
another thrust. My skills reach beyond excellent. I fear only two swords
on Gor, that of the High Master of the Caste of Assassins, and that of
an obscure warrior who, long ago, on the roof of the Central Cylinder
of Ar, bested him."

"Then only one," said Kurik, "for the High Master, bested, defeated,
must have been slain."

"No," said Tyrtaios. "He escaped."

"I see," said Kurik, as the last of the chains fell away.

"I will be quick," said Tyrtaios.

"Doubtless I am expected to be grateful," said Kurik.

"As you wish," said Tyrtaios.

A sword was placed in the hand of Kurik.

"Up, Phyllis," said Kurik. "Aside. We must have room."

I sprang to my feet, and moved to the side. "Do not fight, Master," I said. I did not wish him to be mocked, to appear inept, and foolish. He might, at least, die with a sword in his hand, proudly, arrogantly, not lifted. Too, perhaps Tyrtaios would not strike a man who refused to defend himself. But then I recalled he was of the dark caste. "Master," I moaned. I knew then Kurik of Victoria would fight, no matter the odds. He was Gorean. "Master!" I wept.

"How better to go to the Cities of Dust?" he asked.

"Wait!" said Tyrtaios, suddenly, and backed away some yards, and pointed to our right.

At that point, opposite the stands, where there was a line of soldiers closing off the field, something, apparently unexpected, at least by most, was taking place. The line had parted, allowing the passage of what appeared to be two large Kurii. The first was swathed in chains, and the second, apparently the guard, or custodian, of the first, carried a large Kur ax.

Clearly the men in the stands, and the soldiers about, were not aware of what was occurring. Similarly, it seemed that few of the Kurii, at least at first, understood what was taking place.

"What is going on?" called Kurik to Tyrtaios.

"I do not know," said Tyrtaios. "I have not been informed."

I glanced at the stands. All there, both men and Kurii, were on their feet. Even Decius Albus, half supported by Drusus Andronicus, was on his feet, staring blearily across the field.

The two Kurii who were in the box of Decius Albus, those of high station, who had accompanied Surtak in Brundisium, howled with pleasure and leaped about within the box itself, in what might be some bestial dance of victory, of triumph, of joy. They then desisted, and then, apparently half beside themselves with pleasure, struggling to control their glee, they called out in Kur. There was then a roar in Kur that coursed through the stands amongst the Kurii therein, that was taken up by the Kurii about, on the ground, those apparently waiting for the sounding of the trumpet, to signal the new hunt. Men, in fear, drew apart from the Kurii, as they could. Guards and soldiers, in their lines, looked to one another. Lines wavered as some men moved back, and others leaned forward, bracing their spear shafts in the turf. Officers were silent.

"Behold," called Tyrtaios, from his stance, some yards back. "It is a surprise, arranged by Aelius and Lucilius, to delight the afternoon, the execution of an enemy, the consolidation of their seizure of power."

If larls could speak, how could one transcribe their names in human phonemes? I did not even know, nor, if I knew, could I pronounce the Kur name of Lord Grendel, or that of Lord Agamemnon, or Surtak, or Eve, or Lyris, or others. I had little doubt that the names 'Aelius' and 'Lucilius' had been chosen with political intent, largely to soothe apprehensions in the House of a Hundred Corridors, to suggest a relationship of sympathy and accord that might not exist, to insist on the existence of a bridge where, in reality, one might not exist.

The two seeming beasts, one bound with chains, the other with its ax, approached the center of the small field, opposite the stands, near the stake to which Kurik of Victoria had been fastened.

I suppressed a tiny cry of surprise.

CHAPTER SIXTY-ONE

The one seeming beast, it with the ax, as one would expect, had been rather behind his charge, but, as it came closer, and was less blocked from view, I was startled. So, too, I gathered, was Kurik of Victoria. Its harnessing was not familiar, as the original harnessing had been replaced. The harnessing, now, was much as that of most of the other Kurii about, even festive in nature. But I noted dark stains, brownish red, dried, on the harnessing.

Dangling about the broad, thick neck of the guard was a translator, and, momentarily, I realized it had been activated, for I could hear, relayed, and translated, speech from the box in the stands.

"Bring the wretch forward, closer," commanded one of the Kurii in the box. "Behold, cohorts, the cowardly rogue who would hold truce with the enemy, suspending hostilities, denying us the blood our due, the glory that should be ours. The noble Decius Albus, our esteemed ally, atoning for the loss of a hostage, seizing an initiative, devised a brilliant plan whereby might be brought to fruition the plan of Lord Agamemnon, now regrettably absent, the enlisting or destruction of a foe of significance, Grendel, high in the ranks of the usurper, Arcesilaus. But his plan would be frustrated by the cowardly villain before you, who would continue the hiatus!"

At this point there were righteous roars of indignation, from at least several of the Kurii about, who, I took it, were of the faction of Aelius and Lucilius.

"This cowardice, this dereliction of duty, this refusal to promote an action clearly in accord with the will of, and in the best interests of, Lord Agamemnon necessitated, indeed, demanded, mutiny. Power unexercised is power betrayed. The leader who does not lead is no leader, but a traitor. With grievous reluctance and the keenest of sorrows, choiceless in the circumstances, I and Lucilius did what was called for, indeed, what was necessary!"

Several of the Kurii bellowed agreement.

"It is now only necessary," said the speaker, "to mete out justice." He then called down to the field. "Cut off his head!"

Then Surtak's body swelled in the chains, and the links rustled all about his body. "Come and do it yourself!" he called.

The utterance in Kur was loud, ferocious, and horrifying, but the translator ticked off the translation in Gorean with its customary equanimity.

I shuddered.

For a moment, in the box, Aelius, he I took to be Aelius, as he had referred to the other as Lucilius, remained still, perhaps surprised, perhaps taken aback. Then he called out, "Yes!"

"Wait!" said Decius Albus to him, who, after his recumbency in the box, seemed more in control of his body, less muddled in his mind.

"Do not," said Drusus Andronicus. "Consider your station!"

But Aelius had left the box, and was making his way, lightly, for his bulk, down the tiers of the stand. On the ground level he held out his hand, or paw, and one of the Kurii about placed an ax in that massive, six-digited grasping appendage. He held it as lightly as I might have carried a stick. I would have had difficulty in lifting that lethal tool, let alone wielding it.

"Prepare!" he called to Surtak.

"Do so!" responded Surtak, and, simultaneously, at a flick of the paw of Lord Grendel, the chains, like liberated snakes, leapt from his body, and Lord Grendel handed him his own ax, which he had borne to the field.

"Behold," cried Surtak, his eyes blazing, "you stand within the Rings!"

A hush came over the stands.

Neither men nor Kurii moved, or spoke.

Aelius, ax in hands, stepped back, closer to the stands. But none of his Kur cohorts stepped between him and Surtak. The ground between them had now become different, holy, or ceremonially reserved, I gathered, as a Ring Challenge had been issued. It was not to be intruded upon, I gathered, until the business of the challenge had been resolved.

"I decline to accept the challenge," said Aelius.

"You are within the Rings," said Surtak.

"You must accept the challenge," said a nearby Kur.

There were two rings of reddish iron on the left wrist of Surtak. Leadership amongst Kurii, I gathered, is not easily earned.

"Peace, peace, fellowship!" called Decius Albus, standing in the box. No longer did he seem random or lost. In the way it can be done, by disaster, crisis, or a sudden, freezing recognition of danger, it seemed the reeling heat of his drunkenness had been thrust aside. It may have been there, chemically, as real as the paga in the blood, but it was no longer operative. It was not so much neglected, as shut away. It may have stood at the door of consciousness, but that door was now barred against it. In the presence of a larl or an upraised knife one sobers instantly. "Dear friends and colleagues," continued Decius Albus, "all differences can be negotiated. All viewpoints must be considered. Compromise is always possible. Let us enter into frank, honest, fruitful dialogue."

I sensed that Decius Albus was not certain, given the Ring Challenge, of his Kur allies. Perhaps there were factions amongst them. Might he not endanger himself, his house, and his plans, if he trod blindly in the social and political darkness? Surely he was aware something was suddenly very different. He was confident he could rely on his armed men, the guards, the soldiers. But what of the Kurii? What stance should he take, given what had occurred? The men in the stands, lacking arms, were negligible, at least as of now. They might be formidable in Ar, with their connections, their positions, their influence, and such, but here they amounted to little or nothing. A knife slips as easily into the heart of a Ubar as that of a peasant.

"You are within the Rings!" roared Surtak.

"Hold, hold, my friends!" called Decius Albus. "Do not interfere with the festivities! All disagreements can be resolved amicably. Postpone your differences, at least until the fierce larls of the blood recline. Now, let the games continue! See how I add to them! I have planned a surprise! Look to the gates!"

Decius Albus lifted and lowered his hand, signaling.

The gate on the ground level, through which the verr had been driven out, was flung open, and a collared, Kurlike thing, bereft of harness, was prodded out, into the sunlight.

I recognized it.

"Lyris!" exclaimed Surtak, this name picked up on Lord Grendel's translator, and broadcast about.

Lucilius was standing, in the box. "Behold, a fallen, disgraced one," he shouted out, "a failed one, reduced and degraded, a belonging of the traitor Surtak. We planned, with our esteemed ally, the noble Decius Albus, to have her slain before Surtak, before we did him justice, that he might see her blood before we took his own."

"Lift up your ax!" cried Surtak to Aelius, who had drawn back to the tiers of the stand.

"Throw down yours!" called Aelius. "We will spare her the death of teeth or spears. Your life or hers!"

"Do not, Master!" cried Lyris, rushing to Surtak. She crouched down before him, in Kur deference. "Do not trust them!" she cried. "They will kill us both."

"You have my word," called Aelius. "It is pledged."

Angrily Surtak cast down the ax.

"Excellent, excellent!" called Decius Albus. "Wisdom prevails!"

Lord Grendel made no move to retrieve the discarded ax.

"We will now add to the games," called out Decius Albus, "as being of special interest, two kajirae, one who failed to well serve the House of a Hundred Corridors, a house that is reluctant to accept embarrassment or failure, and one that attests the good faith, the good will, the generosity, the bounty of my house. My house does not stint on the provender of its festive boards, nor on the richness of its gifts to its retainers. So, too, we do not stint on the quality of our sponsored games. In the arena we put upon the sand only the finest of fighters, in the tarn races only the swiftest of tarns, and so, too, here, we do not stint on the quality of our prey animals. You will behold, momentarily, an unusually lovely kajira, a former display slave, a nicely curved item that cost the house a full golden tarsk."

Much attention was then focused on the second gate, that through which we had been hurried, from the girl chute, crowding to the outside, desperate to escape from the heated irons.

Decius Albus again raised and lowered his hand, again signaling.

A blond kajira was thrust stumbling onto the field, her forearm over her eyes to protect them from the glare of sunlight. Then she lowered her arm, looked about herself, and screamed in horror.

Like the rest of us she wore naught but her collar. We are beasts who need not be clothed. We were kajirae, lovely, purchasable brutes who existed for the service of our masters. I did not think the neck of the former, proud free woman, the Lady Alexina, had long been in a collar. I suspected that Decius Albus had welcomed her return to his house, taken pains to allay her apprehensions, and treated her as before, honorably and bountifully, or even better, while contemplating all the while how he might best express his dissatisfaction with her service. Perhaps only today she had been seized, stripped, branded, and collared.

Decius Albus then lifted and lowered his hand again, signaling for the third time to the gate area, and another kajira was thrust into the open.

"Paula!" I cried out, in misery.

"I have this sword," said Kurik. "Do you wish me to kill you, now, quickly, mercifully?"

"It is Paula!" I said, pointing.

"I do not think I can reach her," said Kurik, gauging the distance.

He quickly looked about. Tyrtaios had not approached more closely, but had remained some yards away, muchly at the point to which he had withdrawn, shortly after noticing the arrival on the field of what seemed to be two Kurii, one chained, one with an ax.

Kurik then regarded me.

"Approach," he said. "You will feel little. It will be over quickly. I will do it swiftly."

"Have I displeased my master?" I asked.

"Your friend, Paula, hurries to your side," he said.

A wave of emotion, like a surf of grief, swept through me. How I had betrayed Paula! Happily she knew nothing of my vanity, my treachery, my perfidy. But I knew, and was stricken.

"Dear Phyllis," she cried, tears in her eyes.

"You see the remains of verr, the hides, the blood," I said.

"I know," she said.

"It is the fate intended for us," I said.

"Poor, dear Phyllis," she said.

"There is no escape from the fangs of the beasts," I said.

She put her cheek against mine, and I felt her tears.

"There is an escape," said Kurik. "The trumpet has not yet sounded, the beasts have not yet charged, eager for the feeding. Kneel, both of you, put your heads down, your hair thrown forward, to expose the back of your necks. Two strokes and you have cheated the High Ones, depriving them of the kill."

"You think that a kindness?" I asked.

"Surely," he said.

"A greater kindness," I said, "would be to allow me to die at your feet, lying in your blood."

"And what of you?" asked Kurik, regarding Paula.

"Forgive me, Master," she said. "But you have no right to kill me. I belong to another."

"Decius Albus," said Kurik.

"I had in mind," she said, "another."

"The trumpet will sound any moment," said Kurik, looking about.

"It will not," said Drusus Andronicus, standing with us, his sword drawn, the blade wet with fresh blood. He stood between us and the stands. "Get behind me, worthless slave," he said to Paula.

"Yes, Master!" she cried.

We looked up to the platform of the trumpeter. The great trumpet, in its mount, was not tended. The platform was bare.

Men in the stands looked wildly to one another. Several Kurii in the stands began to descend to the field.

Surtak roared terribly, a noise that might, millennia ago, have shaken forests on a far world, and seized up the mighty ax he had cast down but Ehn ago. Lord Grendel's translator articulated, quietly, as the volume was set, "Yes, the Rings, the Rings." Surtak then, with one massive, clawed foot, violently thrust Lyris to the ground. "Aelius, Aelius!" he cried.

But Aelius, ax in hand, was withdrawing amongst the Kurii, but they were moving to the sides, refusing to shield him, exposing the ground between him and Surtak, producing an open corridor of bloody grass, lined by large bodies.

"I have declined the Rings!" called Aelius, who then cast down his ax, and turned away.

"Command is surrendered!" roared Surtak. "I command!"

"No," came from Lord Grendel's translator, and I saw that this must have picked up, and translated, Kur from the box, for Lucilius was on his feet, an ax brandished, eyes blazing, jaws slavering. "I command!" he cried.

Aelius had climbed toward the box but, before he could enter it, Lucilius, two hands on the great haft, wielded the ax, and the sundered head of Aelius spun far away, a small, dark cloud raining blood, and blood from the decapitated corse, sped by the fierce pressure generated by the frantic pounding of that mighty heart, spurted a dozen feet into the air, reached the height of its arc, paused, and then fell like thick rain, scintillating like a scarlet shower in the bright sun.

"Let the festivities continue!" cried Decius Albus, desperately. "Noble friends, High Ones, mighty allies, do you not hunger? Is a banquet not spread before you? See the soft flesh, the tender, two-legged verr! We set them before you! The feast is prepared. The table is laden. We need no trumpet! Rush forth! Hunt! Eat!"

"No!" roared Surtak. "I will kill the first who should so attack, the first who should so feed!"

"They are humans," protested a Kur.

"My ax is lifted," said Surtak.

"What is your authority?" demanded a Kur.

"The right of command," said Surtak.

"And what gives you the right of command?" asked another.

"The ax," said Surtak.

"Are the Rings closed?" demanded a Kur.

"No!" said Surtak, and lifted his eyes to the box.

"I command!" called Lucilius.

"I command!" said Surtak. "The Rings are open."

"I pronounce them closed," said Lucilius.

"I pronounce them open," said Surtak.

Kurii, those now descended from the stands, regarded one another, banefully. Doubtless some had favored the coup that had supplanted Surtak, and others not. Many, perhaps, had merely accepted it, as done. Surely Aelius and Lucilius were mighty Kurii and awesome leaders. Few would lift an ax against them. Too, they were favored by the House of a Hundred Corridors, the ambitions of which they, in their pursuit of power, were willing to further, which house, undeniably, had been enleagued with Lord Agamemnon. Surely that house had provided him and his fellows with a haven of concealment and support on Gor, and a base of operations in the vicinity of the most populous city in the northern hemisphere of the planet. So the coup, I gathered, had been largely unchallenged. But now Surtak had returned, armed.

The stands were now largely empty. Most men had fled. Most Kurii had poured down to the field, many eager and snarling. Lucilius remained in the stands, in the box, retaining it as a commanding coign of vantage. From it he surveyed the field. One of the few men left in the stands was Decius Albus, standing, white-faced, shaken, clutching the front railing of the box. His white and gold robes were drenched with the blood of Aelius. The soldiers, armed, held their posts, as before, now uneasily, in two lines, closing off the two open edges of the field, that opposite the house, and that opposite the stands.

Men and beasts roiled about.

Confusion, agitation, reigned.

It seemed a tide was uncertain, a storm was poised, undecided, one sensed a silent tumult, a predecessor of movement, one feared lightning.

"I am afraid," I said.

Kurik, looking over his shoulder, addressed Lord Grendel. "I would speak with Surtak."

"Do so," said Lord Grendel. "My translator is activated."

"I think it best that others do not hear what I would speak," he said.

"Kurii?" asked Lord Grendel.

"Yes," said Kurik.

"I deactivate my translator," said Lord Grendel, touching the device. "Whisper to me, and I will whisper to the High One in Kur."

This was done.

And whatever was communicated seemed to meet with the approval of Surtak. He grasped his ax most closely.

Lord Grendel reactivated his translator.

My master turned to me. "I sense looming war," he said. "Our dark friends are disturbed. It is not the way of the Kur to long linger in doubt. Inaction is not tolerable to them. The Kur will act. I do not know how it will act, but it will act. An expression, a word, a movement, may precipitate an attack. They seethe. Many are hungry. They think they have been denied their right to food, to sport. Many do not care for what has occurred. They feel cheated. Surtak could not begin to protect the kajirae if the Kurii should suddenly rush upon them. So we need them to be here. We will ring them, as we can. Hopefully the soldiers will not attack them. In this way we may be able to protect some of them, at least for a time."

"I do not think the time will be long," I said.

"Ah," he said, "you see, you are perceptive, for a pleasure beast."

"I am Master's lowly pleasure beast," I said.

How abject I was before my master!

"I am pleased to own you," he said.

"I am pleased to be owned," I said.

How I belonged to him! How joyful I was to be a property! What woman does not long for her master?

"You are highly intelligent," he said. "It is pleasant to have one such as you in my collar, one such as you subject to my whip."

"Yes, Master," I said.

"Do you fear it?" he asked.

"Very much," I said.

Had I not felt it?

"It will be used on you, unhesitantly," he said, "should you prove in the least bit displeasing."

"Yes, Master," I said. "I am kajira."

"Speak," he said.

"I am yours to whip," I said. "I am your slave, yours to serve, yours to ravish as you wish, yours to love!"

"Beware," said he, "mere pleasure beast."

"Forgive me, Master," I said.

"Surtak," he said, "will advance, suddenly, roaring, then stopping, brandishing the ax. All attention will be directed upon him. It must be. In that moment, dart to the kajirae and tell them, if they would live, to hurry here, closely together, where we might, with good fortune, for a bit of time, fend off the Kurii. I do not think you will be noticed. When the kajirae move they will, of course, be seen. Surtak, then, will interpose himself between them and the Kurii, providing a shield until this position is reached."

He had scarcely said this when Surtak, with a loud cry in Kur, a roar, rushed forward, and then halted, shaking his ax violently at Lucilius, removed in the box, near the distraught Decius Albus.

I sped to the kajirae.

In a moment, they were aflight, hastening to the vicinity of the stake to which Kurik had been chained, where he, Lord Grendel, and Drusus Andronicus had stationed themselves.

The closest Kurii had fallen back, and even Lucilius, in the box, had apparently been startled, presumably anticipating a mad climb on the part of Surtak to the box. He had his ax poised. The headless corpse of Aelius was below the box, sprawled across three of the lowest tiers.

I did not suppose that Surtak, however enraged, given the example of Aelius, would have essayed that climb.

He had, however, clearly suggested that possibility.

The kajirae were well afoot before they were noticed, and then there was a great cry of rage and disappointment from several of the Kurii. At the same time they discovered Surtak had moved to his left, and had placed himself between them and the hastening kajirae. They would then have to deal with steel before they could hope to feed.

One or two of the formerly inert Kurii, who had passed out, or been asleep, had now been roused from their drunken stupor, and were standing, confused, and unsteady, on the field.

A Kur lunged forward, but stopped, snarling, and backed away, threatened by the ax of Surtak.

Surtak now moved to his right, his eyes on the Kurii, and I, and the cloud of kajirae, behind that shield, running, would, in a moment, attain that precarious haven for which we strove, a refuge little superior, I feared, to none at all.

Surtak, of course, had left the vicinity of the stake, to cover the flight of the kajirae, which, of course, exposed the two humans, Drusus Andronicus and Kurik, my master, to attack, and Lord Grendel, as well, who had surrendered his ax to Surtak. Kurii, a life form that tends to be large, agile, swift, fierce, and powerful, tend to be contemptuous of humans, which they commonly regard as an inferior life form. This contempt, on the other hand, is not always justified, as Kurii have learned, in Torvaldsland, the Tahari, the jungles of the Ua, and elsewhere. In any event, I cried out in misery as I saw a Kur, in the absence of Surtak, rush upon Drusus Andronicus, doubtless intent to sweep him aside and seize the slave, Paula, crouching behind him. It reached, snarling, for Drusus Andronicus, and the sword of the latter, like a striking ost, swift, clean, and deep, almost invisible in its movement, penetrated that massive body, only to be instantly withdrawn, that it might be freed for another thrust. But no other thrust was necessary. Clearly the Kur was startled. It wavered, puzzled, confused, and then stiffened, and fell to the earth.

"Beware!" said Lord Grendel.

"It begins," said Kurik, grimly.

For a moment nothing seemed to move on the field. Something of enormity had occurred, and had not yet been fully understood. And the Kurii looked to one another. It had been done. It had taken place. A human, one of that small, slow, fragile, weak, wretched, inferior, almost peltless stock, a small, vulnerable, despicable animal, a thing lacking claws, a soft thing, small jawed, with little in the way of fangs, had slain a High One, a Kur. One does not expect such things. What verr would dare to slay a larl, what tarsk a sleen?

Could such a thing be understood?

Had not nature itself been outraged?

"Peace, peace!" called Decius Albus, in his robes, soaked with the blood of Aelius.

"Kill all humans!" screamed a Kur, and seized a man, tearing off an arm, and biting through the throat, blood running between the fangs, and running like water down its chest.

Men cried out, scattering, fleeing toward the two lines of soldiers. This flight seemed to stimulate many of the Kurii, who, if undecided a moment before, were now precipitate in their pursuit. I saw more than one man dragged down, and fed upon. Some men, wiser, backed slowly away, threatened. Some reached the soldiers, and a Kur, threatened by a forest of spears, would turn away, seeking other prey. Some men remained, frightened, in the stands. Others descended through the tiers and sought to escape, away from the stands and field. Then I saw a Kur attack another Kur.

"Peace!" screamed Decius Albus.

"Hold, hold, stop, stop!" cried Lucilius, from the box, in wild remonstrance, this exhortation picked up by Lord Grendel's translator, and transmitted with impassive alacrity.

"Spare our humans, kill the others!" cried Decius Albus, pointing toward the stake, our small group, and the kajirae clustered about us.

Some Kurii turned toward us, but, wary of Surtak and his ax, did not charge.

I saw another human killed by a half-mad, drunken Kur.

"Traitor, traitor!" screamed Decius Albus to Drusus Andronicus, who stood ready, looking about himself.

"You stood before me, you protected me," cried Paula. "You are my master, my beloved master!"

"Be silent, unless you wish to be put upon the block!" said Drusus.

"I would not perish otherwise than at your feet, my master!" wept Paula.

He spun about and, with the flat of his left hand, struck her savagely to the grass, and was then, again, resolute, in the guard position. She looked up at him, disciplined, reassured, grateful, her eyes shining, put in her place, below him, a slave.

How radiant, how beautiful, was Paula! On Earth she had been nothing, and now, on Gor, she was the slave of a master. How she had longed for this world, and how she now found herself upon it, and as she wished to be, owned, and mastered, a branded, collared slave. Selflessness, and abject surrender, was her joy. Total and uncompromising slavery to her master was her ecstasy.

But how had she dared to speak? Did she not know she had been cautioned to silence? And how dared she use the expression 'my master' to him, when she belonged to another, to Decius Albus?

How tragic can be the lot of a helpless slave!

In her heart she was the slave of Drusus Andronicus, but, in the bonds of stern law, as obdurate as brass, as unyielding as steel, she was no more than another chattel of Decius Albus. A free woman can sell herself, but a slave cannot. She owns nothing, least of all herself. She belongs to her master.

How tragic to find herself longing for the chains of one master, and find herself fastened in the chains of another!

"Officers, men at arms, loyal servitors of the house," called out Decius Albus, to the lines of soldiers, "do not threaten our allies, our Kur brothers." He then pointed toward Surtak, Drusus Andronicus, Kurik, and Lord Grendel. "There are your enemies," he called out. "Turn your spears toward them. Converge upon them, slay them! And do not interfere otherwise. Let our mighty friends, our Kur brothers, have the kajirae!"

"No!" cried more than one man in the ranks.

"Order!" called an officer. "Discipline!"

The two lines of soldiers, closing off the open ends of the field, wavered. In places ranks were broken. Some men would doubtless obey, responsive to the bugles of war, but others seemed recalcitrant. Had they not now noted, this taking place before their very eyes, rampaging Kurii, unprovoked, attacking unarmed men? Who then, or what then, is friend or foe? Might they be the next to fall to those fangs? Surely Kurii had threatened them at the margins of the field. And, too, one does not kill kajirae, no more than one would sully or soil the rugs of Tor, or deface the intricate mosaics of Venna. Kajirae are not free persons, not enemies, no more than kaiila. They are goods, loot, pleasure animals. One does not kill them. One appropriates them, one seizes them, owns them, and enjoys them. Sometimes a free woman's slaves, obedient to the orders of conquering men, will seize, strip, and bind their mistress, and throw her to the feet of the victors, for the collar and iron. And many a free woman strips herself and, in the streets, before victors, as walls tumble and houses burn, performs obeisance, hoping to be spared for the coffle and market.

Decius Albus, his robes bloody, standing in the box, ax-bearing Lucilius wild and snarling at his side, while the field was broken into warring factions, men against Kur, Kur against men, men against men, Kur against Kur, remonstrated again and again with his men, "Peace! Peace! Do not threaten our dark brothers! Do not fight one another! Kill the traitorous Kur, Surtak, so reluctant to pursue the ends of the great Agamemnon! Kill the monster Grendel! Slay his fellow, Tenrik, of Siba! Kill the renegade Drusus Andronicus, murderer of a noble Kur, false to our table, false to his fee! Death to those who would divide us and spoil the festivities! Obey! The kajirae are for the sport of our allies! Do not interfere!"

"Ho!" cried Drusus Andronicus, in a mighty voice. "You have seen the beasts kill men! Do you think you would be spared? Would you have them feed on you, as well as vulnerable, helpless, stripped kajirae? Do you want your blood to fill the goblets of such beasts? They are not your friends, they are your enemies! Fight them and slay them, as you would the wild, ravening beasts of the fields!"

"Order, brothers!" cried Lucilius, his frenzied Kur streaming rapidly but passively through Lord Grendel's translator. "Let Kur not fight Kur! Do not do war upon one another!"

But I feared that few of those Kurii embroiled with one another in that melee, adherents of Surtak or Lucilius, tearing at one another, teeth locked in bodies, rolling in the grass, much attended to the plea of he who had been, but shortly before, their acknowledged leader.

"Differences may be amicably resolved," roared Lucilius, grasping his bloody ax. "Let reconciliation be proclaimed! Let fruitful, gentle peace abide! Traitors may be sought out and slain in a quieter, more pleasant time."

"Return to your posts! Put up your weapons! Heed your officers, those loyal to me!" screamed Decius Albus to the soldiers and guards.

I looked about.

Several knots of war, in moving, violent tangles, roiled in the field. There were cries. Weapons clashed. I saw a man sink to the ground. Elsewhere in the field, and at its edges, men faced one another, many in a threatening manner. Some held Kurii at bay with leveled spears. Many men, clearly, wavered, seemingly confused, surely not knowing what to do, willing neither to obey nor to refuse to obey.

"Soldiers of Ar," cried Drusus Andronicus, "those of you who are men, those of you who are worthy of the Home Stone of Ar, would you let lovely properties that should be yours, and may be yours, perish under the fangs of maddened beasts?"

"No!" cried a man.

"Are they worth only that?" cried Drusus Andronicus.

"No!" said more than one man.

"Discipline!" called an officer.

"Return to your ranks," called another.

"They are not free persons, enemies to be met in battle, enemies who would kill you, enemies who must fear your blades," cried Drusus Andronicus. "They are loot, objects, goods, kajirae, lovely, domestic stock, to be penned and owned, and fitted with chains, and sold."

"Yes, yes!" called more than one man.

"Surely, as men," called Drusus Andronicus, "you can think of better things to do with such goods, kajirae, can you not, than feed them to hungry beasts, better things to do with them than put them to the purpose of a beast's provender."

"Certainly!" laughed a man.

I understood that laugh, the laugh of a proud, free Gorean male.

I think I would have been terrified to have heard such a laugh on Earth. In that laugh was bespoken the truth that there were two sexes, and that one sex was the fit property of the other. Hearing it, I was well reminded not only that I was a woman, but that I was, on this world, aside from the obvious biotruths of a species, a particular sort of woman, that here I was, in full and complete legality, naught but a property, a vendible, purchasable object.

How far I was from my former world!

The kajirae, I amongst them, huddled together, all of us naked, and collared, near the stake to which Kurik, my master, had been chained. We were slaves, female slaves. Our fate was not in our hands. It would be determined by men.

"Albus will summon more men," said Kurik.

"It will take time," said Drusus Andronicus.

"Doubtless he has already done so," said Kurik.

"Possibly," said Drusus Andronicus.

"From the wagons, the guards," said Kurik.

"Quite possibly," said Drusus Andronicus. "Beware the Assassin."

"He remains in position, he does not charge," said Kurik.

"Interesting," said Drusus Andronicus.

"I could not stand against his skills," said Kurik.

"Nor, I think, could I," said Drusus Andronicus. "Why does he not advance?"

"We are two," said Kurik.

"In a moment, given the fire of that sword, we could be none," said Drusus Andronicus.

"He kills for pay," said Kurik.

"Matters are uncertain," said Drusus Andronicus. "Gold moves that blade, not words, not honor. What merchant would part with his goods while lacking the likelihood of recompense? What rational craftsman would sell his services without the assurance of gain?"

My master looked to me, sharply.

"Phyllis!"

"Master?" I said.

"Men are confused," he said. "Gaps may be found in ranks. You are

kajira. Men may be reluctant to strike you. You may be able to make your way to the wagon. Attempt to do so."

I recalled that he had earlier encouraged me to return to the wagon, but I had not been able to do so.

"No!" I said. "I do not wish to do so. Forgive me, but I will remain here. You are in terrible jeopardy. I will not leave you!"

"You will obey," he said.

"I will stay with you!" I cried.

"Go!" he said.

"They will not permit me passage!" I said. Did he think I was a free person? Did he not realize I was kajira?

"Hurry!" he said.

Tears burst from my eyes. I leapt to my feet and raced amongst men, some fighting, toward the perimeter of the field. A Kur turned savagely about, snarling, but I was past it. At the perimeter, I was turned back, resolutely, unhesitantly, as I had anticipated. I was treated identically at the other open perimeter. I was kajira. There was no escape for me. And Kurii fronted the field before the stands. It had doubtless seemed to the soldiers that I was trying to escape. Given the circumstances they would have supposed me to have been, understandably enough, I suppose, frantic with fear. Perhaps that is why they only turned me back, sternly, and did not throw me to my belly and slash the tendons behind my knee on both legs, hamstringing me. Goreans do not look lightly on the foolishness of slaves attempting to escape. And how would one escape, slave clad or stripped, branded and collared? And where could one escape to, in a world in which one could be but one thing, a slave? And why had my master wanted me to reach the wagon? I knew it to be empty. And the guards had determined that to their own satisfaction. Surely he remembered all that.

Miserable in one sense, but far from disheartened in another, cheered that I might return to the side of my master, to be with him, no matter what might ensue, I made my way back toward the stake.

The slaves were huddled there, together. How pathetic they looked. And, in a moment, I must take my place amongst them. I supposed it was much the same when a city falls and its more attractive women are stripped and gathered together, to await what will be done with them. To be sure, the captives would not as yet have been marked and collared. Interestingly, aside from proprietary markings and suitable collarings, it is easy to distinguish between two such groups, one of stripped free women and one of stripped kajirae. There would be a softness and vulnerability, a readiness, an appetition, and vitality, to the kajirae that would not yet characterize the free women. The kajirae have learned that they are women, and slaves. If necessary, they have learned it under the whip. The slave is not a pseudomale. She is a woman, and feminine, extremely feminine. She accepts her femininity, and rejoices in it. It is what she is, and wants to be. In her complementarity to the male, in her yielding to him, in her submission to his dominance, in her slave to his master, she finds herself.

In a moment, on the side rather near my master, I knelt amongst the other slaves. I trusted they would not think that I had been weak, foolish, or stupid, or incredibly naive, that I had essayed an escape, or perhaps they merely thought that I had simply lost my head and fled, that I had hoped, absurdly, to make my way unscathed between the spears.

Could I have been so ignorant, so lacking in understanding?

Did I not know that our only hope of survival lay in the blades of certain men, who might prize us as the goods we were?

I was muchly uneasy.

"Stupid fool," said a slave.

"She is doubtless a barbarian," said another, scornfully.

"I was commanded!" I retorted.

"Give her sandals," said another.

"Better, put her in the Robes of Concealment," said another. "She is not well covered."

"Surely she is a free woman," said another.

"But there is a collar on her neck," said another.

"Then she is a slave," said another.

"But a stupid slave," said another.

"Assuredly," said another.

Paula was in the group, near to Drusus Andronicus, but had not spoken. I saw tears in her eyes. She regarded me sympathetically, tenderly. She would know I had not left the group of my own free will, that I had not deserted it, that I had not tried to save myself, leaving the others to their fate. She would know that the abuse heaped upon me was not warranted. I had not tried to escape. I had not rushed stupidly, hysterically away. She was my friend. Happily she did not suspect how I had betrayed her. I felt guilt, keenly. I had so wronged her! Lyris was near Surtak, crouched behind him. I understood her to be an unusually beautiful female Kur, and yet that was lost upon me. What but another beast, gross and ruthless, agile and powerful, could find her so? The former

Lady Alexina, blond-haired and blue-eyed, now collared, and doubtless marked, wholly stripped, as were we all, knelt toward the center of our group. It is not unusual for slaves to be kept naked; it helps to remind them, like the collar on their necks and the mark on their thigh, that they are slaves. Surely I knew well the joy of being kept naked before my master. I saw Tyrtaios, standing easily, his sword unsheathed, who had not stirred from his earlier position to the side, regard her. She trembled in terror, and put her head down, and tried to hide herself amongst the others, others whom yesterday she might have despised, but from whom she was now no different, merely another kajira.

I looked up at my master. The slave is well accustomed to looking up at free persons from her knees. How right it seems, after a time, that we should kneel before the free. Indeed, we can be terribly uneasy if not permitted to kneel, even terrified not to kneel. I recalled when, on my former world, in the office, he whom I would come to know as Kurik of Victoria, had inquired why I was standing before him. "You should be on your knees," he had said. How puzzled, disconcerted, and then infuriated, I had been. I had not known then that I was a slave and he a master. How swiftly then, had I known these things, I would have hastened to my knees before the will, might, and glory of such a male, so different from the men I knew. How piteously I would have trembled and hoped to please him! Surely one such as he might find some use for one such as I! Had nature not designed us for ones such as he, to kneel naked before them, our necks in their collars, our heads down, our lips to their feet?

"Forgive me, Master," I said, looking up. "I failed."

"I did not expect you to succeed," he said.

"I tried," I said.

"One can do no more," he said.

"Master is kind," I said.

"How so?" he said.

"You hoped," I said, "that I might have saved myself."

"I had hoped," he said, "that we both, and Grendel, and perhaps others, might have been saved."

"I do not understand," I said.

"That you might have reached the wagon, and returned."

"The wagon was empty," I said.

"Then," he said.

"Yes," I said.

"But perhaps not now," he said.

"I do not understand," I said.

"We are lost," said Drusus Andronicus. "Reinforcements have come from the wagons, some tens of guards."

"I feared so," said Kurik.

There were cries of dismay, wails of misery from the kajirae.

"Your foes are there!" cried Decius Albus from the box, pointing toward Surtak, Drusus Andronicus, Kurik, and Lord Grendel. "Deploy! Ready yourselves. Attack upon my signal." He then turned to Lucilius, intent and monstrous, beside him in the box. "Fear not, noble High One," he said, "the festivities will shortly continue, and with appetites yet better whetted!"

Surtak, clutching his ax, looking about, called out to Lucilius, wildly, desperately, his Kur picked up by Lord Grendel's translator. "You are within the rings," he cried. "I pronounce you so! Descend and meet with me."

"I think not," returned Lucilius. "The matter is done. Test the might of your single ax against twenty spears, from twenty sides!"

I saw men encircling us.

"We are armed," said Drusus Andronicus to Kurik. "Now none can deny us the right to die well."

I looked about.

About the edges of the field several soldiers maintained their position. Discipline seemed frayed. Isolated men, backing away from one another, were in the field. Some had fallen, bloodied in the grass. One Kur lay some yards from us, unmoving. Kurii drew back toward the stands. The field seemed strangely quiet. We, the small group at the stake, Surtak, Drusus Andronicus, Kurik, and Lord Grendel, who had no weapon save claws and fangs, and the larger group, the kajirae, were encircled. I saw the eyes of the soldiers about us, but feet away, eyes narrowed, watchful, alit within the apertures of those fierce-seeming helmets, the openings so like a "Y" in shape, the lowered spears, the points threatening us, moving slightly, like the heads of a ring of osts. It was like a trap of steel, a trap from which there was no escape, a trap not yet sprung. I felt sick, perhaps as a tabuk might, with nowhere to run, a tabuk ringed with sleen.

Decius Albus raised his hand.

But then he lowered his hand, looking past us, toward the perimeter of the field, opposite the stands.

Two figures were approaching, that of a small free woman, and, one might suppose, her pet.

The free woman was clad in the full regalia of the Robes of Concealment, and yet, surely to the shock and dismay of some of the soldiers, and the awe or delight of others, had disdained veiling. Who would care to conceal such beauty?

"One side, oafs!" she cried. "Dare not obstruct the path of a free woman, not so much as brushing her sleeve, lest I summon the guardsmen of Ar and have you remanded to the nearest pole of impalement! Aside, all of you, now! I have business here! Stand aside, aside!"

Men moved aside, even officers, lest her robes be touched. And others shrank even farther back, that they not interfere with the large, pelted thing that followed her, light-footed, docile in her wake, which thing bore a large, flat box.

"Do not impede the progress of my pet," said the free woman. "She is high strung, and impatient, and you may lose a hand."

This caution seemed to me unnecessary, as I detected not the least bit of interest amongst the men with respect to blocking the passage of her companion. Aside from the danger that might be involved, I was sure they took the beast for a Kur, which it muchly resembled. The men were naturally wary of the Kurii, not only because of the nature of the form of life, which would be justification enough, but because several were supposedly allies, somehow enleagued with Decius Albus.

"Back, back!" chided the free woman, robes, yellow, red, and purple, flowing serenely between the lines of soldiers, and approaching us across the field.

She also carried a bright, yellow parasol, which I was sure I recognized.

For those unfamiliar with Gorean culture, particularly that of the "High Cities," I think a note of explanation might not be without point. On my former world, where almost all women are "free," there is a sense in which almost no woman is free. For most practical purposes, where all women are free no woman is free, or, indeed, not free. There is no distinction, no important differences, between one woman and another. They are the same. For example, if all women were green or blue, or such, then the distinction between green and not green, or blue and not blue, would be of little practical interest or importance. There would be a conceptual difference, of course, or a logically possible difference, but it would be of little practical moment. Analogously, if everything happened to be, say, red, we might not know that anything was red. Presumably, we would not have a word for "red," or even be aware that other colors might exist. Consider now a culture in which there is a clear, sharp, important, even momentous, distinction between the free and the not free. On such a world, where not all are free, freedom becomes quite important. It is no longer meaningless or immaterial. Associated with freedom is standing, respect, dignity, prestige, status, privileges, and power, and acknowledged claims and rights. One is a person, and, in favored cases, a citizen, and may even possess a Home Stone. The Gorean free woman has a place in society that is far above that of the "free woman" of Earth. She is the pride and treasure of a city, to be elevated and honored, to be exalted and revered, to be defended to the death, unless she should fall slave, in that case, of course, she is then only another animal, to be bought and sold as the stock she then is. Naturally free women, in most cities, in their frustration, as would be expected, make the most of their prestige, caste rights, intelligence, beauty, and such, exploiting such things ruthlessly to consolidate and improve their position in society. Not at the feet of men, and perhaps resentful of that fact, they surround themselves with a mystique of preciousness and power designed to awe, subordinate, reduce, and tame men, perhaps to punish men for denying them the rights and hopes of their frustrated womanhood. In any event, these things are complicated and, I suspect, scarcely understood, as the currents involved are deep and not always easily detected. To be sure, the glory, might, and power, so to speak, of these fine ladies does tend to annoy men, who, upon occasion, perhaps, would like to collar the lot of them and put them to slave use. I understand something like this did take place in one of the "High Cities," Tharna, where every woman except the ruler, a Tatrix, is enslaved. Even free women visiting Tharna must be licensed and put in the custody of a male until they leave the city. Men of Tharna, when outside the city, are recognized by the wearing, in the belt, of two yellow cords, some eighteen inches or so in length. Some women, gazing upon these cords, feel weak, and strangely stirred. Some women follow men of Tharna beyond their own city's gates, begging to be taken to Tharna. Two things might be noted about the "cords of Tharna." First, they symbolize Tharna. That is obvious and important. Secondly they are of a suitable length, and would serve nicely, to bind the wrists and ankles of a woman.

The soldiers doubtless took it for granted that the small, graceful figure passing through their ranks was that of a compatriot, a woman of Ar, one with whom they shared a Home Stone. If they had thought her of a foreign city she might not have made it past the capture straps of the first man at arms. The awe with which the free woman of one's own city is regarded, reinforced by habit, training, custom, and tradition, does not at all apply to the free women of another city, unless perhaps a close ally, nor, indeed, does it even apply to a woman of one's own city, should she have been reduced to bondage. A spurned suitor occasionally has the pleasure of buying a woman who once refused him, for chaining naked to his slave ring. The awe with which the free woman was regarded, approaching, was doubtless not only enhanced by the sumptuousness of her robes, but by her very presence, for, as it might be recalled, no free women were present at the "festivities." What was she doing here, at all, and, in particular, advancing so assuredly amongst them? Too, there is no doubt that her alleged "pet," or companion, so large, and Kurlike, contributed not a little to their apprehension, and astonishment.

They made their way forward, literally piercing the ring of soldiers about us, who drew aside, and continued on, now passing though the other side of that small formation that had encircled us, the men of which, too, parted, that her passage not be arrested.

Free women commonly go, and do, wherever they wish, and whatever they wish.

Decius Albus himself seemed nonplused.

"Ho!" cried the small figure, stopping before the stands, looking up toward the box. "Have I the honor of addressing the noble Decius Albus, trade advisor to Marlenus, Ubar of Ar?"

"Current Ubar of Ar," said Decius Albus. "I am he, Decius Albus."

"I thought you might be," she said, twirling the umbrella. "I had heard he is a heavy-jowled, coarsely featured fellow."

"You are not veiled," said Decius Albus, less than pleased.

"You are perceptive," she observed.

Her alleged pet, bearing the large, flat box, had not followed her to the foot of the stands, but had lingered behind, and was rather close to the stake, near which Surtak, Drusus Andronicus, Kurik, and Lord Grendel had taken their stand.

"Your face is as naked as that of a slave," said Decius Albus.

"And yours is as ugly as that of a tharlarion," she said.

A man somewhere laughed. Decius Albus looked sharply about, failed to note any likely source of the aforementioned mirth, and then returned his attention to the small figure before him.

"Dear Lady," he said, "I do not recall inviting any free women to our gathering."

"Why not?" she asked.

"Perhaps the matter was overlooked," he said.

"That was careless," she said.

"Doubtless," he said.

At this point, Lucilius, his translator slung about his neck, growled.

"Keep your pet quiet," she said.

Lucilius roared in fury.

"Steady, steady," cautioned Decius Albus.

"He is a noisy one," she said.

I feared, for a moment, that Lucilius was going to vault down from the box. But he restrained himself. Perhaps he was not eager to approach Surtak more closely.

"This is no pet with whom I share the box of honor," said Decius Albus, "but a friend, and an esteemed colleague, a rational creature, of a sort with which you may be unfamiliar."

"Do not confuse him with a High One," she said. "I have bitten lice out of the fur of a dozen such beasts who would not permit him to do so much as polish their claws."

Lucilius, shaking with rage, struggled to contain himself. I saw a flush of saliva at the right side of his jaws. He opened his mouth, exposing the forest of fangs within.

"He must be an adolescent," she said, "his fangs are so short."

I myself thought they might snap a stout branch in two. They might have easily bitten an arm from a body.

Lucilius was large and formidable, even for a Kur.

"What are you doing here?" she asked, looking about. "I see slaves. Are you short of tunics? They are not overly dressed, limited to their collars. I suspect you are up to man business. I would not doubt it. Men are such lustful brutes. Throw a sleen a bone, throw a man a slave. But what are the verr, and parts of verr, doing here? One would think this was a slaughter yard."

"Go!" said Decius Albus.

"Shortly, gladly," she said.

"You were not invited," said Decius Albus.

"On the contrary," she said.

"Who invited you?" he asked.

"I invited myself," she said. "That is a free woman's privilege."

"You are a bold little she-sleen," he said.

"Perhaps you think I might look well on a chain," she said.

"Perhaps," he said.

"Beware how you address a free woman," she said.

"Forgive me, Lady," he said. "May I inquire as to what we owe the honor of your visit?"

"Certainly," she said. "Inquiry is the privilege of a free man."

"I so inquire," he said.

"I bring gifts," she said.

She looked back, to where the Kurlike thing that had accompanied her to the field waited, bearing the large, flat box.

"From whom?" asked Decius Albus, warily.

"Perhaps you have heard of a High One," she said, "by name, Agamemnon."

"Lord Agamemnon," cried Decius Albus, "Eleventh Face of the Nameless One! Forgive me, dear, noble lady! I did not know! Forgive me! Welcome! How thoughtful of the noble lord to remember his unworthy servants, and how like him to transmit his gift, or gifts, by means of so wise and beauteous a messenger!"

"Well," she said, "the gifts are not from him."

"But—" said Decius Albus.

"I was merely curious to know if you had heard of such a fellow," she said.

"How is it," asked Decius Albus, narrowly, "that you have heard of Lord Agamemnon?"

"Surely you are interested in the gifts I have brought," she said.

"Of course," said Decius Albus.

"They are not for you," she said.

"For whom then?" he asked.

"Others," she said.

"I trust," said Decius Albus, clutching the railing of the box, "your Home Stone is that of Glorious Ar."

"No," she said.

"Of our ally, Venna?" he said.

"No," she said.

"What, then, is your Home Stone?" he asked.

"I have no Home Stone," she said.

"Kill her!" cried Decius Albus, and one of the Kurii at the foot of the stands lunged toward the small figure, who brought up her parasol between them, and the Kur crashed into it, shook his head, seized it in one hand, or paw, and tore part of the silk away, and then crouched down, jaws opened, fangs wet with saliva, and took a step toward the small figure, its last step as it turned out, for, a moment later it rolled in the grass, writhing, whimpering and choking, flailing about, apparently in great pain, biting at its own body, and then, in a matter of Ihn, it was inert. Its body was contorted, and rigid. The one eye, which it had not torn out in its frenzy, was of a single hue, a sightless wad of dark leather half emerged from the face.

"He spoiled my parasol!" she cried angrily. "For this, I hold you, Decius Albus, responsible."

She still clutched the shreds of the parasol in one hand, several of its spines now exposed, free from the silk.

None of the other Kurii about rushed upon her.

"Sword her, to the blade, strike her!" howled Decius Albus to a man at arms before the stands.

"Noble one," he cried, in protest. "She is a woman, a free woman!"

"She has no Home Stone!" screamed Decius Albus, beside himself in fury. "Kill her!"

"I will do so!" cried a soldier, whipping his sword from the sheath, and raising the weapon, but it fell, almost immediately, from a lost grip, as the man staggered back a foot or so, turned, and crumpled at the foot of the stands, the metal fins of a quarrel clearly visible, the bolt muchly buried in his chest.

"They are armed!" cried a man.

In the bit of time in which the Kur had advanced upon the free woman, had encountered the poisoned spines of the gay, bright-yellow parasol, and experienced the consequences of its indiscretion, the Kur-like thing near the stake had flung open the large, flat box, and Lord Grendel had seized out his ax, and Kurik, of Victoria, had had his foot in the stirrup of the stout bow, had drawn the cable, and set a quarrel into the guide. And in its rest, now, a new quarrel, like a poised bird of prey, like a cartridge in a rifle, lay in wait.

Men drew back from those about the stake. None wished to be the first to die. Lord Grendel roared with pleasure, lifting the ax.

"A shield, a shield!" cried Decius Albus, "and one, as well, for noble Lucilius!"

The large Kur beside him in the box was crouched down, and the broad, double-edged blade of the Kur ax it bore was held across its body, before its chest, covering its heart. Its baleful eyes gleamed over the edge.

Decius Albus drew back a yard in the box, turning white.

The need for shields had not been anticipated.

I now knew why my master had hoped that I might be able to reach the wagon. Surely it had been empty, as had been intended, upon our arrival at the feast, a situation that had been confirmed by suspicious guards, but it had been arranged, clearly, certainly not with my knowledge, for I was a slave, that the Lady Bina and Eve would make their way, in another wagon, to the scene of the "festivities." There they would endeavor to place weapons in the wagon, to be retrieved, if necessary, and if possible, later. In this way Lord Grendel and Kurik might attend the feast in good faith, unarmed, and yet have at their disposal, in case of need, weaponry, should they or another, perhaps even a slave, be able to return to the wagon and retrieve the deposited weaponry. We had not been able to do so, of course. Then, when the weaponry was not retrieved, the Lady Bina and Eve, curious, uncertain as to whether the weaponry was needed or not, and fearing the worst, decided to investigate. Thus they had made their way toward the feast, to ascertain matters, and, if necessary, be of some assistance.

"This quarrel, noble Albus," cried Kurik of Victoria, "is for you! For its residence it would choose your heart! Order your men to throw down their weapons!"

"Men, men!" cried Decius Albus, in terror.

But a snarl of rage burst forth from the shaggy throat of Lucilius, and he, with a wide, violent, fierce, backward sweep of his long arm, struck Decius Albus back in the box, a blow that, I feared, might have broken his neck. The body of the trade advisor, in its robes, stained with the blood of Aelius, lay inert, at the back of the box. I did not know if he had survived the savageness of that blow or not. A stream of hideous Kur emanated from the box.

"We are lost," said Drusus Andronicus. "Your effort, while promising, was doomed from the beginning. On this field power is owned by the beasts."

From various translators about, wild cries and monstrous roars were transmitted noncommittally, as usual, as placid, emotion-free emanations. This made them, in its way, seem even more terrifying, as the most appalling and ghastly of execrations and threats were conveyed with the same colorless neutrality as the ticking of a watch. It seemed one's fate lay at the mercy of a machine, one without the least awareness of, or interest in, what was ensuing. To be sure, even without translators, I think few would have been in doubt as to the significance, the intent and menace, of the affrighting sounds, and emotions and attitudes, about us.

"Behold, men of glorious Ar, noble defenders of her walls, valiant holders of her gates," cried Kurik, "the beast has struck your

leader, your lord, the noble Decius Albus! The blow was treacher-
ous, cruel, and unprovoked! What could be owed to such beasts but
vengeance? Prove yourselves worthy of your fee. Strike blows for the
noble Albus!"

Men milled about. Kurii snarled.

"It seems," said Drusus Andronicus, "the noble Albus is not as
beloved by his men as you supposed. Few, I suspect, would gladly rush
to die for him. No such leader is he. It is not Decius Albus they serve,
but his gold."

"Noble High Ones, Mighty Brothers," called Lucilius, "will you be
befooled by humans, will you waver in your loyalty to great Agamemnon, will you hesitate to be true to the meaning of your fangs and
claws, will you be denied your pleasures, your sport? Behold the game
clustered by the stake, vulnerable and ill-defended. Charge upon it,
and it will scatter, screaming, and you may pursue it and feed upon it as
you did other game, the verr. And who will earn prizes, who will seize
the most meat? Be patient a moment. Our happy allies, the loyal servitors of the noble Decius Albus, with a hundred spears, will thrust aside
any impediment to your hunt." Lucilius then increased the volume on
his translator, presumably that its message might carry throughout the
field, even to the soldiers at the two manned perimeters. "Friends," he
called, "humans, astute and wise, skilled and loyal, beloved allies, you
did note how I intervened to save the life of your lord, the great Decius
Albus, how I, at great personal risk, thrust him aside, away from the
line of a quarrel's flight, just as he was about, boldly, at risk to his own
life, to order you to attack enemies and traitors, the criminal Surtak,
and others. Prepare now to do as he would have then had you do. Prepare now to do death to our common enemies!"

"Meet me!" cried Surtak, lifting his ax.

"Or I!" cried Lord Grendel.

"What of the slaves?" called a man at arms.

At this point, the Lady Bina, still clutching the shreds of the parasol, turned about, and joined us near the stake.

"Tal," she said.

This salute was returned by Drusus Andronicus and Kurik, of
Victoria.

"Look at my parasol," she said, ruefully.

I trusted she would be careful with the spines of that lovely
accessory.

"You are brave to have come here, dear, noble lady," said Kurik.

"Not really," she said. "I underestimated the danger. Had I to do it again, I would have given the matter more careful consideration."

"You may die here," said Drusus Andronicus.

"Look at my parasol," she said. "It is ruined."

"We must have our sport," said Lucilius. "The noble Albus, your brave and hardy leader, so decreed."

I saw many men look at one another.

But Ehn before, this matter had divided men, into those loyal to their fee and those listening to their blood, and what it told them of nature.

"Kajirae," cried Drusus Andronicus, "are to be bought and sold, owned and chained, they are to be worked, commanded, ravished and used, not fed to beasts, unless they are displeasing."

"Yes, yes," said several men.

"Discipline!" cried an officer. "Discipline!"

Drusus Andronicus turned to Kurik. "There is division amongst the men," he said, "as before."

"If the Kurii were wise," said Kurik, his sword in his belt, the bow with its quarrel cradled in his arms, casting a wary glance at Tyrtaios, the Assassin, who still stood to one side, some yards away, "they would forego their sport, and spare the kajirae."

"You do not know them, as I do," said Drusus Andronicus. "Kajirae are muchly irrelevant here. It is now a matter of force, and of what is to be done, and why. The kajirae are now little more than symbolic. Who is to retreat, who is to yield, human or Kur? Whose will is to hold sway? The Kur cannot, and will not, yield."

"Then we are lost," said Kurik.

"My parasol is ruined," said the Lady Bina.

"Perhaps you can buy another," said Drusus Andronicus, his eyes on the soldiers about.

"Do you think so?" she asked.

"Yes," he said.

"Are you annoyed?" she asked.

"A bit," he said.

"Well, beware," she said. "I am a free woman."

"Very well," he said.

She then cast a peremptory, rather contemptuous glance, at us, huddled together, pathetically, kajirae. We took care not to meet her eyes, those of a free woman. If a free person senses the least unwillingness, resistance, or insolence in us we can be punished, terribly. We are quickly taught our collars. We learn them well.

"Kajirae," she said, "who would want them?"

"They sell nicely," said Drusus Andronicus.

"Men are stupid," she said.

"It is pleasant," said Kurik, "to have one curling about one's feet, naked, collared, in sexual agony, her slave fires alit, begging to be used."

"Men," she said, "I gather, would rather have them at their slave ring than fed to Kurii."

"I suspect so," said Drusus Andronicus.

"Dear lady," said Kurik, "with your permission, might you not be less distractive? We are about to be set upon by superior numbers."

"I would not give much for your chances," she said.

"Nor would I," said Drusus Andronicus, impolitely I fear.

"Remember," she said, "I am a free woman."

"Forgive me," he said.

"If I were you," she said, "I would choose a different field, and a different battle."

"We shall give the matter some thought," said Drusus Andronicus.

"If you feel men are reluctant to go about slaughtering slaves," she said, "why do you not take advantage of that?"

"We tried," said Drusus Andronicus.

"We failed," said Kurik.

"These fellows about," she said, "do not appear to be regulars, not members of the common forces of Ar, not soldiers, not guardsmen."

"They are not," said Drusus Andronicus. "These are members of the entourage of Decius Albus, armed retainers, consider their livery, contingents within a small, personal army, a private army, that of the trade advisor to the Ubar."

"They are then," she said, "mercenaries."

"Yes," said Drusus Andronicus.

"There you have it," she said.

"What?" asked Drusus Andronicus.

"I shall solve your problem," she said.

"What problem?" asked Drusus Andronicus.

"Survival," she said.

"I do not understand," said Drusus Andronicus.

"Do not forget," she said, "I am a free woman."

"I have been unable to do so," said Drusus Andronicus.

The Lady Bina regarded us, severely. We kept our eyes down.

"Who here, meaningless, stripped beasts," she inquired, "wants to be free?"

"I, Mistress!" cried the former Lady Alexina, springing to her feet.

"Well," said the Lady Bina, "you are not going to be free. You are a slave, and you are going to stay a slave."

"Mistress!" protested Alexina, the former Lady Alexina.

"Back on your knees, slave!" snapped the Lady Bina, and Alexina sank down, again, frightened, trembling, on her knees, amongst us. "You are all slaves," said the Lady Bina, "nothing but slaves. I can tell by the collars, and your meaningless softness. You are fit for nothing but being owned by men."

"We are women, Mistress!" exclaimed a slave.

"I have seldom seen," said the Lady Bina, "a sorrier platter of collar meat. It is no wonder they want to feed you to beasts. I myself think you would well be bound and fed to urts."

The slaves regarded one another, wildly. I did not doubt but what many of them, as had been Paula, might have been purchased for as much as a golden tarsk. The slaves of Decius Albus were renowned about the city for their beauty.

"Meaningless fluff," said the Lady Bina, "vulos, tastas!"

"Mercy, Mistress!" wept a slave.

It is not easy for a slave to please a free woman. They hate us. No matter how hard we try to be pleasing, it is never enough. They are not pleased. They are never pleased. Why do they hate us so? We are so at their mercy!

"We cannot help what we are, Mistress," wept a slave. "We are collared!"

"You are not a slave because you are collared," said the Lady Bina. "You are collared because you are a slave."

I supposed there were many slaves who had never been collared. And I supposed there were many, not collared, who longed for their collars.

"Seductive little brutes," said the Lady Bina, "I have seen you in the markets, chained on the selling shelves, reaching through the bars of your cages, smiling, calling out, trying to interest men."

We lived in terror of being owned by a woman. We knew ourselves the rightful properties of men.

"What can men possibly see in you?" said the Lady Bina.

From the box Lucilius was roaring. Kurii were inching closer, wary of the axes of Surtak and Lord Grendel. Spears were leveled, swords grasped more securely. Some of the men I sensed were with us, those who would protect the kajirae, but more, by many it seemed, were ready to close and attack. I did not think it had been wise for the Lady Bina to acknowledge her lack of a Home Stone, and, in particular, her lack of that of Ar. I had the sense, rather as when a dam is threatened, that war, long expected, might suddenly burst in upon us.

The Lady Bina then turned away from us, and addressed those about. "Back up, fellows," she said. "Put up your spears, lower your swords. I have something to say to you, and it will not take long. You may then, if you wish, do as you please, drenching the field in blood, cutting one another to pieces, and so on. That is not of great interest to me. I leave it to you. That is man business. First, as I understand it, none of you, even those of you, most of you, it seems, who will obey orders, no matter how stupid and ridiculous, to the death, are enthusiastic about the prospect of having certain vulos in the vicinity fed to unpleasant, ravening beasts. Who knows, if it came to that, you might even object. If I am mistaken in this matter, correct me. I thought so." One Kur crept closer to the Lady Bina, but she lifted her parasol, several exposed spines forward, and it slunk back. "So, second," she said, "I have a counterproposal, one that the noble Decius Albus, to whom you owe your fee fealty, would find congenial, indeed, one he would, if able, embrace with enthusiasm."

"What is that?" asked an officer.

"The girl raffle," said the Lady Bina.

"I do not understand," said the officer.

"It is quite simple," said the Lady Bina, "his life or the girl raffle."

"Surely you can present this matter more clearly," said another officer.

"Certainly," said the Lady Bina, "I am a free woman. I am assuming, one, that the noble and beloved Decius Albus is not currently conscious—"

"He may be dead," said a fellow.

"And two," said the Lady Bina, "that if he were conscious, he would prefer to live."

"Plausible," said an officer.

"Therefore a certain decision must be made for him," said the Lady Bina, "one we would expect him to make for himself, were he able, namely, his life or the girl raffle."

"But he is in no danger," said an officer.

"He is in great danger," said the Lady Bina. "Consider a desperate assault on the box of honor, where the noble Albus lies helpless, unconscious, unable to either flee or defend himself, an assault by several assailants. Surely at least one fellow, from one direction or another, could reach him, and deprive the Ubar of a trade advisor."

"Such an assault might fail," said the first officer.

"True," said the Lady Bina, "but I do not think the noble Albus could count on that. Remember, we must make this decision for him. Do you think he would risk it?"

"No," said Drusus Andronicus.

"A hundred men would defend him!" said a second officer.

"How many of you fellows," asked the Lady Bina, "would gladly sell your life to defend Decius Albus?"

Clearly the response was less than overwhelming.

"Kurii may be wary of my parasol," she said, "and we must consider the blows of two axes, the quarrels of a crossbow, the swords and spears of several fellows who would rather get their hands on kajirae than feed them to monsters, and so on."

"Is the point not clear?" asked Drusus Andronicus.

"It is," said a man.

"The matter is then settled," said the Lady Bina. "Decius Albus, for considerations thoroughly satisfactory to himself, puts up a number of his properties for prizes, in a girl raffle."

"How does this proceed?" asked a fellow.

"Unfortunately," said the Lady Bina, "there are far more men at arms here than there are slaves, so one must have a raffle, but each of you may hope to be lucky. If there are two hundred fellows, say, who wish to participate, though you are under no obligation to do so, we will put two hundred numbers on slips of paper in a helmet, and give each fellow a slip of paper with a number. Then, we will draw one number after another. When your number is drawn, you may have your pick of the kajirae who have not yet been selected."

"Agreed," said more than one fellow.

"Not every slave," said Drusus Andronicus, menacingly, "will serve as a prize." Paula, at his feet, looked up at him, radiantly, and then pressed her lips to his thigh.

Surtak, never taking his eyes from Lucilius, still in the box of honor, not yet having dared to descend, said, "The slave, Lyris, is mine." I did not think any would dispute him in this, not humans, because to them, whatever her outstanding beauty amongst Kur females, she would seem a monster, nor Kurii, fearing the ax of Surtak. Lyris looked up at Surtak, "Give me harnessing," she said. Surtak looked down upon her, and, lifting his ax, said, "On your belly." Lyris then lay prone before Surtak, and Surtak placed his large, clawed foot on her back. "Give me harnessing," she begged. She made a gasping, startled, frightened noise, as she was pressed down into the grass, deeply. She found herself held in place, beneath his foot. She was helpless. She could not move. "There is no harnessing for a slave," he said. "You are now no different from the Kur females who were enslaved following the accession of Lord Arcesilaus to the throne of the Metal World. They are all enslaved, and so, too, are you."

"But," she said, "I favored Lord Agamemnon, your lord."

"You were carried away as easily as might have been a mere human female," he said, reminding her of her abduction by Lord Grendel. "This contretemps was embarrassing, and put plans awry. You are fortunate that parts of you were not nailed to a dozen gates."

"You always wanted me," she said, wildly, accusingly, protestingly. "I saw it in your eyes. You always wanted me, and as a slave!"

"Of course," he said.

"Free me!" she said.

Then she gasped, as the claws of that massive foot, pressing down, dug into her back.

"You were displeasing," he said.

"I was overpowered, carried away," she said.

"We can learn much from our human friends," he said. "A man has the right to enslave a woman he finds displeasing."

This assertion surely required considerable qualification. For example, there is the matter of a shared Home Stone that would militate against such things. Similarly, certain cities are allied, some cities are colony cities founded by emigrants from a mother city, and so on. On the other hand, Gorean males do not respond well to insults, contempt, mistreatment, and such. Offending males may expect to be summoned to a bridge, or field, at dawn; an offending or careless woman is subject to the risk of finding herself naked, chained at a slave ring. This probably accounts for the rather elaborate protocols of etiquette that commonly govern interactions between Goreans of different cities or towns. Contrariwise, friends, male or female, are accorded considerable liberties along these lines. I have heard males insult one another outrageously, with uproarious abandon, and free women bare their claws, so to speak, exquisitely lacerating one another with impunity.

"And what is the right of a mere man," he said, "surely cannot be denied to one who is Kur."

"Mercy!" she said.

"You have been found displeasing," he said.

"You always wanted to own me," she said, "even on the Metal World!"

"And now, in full justification," he said, "it is so."

"You put me in a collar," she said. "I still wear it. I cannot take it off. Remove it!"

She had been collared, I recalled, on the Sleen's Back Bridge, by Surtak, shortly after the exchange, she for Eve, Eve for she, had been effected.

"Collars are appropriate for slaves," he said. "You will continue to wear it. It looks well on you, slave. It, and its meaning, much enhance your beauty, a thousand times, indicating what you now are, and what may be done with you."

"At least," she begged, "give me harnessing!"

"You will be stripped to your collar," he said, "that all, looking upon you, will know you are a slave."

She moaned, held down, beneath his foot.

"You will be well worked," he said, "and I will derive from you extraordinary pleasure, frequently and lengthily."

She moaned, again.

"Do you understand, pretty Lyris?" he asked.

"—Yes," she said.

"'Yes'?" he asked.

"Yes," she said, "—Master."

Surtak then looked up, again, to the box, and he roared in fury, for Lucilius had withdrawn.

"Where is he?" cried Surtak. "I would have him within the rings!"

"He is gone, Commander," said a Kur. "I know not where."

Surtak removed his foot from the back of Lyris, scowled down upon her, and thrust her rolling to the side with his foot. "Worthless slave," he said, "your meaningless beauty distracted me. It could be mine at any time. And I let myself, at this crucial moment, be distracted! I have lost my prey!"

Lyris, from her side, put her head down, fearing to meet the eyes of her master.

Surely she could not be held accountable for the unperceived exit of Lucilius. Was it her fault that her form, and her wholeness, the whole of her, should so disturb, stimulate, provoke, and stir a male of her species, should bring about such mighty feelings, overwhelming and irresistible, of desire, lust, passion, and possessiveness? How was she to blame? Had these realities not been contrived in the innocent corridors of evolution, with no more thought or intention than the tides of Thassa or the orbits of worlds? But she, too, no less than he, was the product of these blind, inexorable processes. I suspect the complementarities of nature are not without explanation. I suspected that my own form, and that of others like me, must be seen in a certain way by men. It must stimulate them with desire, the passion to hold it, to possess it, and own it. And yet, have we not been fashioned by the same dark tools? For one who longs to possess, is there not one who longs to be possessed, for one who desires to own is there not one who desires to be owned, for one who desires to master must there not be one who longs to be mastered? Why should we attempt to repudiate and deny the forces that have fashioned us? We long for the collars of our masters.

"Lucilius has gone," said Surtak. "I am commander. I say it so. I raise my ax. Let those who will, raise another against me. The rings are open."

A Kur to the side growled.

"Do you wish an ax?" inquired Surtak, eagerly. I feared the Kur thirst for blood was on him.

The other Kur moved back, concealing himself amongst his fellows.

"Lucilius has fled the rings," said Surtak. "He abandoned the ax. I have lifted it. Those who would follow him, depart, and seek him out."

Not a Kur moved.

"We shall withdraw from this soiled, ignominious field," said Surtak. "I serve Lord Agamemnon."

"He is served," said several of the Kurii.

"What of feeding?" asked a Kur, pointing toward the huddled kajirae.

"Surely," said Surtak, "think of feeding, but think, too, of the men about, armed humans, who have other uses in mind for the collared she-beasts, men who outnumber you twelve to one. I doubt you could reach the table of your banquet. Feed, yes, but later, if you would live, on less controversial provender."

"What of the human, Decius Albus?" asked a Kur.

"He is gone," said a Kur. "Cohorts bore him away."

I supposed that Master Albus might still be unconscious, reposing in a tharlarion wagon, hastening back to Ar, to the House of a Hundred Corridors.

"Well," said the Lady Bina, imperiously, "bring paper, enough of it, and a marking stick, and a helmet!"

"There will be no slip of paper for this one," said a quiet, menacing voice.

We heard a sudden cry of pain, and a gasp.

We looked about, to the kajirae, and saw, standing amongst them, Tyrtaios, the Assassin. He had pulled one of the kajirae, the former Lady Alexina, to her feet by the hair. He now held her, by the hair, bent over, her head at his left hip, in leading position.

"No, no!" she wept, "no!"

He tightened his grip in her hair.

"Please, no—Master, Master!" she wept.

"Dispute her with me who will," he said.

But none stepped forward.

"You?" he asked Kurik. "No," said my master. "You?" he asked Drusus Andronicus. "No," said Drusus Andronicus.

I had gathered, from earlier in the afternoon, that it was understood that the skills of Tyrtaios were well known, and that he might have easily killed either Kurik or Drusus Andronicus, either singly, or together.

"Perhaps, one day," said Drusus Andronicus, "you will meet your match."

"I think not," said Tyrtaios.

He then departed, the former Lady Alexina stumbling beside him, her head at his hip.

I did not envy her such a master.

"I think he will leave Ar," said Kurik.

"Doubtless several will," said Drusus Andronicus. "Decius Albus, if he survives, will still be mighty in Ar, as the Ubar's trade advisor."

"What of the men about?" asked Kurik.

"I suspect Decius Albus will take them back," said Drusus Andronicus.

"And they will take fee?" asked Kurik.

"Gold speaks," said Drusus Andronicus.

"And you?" asked Kurik.

"Scarcely," said Drusus Andronicus.

"I wish you well," said Surtak.

"Leave the service of Agamemnon," said Kurik.

"He is my lord," said Surtak, "the Eleventh Face of the Nameless One, he who should be Theocrat of the Metal World."

"He is a tyrant, and monster," said Kurik.

"He is my lord," said Surtak.

"Protect him, care for him," said Lord Grendel.

I understood in no way this solicitude for Lord Agamemnon, whom I knew as little more than a voice, hideous and menacing, emerging from what seemed on the outside to be little more than a container, a metal box.

Farewells were exchanged, and Surtak, ax in his grip, turned away.

"Heel," he said to Lyris.

The Kurii then left the field, following Surtak. Lyris was a bit behind him, on the left.

"Good," said the Lady Bina. "Here is paper, and a marking stick, and here the helmet, as well. Be patient, fellows. We will soon raffle away the goods."

"Master!" I wept, at the feet of Kurik. "Master!" I was in terror, and muchly distraught. How well aware then I was that I was only a slave!

"You will return with me to the wagon," he said. "I doubt that Grendel can be torn from the side of Eve, and both may prove to be of assistance to the Lady Bina, and will surely serve to guard her on her return to the wagon, in case any of the fellows recollect she lacks a Home Stone."

"I am not to be raffled away then!" I said.

"We will see how pleasing you can be," he said, "on the grass, in the dirt and ruts under the wagon. There will still be time then, if you are insufficiently pleasing, to return you here, and give you a number."

I pressed my lips to his feet, weeping, kissing them wildly, gratefully, in a slave's joy and submission, repeatedly, again and again. "I will try to be pleasing, Master," I wept. "I will try to be pleasing, so pleasing!"

CHAPTER SIXTY-TWO

S tand there, before us," said Drusus Andronicus, "both of you."

Paula and I rose to our feet, and stood, facing the men.

"Remove your clothing," said Kurik, sitting, cross-legged, beside Drusus Andronicus, he similarly at ease. "You are to be assessed."

"Please, no, Master," I said. "I am so poor a slave, next to her!"

"Oh, no, dear Phyllis," said Paula. "You are far more beautiful than I! We have known that from so long ago, so well, from our former world!"

"Be silent," said Kurik, "and get your clothes off, now, both of you, quickly. Do not dally."

And so we stripped, before our masters. My plea, my protest, had not been heeded. The slave does not demur. She may not. It is not permitted. She obeys.

We had then, commanded, removed our clothing, and stood before them, naked slaves.

In a sense, the command to remove our clothing might have seemed somewhat ironic to one of Earth, for we had both been, as our masters kept us, when permitting us clothing, slave clad. We both had worn only a brief, light, sleeveless garment, of clinging rep cloth, a typical slave tunic of Gor. There would be little chance we could be mistaken for free women. Our necks were closely encircled with our collars. One does not slip the Gorean slave collar. Paula was no longer kept in the relatively modest, opaque, silken tunics she had worn when of the House of a Hundred Corridors, tunics I had then envied her. Little, save her beauty, would now distinguish her from the typical slave on the street. I had become, as one will, in her collar, more brazen. I felt proud, even assertive, in the indignity of a tunic. I was no longer ashamed of my body, but even vain, I fear, where it was concerned. I realized it had value, and had been so desirable and attractive that it had been collared. The brand and collar, of course, are indisputable marks of quality, as might be the stampings on plates and vessels, the tags sewn into the rugs of Tor, and the labels fixed on the cloaks of Turia. How many free women, I wondered, could match the slave in beauty? How many would dare to walk and stand, and move, as a slave, with such casual, unconscious ease, such assurance and womanly grace, the grace of a woman who knows herself so special and prized that she is collared and owned? Did they so, would they be remanded to guardsmen for the collar? Is it a slave's fault that she is a woman, and must now reveal her woman's beauty, and her womanly needs? Is it a slave's fault that men have, whether she wished it or not, put slave fire in her belly? Is it a slave's fault that she now accepts herself as a vital, needful sexual creature, who cannot help her responsiveness to masters, nor wishes to do so, and lives for their touch? It is no wonder that we are sometimes switched gratuitously in the streets, and that the backs of our thighs, and our arms and shoulders, may bear the marks of a free woman's displeasure. Do they envy us the freedom of our collars, the joys of our owned womanhood?

And so we stood before our masters. Tears were in my eyes.

"Paula," said Drusus Andronicus, "brought a golden tarsk."

"That is my understanding," said Kurik, of Victoria. "And were I so abundantly pursed, I might have bid more."

"You are of the blue-and-yellow caste," said Drusus Andronicus. "What do you think your Phyllis might bring?"

The Slavers' colors are blue and yellow. Usually, however, these are worn, if worn, as a pair of chevrons, low on the left sleeve, usually of a darker garmenture. Slavers are often not forward in displaying their caste colors. Such an arrogance might prove indiscreet, and might well put free women ill at ease.

"It is hard to say," said Kurik.

"Be bold," said Drusus Andronicus.

"It would depend on the market, the supply and demand, the time of year, such things," said Kurik.

"Well, this time of year, Ar, a typical market," said Drusus Andronicus. "For example, would she sell in the Curulean?"

I recalled that Paula had been sold in the Curulean.

"No," said Kurik. "She would not sell in the Curulean. In the Curulean they will not even accept a slave, even for a minor block, unless they are sure she will bring at least four or five silver tarsks."

"Phyllis, then," said Drusus Andronicus, "would be sold in a smaller market, a lesser market?"

"Yes," said Kurik.

"She is such a slave?" said Drusus Andronicus.

"Yes," said Kurik.

"What do you think she would bring?" asked Drusus Andronicus.

"A silver tarsk five," said Kurik, "perhaps two silver tarsks."

"Excellent," said Drusus Andronicus.

"Originally I thought she would only do for a pot girl, or a kettle-and-mat girl," said Kurik. "To be sure, there is a market for pot girls, and kettle-and-mat girls."

"It seems she has improved in her collar," said Drusus Andronicus.

"They all do," said Kurik.

"Examination position," said Drusus Andronicus.

We both then spread our legs widely, clasped our hands behind the back of our necks, and raised our heads, looking toward the ceiling. In some cities, the hands are clasped behind the back of the head. To be sure, a slave may be examined in any number of attitudes and positions. The "standard position," on the other hand, at least in the High Cities, as I have been informed, is either the hands-behind-the-back-of-the-neck position or the hands-behind-the-back-of-the-head position. The position is assumed, naturally, while the slave is unclothed, first, that her body be wholly vulnerable, and, second, that nothing interfere with, or impede, the assessment or appraisal. The position of the hands behind the neck or head facilitates appraisal, getting the hands out of the way, and the locking of the hands discourages any attempt on the part of a slave, should she be so foolish, as to attempt to either shield her body or fend away examining hands. The position also lifts the breasts nicely. The raising of the head, fixing the eyes on the ceiling or sky, makes it difficult for the slave to anticipate where, and how, she might be touched. A slave assessment is commonly thorough. After all, money is generally involved. She must, for example, expect her hair, and her nails, of both the hands and feet, to be considered. And she must expect the command to open her mouth, widely, for her teeth to be examined. Many barbarians are characterized not only by a vaccination mark, but by tiny bits of metal in the teeth. The latter, fillings, are sometimes taken, by some Goreans, to be an esoteric form of barbarian adornment. The vaccination mark, on the other hand, is often taken as a subtle brand, this leading some Goreans to suppose that the woman was already a legal slave somewhere, and has only been stolen from, or purchased from, her former master. These misunderstandings commonly occur with Goreans who have been limited to the "First Knowledge," as it is called. There is a

"Second Knowledge," to which intellectuals, and the higher castes, have access. For example, many Goreans limited to the "First Knowledge" do not realize their world is one of many, and think that "Earth," of which they have heard, and from which many barbarian slaves are obtained, is merely a remote country or land falling outside "known Gor." Much of Gor, of course, even for educated Goreans, is *terra incognita*. One might add that it is speculated that there is also a "Third Knowledge," which is limited to Priest-Kings. I know little or nothing of Priest-Kings. They are supposedly the "gods of Gor." I take it that they are men, or some sort of men, perhaps more handsome or godlike than others, with a technology capable, at least until now, of holding Kurii at bay. It seems they inhabit the Sardar Mountains, from which geographical feature Goreans orient themselves and their maps. It might be mentioned that there is no perfectly clear distinction between the "knowledges," as much in the "First Knowledge" is, as would be supposed, included in the "Second Knowledge." The "Second Knowledge," in a sense, "goes beyond" the "First Knowledge." Also, it should be noted that it is not unprecedented for an individual of one of the lower castes to be apprised of the "Second Knowledge." There is nothing secret, or, at least, altogether secret, about the Second Knowledge. On the other hand, this seems not to be the case with the "Third Knowledge," that attributed to Priest-Kings. Indeed, many of the "Laws of the Priest-Kings" seem intended to discourage humans from inquiring into certain forms of knowledge, for example, those leading to technologies by means of which, eventually, after a cascade of steps, a planet might be rendered unlivable, even shattered and destroyed. Men, or common men, may be unaware of what is in their own best interests, but Priest-Kings, whoever or whatever they may be, one supposes, are very much aware of what is in their own best interests. A suspicious, thoughtless, bellicose, territorial, aggressive species is perhaps best limited to clubs and caves. In the "examination position," as noted, the slave stands with her legs widely spread. This anchors the slave in place, so to speak, as it is difficult to move easily from this position. Physically, it increases the slave's vulnerability, and, psychologically, it exponentially augments her sense of, and her awareness of, her vulnerability. In this position she well knows herself a slave, a domestic animal, being appraised as what she is, stock.

The two men stood, approaching us more closely. I felt responsiveness, and heat. I supposed Paula was similarly afflicted, though what a joy to be so afflicted.

We stood before our masters.

Neither Paula nor I had been granted permission to break position.

"May I speak, Master?" whispered Paula. There was a need, and tenseness, in her voice. I recognized that tone. I had heard it often enough in my own voice. It is a tone easily recognized by masters.

"Certainly," said Drusus Andronicus.

The examination position, like bara, nadu, sula, and such, tends to arouse a slave. In a sense, the slave is helpless in such positions. Significance is woven into the fiber of such things. Meaning and symbolism reign. When one behaves like a slave, moves like a slave, and speaks like a slave, one begins to think like a slave and feel like a slave. And one learns one is a slave. In some women the slave begins on the inside, in her recognition of her true nature as slave, and manifests itself on the outside. In others, external forms are imposed from the outside, and the slave becomes real on the inside, as the latent inner slave is discovered and released, and then, now naturally, manifests itself on the outside. In any event, slaves are to be slaves, and there is an entire culture and deportment required by the collar, which culture and deportment deepens and intensifies, whether the girl wishes it or not, her sexuality. She becomes the victim of her needs. Men have seen to it, and will have it so. And yet, are we not grateful, to be so alive, so real, so needful, so slave?

"I beg use," said Paula, tensely.

Her petition was ignored.

Whereas the needs of a slave are commonly noted by a master, they are not always satisfied. Such things are up to the master. It is he who decides whether or not these torments will be assuaged.

"The slaves stand well," said Drusus Andronicus.

"Yes," said Kurik, of Victoria.

Drusus Andronicus glanced to Kurik, who nodded.

"You may break position," said Drusus Andronicus.

Instantly we both knelt.

We looked up at our masters.

"I beg use," said Paula.

"Heads to the floor," said Kurik.

We both went to first obeisance position, kneeling, the palms of our hands down on the floor, beside our head, our heads to the floor.

"I beg use!" wept Paula.

"Nadu!" snapped Kurik.

Immediately we went to nadu, kneeling, back on our heels, our knees well spread, our backs straight, our heads up, the palms of our hands down, on our thighs.

"Master!" begged Paula, of Drusus Andronicus.

"Keep your palms down, on your thighs, not the backs of your hands," warned Drusus Andronicus.

"Yes, Master," said Paula. "Forgive me, Master."

Paula had turned her hands in such a way that the small, soft palms, so open, so sensitive, and tender, were exposed to her master. I did not know if this had occurred inadvertently, or intentionally. It is a begging gesture of an aroused slave. Sometimes the tracing of a master's fingernail, so gently, delicately, in the soft palm of slave's hand, she forced to keep the back of her hand down on her thigh, fixed in place, can cause her to cry out in piteous need. There are many begging signals, from things as simple as tying the loose bondage knot in one's hair to kneeling and kissing and licking the master's feet, whimpering in need. I was pleased that Drusus Andronicus had not cuffed Paula for her indiscretion, whether it was intentional or not. Masters are not always patient in such matters. The pattern traced in the palm of a slave's hand may be as random as the movement of a leaf in the wind, sometimes as clear as the Kef, the most common slave brand. 'Kef' is the first letter of the word 'kajira'.

The men looked down upon us, we both in nadu.

"Excellent," said Kurik, appraisingly.

"I wonder," said Drusus Andronicus, "why the men of Earth do not have their females so before them."

"Doubtless, some do," said Kurik.

This startled me. Could there be something of Gor on Earth? Could there be women there who knew the chain, who knelt, who kissed the whip, who had met men? Surely not! But could it be? I did not know.

"We want our females so," said Drusus Andronicus.

"Of course," said Kurik.

"Women belong on their knees, naked, and collared," said Drusus Andronicus. "It helps them to understand what they are, and what they are for."

"Yes, Master," said Paula.

"Yes, Master," I said.

"You may dress," said Drusus Andronicus.

"Master!" wept Paula.

We drew the tiny tunics on, over our heads, as may easily be done while one is kneeling. It seemed ironic, indeed, to think of donning such a garment as "dressing." Yet, even so slight a garmenture, little more than a wisp of clinging, woven fog, can be precious, particularly in the streets. Do we not beg, fervently enough, to be granted even a rag? The tunicked slave, eyes downcast, hurrying, is less likely to be abused by free women than the slave sent naked into the streets, perhaps even with her wrists bound behind her. Slave garments almost always lack a nether closure. The most notable exception to this is the Turian camisk. The common tunic, for example, has no nether closure, and may easily be thrust up, or pulled off. The point of this is not only to remind the girl that she is a slave and increase her sense of vulnerability, but to make certain that she is always conveniently accessible to the master.

"May I speak, Master?" asked Paula.

"Yes," said Drusus Andronicus.

"What are we to do?" she asked. "What will you do? What will become of us? Master Decius Albus did not die. He is recovering. Surely his power is mighty, and his memory long. His position in the administration of the Ubar is secure. Many men wear his livery. He will not look kindly on the loss of slaves. He did not stint on the slaves he intended to sacrifice to the fangs of Kurii. He has doubtless learned much from the field off the Viktel Aria. He is unlikely to again risk insurrection amongst his cohorts over kajirae. If anything, he will now use them as gifts and prizes, to enhance his image as a generous leader, to consolidate loyalty and assure devotion. He will be stronger, and more feared, than ever. Where, within the walls of Ar, will you be safe? Has Master Tyrtaios, he of the Black Caste, fled the city, with the slave Alexina, or has a pouch of gold changed hands, and he is about, waiting to strike? What of the free woman, the Lady Bina? She has no Home Stone. How is she safe? What of the noble Lord Grendel and his friend, Eve? What is to become of them? What of Surtak, and minions loyal to him? Will they remain in the vicinity of Ar, or depart? What of dreadful Lucilius, who fled the box of honor, on the field? What has become of him? Has he joined forces with Master Decius Albus?"

"Go into the kitchen, and cook," said Kurik.

"Yes, Master," we said.

CHAPTER SIXTY-THREE

The day was hot. We were stripped. We were weary, both of us. Sweat ran down our bodies. The masters had been kind and wrapped our feet in wool, the wool of the bounding hurt, that our feet not be burned by the large, heavy, sun-heated stones of the Viktel Aria. Even so, we could feel the heat through the wool. The wool was held in place by thongs wound several times, tightly, about our ankles. Our wrists were fastened behind us, in slave bracelets, light, but secure restraints. We were helpless in them. That is their purpose, to render their occupant helpless. A chain was fastened about each of our necks, each chain fastened to its ring, anchored in the back of the wagon. The wheels of the wagon were iron-rimmed, and very large. It was a large, closed wagon, with bright, yellow canvas stretched over the high, rectangular frame rising from its sides. The wagon was laden with little in the way of freight, but it did contain a closed bale of some sort of cloth, a box or two, and a cylindrical container. One of the boxes was long, narrow, and rectangular. I had not been informed of the nature of these objects. It is not unusual for slaves to be chained to the back of a wagon or cart. At least we were not harnessed, perhaps with others, to draw the wagon. It is doubtless unpleasant to be switched or whipped when straining in a harness, doing one's best, under the tyranny of a merciless keeper, one of several, soft, slight, two-legged draft animals. How much is to be preferred the pillows and cushions of a tavern alcove, or even a straw mat beneath a slave ring! Looking back, in the far distance, I could see the tops of the high walls of Ar.

I trudged on. The chain was warm on my neck. I could hear the small sound of the links. From somewhere ahead, I heard the sound of caravan bells, coming from the opposite direction.

There was much traffic on the Viktel Aria, moving toward Ar, departing from Ar.

Paula, secured as I was, was beside me.

We were slaves and would be treated as such. There are many ways in which a girl may be reminded that her thigh bears a delicate, distinctive mark, and that her neck is locked in a metal collar.

"Are you hungry?" she asked.

"Yes," I said.

"Shall we have lunch in the cafeteria, with the others?" she asked. Several of us who worked in the same building had often lunched together. The cafeteria was in the same building, and it was convenient. To be sure, the food was not all that scintillating. I had regarded myself the commanding presence at those small gatherings. Paula had been so shy, and quiet, seemingly dazzled by my vivacity and intelligence, seemingly admiring my verve, wit, and charm. "Poor Paula," I had thought. And now I suspected that it had been she who had looked gently on me, making allowances for me, accepting my faults patiently, tolerating my vanity. And she had sold for a golden tarsk, and it was speculated that I might bring in the neighborhood of a pair of silver tarsks, if all went well, on a good day!

"We shall be fortunate," I said, "if they permit us to nibble some cheese from the palm of their hand, while we kneel head down before them, fortunate if they cast us a crust of bread!"

"Of course," she laughed. "We are nothing. We are slaves."

We did not speak for another Ahn.

A kaiila, with a post rider, raced by. News, I supposed, was being brought to Ar. Occasionally we saw a tarn in flight, it, too, with its post rider. Cities maintain their post riders. Too, there are some private companies that supply what might be regarded as a limited postal service, between certain cities. Few, however, can afford their fees. The skies of Gor, particularly in certain areas, can be dangerous, sometimes due to bandit tarnsmen, but more frequently due to municipal patrols intent on protecting a city's territorial claims, which claims are often exaggerated, pretentious and unclear. Borders, in the usual sense of borders, do not exist on Gor. The territory under the aegis of a particular city waxes and wanes with the power of the city. It might be mentioned that some of the great merchant houses maintain their own lines of communication. Interestingly, commerce may be in effect between these houses even when their respective cities are at war. All in all, however, there is, for most practical purposes, no postal service on Gor. Letters, and such, may be entrusted to peddlers, travelers, caravan guards, drovers, and such.

"How are you faring, dear Phyllis?" inquired Paula.

"I feel like a verr," I said. Verr are often tied behind farm wagons.

"There is much similarity," she said. "They, and we, are both domestic animals."

"I was not always a domestic animal," I said.

"But you were," she said. "It is only that you were not then collared."

I was silent. I knew that she was right. On Gor I had learned that I was of the slave sex, that I was a slave, and belonged at a man's feet.

How joyful it had been to acknowledge that, and be at peace with myself!

"Dear Phyllis," said Paula, smiling, trudging beside me, "do you doubt you are a slave?"

"No," I said.

"I love my collar," she said. "I love being a slave."

"That is fortunate," I said, "for the collar is on your neck."

"Would you trade your collar for freedom?" she asked.

"No," I said. "But at times I can lament bondage, and try to tear the collar from my neck."

"But you cannot do so," she said.

"No," I said, "mine is locked on my neck, as is yours."

"Even on Earth," she said, "I thought of us as sister slaves."

"You never told me," I said.

"You would not have understood," she said.

"At times," I said, "I am terrified."

"I, too," she said.

"We are so helpless," I said. "We cannot choose our master. It is we who are chosen."

"We are owned," said Paula. "We are slaves."

"I fear the whip, terribly," I said. "But I love being subject to it."

"We are women," she said.

"Slaves," I said.

"You would not then trade your collar for freedom," said Paula.

"No," I said. "On Gor I have learned myself. I have learned myself at the feet of men. I have learned what I am, and what I want to be, a man's slave. Freedom is precious, but the collar is a thousand times more precious."

We had left Ar well before dawn, by the Viktel Gate. As we were departing, produce wagons, in their lines, were entering the city. This is to bring fresh produce to the morning markets. The larger wagons would leave before light. Heavy wagon traffic, as noted earlier, is not permitted during daylight hours. This is in order to avoid congestion. Where the

streets are wholly closed to traffic, even small wagons, there are often sta-
tions where, if one wishes, and can afford it, sedan chairs and palanquins,
with bearers and attendants, may be rented. Richer individuals, naturally
enough, usually supply their own resources in such matters. Similarly,
individuals with some official status, or official guests of the city, or such,
may be furnished such conveniences at the expense of the state. Most
Goreans, as one would expect, move about on foot.

"Where are we being taken?" I asked.

"We have not been told," said Paula, ruefully.

"Of course not," I thought. Would a herdsman of verr, or a drover
of bosk or kaiila, bother informing their beasts of their destination? A
slave must request permission to speak. She is often kept in ignorance.
Often she does not know where she is to be taken or what is to be
done with her. She is a thing, an object, a beast, a property, a slave. In
a thousand ways she is well reminded of her bondage.

"I hear bells," I said.

"It is another caravan," said Paula.

It would pass us on our right, as Goreans keep to the left side of
the roads, streets, paths, and such. This apparently has to do with the
fact that most Goreans are right-handed, which allows one's weapons,
in case of need, to be most conveniently brought into play. As far as
I know, there is only one word in Gorean for "stranger" and "enemy."
The context usually governs how the word is to be best understood.

"It is a long one," said Paula.

Some wagons were then aligned behind us, waiting for the caravan
to pass.

"It is a caravan of the merchant, Mintar," said Paula.

"Yes," I said.

Neither Paula nor I could read Gorean but we were familiar with
the sign of the merchant, Mintar, which appeared on the side of the
wagons, and on several banners, these raised on wands over every third
or fourth wagon. There would be no doubt as to whose caravan it was.
It must have contained four hundred wagons or more. Surely it took
a very long time to pass. Interestingly, unlike most caravans, it was,
for the most part, unguarded. This was apparently because most brigands or raiders were reluctant to attack a caravan of Mintar. He, rather
as Decius Albus, and certain other high merchants, maintained their
small private armies, which might consist of as many as a thousand
men. He was also noted for the relentless pursuit of any who might
threaten or despoil his caravans. His resources enabled pursuits to be

maintained for years. It was difficult to dispose of his goods. He maintained a large network of informants, from whom intelligence might be gathered, upon whom gold might be lavished. Bribes were tendered, bounties would be paid. His hunters, skilled and patient, were often referred to as "the Sleen of Mintar."

Once the caravan had passed, a succession of wagons that had been behind us began to move past us.

One, however, lingered behind.

On both the left and right side of the road paired ruts were worn in the stone. Clearly the Viktel Aria was a very old road. Major roads, such as the Viktel Aria, are begun as deep, wide trenches, several feet deep. These trenches are then filled with fitted stone until the surface of the ground is reached. They are built like walls, walls of fitted stone, walls that are sunk in the earth. Traffic then makes its way on the top of these "walls." They are intended to last for millennia.

We heard drums in the sky.

"Tarnsmen," said Paula, looking up.

Overhead there was a flight of tarnsmen, perhaps a hundred men and mounts. We could see sunlight flashing from helmets, shields, and weapons. They were perhaps five hundred feet above us, to our right. The tarn drums kept the cadence of the flight, the wings of the great birds beating in unison.

"See the standard," said Paula.

"That of Ar," I said.

There was a blast on a horn, a bugle, trumpet, or such, and the formation, as a single flock, ascended sharply; another signal and it veered to its left; another and it descended to perhaps two hundred feet, far off now, and then veered to its right, and then returned to its original line of flight, toward Ar.

"It is beautiful," exclaimed Paula.

We cried out in fear for there was a sudden sound, striking us like a bludgeon, a sudden snap of wings, great wings, not twenty feet from us, over us, air rushing about us, buffeting us, we covered for an instant by a vast, fleet shadow. We heard laughter, rapidly fading.

"Monster!" I shrieked, after the departing figure.

"It is a joke," said Paula.

"I nearly lost consciousness," I said. "I might have been dragged behind the wagon."

"It is an outrider," said Paula. "Formations are often flanked with them, for purposes of security."

"I trust he enjoyed himself," I said.

"I am sure he did," she said.

"A monster!" I said.

"A man," she said.

"Yes," I said, "a man!"

"Remember, kajira," she said, "we belong to men."

"Yes," I said, jerking at the slave bracelets that fastened my hands behind my back, shaking my neck in the chain that bound me to the ring fixed in the back of the wagon, "we belong to men!"

"Do you object?" she asked.

"No!" I said, angrily.

"Why not?" she laughed.

"I belong in their collars," I said. "I belong in their chains!"

"I, too, dear Phyllis," she said, "I, too."

"He is still a monster," I said.

"It is a man's joke," she said, "a man's prank. Besides, who can blame him for swooping by, and inspecting two naked kajirae? Perhaps he was speculating on how we might look, fastened to his slave ring."

"A tarnsman," I said.

"Of course," she said.

I supposed that it took an unusual man to dare the great tarn. Many, I had heard, died in the attempt. I recalled my flight in the tarn basket. Even in the basket, there had been a joy of flight. Some tarnsmen, I knew, were raiders, raiders for women. In some cities, a young tarnsman's first task is to capture a woman of the enemy and bring her back as his slave. At a feast, before his family and friends, she, once a proud, haughty free woman, must dance, dance as the slave she now is. None may touch food or wine at the feast until he has partaken of each, served, of course, by his kneeling slave. Commonly a marauding tarnsman uses the capture loop. She is then dragged to the saddle apron and tied, belly up, before him. On the other hand, some have trained their tarns to seize the girl in their talons, to be released later at their convenience.

Looking back, I noted that the wagon behind us, some four or five hundred yards back, had neither drifted back, nor approached, and passed us.

"There is a wagon behind us, Paula," I said. "It has been there for some time. It neither drops back, nor approaches."

"Perhaps it is in no more of a hurry than we," said Paula. "Perhaps it is pacing itself off us, thinking we are more familiar with the road. It may even wait to see where we will stop, at some inn, or caravanserai."

"Another is passing it," I said, "and will soon be beyond us."

"I trust the Lady Bina is comfortable," said Paula.

"Doubtless," I said. "Why should she not be? She is free."

The Lady Bina, with Lord Grendel and Eve, were in the wagon, concealed within the yellow cloth. One would not expect a free woman to walk, at least one such as the Lady Bina. Too, Lord Grendel and Eve, obviously, if in the open, would be conspicuous, and would be sure to provoke curiosity. It was better that they be concealed. Drusus Andronicus and Kurik were on the wagon bench, taking turns with the reins. Occasionally one or the other would go back into the wagon, and join the others. Sometimes, someone or other would open a narrow crack in the back of the cloth and peer out. At such times we would keep our heads down, that we not meet the eyes of the free. The wagon was slow and ponderous, seemingly a poor choice if one were interested in effecting a surreptitious escape. The yellow cloth on the frame, too, was easily noted. A wagon such as ours could not easily slip by, unnoticed amongst other wagons. It was drawn, too, by a single, plodding draft tharlarion. What pursuit could it possibly elude? Too, two kajirae, afoot, were chained behind the wagon, and the wagon, thus, must monitor and regulate its speed, lest, secured as they were, they be dragged, and injured, perhaps their necks broken.

"The masters," I said, "do not fear pursuit."

"Perhaps not," said Paula. "Why do you think not?"

"We move on the road," I said. "We move in daylight. We do not endeavor to conceal ourselves or hasten. The wagon is drawn by a single beast. The wagon is large, ponderous, slow, and conspicuous."

"And," said Paula, "two kajirae are attached by leads to two rings, behind the wagon, which assures that the wagon cannot move more swiftly than two secured, tethered kajirae, that they not be lost or harmed."

"That, too," I said.

"How better then, so openly, so conspicuously," she asked, "could one conceal one's presence?"

"Paula?" I said.

"What fugitives," she asked, "would behave so, so foolishly, seemingly frustrating their own designs?"

"I see," I said.

"But perhaps you are right," she said. "Perhaps Kurii, perhaps Decius Albus, do not concern themselves with us, perhaps they do not begrudge us a quiet and unimpeded exit from Ar."

"It seems so," I said.

"Indeed," she said.

"You suspect our tethering," I said, "to be a part of a disguise, suggesting confidence and ease?"

"I suspect so," she said.

"And if it were not," I said, "if no danger threatened, and all was safe, where would we be?"

"Precisely where we are now," she said, "chained to the back of a wagon."

"I see," I said.

"We are slaves," she said.

Many times in the past few days, I had felt the urge to throw myself to my belly before Paula, weeping, and beg her forgiveness for the wrong I had so gratuitously done to her, confessing my miserable attempt to seduce Drusus Andronicus. How grievously I had betrayed her friendship and trust! Clearly Drusus Andronicus had never referred to the matter. It remained, thus, a secret, my terrible secret, a secret that, daily, grew harder to bear.

"—Paula," I said, plaintively.

"Yes?" she said.

"—Nothing, nothing," I said.

"We are drawing to the side," said Paula. "There is a well there, by the pasang stone. Perhaps we will be fed and watered. Perhaps our neck chains will be lengthened, so that we may lie down on the grass, under the wagon."

The wagon rolled from the Viktel Aria, and stopped in the shade of a Tur tree, some yards from the well. We welcomed this. Our neck chains were lengthened, and, as we knelt and lifted our heads, we, by means of a bucket brought from the well, held to our lips, were watered. Kurik allowed some of the water to wash down our bodies, for which we were grateful. Shortly thereafter our wrists were freed from the slave bracelets, and we were given a round, flat loaf of bread, which we eagerly divided between us. We had been attended to by Kurik, while those in the wagon were served by Drusus Andronicus.

"I think we may be allowed to rest," said Paula.

We climbed under the wagon, in the slack of chain allowed, and stretched out, on our stomachs, our bodies damp from the water Kurik had poured upon us, on the soft grass. As we lay, rising a bit on our elbows, we could see the Viktel Aria, and the passing traffic.

"Where will we stop, where will we camp?" I wondered.

"In some public place, I think," said Paula. "The masters seem determined that all should proceed with apparent normality."

Various wagons, some moving toward Ar, some away from Ar, passed. Occasionally one stopped, to draw water from the well.

"What are you looking for?" asked Paula.

"There was a wagon," I said, "that lingered behind, neither exceeding our pace, nor slackening its pace, and falling behind."

"I remember," she said.

"I do not see it now," I said. "I do not think it passed us."

"Perhaps it has turned off the road," said Paula. "There are many side roads."

"Yes," I said.

"Or," she said, "it may have paused, as we are pausing."

"I am afraid," I said.

"It is probably nothing," said Paula.

We continued to watch the traffic on the Viktel Aria.

"I am filthy," I said. "I hope we can soon bathe."

"If we stop at a public camp, or such," said Paula, "there will be arrangements for the washing of slaves."

We suddenly heard the snap of a whip, and a cry of pain. We were startled, and winced. The crack of a whip is a sound slave girls well know. The sound came from the road, from our left.

"Look," I said, "a coffle."

It was moving toward Ar.

"Hold!" called a mounted guard, on a saddle tharlarion, placing his long, slender lance across the bosom of the lead slave.

She stopped instantly, and, with a sound of chain, the coffle arrested its progress.

"They are stopping," I said.

"The shade, and well," said Paula. "They are going to rest and water the slaves." This made sense, as the slaves were all female. Whereas the desiderated attributes of the male slave are stamina, endurance, strength, and such, and male slaves may be driven hard and long, and treated mercilessly, the most obvious desiderated attributes of the female slave are such things as beauty, grace, softness, and femininity. One does not want to bring female slaves to the market exhausted, spent, half-crippled, and burned. The male slave, putting aside the male silk slave, is essentially a work animal. The female slave, though she may be well worked by her master, is essentially a pleasure animal. Accordingly, the marches endured by coffled female slaves are quite different from those commonly enforced on male slaves, for example, in such things as the length of the march, the time marched in a day, the pace of the march, the frequency of waterings and rest periods, and so on. Women are not men. This is something well understood by Gorean slavers, and by Gorean men in general. This is not to deny that coffled women, proportional to their stamina, size, and strength, may not be as weary, worn, driven, and miserable as coffled men. But commonly, after two or three days of rest, water, and food, they are ready for the sales block.

"I think it is a long coffle," I said.

Paula rose to her hands and knees, her head low, under the wagon. "Yes," she said. "Many slaves. I cannot see from here. Perhaps more than a hundred, perhaps considerably more."

The girls were chained together by the neck. In such a way, unshackled, they may be easily moved. They also may be more easily moved when chained together by the wrist. The left wrist is the wrist invariably chosen, rather as, if the chain is ankle-shackled, by the left ankle. Indeed, if a woman is chained to a slave ring by the ankle, it is commonly the left ankle that is selected for the fastening. The most-favored coffle fastening is by the neck. The neck is favored in many chaining arrangements, whether a coffle is in question or not. The neck mount is both aesthetic and secure. Too, a chain on the neck, as a collar on the neck, have their symbolic aspects, each leaving the girl in no doubt that she is a slave. Too, as is well known, chaining, collaring, camisking, tunicking, and such are sexually stimulating, both to the slave and the onlooker.

"To the right," called the coffle guard, and the girls began to cross the road, approaching the well and nearby shade.

"Their feet are not wrapped, not protected, as are ours," I said to Paula.

"Do not be concerned," said Paula. "We were protected, as the stones are hot, and we were following the wagon, which holds to the road. The coffle is marched to the side of the road, on the dirt, the soft grass."

The girls in the coffle were, of course, stripped. That is the common way women are moved in coffle. It saves the soiling of tunics. In this way, at the end of a journey, after the slaves are washed, brushed, combed, and such, they may, if the masters wish, be placed in fresh, well-pressed tunics. Nudity in Gorean streets is rare, and usually reserved for a new slave, usually one who has recently been a free woman, or a slave being disciplined. An interesting exception to this, sometimes encountered, is male laborers, free men, commonly of the lower castes, who might be engaged in heavy tasks. Little is thought of this.

As we watched, we saw some of the girls being ankle shackled. They were then freed from the coffle and sent to the well. Shortly thereafter, with buckets and dippers, some from the following supplies wagon, some from the vicinity of the well itself, they were distributing water. The water is taken by the slaves while they are on their knees. They were, however, permitted to hold the dipper themselves. The slaves distributing the water are not permitted drink until the coffle has been watered. That apparently encourages them to complete their task in a timely manner.

"Your master," said Paula, subsiding again to her stomach on the grass, under the wagon, "is conversing with one of the coffle guards."

"He is of the Slavers," I said.

"What do slavers talk about?" asked Paula.

"I suppose," I said, "business."

"Doubtless," said Paula.

Shortly thereafter, Kurik sauntered over, and snapped his fingers. "Out from under the wagon," he said, "and kneel, here, before me."

Still on our chains, they considerably slackened from when we were fastened closely to the rings on the back of the wagon, we complied.

"You see the coffle," said Kurik.

"Yes, Master," we said.

It now rested, muchly gathered together, in the shade.

The water bearers had now been returned to the coffle, where they had been deshackled.

"It is a large one," he said. "How many slaves do you think are beaded on that particular 'slaver's necklace'?"

"A great many," said Paula, "perhaps one hundred and fifty."

The common coffle seldom exceeds more than a hundred girls. Common coffles usually contain twenty to fifty "beads."

"Two hundred," said Kurik.

"That is very large," said Paula.

"It is moving, of course, toward Ar," said Kurik.

Ar was generally credited with having the most slave markets in the northern hemisphere, a distinction that was held by Turia in the far south. The slavers of Ar also boasted the finest markets in the northern hemisphere, but there were few of the other "high cities" that would not dispute this claim. The most prestigious market in Ar was clearly the Curulean, where Paula, I recalled, not at all pleasantly, had been sold. Two other important marketing centers in the northern hemisphere were the port, Brundisium, and, on the Vosk, Victoria. The latter tended to sell almost as much to slavers, seeking eventual resales, as to private masters. The locations of Brundisium and Victoria had not a little to do, it was speculated, with their economic importance. Brundisium, with its great harbor, did not only command the coast, but was the nearest major port to the island Ubarates of Cos and Tyros, and, of late, to the "World's End." And Victoria, as I understood it, was the largest port on the Vosk, this providing a favored access to one of Gor's major arteries of commerce.

"It should be of some interest to you," said Kurik.

"How so, Master?" asked Paula.

"They are all barbarians," said Kurik.

"Master?" said Paula.

"You did not know?" said Kurik.

"No, Master," said Paula.

"To be sure," said Kurik, "there is little to choose from, between a stripped woman of Earth and a stripped Gorean woman. They all collar nicely."

"Yes, Master," said Paula.

"Yes, Master," I said.

"Surely so many seized slaves on Earth would attract attention," said Paula.

"Not at all," said Kurik. "There are a great many countries on Earth. One can pick a slave here, a slave there. Earth has millions of female slaves, lacking only their collars."

"They would come then from a great many countries," said Paula.

"Indeed," said Kurik, "from dozens of what you call 'countries'. There are slaves from America there, slaves from England, French slaves, German slaves, slaves from Russia, and Japan, and so on. But now they will learn Gorean, the language of their masters."

"They are very beautiful," I said.

"Of course," said Kurik. "One intends to sell them."

"Would that we were as beautiful," said Paula.

"You are," said Kurik. "Otherwise you would not be kneeling before me, on the grass, in your collars."

"I am yours! Have me, Master!" I begged.

"Please tell my master, Drusus Andronicus," said Paula, "that his slave, Paula, oils, oils profusely, and begs to be touched."

"You both stink from sweat and the road," said Kurik.

"Forgive us, Master," said Paula.

"We stop this night at a caravanserai," said Kurik. "Perhaps then you can be washed, and may then belly, and beg use."

"Yes, Master," we said.

"But neither of you have noticed what is most interesting about the coffle," said Kurik.

"What is that, Master?" inquired Paula.

"It is an unusually large, and publicly displayed, coffle of barbarians, moving openly, on a major public road, barbarians, in the midst of daylight. It is not a string of a dozen or so girls, or a handful or two, chained in a slave wagon."

"I do not understand," said Paula.

"The blockade seems porous," said Kurik. "Few ships seem challenged. Have Priest-Kings grown lax? I think something is different, somewhere, perhaps in the Sardar itself."

I understood nothing of this, nor, I think, did Paula.

At this point, Drusus Andronicus descended from the wagon.

"It is time we were on our way," he said.

"The slave Paula," said Kurik, "begs the hands of her master on her worthless body."

"She can wait," said Drusus Andronicus.

"Please, Master," said Paula, "the belly of your slave is afire. It flames with need. I am grievously tormented. Please it. I beg it! Relieve my need, I beg of you!"

"You can wait," said Drusus Andronicus.

"Yes, Master," sobbed Paula, her head down, her fists clutched, futilely.

"On your feet, to the wagon rings," said Kurik, lifting our chains. We then went to the back of the wagon, standing, facing it, somewhat before the rings, while Kurik shortened the chains to a tether link much the same as before.

He then stood behind us.

"Lesha!" he snapped.

We lifted our chins, turning our heads to the left, and placed our wrists behind us. We were then braceleted, and our wrists were fastened behind us, as before.

The lesha command is essentially a "leash" command. Placing the hands behind the body facilitates their tying or braceleting. Lifting the chin facilitates the fixing of the leash. As we were already chained by the neck to the rings on the back of the wagon, and thus, in a sense, were already leashed, the command was essentially one to prepare for a "behind the back" binding of the master's choice. The turning of the head in a particular direction introduces a uniformity into the command. For example, if a line of slaves were given such a command, it would be unaesthetic if some of the slaves turned one way and some another. The lifting of the head exposes the throat nicely for its encirclement. That the lifted head is turned to the left has an affinity with a number of other practices, the shackling of the left ankle, or the left wrist, the heeling of a master on the left, and so on. One heels on the left, presumably, to avoid any possible interference with the master's weapon hand, which, in most cases, is the right hand. I have never seen a girl heel on the right, but I suppose it could be done. A left-handed master does sometimes have the slave heel him behind his back. To be sure, there is latitude in such matters, with respect to distance and location. In pressing through a crowd, for example, almost every slave will heel directly behind the master. In this way, one is less likely to press into, or buffet, free persons. Contact with free women is particularly to be avoided.

"Paula!" I whispered, suddenly. "Look! The wagon! The wagon we feared is not concerned with us, after all. It is passing now. It was not following us. It did not pause, as we paused, not to exceed our pace, not to lose contact with us."

"Yes!" said Paula, relieved.

"We have made our escape from Ar," I said, "cleanly and safely, without incident."

"Our fears were groundless," laughed Paula.

"Yes," I said.

"How foolish we were, and how vain!" said Paula.

"How so?" I said.

"To think that one so mighty and influential as Decius Albus, trade advisor to the Ubar, would be concerned with us," said Paula.

"We did not know," I said.

"That is true," she said.

There was then a creak of the wagon wheels, those of our wagon, and the wagon was turning toward the Viktel Aria.

We felt the chains on our necks lift a little.

It was a good feeling, to know that we were safe, that danger was past.

I was then, following my relief, again stricken, suddenly, miserably, with the guilt I had so long nursed, having to do with my attempt to seduce Drusus Andronicus. I was torn between my desire to tell Paula what I had done and beg her forgiveness, and my fear of her finding out what I had done, and what sort of person I was. How could she ever respect me, or care for me, again, if she should find out what I had done? How could I risk losing her? With what hatred, and loathing, would she view me, if she should learn of what I had done! And yet it seemed I must speak to her. How could she be my friend, if she did not know? And how could she be my friend if she knew?

"—Paula," I said.

"Yes?" she said.

"—Where," I said, "—where do you think we will stop this night?"

"I do not know," she said. "Some camp, some inn, some hostel, some caravanserai. There are many such places on the Viktel Aria, particularly this close to Ar."

"I want to bathe," I said.

"I, too," she said. "I am sure facilities will be provided for such as we."

"For the bathing of kajirae," I said.

"Of course," she said.

"For the washing of animals," I said.

"Certainly," she said.

We were then again on the Viktel Aria, again on our way.

CHAPTER SIXTY-FOUR

I hummed to myself, content, and busied myself with the small fire, kneeling near it, tending it, adding small sticks from time to time. Paula was stirring one of the two pots that dangled from a stout metal rod stretched between two of the three sides of the bricked fire pit.

My training as a slave left much to be desired. Certainly I had not spent much time in the collar house to which I had been remanded by Kurik of Victoria, shortly after my arrival on Gor. I had, however, learned, and well learned, that I was collared. I had not, however, been favored with anything approximating an extensive training. For example, I had not been given much training in what one might have referred to as "domestic tasks," such things as cooking, cleaning, sewing, attending to a domicile, shopping, and so on. On my former world I had been too impatient or vain to concern myself with such things. Such things, if done at all, were for others, particularly women, lesser women, women I implicitly regarded as my inferiors. There were few services, laundering, cleaning, and such, that one could not purchase. Where food was concerned I frequented cafeterias, restaurants, and food shops, where one might be served readily, if not well. One could also purchase varieties of packaged foods that might be conveniently prepared. Paula, on the other hand, at least of women with whom I was personally acquainted, was unusual in this respect, as she could cook and, to some extent, at least, sew. She had even seemed to take a sort of pride in these trivial, homely accomplishments. She seemingly respected them and enjoyed them. Certainly she cooked and sewed. The rest of us, to some degree, looked down upon her, if not scorned her, for such things. Perhaps she was born into the wrong world or wrong century. These interests and skills, such as they were, on Paula's part, were some of the reasons I tended to feel compassion for her. Why could she not, as the rest of us, buy things, and content herself with food that, I would later learn on Gor, was poorly prepared and tasteless? I had never really tasted fresh fruit and fresh bread until I was brought to this world, as a slave, to serve masters. Similarly, I had never realized the gross, poisoned atmosphere of my former world until I had breathed the fresh, clean air of Gor. Goreans, of course, do not even notice such things; they take them for granted, rather as many of my former world do not even notice their familiar, thick, particle-laden, foul air.

"It will be ready soon," said Paula.

Toward the fifteenth Ahn our wagon had drawn into the large cara-vanserai of Hogarth, thirty pasangs from Ar, by the pasang stone, and, already, better than a hundred wagons were housed there. By the eigh-teenth Ahn there must have been more than four hundred. It is said that during the holidays, particularly those associated with the vernal equinox, at which point Goreans begin their year, as many as a thousand wagons might be quartered in the "Hogarth fields," which includes the compass of the caravanserai proper and, beyond that, an extensive over-flow area. Despite the fact that we had arrived fairly early at the caravan-serai, the masters had rented space rather at the edge of the caravanserai, bordering on the enlarged area, which now, at this time of year, was largely vacant. Paula and I were not clear on the motivation for this selec-tion, but we supposed that it had to do either with price or a desire for privacy, most likely privacy, given the fact that our party included Lord Grendel and Eve, the sight of whom would doubtless arouse curiosity, if not provoke alarm. We noticed, shortly after our arrival, as our wagon patiently threaded its way amongst other wagons, on its way to our lot, the wagon we had wondered about earlier. It had apparently arrived well ahead of us. Paula and I felt chagrined. How foolish had been our fears.

"Shortly," said Paula, "you can summon the others."

"Good," I said, stirring the fire with a stick.

The masters had not imposed a ranking between us. I was pleased, and I did not think that Paula had even thought about the matter. I would not have cared to address her, my friend, as "Mistress," and I was sure she would not have cared to be so addressed. Usually, of course, when slaves are together, one is designated as first girl, whom one must then address as "Mistress," and obey, as though she might be free. The first girl supervises work, inflicts discipline, resolves differ-ences amongst her charges, and so on. I supposed that Paula would be first girl, were one to be designated. Certainly she had sold for a much better price than it was conjectured I might bring. On the other hand, we had different masters, in which situation the designation of a first girl might have seemed inappropriate, or, at least, problematic.

"Tur-pah, tur-pah," called a hawker, moving amongst the wagons.

He looked at us, as one looks at slaves, but we were both secure, or, at least, as secure as a slave girl can be, in our brief tunics. We were also washed, cleaned, and combed.

Then the fellow continued on.

"It seems we are desired," remarked Paula.

"Yes," I said.

"I am thrilled to be seen by men as a slave," said Paula.

"I am thrilled to be a slave," I whispered.

"Oh, I, too, so much so," whispered Paula.

"It is what we are," I said.

"Yes," breathed Paula.

As a slave I felt feminine, needful, and vulnerable. I was not only content with my sex, but regarded it as deliciously, wonderfully precious. How can one be more female than in a man's collar?

The caravanserai of Hogarth was extensive, but it was also, in many ways, typical of such enterprises, furnished with amenities, a commissary, and various shops. An administration building was prominent, nearly fronting on the Viktel Aria. It was there that spaces, marked with numbered poles, might be rented. Near the administration building was an inn, where one might eat and lodge, though few of the guests, proportionately, availed themselves of this luxury. On the way through the wagons I noted several kitchens where food might be purchased, a clothing emporium, a barbering shop, two bakeries, four wine shops, two outlets of houses on the Street of Coins in Ar, sheds for wagon repair, an infirmary or clinic, under the green sign of the caste of Physicians, and at least five taverns. Each wagon yard had its tiny corral, or pen, for the housing and feeding of draft animals, whether tharlarion, kaiila, or bosk, and a bricked fire pit. As a number of wells were scattered about the grounds water was readily available, seldom more than a few Ehn from any marked location. Of special interest to Paula and myself was the fact that our wagon yard, which bordered on the periphery of the caravanserai proper, was adjacent to one of the slave pools, these located about the periphery of the caravanserai proper, away from the road. Closer to the center of the camp were private enclosures where free women might refresh themselves, bathing themselves or being bathed by serving slaves. Similar arrangements were available to free men, but were not enclosed. Goreans, on the whole, tend to be concerned with matters of personal cleanliness. In Ar itself, as in many of the larger cities, there are private and public baths. The best known public bath in Ar is the vast Capacian, almost a small city in itself with shops, restaurants, libraries, and gymnasiums. Slave pools, of various sorts, are, as one would suppose, very unlike the baths of the free, with their amenities, servants, and pools of different temperatures. In some baths catering to free women the chamber is perfumed and the water scented. As noted, escape is impossible for the Gorean slave girl, for a number of reasons. It is an almost universal practice to return her to her master, and if, as almost never happens, she eludes one master, she will soon kneel to another, and must expect to be treated as the displeasing slave she has proved to be. Indeed, she often tries to return to her original master, to throw herself to his feet and, on her belly, licking and kissing his feet, beg fervently for his forgiveness. I mention this for it has some bearing on the washing of slaves. The bathing of a slave almost always takes place in a manner that helps her to keep well in mind that she is a slave. Sometimes she is locked in a bathing cell. Sometimes, in the wild, when she would bathe in a stream or pool, she does so on a chain fastened about her neck and padlocked about a nearby tree. If the master, in such a situation, wishes to observe, and supervise, the bathing of the slave, he may keep her on a rope tether. Sometimes the master washes the slave himself, as he might any other domestic animal. One of the things a slave girl is trained to do, incidentally, is the bathing of a man. The bathing pool in which Paula and I were put to clean ourselves had a circular founda-tion of brick, and had a depth of a yard, or so. Rising from this circular foundation of bricks was a conical, barred cage, of a height of some five or six feet. We were conducted to the gate in the cage, following which we eased ourselves into the pool, Paula first. The gate was then locked behind us, with its two locks, and Kurik tossed a bar of yellow, tallow soap through the bars to Paula. We were not permitted the bathing oils commonly utilized by the free. "Clean yourselves well," he said. "When I return I shall bring toweling material, a brush, and comb, and two clean, fresh tunics, that you may not be more offensive to gaze upon than, as worthless slaves, you usually are." He then turned away, and made his way to the wagon area.

"I like that!" laughed Paula. "Perhaps we are worthless slaves, but we are not likely to be given away, except to friends. We cost money. Coins are exchanged for us. The free woman may be priceless, but, being priceless, she is worth nothing. We at least have our worth, what men will pay for us. And worthless, indeed! We are selected for our beauty, our intelligence, our passion, our needs, and our desirability!

And we are clothed, if clothed, in such a way as to display us, to flatter our sex and show it as it can be, as men want to see it, exciting and vulnerable, ready and purchasable! Do not tell me we are worthless! Wars are fought for us! Are we not prime loot? Men risk their lives to get us at their feet!"

"Dear Paula," I said, "use the soap or give it to me. The masters may soon return for us."

"In a moment," she said.

Neither of us wished to be lax in our cleansing. We wished to be well bathed for our own sakes, of course, for we were filthy, but also we wanted to sparkle for our masters. Just as slaves are not permitted to be rudely spoken, or awkward, or clumsy, they are to mind their appearance and keep their bodies clean. A free woman may do as she wishes in such matters, but the slave is not free. Too, she is not eager to feel the lash.

From the slave pool, waiting, standing in the water, I looked out, across the field, away from the caravanserai, into the now-unoccupied overflow area. Our position in the caravanserai was remote. I was certain the masters could have rented a yard much closer to the center of the camp, the shops, and such. "But, of course," I thought, "here, away from things, the presence of Lord Grendel and Eve would be far less likely to be noticed."

I lay beside my master, following supper.

Whereas some food had been brought from Ar in the wagon, some bread, and cold, prepared dishes, the latter for the free, more food had been bought from the shops in the caravanserai, some cubed, salted bosk, and some kes, tur-pah, and suls. In one of the two vessels suspended over the fire, Paula had prepared sullage, a sort of sul soup, or, in this case, given the thickness of the mix, a sul stew, and, in the other, had boiled the bosk cubes, heating and softening them. She had first, as is usually done, washed and scrubbed the cubes in fresh water, which is done to reduce the salt content and make the cubes more palatable.

"Open your mouth," said my master.

I obeyed, and he, from the pan in which the cubes now resided, placed one of the small cubes of bosk in my mouth. I could still taste the salt. We eat what we are given. We are fed well, but not overfed by the masters. As we are animals, our appearance, our figures, are important to the masters. Who knows, they may wish to sell us. Accordingly our diets, as those of other animals, are carefully supervised.

"Be careful," said Drusus Andronicus. "You do not want to spoil her."

I did not think his remark was necessary. He did not own me. To one side, Paula, in the half darkness, away from the subsiding fire, was on all fours, head down, feeding from a pan.

I had been permitted, earlier, to hold a small sullage bowl in my hands, and, head down, feed from it. I did not think my master was weak. Rather, it was I who, when near him, was weak. I always, for some reason, felt weak in the presence of Gorean men. I suppose the projection of their masculinity, so natural, so effortless, so unassuming, so thoughtless, so powerful, so strict, had an effect on my smaller body, my softness, my sensibility, and my awareness. The simple, natural masculinity of such men elicited, or triggered, weakness in me. I felt a natural desire to be on my knees before them. Certainly I was far more stable on my knees before them than I would have been on my feet. I might have shaken on my feet, even lost my balance. Even on my knees, I sometimes, faced with their power, found it difficult to speak. I could not help but feel, kneeling before them, a weakness, a readiness, a desire to yield, a fittingness to serve, a fervent hope to please. I was in my place, before men. There were complementarities in nature, physically, emotionally, and psychologically. Humans constituted a radically, sexually dimorphic species. Even Kurii, merely from the outside, could instantly distinguish between the sexes. Two components, male and female, formed an indivisible whole. Masculinity commanded femininity to its knees, and femininity found itself in its place. How could there be man without woman, or woman without man? How could there be master without slave, or slave without master? I found myself the willing prisoner of my nature, the joyful captive of my sex. I wanted to be what I was, not what I was not. Were the collar not on me, I would have sought it. How desperately I wanted to belong, how desperately I wanted to be owned. And how could I bring myself to respect a man who would not put me where I belonged, kneeling, beneath his whip?

When Paula had finished her repast, she crawled to Drusus Andronicus, and lay lovingly beside him.

He put his hand on her head.

"Master," she breathed.

"Perhaps later, delicious, curvaceous slut," he said.

I lay beside my master, and thought of what Drusus Andronicus had said. On Earth I would never have thought of shy, quiet, gentle, diffident, intelligent, book-reading Paula as a "slut." Surely she projected no such image to the world. That designation would have seemed the absolute opposite of what she was, or, perhaps better, of what she seemed to be. But who knew the interior life of such a person, her dreams, her wants, her needs? Who would know that she wanted to kneel at the feet of a master, in his chains? On Gor Paula had found herself as she wanted to be, collared, and owned. I suspected that in many women there is a "slut," or, perhaps better, and far more helpless and vulnerable, and far more desirable and exciting, a slave?

We spoke softly.

The Lady Bina, sitting on an improvised chair, formed from a box, fastidiously licked her fingers. Most Gorean free women would kneel, their knees closely together. Both Kurik, my master, and Drusus Andronicus, sat about, cross-legged, which is common with Gorean men. In taverns, and most domiciles, at least in the "high cities," the tables are low, and men sit about them cross-legged, and free women kneel at them. Part of our circle, so to speak, the fire pit to one side, restfully crouching, as might Kurii, was Lord Grendel and, beside him, touching him, making tiny loving sounds from time to time, was Eve.

"It is now dark," said the Lady Bina. "Surely it is about time."

I did not understand this remark.

"Patience, dear lady," said Lord Grendel.

The spines on the ruined parasol, once the possession of a Lady Alexina, which the Lady Bina had carried to the amusements of Decius Albus, had been carefully wiped clean of their lethal coating by Lord Grendel and the entire accessory had been discarded. This was thought judicious, given the damage to the object and the attendant risk of an inadvertent contact with the spines. One would not wish, for example, to have envenomed ost fangs lying about in one's immediate vicinity. Too, the Lady Bina refused to carry such an object, in its condition, as it would compromise her ensemble.

Suddenly I noted that Lord Grendel had flicked on his translator.

"Yes," said Eve, her ears lifted.

At the moment this made little sense to me, as he and Eve, at least in our presence, commonly discoursed in Gorean, and, if they wished the privacy of communicating in Kur, there would be no point in activating a translator. Then an instant later the hair on the back of my neck, and on my forearms, lifted, and I was terribly alert, and not a little frightened. Paula, too, was visibly alarmed. The others seemed relatively at ease, Lord Grendel and the men rose to their feet, looking out, into the darkness beyond the slave pool.

I saw a light flash three times, perhaps fifty yards away, and then, a moment later, it flashed three times again.

Clearly, somewhere out there, there was a dark lantern, a lantern whose light can be shielded, or revealed, given the opening or closing of a plate or door on the lamp.

Lord Grendel stirred the fire, and then lifted a glowing brand, and then, three times, slowly, lifted it and lowered it.

We continued to look into the darkness.

Paula and I rose to our knees.

The men made no effort to put out the fire.

Presently we saw a large, dark, rather bent shape emerging from the darkness. Behind it, flanking it, were four or five other shapes, and perhaps more, but they remained back, avoiding the light of the fire. As the first shape approached the light of the fire, the fire was reflected from a broad metal surface, that of the large, double-edged ax it bore. This shape was attended by, heeling it, a somewhat slighter shape.

As Lord Grendel, doubtless for the benefit of the humans present, had activated his translator, we followed much of what occurred.

"Tal," said Lord Grendel.

"Tal," said Surtak.

He gestured, and Lyris, in her collar, lay on her belly, beside him.

"It seems," said Surtak, "you have made your escape from Ar."

"One might hope so," said Lord Grendel.

"I am first amongst others," said Surtak.

"I see it is so," said Lord Grendel, peering out, beyond the slave pool.

This change of command had been effected at the games of Decius Albus.

"I pray you, speak of Ar," said Lord Grendel.

"The trade advisor has recovered," said Surtak. "He recruits men. He has designs on the throne of Ar."

"Perhaps he has forgotten the events of the games," said Lord Grendel.

"That is unlikely," said Surtak.

"He wished to ally himself with Kurii," said Lord Grendel.

"It was hoped," said Surtak, "we might have been mutually helpful."

"Decius Albus," said Lord Grendel, "abetted the ambitions of Lucilius and Aelius."

I recalled Lucilius had slain Aelius when the latter had sought the relative safety of the box of honor at the games.

"Very much so," said Surtak.

"I trust you will not oath to him," said Lord Grendel.

"I would have his throat," said Surtak.

"Are you prepared to oath to Lord Arcesilaus?" asked Lord Grendel.

"No," said Surtak. "Are you prepared to oath to Lord Agamemnon?"

"I think not," said Lord Grendel. "I suspect you are displeased."

"Somewhat," said Surtak.

"I am sorry," said Lord Grendel.

"I owe you my life, and that, too, of this worthless slave at my feet," said Surtak, kicking the prostrate form of Lyris, who lay beside him. "Thus, we need not fight to the death."

"I am pleased," said Lord Grendel.

"Indeed," said Surtak, "I respect you, even as a womb brother, despite your grotesque deformities."

"The noble Surtak is not only generous, but kind," said Lord Grendel. "What of Lord Agamemnon?"

"He is absent, we know not where," said Surtak. "I suspect he is acquiring, and learning, a new body."

"That is a fearful thing to contemplate," said Kurik, from the side.

These remarks made little sense to me.

"Where is Lucilius?" asked Lord Grendel.

"I think," said Surtak, "he fled to Decius Albus."

"An anomalous alliance," said Lord Grendel.

"But a dangerous one," said Surtak. "Particularly for humans."

"The Ubar?" said Lord Grendel.

"I fear so," said Surtak.

"He denied the ring challenge," said Lord Grendel.

"I want him in the rings," said Surtak, "in the rings."

"As he declined the challenge," said Lord Grendel, "you would be denied a third ring."

"I do not want a third ring," said Surtak. "I want his blood."

"Within the rings?"

"Of course."

"Forgive me," said Lord Grendel. "I have been inhospitable. There is still meat in the pot. May we offer you something? *Ela*, we do not have enough for your fellows."

"No," said Surtak, "but permit my homely, worthless slave to serve meat to you and your party."

"Surely not to humans, and to such as Eve and I, supposed monsters," said Lord Grendel. "Consider her former station, her antecedents."

"She is no longer accorded harnessing," said Surtak. "She is collared. She is now a slave, no different from other Kur females embonded on the Metal World. It will be a good lesson for her, that she serve inferiors, that she, once a superior, must now serve inferiors, and that she is now a slave, and now immeasurably inferior to inferiors."

"Dear, noble Surtak," said Lord Grendel, "Eve and myself, and the humans here, putting aside the slaves, do not regard ourselves as inferiors."

"Oh?" said Surtak.

"No," said Lord Grendel.

"But, is it not obvious?" asked Surtak.

"No," said Lord Grendel.

"Interesting," said Surtak.

"Not particularly," said Lord Grendel.

"As you wish," said Surtak. He then scowled down at Lyris. "Serve, Lyris," he said.

"Please, no, Master," she begged.

"Be about it," he said.

"Yes, Master," she said.

Lyris then, head down, took the pan of cubical chunks of meat, and held it, first, to the Lady Bina.

"Long ago," said the Lady Bina, selecting a cube of meat from the pan, "I was a Kur pet, and groomed my master, and bit the lice from his pelt. Now I am served by a Kur, before whom, once, I would not have dared to raise my eyes."

"I am now a slave, Mistress," said Lyris.

"You may now serve the men," said the Lady Bina, indicating Drusus Andronicus and Kurik, of Victoria.

"Yes, Mistress," said Lyris.

She then brought the cubes to Drusus Andronicus and Kurik, of Victoria. Each selected a cube of meat, but paid her no further attention, as she was a slave.

How that would have hurt me, and yet I knew I deserved no better. I was a slave.

Lyris looked up, agonized, at Surtak, but Surtak gestured impatiently toward Eve and Lord Grendel.

Lyris approached Eve, and head down, held up the plate.

"You are very beautiful," said Eve kindly, taking one of the cubes of meat.

"I am a slave, Mistress," said Lyris, gratefully.

Did Lyris not know slaves were beautiful? Did she think there was no relationship between being beautiful and being fastened in a collar?

Lyris then approached Lord Grendel, and, offering him the meat, looked up, her eyes wide, and a soft, begging noise escaped her.

I was startled. It was not unlike a slave whimper, a plea to be found pleasing. Are masters not familiar with such sounds, from a slave at their feet?

There was a sudden, ferocious shriek from Eve and she leaped upon Lyris, seized her, the pan of meat flying away, and hurled her to the ground on her belly, pushed her head down to the dirt, and snapped at the back of her neck. In unweaponed combat amongst Kurii each goes for the other's throat or neck. It is a common martial tactic to attempt to get behind the opponent, slipping to the side, or such, for then it is difficult for the opponent to protect himself. From this position the back of the neck can be conveniently bitten through, this breaking the connection between the spinal cord and the brain. A sound of furious frustration escaped Eve as her fangs closed, scratching, about Lyris' collar. Lord Grendel had leaped up at almost the same moment that Eve had left her position, taken hold of Eve and pulled her back, and away, from the helpless, terrified Lyris. He held Eve back, off the ground, by the arms, she squirming, snapping, hissing, and snarling at the distraught, imperiled Lyris. "No," he said, "no, sweet, gentle Eve! Desist. Do not kill her!"

I then realized that it was not only Lord Grendel who carried in his veins the dark, fiery blood of the Kur, but Eve, as well.

Never had I seen Eve so provoked, so wild, so bestial.

"Steady, steady, my sweet, my gentle, precious beloved!" said Lord Grendel, softly, soothingly.

Lyris scrambled up, and hid herself, cowering, behind Surtak.

Surtak himself leaped up and down with pleasure, and slapped his thighs, again and again, with delight. A roar of staccato noises escaped him, like an avalanche of uncontrolled sound. Lord Grendel's translator appeared to emit nothing but unintelligible static. I shuddered. I was in the presence of what I recognized, half fainting with fear, as Kur merriment. Surtak was beside himself with mirth.

"Forgive her, noble Surtak," begged Lord Grendel. "It was but an impulse, the matter of a rash moment."

Surtak struggled to regain his composure.

Eve, now released, had returned to her place, but she continued to regard Lyris balefully, and, from time to time, uttered what could be nothing but a menacing growl.

"I am sorry," said Lord Grendel.

"I trust your friend did not injure her fangs," said Surtak.

"I am sure all is well," said Lord Grendel.

There was a bit of blood on the left side of Eve's jaw. It was clear her fangs were unharmed, as one could make out, from her occasional baring of them in the direction of Lyris. I think she had cut the side of her jaw on the collar.

"I am pleased," said Lord Grendel to Surtak, "that you managed to keep our prearranged appointment, at the agreed-upon caravanserai, that we might be apprised as to what has ensued in Ar."

"I owe you much," said Surtak. "I like you. You will make a fine enemy."

"And you, too, I fear," said Lord Grendel.

Surtak then looked down at Lyris, at his feet. She quickly put her head down.

"And you, beautiful slave," he said, "we will see if you like the way you are chained tonight."

"Yes, Master," she said.

"We shall now leave," said Surtak. "We have far to go before light. It pleases me you have made good your escape. I feared it might not be so. You are now safe."

"I wish you well," said Lord Grendel.

"And you are so wished, as well," said Surtak.

He then turned about, and moved away, into the darkness beyond the yard. The others, in the night, his cohorts, had apparently withdrawn farther. He, in his departure, was heeled by Lyris, his slave. We could then see them no more.

"A fine Kur," said Kurik.

"Would he were of our faction," said Lord Grendel.

"In one respect, he was seriously misinformed," said Drusus Andronicus.

"Yes," said Lord Grendel.

"May I speak?" I asked.

"Certainly," said Lord Grendel.

"In what respect," I asked, "was Master Surtak misinformed?"

"In that we had made good our escape, that we are safe," said Lord Grendel.

CHAPTER SIXTY-FIVE

M aster?" I asked.

"Strip," said Kurik, "bathe, both of you."

"We have already bathed," I said.

I was held by the hair, and cuffed three times, once with the palm of his right hand, then with its back, and then, again, with the palm. I tasted blood at my lip.

"Forgive me, Master," I said. I had been slow to obey.

Paula had already slipped from her tunic.

I hastily pulled off the tunic.

Kurik then stood between us, and took us by the hair. His left hand was tight in my hair and his right hand was doubtless the same in Paula's hair. I winced. Then our heads were thrust down. We were bent over, our heads at his waist. We were in leading position, one on each side of the master.

Long hair is favored in slave girls, for several reasons. Doubtless the first reason is aesthetic, as such hair is lovely in a girl. Certainly long hair tends to raise the price of a slave. Too, in the furs, much can be done with long hair to please a master, it brushing against him, and such. Too, as in leading, long hair makes it easier to control the slave. Indeed, sometimes a slave is bound with her own hair. Too, of course, a girl, if only in her vanity, wishes to retain her hair, and will do much to keep it. A shaved head not only punishes a girl but marks her out to other slaves as having been a displeasing slave. She is then likely to be the object of much derision and contempt. Lastly, it might be noted that the shorn hair of slaves, commonly marketed as the hair of free women, may be used by free women for various cosmetic purposes, such as wigs and falls. Woman's hair, too, makes the best catapult cordage, being resilient, strong, and weather-resistant. Indeed, when a city is besieged, even free women may donate their own hair for such a purpose.

We were led, half stumbling, by Kurik, my master, toward the slave pool, with Drusus Andronicus now preceding us. He undid the gate, and we were thrust through the gate, into the water, and almost before we could turn, standing in the now-cold, waist-high water, we heard the gate close and the snap of the two heavy locks that held it in place. We were again locked in the domed, cage pool. It was dark about, but we could see into the yard, illuminated by the fire pit, now containing a smaller fire, see the Lady Bina, still seated, and, closely behind her, the wagon. All this was within a few yards.

"Kajirae," said Drusus Andronicus.

"Master," we said, acknowledging that we were to be spoken to.

"You have been caged for your own protection," said Drusus Andronicus. "The bars should protect you. In the heat of what may ensue, perhaps abruptly and unexpectedly, you might be injured. If I were you, I would endeavor to remain relatively unobtrusive. Do not call attention to yourselves. We will brook no interference. You should survive. You are not free. Your collars should protect you."

"Release us, Master," I wept, standing in the water, clutching the bars.

"They know you are of our party," said Drusus Andronicus. "They will search for you. So, let them learn where you are. If you were loose, and fled, you would be soon apprehended, and might be hamstrung as fugitive slaves, if only by the guards of the caravanserai."

"What is going on, Master?" begged Paula, plaintively, but Drusus Andronicus had turned away from her.

The two at the gate, Drusus Andronicus and Kurik, of Victoria, were joined by Lord Grendel.

"Might it not have been wise, dear Grendel," said Kurik, "to have solicited the aid of Surtak, and those with him?"

"I am sure they would have looked favorably on such a request," said Drusus Andronicus.

"No," said Lord Grendel. "All might have died. Their participation would have been anticipated by Decius Albus and Lucilius, and the intruders will be prepared, equipped with bows and quarrels. An ax is small protection against a quarrel flighted at a pace's distance. Too, Surtak and his cohorts, despite their reservations pertaining to Decius Albus, are oathed to Lord Agamemnon. I think their participation, ill-fated as it would have been, would have compromised their oathing."

"Then we are alone," said Kurik.

"We have an ally," said Lord Grendel, "the fear of those who will breach the camp."

"Let us put our plan into effect," said Drusus Andronicus.

"I shall prepare the wagon," said Kurik.

"Master!" I called.

He turned back to face me.

"You fear an attack," I said.

"Surely," he said.

"Perhaps you are mistaken," I said. After all, the minions of Decius Albus would not know we had left the city, or when we might have left, or what route we might choose. Too, there had been no obvious evidence of pursuit. The trip had been uneventful. And Surtak had supposed our exit from Ar had been successfully effected.

"I suspect not," said Kurik. "Decius Albus has spies. He is well informed."

"Still," I protested.

"There was a wagon," he said, "that soon followed us from Ar, a fine brown wagon, long-bedded and wide, lacquered, with two lanterns, drawn by two fine tharlarion, displaying the selling banner of itinerant cloth workers."

I knew nothing about a selling banner of cloth workers, itinerant or otherwise, but I knew the wagon, for Paula and I, earlier in the day, had noted its presence, with some concern.

"It matched its pace to ours, despite the traffic. This was easily determined, from the back of the wagon. When we rested, it ceased to move, and so on."

"Paula and I noticed such a wagon," I said. "But these congruences were a matter of coincidence."

"Cloth workers do not sell from such a wagon," said Kurik. "Itinerant cloth workers are peddlers. They would have a smaller wagon, or, more likely, a cart, not so fine a wagon. It would be unusual peddlers, indeed, who could afford so splendid a wagon and such a brace of prime tharlarion."

"Coincidence, Master," I said, "surely coincidence."

"I should hate to trust my life to your coincidences," he said.

"The wagon passed us," I said, "and came to lodge at the caravanserai, before we arrived."

"The road could be watched," he said. "If we passed the caravanserai, it would be a simple matter to renew the pursuit. If we did not pass, how better to conceal the pursuit, than by appearing independently lodged, thus suggesting indifference or disinterest?"

"It could still be a coincidence," I said.

"Certainly," said Kurik. "Now, if you will excuse me, I must prepare for the attack."

He then turned about and went across the yard, and began to busy himself about the wagon.

"I do not understand what is going on," I said. "If some attack is imminent, and we are likely to be outnumbered, surely we should flee."

"And be again pursued?" said Paula. "And again, and again, always fearing small sounds, an unrecognized step, an unfamiliar face? They will take a stand, one calculated to discourage pursuit."

"I see no hope in this," I said.

"Who would walk blindfolded amongst osts?" she said.

"The water is cold," I said.

"Hsst," whispered Paula.

"Yes," I whispered.

Perhaps half an Ahn had passed since we had been locked in the cage of the slave pool.

We saw torches approaching through the wagons, approaching the yard where we had camped.

"I count eight torches," said Paula, "and each torch bearer illuminates the way for a bowman."

"The other shape," I said, "with the great ax, hideous amongst them."

"Kur, kur," said Paula.

"Lucilius?" I said.

"Doubtless," said she.

"We should have fled," I moaned, softly.

"It will be done with us as men please," said Paula. "We are caged. We are beasts, slaves."

I, standing in the water, clutched the bars, looking out, through them. We could not affect the outcome of what might ensue.

"We must stand by," I said. "We can do nothing. We are helpless."

"We are only beasts, slaves," said Paula.

The Lady Bina remained as she had been, sitting, near the fire, the wagon a yard or two behind her.

"We must call out," I said.

"No," said Paula, "remember the instructions of the masters."

"But the Lady Bina," I said.

"She is as aware as we of the torches, the men," said Paula. "They make no effort to conceal their presence."

"She is alone," I said. "She has been deserted."

"Seemingly so," said Paula.

There was no sign of Lord Grendel, or Eve, or of Drusus Andronicus, or of Kurik, my master, in the camp.

"The others have fled," I said. "Leaving the Lady Bina, a free woman, to the intruders, to the mercy of the minions of Decius Albus."

"Then we, as well," said Paula.

"We can effect nothing critical," I said. "They were outnumbered. Their opponents have bows. Flight is rational. It was wise to flee."

"And abandon the Lady Bina, a free woman?" she asked.

"It seems so," I said.

"Why would they not take her with them?" she asked.

"She might encumber their flight," I said.

"Then," she said, "they are cowards."

"How can it be otherwise?" I said.

"I know little or nothing of he whom you call 'Lord Grendel', and she whom you call 'Eve'," said Paula, "but Drusus Andronicus and Kurik are Goreans, masters."

"They have left the Lady Bina," I said.

"No coward is worthy of owning a woman," she said.

"On this world," I said, "it is easy to buy a woman."

At that point, Lucilius, bearing his ax, entered the yard. He was flanked by two torch bearers, and two bowmen, quarrels readied in guides. The others, torch bearers and bowmen, appeared, alert, ranging about. The yard was well illuminated. The humans were not in the livery of Decius Albus. Their projected action was apparently to be accomplished anonymously. About the neck of Lucilius was a translator, doubtless that he might communicate with his fellows.

Lucilius looked about.

"Are you not late?" inquired the Lady Bina.

"Where is Grendel, the beast, the beast, Eve, the loathsome humans?" demanded Lucilius.

"I have been waiting for you," said the Lady Bina.

"No," said Lucilius, "you are taken unawares, surprised."

"Scarcely," said the Lady Bina.

"Astonished," said Lucilius.

"We have been aware of your presence since early this morning," said the Lady Bina. "It would have been easier to overlook the presence of a sleen in a vulo coop, or that of a draft tharlarion in a slave market."

"Where is Grendel, who would not oath to Lord Agamemnon,

Grendel, who freed the traitor, Surtak, Grendel, who disturbed the games of Decius Albus? Where, too, are the others of your party, the monster, Eve, and the two humans?"

"They will return shortly," said the Lady Bina.

"Good," said Lucilius. "We shall wait."

"Are you sure you wish to wait?" she asked.

"Yes," said Lucilius.

"What is your business with sweet, gentle Grendel?" asked the Lady Bina.

"I will meet him, ax to ax," said Lucilius.

"Excellent," said the Lady Bina. "Then dismiss your bowmen."

"They are with me," said Lucilius.

"Once," said the Lady Bina, "when I was in dire straits, dear Grendel was kind enough to stand as my champion, in an arena, on the Metal World. Perhaps you witnessed the events of that afternoon, or are familiar with an account of them."

"I do not fear him," said Lucilius.

"Neither would I," said the Lady Bina, "if he were pierced by eight crossbow bolts, before he could lift his ax."

"We will wait," said Lucilius.

"You may be prepared to die," said the Lady Bina, "but your fellows may be less willing to do so."

"I do not understand," said Lucilius.

His men looked about, and at one another, uneasily.

"You have led your men, poor fellows, unwittingly to be sure, so they should not really blame you," said the Lady Bina, "into a lethal trap."

The torch bearers and bowmen stirred, looking apprehensively about.

"Stay where you are, do not move!" said Lucilius.

"I suggest," said the Lady Bina, "that some of you fellows bring those torches a bit closer and lift them higher. That done, please examine the wagon, in particular, the emblem with which it is emblazoned, and the banner it flies."

There were cries of dismay from several of the fellows about.

"The sign of Mintar, Mintar of Ar!" cried a man.

"Anticipating our meeting," said the Lady Bina, "we arranged with the house of Mintar to transmit some parcels on his behalf to Besnit."

I was sure this was false. But Lucilius, and certainly his cohorts, might be less certain of the matter.

I now suspected the nature of some of the mysterious objects carried in the wagon, paint, perhaps, in the cylindrical containers, and, surely, the pole and banner, which must have resided in the long, rectangular box.

"Further," said the Lady Bina, "we informed the agents of the great merchant, Mintar, that we anticipated the appearance of caravan bandits."

"We are not caravan bandits!" cried a man, clearly alarmed, looking about.

"Then I regret that a tragic misunderstanding has taken place," said the Lady Bina. "I am very sorry."

At that point, from the darkness, a voice called out, "Deploy, Sleen of Mintar, the urts are in the trap!"

Lucilius may have understood little of this, but the men with him were only too aware of the might of the merchant, Mintar, his vast web of agents and informants, his generous rewards for the apprehension of those who might be so foolish as to harrow his wagons, and the numbers and tenacity of his hunters, trained killers known for the relentless pursuit of their quarry, pursuits sometimes prolonged for years. More than one road had been lined with the impaled bodies of their prey. Too, it was rumored that Mintar had access to the resources of the state, as well. Surely it was clear that he was highly placed in the estimation of the state. It was said, even, that he occasionally enjoyed a game of kaissa with Marlenus, the Ubar himself.

Then another voice called out, from the opposite side. "Guardsmen of Ar," it called, "prepare to do justice to those who would endanger the great road. And, guards of the caravanserai, unsheathe your thirsty swords, to drink the blood of those who would rob within the protected precincts of the caravanserai of Hogarth!"

Those with Lucilius looked wildly about. Some thrust their torches in the dirt.

"Upon my signal," cried the first voice, "loose your quarrels."

"No, no! Wait, wait!" cried a man. "Hold your fire! We are not bandits! We are not bandits!"

Men thrust torch after torch into the dirt, extinguishing them. And, in a moment, the yard was in darkness, save for the light from the fire pit.

"Close the ring," called the first voice. "None shall escape!"

"This is all a mistake," called one of Lucilius' fellows from the darkness. "Robbery is not our work!"

"We have no intentions on the goods of Mintar!" cried another.

"We knew not the wagon his!" cried another.

"We are innocent, innocent!" cried another.

"Be silent!" came from the translator of Lucilius, the volume increased well beyond the normal level.

"We are not bandits, we are not robbers!" cried another voice, from the darkness.

"Glory to Mintar!" called another.

"May he prosper!" called another voice.

"We are innocent, innocent!" cried another.

"We are patient," called the first voice, that which had originally alarmed the intruders. "We can wait until morning, and then, at our leisure, with a thousand quarrels, slay these thieving urts with impunity. In the meantime, keep the circle closed!"

"It will be done, Commander!" answered the second voice, that which had been supposedly associated with road patrols, with guardsmen of Ar, and the supposed guards of the caravanserai itself.

"None will escape!" called the first voice. "The caravanserai will furnish the impaling poles!"

"We are innocent!" cried one of Lucilius' followers from the darkness.

"It is a mistake!" cried another.

"Mercy, mercy!" called several terrified voices.

"Be silent, be silent!" came from Lucilius' translator.

"Hold!" called the Lady Bina, whose voice, despite its diminutive, exquisite housing, carried in it all the majesty of a Gorean free woman. "I am a free woman, and I am speaking, so attend me, and well! I think these fellows were honestly misled. What thief in his right mind would risk the impaling poles of the great Mintar? I am sure they did not know a cargo of Mintar was in question."

"No, no!" cried several men.

"We did not know," called others, plaintively.

"Be quiet," said the Lady Bina. "A free woman is speaking."

There was, instantly, silence.

"Reluctant as I am to interfere in the activities of men, riddling bodies with quarrels, lopping off arms and heads, stabbing with knives and spears, splashing blood about, and such," she said, "such activities are, I gather, most enjoyable when properly motivated."

There was silence.

"I am convinced," she said, "Sleen-of-Mintar fellows, Guardsmen, guards, and others, whosoever they may be, out there in the darkness, that this evening's business is founded on a misunderstanding. I do not think these fellows had any designs on what did not belong to them, in particular, anything that might belong to Mintar, the merchant, whom we all respect, and of whom we are all fond."

"That is true!" called one of Lucilius' cohorts.

"Please," said the Lady Bina, annoyed.

There was, again, silence.

"Accordingly," said the Lady Bina, "I have a proposal to make. Unless you are bent on pointless, gratuitous slaughter, which is, of course, your business, man business, I suggest, under the circumstances, you spare these fellows, provided they throw down their weapons, and hasten away, into the darkness."

"Yes, yes!" cried several of Lucilius' men.

"Please, at least, consider the matter," called the Lady Bina.

There was a lengthy pause, and then the voice that had first called out from the darkness, that which had supposedly been associated with the "Sleen of Mintar," said, "We will consider it."

At this point, the Lady Bina resumed her seat. "Now, fellows," she said, "we will wait, and find out whether you will live or die."

I heard some weapons being cast to the ground.

Something like a quarter of an Ahn later the first voice called out from the right, in the far darkness, from outside the yard. "We have considered it."

"And what have you decided?" called the Lady Bina, again rising to her feet.

"We are reluctant—," said the voice.

"But?" called the Lady Bina.

"We accept your proposal," said the voice.

"You had better," said the Lady Bina, "as it is the proposal of a free woman. Otherwise you would certainly hear about this."

I heard cries of joy, and the sound of weapons being cast to the ground.

"No, no!" came from Lucilius' translator. "Stay! Remain!"

"Open the ring of death!" called the Lady Bina into the darkness.

"It is open," called the voice from the left, which had supposedly been associated with the guardsmen of Ar, and caravanserai guards.

"Stop, stop!" cried Lucilius, as men rushed about him, in the darkness, hurrying from the yard.

Then he was alone in the yard, save for the Lady Bina, who had resumed her seat.

"You," snarled Lucilius, the menace clear in Kur, "you unveiled, shameless she-sleen, with one blow of my ax there will be two of you."

"You have enough difficulty dealing with one," she said. "What would you do with two?"

Lucilius, with a cry of rage, lifted the ax.

"I would lower my ax, if I were you, fellow," she said, "for, by now, you might have a quarrel between your eyes."

Kurik, my master, stepped forth from the shadows, his bow lifted, and aimed.

Lucilius, snarling, lowered the ax, and stepped backward.

"I have a friend," said the Lady Bina, "who has been looking forward to meeting you."

"Tal," said Lord Grendel, appearing out of the darkness, ax in hand. Behind him was Eve. Then Drusus Andronicus appeared from the right.

"You see," whispered Paula to me, "they did not desert the Lady Bina, they did not leave, they did not flee."

"No," I said.

"They are Goreans," she said, "masters."

"Yes," I said, contrite, holding the bars of the cage, half sick, much ashamed of the doubts I had entertained, however plausibly, however naturally. The Lady Bina had been alone. I had not seen the others.

"Would you care to belong to lesser men?" asked Paula.

"No," I said.

"You will serve your master well, will you not, Phyllis," she said, "and as the slave you are?"

"Yes," I said.

"—If he keeps you," she said.

"—If he keeps me?" I said.

"You have much to atone for," she said.

"You will not tell him of my doubts," I begged.

"You will do so," she said.

"No," I said.

"Then I will do so," she said.

"No!" I said.

"It is in your best interest," said Paula. "Otherwise I would not speak to him."

"Do not speak to him," I said. "I will do so."

"Good," she said. "A slave is to be completely open to the master. There are to be no secrets between a master and his slave."

"What will he do with me?" I asked.

"I do not know," she said. "But he will understand you better, as a weak, shallow barbarian slave, clever and superficial, who doubted her master's honor."

Standing in the water, naked, clutching the bars, I felt miserable.

"Honor is important to Goreans," she said.

"I know," I said. "I know."

"Tal," had said Lord Grendel, who had appeared out of the darkness, ax in hand. Behind him had been Eve. And then Drusus Andronicus had appeared from the right.

"Doubtless you are pleased to see Grendel," said the Lady Bina to Lucilius.

"Of course," said Lucilius.

"You might say 'Tal' to him," said the Lady Bina.

"Tal," said Lucilius.

"Your bowmen are absent," observed the Lady Bina.

"There is no wagon of Mintar," said Lucilius. "You are not in league with him. You carry no cargo for Mintar. The emblem on your wagon, the banner, are fraudulent."

"Quite so," said the Lady Bina. "And it would be wise on our part to remove the emblem and banner before we exit the caravanserai."

"You have perpetrated a hoax," he said.

"A useful one," she said, "one that served its purpose."

"I want blood," he said.

"Do not interfere," said Lord Grendel to Kurik, with his leveled bow, he, my master, and to Drusus Andronicus, Paula's master.

"As I recall," said the Lady Bina, addressing herself to Lucilius, "you wished to meet sweet Grendel, ax to ax."

"Very much so," said Lucilius.

"Even without bowmen?" she asked.

"Surely, splendid lady," said Lucilius.

Eve was trembling in the background.

"But I suggest," said Lucilius, "if we are to do without bowmen, you might ask that fellow to lower his bow."

Kurik, of Victoria, lowered his bow.

"And remove the quarrel from the guide," said Lucilius.

Kurik turned his head, slightly, toward Lord Grendel.

"Do so," said Lord Grendel.

Kurik then removed the quarrel from the guide.

"Now, if you will, dear lady," said Lucilius to the Lady Bina, "count to three, slowly, and then we shall engage."

"Very well," said the Lady Bina. "—One."

Lucilius roared with rage and leapt at Lord Grendel, with a mighty stroke of the great ax, but Lord Grendel crouched down and, lifting his own ax, gripped in two hands, or paws, struck upward, bringing the blade of his own ax into play, against the higher end of the shaft of the descending ax, and the head of the shaft, splintered, shattered, spun aside, to the dirt, and Lord Grendel, with the butt of his own ax, struck Lucilius, then unarmed, a heavy blow, against the side of the head, and Lucilius fell to the ground, dazed, hardly aware, I suspect, that Lord Grendel, with his foot, had turned him to his stomach, before him.

"Two," said the Lady Bina.

Lord Grendel then placed his foot on Lucilius' back, his ax lifted, pressing him to the ground.

"Three," said the Lady Bina.

"Mercy, mercy!" said Lucilius.

Lord Grendel then removed his foot from Lucilius' back, and stepped back.

Lucilius did not dare to move.

"One blow," said Lord Grendel, "will take the right foot, a second blow the left foot, a third the right hand, a fourth the left hand."

"No," said Lucilius. "Do not! Do not!"

"If you thrust the bleeding stumps, as you can, into the dirt," said the Lady Bina, "that will slow the loss of blood, and you may live a little longer, to consider matters."

"Have mercy!" begged Lucilius.

Lord Grendel stepped back, lowering the ax.

"Another wants your blood," said Lord Grendel, "not I. Indeed, I do not care to stain my ax with your blood, lest the blade be dishonored."

Lucilius, prone, prostrate, did not move.

"May I go?" he asked.

"But without harnessing," said Lord Grendel.

"No!" said Lucilius.

Lord Grendel, then, with a grasping paw, or hand, pulling against the leather, lifting it, employing the blade of his ax, cut away the harnessing of Lucilius.

"And now," said Lord Grendel, "you may hasten, as you are, to Decius Albus and inform him of how your cohorts deserted you and how, despite your vigor and bravery, you were overcome by overwhelming numbers."

Lucilius, trembling with fear or rage, or both, lay in the dirt, at Lord Grendel's feet.

"Go," said Lord Grendel.

Lucilius scrambled up, and on feet and knuckles, fled away, into the darkness.

Eve hurried to Lord Grendel. I observed them embrace.

A bit later, Kurik and Drusus Andronicus approached the slave pool. Kurik carried the key to the locks and Drusus Andronicus held a pair of blankets. We kept our heads down, hearing the movement of the keys in the locks, and the rattle of chain. When the gate was opened, we exited the pool and knelt before our masters, our heads down. How helpless we had been, put to the side, while the free had conducted their business.

Each of us was given a blanket, which we accepted gladly.

I saw Paula cast me a sharp, meaningful look.

"Master," I begged, "may I speak?"

"Yes," he said.

The blanket partly about me, I went to the first obeisance position, kneeling, head to the ground, the palms of my hands at the sides of my head.

"When in the pool," I said, "I thought you and the others had fled, abandoning the Lady Bina. I thought ill of you. I thought you were cowards."

"That is natural that you should think that," he said. "What else would one such as you, from Earth, with its ethos of selfishness and gain, with its smug contempt of honor, have thought?"

"Paula did not think it," I said.

"Paula," he said, "went for a golden tarsk."

"I am sorry, Master," I said. "Forgive me. I await my punishment."

"No punishment," he said. "Dismiss the matter from your mind. Besides, not all Goreans are brave, or honorable. And sometimes a man may be brave, and at another time not brave; sometimes a man may be honorable, and at another time not honorable. And how could one know about such things?"

"I thought badly of my master," I said. "I am not worthy of my collar."

"That is for me to decide," he said. "In any event, worthy or not, you are in it."

It was surprisingly warm under the blanket.

"I suspected as much, of course, that you would doubt," he said.

"The inference is persuasive. You should have told me, of course, as you did. That was proper."

I glanced at Paula, who smiled approvingly. I wanted her to know that I had openly confessed my doubts to my master. There are, I recalled, to be no secrets between a master and his slave. I felt gratitude, and relief. Then I recalled the wrong I had done to Paula, how I had attempted to steal the affections of Drusus Andronicus, not because I wanted him, but because, in my vanity, I had been jealous of her. I had been punished for that. Even now, when I thought of it, I could feel the fire of the whip.

"Hurry, fellows," called the Lady Bina. "We must remove the emblem of Mintar from the wagon, take down the banner, change the canvas to brown, harness the tharlarion, be on our way."

"A free woman speaks," said Drusus Andronicus.

"They often do," said Kurik, my master.

I now understood the contents of the one sack, large, and seemingly filled with cloth, which had puzzled me earlier. With so small a change as the canvasing, our wagon, so conspicuous before, would become only another vehicle on the Viktel Aria.

CHAPTER SIXTY-SIX

Paula and I sat in the back of the wagon, on a blanket, naked, amongst the boxes, shackled, hand and foot.

We spoke softly, that we not disturb the masters, Drusus Andronicus and Kurik, of Victoria, who rode together on the wagon bench, Drusus Andronicus handling the reins. We felt comfortable, and meaningful, in our chains. We felt, and were, deliciously helpless, and wholly owned. How ancient and deep was our understanding of our sexuality, and how jejune and shallow then seemed to us the engineered distortions and strained falsities of our former world, distortions and falsities dictated by political agendas subservient to one tyranny or another. Why, I wondered, can one not be left alone, to learn oneself and find oneself? Is that so terrible, to be what one is? Some profit, I supposed, from laws that would make nature illegal. Is that not to the advantage of those who fear nature, who regard it as threatening their ambitions? But why should the goals of one be imposed as demands on others? Why is prescription superior to need and desire? If one desires to submit, to kneel, to serve, and love, why should one not do so? Who is to tell us that our blood is mistaken? How empty and ugly is a road to power that would deny one to oneself!

"I feared Lord Grendel and Eve," said Paula, "but I wish them well."

They had left us, left, too, with the Lady Bina. Apparently they would return to Ar. Few Kurii would dare to roam the streets of Ar at will, and more, I was sure, would fear the ax of Lord Grendel. I did not think they were muchly unsafe. There seemed to be, on their part, on the part of Lord Grendel and Eve, two main motivations for their return to Ar. First, they wished to please the Lady Bina, who was fond of the sights and sounds of Ar, and, second, they wished to provide Lord Arcesilaus, the lord of some metal world, with an eye and an ear, an agent and an informant, in Ar.

One might note, at this point, in passing, that the Lady Bina seemed to regard herself as responsible for Lord Grendel and Eve, that they were somehow her charges, and that she must look after them, while, on the other hand, it seemed, contrariwise, that Lord Grendel, and Eve, were muchly concerned about her, and hoped to look after her, and protect her.

We continued on.

I was pleased that we had the cushioning of the blanket, little as it was.

"At least," I said, "we are not chained behind the wagon."

"And the wagon is closed," said Paula. "No one would know it contains two kajirae."

"Who would have thought," I said, "that we, once two women of Earth, our former world, would one day have found ourselves naked and collared, on a far world, shackled, owned by men?"

"I am pleased to be a commodity, a property, an owned beast," said Paula.

"I, too," I said. How free, simple, natural, rightful, and fulfilling I found my lot.

Paula moved her wrists and ankles a little, moving the shackles.

I stirred, too, relishing my helplessness. How I delighted in the small sounds of the metal, the rustle of an obdurate linkage. How wonderful felt the weight on my limbs. I supposed few women of my former world realized how reassuring it can be to be chained, how secure one can feel, say, lying in a slave cage, owned.

"We are well chained," I said.

"When a woman is chained," said Paula, "she knows she is desired."

"Why do the men of Earth not put collars and chains on their women?" I asked.

"Perhaps some do," she said.

"Perhaps," I said, "they do not desire them enough to do so, desire them enough to claim and own them, do not want them so much, so fiercely, so uncompromisingly, that they will make them their slaves."

"When one truly desires an object," said Paula, "it is natural that one wishes to own it, to protect it, and keep it."

"I wonder why women respond so, in the collar," I said.

"Because," said Paula, "they know they belong in it."

"What of Lucilius?" I wondered.

"I would suppose he has returned to the keeping of Decius Albus," said Paula.

Of what use, now, I wondered, could Lucilius be to the intentions and plans of the trade advisor?

"The Lady Alexina," I said, "was seized by Tyrtaios, the Assassin."

"No," said Paula, "the slave, Alexina, was seized by Tyrtaios, the Assassin."

"What of her?" I wondered.

"I did not much care for her," said Paula. "Let her kneel to an Assassin, covering his feet with tears and kisses, hoping not to be beaten."

I sat back, leaning against the side of the wagon bed. I wondered of Gor, the Priest-Kings, and Kurii, the slave routes, the affairs in Ar. I hoped the best for Lord Grendel, his consort, Eve, and the troublesome, wayward, outspoken, opinionated Lady Bina, their mistress, or ward. What of Surtak, and Lyris, and those Kurii who had followed him? What of Lord Agamemnon, so mysteriously absent? What could they mean, that he might be searching for, seeking, or intent upon obtaining a body, or such? What could that mean? Surely it was unintelligible.

After a time, we had been on the road for six days. At nights we had stopped at one camp or caravanserai or another. Sometimes we made our own camp, off the road. Occasionally, when the masters stopped at an inn, they resided within, and we were chained in kennels, in the inn yard. Slave biscuits and slave gruel were furnished, as part of our board. In these days and evenings, frequently, when we were not kenneled, we pleased our masters, in the many ways of a Gorean slave girl.

At one of the caravanserais, returning from the cluster of slaves about one of the wells, I hurried to Paula. "I have heard," I said, "that the muchly sought, fugitive Ubara, Talena, has been apprehended!"

"I doubt it," had said Paula. "There are many such rumors. Put them from your mind."

"Here is the water, fetched from the well," I said.

"Good," she had said.

I was again overcome with misery and guilt, that Paula knew nothing of my indiscretion, or betrayal, when I had attempted to sway the manhood and lust of Drusus Andronicus in my favor. How I despised myself. I wanted to speak to her, but did not dare to do so.

"You are very beautiful, Paula," I said.

I did not think I had seen her so, until after my being scorned and bound by Drusus Andronicus.

How the blood of a man might demand the ownership of such a woman!

"Nonsense," said Paula. "You are far more beautiful than I. Now let us attend to the supper. The sooner the masters eat, the sooner, too, we will eat."

"Paula," I said.

"Yes?" she said.

"I fear we will part," I said.

"My master spoke of it to me, days ago," she said. "I was reluctant to speak to you."

"Paula?" I said.

"Tomorrow," she said. "I am sorry."

I burst into tears.

"They cannot stay together," she said, holding me. "It is dangerous. Their Home Stones differ. They do not share caste. Each must go his own way."

"Paula," I wept.

"In secrecy," she said.

"Paula, Paula!" I wept.

"Our paths may cross," she said, consolingly. "Until then, each must heel his own master."

"Paula," I wept.

"Hush," she said, "dear, precious Phyllis, supper is to be prepared."

CHAPTER SIXTY-SEVEN

Please, please, Master!" I begged.

"Very well," he said, and unsnapped the ring on my leash, and I leaped to my feet and ran after Paula, who was heeling Drusus Andronicus.

"Paula, Paula!" I cried.

We were both naked. Slaves are often kept naked indoors, and, often, in the wild, so to speak. We were now in the informality of a wagon camp, that which we had reached yesterday afternoon. Many slaves about were naked.

Hearing my cries, Drusus Andronicus stopped, and turned about.

I threw myself to Paula's feet, weeping, my head down. "Forgive me, Paula," I wept. "I betrayed our friendship! I was vain, foolish, jealous! You sold for more than I! You were found of much greater interest than I, by many masters! I wanted to prove myself your equal, indeed, your superior! If you could interest a master such as Master Drusus, could I not do so, as well? I sought to interest him, as what I was, as you, a slave! I would have been pleased to turn him from you! I tried to do so! I failed! I was rightfully scorned and bound. I was punished. Forgive me, dear Paula. Please, please, forgive me!"

"Dear Phyllis," she said, looking down at me, at her feet.

"I dared not tell you," I said. "Now, I have spoken. Despise me, scorn me, hate me, as you will!"

"I do not hate you, scorn you, despise you, or such," she said. "You are dear to me, you are my friend."

"I could no longer bear you not knowing," I said.

Kurik, of Victoria, my master, had now joined us.

"But I knew, all along," she said.

"Paula?" I said.

"Certainly," she said, "my master informed me of the business that very afternoon."

I could not speak, I was shaken.

"I told you so," said Kurik. "Of course Drusus Andronicus would inform his slave of the incident. Why should such intelligence be withheld from her? Surely she should be informed."

"I did not know you knew," I said, weakly, to Paula, on my knees. "You gave no sign, not the least indication that you knew."

"We must be on our way," said Drusus Andronicus. "We have a wagon to be bargained for, tharlarion to purchase."

Paula knelt by me, and embraced me. "I wish you well, dear Phyllis," she said. "Perhaps we shall meet again."

"I wish you well," I wept. We kissed, quickly, and Paula sprang to her feet. "Forgive me, Master!" she called after Drusus Andronicus, and hurried to heel him. She turned once to wave, and I waved back, tears streaming down my cheeks. At the same time I heard a snap, and my master's leash had been again fastened to the ring on my leather leash collar, fitted over my regular collar.

"She is such a dear, wonderful thing," I said.

"She went for a golden tarsk," he said.

"She gave no sign she knew what I had done," I said. "She knew all, and yet forgave me. She would not allow my act to impair our friendship. She was willing to give up Drusus Andronicus, if he preferred me. She would have stepped aside, nobly, sacrificing herself, thinking only of him, that he might be happy."

"You think so?" asked Kurik, my master.

"Surely," I said, "Master."

"You seem to think of her as more than human, or as somehow other than human," he said.

"I suppose so," I said. "I had not thought of it in that way."

"As some sort of paragon," he said.

"Perhaps," I said.

"Mindlessly obedient to absurd prescriptions," he said. "Smiling while being robbed, offering her throat to the knife, turning her back on what means most to her?"

"Perhaps," I said.

"Well," he said, "foolish, naive kajira, know that she is far more worth being your friend than you think, that she is no icon of idiocy, but a living, breathing, feeling creature, a living, loving animal, profoundly and deeply human. Drusus Andronicus recounted the business to me, which he found quite amusing. Your friend, Paula, was furious. Drusus Andronicus had to bind her to keep her in place. She wanted to tear the skin from your body, pull out your hair, and scratch out your eyes. How she squirmed in her bonds, shrieking with rage. He did not dare let her out, into the street, lest she would have sought you out, and perhaps irreparably impaired your value on a slave block."

"I did not know," I said.

"He had to switch her to silence."

"I see," I said.

"She was somewhat mollified, of course," said Kurik, my master, "when he informed her of how he had rejected your offer, and left you bound on the street, his rejection of you inscribed on your bared left shoulder with a marking stick, for all to see. She was further mollified when she learned of your lashing."

"She gave no sign she knew of my deed," I said.

"She was instructed not to do so," said Kurik, my master.

"How she must have seethed with hatred," I said.

"Not at all," he said. "She soon calmed down, reassured of her master's rejection of your advances, and having been apprised of your condign punishment. She has always, doubtless, despite what I think is her profound and genuine affection for you, regarded you as weak, shallow, and vain."

"I see," I said.

"When one cares for a person," said Kurik, of Victoria, "one cares for the whole person. Even their weaknesses and faults become precious, and dear."

"Perhaps I am less weak, shallow, and vain than I was," I said.

"I doubt it," said Kurik. "But we must prepare the wagon. We must soon leave."

"What is our destination?" I asked.

"Curiosity," said he, "is not becoming in a kajira."

"Yes, Master," I said.

"Down on all fours," he said.

"Master?" I said.

"You are now in the modality of the she-sleen," he said.

I went down to all fours, looked up at him, and whimpered, questioningly. One can do much with noises, expressions, and attitudes of the body. Does not any pet animal know that?

"Yes," he said. "You are now in the modality of the she-sleen."

I put my head down, on the leash.

I was now in the modality of the she-sleen. One is denied an upright posture. One moves on all fours, or squirms on one's belly. One may kneel, but not rise to one's feet. One is denied human speech. One sound or whimper, as in gag signals, signifies "Yes," and two sounds or whimpers, again, as in gag signals, signifies "No." One feels very help-less in this slave modality. And few slave modalities better convince one that one is a slave. It can be terribly frustrating, trying to communicate in this modality, a frustration that is doubtless shared by many pet animals. Needless to say, as well, one is naked in this modality, as I was; one feeds and drinks from pans, head down, not permitted to use one's hands; and when one is put to use in this modality, it is done as one might expect.

"You are pleasant to regard in the modality of the she-sleen," he said, "or, perhaps, in your case, that of the she-tarsk. When you were so unpleasant in your office that afternoon, on your former world, I speculated how you would appear in this modality. I am not at all disappointed."

I shook with anger, helpless on my leash.

I was then led through the camp, on all fours, on the leash, as we returned to the wagon.

After a time, I was no longer angry. I realized I belonged on his leash.

CHAPTER SIXTY-EIGHT

You are a slave, Phyllis," he said.

"Yes, Master?" I said.

There could be little doubt of that.

"Are you content as a slave?" he asked.

"Very much so," I said.

He rose, went to the side of the room, removed the whip from its peg, and cast it to the floor, a few feet away. "Go to the whip," he said, "on all fours, put your head down, lick and kiss it, and then lift it in your teeth, and bring it to me, on all fours."

I did so.

I belonged to him.

He could do with me as he wished. I would have it no other way.

He then sat down, cross-legged, and put the whip to the side.

I then knelt before him, in nadu.

"Is freedom not precious?" he asked.

"Surely," I said.

"Do you not desire freedom?" he asked.

"No," I said.

"Why?" he asked.

"My collar," I said, "is a thousand times more precious."

"You were once free," he said.

"Yes, Master," I said.

"Now," he said, "you can be bought and sold."

"I am a slave," I said.

"I am troubled," he said.

"Master?" I said.

"I fear I may grow fond of you," he said.

"Do not sell me!" I begged.

"You know my caste," he said.

"Yes, Master," I said.

"I have assisted in the acquisition, and processing, of hundreds of women," he said. "I have had my pick of them, and enjoyed them frequently, and as I pleased."

"Of course," I said, "they are slaves, or soon to be slaves."

"But now," he said, "I am thinking of withdrawing from the work of my caste."

"Master?" I said.

"At least temporarily," he said.

"I do not understand," I said.

"I was searching," he said, "for my slave."

"It is my hope," I whispered, "that you have now found her."

"I am thinking of freeing you," he said.

"Do not," I said, frightened. "I am a thousand times more content, and free, in my collar, than I ever was, or could be, as a free woman. Let them have the emptiness and bondage of their freedom. Let me keep the fullness and riches of my collar. Let me keep my rightful subservience, my welcomed subjugation, the privilege of my joyful submission."

He regarded me.

"Here, on this world," I said, "I have found myself. Do not, I beg you, take me away from myself! I wish to be a man's belonging. I want to love and serve, selflessly. I want to be owned, and mastered!"

"Why is that?" he asked.

"Because I am a woman," I said.

"Serve me wine," he said.

"Yes, Master," I said.

It was late in the evening.

I will not specify our location. It could be any one of hundreds of cities and towns. Too, we were not, as I understood it, to remain long in this place. Similarly, I will, from time to time, omit details that might, if one were to investigate, supply clues as to our location, or route.

"In this restaurant," said Kurik, my master, "you will note that the waitresses are briefly tunicked."

"No less so than I," I said.

Kurik sat at the small, rather private table, to one side of the broad, pillared, low-ceilinged dining room. A single candle was on our table. I knelt by his side.

"Thus, as in a tavern," said Kurik, "free women are not permitted."

"We would not wish to scandalize them," I said.

To be sure, I did not mind scandalizing them. Let them, in their fine robes and veils, fume and fret. Let them wonder what it might be, to be so beautiful, so desirable, to be wanted so fiercely, that men would take away their clothes and dress them, if they chose to dress them, for their pleasure, to have them before them as they wanted them; let them wonder what it might be, to be so wanted that men would seize them and turn them into properties, into will-less, right-less possessions; let them wonder what it might be to be so wanted that they would be seized, taken in hand, stripped, collared, and branded, and put to a man's feet, in their place in nature, where they belonged, owned and mastered.

"Sometimes," said he, "a bold free woman will insist on entering a tavern. Sometimes they even disguise themselves as slave girls. Not unoften then they are seized, and enslaved, and sometimes they discover themselves as collared paga girls in the very tavern into which they sought, illicitly, to intrude."

"There are many ways to court a collar," I said. "What woman, in her deepest heart, does not long for her master?"

"There is something interesting about the waitresses here," said Kurik.

"What?" I asked.

He then explained to me that this city, in which was the restaurant, had been long at war, for generations, with another city. I shall not specify the names of the two cities. There are many cases of such instances on Gor.

"So, what is interesting, Master," I asked, "about the waitresses here?"

"They all have something in common," he said.

"What?" I asked.

He then explained to me that they had all once been free women of the enemy city.

The free women of the enemy are always accounted high amongst the loot of conquerors. What better loot can one have than the women of the enemy, naked, and chained at your feet as slaves?

"I should think," I said, "that men would fear to eat here, lest the waitresses, who may have access to materials in the kitchen, say, knives, might attack them."

"It would be difficult," said Kurik, "for a slave to conceal a weapon in a tunic, or, better, if she is naked to the collar."

"Doubtless," I said.

"Being served by such women," said Kurik, "adds a piquant sauce to the food. Too, it is pleasant to consider their feelings, as they now, as degraded, abject, meaningless slaves, must serve those who, from childhood, they have been taught to despise and regard as inferiors."

"I would suppose so," I said.

At that point, a briefly tunicked brunette, of the sort that men, the beasts, might regard as luscious, knelt before our table, and, head down, placed her tray on the floor, and then began placing the plates, utensils, and cups on the table.

"Girl," said Kurik.

"Master?" she said, not raising her head.

"Did you mix a bit of gravy in my slave's gruel?" he asked.

"Yes, Master," she said.

My master was often thoughtful. I muchly loved him, and I suspected he might care for me, at least a little, but it was not wise, of course, to enter into such matters. I would not have cared to be hooded and led to a market.

So much I loved him; so much I was his!

"My slave," he said to our waitress, "is a barbarian."

The waitress, on her knees, stiffened in anger.

"Serve her," he said. "Lift up the bowl, and hand it to her."

"That is not necessary, Master," I said.

"Be silent," said Kurik.

"Yes, Master," I said. "Forgive me, Master."

"Say," said Kurik, to the slave, "'I, once a free woman, of the high city of —'," and here we omit the name of the city, "'now a slave, serve, as a slave, on my knees, another slave, a barbarian slave'."

The slave repeated the words.

"Do you hesitate?" asked Kurik. "Shall we summon the manager and report your hesitation? Perhaps you have been roped and whipped before."

"I do not hesitate," she said, quickly, handing me the bowl. In it was a spoon. That, like the gravy, had been specified by Kurik, and was, surely, another indication of his thoughtfulness. I feared he might grow weak with me. He must not do so. He must not do so!

"Speak," said Kurik, sharply.

"Your supper," said the slave, lowering her head.

"Speak," said Kurik, even more sharply, more menacingly.

"Your supper, *Mistress*," said the slave.

"Go," said Kurik to the waitress. "Then return, and kneel, from time to time, to see if we would be further served."

"Yes, Master," she said, frightened, and swiftly withdrew.

"Was Master not hard with a slave?" I asked.

"She does not yet realize she is a slave," said Kurik.

"She probably does not yet have a private master," I said. How frightful, I thought, to be on a common chain, uncared for, uncaressed.

"She is probably stupid," said Kurik. "It takes a stupid girl longer to learn her collar, as they are slower to learn anything."

"I do not think she is stupid," I said. I suspected it took longer for some women, particularly Gorean free women, with their pompous, exaggerated self-image, their ponderous, inculcated sense of self-importance, to realize that there was now a collar on their neck. The whip, of course, makes such lessons much easier.

"A woman may maintain for weeks the delusion that she is somehow free," said Kurik. "Then one night she goes to sleep, thinking she is somehow free, and, in the morning, awakens, knowing that she is truly a slave."

"If they would only listen to their blood, their heart," I said.

"There are layers of lies," said Kurik. "Much must, in some cases, be broken through, gross husks to be peeled away, one after another, until the true woman, soft, vulnerable, open, needful, ready, hoping, is revealed."

"I am grateful for my warm, flavored gruel," I said. "I am grateful to have been permitted a spoon. I am pleased that my master has brought me here, that he has let me kneel so close to him."

Indeed, he could have reached out and touched me.

"Keep your knees spread a bit," he said.

"Yes, Master," I said.

Perhaps this was a subtle thing, but it helped to remind me that I was not only a slave, but a particular sort of slave, a pleasure slave. What girl does not wish to be her master's pleasure slave? How this position reassures a girl of her master's interest; and how she must tremble when he allows her a laxity in such matters. Must he not then be thinking of ridding himself of her? Must he not then be thinking of giving her to someone, or taking her to a girl exchange or market?

"Would you like a honey cake, and a small vessel of ruby ka-la-na?" he asked.

"It will be as Master pleases," I said.

There was a snap of a whip from the kitchen, and a cry of pain.

"Master?" I said.

"I suspect a waitress has been encouraged to be more attentive to guests," he said.

"Oh," I said.

A moment later our waitress reappeared, tears on her cheeks, her hair half obscuring her countenance, and knelt at our table, inquiring if we might desire aught else.

"You are learning deference," said Kurik.

"Yes, Master," she said.

He then specified some items, with which we might conclude our pleasant, but modest repast.

"Such waitresses," said Kurik, "other than those to whom you were accustomed on your former world, do not expect tips. They hope, rather, not to be beaten."

I was silent.

Later, we left the restaurant, and were walking back, to our rental. It was about the eighteenth Ahn. I was not leashed.

"Would you like to walk beside me?" he asked.

"No, Master," I said. "It is the place of a slave to heel her master, or, if he wishes to display her, as on a promenade, to precede him, leashed."

"Would you like to be so displayed?" he asked.

"I am not a display slave," I said. I thought of Paula, of course. She had been purchased in the Curulean, to be a display slave. Only on Gor had I come to realize how beautiful Paula was, with her high intelligence, her passion, her profound slave needs. "I am better behind you," I said, "in heeling position."

"You are not a bad looking slave," he said.

I could still relish the taste of the tiny honey cake, and the sips of ka-la-na I had been allowed. When one is a slave, small things can be important, and precious, to one. I suspected that a slave might value such things, small things, a pastry, a candy, a bit of honey cake, more than a well-to-do free woman, particularly of a high caste, might the expensive delicacies and sumptuous fare that were at her disposal, and to which she might be accustomed.

"Master has seen to my figure, and my posture and carriage," I said.

Indeed, a slave is expected to appear as, and walk as, a slave. It is no wonder free women so hate us. They do not dare present themselves as a slave must, or be punished, a way in which we soon revel, as women.

We learn grace, and deference, and our diction is to be soft, clear, and modest, suitable for slaves.

It had been a cheap ka-la-na, as ka-la-nas go, but even so the taste and bouquet had been exquisite, surely as good, or better, than any wine I had known on my former world, at least before my acquisition. I had had a similar experience, startling me, in the holding of the slavers, before I had been shipped as stock, as cargo, to Gor.

A slave, apparently bent on an errand, hurried past, but turned, to look after my master. "Keep your eyes to yourself!" I hissed at her. "That will be enough of that," said my master, and then I cried out in pain, for my master had put his hand in my hair, and I was bent back, helplessly, in the position of the slave bow, which position well accentuates a slave's figure. It is often used in auction houses and on slave shelves. The slave laughed merrily, and spun about, hurrying on.

"Excellent," said a passing fellow, regarding me, helpless, in the slave bow. "I will give you a quarter of a tarsk-bit for her."

Kurik laughed and put me in leading position, his hand in my hair, my head held closely at his hip. One is not only helpless in this position, but it is awkward, and humiliating. In it, one is well reminded one is a slave. "She looked at you, she looked at you!" I said.

"And so men look at you," he said.

"I am a slave," I said. "I am collared. I am meant to be looked at, assessed, and appraised!"

"I am pleased that men look at you," he said, "and envy me a hot, squirming, helpless, begging, little beast at my slave ring."

"But she looked at you," I said, my head at his hip, "you, my master!"

"I do not mind," said Kurik. "A fellow is flattered. Why should he not be? Just as a man may look at a woman and wonder what she might look like at his slave ring, so, too, a woman may look at a man, and wonder what it would be, to be at his slave ring."

"May I be released?" I asked.

"Will it be necessary to leash you?" he asked.

"No, Master," I said.

"Very well," he said.

He then released me, and we continued on, toward our rental, I heeling him.

"Surely I am worth more than a quarter of a tarsk-bit," I said.

In fact, as far as I knew, there was no such coin. To be sure, there is a welter of currencies on Gor. Much depends on the city. I would later learn that the phrase most often functions as a figure of speech. In many markets, scales are used, particularly if gold or silver figures in the transaction. Coins can be debased, shaved, or such. Scales are particularly important if, say, a silver buckle, or a scrap cut from a gold vessel, should be in question.

"Possibly," he said.

"Master!" I exclaimed.

"That was a joke, a joke," he said, not looking back.

"A master's joke," I said.

"Surely," he said.

"I did not find it amusing," I said.

"I thought it clever," he said.

We continued on for some Ehn.

Many lamps were in doorways. We were once passed by a palanquin, preceded by a torch bearer.

"Master," I said, "that dangling cage!"

It had not been there when we had approached the restaurant, earlier in the evening.

It was a small slave cage that hung on a chain from a projecting beam. This beam extended, fixed in braces, from a window in the third story of the insula we were passing. The window had two lamps. These were fixed in the outer wall, one on each side. The wall was a pale yellow, in the twin pools of lamp light. In daylight it would have been a bright yellow. It is common for Goreans to enhance their surroundings with color, the exteriors of buildings, the interiors of rooms. In the cage was a camisked female slave. In many cities, camisks are not allowed on the streets during the daylight Ahn, as a concession to the sensibilities of free women. Some regard the camisk as more provocative than nudity. To be sure, such things, given rulings in councils, shifts in mores, and such, change from time to time. I refer, of course, in these remarks, to the common camisk, not the Turian camisk, which, however revealing, is generally considered less objectionable, more restrained, or refined.

The camisked girl in the cage, kneeling, holding to the bars, looked down at us, and called down to us. "Handsome Master," she called. "This is the exchange house of —. I bid you enter!"

"Let us hurry on," I suggested.

"Are you on the Exchange Wheel?" called my master.

"I can be placed on it," she called down. "Inquire within."

"It is late, Master," I said. "Perhaps we should best continue on."

He turned about, laughed, and shook my head, roughly, his large hand in my hair. "Very well," said he, to my relief.

An "Exchange House" is much what the name suggests. In it slaves may be exchanged. I suppose it is a market of sorts as, in it, one may use one slave to, so to speak, buy another. Slaves are the primary currency, rather than coins. Sometimes, however, an exchange is not an even exchange, slave for slave, or two slaves for one slave, or such, but a certain amount of money may also be involved. For example, a slave, say, A, might be exchanged for a slave B, but only if, say, A's owner or B's owner adds in, say, a number of copper tarsks. One slave might go then for, say, another slave, and twenty copper tarsks. The owner of the establishment often involves himself, to his profit, in some speculative trading, but, for the most part, he earns his living by, first, charging for access to the premises, and, second, receiving a small honorarium for every slave placed on the wheel.

We prepared to proceed when the door to the exchange house swung open, and two fellows emerged. During the moment the door was ajar, I saw lamps within, and some men milling about. Two held goblets, probably of paga. There was also a screen. I heard some music, a czehar, tabor, and flute. I could not see the musicians. They and, I supposed, the wheel, were behind the screen.

We paused, viewed. I tried to stand well, my head down.

"Are you taking her inside?" asked one of the fellows of my master.

"Not tonight," he said.

"I do not blame you," said the second fellow, who had accompanied the first from the house. "You would do better with her in an auction house."

"What do you think she would bring?" asked my master.

"Two silver tarsks," said the first fellow.

I was somewhat annoyed that there seemed to be general agreement, or nearly general agreement, amongst masters as to what I might bring off the block. Doubtless subjectivities were involved, but the relative uniformity of these subjectivities was annoying, extremely annoying. Could a master simply look at me, and see me as a "two-tarsk" girl? Is that what I was, a "two-tarsk" girl? To be sure, many girls did not go for as much as two tarsks. Two tarsks was not a bad price, I had been given to understand, for a girl.

"I would say," said the other, "four silver tarsks."

I trembled. I almost lifted my head. "That is more like it," I thought to myself. "Let Kurik of Victoria hear that!"

"I wish you well," said Kurik of Victoria.

"And we, you," said the first fellow, and then they took their leave, moving in the direction from which we had come.

As we continued on, toward our rental, I, though I had a standing permission to speak, explicitly requested this permission. I thought that that would add some point to what I had to say.

"No," said Kurik.

"Master!" I protested.

"Very well," he said, affably enough.

"—Four silver tarsks," I said. "*Four silver tarsks.*"

"Possibly," he said.

"Master!" I said, startled.

"Yes," he said.

"Would you pay so much?" I asked.

"I would be a fool to do so," he said.

"But would you do so?" I asked.

"Are you asking me if I am a fool?" he asked.

"My master is not a fool," I said. Of that I was sure.

"I might," he said.

I went instantly to my knees, and pressed my head, gratefully, against his thigh.

"If you are worth four," he said, "I might be able to get five for you."

"Oh," I said, removing my head from his thigh.

At that point we heard two men approaching, moving rapidly, a sound of bootlike sandals, a jangle of accoutrements, of weapons and chains.

"Up," said my master, looking back, toward the sound.

I rose, standing rather behind him.

The men stopped, some yards off. One held a lamp. I saw they were guardsmen. "Hold," called one of them, he with the lamp.

We remained where we were.

I knelt.

Then they were with us.

"May I see your slave?" said one of the guardsmen.

"Surely," said Kurik. "Stand, Phyllis, lift your head, hold your right wrist behind you, with your left hand."

I closed my eyes, against the glow of the lamp.

"What does this collar read?" asked the guardsman with the lamp.

"'I am the property of Tenrik of Siba'," said my master. We had not changed the collar.

"Forgive me," said the guardsman.

I gathered that I might now kneel, and so did so. A slave seldom remains standing in the presence of free persons. I looked up at the guardsmen, subtly, furtively, that I might the better comprehend their intent and attitude. It well behooves a slave to be aware of such things, moods, temperament, dispositions, and such, in free persons. That can be important when one is a slave. When one of the guardsmen glanced down at me, I lowered my head, quickly, humbly. It can be dangerous to meet the eyes of a free person. Some free persons regard that as an audacity or insolence. It can bring a lashing.

"I gather that a slave is missing," said Kurik.

"From the restaurant of —," said the guardsman, "a brunette."

That was the very restaurant at which we had just dined.

The guardsmen then proceeded on their way.

I was very much afraid.

"You may rise, Phyllis," said my master.

I regained my feet.

"To run, what a fool," said my master.

"Be kind, Master," I said. "She was probably frightened. Perhaps she could not help herself. Perhaps she thought it possible to escape."

"You have never run, have you?" asked Kurik.

"No, Master," I said. "I know that I am a slave, and that escape is impossible for me. Too, I do not want to run."

"Why not?" he asked.

"I do not wish to be hamstrung," I said. "I do not want my feet to be cut off. I do not want to be fed to sleen. I do not want to be thrown naked to eels, or leech plants."

"Is there no other reason?" he asked.

"Please do not make a helpless girl speak," I said.

"Speak," he said.

"I am not only a slave, but I want to be a slave," I said. "I want to be in a collar and chains. I want to have no choice but to submit and obey, to love and serve my master."

We were later passing the entrance to an alley, one of several off the street, when we heard a small sound, to our left, coming from the alley.

Kurik turned to the alley, abruptly.

"Come out," he called, "with your hands clasped behind the back of your head, and kneel before me."

We waited.

"There is no one there," I said, "or it is an urt, fishing in a garbage can."

"I have no doubt that it is an urt, fishing in a garbage can, doubtless half starved," said Kurik, "but it is a foolish urt who will make a sound within the hearing of a free person."

The alley was quiet.

"You are discovered," called Kurik. "There is no escape for you. Come out."

Again there was only silence, and darkness.

"Where will you go in the light of day?" called Kurik.

I thought I heard a sob from the darkness.

"Guardsmen are about," called Kurik. "Would you prefer to fall into the hands of guardsmen?"

Then, emerging from the darkness, there came a small figure, approaching us, its hands clasped behind the back of its head. It knelt before Kurik, keeping its hands clasped behind its head.

"Master," I said.

"Yes," he said.

It was the waitress from the restaurant of —.

Kurik then took her by the hair and put her to her belly, and then, with binding fiber from his wallet, he bound her wrists behind her back, and then he crossed her ankles, and lashed them together, as well. Then he turned her to her side, before us.

"There she is, the fool," he said. "Now you may have your vengeance on her."

"I do not want vengeance on her," I said.

"She was once a free woman," said Kurik.

"So, too, legally, was I," I said.

"She scorned you," he said.

"What will be done with her?" I asked.

"As she is not a privately owned slave," he said, "and she means little or nothing to anyone, I would suppose an example would be made of her, perhaps casting her to sleen."

The slave sobbed, and squirmed, helpless at our feet, tied by a Gorean male.

"Surely not," I said.

"I will cut her tunic away," he said, preparing to reach down and grasp the tiny garment.

"Leave her her tunic, please, Master," I said.

"She was displeasing," he said.

"Even so," I begged.

"We will leave her here, bound hand and foot, for guardsmen," he said.

"Be merciful," I begged.

"I am being merciful," he said. "Here she is helpless, incapable of resisting, of running. If she were taken afoot, the guardsmen might well hamstring her, before returning her to her master, for sleen feed."

"Poor slave!" I said.

"Do not feel sorry for her," he said. "She is only a slave."

"I, too, am a slave," I said.

"And do you wish to be whipped, to remind you of it?" he asked.

"No, Master," I said.

"Why did you run, little fool?" said Kurik.

The slave only sobbed.

"Perhaps she thought," I said, "to somehow make contact with one of her own city, who might abet her flight."

"No," said Kurik. "She is now a slave. Those who were her fellow citizens would now see her as only that. If she were so unfortunate as to be returned to her former city, she would be treated as the least of, and the most abject of, slaves. Her own family would lash her, and sell her as soon as possible out of the city, as she has humiliated and dishonored them. She is now a domestic animal, purchasable and meaningless. Her very presence would be a source of embarrassment and shame to them."

"May I speak to her?" I begged.

"Very well," said Kurik.

I knelt beside her, and spoke to her, softly, earnestly. "Love your collar, your marking," I said. "They show that you are, of all women, the most exciting, and desirable. Pity free women. You can be a raw, and perfect, female. This is your fulfillment, to be owned, and to have no choice but to serve, and be pleasing. It is what we, as women, are for. It is what we want to be."

"You are a barbarian," she sobbed.

"So I am a thousand times less than you," I said, "but we are sister slaves. Do you think the collar is on your neck less than mine?"

"No!" she wept. "It is on my neck as much as yours."

"Surely you wish a private master," I said, "before whom you might kneel, whose feet you might cover with kisses."

She squirmed, and sobbed, uncontrollably.

"Is it not true?" I said.

"Yes," she wept, "even in my robes and veils, I thought such things, and in countless dreams I found myself so."

"In a restaurant, as in a tavern," I said, "you have an opportunity to present yourself, humbly and hopefully, beautifully, before men. Do you not think some of those men would wish to lead you home with them? Might not a man offer your master coin for you, coin that he would be unlikely to refuse?"

"It is too late," she said. "I am caught. I am bound."

"I see the lamp of guardsmen, afar," said Kurik. "They return."

The slave put down her head, and moaned.

I looked up to my master, my eyes, I fear, bright with tears. "Dear Master," I said, "in the restaurant, you inquired of this slave if there were an Exchange House in the vicinity, and having been informed that this was so, you commanded her to slip from the restaurant, and, meeting outside, to conduct you there personally, to be returned to the restaurant when this errand was completed."

"Oh?" said Kurik.

"Yes," I said.

"Who would believe that?" he asked.

"Who would doubt the word of a free man?" I asked.

"Is this what you want, Phyllis?" he asked.

"Yes, Master," I said.

Kurik then bent to the bonds of the slave, and freed her, wholly.

"Now," I said. "We are going back to the restaurant. Get up, and walk along with us, nicely."

"Do so," said Kurik. "You may live. And if you live, you owe your life to a barbarian."

The slave, unsteady, trembling, rose to her feet.

"There is nothing out of the ordinary in this," I said to the slave. "Our pace is leisurely."

I looked back.

Happily the lamp of the guardsmen was far behind.

In a few Ehn we were near the main portal of the restaurant, that giving access to the restaurant from the facing street.

Some four or five individuals were outside the portal. Two held lamps.

"Open your mouth," said Kurik, my master, to the slave.

She did so, and Kurik slipped a coin in her mouth. This is not that unusual or unseemly; slave girls, and even many free persons, often carry coins in the mouth. Slave tunics lack pockets and so, too, do most Gorean garments, a prominent exception being the tunics of craftsmen. A slave girl shopping, for example, will almost always carry the buying coins in her mouth, or clutched in her hand, perhaps wrapped in a handkerchief or, in the case of some coins, threaded on a string. The disadvantage of carrying the coins visibly is that their obvious presence might encourage buffeting and theft, particularly where slaves are concerned. Most free Goreans will carry a purse, or wallet, usually slung on a string, strap, or cord, commonly attached to a belt, or girdle. Some thieves are proficient a cutting such attachments, or, even, the purse or wallet itself.

"What are you doing?" I asked my master.

"That is a tarsk, a whole copper tarsk," said my master, apparently determined that I might not overlook the extent of his generosity, "a gratuity for the use of the slave."

"Ho!" called a fellow, stepping forth from the group. "I see you have caught —."

"Not at all," said Kurik. "I am merely accompanying her, to see that she reaches your chains safely. I would not wish her, after her aid to me, on your behalf, to be seized in the darkness, and carried off."

"I do not understand," he said.

The fellow cast a proprietary glance on the slave, who lowered her head, and I assumed he was her master.

Both the slave and I then knelt, as we were in the presence of free persons.

"She ran away," said the fellow.

"Certainly not," said Kurik. "I was interested in visiting a local Exchange House. As the slave knew of such an establishment I thought it would be convenient to prevail upon her to guide me to it, which I did."

"How dared she act so?" demanded her owner.

"How could she dare not do so?" inquired Kurik. "Would you have her, on your own premises, deny a legitimate command issued by a free person?"

"I should have been informed," said the man.

"Doubtless," said Kurik. "The fault is mine. I commanded instant obedience. What choice had she? Surely your slaves understand instant obedience."

"They do," said the fellow.

"I am sorry that I did not realize that her absence, so brief, might have been of concern," said Kurik. "For that I apologize. On the other hand, I appreciate the use of the slave, and am pleased to show my appreciation."

"Oh?" said the fellow.

Kurik snapped his fingers, and the girl dropped the coin from her mouth into the palm of her hand, and, head down, lifted it to her master.

One of the fellows whistled, softly.

It was not a tarsk-bit, or two, but an entire copper tarsk.

"For such a gratuity," said her owner, "I would let her run all over —."

Some of the fellows with the master laughed.

"She is quite beautiful," said Kurik. "If I were you, I would have her wait on prime customers, serve at the better tables, and so on. You might, in time, make a nice profit on her, even though she is from the loathsome city of —."

"May its gates break from their hinges," said a man.

"May its walls collapse," said another.

"May its wells go dry," said another.

"May its women grace our coffles," said another.

"I wish you well," said Kurik, pleasantly.

Such wishes were mutually proffered, amongst all present.

"—," said the master, "it is late, time to retire."

"Yes, Master," she said.

"You are a pretty thing," he said, "despite your origin. I think I will change your station tomorrow."

"Thank you, Master," she said.

She was then alone with us, on the sidewalk.

"Thank you," she said, putting her head down, to Kurik's feet.

"You might thank another, as well," said Kurik.

The slave knelt up, and, tears in her eyes, kissed her fingertips and pressed them lightly on my left cheek.

"I am a barbarian," I reminded her, tears in my eyes.

"I wish you well," she said.

"I wish you well," I said.

"I must to my cage," she said, and sprang up, and hastened within the restaurant.

Kurik looked down at me, and smiled. "What a weakling you are," he said.

"Yes, Master," I said, happily.

At that point the two guardsmen, one with the guardsman's lamp, arrived.

"The slave is back," said Kurik to them. "She did not run away. It was all a misunderstanding."

"I thought so," said one of the guardsmen. "I would hate to think that any slave was so stupid that she thought she could escape."

On this world, it is true, I thought, there was no place to which she could escape.

The guardsmen then continued on their way.

Kurik, my master, then turned away, to return the way we had come, and I heeled him. As I followed him, I tied the loose, simple bondage knot in my hair. When we reached the domicile, I trusted that he would notice.

CHAPTER SIXTY-NINE

Thank you, Master," I said, grateful for the pleasure he had given me.

"You did not wish to see the slave, the restaurant girl, suitably punished?" he said.

"I did not want her to be slain, or hamstrung," I said.

"I was testing you," he said.

"Master?" I said.

"You were a sly, clever, inventive little slave," he said. "That is one of the dangers of having an intelligent slave. Indeed, some are so clever, they sometimes manage to elude the whip, though seldom for long."

"It is not pleasant to be whipped," I said. "Am I to understand that you would have disapproved of having had the slave fed to eels, or such?"

"Certainly," he said. "Why not? Few men could not think of something better to do with a lovely slave than feeding her to eels."

"Doubtless," I said.

"Of course," he said.

"Had I not proposed my plan," I said, "might you have thought of intervening?"

"Possibly," he said.

"Oh?" I said.

"If one were interested," he said, "there are many ways in which one might intervene, or attempt to do so. One might claim capture rights; one might index a recovery fee to conditions as to the slave's punishment, and so on, a high fee, even a prohibitive or exorbitant one if a severe punishment was in prospect, which an owner would be unwilling or unable to pay, a low fee if some lenience were granted. Such agreements are put in writing, of course, before a praetor's man. One could even keep the slave, or hide her and then sell her privately. If one were a warrior, one might even issue a challenge, a challenge in virtue of sword right, the right of beauty to be claimed by means of the sword. If worse came to worse, one might even consider buying the slave."

"So extreme a course of action?" I asked.

"It is an interesting fact," he said, "how a slave's value goes up when one is interested in buying her."

"As high as four silver tarsks?" I asked.

"Beware," he said.

"Forgive me, Master," I said.

"But clearly," he said, "flight is unacceptable. Many punishments are condign. Whippings, close chains, onerous tasks, restriction of diet in quantity and quality, or both, unpleasant slave modalities, shaving the head, denying clothing, public nudity, and such. Afterwards, of course, if the offense should be repeated, one can always think of hamstringing, the removal of feet, the feeding to eels or sleen, or such. One of the best discouragements of flight, of course, is prompt recapture, this convincing the slave that flight is pointless, and impractical. Too, of course, there is always the danger, if one manages to elude one master, of falling into a more severe, more grievous bondage, which is almost certain to be inflicted on an apprehended fugitive slave."

"You would disapprove of eels, and such," I said.

"Yes," he said. "That would be a waste of slave. Too, not that it matters greatly, it would deprive the slave of her eventual fulfillment and joy. More importantly, it would deprive some master of her service, and the many pleasures to be derived from her body, her mind, her imagination and feelings."

"You said, on the street, that I was a weakling," I said.

"Yes," he said.

"Well then," I said, "are you not a weakling, as well?"

"Perhaps," he said, "but a slain slave has no value. One wants to make money from the sale of women. Throwing a girl to eels or sleen scarcely improves her value."

"I think you are kind," I said.

He glanced to the whip, on its peg.

"Forgive me, Master," I said.

He put his hand on my collar.

"Prepare yourself to serve your master's pleasure," he said.

"Yes, Master," I said.

"You may please me," he said.

"Thank you, Master," I said.

I lay at the foot of his couch, on the blankets spread over the mat, on the floor, chained by the neck to his slave ring.

Then I rose up, to kneel at the foot of the couch.

"May I ascend the couch, Master?" I asked.

"No," he said.

I lay back on the blankets, on the mat, on the floor, restless.

I lay there for some time. I clenched my fists. I squirmed in the chain's collar. "May I speak?" I whispered.

"Yes," he said. He was awake.

"Touch me," I said. "Caress me. I am a slave. I am afire. I beg the hands of my master on my body!"

He left the surface of the couch, and knelt before me, and pushed me to my back. He held my ankles up, and parted. So held, I could not approach him.

"You are my property," he said.

"Yes, Master," I said. It was true, in full law.

"It is pleasant to have a woman as a property," he said.

"A girl is pleased to be the property of her master," I said.

He then turned me about, to my stomach.

Afterwards I turned to my side, facing him. I brushed my sweaty hair back, away from my face.

I bit my lip. "I fear," I said, "you do not take me seriously."

"I do take you seriously," he said, "as a slave."

He then reached for me, again.

"Yes," I said. "Yes!"

I was then enraptured again with the joy of being my master's rightless slave.

The next morning I served him breakfast.

After we were finished, and I had cleared the table, and washed the ware, I knelt, before him, but a bit to one side, that he need not look upon me if he did not wish to do so.

"I am at Master's disposal," I said.

"A slave is always at her master's disposal," he said.

"Am I to be permitted clothing today?" I asked.

"I have not decided," he said.

"Yesterday," I said, "Master purchased me a lovely yellow tunic, though unnecessarily brief."

"It will go nicely with your dark hair and eyes," he said.

"It was slit to the hips," I said. Being slit at the left hip, it might be easily brushed aside, to examine my mark. Slitting the garment at the right side, as well, is presumably done for a variety of purposes, to achieve balance, symmetry, and such. Also, of course, it shows more of the slave. There are various branding sites on Gor, but, by far, the most common is on the left thigh, below the hip. That is where I had been marked. Similarly, there are many slave brands on Gor, but the most common, by far, is the small, delicate, tasteful cursive Kef. It is small, and not obtrusive, but it means so much! How dramatically different I had become when it was put on me. 'Kef', as earlier mentioned, is the first letter of the Gorean word 'kajira'.

"Surely you do not object," he said.

"I may not object," I said. "I am a slave."

"Your body is public," he said, "as much as that of a tarsk or kaiila. You know that much from Merchant Law. Whether it is clothed or not, and to what extent, is up to the master."

"I understand," I said.

Then he looked at me fully, and, I think, appreciatively. It much pleases a slave to be looked upon appreciatively.

"You kneel nicely," he said.

"I have been trained by my master," I said. I was in nadu.

"You look well in your collar, Phyllis," he said.

"Thank you, Master," I said. A kind word, a touch, a caress, can mean much to a slave.

"I knew you would," he said, "even on your old world, when I first saw you, clothed, in the quaint fashion of your former world. I conjectured how you might look, clad only in a slave collar. And I was not disappointed. It is interesting, a woman clad in the silly raiment of your world and a fine Gorean woman, resplendent in the full robes of concealment. Removing the clothing from both, they are the same. And surely both would wear a collar well. There seems little to choose between them. Both are women. That is the most appropriate clothing for a woman, nothing but the collar of a slave. What clothing needs she other than that?"

"None, Master," I said.

"May I speak?" I asked.

"Yes," he said.

"I think," I said, "Master cares for his slave."

"Remain in position," he said.

I did so.

"You think I might care for you?" he said.

"Yes, Master," I said. "Do not sell me."

"Freedom is precious, is it not?" he asked.

"Doubtless," I said. But how could freedom compare with the collar, with being owned, with being a belonging, with the helpless love of a slave for her master?

"Surely you desire freedom," he said.

"No," I said. "I am a woman. I want bondage."

"Perhaps, before," he said, "when I said I was thinking of freeing you, you thought me jesting."

"I feared you were not," I said, uneasily. "I hoped you were."

"I was serious," he said.

"Only a fool frees a slave girl," I smiled. It was a Gorean saying. What rational man, fortunate enough to own a desirable woman, would let her out of his collar?

"I am serious," he said.

"I am not a man," I said. "I am a woman!"

"I can have you manumitted," he said. "We can see a praetor tomorrow. I can buy you slippers, veils, robes, suitable raiment."

"No!" I said. "No! Do not deny me my collar!"

He regarded me, angrily.

"Do not despise me for what I am," I begged. "Or, if you will, despise me for what I am, a slave!"

"Slave!" he said.

"Yes, slave!" I said.

"How can I respect you, as a slave?" he said.

"I do not want to be respected," I said. "I want to be owned, subdued, put to work, mastered, used as a vessel for your lust, a meaningless toy for your pleasures."

He rose to his feet. His fists were clenched.

"Do not try to make me be like you!" I said. "Do not try to impose your values on me. I have my own values, my own nature and needs! Surely you do not want me to be what you are. I do not want to be what you are. I want to be what I am, and want to be, a woman, a slave!"

I could not see his face for he had turned away.

"Be kind," I said.

He did not respond.

"Phyllis is a slave," I said, "and she would be your slave!"

He continued to face away from me. Then he spoke. His voice was cold. "Do you wish to be freed, or sold?" he said.

"I do not want to be sold," I said.

"Then," he said, "you want to be freed."

"No," I said. "If you must either free me or sell me, sell me."

He turned about, abruptly, startling me, his fists clenched, strode toward me, and stopped before me, looming over me, looking down at me. I averted my eyes, instantly. I did not think I had ever seen an expression so wild, so possessive, so claimant, so fierce, so exultant. "You Earth bitch!" he cried. And it took me a moment to realize he had spoken in English. "Yes, Master," I responded, unthinkingly in English. "You are a slave," he said in Gorean. "Yes, Master," I said, in Gorean. "Free you?" he said in Gorean. "Free you, never! Who would be fool enough to free a slave? You are in a collar, and you belong in a collar, you Earth slut, and you will stay in a collar!"

"You want me as a slave, do you not?" I said.

He then went to the side, to the wall, and ripped the whip from its peg, and, returning to me, he took my hair in his left hand, and, by the hair, hurled me from nadu to my stomach on the floor, and then I was lashed.

He then returned the whip to its peg.

"The matter is now closed," he said. "It is to be heard of no more."

"Yes, Master," I said.

"And," he said, "if, when you are worn and neglected, when you are scorned and humiliated, when you are chided and berated, when you are derided and mocked, when you are tired of sleeping on a rug or mat with only a sheet to cover you, when you are tired of slave gruel, lapped from a pan, in the shadow of a whip, when you smart from the switch, improving you in your lessons, when your chains are heavy and you cannot go where you wish to go, and you cannot move more than a yard from your slave ring, if I even suspect you are even thinking of freedom, you will be lashed again, and well lashed again, and as the slave you are."

"Yes, Master," I said.

"Now," he said, "please me, and as the slave you are."

"Yes, Master," I said.

I was once Phyllis Rodgers, a free woman of Earth. I am now simply 'Phyllis,' and the name has been put on me, as a slave name, for the convenience of masters. Slaves have no names in their own right. Indeed, we have no rights. We belong to our masters. I was captured, and brought to the planet Gor. Here I am a branded, collared kajira, or slave girl.

Here, on this world, I have found my master.

Here, on this world, I have found my identity.

I am a slave, and it is what I want to be.

Scorn me if you wish.

I am complete.

I am happy.

I wish you well,
Phyllis

ABOUT THE AUTHOR

John Norman is the creator of the Gorean Saga, the longest-running series of adventure novels in science fiction history. He has also produced a separate science fiction series, the Telnarian Histories, plus two other fiction works, *Ghost Dance* and *Time Slave*; a nonfiction paperback, *Imaginative Sex*; and a collection of thirty short stories, *Norman Invasions*. *The Totems of Abydos* was published in 2012. Norman is married and has three children.

For more information, visit Norman's website, gorchronicles.com, which has been specially created for his tremendous fan following and where one may read everything there is to know about his work.

GOREAN SAGA

FROM OPEN ROAD MEDIA

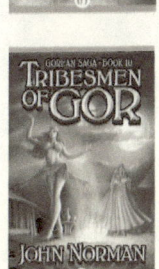

INTEGRATED MEDIA

INTEGRATED MEDIA

Find a full list of our authors and
titles at www.openroadmedia.com

FOLLOW US
@OpenRoadMedia

www.ingramcontent.com/pod-product-compliance
Lightning Source LLC
Chambersburg PA
CBHW020241030726
47499CB00001B/14

* 9 7 8 1 5 0 4 0 3 4 0 6 7 *